Spirit of Love

Sue Langford

ISBN: 1499239505
ISBN-13: 9781499239508

DEDICATION

For the ladies who came before us, the ladies who are with us and the ladies we'll be in our future. Thank you for your strength, your advice, your shoulders and your loving words.

To Ms. Patsy Cline, my dear girlfriends that I could never live without, and to all the ladies who ever asked for advice from anyone. Never doubt the advice that people you love give you.

To Nashville, for being my inspiration, my dream and my hope. To my true inspiration, thank you for reminding me that things are worth fighting for.

The Story

I can remember the first time I came across Patsy Cline's music. I always loved the music I heard, but I never really heard it all. It wasn't until I went down to see the Patsy Cline exhibit at the Country Music Hall of Fame in Nashville, Tennessee that I understood why I'd always loved the music. Patsy was not only a country music legend, but she was part of what made people dream of Nashville. She went to Nashville and made her dreams come true.

It's a legend about the circle on the Grand Ole Opry stage. That's where the idea came from. Legend says that if you stand in the circle on that stage, you'll feel spirits around you. Whether it be Patsy, Hank or any of the major greats, you'll feel all the inspiration that all those greats had swirling around you. My ritual was always to have a few quiet moments in the Opry to absorb all the history and inspiration. This year during that quiet time before a performance, I came up with the idea for this story. It wasn't until I learned more and more about Patsy, that I fell in love with the idea for this story.

I was honored when I learned so much about Patsy Cline. She is and always will be an amazing woman. She has strength and power that nobody could really top. She has some amazing children who I know miss her. I hope they understand that I think somehow some of the words that the character of Patsy Cline says in this story might just be advice that their mom might have given. It comforted me in knowing that somehow they might get some comfort in this story. I know I have, and I will never forget, one of the most amazing country songstresses in the whole world. Patsy Cline..... this book is for you, for your heart, for your family and for your memory that will be with all of us for a lifetime. Thank you for being Patsy.

Chapter 1

"You aren't walking out that door Faith. Don't even think it," Evan said. "Says who? I'm walking out that door. Nothing you can do about it," Faith said. She grabbed her bag, sliding the strap of her bag over her shoulder and he tried grabbing it away from her. "Faith, get your ass back in here," Evan said. "Let go." It was the same every time she tried to leave. He'd fight her, she'd end up with a handgun or rifle to her face and would have no choice but to give in. This time, there wasn't going to be any giving in. This time she was leaving once and for all.

"I said, sit your ass back down on that damn sofa before I shoot it off," Evan said. "Really? Sorta like the air conditioning I'm putting in that oversized ego," Faith said pointing the 9mm she'd bought straight against his forehead. "You didn't even load it right. You ain't doing nothing," Evan said. One shot went off, putting a hole in the roof of his double wide trailer. "What the hell are you trying to do," Evan said. Faith walked out the door, threw her bag in the backseat of the truck and saw Evan heading straight to her. She locked the other doors and hopped in. She was gone from the driveway before he made it around her side. Taking off was the easy part as far as things were concerned with Evan. She'd never managed to get out of town. As far as Faith was concerned, that was the last time that she was giving in. The last time she was letting him talk her into staying somewhere she never should've been in the first place.

Faith Andrews had been in a relationship with Evan James for over a year. Not one day in that relationship passed that she didn't wish she'd never left home. Faith could've had any man she wanted. She was almost 5 foot 6, and had an hourglass figure that made some guys follow her like lost puppy dogs. The long blonde hair and blue eyes made her a teenage boy's dream. Instead of being with the guys she deserved, she ended up with Evan - A no-good lying psychopath who scared the crap out of her on a regular basis just to keep her in line. Little did he know, that one trip he'd taken her on to the gun range in the mountains would mean he wasn't the one in charge anymore. Faith was determined, stubborn and was a fighter, although Evan never let her. He wouldn't let her have any control. Faith was determined to get out of there, and she was gonna succeed.

Evan James was a piece of work to say the least. He gave himself the military haircut, but as Faith found out, everything he'd ever said was a lie. His military background was a split personality and not one ounce of it had ever been true. He wasn't the sharpest tool in the tool shed, but he was convincing enough to have distracted her heart into falling hard for him. He was almost 6 feet, around 250 pounds and had a mean streak that could scare anyone. He was notorious for pulling out a gun or even a samurai sword to make his point. His family had been in denial about him for years. The only woman that had the guts to stand up to him, was standing in front of him about to walk right out that door.

Faith made it as far as the highway before she saw Evan's daddy's truck following her. She made one move. One amazing move and Evan was stuck. Faith pulled into the police station off the highway after driving like hell down the shoulder. "What's wrong Faith," the officer asked. "The jackass threatened me. He's tailed me all the way here. Just do something so I can get out of here. Please," Faith asked. The officer went outside, grabbed Evan's keys and Faith took off. The fact that there wasn't a red truck tailing her had her being able to breathe for the first time. It felt like a weight had been lifted. She knew the feeling was bound to return, but she was darn happy that for now it was behind her.

"Why the hell did you have to do that? I'm gonna lose her," Evan said as his police officer friend said. "Let her go Evan. If she loved you she wouldn't be leaving. Let her go and find someone who won't want to go. Be with someone that you aren't fighting with all the time. You shouldn't have to hold the woman hostage in your damn trailer to get a woman to be with you," his officer friend Jake said. "You don't get it. She was the one Jake. The one I'm supposed to be with." "Then she'll be back. Let go Evan. Before I have to arrest you," Jake said

Faith drove until she was too tired to drive. The minute she saw the sign that said Nashville Tennessee, she got a grin ear to ear and got her second wind. Faith pulled into the first hotel she found and checked in.

She had her truck parked in the covered parking garage and had herself unloaded in minutes. She grabbed the first paper she'd found and started hunting down a job. Faith turned her cell phone on and her mailbox was filled with messages from Evan. She deleted them all and changed the number. She called the important people and gave them the new number, making them promise not to say a word to Evan. She called her friend Emma and instead, got a mouthful and a half of 'I told you so'.

"Girl, why didn't you just tell me you were doing this? I could've come and kicked his butt and helped you get out of there," Emma said. "Right. Like I can even say a word when he's there. You know that. He's listening to everything Emma. Always has. I needed out," Faith said. "Girl, tell me where to go and I'll help you," Emma said. Faith gave her the address and went and had a long hot shower. Not 20 minutes later, Emma shot her a message with the flight info. Faith had 5 hours until Emma was gonna land. She looked in a mirror. She saw the bruises, the stress and the crap that Evan had caused. The only thing she knew was that she was happy as hell that she was gone. The fact that she didn't have to sleep with a gun to her head and a threatening word or comment had her out cold in minutes.

Faith woke up 3 hours later, got changed and took off to the airport to pick Emma up. The minute Faith saw her, she started tearing up. Emma hugged her. "He's not getting near you now. Jamie's coming too. I'm not taking any chances Faith. He wanted to get you out of all of this," Emma said. "Emma, I get you're trying to help, but bringing him here is just gonna make it harder to hide out," Faith said. "You aren't hiding anymore. He got you an interview at the label," Emma said. "Great. And me being there isn't going to be out in the open at all," Faith said. "I know you're scared. Just let him help you," Emma said. Jamie headed out, got the truck loaded up and headed to the hotel that Faith was staying in. "You can't stay here," Jamie said. "And why not," Faith asked. "Because he knows you're here. He made a comment to someone and he knows you're here. We're checking you into a hotel somewhere else. I'm putting it under my name," Jamie said. He got her truck loaded and checked her into a hotel with top notch security. "Jamie," Faith said.

"You're staying safe and that's it," he said with a smirk. "He's not getting you back. Not now."

Jamie Gilbert was the perfect southern boy. He was born and raised on country, or what he considered country at the time. He'd been playing guitar since he was a kid and had always had that musical talent. He was around 6 foot 2 and had those sexy blue eyes that women drooled over. The blonde hair didn't exactly help. He had muscles, a smile that could melt women and always had the popularity. When he first hit the country music industry, they'd welcomed him in with open arms and he'd slowly started to rise to the top. He had few regrets in his life. The one he knew he'd always regret – Letting Faith leave and be with Evan. He'd fought his feelings for so long that it was almost second nature. One problem with that – He had a fierce protective nature. He'd been shooting since he could hold a gun, and had always defended women, especially Faith, from predators. He didn't know how to tell her, and he wasn't letting anyone get near her. He had his chance. A chance that God had handed him on a silver platter. He wasn't about to lose it to anyone. He was taking care of her like he should've all that time ago.

After a week or so, Faith heard back about a job at the label and headed in for another interview. "So, what we need is for you to work with some of the artists. They need to be set up with a fan club and an online presence. Until they get well known, you're in charge of the online stuff. You think you can handle that," Patrick asked. Emma nodded. "Then it's yours for now. We're gonna set you up with a cell phone tomorrow. Where are you staying," Patrick asked. "For now a hotel. Long story," Faith said. "Well, you should be okay for a little while. When the address changes, let me know." Faith nodded. She signed the papers and headed back to the hotel. She walked in and saw Emma curled up on the sofa with Jamie. "So when do you start," Jamie asked. "Tomorrow mornin. I appreciate the help Jamie," Faith said. "Talked to a buddy of mine. Evan's done lost his mind. Doesn't matter. You're here. You're safe. Unless you wanna go back to the third floor of hell, it won't matter," Jamie said. "I'm not going back. I almost want to change my name just to get away from there," Faith said. "If that's what you want, say the word baby girl," Jamie teased.

They went out for dinner and celebrated, had a drink at the bar and Jamie drove them back to the hotel. They took Emma back to the airport then headed back downtown. Faith went for a walk for a while and stopped at a few honky-tonks on Broadway. One specific performer caught her attention. Once people saw him there, the bar was rammed. Faith was front row. The minute the man finished his set, he walked off the stage and grabbed a drink, starting right at Faith. A few people asked for an autograph and then left the bar. As soon as the room cleared out a bit, he walked over to Faith.

He whispered, "Come with me a minute," and Faith was hand in hand with him heading to the upper level to the VIP seating. "What are you doing," Faith asked. "Getting a minute to talk to the sexiest woman in here," he said. "And you are," Faith asked. "Deacon Hart," the man said. "And what a stage name that is," Faith teased. He pulled out his ID and showed it to her. "That's you're actual name? Well my goodness. Don't even have to change it," Faith teased. "And what's your name," Deacon asked. "Faith Andrews," Faith said. "How on earth did I get this lucky that I met a girl like you," he asked. "Extremely lucky," Faith teased. They talked a while, she had a soda and he walked outside with her. "Where you stayin," he asked. "Why? Because you think you're getting into my room," Faith joked. "Because I wanted to make sure you got home okay," Deacon replied. "Just across the way. It's fine," Faith said. He walked her into the hotel anyway, with a grin ear to ear, and up to her bedroom door. "What you doing tomorrow night," Deacon asked. "Sleeping," Faith joked. "I'll come take you to dinner," he said. "I appreciate the idea, but I'm starting a new job tomorrow and I'm...." He kissed her. "Just say yes," he asked. "Fine, but after..." He kissed her again and she went into her room. Deacon wrote down the room number and headed back to the elevators with a grin ear to ear.

"So where'd you disappear to," Jamie asked. "Walked around on Broadway a bit. Went in to hear a little music at Tootsie's and watched a show." "So who's the guy," Jamie teased. "Deacon." "Faith, just keep an eye out. I don't want to have to save you again," he teased. "Funny," Faith said. Jamie hugged her goodnight, went into his room and left Faith to relax before bed. Not even 10 minutes later, the room phone rang.

"Hello," Faith said. "Well hello back there beautiful. So, about that dinner idea. Was thinkin we could do breakfast instead," Deacon said. "You were thinkin that were you? What makes you think that I don't have plans," Faith asked. "Because I'm persistent. I'd have to follow you around like a puppy dog until you agreed." Faith couldn't help the smirk starting across her face. "So, that a yes," Deacon asked. "I have plans tomorrow morning." "Then we're going Friday morning. No excuses allowed." "Deacon." "Nope. Can't back out on it." Faith shook her head. "I'm staying with a friend. I can't guarantee…." "Write this down." He gave Faith his cell and house number. "Get some sleep baby. You don't need the beauty sleep, but you're gonna need rest to keep up with me," Deacon joked. "Well goodnight to you too," Faith joked.

Deacon was almost 6 foot 3 and was gorgeous. He could've been a model with just a change of clothes. Any woman would've fallen over herself to get just one look from him. Working out 7 days a week did his body something good, his blue eyes that were almost a smoky blue had women drowning themselves in the pools of blue in his eyes. He had a perfectly chiseled jaw, the perfect chicklet teeth and was too gorgeous for words. He had a voice like a dream and knew it would pay off. He'd been single on and off for years and never found the dream girl that he'd always wanted. When he saw Faith, he couldn't stop staring. He was determined and had a way into any woman's heart. Faith wouldn't be that hard to get, at least not in his mind.

Faith curled up in the pillowy bed and couldn't wipe that grin off her face. She finally fell asleep. She woke up more than once with nightmare after nightmare. When she woke up at 6am in a cold sweat, Jamie came in and put a cool towel on her neck. "I heard you screaming in the other room. You alright," Jamie asked. Faith shook her head. "When is it gonna stop," Faith asked. He hugged her and she tried to go back to sleep. "You sure you're okay," Jamie asked. Faith nodded. "Baby girl, it'll go away. Getting out of that place was just the first step. You're safe here. Nobody is hurting you again," Jamie said. He kissed her cheek and turned her light back out. He went back into the sitting room area and went back to his morning paper.

Faith got a few more hours of shut eye, had breakfast and went downstairs to the gym to work out. She came back upstairs and there were white and sterling roses on the doorstep of her room. She looked at the card and had a smirk ear to ear again. The card read:

Hope you got shut eye beautiful. See you tonight. – Deacon

She went inside, showered and got changed. Jamie knocked on her door. "What's up," Faith asked. "You got this in from the label. They want you to check out two or three of the new artists and work with them to set up websites. That last one is from that show you like. The guy is branching out into the music industry," Jamie said. "And you just know everything don't you," Faith teased. "Look at who it is, then you can thank me," he teased. Faith went through everything and saw that name. "He's actually singing? He's so good on that show though. Why this," Faith asked. "Go talk to him and find out," Jamie said. "Where you headed?" "Studio. Have to do rehearsals before we head out next week. You sure you're gonna be safe here," Jamie asked. Faith kissed his cheek, hugged him and headed off.

Faith made a few calls, got the artists to come in to go over what they needed to and got settled into her office. An hour or so later, Faith was about to walk into the boardroom when she got the feeling someone was watching her. She set up for her meeting and turned to see Deacon walking past the meeting room and heading into a meeting with her boss. She took a deep breath, poured a glass of water and her first meeting started.

"So we need to update the website. We got these in as an example of the new designs. What do you think," Patrick asked. "Sounds good to me. I kinda like this one," Deacon said slipping a ball cap on his head. "Figured you'd like that one. I'll bring in the team to start work on the site," Patrick said. Faith had just finished going through the meeting with the last artist and saw Deacon. He looked right at her with a grin ear to ear. "Faith, this is Deacon Hart. Deacon, this is Faith. She's gonna help you out with the website additions. If you want to change anything on it, say the word," Patrick said. "Thanks," Deacon said. Patrick went back to his office and Deacon walked over to Faith. "Now what do you know. I bump into the prettiest girl in the city and my stomach's growlin. When we're done this, we can go to lunch," Deacon suggested. "Working?! I told you…" Deacon closed the blinds, locked the door and pulled her into his arms, kissing her and almost sweeping her feet out from under her.

They came up for air and Faith almost forgot where she was. "This is my workplace Deacon. Stop," Faith said trying to remain professional. She backed away and went to sit down. He pulled out her chair for her. "I mean it Deacon," Faith said. "Not a word about how sexy you look right now then," he teased. "So professionalism isn't gonna happen today," Faith asked. "You're too damn sexy to concentrate," Deacon teased. Faith made the changes to his website that she'd envisioned and showed him. "Damn woman. That looks perfect," Deacon said. "Good." Faith got up, grabbed her laptop and went to head to her office. Deacon slid his arms around her waist before she got out the door. "Faith." "Let go. I have work to do Deacon," Faith said. He slid her laptop out of her hands, laid it onto the table and slid his hand in hers. "What," Faith asked. He kissed her with a kiss that turned the heat in that room up to 150. It was truly the perfect kiss. Faith broke the kiss, grabbed her laptop and walked out and into her office. Just as Deacon was about to walk in, her next appointment showed. "I'm waiting right here," Deacon said sitting down in her office. "Out," Faith said. "Darlin, what are you so worried about? I'm gonna play around with my site while you're in your meeting," Deacon said. Faith shook her head. "What," Deacon asked. "Dinner. End of discussion. I have to finish…" Deacon closed her blinds, locked the door and kissed her again, leaning her against the door. "All I gotta say is that we're lucky if we make it into the restaurant," Deacon said. Faith slid away from him and went into her meeting.

Three hours later, Faith made edits to the websites and started on the problems of the sites. She had something quick to eat and by the time 5pm hit, her phone was buzzing. She locked up everything and headed back to the hotel. She walked right past Deacon in the lobby and went up to her room. She slid into a hot shower. Minutes later, she heard her phone buzzing. She ignored it, finished her shower and started getting changed. When there was a knock at her door, Faith slid into her jeans and t-shirt and answered the door.

"Think you're running late," Deacon said. "I'm not going. Not after that today. That's what you want, find someone who isn't gonna want you in the morning," Faith said. He kissed her, leaned her against the wall just inside the doorway, kicked the door closed and grabbed a shirt and her boots and handed them to her. "I'm not going anywhere," Faith said. "Why," Deacon asked. "You don't know me Deacon. I don't know you. After the crap you pulled in that office, the date is off and so is anything else you dreamed up," Faith said. She went to the door and he kissed her again. "Stop being silly," Deacon said. "Out." She pushed him out the door. "One drink," Deacon asked. "I don't mix business and personal. End of discussion," Faith said. She closed the door. Faith changed into her sweater and her beat-up jeans, did her hair and makeup and went to head out when she saw Deacon waiting in the hall. "What are you still doing here," Faith asked. "Waiting. I get you don't want to mix, but it's a little late now," Deacon said. "I'm not going anywhere with you," Faith said. She walked over to the elevator, went downstairs alone and was gone from the hotel before he even got downstairs.

Faith headed over to a ranch that she'd heard wild stories about from Jamie. She got a horse and went off for a ride. Being cooped up with Evan meant that the horseback riding she'd dreamt of was impossible. For once, she was safe and away from any more stress. When she came into the barn an hour and a bit later, she fed the horse and brushed him down then headed to grab dinner and made her way back to the hotel. She walked into the lobby and Deacon was talking to Jamie. "I'll talk to her," Jamie said as Deacon spotted her. Faith walked past both of them and went upstairs.

Jamie came in a little while later. "Don't try to take his side," Faith said. "He wants to go out with you. Stop being so hard on him," Jamie said. "Just don't. He walked into my office and kissed me and practically tried to have sex with me in the boardroom. That's just stupid as hell." "Faith, give him a chance. He isn't gonna push that hard. I talked to him and told him to quit it. If he didn't, he deals with me. You'll be alright." "And when I'm not? You're gonna be on tour Jamie. I can't just hide out forever, but I'm not putting myself into that situation and screw up a job like this," Faith said. "Woman, this is Nashville. Half the damn town is in the music business. Faith, he's a good guy. He's not causing crap. Just go and have dinner with him. I'll have this," he teased taking her dinner out of her hands. She shook her head, washed up a bit and changed, then headed downstairs.

Deacon was still sitting in the lobby where Jamie left him. "My stomach is growling," Deacon teased. "One rule first. No more attacks in the office. They're staying separate period. No more bullshit," Faith said. "Then can I do one thing first," Deacon asked. "No," Faith said. She headed into the valet area and Deacon slid his hand in hers. "Deacon." He kissed her cheek, grabbed his truck and hopped out to open her door for her. "Where are we going," Faith asked. "Best restaurant in Nashville," Deacon replied. They drove and 45 minutes later, they pulled into the Loveless Café. "Deacon." "Best food. I love this place. I can't help it," he joked. Faith shook her head.

They headed in and were seated off at a quiet table in the back. "And why are we here," Faith asked. "Quiet time. Nobody is disturbing us, nobody is in the middle of it all and we have privacy," Deacon said. They ordered dinner and talked a while. Faith still wasn't convinced. "What," he asked. "You realize that what happened today isn't happening again right? I just got out of a relationship Deacon. I'm gun-shy. Just back off a bit," Faith said. "Baby girl, I could barely sleep last night. I kept hoping I'd see you. I made a mistake. I get it," Deacon said. "Then you aren't gonna be mad when I say this isn't gonna work." "Faith." "You can't just change my mind Deacon. I just got out of the third level of hell. Being with anyone isn't gonna happen." They finished dinner and Faith thought they were going back to the hotel. "Where are we going now," Faith asked. "For a drive so we can talk," Deacon replied.

They drove a while as he showed her around his version of Nashville. They pulled into a gated neighborhood a little while later. "Deacon." He pulled into his driveway, turned the truck off and came around to open her door. "Where are we," Faith asked. He helped her out of the truck.

He unlocked the front door and Faith shook her head. "Take me back to the hotel," Faith said. "Woman, stop. I thought we could hang out here so we could have privacy. That's it," Deacon said. Faith went to walk back outside and he slid his hand in hers. "I get why you're worried, but I just wanted somewhere quiet that we could talk. That's it." He walked her into the huge gourmet kitchen and grabbed the bottle of Jack Daniel's and two glasses. "I'm not drinking," Faith said. He poured the whiskey into both glasses, added ice and cola to hers and handed it to her. He walked her outside, turned on the fire pit and sat down on the chaise. "Just come sit so we can talk," Deacon said.

She sat down and sent a text to Jamie letting him know where she was and turned on her GPS function so he could find her if anything went down. "What's wrong," Deacon asked. "You keep pushing. You walked into the office and embarrassed me. You can't just walk in and kiss me like that," Faith said. "What did he do to you?" "Deacon." "What did he do that scared you off that easily?" "Deacon, stop." "What did he do? Tell me and I'll stop asking." "He held me hostage. He forced me into being his slave practically. That's what," Faith said. She finished her drink and walked into the house. Deacon walked over to her and kissed her hand. "He screwed up. I'm not like that Faith. Never have been. I just met you and I couldn't get you off my mind. I normally never have a fight when I want a woman in my arms but you won't give in even a little," Deacon said. "It isn't gonna happen Deacon." "Give me one reason why not that has nothing to do with work," he teased. "Stop being a pain in the…" "Can't think of one can you," he asked. "Stubborn," Faith asked. He kissed her. Faith pushed him away and walked out the front door, went down to the gate and hopped in the truck with Jamie.

"What happened," Jamie asked. "I swear. Either he doesn't comprehend English or he's just an idiot. I said it wasn't happening and he made a move anyway. He drives me nuts," Faith said. "He made a move on you," Jamie asked. Faith could see that he was about to shoot steam out his ears. "After what I already went through I'm not jumping in another stupid relationship like that," Faith said. Jamie u-turned the truck, parked it at the gate, hopped out and went straight to Deacon's house.

"Where did Faith go," Deacon asked. "You made a move on her. What the hell were you thinking," Jamie asked. "I like her. Have since we met. I kissed her. We were just sitting here and I asked her why she was so worried. She said I was being stubborn. I kissed her." "Keep your damn hands off her. You make one more move towards her, you'll be black and blue. End of discussion," Jamie said. He walked out and went back to his truck. He took Faith back to the hotel, got her checked out and took her to his condo. "Don't tell anyone where you're staying. Got me," Jamie said. Faith nodded. "He makes another move on you he's a dead man," Jamie said.

Faith went and had a hot bath then came downstairs and saw Jamie trying to calm down. He was in a video game battle with his buddy Andrew. "Andrew. You remember Faith right," Jamie asked. Andrew looked over. "You mean the little sister," Andrew teased. "Don't push it. You're in more shit if you even think it," Jamie said. Faith walked upstairs and curled up in bed with her laptop. A half hour later, she got a text from Deacon:

I need to talk to you. Call me. I'm sorry for going too far. I met you and the loneliness got the best of me.

She shook her head. The fact that Jamie had already ripped him a new one hadn't deterred him. Nothing had. Getting involved with a man from work wasn't a smart move. Getting involved with a musician was gonna be worse. She could see it now. The minute he was on tour, he'd be going from woman to woman then come home to her and play house until he could go back to the single road life. That wasn't happening. Not on her watch. She replied back:

Not signing on for a relationship where there's no fidelity. No thanks.

Not even 2 minutes later, Deacon replied:

Haven't had a relationship period in years. I figured people were after me for my music connections. I know that's not what you're about. That's why I wanted the chance. Please.

She couldn't do it. Not after what she'd gone through. A little while just having peace and quiet is what she needed. Besides, Jamie would kick Deacon's ass to china if he hurt her. She couldn't. Her phone buzzed again.

I need to know that I still have that chance Faith. I really wanted for us to just have privacy so we could talk. Please.

Faith shook her head. She put her phone on silent, turned the laptop off and curled up in bed. An hour later, she opened her eyes and saw Jamie putting on his leather jacket and grabbing his bike keys. "Where are you going," Faith asked. "I warned him. That little punk," Jamie said. "Who," Faith asked. "You don't think I knew he'd messaged you? He doesn't get to disrespect you. Not on my damn watch." "Jamie, sit down," Faith said. "Why," Jamie asked. He sat down on the side of the bed. "If I get in over my head, I know you're gonna be there. I appreciate the help with him tonight but I don't think he's gonna cause any more trouble." "After what he just said in that text…" Faith grabbed the phone out of his hand and read the text:

I want to see you. I can't just go to sleep knowing that I did that. I'll come meet you. Please.

"Jamie, sit down and breathe. He's not doing anything. He knows where I stand. He scared the crap out of me earlier alright. I didn't know what to do." "What happens when I'm on tour? I need to know you're safe," Jamie said. "You need a girlfriend to worry about," Faith teased. "What if you just came with me on the tour," Jamie asked. "Are you going into panic mode?" "Faith." "I know. You have to take care of you like you're taking care of me. Don't make me kick your butt," Faith teased trying to calm him down. "Woman, you wouldn't know where to start," he teased. "Bike keys," Faith asked. He handed them over and Faith hugged him. He kissed her cheek and headed back downstairs. He got some shut-eye and tried to calm himself down.

17

Chapter 2

The next morning, Faith woke up and did her workout then made breakfast for her and Jamie. "What time you heading in," Jamie asked. "Half hour. I have to work on those websites this afternoon. I'll be surprised if I even remember lunch," Faith joked. "Then I'm bringing you lunch." Faith laughed. They had breakfast and she headed off to work. When she got there, a bouquet of a dozen sterling roses was on her desk. There was a note from Deacon with them:

Dinner. I promise I'll behave.

She shook her head and got down to work on the changes to the websites. She got all the way through the first two then started working on Deacon's. She played around with the background, the photos, and the cover page then added a few new ideas to get attention. She handed off a few new design ideas to the artists via email and sent Deacon his. Within minutes, she got an email back from Deacon:

What. No reply? I love the new stuff. Way to go. That mean that I get you for lunch? Joe's at 2.

Faith smirked. Another email from him came in.

Sexy little smirk. You look gorgeous today sexy.

She looked up and he was in a meeting with her boss with a smirk ear to ear. She shook her head and finished up on some of the other changes. She put the site back up with the changes and got up. She handed off the pictures of the changes and her boss pulled her into the meeting. "So with those changes, we can do the re-launch and do a few appearances. We're thinking of adding him onto the tour for a few dates with Jamie. What do you think Faith," her boss asked. "Totally different fan base. Jamie is more heavy stuff. They're not quite the same," Faith said. "Doesn't mean no," Deacon said. "Then y'all are running it by Jamie. I'm not touching it," Faith joked. "Well, here's an idea. What if you went

18

with them for those dates? Can you handle that," Patrick asked. "I'm not bringing it up to him. That's not my place. You want me there to ensure that the fan experience works with the new websites, fine. I'm not refereeing them." Deacon smirked. She went to get up and Deacon slid his hand over hers on the armrest of the chair. "Can you get Jamie on the phone for me," Patrick asked. "He's in the studio a bit. I'll text him and get him to call you," Faith said. She got up, went into her office and texted Jamie telling him all the details.

Not even 10 minutes later, Deacon texted her:

Didn't get an answer. You trying to drive me crazy in here?

Faith grabbed her purse and headed out the door. She walked over to Joe's and sat down and ordered lunch. She was just getting her meal when Deacon walked up behind her. "Guess that was a yes," he teased. He sat down with her and they had lunch together. "So what did you want," Faith asked. "My date. Me and you. We can go down to the Bridgestone and go to the Aldean concert. I got tickets for us," Deacon said. "Presumptuous. What if I said no," Faith asked. "Have to talk you into it. We're in a public place. No making out on my back porch. Promise." "What are you trying to do?" "Make you understand that you don't need to worry. I'm not making a move Faith. I just wanna spend some time with you." Faith got up and Deacon paid for lunch. He slid his hand in hers and walked her back to work. "Deacon." "I'll come get you at the hotel at 6," he said. "Not staying there." "I know. I'll meet you at the hotel." Faith shook her head. "Then I'll meet you at the front door of the Ryman on 4th street. Deal?" She smirked. "Alright then." He looked her in the eye. "What," Faith asked. "I wanna kiss you so bad right now I can taste it." Faith walked upstairs to her office.

Around 4:30, Faith headed back to the condo. Jamie left her a note that he got a last minute request to be one of the openers for the concert. Faith smirked. She got changed, put her boots on and fixed up her makeup. She headed downstairs, walked over to the Ryman and saw Deacon's truck. She saw him sitting inside at the Ryman with a half-dozen sterling roses. He walked out to her. "About dang time. Where were you," Deacon asked. "Getting changed," Faith replied. "You gonna get mad at me if I kiss you," he asked. "We…" He kissed her. The kiss had the heat sliding from her head right down to her toes. She broke the kiss and they headed over to the concert.

They walked in and Jamie was pacing backstage. Deacon handed Faith a drink and kissed her cheek. Security walked over to Faith and handed her a backstage pass. "I guess Jamie needs me," Faith teased. Deacon went to kiss her and she stopped him. She walked backstage and saw Jamie losing it. "What's wrong," Faith asked. "What in the hell are you doing here with him?"

"Don't you have other things to worry about," Faith asked. "You aren't going back down there. Stay back here and watch the show then I'm taking you home. End of discussion." "Jamie, stop. I'm watching the show, having a drink with him and coming back to the house. Period." "I didn't know I had to ask you permission," Faith said. "Woman, I'm keeping you safe. After what that idiot did, you're putting yourself back in danger and you know it. Stay back here. I'll get you home safe and…." "Jamie, go on stage and do your thing. Stop trying to tell me what to do. I can handle it. When I can't, you'll be the only one I call. I get it Jamie." He hugged her. "Now go kick ass and have a good show. You're living this dream. Go work it." He kissed her cheek and Faith went to go back into the stadium. "Stay back here," he asked. Faith nodded. He headed on and Faith smirked at him. A minute or two later, Deacon messaged her:

Get your butt down here.

Faith walked down and sat with Deacon. He had his arms wrapped around her most of Jamie's set on stage. When he intentionally ended with "Hands off" – the song he'd written about Faith and Evan – she knew. Deacon wasn't gonna be able to be with her. Not that night anyway. "Why are you so stiff," Deacon asked. "I had to hold him back from kicking your butt last night," Faith said. "I don't need you to protect me. Faith, I meant what I said. I just wanted us to have privacy. That's all." "Deacon, it's not gonna happen alright? He's never gonna allow it."

"I didn't know I needed his permission." Faith went to walk off. "Stay," Deacon said. "He's gonna snap if I don't go…." Deacon kissed her. "Stay." Security walked towards her. "I have to go," Faith said. "No. He wants to kick my ass, he can kick it," Deacon said. Faith went to walk off and Deacon grabbed her hand. "He wants you back there, I'm coming with you," Deacon said. "I can't referee between you two. I'm not getting into a fight with him over this. He's been there when nobody else was Deacon. He's my best friend." "Guess you made your decision." Faith walked off with the security person. It killed her to walk off, but…. Faith walked back over to Deacon. "You think making me choose between you is right? Kiss my ass Deacon," Faith said. She walked off and went backstage.

Jamie was standing there talking to Jason when he saw Faith. "Jason, this is Faith. She's the reason for all those over-protective big brother songs," Jamie teased. "Nice to meet you," Jason said. Faith shook his hand and Jason headed on stage. "What you two fighting about," Jamie asked. "You being a pain in my backside. I get you're mad Jamie, but you have to let me make up my own mind," Faith said. "He's just like all those other guys Faith. They aren't helping you to be a better you. They're trying to keep you like they're little pet," Jamie said. "And what am I supposed to do Jamie? Wait for you to find me the right one?" He hugged her and they watched the show from the side stage. Part way through, Faith got a text from Patrick that Jamie hadn't replied. He needed her to talk to him. "What," Jamie asked. "Patrick. He texted you earlier. He has an opening act for the tour. He also wants me there with both of you," Faith said. "Who," Jamie asked. "The person you want to knock out," Faith said. "Then I'm not doing the tour," Jamie said. "Then screw yourself. Both of you are good whether you like him or not. He needs it as much as you do Jamie. Either accept it or don't, but I'm not the damn excuse," Faith said. She walked out. Jamie went after her. Deacon saw her leaving and went after her, bumping right into Jamie.

Jason Cane was one of the top country artists. Faith had been a fan for years and Jamie's dream always was to be on tour with Jason. He wasn't sure what dream was gonna come true first. Jason was almost 6 feet tall, had green eyes you could get lost in and that perfect sandy brown hair.

He had the swagger, the build and the attitude, but his mom raised him right. She taught him everything a southern man needed to know, but sometimes that wasn't enough. When he wanted something that bad, there was no stopping him. Whether it was an award, a venue or even a date. Fact was, that moment was the moment that changed everything for them. The moment where he realized what he wanted – or who.

"What part of stay away from her didn't you get," Jamie asked. "The part where you run me off. She gets to make her own damn decision," Deacon said. They were fighting and barely even noticed that Faith left. She drove back to the house, took her makeup off, got undressed and slid into a hot bath.

Jamie came back into the house an hour later with a split lip. Faith came into the kitchen in her satin robe and saw him. "What the hell? What happened," Faith asked grabbing an ice pack out of the freezer and wrapping it in a towel. "Deacon. That's what happened," Jamie said. "How bad does he look," Faith asked. "He's staying the hell away from you period. I know what he's up to. Faith, the man isn't up for a real relationship and he sure as hell doesn't want the best from you." "Jamie, when are you gonna get it? I'm an adult. I get to make my own choices remember," Faith asked. "Not with him you don't," Jamie said. "Thanks big brother," Faith said sarcastically. "Get back over here," Jamie said following her. "Why?" He grabbed Faith's hand and walked her to the sofa. "What," Faith asked. "He's not good enough for you. Faith, I know him. He's not a good guy. He's a user period. You deserve better." "Jamie. You're always gonna say that. Nobody can be good enough," Faith said. "I need you to be safe. Do you get that?" "Yeah. I get it. Doesn't mean you run my life," Faith said. He kissed her. "Jamie, what are we doing," Faith asked pushing him away. "I just…" Faith walked upstairs, got changed and started packing her bag. "Faith," Jamie said. "Now you make a move on me? Seriously?" Faith zipped up her bag. "Faith, you aren't going." "I'm not sitting here while you stand in my way with every man in the planet. Deacon isn't good enough? You sure Jamie? You sure it wasn't just that you wanted…" "Faith, I need you with me. When you go off and do your own thing, you suck at choosing guys. The only thing standing between you and you being happy is being with someone who accepts you the way you are. I've always been that." "So that's why you flipped at him?" "Faith." "I'm leaving. Don't stop me," Faith said.

Jamie walked towards her, slid the bag out of her hand and pulled her to him. He kissed her, pinning her against the door. He picked her up and wrapped her legs around him. He didn't let her up for air. He carried her to the sofa and still didn't let her up for air. They made love on the sofa and it was like they were floating on air. She didn't know what to think, what to do or how to feel. She was with the one man she'd known for a long time. He knew her better than anyone. He also knew better than to put them in this position. He didn't let her up for air. When they finally quieted down, he curled up with her. "We can't do this," Faith said. "Faith…" She tried to get free of him. "Faith, please." She got up and walked upstairs. She laid down in that bed. "Faith," Jamie said standing in the doorway. "What," she said barely able to look him in the eye. "I'm not doing that tour without you there." "Jamie." "You're coming. Please just come with me. Please." "I don't have a choice. Patrick wants me on that tour." He walked in and sat down on the edge of the bed. "I want you to be safe Faith. Just let me keep you safe." "Jamie, whatever you're thinking that we're doing here…" He kissed her again.

Faith got up the next morning and Jamie's arms were still wrapped around her. She went to slide out of bed and Jamie pulled her back to him. "I have to go to work," Faith said. He kissed her and Faith got up. Her things were back in the closet and where they were before she packed them up. She showered, got dressed and left. She walked into the office. Deacon was sitting in her office. Faith walked in, closed the door and sat down. "Where'd you take off to," Deacon asked. "Just go." "Faith, answer me," Deacon said. "I went home. I'm not watching you two act like children. I went and slept." "So what else is going on with you," Deacon asked. "You need to go," Faith said. "I'm opening for him. You're coming on the tour with us. One way or another we're gonna end up talking about this," Deacon said. "I have work to do Deacon. Second off, why are you here so damn early," Faith asked. "Signing the contracts and we're going through the merch for the tour. Deal?" Faith shook her head, took a sip of her coffee and Deacon headed out. Not even 10 minutes later, Faith was called into a meeting. She walked in and Jamie was sitting down. He pulled an empty chair over to him and she sat down. He wrapped his arm around her back.

They went through the merch ideas for the concerts and the tour dates then signed Faith onto the tour for the PR. Jamie wouldn't let her back out. Once the meeting was done, Faith went back into her office and locked the door. The last thing she wanted was to be in the middle of all of this. Now she was in the middle of it period. Faith went back to the house to start figuring out what she was gonna need for the tour and saw a note sitting on the bedside table:

Take this. Whatever you need, just get it. I don't regret a damn thing about yesterday.

Faith saw his credit card. She called him. "So which jean place are you heading to? Might want some shorts and a new pair of boots or two. Can you do me a super huge favor and grab me a couple black tanks and tees," Jamie asked. "We need to talk," Faith said. "I'll meet you at the house tonight. I'll grab Joe's." "Jamie." "I know. I'll be back at 8." "Okay," Faith said. They hung up and Faith went off to the mall. She grabbed the tanks and shirts for Jamie, got her boots and some clothes for herself and a few extra things to distract herself from boredom and headed back to the house. She walked in and put Jamie's things in his tour bag. She walked downstairs just as Jamie was coming in.

"Hey baby girl. How was your day," Jamie asked like nothing was wrong. Faith handed him the credit card and the receipts and walked back upstairs. "Faith," Jamie said following her. "Last night was a mistake Jamie. I'm not ruining our friendship over something like that. You weren't thinking straight and…." He kissed her. "I'm thinking crystal clear," he said as he kissed her again. She broke the kiss and backed away. "What happens when it goes wrong? I lose my friend. I lose everything all over again. I'm not jeopardizing that Jamie." "And you think dating him is a good move? Faith, the man wants a piece of ass and he's walking away. I want the woman I've known forever. I want you." "I need to move," Faith said. "No." "Jamie, I didn't ask your permission.

I'm moving out once I find…." He kissed her and picked her up, leaning her onto the window seat. "Watching what Evan did to you about killed me. Faith, I can't let something like that happen again. The minute I saw what Deacon did, I wanted to kill him. You deserve respect. Evan blew it and I had to step in. Fact was I realized then that I was in love with you. I should've said something then but I couldn't. I needed to know you were okay." "And you think sleeping with me was going to make sure I was okay? Seriously? Jamie, you pushed our friendship into something else. I need my friend. I can't lose that," Faith said. "You aren't going. Please say you won't go," Jamie asked. He kissed her again and ended up leaning her back onto the bed. "Jamie." "Can't help it," he teased kissing the tip of her nose. "Dinner first then," Faith said. He kissed her with a kiss that was so intense and so hot it would've burned the house to the ground.

"Jamie," Faith said. "I want you. So kick my ass," he teased. "Let me up," Faith asked. "Not until you let go and just give this a chance." "Right. I'm gonna be dating the one guy that every woman in the planet is drooling over and begging to date. I get to be the one fighting them off? Forget it," Faith said. He kissed her again and undid the buckle of her belt. "Jamie." He unzipped her jeans then kissed down her torso. He looked up at her with those killer blue eyes and she couldn't say no. "We can't keep doing…" He kissed her with a kiss that made her lose her words and her restraint. He kicked her jeans to the floor, she helped him with his and that was all there was to it. She couldn't say no, and he was never going to let her. Fact was, Faith had always had a thing for him. The thought of losing his friendship when a relationship went bad was still in her mind. If he wasn't worried, the question remained – why was she?

When they finally came up for air an hour or two later, Faith went to get up. "What," Jamie asked. She shook her head and slid a tank and her shorts on and walked downstairs. Jamie got up, pulled his blue jeans on and walked downstairs. "What's wrong," Jamie asked. Faith shook her head. "Faith, stop thinking it. We aren't losing each other. No matter what happens, we're gonna be alright," Jamie said. "And when you go on that tour and start with all the stuff that goes with it…" He kissed her. "Always had eyes for one woman at a time. You're that woman." "Stop alright? I know better Jamie. I know what happens on a damn tour. Don't forget that," Faith said. He warmed up dinner and they sat at the counter. "I'm not looking anywhere else. Don't want to. I'm blind to other girls Faith. You know better. Stop being worried." They relaxed and ate then he walked her upstairs and curled up with her in bed and turned on a movie.

Faith sat there all night thinking about what Jamie had said. Around 7am, Faith got up and got dressed. "Where are you going," Jamie asked. "For a run," Faith said. She went to leave the bedroom and he grabbed her hand and pulled her towards him. He kissed her and pulled her to him. "Jamie." He pinned her to the bed. "What," he asked. "I'm not losing a friendship. I'm not losing it to one stupid moment Jamie. We need to leave us as friends and not do...." He kissed her. "You trying to say that you don't want me? That you didn't? I know better," Jamie said. She got out from under him, grabbed her iPhone and her iPod and left for her run. She got 20 minutes into it and saw Deacon. She shook her head and went a different way.

"Faith," Deacon said. She kept going. "Fine. I get why you're pissed off," Deacon said. "I'm not getting between two guys who act like 2 year olds. Just go away," Faith said. He still followed her. She stopped and grabbed a refill in her water bottle and Deacon leaned her against the wall. "What," Faith asked. "I'm asking it and I want a straight answer," Deacon said. "What," Faith asked. "Do you want me or don't you," he asked. "Goodbye Deacon," Faith said. He kissed her. Faith pushed him away and left. She ran back to the house and walked in to see a white rose sitting on the steps leading upstairs. Faith grabbed her change of clothes, grabbed a shower and got changed. She walked upstairs, did her hair and makeup and as she finished brushing her teeth, she saw Jamie's hands pinning her to the counter.

"What," Faith asked. He kissed her neck. "How was the run," he asked. "If I hadn't bumped into Deacon, it would've been great," Faith said. "Guess he was pissed when you told him we were together now," Jamie said. "I have to go to work Jamie," Faith said. "You told him right," Jamie asked. Faith slid out of his arms and grabbed her purse. "Faith." "I'm going to work," Faith said. He kissed her. "This isn't a damn game Jamie. If that's why you're doing this then I'm out." She walked out the door and went to work.

She went through websites, questions from fans and a few additions or changes that the artists wanted. By the time lunch came, she was up to her eyeballs in work. An email came up and Faith ignored it. She kept working. A half hour later, a bag was plopped onto her desk with the smell of lobster Alfredo. She looked up and Jamie was locking the door and closing the blinds. "What are you doing here," Faith asked. "Making you eat lunch. Getting a straight answer about something and reminding you who's never leaving your damn side. You're that worried that we're gonna mess things up? Faith, I know you alright? Emma knows you too. She's the one that told me that we belong together. Faith, I can't just let this go. I don't want you being hurt anymore. I just want you. Is that so wrong?" "I'm working. Jamie, stop alright? You and Deacon are acting like little kids on a damn playground. I'm not a damn toy for you two to fight over. Just stop alright?" "I want you to myself. I'm not fighting him to have you in my life. He wants the game, he can play it alone." "Jamie, I need to finish this work up." He walked around her desk and kissed her, tipping her chair back. "Stop over-thinking everything. It's this simple babe. Have a little faith in what we're doing," Jamie said. "What are we doing? Ruining the friendship we've had all this time? Jamie, I can't just..." He kissed her again. "Stop over-thinking. Just go with it. We'll be find baby. I promise you," Jamie said. He kissed her again and let her up. "I'll finish packing up for the tour. We're leaving in the morning. Is there anything else you need," Jamie asked. "For my mind to stop thinking," Faith said. He kissed her. "I'll see what I can do with that," he teased. Faith smirked. "I'll see you at home," he said. A quick peck and he headed out. Faith sat back down and finished up, backed up the work to the laptop and went in to talk to Patrick.

"What's up Faith," Patrick asked. "So, I'm doing this tour thing starting tomorrow with Deacon and Jamie. You do realize those two are like fire and lighter fluid right?" "Faith, they're on separate sides of the hotels. For now, they're on separate tour buses. There's 20 weeks of the tour. Mondays and Tuesdays we can do a conference call to work on anything that comes up. That okay with you?" Faith nodded. "I just keep wondering what happens if something doesn't work out right. Do we have a backup to replace Deacon if we need it," Faith asked. "There's a few shows he can't do and we're putting someone in his place for those. I'll keep you posted. If you need anything, just say the word," Patrick replied. "If I give you a name can you make sure he doesn't get in to any of the shows," Faith asked. Patrick nodded. She handed him Evan's info and took her laptop. "Faith, don't forget this," Patrick said handing her the paycheck. "What's…" "This is the paycheck for the work you've done plus for the first month of the tour. If you need anything, say the word. We'll keep in contact," Patrick said. Faith nodded. She headed out and saw Jamie's truck at the door.

She shook her head and the passenger window opened. "What are you doing here," Faith asked. "Took your truck into the shop and they said that it's not a safe truck anymore. There was damage to the brakes. You aren't driving a truck that's been tampered with. We'll find you something else. We're bringing this on tour with us. Do you need anything else before we leave," he asked. "Sweater, leggings, a shield for the amount of crap he's gonna throw at me," Faith said. "Babe, that's what I'm here for. He's not getting anywhere near you," Jamie said. She got out of the truck, grabbed her laptop and walked back to the house. She walked in and Jamie was sitting on the steps.

She walked into the kitchen, got herself a drink and sat down outside. "Faith," Jamie said. "Want to make sure that you put your name on me? Since I'm just a damn possession to half the damn men in this planet. Have a good damn tour. I'm not going on that bus with either of you," Faith said. She finished her drink and went to walk inside. "I get that you're pissed off alright. He's not gonna cause shit or he's getting in shit from Patrick and not me. I don't want him bugging or hurting you. That's what I meant," Jamie said. She walked past him and went inside. She packed her things and he saw her looking through the real estate section. "Don't even bother to think it. Faith, pick a damn fight with me if you want to. You need to be safe and not being here isn't gonna happen. Faith, please," he said. "I'll meet you at the meet up spot," Faith said. She went to walk downstairs and he pulled her to him. "Faith." "No. I'm going. I have no choice but to go with you. I'm not playing this stupid ass game Jamie. Do whatever the hell you want, but just leave…." He kissed her. He picked her up, wrapped her legs around his waist and leaned her against the wall in the hallway. Her shorts hit the floor and so did his jeans.

He kissed, nibbled, bit and licked her neck. He kissed her until she begged to come up for air. He didn't stop and he didn't want to. When they hit that point where both of them were about to crumble, he walked her into the bedroom and leaned her onto the bed. They curled up and kept going until her legs were dead weight and neither of them had any strength left. She curled up in his arms. "We aren't breaking this off Faith. There's so few people that either of us trust enough to let go. I need you. I want you more than anything in this planet. Don't just walk away." He felt a tear slide over his shoulder. "Baby," he said. "Life is never gonna be normal again is it," Faith asked. He could feel her lip trembling. "It's a different normal Faith. One that both of us are gonna be okay in. Knowing what he did killed me too," Jamie said. "I wanted to start over Jamie. I can't when the past is still here," Faith said. "Meaning what," Jamie asked. "No more talking about him. Just let me figure myself out again," Faith replied. He kissed her. "I'll be back in a sec," Jamie said. He got up, cleaned up a little and was gone. The house was dead silent and Faith fell dead asleep.

Faith woke up an hour later from a nightmare. She looked all over and Jamie still wasn't there. She looked downstairs and the truck was gone. She was stuck. She wasn't gonna be able to leave, and she was stuck. She called Jamie and he didn't answer. Faith turned around and swore she saw Evan. She called Jamie again. "What's wrong," Jamie asked. "Where are you," she asked. "Pulling in the driveway." Faith hung up. She walked to the front door and Jamie came inside. She almost jumped into his arms. "Nightmare," he asked. Faith nodded. He kissed her and handed her a bag. "What's this," Faith asked. He kissed the tip of her nose with a smirk ear to ear. She opened the bag and saw the only thing that was going to make her laugh. "Are you seriously kidding me?" Faith pulled out the picture that Jamie had taken with her over a year ago when they were hopped up on sugar and sodas. "Jamie." "That's who you were before this. That's the woman you've always been. He's the only one that didn't want it to be that way. He's what changed you. This is the woman you were before him. You're scared of ghosts Faith. You're scared he's gonna come after you. He's not. I am keeping you safe no matter what. Second off, I love you. Got it?" Faith nodded. "Now, under that was your dinner. Get your butt over here and eat," Jamie said. She looked and saw the angel hair pasta with crab that she'd made him a million times. "Jamie," Faith asked. "What beautiful?" "Can I erase him," she asked. He kissed her. "Already have." They finished dinner, finished packing up and curled back up in bed together.

Chapter 3

Jamie got up the next morning with Faith and they got ready to head out. "No more worrying," Jamie asked. Faith shook her head. "What," he asked. "What happens if Evan shows at one of the stops," Faith asked. He kissed her. "Then you grab my glock and do what you have to," Jamie said. "I don't have a…." "You know how to shoot it right," he asked. Faith nodded. He kissed her. "We're gonna be alright. Nobody is hurting you, and nobody is ever laying a hand on you like he did. We're gonna be okay babe. I promise." Faith hugged him. He grabbed the bags, threw them in the truck and they headed off to meet everyone. He got them each the biggest Starbucks coffee that he could get for each of them and they hopped on the tour bus. The truck got loaded onto a trailer and they were off. Faith fell back asleep in Jamie's arms. He let her sleep a while and when they made a pit stop for fuel, the guys hopped off and grabbed a snack and Jamie kissed Faith and woke her up. "What," Faith asked. "Come with me," he teased. They got up and he walked her into the state room. "Jamie." He kissed her and closed the door. "What?" He wrapped his arms around her. "Trust me," he asked. Faith nodded. He leaned her onto the super soft bed and curled up with her. "What are you up to," Faith asked. He slid her belt off. "Jamie." He nibbled her lip. "What are we doing," Faith asked. "Being you and me," he replied.

They made love in the state room and curled up together. "I'm still scared," Faith said. He grabbed something from the pocket of his jeans. "What are you doing," Faith asked. He slid the silver band onto her ring finger on her right hand. "Jamie." "When you get scared, look at it. Remember that I'm gonna be there for you. Just give us a chance," he asked. Faith nodded. She didn't really know what else to do. In one move, he'd made her feel that much better. "I'm not leaving no matter what you think," Jamie said. She kissed him. A little while later, one of the guys knocked saying that Jamie had a call. He kissed Faith, devoured her lips and teased the hell out of her then got up, pulled his t-shirt and jeans on and walked into the sitting area and grabbed his cell.

Faith walked out and heard Jamie screaming at someone. "I said don't call her. That meant don't call. It didn't mean come after her and start being an idiot. You want your backside 20 feet under, keep doing what you are. Leave her the hell alone," Jamie said hanging up. Faith looked at him and he went straight to her. "Babe," he said. "Don't even think it," Faith said. She went around him and sat by herself. "Faith," he said. She put her ear buds in and turned her music up then started going through her emails on her laptop. Not even 15 minutes later, he grabbed her laptop and her hand. "What are you doing," he asked. She took her laptop back in her hand and walked into the state room, locking the door. She got her emails done, make the tweaks on the websites that were requested and then an email came through from Deacon:

I need to talk to you.

Faith replied back to him:

So that's who he was yelling at. Might not be a smart move. He already wants you 20 feet under. I can't do this Deacon. I'm not a pawn in your chess game.

She turned her laptop off just as the bus was stopping. Seconds later, Jamie walked in. "What," Faith asked. He put her laptop in the bag, took her hand and lead her outside. "What," she asked again. They went into the interview and he wasn't letting Faith out of his sight. He got changed and the second he went to head in, he kissed Faith. "Stop," Faith said pushing him away. "We're talking about this tonight," Jamie said. He walked into the interview and didn't take his eyes off Faith.

As soon as he was finished, Faith walked out and went down to the tour bus. In seconds, Deacon was dragging her to his bus. "What," Faith asked. "You're letting him make the decisions for you now," Deacon asked. "Just leave me be," Faith said. She went to walk away and Deacon grabbed her. He pulled her up the steps onto his tour bus and into the state room away from everyone. "Let go of my damn arm," Faith said. Deacon kissed her. "You aren't gonna be happy with him and you know it," Deacon said. She went to walk out and he grabbed her, pulling her to him and onto the bed. "We belong together. End of damn discussion," Deacon said. One kick and Deacon let go of her. She got out of the room, off the bus and directly into Jamie. "You alright," Jamie asked. Faith looked at him. "Go get on the bus," Jamie said. "You start anything you're sleeping alone," Faith said.

She walked back to their tour bus, hopped on and the guys distracted her. When Jamie came back 45 minutes later, Faith walked into the state room and locked the door. Jamie sat and worked on music with the guys and when they finally pulled into the hotel, Jamie went into the state room to talk to her. "We're checking in. Come on," Jamie said. "If I'm not getting my own room, forget it," Faith said. "Woman, stop being a pain in my ass. Let's go," Jamie said. They walked into the hotel, got their room keys and went up to their room. He walked her into the room and Faith fought him. "What," Faith asked. "Quit thinking that this…" "Let go Jamie. You think pushing him around is gonna end this? You either trust me to do the right thing or there's no point in being anywhere near you," Faith said. She grabbed her bag, grabbed one of the other room keys and went and got settled in her room. She finished up her emails, got some work done and went to go downstairs to get dinner. As she was walking towards the elevators, Jamie grabbed her hand and walked her back to his suite. "Let go," Faith said. He sat her down and dinner showed up at the suite.

She took her dinner and sat on the sofa. "Woman, get over here," Jamie said. "You decided kicking his butt was more important. Have a nice sleep alone," Faith said. She took her dinner to her room, locked the door and turned on a movie. A half hour later, Jamie walked into her room. "What are you doing Jamie," Faith asked. He took the dishes and put them on the counter. He walked over to her and kissed her. He pinned her to the bed, kicked his jeans off and leaned into her. "Jamie, quit it," Faith said. "We aren't getting in a fight over a pain in the ass. He wouldn't back off so I went and told him straight out that we were together. That he needed to back off or the whole tour with him was done. That's why I went there." "Just leave me alone," Faith said. He kissed her again. She got up and walked off. "Woman, why do you have to be so damn infuriating?" "Because I'm the only one who's gonna ever stand up to you," Faith said. She got changed and went down and sat by the pool.

Jamie came downstairs a half hour later, grabbed Faith's hand and walked her upstairs. "What," Faith asked when they hit the elevator. He kissed her. "I love you. Quit picking a damn fight with me," Jamie said. "Then quit telling me who I can and can't talk to and what I can and can't do. Just leave me be," Faith said. They walked off the elevator and Faith went to go back to her room. "Your stuff is back where it belongs," Jamie said walking her back to his room. "Can't just let me do what I want," Faith said. They walked into his room and she saw sterling roses. Sucking up was always one of Jamie's specialties. "You just don't get it do you," Faith asked. "I get that you can't just accept a compliment. I love you. I get you're mad at me about him but I just explained to him that he was getting in over his head. That he needed to leave you alone." "Right. Did that involve you putting your hands on him? Jamie, let me deal with my own things on my own," Faith said. "Stop. I went and talked to him and went through a few tour rules that we've always had. I am not going through this again with you. I love you. Nobody is getting in our way." "You done," Faith asked. "Nope," he replied. He kissed her. He picked her up, wrapping her legs around his waist and leaned her onto the king sized bed. "Would you just pay attention for five damn minutes," Jamie asked. "What," Faith asked. He handed her a rose.

"What are you trying to do," Faith asked. He kissed her. He devoured her lips until they felt like they were his. They didn't come up for air for over an hour. "I love you. Whether you want to be here or not, that isn't changing. I don't want to lose you," Jamie said. "Then stop trying to make me do what you want. Jamie, let me make my own decisions." He kissed her again and ended up making love to her. Making love wasn't even the right words. Devouring each other and becoming one was more like it. They didn't come up for air until almost 1am. By then, they fell asleep curled up together. Jamie's phone buzzed at 2:

Jamie, I know you're in town. I want you.

Faith saw it. She got up and slept on the sofa. She set her phone to wake her up before Jamie would be up and went back to sleep.

Jamie woke up around 9 and saw his phone on the pillow. The only thing on the screen was the text he'd got. He got up and Faith's things were gone. He walked into the TV room and saw her sitting on the sofa. "Faith," he said. "I'm staying in my own room. That's the end of it," she said. Faith got up and went to walk out. Jamie stopped her. "Doesn't mean I'd go," Jamie said. Faith shook her head. He got her bags and put them back in the bedroom. "Come on. We're going to squash this right now," Jamie said. "You have to be there for interviews at 10. Try again," Faith said.

He walked in hand in hand with Faith and got ready for the interview. As soon as it was done, Faith posted pictures she'd taken and one clip that the camera team had given her. A half hour or so later, Jamie snuck up behind her, wrapped his arms around her waist and walked her into the stadium. "What do you want," Faith asked. He walked her out to the stage. "Jamie." He kissed her. "Don't care if the entire planet knows it. Someday I'm gonna talk you into something more than this you know. I want you with me Faith. Whatever I have to do, I want you with me." "Jamie." "I hate being without you. I can't sleep, and I damn well can't concentrate. Just give me the chance Faith," he asked. "I have to go back Monday. I have a doctor's appointment," Faith said. "Then we go back for Monday," Jamie said. "Alone," Faith replied. "I'm playing the Opry on Tuesday night. Come with me," he asked. "You gonna stop talking crazy," Faith asked. He kissed her. It was a kiss that could've melted metal. "Keep doing that I'll forget why we're here altogether," Jamie said. He kissed her again then started sound check.

Faith went and tried to get some work done and ended up face to face with Deacon. He grabbed her hand and walked into his dressing room. He locked the door. "What are you doing," Faith asked. He pulled her to him and kissed her. "What are you doing," Faith asked. "Taking back what's mine," Deacon said. "You want to get your ass kicked don't you," Faith asked. He kissed her again. "I want you back. That's what I want," Deacon said. "Well this isn't gonna be the right way to do it. Deacon, we're together. That's it. No matter how many times you make a stupid move it's not changing," Faith said. She went to walk out and he grabbed her hand. "Faith," Deacon said. "Just don't. I've had enough of everyone fighting Deacon. I need to go do what I need to. I need to take care of me first," Faith said. She walked out and went back to Jamie's dressing room area. She tried to relax but there was no point. Stress was following her. Somehow she had to do something to end all of the bull crap between Deacon and Jamie. An hour later, Jamie walked into the dressing room.

"What you doing in here," Jamie asked. "Needed some peace and quiet," Faith replied. "Baby girl. I know something's wrong. Just say it." "Deacon. He's not letting up," Faith said. She could see it in Jamie's eyes that he was itching to kick Deacon's butt into the next solar system. "What did you tell him," Jamie asked. "That we were dating. That he needed to quit starting trouble." "Good." Jamie kissed her and pulled her to her feet. "What," she asked. He kissed her and held her tight. "Anything new on the work stuff," Jamie asked. Faith shook her head. "Then come with me. We're going back to the hotel for a little bit," Jamie said. "Why?" He kissed the tip of her nose and walked her out.

They got back to the hotel and walked into the room. "Now what was it that…." Jamie picked her up, leaned her onto the sofa and curled up with her. "This is what you were planning was it," Faith asked. "Privacy. Hell yeah. I get he wants to be with you but he's acting like an idiot," Jamie said. "And you acting like an over-protective big brother means what," Faith asked. He kissed her. "Means that I love you. It means that I don't want anything happening to you. After what you went through, I need to know that you're okay. You get that right?" "Jamie, enough. He's the history remember," Faith said. "He showed up at the venue," Jamie said. "So that's why you brought me back…" He kissed her. He got up, grabbed her hands and pulled her to her feet, walking her back into the bedroom. "You have…" He picked her up, kissed her and leaned her back onto the bed. "Jamie," Faith said. "We have a few hours left until we have to be back," Jamie said. He kissed her. Minutes later, his phone buzzed. Faith laughed and he muffled it with a kiss. "Phone," Faith said. He kissed her again and grabbed it. In seconds, he jumped up. "What," Faith asked.

"Stay here. Don't leave the room," Jamie said. "Tell me he didn't," Faith said. "Stay here. No causing shit and being a pain in the butt." Jamie walked out. An hour later, he walked back in, grabbed her hand and they got in a truck and headed straight to the tour bus.

"Are you gonna tell me what happened," Faith asked. "Security is staying with you. As soon as the show is done, we're leaving," Jamie said. "So I was right," Faith asked. He could see the panic hit her. "Faith." "I need to go Jamie," Faith said. He shook his head. He locked them into the state room and grabbed his 9mm gun out of his lock box. "Jamie," Faith said. He looked at her and saw the tears start. "He's not getting near you. That's all there is to it," Jamie said. "He's gonna keep coming until..." He kissed her and leaned into her on the king sized bed. "Jamie." He peeled her jeans off, kicked his off and snuggled in close to her, not letting her up for air. "We can't just..." He kissed her again and heard the door to the tour bus opening. "What..." He kissed her. He got up, pulled his jeans on, grabbed his gun and walked into the sitting area.

"He disappeared. We had him and he took off Jamie," the security guard said. "Do you realize how dangerous he is? Call the damn army if you have to. Keep him away from her and from me. If he does something stupid as shit, I'm not responsible for my actions. Got it," Jamie asked. "He's gonna take off. He's trying to avoid you. What do you want me to do Jamie?" "Get us out of here right after the show. I'm not staying around so he can find her and hurt her again." Security left and Jamie walked back into the state room. Faith was dressed and in his sweat shirt. "Faith," Jamie said. "Why won't he leave me alone? I didn't do anything to deserve this," Faith said. "Babe," he said trying to comfort her. She shook her head, walked past him and got off the bus. "Faith." She shook her head and walked back into the venue and sat in the dressing room. Jamie walked in a little while later.

Faith had most of her stuff packed up. "You aren't going back to the house alone," Jamie said. "At least I'm safe there. He doesn't know where..." "You're safer here with me. I promised you that you weren't gonna need to be scared anymore. I'm sticking to that promise Faith. He's not hurting you again." He sat down with her and she just curled up in his arms. "He's never gonna stop." "I know you think he won't but he will. I promise you," Jamie said. They relaxed a while, he tried to calm Faith down and she fell asleep in his arms. He got up a little while later and checked on updates from security.

"Anything," Jamie asked. The officer he talked to shook his head. Jamie walked around then came back to the dressing room. The door was locked. He got security to open it and saw Faith on the phone. "He's shown up in more than one place. I just need him to stop. Whatever you have to do," Faith said. "The papers were served on him 48 hours ago. If he steps foot near you, contact the police," the officer said. "What happens if he makes a move," Faith asked. "Meaning if he causes you harm? Self-defence," the officer said. "My boyfriend was trying to protect me but Evan's lost his mind. I don't want anything…." "Keep in contact with us alright? No matter what," the officer said. They hung up and Faith looked up at Jamie. "I'll stomp his ass before he puts a hand on you again," Jamie said. "And you'll end up in jail. Jamie, I'm not safe here alright. You aren't." He walked over to her and kissed her. "We're gonna be okay." "What…" He kissed her again and walked her outside to catering to have dinner. She barely ate. Jamie grabbed her something and put it in a container for later. He walked her back to the dressing room and grabbed his bag then walked her out to the tour bus.

"Jamie," Faith said. He dropped his bag, picked her up and walked her back to the state room. They made love on that bed without a disturbance, without any interruptions. He would've done anything to get her to feel better. He curled up with her until her heart calmed. "Remember what I said. Nobody is hurting you," Jamie said. Faith kissed him and for the first time in a long time he thought she might just be alright. He got changed, showered and Faith kissed him for luck. She walked him inside hand in hand right past Deacon. Jamie kissed her and Faith sat at the side of the stage watching him.

"I need to talk to you," Deacon said coming up behind her. "Just stop. He's on stage. Don't cause more crap," Faith said. Jamie walked over to grab his other guitar, kissed her and walked back on stage. "This is what you want? Someone who tells you what you can and can't do," Deacon asked. "Someone who's had my back through everything. Someone that I know better than most people. Deacon, just stop trying to get in the middle of all of this," Faith said. "I want you back. Faith, what the hell did I do so damn wrong," Deacon asked. "You don't want to know Deacon. I have my reasons and I made a decision. That's all you need to know," Faith said. Jamie looked over at her as he sang the one and only song he hoped would remind Deacon to back right off. When he finished, the crowd was screaming for Jamie and he waved goodbye and walked straight to Faith, picking her up and kissing her. They walked back to the dressing room and Jamie grabbed his things. They hopped on the tour bus and took off.

"So what did Deacon want this time," Jamie asked. "Don't know. Wasn't paying attention," Faith said. He kissed her and they hung out together and watched a movie. The guys all teased her and they were giggling and joking around on their way to the next stop. "Still don't know why we had to leave so damn soon," Greg said. Greg was the over-spoken guitar player who Jamie considered family. Only thing was that Jamie wouldn't tell Greg a thing about what was going on. "So what were you running around all afternoon for," Greg asked trying to get a shred of info out of Jamie. "Just a bit of personal stuff. Nothing major," Jamie said. "Dude, if this tour is lasting that long we need to know," Greg said. He held Faith a little tighter. She shook her head.

Faith got up a little while later and went and sat in the state room going through emails. When she got one from Patrick saying what a great job she was doing, she almost wanted to say something to him. Instead, Jamie came into the state room and they curled up together and got some sleep. Somehow the feel of his arms wrapped around her had her fast asleep. The first descent night of sleep that she'd had.

She woke up the next morning to the feel of Jamie kissing her neck and her shoulder. "Can't just let me sleep," Faith asked. He nibbled her neck. "Sleep," Faith asked. "Better idea," Jamie said. He undid her jeans. "Jamie." "You are just too damn cute when you're sleeping," Jamie whispered causing goose bumps up and down her body. "What are you up to," Faith asked. "Seducing my woman. That allowed," he asked.

"Depends," Faith teased. He kissed her and his warm hands slid down her torso. They had sex. Toe-curling, hot enough to steam the mirrors sex that they almost had to muffle each other with kisses to drown out the noise from. Her body was shaking in his hands. "What are we doing," Faith asked. "Being you and me. Being what I wanted us to be. Being what we deserve to," Jamie said. He didn't let her out of his arms and he wasn't about to move. "You know how silly this is," Faith asked. He kissed her and held her close. They barely made it out of bed when he felt the bus stop. He smirked. "What," Faith asked. He kissed her again and they had round 2. Finally they came up for air and her legs were shaky. So were his.

"We have to…" "No we don't. We're gonna be on the bus for two days getting to the next stop. You and me," he said. "Jamie, we can't just stay in…" He kissed her. Faith pulled on her shorts and his sweater and went to grab something to eat. "About time y'all woke up," Greg teased. "We were up talking," Faith said. Jamie walked in 10 minutes later, wrapped his arms around her and sat down behind her wrapping his arms around her and pulling her into his lap. "Y'all need to just get a room. You're making us sick," Greg said. "Funny," Jamie teased. They hung out, the guys worked on some music and Faith tried getting some work done on a few more websites.

By dinner time, they were at the next stop and checking into a hotel. "Finally. I don't have to hear y'all," Greg teased. Jamie threw the hand towel at Greg. They got their bags and headed up to the room. They checked in, Jamie and Faith had dinner and curled up on the sofa. Jamie was working on some music and Faith had a long hot bath in the Jacuzzi tub. He walked in an hour later with a Jack and cola for Faith and sat down on the edge of the tub. "How's the music going," Faith asked. "Needed some inspiration," he said. "So what are you doing in here again," Faith asked. He kissed her. He peeled his shirt off. "Don't you dare," Faith said. "Don't I dare what?" He splashed her with the bath water. "You little…" It ended up in a water fight that soaked the floor in the bathroom. She chased him into the bedroom wearing one of the hotel fluffy robes and he tackled her to the bed.

"What are you up to," Faith asked. "So, since we're way out here in the middle of nowhere, I had an idea," Jamie said. "Which is what," Faith asked. "Going down to one of those little chapels," Jamie said. "In a church mood? Have a blast," Faith teased. He kissed her. "Come with me," he asked. "What are you trying to say," Faith asked. He grabbed his leather jacket and pulled out a little black velvet box. Faith shook her head. "Babe," he said. "You aren't asking what I think you are. Jamie we haven't been together that long. Stop rush..." He kissed her. "Well," he asked. "Well what," Faith asked. He opened it. "I designed it for you," Jamie said. "When did you do this," Faith asked. "A month after we met. When you first got together with stupid idiot. Say yes," Jamie asked. "Can't just wait," Faith asked. He kissed her. "Baby," Jamie said. "Quit. We just got together," Faith said. He slid it on her finger. "Jamie," Faith said. "Marry me," he asked. "The tour just started. You might change your mind," Faith said. One kiss and she was back to being putty in his hands. "Say it," Jamie asked. "If you wait until we really know each other than fine. If you're thinking tomorrow, answer is no," Faith said. He kissed her. "Next summer," Jamie said. "Jamie." "Say yes," he teased. "Why?" "Because I made you a promise. Nobody is hurting you ever again," he said. "And a ring has super powers does it," Faith teased. He kissed her. "Say yes." Faith kissed him. She nodded. A smile went across his face so wide a tractor trailer could've driven through. They spent the rest of the night curled up together in that giant bed.

Faith got up the next morning and her fingers were linked together to Jamie's. "Morning beautiful," he said. "Morning yourself. Am I allowed to get up," Faith teased. He kissed her neck. "Depends," he teased. Faith kissed him and got up. She ordered breakfast for them then hopped into the shower. When she came out, Jamie was on the phone.

"Just make sure that it's secure this time. Hiding out in the damn tour bus isn't a smart move and y'all know it," Jamie said. "The cops have him in custody Jamie. He's not getting out," the man said on the other line. "Then if I see him I can kick his ass right," Jamie asked. "Understood. Just take care of that fiancée of yours," the man replied. They hung up and Jamie noticed her in the doorway. "What's up sexy," Jamie asked. "Who were you talking to," Faith asked. "One of the security guys. He's supposed to keep an eye out for Evan. That's all he was there to do," Jamie said. "Stop blaming him being an idiot on someone else," Faith said. Jamie got up and kissed her. "Seriously," Faith said. "I'm just worried that he's gonna pull something stupid," Jamie said. Faith kissed him. "Stop worrying. Whatever he tries to do we can deal with it," Faith said. He kissed her and hugged her. "I have to do an interview at noon. Do you want to go for a walk for a bit," Jamie asked. Faith nodded. He kissed her, smacked her butt and went to hop into the shower. Just as he was stepping out, breakfast showed up. Faith signed for breakfast and sat down to see the newspaper. She flipped to the entertainment section and there were pictures of her with Jamie. The headline read:

JAMIE GILBERT SPOTTED OUT WITH NEW LADY

Faith put the paper on the bed. Jamie came out in his jeans, pulling his shirt on and had a grin ear to ear. "That what the ring thing was all about? Jamie, I swear if you…" He kissed her. "That's not what it was," Jamie said. She finished getting dressed then went and did her makeup. "Faith," Jamie said. "If that was your real reason I'm kicking your butt home," Faith said. He kissed her neck. "It isn't. Faith, the day we met the first time I wanted you. I always have ever since." "Jamie." He kissed her.

* * *

Fact was, that day all those years ago that she came face to face with Jamie, she had a crush on him. She always had. She met him in a little bar in Athens Georgia. She walked in and he looked right at her. After hours of trying to send her drinks and notes she finally gave in. He walked over to her just as she was getting ready to leave. "One drink," Jamie begged. "You could be with anyone that was here. Why me," Faith had asked. "Because I don't want just someone. I want the one," Jamie had said. "And you think you're meeting her right now," Faith teased. "Come sit with me," he asked. They had a drink or two and talked for what seemed like hours. "Why me," Faith asked. "The only woman who wasn't drooling and staring at me. You listened to the lyrics. You understood them. That's why," Jamie said. "Cute," Faith said. "I try.

Those girls you came with left. Did you need a ride home?" "Jamie, I appreciate it but..." "Guys I'm driving her home. Be back in an hour or so," Jamie said. He walked her out, opened her door for her and they got in the truck. "So where to," Jamie asked. "You're serious?" "Address," Jamie asked. He pulled out a little bit later and started driving her home, intentionally going the long route so they had time to talk.

From that day on, they were friends. He'd had a thing for her from that first day on but he knew that she deserved someone who would be at her side. He wanted more than anyone to be that man. When Faith first met Evan, it almost killed Jamie. "Why would you go all the way to Virginia to be with someone like that? Faith, just give me a chance," Jamie had said. "Why? Because you want me soooo bad?" "Because I have a feeling you're getting in over your head. Something doesn't sit right with me about him," Jamie said. "He's not you. That's what bugs you," Faith said. "Faith, you won't even let me get him checked out," Jamie said. "If I screw up, you can have your way Jamie. I'm making my decision and I'm staying with it," Faith said.

He had talked her into one last date before she left to be with Evan. It was his only chance to get her to see him as her man. He took her out for dinner to one of her favorite places. After dinner he took her for a walk and they had a few drinks. By the end of the date, both of them were tipsy. They went to a hotel and ended up in the longest kiss they'd ever had. It went from the hallway, to the sofa and into the bed. They made love for what seemed like hours. Jamie fell asleep at 3am and Faith snuck out at 5 and went home. She packed up and was gone by the time Jamie woke up. He saw the empty bed and it killed him. When he started that tour, he was determined that he was gonna find her. Thanks to Emma he did, but not the way he'd wanted.

The minute their eyes met again he was in deeper than he thought he could ever be.

*　*　*

"The minute we met the first time, I kicked myself for not putting it on your finger. I designed it and got it made on the off chance that we'd be together again. That's why I put it on your damn finger," Jamie said. "I was with him for over a year Jamie. Why…" He kissed her. "I never gave up on my music and I damn well never gave up on you. I haven't even dated since then Faith. Try to remember back. I'm the one that got left behind. Not you." Faith walked down to the elevator. "You expected me to choose. You knew I was going Jamie. Fine. It was a stupid move that I'll kick myself for, but it was my decision," Faith said. "And I promised to stand by you no matter what. The minute he made you cut off contact was when my buddies came and stayed in the park. They kept an eye out because I was scared stiff that he was gonna kill you. He would've," Jamie said. "It was a mistake alright," Faith said. He kissed her. "That's why you're staying safe from now on," he said. He didn't let go of her hand the rest of the morning.

They walked and talked and walked some more then headed over to the venue to do sound check. "Pick a song babe," Jamie said. "Cuffs," Faith teased. He kissed her. "Girl after my heart." Jamie kissed her again and headed into sound check. He couldn't help but smile when he saw Faith sitting front row. When security walked over to her and handed her a note, he about snapped. "What do you mean he wants to talk to me? I thought he was in jail," Faith said. Jamie had become pretty good at reading lips. He looked at Faith and shook his head. When her hands went through her hair, he stopped and hopped down, coming straight to her. "What," Jamie asked. She handed Jamie the note. "You're not moving from this spot. Jamie made a call and a half hour later his buddies showed. "He's at the damn gate Jamie," his buddy Andrew said. "And," Jamie asked. "Done. He's scared crapless. Second he saw us he took off," Jamie's other buddy Jake said. "Just watch for him. He comes near her I'm picking the little shit off myself," Jamie said. Faith shook her head and wiped the tears away. Jamie picked her up and carried her back to the dressing room.

Chapter 4

"He's not getting that close to you Faith," Jamie said. "He's supposed to be in jail too Jamie. He's not gonna leave me alone. I'm the only one that had the balls to take off," Faith said. "And you're the one that's gonna be safe. He's not gonna get in here and he's not getting one step near you without a bullet in his damn head," Jamie said. "I just wanna go home," Faith said. "Babe, running away is only gonna make it worse. You're not gonna be alone until he's in custody. When I'm on stage, these two knuckleheads are staying with you. That okay," Jamie asked. Faith nodded. He kissed her again. "Nobody is getting a hand on you tonight. Not on my damn watch," Jamie said. He kissed her again and they walked back out to the stage. Faith sat down on the edge of the stage and Jamie finished his sound check. As soon as he was done, they went out to the catering area, grabbed dinner and went and sat back on the bus together.

A half hour later, the guys walked on the bus. "Why do you look worried," Jamie asked as Andrew walked on. "He's out on bail and followed you here. He's not gonna back off Jamie. Nobody can find the idiot. He went and died and chopped his damn hair," Jake said. "Then find him. If he's here, he won't be that hard to track down," Jamie said. They put his picture in the hands of every ticket taker in the stadium. If he showed, Evan was going down. Faith barely said a word the rest of the day. She came out and watched Jamie's show and Deacon was a foot behind her still trying to figure out what was wrong. When he was about to make his move, Jamie walked over to Faith and kissed her. "Come," he whispered. Faith shook her head. He kissed her and grabbed her hand walking her on stage. "This is my fiancée Faith. I promised y'all a new song. She's who I wrote it about," Jamie said. It was the song that he'd been humming in the shower and had been working on every night when he couldn't sleep. It was the story of when they met. When he walked until he couldn't anymore and kissed her when he couldn't restrain. The ending was hearing yes. He kissed her and everyone cheered. "The only woman I'm ever gonna marry y'all. He kissed her and Faith waved and headed off.

"You're marrying him," Deacon asked. "He asked me last night. Deacon, I know you aren't gonna understand this, but it's right. Please just don't stand in the way," Faith said. "Why him," Deacon asked. Not even a minute later, Jake came and grabbed her hand and walked her back to the dressing room. "What," Faith asked. "Stay here. Don't freak out. Don't move," Jake said. Faith started shaking. Security was posted outside the door. She heard their radios saying they'd spotted him finally. He went on a damn rampage when he heard that Faith and Jamie were engaged. A half hour later, Jamie came down to the dressing room, packed his bag up and walked her out to the tour bus. The door was locked and guarded with 4 guards.

"Jamie," Faith said. "They have him. Jake and Andrew have him baby. You're safe," Jamie said curling her into his arms. "Is that why you announced…" He kissed her. "I'd scream it from every mountain if I could. That was sharing with the fans. They know me baby. I did write that song for you," Jamie said. Faith kissed him. Jamie kicked the state room door shut. "Just promise me that nobody is getting hurt," Faith said. His arms wrapped around her and his body leaned into her. "Nobody is hurting you again. I love you," Jamie said. That kiss lasted a while until it led to more. Fact was, being curled up in his arms was the only place she felt safe until she knew that Evan was in custody for good. Jamie made love to her and they fell asleep curled up together,

Jamie woke up an hour later with Faith's arms still wrapped around him. He pulled his t-shirt and jeans on and walked back out to see what was going on. Jake came back bruised and so did Andrew. "And," Jamie asked. "Busted a rib and got a black eye but the cuffs and shackles are on him. He's in maximum lockup. He's not coming back," Jake said. "You two okay," Jamie asked. "Doc said yeah. Just need ice and TLC," Andrew said. They hopped on the bus with Jamie and Faith and fell asleep in the bunks. He went back into the bedroom, locked the door and slid back into bed with Faith. "Where did you go," Faith asked. "It's over. He's in custody. The guys are a little bumped up but you're safe baby. No more worrying," Jamie said. "Promise," Faith asked. "Get some sleep beautiful. We have one more stop and we're going home," Jamie said.

They got home Monday morning super early. They finally got sleep in their own bed and Jamie slept like a baby. Around 10, Faith got up and went downstairs to check in with her boss. "So we got some great comments with the new websites. Everyone loves your changes and the updates. How is the tour going with Deacon and Jamie," her boss asked. "Good. Deacon is holding his own and Jamie keeps impressing the heck out of his fans. Think that the mid-concert updates I started for his tour are kind of impressive. The fans are liking them. Gets them a little closer to him I guess," Faith said. "We're gonna try to do that for all the artists we have and see what the result is. That was a great idea Faith," Patrick said. "Thank you," she replied. "And I hear we have congrats to share. We heard that Jamie proposed on the weekend. Since when were you two together," Patrick asked. "We dated a long time ago. When I came back here and started working here we just picked up where we left off. We've been best friends a long time," Faith said. "Well we wish you an amazing life together. I hear he even got a song out about you two. Any chance he's willing to perform it at the Opry tomorrow," Patrick asked. "I'll talk him into it I'm sure," Faith replied. They went through some more work and then they were done for the day. Jamie came walking downstairs and got them both a coffee. He headed into the office and handed one to Faith.

"And what did everyone think of the ring," Jamie asked. "They just said congrats. Was more a business meeting," Faith said. "Still worried," he asked. "Now that he's in custody, no. Still making you slow down," Faith teased. He kissed her. "And what about the mid-concert ideas," he asked. "They loved them. Makes people really want to be at the show. May sell out more concerts," Faith replied. He kissed her again. "Then come have breakfast with me," Jamie said. They got up and went into the kitchen, made breakfast and curled up together on the chaise outside. "Think you should probably call your folks and tell them," Jamie said. "What about your parents," Faith asked. "Told them I was gonna do it. They love you and you know it," Jamie said. "Nice," Faith said. He dialed her mom and dad's house line and put the phone on speaker. He kissed her. He came up for air just as her mom was answering.

"And how's the most amazing daughter in the planet," her mom asked. "Jamie's here too mom," Faith said. " So he talked some sense into you did he," her mom teased. "Sorta found each other. Anyway, I meant to call you. Um, Jamie and I are..." "We got engaged on the weekend," Jamie said. "Well, welcome to the family," her dad said chiming in. "Thank you. I promise I'm gonna make her happy," Jamie said. "You better. As long as she has that smile ear to ear we're all good," her dad said. "Promise I will. We're not gonna even start planning until next year," Jamie said. Faith took the phone off speaker. "You sure you're okay baby girl," her dad asked. "I left Evan. Jamie helped. I'd probably be dead without him," Faith said. "Evan called here looking for you. I told him to stay away. You sure you're safe," her dad asked. "Now I am. I'm just glad Jamie was there," Faith said. "If you need us, say the word alright," her mom said. "I will. I love you guys," Faith said hanging up. Jamie kissed her. "What do you want to do," Jamie asked. "Are you singing my song tonight," Faith asked. "Tomorrow night. Private two person show tonight," he teased.

He rehearsed with the guys a while then went and checked on Faith. "I'm heading out to the store for a few. Do you need..." He kissed Faith. "I love you," he said. "Love you too. I'll be back in an hour. Promise," Faith said. He kissed her again and almost knocked her purse from her hands. "I need to go before the traffic..." He kissed her one last time then looked in her eyes. "The fear's gone," Jamie said. Faith nodded and hugged him. He kissed her cheek. She headed out and went down to the mall.

Faith grabbed a few things for herself, a couple things for Jamie and a few things that they still needed at the house. She grabbed something to wear to the Opry the next night then headed home. She walked in and saw candles and heard some of Jamie's romantic slow songs. "What are you up to," Faith asked. She heard him on the phone. She walked into the kitchen and another woman was there. "Great," Faith said. She heard Jamie's phone drop and he ran upstairs after Faith. "Baby," he said. She shook her head.

"What can you possibly use as an excuse? We've been engaged for what? Four days? Surprise you lasted that long," Faith said. She went to grab her bag and Jamie blocked her into the walk in closet. "Move," Faith said. "She showed up here and wouldn't leave. It's not what you're thinking. The candles and everything was for you," he said. She pushed him out of the way and started putting her things in her bag. "Faith," he said. She grabbed her things from the bathroom and what clothes she had. "You can't just leave." "Watch me," Faith replied.

She walked down the stairs and Jamie grabbed her hand. "Faith, don't do this," Jamie said. She went to take the ring off and he stopped her. "You go, I'm coming with you," Jamie said. "You have…" He kissed her. "I'm not letting you leave. Faith, she showed up. I swear that it isn't what it looks like," Jamie said. "Whatever Jamie. I'm not getting between you two Jamie. Have fun," Faith said. He kissed her again, picked her up, wrapped her legs around him and walked up the stairs. He leaned her back onto the bed. "Get off," Faith said. "I'm not letting you leave like this," he said. "You don't get up you'll be on the floor. Move," Faith said. "You're not walking out." "Watch me," Faith said. She got up and he wouldn't let go. "Jamie." "I love you. You can't just leave," Jamie said. She walked away, went downstairs and walked out the front door. She threw her things in his truck and left.

Jamie went into the garage and got in the other truck and took off after her. He caught up to her and after 20 minutes of getting her to pull over, she finally did. "What do you want Jamie? You want me to sit there and put up with some other woman being in the house? You put a damn ring on my finger and you think you own me. Jamie, leave me alone. Take the stupid…" He wouldn't let her take it off. "Faith, stop. Just come home. She showed up on her own Faith. There's nothing I could do to shut her up and get her out. She intentionally tried getting in the middle. She found out we were engaged and hit the roof. I didn't and I damn well don't want her there. Babe, come home. Please," Jamie said. She went to get back in the truck and he grabbed her and pulled her to him. He kissed her with a kiss that she couldn't shake. He picked her up and sat her on the tailgate. "I can't do this without you. Baby, please," Jamie said. He kissed her again and held her so tight he could feel the air coming in and out. "I can't lose you," he said. "I'll meet you at the Opry tomorrow..." He wasn't about to take that. It wasn't enough. "Follow me home," he begged. "She gone," Faith asked. "Yeah she's gone. She didn't belong in our house. She's not welcome there either," Jamie said. "One..." He kissed her. "Home," he asked. Faith nodded.

They started driving back. Faith started wondering if all of this was right. She needed to know what happened. She needed to know that she had no reason to worry. She needed to know that once and for all she was gonna have him all to herself. She'd played the game before when Evan tried to talk her into an open relationship. He'd forced her hand, forced her into it and had a gun to her head making her stay. Her life was in jeopardy the entire time she was there. Every time she attempted to walk, her life was in jeopardy. Either there was a gun to her head or she was getting run off the road. Faith got to the gate and something told her that she shouldn't go back.

She went to back up and there was another car behind her. Pushed into it was an understatement. She pulled in, pulled into the driveway and still hadn't got out of the truck. "Faith," Jamie said. He reached in and grabbed the keys. "Come out of the truck," Jamie said. "She gone," Faith asked. "Babe, please," Jamie said. She grabbed her purse and her bag and got out. She shook her head and started walking towards the gate. He ran after her and picked her up, carrying her into the house. "Put me down," Faith said. He put her down onto the bed upstairs. "Jamie," Faith said. "I can't let you go," he said. She broke away from him and walked downstairs. She got something to drink and saw that whoever it was left something for Jamie. She went and sat outside and turned the outside gas fireplace on. She curled up on the chaise and had her drink. Jamie came outside with a glass of Jack and topped hers up with the bottle.

"It's not gonna get me back on your side," Faith said. "She showed up on her own. Faith, there is no way in hell that I would voluntarily invite her over. Babe, you're the one I've wanted. You're the only one I ever wanted. Please," Jamie said. Faith took a big gulp of her drink. "Faith," he said. The worry started kicking in. "I walk in and you're sitting there with some woman. What do you expect? That I'm gonna jump you in front of some random stranger?" "Baby stop. I had nothing to do with it." "You let her in Jamie. She walked in the door and wouldn't leave. Please. I love you. I wouldn't jeopardize us ever. Please," Jamie said. "So you let her in the damn house? She had to get through the gate Jamie. Someone had to authorize it. Don't pull that with me," Faith said. "I was doing something romantic for us," he said. "And? Looks like that's not happening," Faith replied. She guzzled the rest of her drink and went inside. "Faith," Jamie said. She walked upstairs and went and had a hot shower. She tried washing the pain away. Instead, he walked into the bathroom and slid into the shower with her. He kissed her neck and wrapped his arms around her. "Jamie," Faith said. He turned her towards him and kissed her. She pushed him away and stepped out, wrapping herself in a towel.

Faith changed into a t-shirt and fuzzy socks and slid into bed, turning the light off. Jamie came out of the shower, wrapped a towel around him and walked into the bedroom. "Just talk to me," Jamie said. "What do you want me to do Jamie? Forget that I walked in to another woman trying to make a move on you? If you want me to let go of it then give me time to," Faith said. He slid into bed beside her. His arm slid around her and he tried to sleep.

Jamie got up the next morning and Faith was gone from the bed. Her things were still there at least. He pulled his track pants on with a tank and walked downstairs. She was doing yoga outside. He made coffee and breakfast and brought it outside to her. He waited for her to talk and say something, anything, but she didn't. When she finished her yoga, she grabbed breakfast and went to go back inside. "Faith, please," Jamie said. "What? Want me to forget it," Faith asked. "Forgive," he asked. She sat down. "How am I supposed to do that," Faith asked. "Kick her ass," he replied. He was trying to make her laugh. "I'm going to the gym," Faith said. "Then I'm coming with you," Jamie said. He got up and kissed her. They had something to eat then headed off to the gym together. He opted to take her straight to the kickboxing bags. An hour later, they were both laughing. "Told ya kicking her butt would make you feel better," he joked. They got changed and headed home.

They got to the house and headed inside. "You coming to sound check," Jamie asked. "Opry night. Hell yeah I'm going. You know I love that Opry house," Faith said. "Sound check is at 3. Lunch before?" "Jamie." "Come on. Baby we're playing the Opry. Just come with me. It's not like I'm asking you to marry me on stage," Jamie said. Faith walked upstairs, showered and got changed. Jamie walked into the bedroom and walked up behind her. "What," Faith asked. "What you wearing tonight," he asked. "Blue jeans," Faith said. He shook his head. "I'm not the one going on stage Jamie." "The black dress," he said. Faith walked away. "Fine. The pale pink one," Jamie said. "Putting me on display? Jamie, enough." She walked downstairs, grabbed a bottle of water and headed outside. "Where are you going," Jamie asked. "Opry Mills. I'll meet you there," Faith said. He took his truck keys back. He walked upstairs, put her dress and his change of clothes into his bag and came downstairs walking out the door hand in hand with her.

They left their stuff at the Opry and went and walked around the mall a bit. "Can't just walk around on my own can I," Faith asked. He walked her into a few places, got a few things that he thought she loved then had a quick snack and headed back to the Opry. "Jamie, I can't keep…" He kissed her and walked her onto the Opry stage. "Tell me why I want you here. Try singing something. Tell me how easy it is to do this on my own," Jamie said. "I can't just hold your hand," Faith said. He kissed her. "Be here. That's all I need," he said. "What about what I need," Faith asked. "Name it," Jamie said. "To believe that I can trust you. To believe that the next time I walk in that door I won't be walking into that. I told you before Jamie. You want the single life while you're on tour, I'm not gonna be there. I'm not gonna watch you do whatever…" He kissed her, devouring her lips until her toes curled. "What are you…" He kissed her again. "I want you as my wife. The single stuff is long ago over. I don't want anyone else," he said. Faith looked down and they were standing in that sacred circle on the stage.

Everyone before that moment had been in that exact spot. From Patsy Cline to Tammy Wynette. From Jason Aldean, Luke Bryan and Rascal Flatts to George Jones and George Strait. The sacred circle was an understatement. He wasn't letting go. She got a feeling surrounding her telling her that someone was listening. "I don't want anyone else Faith. You're the only one I want. She was an old friend who started shit. That's it baby." Faith went to walk away and she couldn't. "Faith," Jamie asked. "What?" "Do you love me or don't you," he asked. She nodded. He kissed her again. He walked her backstage and into one of the dressing rooms. "No more worrying. No more thinking that some idiot woman can get between us. Nobody, not even a cement truck filled with 1000 feet of concrete can do that. We're together for a reason. We're here for a reason. Please," he asked. "Fine. If you start shit again…" He kissed her and held her tight. She went and sat down while Jamie chilled and did sound check.

Faith sat down second row. Once she did sit, she felt like there was a breeze going past her. She slid her sweater on and if felt like someone was holding her hand. It was almost creepy, but somehow it was comforting. Jamie did sound check and was amazing as always, but something didn't seem right with Faith. She got up and walked into the back, wandering through the halls of the Opry. It hit her that there was too much history to not treat it right. When she came back to the dressing room, Jamie was sitting there waiting for her.

"Where'd you go," Jamie asked. "Was just walking around a bit," Faith said. "We goin to dinner," Jamie asked. Faith nodded. They headed over to the restaurant, had a relaxing dinner and headed back to the Opry. Faith did her hair and makeup then got changed and helped Jamie get ready. "You okay," he asked. Faith nodded. "You haven't been that quiet since we were moving into the house. What's going on Faith," Jamie asked. "Just got a creepy feeling while I was sitting down there," Faith said. Jamie kissed her. "You aren't sitting down there tonight. This is that day," Jamie said. She kissed him and sat down side stage with him until he had to go on for his first set.

When Jamie went on, he still stared at her. Faith did her best to relax. The co-ordinator came over to talk to her. "Jamie asked me to come over. He had an idea about doing the ceremony here. That okay with you," she asked. "When did he suggest," Faith asked. "May next year," she said. Faith left the stage and went and sat in the dressing room, putting her feet up. Again, the feeling that someone was with her had her creeped out. She went to get up and the door wouldn't open.

Jamie came in a little while later. "You okay," he asked. Faith nodded. "Then why are you being so quiet? You didn't even watch the set," he said. "Got a really weird feeling. Decided to come in and lay down for a little bit," Faith said. Jamie sat down with her. "Babe," he said. Faith kissed him. "We okay," he asked. Faith nodded. He went and got them a drink. When he came back in, Faith was shivering. "What's wrong," Jamie asked. "Why do I keep feeling like someone's in here other than us," Faith asked. "It's the Opry. There is someone other than us. It's a full house tonight," Jamie teased.

Jamie went on to do his other set and things got quiet backstage. Faith felt an arm around her. "Trust him. Nobody is gonna love you like that," a voice said. "Who are you," Faith asked. "Take him back once. It happens again, run," the voice said. "Who are you," Faith asked. "The Cline," the voice said. All of a sudden Faith could hear Jamie on stage again. Faith looked around and whoever it was talking to her had left. Jamie walked over to her. "You okay," he asked. Faith nodded. She went and sat down and waited for Jamie to finish getting packed up.

"I don't know what to do anymore. Am I supposed to trust him? He could be gone with anyone. What happens when I get left behind," Faith said. "He forgets that he has you, remind him he does. He cheats, get revenge," the voice said. "What if it doesn't work," Faith asked. "Unless he's ignoring you, stand by him. That's what Tammy's song said," the voice replied. Faith looked up and Jamie was sitting on the edge of the stage. "You okay," he asked. Faith nodded and he took her out to Tootsie's for a drink.

Faith walked in and those words and wisdom were still repeating on a loop in her mind. They had a drink and headed home. "You sure you're okay," Jamie asked. Faith nodded. "Was just thinking about all the history of being in the Opry. Sorta caught up with me," Faith said. He kissed her. They went home and that conversation she'd had with whoever it was at the Opry had her freaked out. Jamie curled up with her in bed and Faith turned towards him. "What's wrong," he asked. Faith kissed him. "Babe." "What was up with asking that lady about having our wedding at the Opry," Faith asked. "Was an idea I was throwing around," he said. "Wedding is about two people, not one," Faith said. "It was an idea," he said. Faith rolled over and went to sleep.

Faith woke up the next morning and sat downstairs. She looked through her emails, worked on the other websites and checked fan reaction to the Opry performance. She added stuff on to Deacon's site and in minutes he emailed her:

You're up this early and working? Couldn't sleep or what?

Faith replied back:

Shouldn't you be working on music or something?

She finished up the changes, packed up and got ready to head back out on the road. Not even 15 minutes later, her phone was ringing. "What," Faith asked. "Obviously something's wrong. Change your mind about marrying him," Deacon asked. "When you decide to grow up and leave me to make my own decisions let me know. I'm done Deacon. Quit starting crap," Faith said. "You looked spooked last night. I'm allowed to be worried," he said. "Was just trying to make a decision. I'm fine," Faith said.

Jamie came down the steps and heard Faith on the phone.

"What was the decision," Deacon asked. "A lot of stuff. Decisions to make on what to do with the websites. What to do with my life. A lot of stuff Deacon. I have to figure out what to do with a lot of stuff. I have to make sure that the history stays there," Faith said. "What's really going on with you," Deacon asked. "Nothing other than an ex who wants me dead." Faith heard the step creak. "If you need me, just say it," Deacon said. "Appreciate it. I gotta go," Faith said. "Dinner when we head back out," Deacon asked. "Maybe," Faith replied. She hung up.

"Deacon," Jamie asked. Faith nodded. "What are you doing up this early," Jamie asked. "I couldn't sleep. Mind was racing all night," Faith said. "Talk," Jamie said. "Why didn't you ask me about doing the wedding at the Opry," Faith asked. "It's full of history. I told you once that I was gonna be there someday. It was a dream Faith. How messed up is it that when we finally get back together I'm standing in that circle," Jamie asked. "I know. Still would rather do it the right way," Faith said. "We could just do something simple just us then have the big...." "No," Faith said. "Baby, we've been together or in each other's lives for years. I just want us to to what we want to. Everyone's expecting a huge fancy thing. That's not us Faith," Jamie said. "I'm not getting married more than once. We either do it right or we don't do it at all." "Can't even talk you into it," Jamie asked. "No," Faith replied. She got up and refilled her coffee cup.

"Faith, we can survive almost anything. We already have," Jamie said. "We haven't done anything but make it through Evan. Even so, he's not gone forever. He's still here," Faith said. "He's in jail. He isn't getting out. If he does, he isn't getting near you. I'm with you. He's not touching you," Jamie said. Faith shook her head and walked upstairs. She slid into the shower and when she stepped out, she saw Jamie sitting on the bed. "What's wrong," Jamie asked. "Got a stupid idea in my head. Started off as a nightmare that Evan came after us and had us at point blank range," Faith said. "He's not getting that close again," Jamie said. "And you think that getting engaged was gonna calm him? He's gonna go postal," Faith said. "Babe," Jamie said. Ten minutes later, the cops were at the door.

"You're Faith Andrews. Am I correct," the officer said. "Yes sir. What's wrong," Faith asked. "Evan James is your ex-boyfriend. That correct," the officer asked. Faith nodded. "He's disappeared from the lockup. He got out and we didn't even know until now. Someone posted his bail," the officer said. "Who," Faith asked. "We don't have a name. It was a large number. I don't know what to say ma'am," the officer said. "Say that someone is trying to find him. If he's out, I'm in danger. I could be killed," Faith said. "We just wanted to let you know. We're adding more security onto the tour. You're gonna have to have a bodyguard with both of you. He's made threats against Jamie," the officer said. "Great," Faith replied. "If you need us, here's the numbers," the officer said handing her a business card. Faith nodded and headed back inside. "Who in their right mind pays that kind of bail to get him out," Jamie asked. "Good question. Since I'm not going on the rest of the tour…." He kissed her. "Yeah you are. I'll be there with you. Nobody is hurting you. The 9 is still on the bus. He's not getting that close," Jamie said.

They spent part of the morning at the gun range as he showed Faith how to shoot. "We're getting you a permit. If we have to get you your own…" "Stop. Jamie, I can't do this," Faith said. "Why? Because you're gonna let him win? You're gonna let him come after you? Faith, you have to protect yourself," he said. "Jamie, I'm not carrying a damn weapon. This is insane," Faith said. They headed home and saw police cars out front.

"Stay in the truck. Seriously. Lock the doors and stay here," Jamie said. He parked and kissed her then hopped out and talked to the cops. "He got through the main gates and busted in before we found him," the officer said. "And? Where is he," Jamie asked. "He took off. He ripped the bed in the master bedroom to shreds and destroyed some of Faith's clothes." "I'm going to get what's left of her stuff and we're going on tour. Find him," Jamie said. He went inside, packed his things and Faith's, threw the bags into the back and drove to the Opryland Hotel.

"Why are we staying here," Faith asked. "Doesn't matter. We're leaving tomorrow morning," Jamie said. "Say it," Faith said. "I'm not scaring you," Jamie said. "He got in the house," Faith asked. "It's handled," Jamie said. He went up to the suite and Faith walked off. She went over to the Opry and was given permission to just sit.

"He'll protect you," Faith heard. "I can't be safe anywhere. He destroyed my things," Faith said. "He can't destroy you. Those are things. Nothing a store can't fix," she heard. "He's coming after me." "He hits once he'll hit again," the voice said. "You really Patsy," Faith asked. The voice disappeared. Faith got up and headed out. She walked out the front door and saw Jamie sitting there. "You've been in there for 3 hours," Jamie said. "Needed time to think," Faith said. "The doors were stuck. I tried to head in," Jamie said. Faith kissed him. He drove her back to the hotel and they had dinner. They had a long hot bath and curled up together in bed. "What did you go back to the Opry for," Jamie asked. "I swear, I heard Patsy Cline talking to me," Faith said. "You were in the Opry house Faith. They always said it was haunted," Jamie said. "I can't be talking to her. She passed away years ago," Faith said. He kissed her. "As long as she likes me," Jamie teased. They snuggled up together and went to sleep.

Faith had the oddest dream. She was sitting on a stage with Patsy Cline. She was telling her about the things she learned in her lifetime. "He put his hands on me and I should've left. You did. You are with a man I wish I had. He puts hands on you leave. He doesn't, hold on. I love my babies, but if I'd had a man like that I wouldn't have had to over-work myself. Hold on tight or you'll lose him to one of the new people. You'll lose him altogether. There are girls like me everywhere. I've done it. Watch your back," Patsy said to her. Faith woke up minutes later. Jamie was on the other side of the bed. Faith slid over and wrapped her arms around him. He turned towards her and kissed her. "I missed you," he said. He made love to her until they were almost late to the tour bus. They hopped on and he didn't let go of her hand once.

Chapter 5

After a few more weeks of touring and house hunting, Faith and Jamie finally pulled into the new house. Everything was back the way it was supposed to be. "So now that we have the house," Jamie said. "Don't start suggesting getting married right now. Jamie, he's still out there alright? Neither of us are safe period. You know it and I do," Faith said. "Baby, we need to pick a date. Then we can schedule the tour around it. Every interview I have they ask. Please," Jamie said. "There's no rush Jamie. We got all the time in the world," Faith said. She kissed him and got up to head into a meeting.

She walked in and Patrick was waiting for his next client to come in. They went through changes to some of the other websites and his next artist came in. "Faith, this is Evan James," Patrick said. Faith looked at him hoping that he wasn't one and the same. The second she saw him, Faith got up and went into her office then took off. Jamie got up, saw Evan and snapped. "You aren't welcome here Evan. Leave her the hell alone," Jamie said. "Right. I'm signed to the label. Guess she's gonna have no choice," Evan said getting nose to nose with Jamie. Patrick walked Jamie into the office, demanding an explanation.

"Talk Jamie," Patrick said. "He's been stalking her since she left Virginia. He won't leave her alone. He pulled guns on her and threatened her the entire time they were together. She has a restraining order against him. If he's here, she isn't gonna be," Jamie said. He walked out and went after Faith.

He pulled into the new house and saw her sitting in the truck in the driveway. "Babe, he's not gonna be there anymore. I talked to Patrick," Jamie said. "I told you. Even if we did run off and get married he'd still show and come after me. Jamie, no matter where I go he's never gonna leave me alone," Faith said. "Come out of there," Jamie asked. She hopped out and Jamie wrapped his arms around her. "Nobody is hurting you with me here. They're gonna have to kill me first," Jamie said. "I know you want to get married Jamie, but with everything…" He picked her up wrapping her legs around his waist. He leaned her against the driver side door of the truck. "We can get married any time we want. He's not making us wait or hurry. We do it when we want to. You want to wait, I'll wait. I'm not losing you, and I'm damn well not letting him hurt you," Jamie said. He kissed her and carried her inside.

They curled up on the bed together and Faith couldn't help that feeling like something was wrong. "Okay. No more freaking out about him. Happy thoughts. Valentine's Day," Jamie said. "One track mind," Faith teased. "We'll be doing the last show in Texas. It'll be warm and sunny. What do you think," Jamie asked. "What makes you think I won't kick your butt to the curb by then," Faith teased. He kissed her. "You won't. Can't live without me that long," he teased. They were kissing and being silly like always when Faith's phone rang. Jamie looked at the caller.

"Hey Patrick," Jamie said. "We still want him on the label. He's a good artist," Patrick said. "She has a restraining order against him. She's not going near him. She's that scared Patrick. Find someone else to work on his stuff. Please," Jamie said. "The sites for you and Deacon are taking up most of her time anyway. What if we put you two on just with Faith? Y'all can do the tour together and she can keep the updates going. We can hire someone else to work on Evan's work. What do you think," Patrick asked. "Talk to Faith. As long as she has no dealings with him she'll be alright. The man is bad news all way around," Jamie said. "I'll keep that in mind. Just make sure she's alright. I'll see y'all Monday at the meeting," Patrick said. They hung up and Jamie curled back up with Faith.

"Thank you," Faith said. He kissed her cheek. "I'm taking care of my baby. Promised to do that a long time ago," Jamie said. She slid her fingers to entwine with his. They went back to sleep and Faith ended up with another dream like she thought she'd had when she was at the Opry. "What are you saying Patsy," Faith asked. "I remember the part about promising to keep me safe. Didn't get me anywhere. Did he mean it with you," Patsy asked. "I think so. I love him. I just don't know what to do next," Faith said. "Never needed a man to keep me safe. I needed me and mama. She was the one who kept me safe," Patsy said. "Am I in danger," Faith asked. "Just watch your own back," Patsy said. Not 10 minutes later, Faith woke up. She went to take a sip of ice water and saw Jamie's 9mm on the bedside table.

Faith tried to go back to sleep and couldn't. She looked over at the clock and it said 6am. She went to slide out of bed and Jamie pulled her in close. "Let go," Faith asked. "You're not getting up to start worrying all over again. Close your eyes and get some more sleep," Jamie said as he kissed her neck. "Why's that out," Faith asked. He reached over her and put the gun in the drawer. "Heard something last night. Double checked and everything's fine," Jamie said. Faith nodded and got up. "Baby," Jamie said. Faith went in and washed up, had a hot shower and threw on her yoga stuff and did yoga outside. When she finished, she got changed and headed into the office to grab some paperwork she needed to finish up. She came back and Jamie started loading the truck up. "Was wondering when you were coming back inside," Jamie said kissing her. "We have to be there in an hour," Faith said. He grabbed her hand. "Faith," Jamie said. She threw her bag in the back, grabbed the last of her things that she needed and turned the alarm on and locked up.

They headed over to meet up with the tour bus and Faith was way too quiet. "Say what you need to," Jamie said. "I can't wake up to that Jamie. Not after what I already have," Faith said. "I was trying to help baby. I get you're freaked. So am I. That's why I got up the second I heard it. He's gonna leave you alone, no matter what I have to do," Jamie said. She tried to break away from him and he wouldn't let go of her hand. "Did you think about that idea that Patrick suggested," Jamie asked. "Cut off half my work because of him? Right. That's like letting him run my damn life. He needs to stay away from here. He's not allowed near me. Someone keeps him out of my way and out of that office when I'm there and I'm fine. They ask for a site for him, I'm not doing it. Not unless I get to say what I want to about him," Faith said. He kissed her. "I'll do the worryin. Too sexy to be stressed," Jamie said. He kissed the tip of her nose and walked her onto the bus.

Faith attempted to get work done and Jamie kept teasing her. First it was paper balls. When that didn't distract her enough, he sat down with her and laid her legs over his lap and started singing. "What are you up to," Faith asked. "Distracting my woman," Jamie teased. They ended up cracking jokes and being silly the rest of the afternoon. They stopped for dinner and once everyone was just finishing up dinner, he walked Faith into the parking lot and asked her to dance. "I love you. Nobody can be this lucky," Jamie said. "I'm still gonna worry about it," Faith said. He kissed her. "That's what I'm here for baby," Jamie said. He kissed her again and they headed back on the tour bus. They curled up together in the state room for a while then came out and watched a movie with the guys. Faith fell asleep in Jamie's arms.

"Don't keep counting on everyone else to take care of you," Patsy whispered. "What am I supposed to do? Let him come after me? Let him kill me," Faith asked. "Put you first instead of him. You want something, get it. When you get that feeling that something isn't right, follow your gut. When something goes wrong like it's gonna, remember this Faith. I chased my dream and won. I got everything and found out I had nothing. You have nothing when you lose yourself in the dream. Keep both feet on the ground Faith," Patsy said. "Meaning what," Faith asked. "Meaning you know what that dream is. Don't let his dreams outshine yours." "Why me Patsy," Faith asked. "You're the only one that understands Faith. I started the same as you. I want you to have a better life than I did. If I can help you then I did someone right Faith." Minutes later, Faith woke up.

Jamie was still out cold. She got up and grabbed some juice and went through her emails. Jamie came in a little bit later and kissed her head. "What you doing in here so early," Jamie asked. "Couldn't sleep. I swear I am hearing things when I'm sleepin," Faith said. "I used to have conversations with Johnny Cash," Jamie said. "Liar," Faith teased. "Told me to be who I am and never change for anyone. That when I met my June that I'd know. To never let go of her when I find her. When I started listening to it is when I saw you again," Jamie said. "Nice try," Faith teased. "Seriously. He said not to screw up like he did, to not get caught up in the drugs and alcohol and to be a good husband. I love you Faith. Always have babe," Jamie said. "Remember when we talked about that silly dream I had about writing music," Faith asked. Jamie nodded. "What if I tried it," Faith asked. He kissed her. "Your dreams are just as important as mine. I want your dreams coming true too baby," he said. Faith kissed him. That one kiss led to making out like teenagers and the two of them curling up in the state room and making love.

When Faith and Jamie woke up 4 hours later, they were just pulling into the venue. Jamie kissed her the minute her eyes opened. "Morning beautiful," Jamie said. "More like afternoon," Faith joked. He kissed her again. "I love you," Jamie said. Faith kissed him and got up. She pulled on her shorts and t-shirt and went and grabbed a shower. She came out, got changed and Jamie leaned her against the door of the state room. "What," Faith asked. Jamie kissed her. "Marry me," he asked. "Already said yes once," Faith teased. "Tomorrow," he asked. She kissed him and pulled her hair into a ponytail. "I'm marrying you," he teased. He kissed her, devouring her lips. Faith went and sat down with the guys and went through emails while Jamie was getting changed.

A little while later, they all headed off and went into sound check. Jamie got a few interviews done and couldn't help the silly grin from ear to ear. Just as Faith was finishing up some changes to a few sites, Jamie hopped off the stage and walked over to her. "What," Faith asked. He kissed her, grabbed her hand and pulled her to her feet. "What," Faith asked. He slid her laptop into her bag and walked her back to the dressing rooms. "Where are we going," Faith asked. He took her outside, into a waiting SUV and they took off. "Where are we going Jamie," Faith asked. "To put an end to the bullshit with Evan," Jamie said. "Meaning what," Faith asked. "Meaning he made threats. That's what," Jamie said. "What kind of threats," Faith asked starting to get shaky. "That we weren't getting married if he had his way. He's not standing in our way. If we go do this tonight…" The minute the SUV stopped Faith stepped out. She walked off on Jamie. "Babe," he said. She got in a cab and went back to the venue. She grabbed her bags and went to the airport before he had even made it back. She was pulling out when he was pulling into the parking area. He ended up tailing her to the airport. Faith got out, got her ticket and was about to go through security when he got there. He grabbed her hand and pulled her out of the line.

"What," Faith asked. He kissed her. "I just want…" "You want what you want Jamie. Go do the show and I'll be home." Faith went to walk off and he kissed her. It was a kiss that had her melting in her shoes. She broke away and went through security and headed home.

Faith walked in the door of the house and sat down to relax. Minutes later, Emma called her cell phone. "Something's wrong. Spill it. I saw your email," Emma said. "He asked me to marry him. We agreed next year and now he's pushing. He's trying to push the envelope and push me into doing all of it now. What am I supposed to do Emma? Give in? Jump into something I'm not ready for," Faith asked. "Just promise me that you'll stay safe. He needs you Faith. I get it. Rushing into a marriage is just silly. What makes him think that's gonna solve everything," Emma asked. "Exactly," Faith said. "Just promise me you'll be safe. I don't want you ending up in an altercation with Evan alone," Emma said. "What's the big deal Emma? He's in jail," Faith said. "I guess Jamie didn't tell you that he's out. Faith, promise me you'll stay safe," Emma replied.

Faith locked and triple checked the doors, slid into a hot bath and in minutes of Faith closing her eyes her phone rang. When she saw the 540 area code, she pressed decline and the iPhone slid out of her hand to the bath mat. She finally slid out of the tub, pulled on one of Jamie's t-shirts and slid into bed. She flipped the TV on and found a movie then caught up on some emails. She had email after email from Jamie. It's when she started getting messages from people that were in Virginia that she started to panic. She was just about to get up when she heard a truck pulling into the driveway. Faith looked and saw the Virginia license plate. She called Jamie.

"You're safer here and you know it. Call security and I'll get in touch with the bodyguard. Baby, please just come back," he said. Faith hung up, called security, called the bodyguard she knew and seconds later, they had whoever it was in custody and they left the area. Jamie's head of security when he's home showed at the house and got Faith packed. "I'm not going back when he's…" "He said to get you out of the house. That you're safer there. The label is flying you out on the jet. End of discussion," the security officer said. He was about to walk her to the waiting SUV when she saw someone coming back up the road. "Now," the security guard said. The license plate on the vehicle speeding towards them was a Virginia plate. She got in the SUV with her things and they headed off to the airport.

Faith fell asleep on the plane. When they landed, Jamie hopped on and walked over to her. He kissed her. "Morning," Jamie teased. "I was tired," Faith said. He kissed her again and walked her out. "I was perfectly fine being at home," Faith said. "Then help me to not be worried. Can't do a proper show without you anyway," he said. They hopped off the plane and he walked her to the SUV that was waiting for them. "When are we headed back home," Faith asked. He kissed the tip of her nose. "Next week. Sunday night after the show. We can just spend time together without anyone bugging us. The guys are flying home. They have to be back for some extra stuff they're doing. Babe, we're gonna be fine," he said. "You gonna stop talking about getting married now," Faith asked. He kissed her. "If I could we'd be going off and doing it tonight. I get why you're nervous Faith. We're gonna be alright. Whether we wait or whether we don't, we're not gonna end up apart," Jamie said. "I'm not rushing a wedding Jamie. You should know better," Faith said. He kissed her. "We're gonna be alright babe. If we do it now we…" Faith shook her head. They got to the tour bus and Faith walked right past the guys and walked into the state room. Jamie followed her.

"What's wrong with that," Jamie asked. "Forget it," Faith said. "Babe," Jamie replied. "We're not doing this now alright? You got me back on the damn tour bus. Let's just go," Faith said. "Baby," Jamie said trying to reason with her. She tuned him right out. He sat down on the bed beside her. He slid his arms around her. "Fine. I'll stop until we're both okay," Jamie said. "I'm not jumping into a wedding Jamie. I can't," Faith said. He kissed her. "Okay," he said. "Just let me deal with the other crap before we jump into getting married alright? Evan isn't gonna get better if we run off and do this. He's gonna get worse. When he does…" "Shh. He's not laying a finger on you. Not on my damn watch. I don't want him getting you upset ever again," Jamie said. "He's never gonna stop. The sooner we get used to it, the sooner he starts worrying about us coming to get him. He isn't stopping until we stop him Jamie. She's never gonna end it until he's in a permanent cell whether it's padded or not," Faith said. "Fine. I get it. We can't keep trying to outrun him and use him as a reason for us to not move on? We need to take care of us Faith. You and me," Jamie said.

They curled up together a while and tried to get some sleep. Instead, Jamie was out cold. Faith got up, went and sat down at the table and worked on emails. Jamie got up an hour or two later. He walked into the sitting area and smirked. "What," Faith asked. "Sleep," he replied. He turned her laptop off and walked her back to bed. "I'm not…" "Just come and curl up with me then. It'll make me feel better if nothing else," he said. He kissed her and they curled up together on the bed. "No matter what happens we're gonna be together. He can't change that," Jamie said. "What happens when he tries to? Whether he's in jail or he isn't he's never backing off. If he can get past the gates," Faith said. "It wasn't him. It was some girl he was dating. He talked her into doing something for him. Babe, I know you hate the gun range, but you have to go. Just so I know you're okay. Please," Jamie asked. "We'll talk later," Faith said. "You're going," he said. Faith kissed him and tried to sleep.

They woke up a few hours later and Jamie was checking gun ranges. "I'm not doing it," Faith said. "Yeah you are. If he makes a damn move on you, I want you knowing how to get a shot. You need to do this. Even if it's just for me. Please," Jamie asked. "Fine, but don't start thinking that I'm gonna keep one on me. It's not safe," Faith said. He kissed her. "We're gonna be fine. You know that," Jamie asked. "I want my damn life back," Faith said. He curled back up with her. "You do," he replied. "Right. He hunts me down like I'm some crazy animal. That's getting my life back," Faith asked. "If you could choose anything, what would you want," Jamie asked. "Him long gone. Not having to worry anymore. Not worried that if we ever have a daughter that she'll have to go through this. That's all I ever wanted," Faith said. "If you can have anything in the world for you," Jamie asked. "Writing music and never having to watch my back again," Faith replied. "Part one is done. Now you can write. Do it for you. I'll help you with the music and I can even put some on my CD."

Faith worked on music and Jamie rehearsed a while with the guys. He came in and saw her working on the music and she finally had something else to concentrate on. Jamie walked over and kissed her. "What," Faith asked. "I love you," Jamie said. "I'm not running off and marrying you," Faith teased. He kissed her. "Soon enough you will. I love that smile on your face," Jamie said. "What you sucking up for now," Faith asked. He slid onto the bed behind her, wrapped his arms around her and kissed her neck. "Jamie," Faith said. He closed the door and locked it. "Don't even think…" He kissed her, slid her laptop onto the counter and pulled her legs around him. "The guys are ten feet…" He kissed her. "Then we should probably be quiet," he teased. "Jamie," Faith said. He kissed her again, devouring her lips and slid her jean shorts off.

He kissed her again, silencing any objection she could possibly have. In minutes Faith almost forgot where she was. They made love and both of them forgot time even existed. He kissed her lips then kissed, licked and nibbled his way right down her torso. When he saw her toes curling he kissed her with a kiss that could have torched the bus in seconds. When they came up for air a half hour later, Jamie had a grin ear to ear. "What," Faith asked. "Kinda glad you're here," he teased. "I bet," Faith teased. He kissed her again. "Don't you have somewhere to be," Faith asked. One more kiss and they got up and got changed and cleaned up and headed into the venue hand in hand.

They had a quick dinner, Jamie got ready for the show and Faith walked him to the stage. He kissed her again. "I'm sitting in the tour bus," Faith said. "Babe," he said. "What?" "Stay," he asked. "I'm not…" He kissed her again and went onto the stage. Deacon slid up behind Faith. "You know you'd be safer with me right," Deacon said. "Leave me be Deacon." He slid his hand in hers and pulled her towards him. "What do you want," Faith asked. He pulled her to him and walked her back to the dressing room. "Deacon, enough. You don't want to piss him off tonight alright," Faith said. "I want you back. Am I not allowed now," he asked. Faith tried to walk off and he grabbed her arm. "You don't need to be with him Faith. He's only causing shit," Deacon said. Faith broke away from him. "I'm doing what I want to. You don't get to make a decision for me. Got it," Faith said. She walked off and went back to the side stage. Jamie looked over and saw her and winked at her. He came over to change guitars and kissed her. "I'm going," Faith said. He kissed her again and walked out to the tour bus with the security guard.

Faith checked emails and relaxed a while then slid one of Jamie's t-shirts on and turned on a movie. When she heard what sounded like a fight outside, she slid her shorts on and went outside. "He doesn't get to run her life. She belongs with me period," Deacon said to the security guard. "Then take it up with Jamie. Leave her be. End of discussion," the security guard said. "Faith," Deacon said. "Just go and leave me alone," Faith said. Deacon grabbed her arm. He started walking her back towards his trailer. Faith ended up in a fight with him. Jamie finished his set and was just heading out and saw it. "Just leave me alone," Faith said. Jamie walked over towards them and laid one punch on Deacon. He ended up letting go of Faith and went to punch Jamie. Faith took off and walked towards the tour bus.

She got on and locked the door of the state room. She turned her iPod on and went through emails on her laptop. Jamie came in not 15 minutes later. Faith got up and handed him a bag of ice. "Baby," he said as he put the ice on his hand. "I'm not doing this. You wanna fight the planet, go ahead," she replied. Faith went to walk back into the state room and Jamie grabbed her hand. "Baby, please. He was hurting you. You don't need that after everything you've gone through." "Jamie, let me fight my own damn battles. I can do things on my own and you know it," Faith said. He kissed her. "You shouldn't have to. I told you before," he said. Faith shook her head and walked into the state room. "Faith, nobody gets to put their hands on you. Nobody gets to hurt you," Jamie said. "Everyone does anyway," she replied. Faith went back to sleep on the bed and Jamie walked in and laid down with her. "Babe," Jamie said. "What," Faith replied. He kissed her neck. "Come here," he asked. She turned towards him and he wrapped his arm around her. "Tell me what you need me to do," Jamie said. "Let me be me. I get that he wants me with him but I made my choice Jamie. You're on tour with him. Throwing punches isn't gonna fix anything. It's gonna make the stupid tour hell for both of you. Just stop," Faith said. He kissed her. "The sooner he gets used to the fact that he can't make a move the better. I'm sorry," Jamie said. Faith kissed him. "So what if we used the days off and did something just us," Jamie asked. "As long as you don't talk Las Vegas fine," Faith teased. He kissed her. "How about a little chapel in the middle of nowhere," he teased. "Determined to sleep alone," Faith joked. He kissed her.

Faith got up the next morning and Jamie was already up. She could hear him playing guitar and working on a song with the guys. She got dressed and walked in and sat down with the guys. "What do you think of this part," Jamie asked singing the song to her. She kissed him. "That good or not," he asked sarcastically. "Good," Faith replied. She grabbed some breakfast and sat down at the table. "Babe, did you come up with any lyrics yet," Jamie asked. "Right. It's called work," Faith said. He kissed her. "You need to relax and have fun for a while," Jamie said. He kissed her and pulled her into his lap. "What you want," Faith asked. He kissed her. The bus made a stop and Jamie piggy backed Faith into the store to grab some snacks. They hopped back on the bus and they all hung out. Faith finished up some emails and Jamie finished working on some music. Faith came up with a few lyrics and wrote them into a notebook Jamie had. She made a few calls making sure that any new changes were documented to the various websites, checked in with Patrick and got news she wasn't expecting.

"We're sending over the list of your clients. We're dividing it up between you and one of our other website creators. The man you were concerned about was dropped by the label. He tried to break into your office. We realized he was exactly what you thought." Faith's hands started shaking. The call went on for another half hour and then Faith hung up and worked on the song lyrics.

Jamie walked back to the state room and saw Faith writing. "What you doin back here sexy," Jamie asked. "Writing," Faith replied. He kicked the door shut and leaned into her. He almost had her pinned to the bed. "What are you up to," Faith asked. He kissed her neck, nibbled her neck and kissed her. "What are you up to," Faith asked. "Teasing my woman. I'm not allowed," Jamie asked. "Depends on what you're really doing," Faith said. He slid her shirt up. "Jamie," Faith said. "What," he asked.

He went for the buckle of her jeans. He kissed her neck. "Jamie," Faith said. He slid her jean shorts off and nuzzled her neck. "What are you doin," Faith asked. "Making love to my woman," he said. They had sex until both of them were almost shaking.

"I love you," he said. "I love you too," Faith replied as she curled up in Jamie's arms. "What you writing," Jamie asked. "None of your business," Faith replied. He grabbed the notebook and no matter how many times Faith tried getting it out of his hands she didn't win that tackle fight. "Babe, these are really good," Jamie said. "A bunch of silly stuff I came up with," Faith said. "They're good," Jamie said. Faith slid her t-shirt back on and Jamie pulled her into his lap. "What," Faith asked. "I love you," he said. Faith kissed him. "Seriously. The lyrics are good," Jamie said. Faith nodded and got up. She slid her shorts on. "Faith," Jamie said. She went out to grab herself a drink, closing the door behind her.

Jamie got up and got dressed and came into the sitting area with her notebook in hand. "Jamie," Faith said. He started working on the music part of the song. "Jamie," Faith said. He kissed her and pulled her over to the sofa with him. She shook her head. He sang the song to her. Faith got up. She made something to eat and Jamie took a monster sized bite of her sandwich. They finally got to the next stop and checked into the hotel. Jamie walked her upstairs. "What," he asked when they got to their room. "You don't need to help me with the song," Faith said. He kissed her. "I know where it came from Faith. You could even make it into a duet you know," Jamie said. "Jamie," Faith said. "What," he asked. She shook her head. "What's wrong," Jamie asked. "You read them. You singing them isn't a good idea," Faith said. He kissed her. "Stop worrying about it and just keep writing," Jamie said. "Right. I'm supposed to just write about that? Jamie it's not..." He kissed her. "It's good," Jamie said. "It's something I had stuck in my head," Faith said. He kissed her. "That worried that he's coming for you aren't you," Jamie asked. Faith nodded. "He's not touching you. Never ever again," Jamie said pulling her into his arms.

They finally got to the next stop and Jamie walked Faith upstairs. "I'm not feeling like going to..." Jamie kissed her. "You have to. You're the only reason I can sing those love songs. Always will be. He's not getting near you Faith. Nobody is ever hurting you. Not on my watch," Jamie said holding her in his arms. "He's never gonna stop," Faith said. "Yeah he will. He knows that fighting us is just plain stupid. Babe, he's gonna find someone else to come after. As long as we're together, we're safe." "And what happens when he tries to hurt you? I couldn't live through that," Faith said. "That's what you're scared about," he asked. Faith kissed him. He wasn't fighting anymore. There was no reason to. He knew what she was really scared for. They relaxed a bit then headed over to the venue. He was hand in hand with Faith. Now that he knew what the fear was about, he wasn't letting it come true. He did sound check singing straight to her.

When they finished up sound check, Jamie took her over to grab some dinner. The more he thought about it, the more he wanted to marry her. Right at that exact second, he was more in love with the woman who didn't hold anything back. He was so in love with her that nothing else mattered. They talked and hugged. They kissed and they were totally honest for the first time in a long time. "He why you didn't want to get married yet," Jamie asked. "He's dangerous. I don't want him hurting you," Faith said. He kissed her and got up and walked her back to the tour bus. "What," Faith asked seeing that look in his eye. "He's never hurting me, and he's never hurting you ever again. You need to stop worrying," Jamie said pulling her into his arms. "He's never gonna stop. Putting you in the middle of everything means you could get hurt. I know you aren't planning to get hurt, but he…" Jamie kissed her. "Is that all you're worried about or is there something else?" "What if we're rushing into everything," Faith asked. "Then we rush into the rest of our lives. Faith, I'm marrying one woman in my life. You're it. There isn't gonna be a divorce or a separation. Just you and me and a mess of kids. That's all," Jamie said. "So convinced," Faith teased. "That I get to have you in my arms and in my life until we both take our last breath? Hell yeah," he replied. Somehow just the thought of it calmed her.

Jamie did the show with Faith watching him. Nothing was distracting that connection. Every love song was dedicated to her and every chance Jamie had, he walked straight to her and kissed her. The minute the show was done for the night, he walked straight to Faith and kissed her, picking her up in his arms and wrapping her legs around his waist. They curled up on the tour bus on the bed and he was back where he belonged. "Promise we won't fight ever again," Jamie said. She laughed. "Nice guarantee," Faith teased. "Next time you're scared just say it. I'd never hurt you Faith. Never," Jamie said. "He's…" Jamie kissed her. "We have plans tomorrow," he said. "Oh really," Faith replied. "We're going out tomorrow just you and me. We have tomorrow off remember," he teased. "And just what do you have planned," Faith asked. He kissed her with a kiss that had her melting into his arms. "We're busy. No cell phones, no computers allowed. You and me period," Jamie said.

Chapter 6

Faith got up the next morning and had a hot shower and started getting changed. "Where you goin," Jamie asked. "Up," Faith teased. He handed her a jean skirt from her bag. "Jamie," Faith said. He had a devilish grin that told her to be very very worried. "What are you up to," Faith asked. He kissed the tip of her nose and slid into the shower. Faith went and walked into the sitting area and saw that the guys weren't there. Faith grabbed breakfast and made something for her and Jamie. He came out and had breakfast with Faith then they left in an SUV. "What are you up to," Faith asked. They stopped at a dress shop. "Jamie," Faith said. He kissed her and walked her in as they closed the store off to anyone else and blocked the windows from prying eyes. "We have a few dresses put aside for you," the saleswoman said. Faith looked at Jamie. "Have an errand to run. You chill here," Jamie said kissing Faith. "Jamie," Faith replied. He smirked. She shook her head. Jamie took off out the back. Faith went into the dressing room and saw the white dresses. She shook her head. That was one hell of a sign that he was making.

Faith found one that was beyond beautiful and it fit like a glove. She came out and the saleswoman was in shock. "Oh my goodness," the saleswoman said. It had the perfect antique lace, was flowy where it should be and had just the right amount of sexy. "Tell me you're choosing this," the saleswoman said. "Depends on what it's for," Faith teased. Faith slid out of the dress and came out. The sales woman put the dress into a suit bag. Jamie came back in and the saleswoman handed him the suit bag. "Thank you," Jamie said. The woman had a smile a mile wide. Jamie paid for the dress and walked Faith out the back. "Jamie," Faith said. He kissed her in the alleyway. They got back in the SUV and were at the airport a short while later. "Where are we going," Faith asked. "Home," he replied. "Are you telling me what we're doing or not," Faith asked. "Had an interview while you were shoppin. Plus I was finishing organizing the surprise," he teased. "What are you up to?" He kissed her and they started flying back.

They landed a while later, hopped off the plane and were rushed into a waiting SUV. "Jamie," Faith said. He kissed her. "Quit worrying. No more stress remember," Jamie said. "Tell me you aren't trying to pull off a surprise wedding," Faith said. He smirked and kissed her. "Figured we could go hang out at the old Opry," Jamie said. "What are you up to crazy man," she joked. "Reminding you why I fell in love with you the first second we met," Jamie replied. He kissed her and the second the SUV stopped, they were in front of the Ryman. "Jamie," Faith said. He grabbed the suit bag. She shook her head. The minute they walked in, Faith saw a sign that said:

Closed for Private Event

She shook her head. "I'll be back in a sec," Jamie said. He kissed Faith and went off to talk to someone. A few minutes later, she saw the hair and makeup team come towards her. "Tell me he isn't doing what I think he is," Faith said to herself. They walked Faith off to a quiet area that had been blocked off. "What are y'all doing here," Faith teased. "Jamie wanted us to come by," her favorite makeup artist said. They did Faith's hair and makeup and she slid into that perfect dress and a pair of heels that looked like they were covered in diamonds. Just as she was almost dressed, Emma came in with Faith's mom and Jamie's. "What are y'all doing here," Faith asked. "Jamie invited us," her mom said. Faith knew what he was up to. She chatted with everyone a while then they left her be for a few minutes.

"Don't let anyone talk you into anything. Never do what your heart isn't in. I did and ended up divorced," Faith heard. It was the same voice she'd heard at the Opry house. "I love him. That won't change," Faith said. "I thought so too. He's as jealous as my husband. Look where that got me," Patsy said. "He's not like that. He's not jealous. He's protective," Faith said. "Don't ever do something because you want to make someone else happy or because you think you should. I was a fighter too but I never gave up. He may say he's helping you but what happens when your dream gets put on the back burner," Patsy said. "They won't. He won't let them," Faith replied. "Listen to your heart baby girl. If it's not with him don't marry him. Make your dreams come

74

true first," Patsy said. "They already are," Faith replied. There was no reply.

Faith's dad walked in with her brother. "One question. When did Jamie call you," Faith asked. "Yesterday. He flew us into Nashville last night," her brother said. Her dad and her brother hugged her. Her dad walked her out to the seating and she saw Jamie on the stage with the minister from the church across the street. She smirked. Her mom handed her the bouquet of sterling and white roses. She shook her head. "I know what he's doing," Faith said. Her mom's eyes started welling up. Faith hugged her and she walked over towards Jamie. "Surprise," Jamie teased when they were face to face. "Never heard of slow," Faith teased. "Never has been with us," he teased winking at her. It took every ounce of will power he had to not kiss her right there and then.

They started through the ceremony and when it came time for the vows, Jamie did what he'd always done best. "I have loved you since that first look. I looked in those blue eyes and was lost in them. I never stopped loving you. No matter where you were I was there. I've always been there. When you came back into my life I knew I could never let go. You are my everything Faith. You always will be. I promise to dry every tear, steal away every fear and never let you hurt like that again. The only tears I want to be shed are tears of happiness. Until the last breath I will be in love with you." Faith brushed a tear away. He slid a pave diamond band onto her finger. Faith shook her head.

Faith looked in Jamie's eyes. Winging it had never been something she was great at but she had no choice. "The day I met you it was like a hurricane hit. All the things I had wanted included you. When you saved me that day I knew that I'd never be the same. I know you better than I thought I would, love you more than I thought possible and my life has changed since you became part of it. The thought of being with you forever doesn't even scare me anymore. I promise to love you, always tell the truth and never hide a secret from you. I promise to make your dreams come true and to always surprise you. I never knew what to think of what you do to me, now I know. Forever and forever," Faith said sliding a matching band on Jamie's finger. Jamie had a smirk ear to ear.

"If there are no objections," the minister asked. Everyone was quiet until Faith heard a commotion in the hallway. "I'm not letting her…." Faith looked at Jamie. He shook his head. "I now pronounce you husband and…" "You can't do this," Evan said. "Wife," the minister said. Jamie kissed Faith. "Couldn't wait," Faith teased. "Not another second," Jamie said. He kissed her again. They signed the one and only thing they needed to and he walked Faith down the steps. "Surprise," he teased. She shook her head. "I love you," Jamie said. She hugged him. He kissed her and went to deal with Evan.

"What," Jamie asked closing the door so nobody would be disturbed. "You can't marry her," Evan said. "Just did. What's your excuse Evan," Jamie asked. "We're married. That's why," Evan said. "Really? A legal marriage or one of those fake ones you have," Jamie teased. Evan went to take a swipe at him and Jamie leaned back. "That's what I thought," Jamie said. The police showed a few minutes later and took Evan away. Jamie walked back in and saw Faith walking towards him. "It's fine," Jamie said. "What did…" Jamie kissed her. "I love you. He doesn't matter anymore. He's not hurting you," Jamie said. He had his arms wrapped tight around her. "Couldn't wait could you," Faith asked. He kissed her again. "Nope. Hate waiting," he teased. "Jamie," Faith said. "Just smile and be happy. Today is you and me. No phones, no computers. Just you and me and the moonlight," Jamie said leaning in to kiss her. They all headed out and went off to the Opryland hotel and into a private suite he'd organized. "And just when did you find all of this spare time," Faith asked. Jamie kissed her. "Emma," he replied. He kissed the tip of her nose.

They had a beautiful dinner, had a little celebration and Jamie got her on her feet for the perfect first dance. Jamie talked one of Faith's favorite artists into singing for them for that first song. Jason came in and surprised Faith. He sat down with one of his guitarists and started playing. While Jason sang 'Staring at the Sun', Jamie slow danced with Faith. "Still can't believe you did all of this," Faith said. Jamie kissed her. "We're gonna be alright babe. I promise. You're never gonna be scared again," Jamie said. She shook her head. "He's not coming back to hurt you," Jamie said. Faith kissed him. "I love you for trying," Faith said.

They finished the dance, Faith danced with her dad and Jamie danced with his mom then they all sat around chatting. They finished their cake and coffee and everyone headed back to their rooms leaving Faith and Jamie surrounded in candlelight and roses.

"Why now," Faith asked. "Because nothing else has got in our way. This was about us Faith. Nobody else," Jamie said. He danced with her and flipped on another song. It was a secret surprise gift from Jamie just for her. He sang to her and Faith was almost in tears. "That's what you were doing," Faith asked. He kissed her. "I've been working on it since we met. Never figured out the end until now," Jamie said. Faith kissed him. "Now I get to give you the other surprise," Jamie said. "Which is what," Faith asked. He kissed her and walked her down the hall to the honeymoon suite. They walked inside and she saw candles, roses and an envelope on the bed with a ribbon on it. "Jamie," Faith said. He kissed her and handed her the envelope. She opened it and saw two plane tickets. "Jamie," Faith said. "You and me and nobody else on that trip. No phones, no internet and nobody else. Only way we can get there is by boat. Total privacy from everyone and everything," Jamie said. Faith kissed him. "You're never hurting again. Not with me here. Never ever again," Jamie said as he held her tight in his arms. A single tear fell from her eyes.

She saw her suitcase beside the bed and knew he'd had it planned for weeks. Jamie undid her dress and she slid out of it and into his arms. He kissed her and picked her up, wrapping her legs around his waist and leaned her onto the massive bed. "Mad," Jamie asked. "Knew you weren't gonna be able to wait," Faith joked. He kissed her again and Faith undid the buttons of his shirt. He kicked his clothes off, curling up in her arms. They made love on the oversized bed as he devoured her. He ravished her with kisses and nibbles until every inch of her was humming a song only he could hear. For the first time in forever, Jamie wasn't letting go. There wasn't a thing anyone was gonna do that could ever hurt her again.

The next morning, Jamie and Faith got up first thing and got dressed then headed straight to the airport. Half way there, they got stuck in a massive traffic jam. Faith heard a voice that she knew had to be Patsy. "Things happen for a reason Faith. You listening to me now?" Jamie kissed her hand. "What you thinking wife," Jamie asked. "Just thinking about how Patrick is gonna react," Faith said. "He said congrats," Jamie teased. "So you told everyone but me," Faith asked. "I know how you felt about rushing this. Faith, it doesn't matter when we did it. Just matters that I love you and you love me." Faith shook her head. "Babe," Jamie said. "I said that because a marriage that lasts forever means that we're best friends and we worked on us. Jamie, you don't know me. You only know from Evan on," Faith said. Jamie leaned over and kissed her. "Woman, stop worrying about what happens 20 years from now. We're okay and we always will be," Jamie said. Faith shook her head. "What," Jamie asked. "Can predict the future now," Faith asked. "Say what you want to really say," Jamie replied. Faith shook her head. They pulled into the airport parking and parked, Jamie hopped out and grabbed the bags and Faith's hand and they headed into the airport. Within 10 minutes they were on the plane and about to take off.

"You worried that things aren't gonna go the right way," Jamie asked. "I'm worried that we're gonna look back on this and wish we hadn't rushed into it. We deserved the big wedding. The fact that you didn't want to wait just makes me worry that there's another reason behind it that you don't want to tell me," Faith said. He shook his head. Faith went to slide her ear buds in and Jamie stopped her. "A wedding isn't about everyone else Faith. It's about us. Neither one of us wanted that massive wedding. I get that everyone's gonna be expecting it, but this was for us and only us. Baby, There aren't any secrets. I love you. I always will," Jamie said. "And if I find out that you're hiding something," Faith asked. He kissed her. It was a kiss that heated her from the inside out and made every nerve boil. He held her face in his hands. "Nobody will ever love you like I do. That's why we're never gonna lose each other. I loved you from that first day that we met. When you got with him it killed me. Every damn guy I worked with said they thought I was gay or something. I never wanted anyone else Faith. I never will," Jamie said. He kissed her. He slid the arm rest up so he could snuggle Faith. "Why are you so darn worried," he asked. Faith shook her head. "Say it," Jamie said. "Because I didn't have time to do this before we got married.

You sprung a wedding on me," Faith said. He kissed her. "You looked beautiful," he said. "Suck up," Faith said. He kissed her again and they relaxed on the flight. "So where are we headed anyway," Faith asked. He kissed the tip of her nose and they snuggled up the rest of the flight.

"What do you mean she got hitched," Evan said. "She married the dude. You have to stay away," Evan's new girl Maggie said. Evan about threw a fit. The sex was rough and the minute it was over, Evan got up, cleaned up and stormed out, hopping in Maggie's truck and took off to Nashville.

"Where are we," Faith asked. Jamie kissed her. "One more flight," he said. They hopped on a tiny plane and a short flight later, they landed on a little island. "You weren't kidding," Faith joked. They hopped off the plane and were at an island alone. There was no cell service, no internet and no distractions. Jamie kissed her. "Said I'd find somewhere," he teased. They walked into the massive villa and saw sterling roses and lilac candles everywhere. "You, me and the water," Jamie said. Faith went to go upstairs to get settled and Jamie followed her, wrapping his arms around her waist. Faith laid her bag onto the foot rest and Jamie kissed her neck. "What are you up to," Faith asked. He undid the button of her jeans, unzipped the zipper and started peeling her shirt off. "Jamie," Faith said. "What," he asked. She felt his hand slide up her shirt and felt the warmth of his hands on her breasts. "Jamie," Faith said. "We're alone. Just you and me," Jamie said. "Permanent one-track mind," Faith teased. "Knowing that you had on the barely there black lace drove me nuts that entire flight," Jamie teased nibbling her ear.

Faith turned towards him and he leaned her onto the massive soft bed. "I missed you," he joked. "Ten hours," Faith joked. He kissed her, devouring her lips and peeling her things off. She had his clothes in a pile with hers in minutes. He made love to her like it was the last time he'd have her in his arms. "And just think. You get me all to yourself for a whole week," Jamie teased. "Guess it's a good thing I got sleep the other night," Faith teased. He kissed her again. Three hours later, they finally came up for air. Faith got up and slid into a hot shower and seconds later Jamie was in there with her. The steam from the hot air steamed up the mirrors and fogged up the windows. They had sex again in the shower then Faith slid out and pulled on a bathing suit and a sweater she'd found in Jamie's bag. She went for a walk along the beach looking out at the boats. A half hour later, Jamie came outside with a snack for them both. They sat on the patio in the massive Muskoka chairs and he didn't let go of her hand for a second. "What," Faith asked. "See? Forgot what life was like without cell phones," Jamie joked. "No. It's just nice having peace and quiet," Faith said. They had dinner in those chairs. Jamie lit torches and their feet sunk into the perfect sand of the beach. "Aren't gonna want to go home," Jamie said. Faith kissed him and got up. "Where are you going," Jamie asked. She let go of his hand and headed inside.

They had more than their share of romantic moments that week. There were candlelight dinners and peace and quiet. It was hard as hell getting used to. By the time they were ready to leave, Faith had fallen asleep in Jamie's arms every night and woke up with his arms around her and kisses up her neck. "Now what," Faith asked as they headed back home on the plane. "Now we go back on the tour," Jamie said. Faith nodded. Now she knew what Patsy had been saying.

They got home and Jamie was on the phone minutes later. Faith walked upstairs and got changed back into her blue jeans and t-shirt and unpacked. She threw laundry into the washer and came back downstairs to find Jamie still in the midst of a call that was obviously stressful for him. He looked like someone was completely biting his head off. Faith went and grabbed them each a drink and handed one to him. Jamie put it down and pulled Faith into his lap. "I'm not doing it. You can't tell me I'm supposed to leave her here alone. We just got married," Jamie said. Faith kissed his cheek and went to get up but he held on. "Patrick, I get it but I'm not going without Faith. I get you need her at that office but I'm not doing it. Not when Evan is signed to the damn label," Jamie said. Faith got up. "I'll talk to her, but if I'm not in town she's getting heavy security with her at all times." Faith shook her head. She went and sat down outside and finished her drink. Jamie walked outside a couple minutes later.

"Babe," Jamie said. "If you have to go then go," Faith said. "Not when he's this close. You're more important than a stupid show in the middle of nowhere," Jamie said. "You have to do the show. I'll be fine here. I'll get Emma to come over," Faith said. "It's in the UK. Emma being here is great, but I'm too far away. If he does something stupid…" "He's not going to. I can handle things. Stop worrying," Faith said. He sat down on the chaise behind her and wrapped his arms around her. "I know you can. I'd miss you way too much," he whispered as he nibbled her earlobe. "I love you too," Faith replied. He nuzzled her neck, kissing and nibbling. Not 2 minutes later, the phone rang again. Jamie laughed. Faith answered it.

"Okay. We have security set up. He has a show this weekend then Sunday he has to go. I can see what I can do about getting you on the trip with them, but…" "It's fine. We can figure something out. I'll be alright Patrick," Faith said. "Was gonna say we needed to put him on a super early flight if he wanted you there. I get him freaking out because of Evan, but you can't be at every stop with them," Patrick said. "We just got married. He isn't letting go that easy," Faith joked. Patrick laughed. "Gotcha. I'll see if I can get the jet for that flight. I'll email later with confirmation," Patrick replied. Faith said her goodbye and hung up as Jamie was about to undo her jeans. "What are you up to," Faith asked. He kissed her and her toes went numb.

It's like time stopped when he kissed her. There was no such thing until they came up for air. She was so in love with him, she forgot where she was altogether. He picked her up, still lip-locked and carried her inside and barely made it to a sofa. He peeled her t-shirt off and slid off her jeans and his and leaned into her. "I love you," Jamie said. "I love you too," Faith said. He kissed her again and made love to her on that sofa. Her body was almost humming. A nibble here, a kiss there and her knees started going numb. They fit together like a hand in the perfect glove. "I'm never losing you," Jamie said. Fact was, she needed him as much as he needed her. Her entire life had changed the day they finally had that overdue date. When they came up for air an hour later, Jamie was smiling at her. "What," Faith asked. "I swear I'm the luckiest man in the world. I never thought this day was gonna come," Jamie said. "Thought

I'd say no," Faith teased. "Never thought I'd have you in my arms. Dreamt it, but I never expected it to happen," Jamie said. Faith kissed him.

After an hour or two of snuggle time, Jamie and Faith finally got up and had some dinner. Just as they were cleaning up, the guards at the security gate called. "There's a visitor here for you. His name's Evan," the officer said. "He's not allowed in here. He's on that list I gave you," Jamie said. He hung up and walked over to Faith, sliding his arms around her waist and washing the dishes. "Trying to do two things at once," Faith teased. He kissed her neck again. "Dishes first," Faith teased. He turned the water off, picked her up and carried her upstairs.

They curled up in bed together and went through the schedule for the next few weeks. "See why I wanted you to come with me," Jamie said. "Gives you time to miss me," Faith said. He bit her neck. "Oh yeah," he teased. "I can handle being here alone," Faith said. "I'd miss you way too much," he said. Faith was beginning to wonder what the real reason was. Was it that he didn't trust her to take care of things, or was he really afraid that Evan was going to get to her? Either way, she knew why he had always carried that handgun, and she knew that even if it meant having to use it herself Evan wasn't hurting her again. "Why are you so quiet," Jamie asked. "Just thinking," Faith said. "If you don't want me going I'll tell them no," Jamie said. "You're going. Patrick already agreed to it," Faith said. "Then what's with the tension that just doubled in your shoulders?" Faith went to get up and he pulled her back to him. "You're scared of him. I get that baby. That's why you're getting your permit," Jamie replied. "So I'm supposed to walk around with that everywhere we go? Jamie, it's not realistic. We can't do that," Faith said. He kissed her. "Won't need to. We're getting security," he replied. Faith nodded. "So we have a break for a few weeks around middle of November. Just in time for Thanksgiving. What did you want to do," Jamie asked. "Dinner with the family," Faith said. He kissed her neck. "There or here," he asked. "Wherever," Faith replied. "Babe, something's eating at you. Just say it," Jamie said. She kissed him and got up.

She went downstairs and grabbed a glass of ice water and her phone buzzed. She looked over and saw a text from an unknown number. The second she opened it, the phone dropped to the floor. Faith sat down on the sofa, staring at the phone. Jamie came downstairs and saw the phone on the floor. "What's wrong," Jamie asked seeing her dead scared on the sofa. Faith shook her head. He grabbed the phone and saw the photo in the text message. He forwarded it to the security officers and the police officers that he'd spoken to. Jamie made sure any tracking was off so Evan couldn't find her and sat down beside her. "He's never leaving me alone Jamie. Ring or not," Faith said. He tried to comfort her and could tell in a matter of minutes that he wasn't gonna be able to succeed. "Tell me what you need me to do," Jamie asked. She leaned into his arms. At that second, it was the only safety that she knew. He carried her upstairs and curled up on the bed with her. Once she fell asleep, Jamie locked up and double armed the alarms. He loaded his handgun and put it in the drawer in the lockbox.

"You have to watch your own back. Nobody keeps you safe but you," Patsy said. "I'm scared," Faith said. "He loves you, but he isn't the only one that can keep you safe. I learned to take care of me. Be strong. Don't let him be your only strength. My husband hit me. Doesn't mean I couldn't handle him myself," Patsy said. "What now," Faith asked. "Concentrate on your dreams. Stop putting them aside. Get your mind on it and off the past." Faith woke up and Jamie wasn't in bed. She saw the bedside table drawer open and the empty gun case. She went to walk downstairs and heard Jamie talking to someone.

"He needs to leave her alone. I don't care what you have to do. Just keep him away from us. She's shaky for god sakes," Jamie said. She saw him on his cell. "I don't care what it takes. Put it on my damn tab. She's staying safe and that's the end of it. If I go and she's here, someone is damn well staying with her. Whoever stays is keeping that gun on them. She doesn't need to be scared anymore." He turned and saw Faith going into the kitchen and came inside. "Baby," Jamie said. "I don't need the kid gloves alright? I'll go see my folks for a…" "No. You can stay here if that's what you wanna do. I just need to know that you'll be safe. I told a few of my buddies to keep an eye out," Jamie said. "Just what I need.

More people telling me that I can't be here by myself. If he wants to find me, he will. He wants to get to me, he'll find a way Jamie. Bodyguard or not, he's gonna do what he wants to," Faith replied. "Then you're staying with me," Jamie replied. Faith got a drink and headed back upstairs. "Baby," Jamie said. She didn't reply. He walked upstairs and saw her sitting on the edge of the bed. "Tell me what you want me to say. It would kill me if anything ever happened to you. Baby, please. Please just let me take care of you," Jamie said. Her hands started to shake. "Faith," Jamie said. "I'm staying," she replied. He walked over to her. "If that's what you want to do then I'm not fighting you on it. Just promise me that you will tell me if something goes wrong," he said. Faith nodded. He kneeled down in front of her, wrapping his arms around her waist. "I mean it. You're my world baby. I don't know what I'd do without you," Jamie said. He kissed her. They curled back up together in bed. That gun was still on him.

Faith woke up the next morning and saw the gun on the bedside table. Jamie's arms were still wrapped around her. She got up and within seconds felt like she was gonna puke. She got up and ran for the bathroom down the hall. She was sick. Really sick. An hour later, she came out and Jamie was still out cold. She freshened up and went downstairs and turned the coffee on. She was about to make breakfast when she was sick all over again. Finally, the nausea passed and she made breakfast, making herself toast.

Jamie came downstairs a little while later and saw her curled up on the sofa with tea and toast. "What are you doing up so early," Jamie asked. "Couldn't sleep," Faith said. He kissed her and grabbed a massive mug of coffee. "Heard you this morning. Flu," Jamie asked. Faith shrugged. He smirked. He curled up on the sofa with her. "What you gotta do today," Jamie asked. "Have to upload some stuff from Deacon's shows. Going over a few changes with him," Faith said. "I have to go into the studio and finish up a few songs. Come meet me," Jamie asked. "I'll see how long it takes for me to finish up," Faith said. Jamie kissed her. "What's with the smirk," Faith asked. "Thinking I know why you were sick," Jamie teased. Faith shook her head. She put her dishes into the dishwasher then headed upstairs. She had a shower and started getting dressed.

"Babe," Jamie said standing in the doorway. "Don't even think it," Faith said. He kissed her again and went and hopped into the shower as Faith did her makeup. He slid out, smelling like his shampoo that Faith loved. "What," Jamie teased. "Stop thinking what I know you are," Faith said. He kissed her neck. "Quit it before I'm late," Faith said.

Faith went off to the office and Jamie went down to the studio. She loaded up the new photos for Deacon and just as she was about to finish loading them, Deacon walked into her office. "I'm thinking you needed this," Deacon said handing her an over-sized coffee from Starbucks. Faith ran into the bathroom and was sick. She came out a few minutes later and headed back into her office. "You okay," Deacon asked. Faith nodded. She finished up her work with Deacon and made an appointment to go to her doctor. "I can go with you if you need me to," Deacon said. "The press is gonna be all over me. I'll be fine," Faith said. One of Jamie's friends came into the office and walked over to Faith's desk. "What are you doing here," Faith asked as Alan walked in. "Jamie said he wanted someone with you. That's all baby girl," Alan replied. "I have a doctor appointment and if you say one damn word…"

Alan took Faith over to the doctor's appointment and Faith took custody of his cell so he couldn't call Jamie. One quick test later and the doctor headed back into the exam room. "Well," Faith asked. "Here's the vitamins. I'll see you in a month," the doctor said. "Not a word," Faith said. She nodded. Faith headed out and Alan took her back down to the office to get her truck. She dropped it off at the house and Alan took her to the studio to meet up with Jamie. "And what did the doctor say," Alan asked. "She said none of your dang business," Faith replied. Alan laughed.

Faith walked into the studio and heard Jamie singing. It was an amazing song that she knew she'd never heard. It was all about a man protecting a woman and defending her honor. Faith sat down with Alan and Jamie saw her. The true meaning of the song showed. He finished up and came in to listen. He curled up on the sofa beside Faith and wrapped his arms around her. "Well," Jamie asked. Faith nodded. Alan was smirking. "Quit it," Faith said punching Alan's shoulder. Jamie kissed her neck. The song turned out amazing. They finished the last little adjustments, got two more songs in and they were done. "You have one track left. Did you make a decision on it," the producer asked. "Got a head start on it. Not done it yet though. We done for tonight," Jamie asked. The producer nodded and Faith headed home with Jamie. "What was the punch about," Jamie asked. "Nothing," Faith replied.

They got back to the house and Faith saw Jacob and Zach sitting on the front porch. "What's going on," Faith asked. He kissed her neck. "Come on inside," Jamie said. "No. Say it Jamie," Faith said. He kissed her. "Just to make sure things stay safe," Jamie replied. Faith shook her head and went inside. "Babe," Jamie said. "Talk," Faith replied. "He threatened you. He made a stupid ass threat. They're here to handle things," Jamie replied. Faith walked upstairs. "What," Jamie asked. "Just say it," Faith replied. "He said he was gonna find you and steal back what I took. I can't…" Faith kissed him and pulled on a sweater. "He's not hurting you. The other reason is the guys wanted to go hunting. I told them I couldn't and…" "You're going," Faith said walking into the bathroom. She was almost sick again. Jamie came in behind her. "Say it," Jamie said. "Say what?" "Whatever you're trying to say Faith. You want me to back off? What?" Faith shook her head. She went downstairs. "Faith," Jamie said. She poured herself a ginger ale and sat down. "Still feeling sick," Jamie asked. "Will be for a while," Faith replied. Jamie smirked. She went through emails. "Is it what I think," Jamie asked. "I don't know yet. Just go hunting with the guys. I'll be fine here," Faith said. He walked back over to her. "Are we," Jamie asked. "Go hunting," Faith replied. He kissed her. He nodded and she nodded back. "Seriously," he asked. Faith nodded. He kneeled down and wrapped his arms around her. He kissed her and ended up in a kiss that had her forgetting where she was and who else was there. Just as they were coming up for air, one of Jamie's buddies knocked at the door.

Chapter 7

"What's up," Jamie asked as he answered the door. Alan motioned towards the gates to the area. "Oh hell no he isn't," Jamie said. "Jacob's down there now," Alan replied. "Stay here with Faith," Jamie replied. He walked down to the gate and pulled his 9mm out of his back. "What part of leave my wife the hell alone don't you understand," Jamie asked. "The part where she can't be married to you and me at the same damn time. We're married," Evan said. "No you aren't. Stay away from my wife and keep your distance from me or you're getting 50 against one," Jamie said. "Just try it country boy," Evan said. Jacob had to hold him back from pummeling Evan. "Leave before I let him loose," Jacob said. "Like his punk ass is gonna do anything," Evan replied. Jamie had the gun to Evan's forehead in a split second. "Now. Just leave her the hell alone before I put a bullet in that stupid head of yours," Jamie said. Security pulled Evan back and the police put him in cuffs. Jamie walked back down to the house and saw Faith curled up on the porch swing.

He walked towards her and Faith went inside. "Babe, he's gone," Jamie said. Her hands were shaking. She went upstairs and Jamie followed her. "Faith," he said. She closed the bathroom door and was sick. Jamie walked in behind her. He picked her up and carried her back to bed. He knew she was still shaking. "You'll be alright," Jamie said. "He's never going away. He's gonna keep coming until he get me back Jamie," Faith said. He kissed her. "I love you. Until the sun stops rising, I'm never leaving your side. He can't have it all back the way it used to be Faith. He doesn't win. The bad guy never does," Jamie said. He laid down beside her and pulled her back into his arms. "You're coming with me on that trip. No more bullshit," Jamie said. Faith was almost pulling away. He sent a text to his lawyer to double check and make sure that Evan was wrong.

He didn't let go until he knew Faith was asleep. Just as he was closing the door, his cell buzzed. Jamie answered the call. "And," Jamie asked. "Not a legal one, but he had a license drawn up. Only had his signature on it.

I'm looking into it, but I have to request the Virginia state records," his lawyer said. "Do whatever you have to," Jamie replied. He went and grabbed Faith a ginger ale and soda crackers, slid them on the counter by the bed and went outside to talk to the guys. "That little punk ass is getting my size 12 up his backside next time he pisses me off," Alan teased. "Someone is staying here with her if we're going to the ranch. Either that or she's coming. I'm not letting that jackass scare her again," Jamie said. "We'll all head up there then. She's safer surrounded by rednecks with ammo," Alan teased.

Faith woke up a little while later and saw the ginger ale and crackers. She took a sip and walked downstairs. She went in and put something on for dinner. Just as she was going to sit down, Jamie came back inside. "What," Jamie asked. "What were you doing out there," Faith asked. "Talking about my sexy wife," he teased as he leaned in to kiss her. "So when do you go," Faith asked. "You're coming. We're going up to the ranch for a day or two before we head off to do the shows this weekend," Jamie said. Faith shook her head. "And what smells so damn good in here," Jamie asked. "Dinner," Faith replied. He kissed her neck. "I love you," Jamie said. "I love you too," Faith replied. They curled up on the sofa and went through emails Jamie had received from fans. They laughed and joked around all the way through them then told the guys to come in and have dinner.

The guys had dinner and they were all full of compliments for Faith. "Woman, you are one heck of a cook," Alan said. "Thanks," Faith replied. Jamie kissed her and helped to clean up once dinner was done. "Faith," Jamie said. "What?" "Still not allowed," he teased. "Don't make me kick your butt," Faith teased. He kissed her again. The guys headed out and left Jamie alone with Faith for a while. "Babe," Jamie said. "I'm going to the ranch," Faith said. "Good. Can't sleep without you anyway," Jamie teased. He kissed her neck. "You have to let me take care of me," Faith said. He kissed her. "Whatever you want," Jamie said as he leaned in and kissed her again. The kiss turned into making out on that counter. He picked her up and they ended up on the sofa by the fireplace. He barely let her up for air.

Clothes slid to the floor and Faith's arms slid around him. They curled up together and made love on the sofa. He wrapped his arms around her and felt like their bodies meshed. They always would fit together. He didn't want to stop kissing her lips. "I love you," Jamie said. She curled up into his arms. "Promise me something," Jamie said. "What," Faith replied. "That we're always gonna find our way back to this," he said. Faith kissed him and they went back to making out and reminding each other that they were going to be in each other's arms forever.

Jamie woke up around 2am. Something wasn't right. He walked outside and Jacob was standing up. "What," Jamie asked whispering. "Just escorted Evan's cousin out of here. The man can't keep pulling this crap," Jacob said. "Just keep things as quiet as you can. She's sleeping in the TV room," Jamie said. Jacob nodded and Jamie headed back inside.

Faith got up the next morning and slid out of Jamie's arms. She went in and tried to make breakfast without being sick. She ended up being sick more than once, but made something for both of them for breakfast, opting for oatmeal minus any scent. "So what are you doing up so dang early," Jamie asked. "Wasn't feeling great. I'm fine now," Faith said. He kissed her neck. "Baby, if you aren't feeling well..." "Him showing up here didn't help," Faith said. He kissed Faith's neck and checked to see if the guys were there. "We're going tomorrow up to the cabin. Are you coming with me or am I sneaking you in via my suitcase," Jamie teased. Faith kissed him. "I'm staying here. I have a ton of..." He kissed her. "Have to," he replied. "Guess there was no point in asking me then," Faith said. She walked back upstairs. She went and had a hot shower and when she came out, Jamie was sitting on the edge of the bed. "What," Faith asked. "Say what you want to say Faith. You're pissed that he's practically started holding you hostage. Babe, I get it," Jamie said. Faith got dressed. "Baby, stay. I get you're mad," Jamie said. "Way past it," Faith said. She finished getting dressed, did her makeup and pulled her hair into a ponytail. "Baby," Jamie said. "I'm going for a drive," Faith said. "Babe," Jamie said. Faith grabbed her phone and her purse and walked out. She took off in the truck a couple minutes later.

Jamie showered, got changed, packed up for the night for him and for Faith and they headed off to the ranch. Jamie tried calling her cell more than once and got her voicemail. He sent her a text with the address and he kept trying to call. Finally, as they were pulling into the ranch, Faith called back. "I went for a drive," Faith said. "Come down to the ranch," Jamie asked. "I'll grab some food and be down there in a couple," Faith said. "Babe, please," Jamie said. "I get you're scared. At some point I'm gonna be handling all of this alone Jamie. Just relax for ten minutes," Faith said. "I love you," Jamie replied. "Love you too," Faith replied then hung up.

Jamie tried to chill with the boys, but he couldn't help but watch the door. He was dead scared something was gonna happen. Alan pulled out Jamie's guitar and handed it to him, knowing full well it was the only distraction that was gonna work. He was half way through his third song when he heard a truck pull in the driveway. He almost jumped. Faith came in with the groceries and Jamie was finally able to relax. Faith put things away then answered a call and headed upstairs. Jamie kept joking around with the guys and played through songs. They divided up where they were hunting on the property and Jamie headed upstairs. He saw Faith sitting on the bed.

"Babe," Jamie said. "What," Faith replied. "What's wrong," he asked. "He showed up at my mom and dad's," Faith said. "What do you need me to do," Jamie asked. Faith shook her head. "Nothing either of us can. He's going after them to get to me. He even told my mom that if she didn't get us to call off the sham of a marriage, he'd haunt them for the rest of our lives," Faith said. "He's not going to," Jamie said. "Is that why we rushed? So he couldn't..." Jamie kissed her. "I married you and I fell in love with you. He doesn't get to stand between us Faith. He lost because he's nuts. Because he treated you like crap. He's grasping at straws and we both know it." He brushed the tears away and pulled her into his arms. "He's not hurting us anymore. He can't. I love you Faith. He can't hurt us anymore," Jamie said. "I just want it to stop," Faith said. He kissed her. "It will. Give it a little time," Jamie said. He was damn glad she was there, and determined as hell to get back at Evan. He was putting an end to all of it once and for all.

Faith came downstairs with him a little while later and they all started cooking up something for everyone for dinner. Jamie couldn't stop trying to make sense of all of the drama. Kicking Evan's butt into a hole somewhere was the only thing that he wanted to do. Once the guys sat down to dinner, Faith went and called her folks.

"What is he doing all of this for," her dad asked. "He can't get me back. He keeps coming after me and he's not backing off. I called the police and Jamie's been on edge for days. We need to do something. Anything," Faith said. "The police here put him on a bus home. We got a restraining order put together and it's holding. Just tell me you'll be safe," her dad said. "We will be. Got a house full of hunters," Faith joked. "Keep in touch okay? If anything happens we need to know," her dad replied. "I will. I love you guys," Faith said. "We love both of you two. Stay safe baby girl," her dad said hanging up. Jamie came in, shutting the door and kissed her. "What," Faith asked. "I love you," Jamie replied. He kissed her again and picked her up, locking the office door. He locked the door and pinned her onto the desk. "Jamie," Faith said. He kissed her again, pulled her jeans and shirt off and they had sex on the desk. It was down and dirty, barely a word said between them sex that had his legs almost shaking. When they came up for air, Jamie pulled her into his arms. "What," Faith asked. "I love you," he said. Faith kissed him and got dressed. He walked back out to the dinner table and finished dinner. Once dinner was done, they got cleaned up and Jamie sang a few more songs before they all headed to bed.

Faith went upstairs and showered and Jamie slid into bed with her. "Get some sleep," Faith said. He kissed her. "Can't sleep without you," Jamie said. "It's 8:30. I'm barely even…" He kissed her. "I love you," Jamie said. "I love you too," Faith replied. "If you need me tomorrow, just text alright," Jamie said. Faith nodded. He nibbled her ear. "Sleep before you never get any sleep. What time are you guys getting up," Faith asked. "5 a.m." "Then you should be sleeping," Faith said. He kissed and nibbled her neck. She snuggled up with him and tried to fall asleep.

Jamie woke up the next morning with the guys and made sure to kiss her before he headed out. "If you need me," he said. Faith kissed him again and he headed off with the guys. Faith was in the bathroom sick again and again until almost noon. She had lunch, had a long bath and her phone rang. "Yep," Faith said answering. "You know that marriage isn't legal. I have our marriage license," Evan said. "And I have a restraining order," Faith replied. She hung up. Faith turned the security alarm on and went back to the bathroom to finish her bath. When her hands wouldn't stop shaking, she gave up. Faith got dressed and went downstairs to put something on for dinner for the guys.

Jamie came back in later that evening with the guys. He went upstairs to find Faith going through emails. He leaned over and kissed her. "What," Faith asked. "Why are you all damn shaky," Jamie asked. "Doesn't matter," Faith said. "Yeah it does. What did he do," Jamie asked. "Said that he has a marriage license to prove it. That's the only reason and I know it," Faith said. He kissed her. "I'll put my lawyer on it. Faith, he's not coming after you without something behind it. What aren't you telling me," Jamie asked. Faith shook her head. "I know it's not true. Jamie, I don't remember any of it. If I could, I'd permanently delete it from my brain," Faith said. Jamie kissed her. He called his lawyer, sent him all the info that they had. "I'll get back to you by the end of the day tomorrow," his lawyer said. "Thanks. All I need to know is that he's full of it," Jamie said. "Will do," the lawyer said. Jamie kissed Faith. "Come down and eat," Jamie asked. Faith nodded. "Ate already but yeah," Faith said. "Babe, please," Jamie said. He slid his hand in hers and walked her back downstairs.

They all had something to eat, even if it meant force feeding Faith. The guys headed back out and Jamie and Faith curled up together on the sofa and he flipped on a movie for them. Faith was still shaky and he could tell a mile off. He kissed her neck. "I know you're trying to help," Faith said. "I'm being in love with my wife. If something is bothering you, just say it," he replied. "What if he's right," Faith asked. "Look at me," Jamie said. Faith turned and looked at him. "Forever. Not one day more, not one day less. I love you. Faith, if that happens, it gives us another reason to have that huge wedding. Nothing is getting in our way," Jamie said. "But...." He kissed her. One kiss always became more. "I love you. Nothing is gonna change. Whether you're with him or you aren't, we're married. Faith, nothing is shaking this. Nothing is breaking us up. Not now. Stop worrying," Jamie said as he leaned in and kissed her again.

After a long night of Jamie trying to distract her over and over again, Jamie carried Faith upstairs and curled up in bed with her. She curled up in his arms and he serenaded her to sleep. Fact was, the song hit him at that exact moment. It was on the fly, and a song he never thought he'd be singing. Faith finally fell asleep a while later, and just as Jamie was nodding off, his cell buzzed. "Jamie, bad news," the lawyer said. "Tell me it isn't what I think," Jamie said. "He forged her signature on one. He tried to have it filed and since he was related to the judge, he put it through. I can fight it, but it's been filed since they first got together. What do you need me to do," the lawyer asked. "Fix it. That's it. Just fix it," Jamie said. He hung up and managed to stay quiet. "I heard you," Faith said. "Wasn't about..." "I know it was Jamie. What did your lawyer guy say," Faith asked. "He can fix..." Faith was almost sick. "Babe," Jamie said. She got up, running for the bathroom and was sick. "Baby, he's fixing it. He forged your name on it," Jamie said. Faith was sick again.

Jamie woke up at 5am. He tossed and turned most of the night. Knowing that Evan still had that hold on her was killing him. He called the lawyer. "Well," Jamie asked. "I put in a request with the court office. Jamie, she's gonna have to go up against him in court. You know that right," the lawyer said. "Do whatever we have to so she won't have to. She's a mess as it is. I don't want him getting any info that he doesn't need. We have to find a solution," Jamie said. "I'm working on one. I'll do what I can, but you may have to go back to put a complete end to it," the lawyer said.

Jamie did a workout then headed upstairs to have a shower and saw Faith with a smirk ear to ear. "What," Jamie asked. "Nothing," Faith said. He walked over to her and kissed her then grabbed her hand. "What," Faith asked. He walked her into the bathroom, pulled her shirt off and pulled her into a hot shower with him. He kissed her, devouring her lips and didn't come up for air until the water turned cold. They made love in the shower then he washed her back and she washed his. Letting her waste one more minute on that stress wasn't an option. When they finally did come up for air, Jamie's cell was buzzing. "Don't even think it. He's not getting you back Faith," Jamie said. "What happens when he won't leave me alone," Faith asked. Jamie kissed her. "Remember who isn't letting you get hurt ever again. You have me and the guys. Nobody is getting that close except me," Jamie said. He kissed her again with a kiss that knocked the wind right out of her. "You're my wife. Not his. Never will be his. Whatever it takes Faith, he's never getting near you. Never," Jamie said. She could see his blood boiling. She started getting changed. "Faith," Jamie said. "What," she replied. "I put your gun in your bag. He makes one move near you, shoot," Jamie replied. Now she knew he'd tipped over the edge.

She finished getting ready and Jamie started packing their bags to head back out. "I get you're flipping out, but there's nothing else we can do," Faith said. Jamie kissed her again. "There always is," he replied. He kissed her and packed up the rest of their things. "Jamie," Faith said. "Finish getting that sexy ass ready. I got this," Jamie said. He smacked her butt and went and finished packing. He was playing stupid or ignoring it all. Faith knew better than to push, but something was going on with Evan and she knew Jamie well enough to know he wasn't standing for it. They finished getting ready, he grabbed the bags and they all headed down to the tour bus. The guys hopped on with Faith and Jamie and Jamie walked her straight back to the stateroom.

"If you see him or he tries calling, you need to tell me. I know you don't want…" "You aren't doing anything stupid. Jamie, you have a career that you need to concentrate on. Stop letting him ruin things," Faith said. Jamie kissed her. "He's never ruining us," Jamie said. One kiss that had both of them forgetting what they were doing and where they were. One that had her heart racing. "Nobody is ruining us," Jamie said. It was a rough kiss, but one that had her knees going weak. He wrapped her legs around him and pinned her into the wall. "Jamie," Faith said. Her jeans dropped and he made love to her against that wall. A half hour later, they came up for air and he walked out of the stateroom. Faith got dressed and sat down on the bed with her laptop. She heard his phone buzz. She saw it and saw a text from Jamie's ex:

Just come over. We can talk about what's bugging you. Love you.

Faith walked out and handed Jamie his cell then walked back into the stateroom and tried locking the door. Jamie walked in. He locked it behind him. "What," Jamie asked. "Go call her back," Faith said. "Woman," Jamie said. She walked past him with her laptop in hand. She put her iPod on and slid her earbuds in and tried to get work done. Jamie came out 10 minutes later and handed her his phone. It was open to his reply to his ex:

I married Faith. I love her more than you could ever even understand. I'm fine. PS The I love you crap can end now. Didn't matter then and it has no meaning now.

Jamie sat down and got some of the song he'd sung to Faith the night before on paper. He sat and stared at her, wondering what was running through her head. Finally, after an hour and a half of her being silent, he started throwing paper balls at her. She took her ear buds out and threw them back at Jamie then walked back to the stateroom and closed the door. They made a pit stop a little while later. The guys hopped off to grab some drinks and Jamie walked back to the stateroom, grabbed Faith's hand and walked her down to the little shop. He grabbed them some snacks and something to drink and started walking around the back. "What," Faith asked.

"I love you. He's not ruining us. Either is my ex. No matter what she says or what happens, nobody is causing trouble. You have to let me deal with him. I get that you don't want him coming after either of us, but he's going to no matter what Faith. He's not the type to leave it be," Jamie said. "Then stop scaring me and trying to put your mark and take possession," Faith said. She walked off and Jamie pulled her back to him. He kissed her and cradled her face in his hands. "I'm handling it. We will handle it," Jamie said. "Then do what you want," Faith replied. She walked back onto the bus and sat back down in the stateroom and worked on emails. Jamie worked on the music a while longer then closer to dinner, he walked back down to the stateroom.

"Come," Jamie said. "Not hungry," Faith said. Jamie pulled her to her feet and kissed her. "Dinner," Jamie said. They walked down the aisle and headed into the restaurant for dinner. He didn't let go of her hand until their dinner came. They had dinner with the guys, paid and hopped back on the bus for the last hour or two. They finally pulled into the hotel and Jamie headed up the back with Faith. His buddies were posted on the floor with them. As they were getting settled, Jamie's lawyer called. "Well," Jamie asked. "He's standing by the idea that she signed it. I put her actual signature beside it and they were completely different. The judge wants them both in a courtroom. They have to hash it out. He won't back off on it," the lawyer said. "She's not going. Find a way around it," Jamie said. "I did. There isn't one. We set the court date for Wednesday. I'll send you the address," the lawyer said. "Double up security. See if we can make them both separate. I don't want them in the same room. Got me," Jamie said. "I'll do my best," the lawyer said.

"What," Faith asked. "Nothing," Jamie replied. "Spill it," Faith replied. "The judge wants you both in the same room to discuss it. He's trying to get it so you two talk to the judge separately and you don't get stuck in a room alone with him. You're not safe if you are," Jamie said. "I'm not doing it without you. I'm not walking in that room without you with me." "I can't just let him get in the middle of us. You get it right," Jamie asked. Faith kissed him. "Nobody is doing that. Just try to concentrate on that ring on your finger Jamie. I said yes to you. I said no way in hell to him." He kissed Faith. He picked her up, wrapping her legs around his waist and leaned her onto the bed, pinning her arms down. "Jamie," Faith said. He kissed her again, devoured her lips and peeled her clothes off. He kicked his off and they ended up in a pile together at the bottom of the bed. He made love to her and they ended up entwined the rest of the night. He didn't let go, even when his phone buzzed.

The next morning, Jamie woke up still curled up with Faith. He kissed her neck and reached for his cell. He saw the text from the lawyer:

Judge agreed. Said you can do video conference instead. 10am Nashville time.

Jamie looked at Faith's watch and they had a half hour left. He kissed her neck, nibbled her ear and kissed down her shoulder. "Good morning to you too," Faith said. "Video conference with the judge in a half hour," Jamie said. He kissed her. They got somewhat dressed and Jamie logged into the video conferencing.

"So are you sure that you didn't sign anything regarding a marriage between yourself and Evan James," the judge asked. "I feared for my life every day I was there. Marrying him wasn't an option. Never has been. He did something stupid and tried pulling out stupid fake vows. I said no more than once to him. I wouldn't have married him ever," Faith said. "And signing this form," the judge asked. "I wouldn't have and I know I didn't sign anything. He racked up my damn credit card. I wouldn't have married him." She heard Evan grumbling. "She signed it. My folks witnessed it," Evan said. "Your parents? Right. The ones you have in your pocket? You got them to go along with it. I didn't sign it," Faith said. "You can verify that you didn't," the judge asked. Faith nodded. "The signatures don't match even partially, but," the judge said. Faith shook her head. "I didn't sign it," Faith said. "We can't prove you didn't." "Yeah I can. The minute all of it was happening, I was trying to leave and he wouldn't let me. I had a damn gun to my head. Signing that wasn't happening if it meant being tied to him," Faith said. "We can't verify either way, so as far as things are concerned here, the license isn't valid." Jamie turned off the video conference and kissed Faith. She got up and showered. Jamie came in and slid in behind her. "Faith," Jamie said. She rinsed off the last of her conditioner and stepped out. She dried off and went and got changed.

Faith got dressed and started doing her hair and makeup. Jamie slid out. He wrapped a towel around him and walked over to her. "Faith, stop," Jamie said. She brushed him off. "Faith," he said. She finished getting changed. "What's going on," he asked. "Nothing," Faith said. She ordered breakfast for them and sat down by herself and went through emails. Jamie got half-dressed and walked into the sitting area. "Faith, I get that he's pissed you off more than once, but you won. You're free from him," Jamie said. "Right. Like he's gonna stop. A judge says he can't win and you think that's gonna stop him?" "He's not hurting you and a judge said he has no right to you. That should be enough," Jamie said. Faith shook her head. Breakfast came. Jamie paid off the room service and they had breakfast. "He's not coming near you," Jamie said. "Right. He's not? He's gonna get ten times worse Jamie. Now he isn't gonna back off. He's gonna go off the damn deep end," Faith said. She finished breakfast, got up and went into the bedroom. "Faith, quit walking off. I get you're mad. I love you. He doesn't get to hurt you and he damn well doesn't get to steal you away. Stop," Jamie said.

Faith grabbed her laptop, her purse and her cell and went to walk out. "Faith," Jamie said. She walked out the door and Alan was standing at the door. He followed Faith and Jamie caught up to them. "Woman, where the hell are you going," Jamie asked. Faith got to the waiting SUV and hopped in. Not even a second later, Jamie hopped in beside her and Alan hopped in the front. They headed over for sound check. "Faith," Jamie said. She shook her head. They got over to the venue a while later and Faith hopped out before Jamie even noticed they'd stopped. She walked in and went over to the dressing room. She locked the door behind her.

Jamie came in the back way. "Gonna tell me why you're pissed off? Thought everything was alright," Jamie asked. "And I needed to go back and tell the judge all the bullshit he caused? Jamie, the man put me through hell. I can tell you he isn't gonna stop," Faith said. He kissed her. "I love you. Stop worrying about what he's doing next. We're having a baby Faith. Something that is you and me." He kissed her again. She tried to pull away, but he slid onto the sofa with her and wrapped his arms around her. "What are you worried about?" "That he isn't backing off. That he's gonna do something stupid to get back at us," Faith said. He kissed her. "He's not going to. He can't hurt either of us Faith. Not anymore," Jamie said. "I just need some time to relax," Faith said. He kissed her. "No more worrying alright? Faith, you have a baby to think about too," Jamie said. Faith got up and the minute she did, a pain shot right through her. "Baby," Jamie said. "Ow," Faith said. Jamie picked her up, unlocked the door and took her to the SUV. "Hospital. Now," Jamie said as Alan hopped in and drove them to the closest hospital.

Jamie was pacing the hall and Alan came over to him and handed him an oversized coffee. "You okay," Alan asked. Jamie looked at the hospital room door and saw the doctors coming out. "Well," Jamie asked. "You can go in now," the doctor said. Jamie ran in to her side. "What did the doctor say," Jamie asked. Faith looked at him and her eyes were almost a glowing blue. "Faith," Jamie said. She turned away from him. Jamie slid onto the bed with her and wrapped his arms around her. "Faith, please. We can try again," he said. Faith started crying all over again. Jamie didn't let go. "We're gonna be okay," Jamie said. "Do you want me to call the venue," Alan asked. Faith shook her head. "You're not staying here by yourself. Not when he's on the rampage," Jamie said. "I'll stay here and we'll rotate with the guys. She'll be fine," Alan said. Jamie kissed Faith and went out to talk to the doctor.

Chapter 8

"If I get her somewhere safe that she can just relax, can she come home," Jamie asked the doctor. "Once we know she's alright, she can go whenever she wants," the doctor said. "What's left before I can take her home," Jamie asked. "A small procedure. An hour or two at most. She just can't be left alone. If anything else happens, she has to be close to a hospital. No flying," the doctor said. Jamie nodded. The nurse wheeled Faith out. Jamie went to go with her. "She'll be fine. You can't be there," the doctor said. Alan went to guard the room. Jamie paced the halls until she came back. Alan was right beside her. She got back to the room and Jamie curled up with her. "I'm not going anywhere without you," Jamie said. "You have sound check," Faith said. "I'm not going there without you," Jamie said. Faith knew there was no point in fighting with him.

He talked the doctor into letting her go home, but had to promise that she'd be near a hospital in case anything happened. "She'll be at the hotel we're staying at. She's going to be guarded. Deal," Jamie asked the doctor. The doctor nodded. Jamie took her back to the hotel. "I'm fine," Faith said. "Alan is staying and so is Callon. End of discussion. No fightin," Jamie said. Faith nodded. He kissed her. "If you need me, say the word. I promise," Jamie said. Faith nodded. "Babe, we're gonna be alright. We can try again," Jamie said. Faith rolled over. Jamie curled up with her. "We're gonna be okay," he said. Faith curled up on the bed. "Baby, it's gonna be okay. As long as you and me are okay, we'll be alright," Jamie said. She didn't say a word. "Faith," Jamie said. "Just go," she replied. He kissed her. "I love you," Jamie said. "I love you too," Faith replied. Jamie headed off and went down to sound check, but his heart wasn't in it.

He kept calling to check on Faith. "She's fine. She's sleeping Jamie. I'm sitting right here. I can see her," Alan said. "Just make sure she's okay. That's all I need," Jamie said. Alan walked over to Faith and handed her the cell phone. "Aren't you supposed to be doing a meet and greet or something," Faith asked. "Miss you. It's not the same without you," Jamie said. "You lived without me before," Faith said. "Promise me something? Promise me you'll get some sleep. I'll come snuggle you the minute I'm done here. I love you," Jamie said. "I love you too. Go kick some serious butt," Faith said. "Chocolate or strawberry," Jamie asked. "What," Faith asked. "Milkshake," he teased. "Vanilla," Faith replied. "See you in a couple. I love you," Jamie said. He hung up and went to get ready for the show. He got one of the guys to video part of it.

Jamie hit the stage and 3 or 4 songs in, dedicated a song to Faith. "This one is going out to my gorgeous wife Faith. I love you baby," Jamie said. Cameron sent it to Faith and it put a smirk on her face. "Now will you eat," Alan teased. "Thank you," Faith said. "Baby girl, he's in love with you. Nothing is happening. That punk ass isn't hurting you when any of us are here," Alan said. Faith ordered something to eat and curled up on the bed.

Jamie came in around 11:30 and Alan was out cold on the sofa. Faith was checking through emails. "What part of you are supposed to be resting didn't you get," Jamie asked. "Cabin Fever. Went for a walk with Alan for a bit. Went and chilled in the hot tub for a while then I came back up here. I was antsy," Faith said. Jamie walked over and slid the vanilla milkshake on the bedside table. "Thank you," Faith said. He kissed her. He curled up on the bed with her. "Stomach still hurt," Jamie asked. "It does, but it's going away," Faith said. He kissed her and kicked his jeans off. "Jamie," Faith said. He closed the bedroom door and slid back into bed with Faith. He put the laptop in her bag and snuggled up to her.

The next morning, Jamie woke up and the bed was empty. "Faith," Jamie said. "Yep," Faith said from the sofa. "Woman, don't scare me like that," Jamie said. He got up and walked over to her and saw Faith going through emails. All of a sudden she stopped. "Babe," Jamie said. He looked at the email:

Start watching your back. Can't run forever Faith. One stupid move and you're mine.

Jamie put a trace on the email. "We're leaving. Now," Jamie said. They packed up and were out of the hotel in a matter of minutes. They got on the tour bus with the band and were gone within the hour. He curled up with Faith and tried to get her calmed down. "I told you," Faith said. He kissed her and sat with her until she calmed down. Once she fell asleep, Jamie went in to explain to the guys what was going on.

"What do you mean the jackass came after her? He can't just break y'all up," Greg said. "Tell him that. We just had world war three with him. Tried to pull off a fake marriage license. She's gonna be safe one way or another," Jamie said. "Don't do something stupid. Y'all need to stay away from his crazy ass if that's how nuts he is. You can't keep running," Greg said. "He's the one that's gonna be runnin. He's staying away no matter what we need to do. When we have to go, we need to go. She's safer at home but we can't hide out. He needs to leave us alone and putting him in a jail cell is just the start of it," Jamie replied. "What do you want us to do," Greg asked. "You see her panicked, do something. Come find me. We got the guys doing security, but nobody can be there all the time," Jamie said. "That's what you want, you got it," Dean said. Jamie went to go back down the hall and saw Faith. She walked down the hallway and grabbed a drink. "Babe," Jamie said. She walked past him, checked how far along they were and went back to the stateroom. She closed the door and locked it. Jamie sat down. He took a deep breath then walked back down the hall and unlocked the stateroom door. He stepped inside and closed it behind him.

"Faith," Jamie said. "I'm flying home," Faith replied. "You can't fly. Doc said you can't," Jamie replied. "Then I'll find my way back," Faith replied. Jamie walked towards her and went to kiss her and Faith brushed him off. "What," he asked. Faith sat back down. "Babe, you can't..." "I'm going home," Faith replied. The tour bus stopped 15 minutes later. "You aren't leaving. Faith, you aren't gonna be safe," Jamie said. She put her things into her bag. "You can't just leave," Jamie said. "I can do whatever the hell I want to. I'm going home," Faith said. She got off the tour bus and Jamie grabbed her bag. "We're not doing this Faith. You're staying with us. I can't just..." Faith went into the car rental and went to rent a car. Jamie grabbed her hand and walked her out, grabbed takeout for them and walked her back onto the tour bus. "I'm going..." He kissed her and walked her back into the stateroom. "No more fighting. I get you're scared Faith. I love you. I'm not letting him hurt you again," Jamie said. Faith grabbed her bag. He took it back out of her hand. "You can't," Jamie said. The tour bus headed back out. "Happy now,' Faith asked. "I get it alright," Jamie said. "When we get to the next stop, I'm going home," Faith said. "Emma's meeting us. Thought you'd like to get some time to hang out with her. Faith, please just stop worrying," Jamie said. She shook her head. He handed her the takeout Chinese she loved and sat down on the bed with her. "What," Faith asked. "Stop worrying. Faith, he's not hurting you and he's not getting close enough to try anything," Jamie said. Faith shook her head and walked back into the sitting area.

Jamie followed her and curled up on the sofa with her. "So what you think about that new song," Greg asked. "Sounds good. Still don't know where it came from," Faith said. "Jamie came up with it. We just ran with it," Dean said. "I get it," Faith said. Jamie tried to hold her hand and she wouldn't let him. "Plus, I found some of those lyrics you were working on babe. Put your stuff to music," Jamie said. "I bet," Faith replied. He slid his hand in hers and kissed her hand. He slid her arms around him. "Feeling any better," Greg asked. "Sorta," Faith replied. Jamie wouldn't let go no matter how much Faith fought him. "So what other lyrics did you save in that computer of yours," Alan asked. "A bunch of stuff. I have a pile of stuff I was working on," Faith said. "Guess that means a heck of a lot more love songs there Jamie," Greg teased. "Dude, she wrote part of that Chains song. They aren't love songs," Jamie replied. "Then you're gonna have a dang CD full by the end of the month, Greg joked. They pulled into the next hotel a few hours later. Faith went to walk off the bus and Jamie stopped her once everyone was off. "What," Faith asked. "You aren't leaving Faith. I need you as much as you need me. Please," Jamie said. "Going home doesn't mean I don't love you. It means I want to just go home and try to relax. I need to...." He kissed her. That one kiss turned into a steamy make out session. He walked her off the bus and into their suite and they barely came up for air. An hour later, he let her up for air. "Jamie," Faith said. "Stay. Please baby. Stay here," he asked. "I need to go...." He kissed her again.

He curled up with Faith the rest of the night. It killed him knowing that Faith was that worried. There was nothing he could do to change anything that was going on. He got a text from Alan that said he'd found Evan. He was being handled. Jamie finally managed to fall asleep. He curled back up to Faith and kissed her neck. "What," Faith asked. "I love you," he said. Faith tried to squirm away and Jamie linked their fingers. "You're not picking a damn fight in the middle of the night," Jamie said. "You letting me go home tomorrow," Faith asked. He kissed her neck. "I hate doing shows without you. The doctors said that they didn't want you flying. We're going home after the show Sunday," Jamie said. "Then it won't be that long apart," Faith said. He turned her towards him. "Picking a damn fight," he said. "It's not a fight. I'm going," Faith replied. He kissed her. "I love you woman. I get you're miserable and upset. I can't go back and change it. I can't stop you from losing the baby. I love you," Jamie said. "I just need to handle this my own way," Faith replied. ""Tell me what you need me to do," Jamie said. "I need to go home and relax. I'll stay with Emma," Faith said. "You can't fly," Jamie said. "Then I go home with..." Jamie kissed her. "I can't do that show without you again," Jamie said. "I'm supposed to tour with you the rest of my life," Faith asked. "Please," Jamie said. "I can't just put me on hold for you," Faith said. "If you make sure that you're safe then its fine. I just need to know you'll be safe. Please," Jamie said. "I will be. I need quiet," Faith said. Jamie kissed her. "Promise me something," Jamie said. "What," Faith replied. "That you won't take off and walk off from the guys. I need to know you're safe or it's gonna drive me nuts," Jamie said. "I'll be alright. I'll be with Emma," Faith said. "And you'll have security no matter what," Jamie replied. Faith nodded and he leaned in and kissed her. "Even if he tries proving that the marriage isn't legal again, I'd marry you a thousand times over. You know that right," Jamie asked. Faith kissed him.

They headed into the venue and a half hour later, Faith saw Emma heading in with security. Jamie had his arms still wrapped around Faith while the guys were starting to get warmed up a bit. "We can try again," Jamie said. "I don't want to talk about it Jamie. Just stop," Faith said. He kissed her. Faith walked off. "Babe," Jamie said. Faith hopped off the stage and walked over to Emma and hugged her. "You okay," Emma asked. Faith shook her head and walked off with Emma. "What happened," Emma asked. Faith went off to talk to Emma and told her what had happened.

"So what's going on with Faith," Greg asked. "She's just upset," Jamie said. He blew it off and started sound check. When he started the song he knew would catch her, he saw her walking back in with Emma. "So what if the license ends up being real," Emma asked. "Then I have to be in a courtroom with him. I have to fight him and prove that I didn't. That plus losing the baby is killing me," Faith said. "All the more reason to go back to Nashville. He deserves to have all of you and not just the part that works Faith. He married all of you," Emma said. "And the fact that my heart was ripped out and ripped to shreds, put back in and then toyed with means what Emma? I should've just gone home," Faith said. "So now you're regretting marrying Jamie," Emma asked. "I'm regretting being anywhere near Evan. Walking away when I should've just been with Jamie in the first place. I screwed everything up," Faith said. Emma hugged her. "The second you said you'd marry Jamie was erasing it all Faith. He loves you," Emma said. "I'm not worthy of it and never have been. I sat out in that stupid..." Jamie walked towards them. "Come down and grab some dinner," Jamie asked as he approached the ladies.

Jamie slid his hand in Faith's and wrapped his fingers in hers. "Okay," he asked. Faith nodded. Telling him what she'd just told Emma would kill him. Greg came up and showed Emma to catering and gave Jamie a minute with Faith. "Why do I get the feeling that y'all were talking about me," Jamie asked. "We were talking," Faith said. He kissed her. "No matter what happens with that other Evan stuff, we're gonna be alright," Jamie said. "If I had just not bothered to..." Jamie kissed her. "We all make mistakes Faith. We ended up together. That's all that matters. You know that," Jamie said. "Also shows I suck at decisions. I made more than just one," Faith said. He kissed her. "I know one neither one of us made. Faith, stop beating yourself up about everything. Baby, I love you. We love each other. We're fine," Jamie said. Faith nodded. He kissed her again. He wrapped his arm around her and walked her down to catering. The chef had made her favorite at Jamie's request. On top of it, he made a dessert that he knew Jamie and Faith both loved. They had dinner back on the tour bus alone while Emma ended up flirting through dinner with Greg.

"Just because we made mistakes doesn't mean this is one of them," Jamie said. "I lived with a psychopath. For all I know, he drugged me into signing it," Faith said. He kissed her. "Stop worrying about what he's doing and concentrate on us. We'll be alright," Jamie said. "I know, but I might have…" He kissed her again. "You didn't do anything," Jamie said. "What if I did Jamie? What if I just screwed everything up altogether," Faith asked. He pulled her into his arms. "You didn't do anything," Jamie said. Now it hit him. All the need to go home, to hide, to fight everything was because of Evan. Baby, you can't keep letting him get to you," Jamie said. "What am I supposed to do Jamie? Forget that it was the worst mistake I ever made? Forget that he destroyed my life," Faith said. Jamie kissed her. "I love you. Faith, you can't keep beating yourself up. Please," Jamie said. "He's never gonna leave me alone," Faith said. Jamie tried to comfort her and she brushed him off. Faith went and cleaned up and got changed and just as she was stepping out of the stateroom, Jamie was in the aisle. "What," Faith asked. He kissed her. He picked her up, walked her back into the state room and leaned her onto the bed. "Jamie," Faith said. He kissed her. He slid her shirt off, her jeans and everything in between. They made love in that bed. "Never loving anyone else. We were meant to be together Faith. I love you," Jamie said. Faith kissed him. "You do have a concert you know," Faith said. He kissed her again, they both got dressed and cleaned up and then headed inside. Jamie kissed her with a kiss that could melt metal and headed into the meet and greet. Faith just stood at the door. She was the only thing making him smile at all. As soon as he finished, he grabbed her hand and kissed her and they headed towards the stage. "What," Faith asked. "Never ever think that we don't belong together. I love you," Jamie said. He kissed her and headed on.

Emma wandered over to her. "So I guess you're feeling better," Emma said. "I need to know I can be free of him altogether. All of it is gonna haunt me forever," Faith said. "Look at him Faith. He loves you. He's never letting go Faith. You can't just leave," Emma said. "I'm handling all of it. He's not even getting it Emma. The fact that Evan is gonna keep coming is making it all worse. I need my life the way it should be. I want to be able to be happy Emma. I can't do it watching over my shoulder," Faith said. "Don't even think it," Emma said. "I have to," Faith replied. They watched the show. "Don't do this," Emma said. Faith heard the last song from the hallway as she made her way out the door. "Faith," Emma said.

Jamie headed off the stage and saw Emma. "Where is she," Jamie asked. "Jamie," Emma said. He ran down the hall and saw Faith getting in one of the SUV's. "Faith," Jamie said. She got in the SUV and left. Jamie grabbed his cell and called the driver. "Don't take her to the airport. She's not allowed to fly. Circle back," Jamie said. "We can't circle back. We're in a traffic jam now," the driver said. "Pull over. I'm coming," Jamie replied. He took off in the other SUV and drove straight towards where Faith was. He pulled in behind the SUV Faith was in and hopped out. He walked over towards the other SUV and got in the passenger seat.

"Jamie," Faith said. "You're not leaving. Faith, please," Jamie said. "I need to end all of this crap Jamie. Just let me do it," Faith said. He kissed her. The police escorted them back to the tour bus. "Jamie, I need to do this," Faith said. "You're not doing it. Not alone," Jamie said. "I'm doing it my way. Please," Faith said. "No. You take Alan with you. Anyone," Jamie said. "I'm doing this my way Jamie. I have to. I got myself into it. I have to be the one to finish this," Faith said. He kissed her. "No. Not after everything he did. You barely made it out of there. No," Jamie said. Faith could barely say a word the rest of the night. "You can't do this," Jamie said as the tour bus took off. "Stop telling me what I can and can't do. I'm doing this Jamie. I brought all this crap on us. I'm putting an end to it once and for all," Faith said. "No," Jamie replied. "So now you're the boss of me," Faith asked. "Stop. Stop throwing yourself under the bus. I love you. Faith, I married you knowing that Evan is a psychopath. You can't keep doing this. You're safe with me. I love you," Jamie said. "I love you too, but I need to do this for me. I love you but I'm not letting him get back at you. He was pulling loaded guns on you. I can't let you walk into that again," Jamie said. "I'm going Jamie. I need to," Faith said. "Then take Alan with you," Jamie pleaded. Faith walked into the stateroom alone. "Faith," Jamie said. She went to close the door and he blocked it. He walked in and locked the door behind him.

"Faith, please just stop. You don't need to keep doing this. You left. That's what matters. That's all that matters," Jamie said. "You don't get it do you," Faith said. "I get that you don't think that you deserve to be happy. You can't get past what happened. That doesn't mean you walk back into that hornet's nest. Faith, he had you at gunpoint. He almost killed you more than once. I love you. I've never ever laid a hand on you. Don't do this," Jamie said. "Stop. Jamie, I'm doing it whether you agree or not. I wasn't asking your permission." He kissed her. He picked her up, wrapped her legs around him and pinned her to the bed. "Stop picking a damn fight," Jamie said. He peeled her clothes off then his and devoured her. They made love in that bed until both of them were exhausted and out of energy. "Don't leave," Jamie said. Faith turned away from him. Jamie's arms wrapped around her and they both went to sleep.

Faith got up the next morning and everyone was out cold. They'd stopped at a truck stop that was all of an hour away from where hell was. Faith snuck off the tour bus quietly, leaving Jamie a note and got a taxi to a car rental. She got a black pickup with tinted windows and drove straight back to the trailer she'd been living in with Evan. She pulled in and not seconds later, Evan stepped out. "Came to your senses," Evan said. "Say what you want to say Evan. Get it out of your system," Faith said. Evan grabbed her arm and dragged her in the door. First thing Faith did was make sure her gun was in her purse.

"What the hell? You let her walk out," Jamie said. "We were all sleeping," Alan said. "She's gone. She went back to that stupid ass trailer. She could be killed," Jamie said. "What do you want us to do," Alan asked. "Go down there and make sure she's okay. Get her out of there," Jamie said. The guys headed off in one SUV, Jamie headed there in another.

"I knew you'd come to your senses," Evan said. "Say what you wanna say Evan. Just spit it the hell out," Faith said. "You think you can walk away that easy? He doesn't get to take what's mine," Evan said. "I'm not a damn possession. When you get over that, let me know," Faith said. "I want you. Now. Here. In that damn bed that I made you mine. Walk," Evan said. "You're not..." He slapped her. "Walk," Evan replied. He pushed her down that hallway. She was shaking. "I'm not doing it," Faith said. Evan pushed her and almost knocked her to the floor.

"You don't get to walk out on me. You don't get to push me away and you damn well don't get to marry someone else," Evan said as he locked the bedroom door. "I married him. That's not changing. You don't get to just try to pull out some fake marriage license. I never would've married you. Not even if I was on drugs would I have ever said yes to living with the damn devil," Faith said. Another slap. "You don't get to talk. Do what you're supposed to do. Take off the damn clothes he bought you and you're getting what you came back for – me," Evan said. Faith's hands were shaking. "You faked my signature," Faith said. "And," Evan said. Faith pulled her gun out of her purse and pointed it. "Right. Forget that I know how to dismantle it," Evan said. He almost busted Faith's hand and ended up with a shotgun to the back of his head. "Drop it," Alan said. He almost broke Faith's wrist. She pushed Evan away, grabbed her things and ran. She got out the door and ran into Jamie. He picked her up, put her in her rental truck and drove her to the tour bus.

"Jamie," Faith said. "He put his damn hands on you. He can't just hurt you Faith. Not without getting his ass kicked. You shouldn't have left," Jamie said. Faith didn't say a word but he saw her brushing tears away. "Baby," Jamie said. The second the truck stopped, Faith got out. She got on the tour bus and locked herself in the stateroom. She started crying. It killed Jamie to hear any of it. The bus headed back out and Jamie was still pissed.

When they stopped for dinner, Jamie went back to talk to Faith. She wouldn't unlock the door. He left Emma on the bus with her. "Faith, it's just me. Come out," Emma said. She unlocked the door. The minute Emma saw the bruises, she walked Emma off the bus and grabbed ice. She grabbed them something to eat and walked back onto the bus with

Faith, putting ice on the bruises. Faith had dinner alone in the stateroom and Emma went to talk to Jamie.

"What's going on," Jamie said walking towards Emma in the parking lot. "He did more than put his hands on her. She has bruises Jamie. She's scared and she's hurt. He scared the living hell out of her. Jamie, she needs somewhere to just breathe. She needs to be able to be mad without being in the public eye. She can come back to Dallas with me for a few days," Emma said. "No. Not after what he did. I don't wanna lose her to a bad memory," Jamie said. "You aren't." "I am. Emma, he's learned his damn lesson at her hand. She's gonna take more than days to get through this. We need to deal with this together," Jamie said. "She wants to be alone Jamie. I'll stay with her. Alan can come with us if it makes you feel better," Emma said. Jamie walked past her and walked onto the bus then opened the stateroom.

The second he saw the bruises, his blood started to boil. Jamie walked over to her and wrapped his arms around her and pulled her into him. "Why didn't you tell me," Jamie asked. Faith shook her head. "Baby, you can't just run. You can't keep thinking that you don't deserve what we have. I love you. I loved you the day that we met. I helped you because you deserve a hell of a lot better. You deserve better than him and a hell of a lot better than Deacon. Just be happy. Let me help you," Jamie said. Faith shook her head. "Baby, please," Jamie said. Faith squirmed away from Jamie. He kissed her. "I love you," Jamie said. He didn't let go of her until they stopped at the hotel. He got the key, picked Faith up and carried her up to the suite. He laid her on the bed and went and got ice. He came back and put it on her bruises, ordered dinner for them both and curled up on the bed with her. "You're gonna be okay," Jamie said. He didn't let her go for even a second.

That night, Jamie fell asleep curled up with Faith. An hour after they'd fallen asleep, Faith woke up with a nightmare. Jamie got up with her. "Baby, you're gonna be okay. I'm here," Jamie said. "He…" The more worried she was, the more scared he was. Whatever happened in that short time was enough to scared the crap out of her. "Tell me what happened," Jamie said. Faith got up and walked into the TV room. She grabbed some milk and curled up on the sofa. She grabbed a blanket and curled up with her laptop. Jamie came out a couple minutes later. "Faith," Jamie said. "What did he do," Faith asked. "Who," Jamie replied. "Alan," Faith answered. "Doesn't matter. Evan isn't hurting you anymore," Jamie said. Faith went and grabbed her things. "Faith," Jamie said. She packed. "Faith, where are you going," Jamie asked. She walked out the door. Before she even made it to the elevator, Alan stopped her. "You aren't going," Jamie said. "Leave me alone," Faith said. She walked out, got a cab and went to the airport and was on the first flight home before Jamie even got there.

Faith got the truck and headed back to the house and found Alan, Callon and Jake sitting on the front steps. "Tell me he..." "He's finishing the last few shows. He wants you back there," Alan said. Faith walked past him and went inside. "Faith, he's worried," Alan said. She shook her head. Faith walked upstairs and drew herself a hot bath. "Faith, I get you're upset, but you scared the crap out of him," Alan said. Faith locked the bathroom door and soaked in the tub with her iPod blaring. An hour later, the door opened and Jamie handed Faith a towel. "What are you doing here," Faith asked. "We're leaving in 20 minutes," Jamie replied. Faith got up, wrapped herself in a towel and walked into the bedroom. He handed her a pair of leggings, her leather boots and a shirt. "I'm not going," Faith replied. He packed her some extra clothes. "Jamie," Faith said. "You aren't staying here by yourself. Get dressed," Jamie said. She got changed. "Let's go," Jamie said. He grabbed her bag, her purse and anything else she was going to need and walked her outside. "Jamie," Faith said. "I get you're upset alright? I love you. The man doesn't deserve oxygen. You have to stop Faith. Stop thinking that you don't deserve what we have. That he's gonna haunt you forever. He's going away for a damn ass long time. He's never hurting, breathing or touching you ever again," Jamie said. "I need to be alone Jamie. I need to get the other things that happened off my mind. Walking back onto that bus and having no peace and quiet isn't gonna help," Faith replied.

Jamie pulled her to him and kissed her, leaning her against one of the posts on the front porch. It was a kiss that got more and more intense with every breath. He picked her up, still keeping that kiss, and wrapped her legs around him. He pinned her arms to that post. Not 15 minutes later, they came up for air. "You're getting on the plane. I'm not gonna be able to even do a damn show without worrying about you. Please," Jamie said. He kissed her again and finally let her up for air. "Jamie," Faith said. He put her down and walked over to the truck and threw her bag in. He walked back towards her, picked Faith up, flinging her over his shoulder, and put her in the truck with him. They pulled out and Alan and the guys got the house locked up and followed them to the airport. A half hour later, they were in the air.

Jamie walked Faith to the back of the plane and closed the door so they could talk. "What," Faith asked. "You're scared. I get that. He made your life a living hell. He scared the shit out of you and hurt you. Faith, stop torturing yourself. Stop scaring both of us and let the damn authorities take care of him," Jamie said. "He's never backing off alright? He's determined to scare the shit out of me until I die," Faith said. "I love you. Do you understand that," Jamie asked. "I get that. Jamie, I'm scared. I've been scared since he came after me. I need to have the time to handle this," Faith said. "Not alone. Faith, I would die if something happened to you," Jamie said. Faith shook her head. "Faith," Jamie said. "He's gonna kill me. He's gonna keep coming until he gets what he wants," Faith said. "And he's gonna meet the business end of my shotgun," Jamie said. He kissed her again and knocked the wind out of her. He picked her up, pulling her boots off and her leggings and they had sex in that little room. He barely let her up for air. Nobody even heard a word. When they finally came up for air, there was only one thing he needed to say. "I love you. No matter what happens, I'm gonna love you until the end of time," Jamie said. Faith kissed him. "No more running," Jamie said. Faith kissed him and they both got dressed. They laughed and he walked her back to the sofa on the plane. They curled up together the rest of the flight. Nobody asked why.

They landed and went straight to the venue. Jamie put Faith's bags on the tour bus and they headed inside. Jamie did sound check with the guys later than planned, but it was done. Jamie didn't let Faith out of his sight the rest of the afternoon. Even when it came time for the meet and greet, she was in eyesight. As soon as he finished, he slid his hands in hers and walked her towards the stage. "What," Faith asked as they listened to Deacon on the stage. Jamie kissed her. "Don't leave. Please," Jamie said. "I just…" He kissed her again. "Don't…. leave…..ever," Jamie said between kisses. Faith smirked. "Besides. I'm not done with you yet," he teased. Faith kissed him and he headed on with the guys.

Chapter 9

As soon as the show was finished, Jamie walked Faith straight back to the tour bus. "What," Faith asked. Jamie had a grin that made her wonder what the look was for. He grabbed her a drink, handing it to her and walked her back to the state room. "What are you up to," Faith asked. He kissed her then kissed the tip of her nose. "What," Faith asked. "Stay here for a sec," Jamie said. He went back into the main area. "I guess y'all quit fighting," Alan teased. "We driving or hotel," Jamie asked the driver. "Have to be at the next venue in the late morning tomorrow. We have to drive," the driver said. Jamie nodded. "I'm going to talk to Faith. If we end up screaming, we do. Don't let her leave this bus. I don't care if it means sleeping in shifts," Jamie said. Alan nodded. Jamie grabbed the bottle and walked back to the stateroom.

He topped up Faith's drink. "What are you up to," Faith asked. "We're talking until it's done," Jamie said. "Meaning," Faith asked. He leaned her onto the bed and undid her boot, sliding it ever so slowly off her leg. "Jamie," Faith said. "Why," Jamie asked. "I know him Jamie. He's not backing off until I put an end to it. He's not gonna let me walk away," Faith said. "And what if I fixed it so he would leave you alone," Jamie asked. "I'd lose you. You'd end up in jail," Faith replied. He topped up her drink. "Jamie," Faith said. He kissed her and leaned over to undo her other boot. "Jamie," Faith said. "Sip," he replied. "Getting me drunk," Faith asked. He kissed her. "I would never," he teased. She took a gulp of her drink. He kissed her again. "Why can't you let me take care of it? He's pushing every button he knows to get you back there. Then you just fall for it," Jamie said. "I went back so he'd leave us alone. He's never backing off," Faith said. "And what would've happened if he hurt you? Who was gonna help you," Jamie asked as he topped up her drink. He kissed her, knocking the wind out of her again. "Jamie," Faith said. He topped up her drink and kissed her. "Who would've helped you Faith?" "Fine," Faith replied. "He put hands on you," Jamie replied. Faith finished her drink and went to get up. Jamie kissed her. "If he had touched one inch of you I would've killed him. Faith, you need to let me take care of him," Jamie said. "You aren't doing something that will get you in trouble," Faith replied. Jamie handed her the drink and topped it up. "I love you. Let me love you," Jamie said. He kissed her and peeled her leggings off. "Jamie," Faith said. "Let me be me Faith. Let me protect you," Jamie said. "He's not gonna listen to you," Faith said. He kissed her, knocking the wind out of her. "Every inch of you is under my protection. Deal," Jamie asked. "And getting me drunk or trying to means," Faith asked. He leaned into her. "Deal," Jamie repeated. "Or what," Faith asked. "Finish your drink," he said. "Jamie," Faith said. He slid her shirt off then nibbled his way down her torso. She drank the drink and put the glass on the counter. He peeled her lace underwear off, peeled her bra off and kicked his clothes to the floor.

"No more running off. No more thinking you can handle him alone," Jamie said. "Intentionally taunting me," Faith asked. "Nope. This would be taunting you," Jamie said as he nibbled at her hip. "Jamie, quit," Faith said. "I can do…. Whatever… I…want…..I….married….you," Jamie said as he kissed her hip. He kissed her and wrapped her legs around him. "Faith," Jamie said. "Alcohol isn't gonna get me to back down," Faith said. "Admit it then," Jamie said. "What," Faith replied. "That me taking care of Evan turns you on," Jamie replied. He got that devilish grin again. "Jamie," Faith said. He kissed her and made love to her. It was almost a primal urge. Fact was, taking care of Evan was the one thing he craved but he wanted Faith more. For that night, Evan was on the back burner. The only person he wanted any part of his mind or body concentrating on was in his arms.

Jamie got up the next morning and still had his arms wrapped around Faith. He nibbled down her neck. "You are like the damn energizer bunny," Faith said. "I could prove that theory," Jamie whispered. "I need sleep," Faith said. "It's almost 10am," Jamie said. "Intentionally tried getting me drunk? Nice. Too tired to…" Jamie kissed her. They made love again. "Don't forget what you promised," he said. "Jamie, I know you want to handle him alone, but…" he kissed her. "Quit causing a problem," he teased. Faith kissed him. She got up. Jamie pulled her back to him. "What," Faith asked. "I love you. I always have and I always will," Jamie said. "Why do I get the feeling that you're doing something bad," Faith asked. He kissed her. "Making you happy is never and will never be a bad thing," Jamie said. They showered and got dressed and came down to grab something to eat. The guys were in the restaurant at the hotel. Jamie kissed Faith and picked her up, carrying her down the steps to the back entrance. They went in and had breakfast together, checked into the hotel and got settled in the room. "What," Faith asked as she noticed the smirk on his face. "You better remember that promise or I'm having a do-over from last night," Jamie teased. Faith smirked. Jamie's arms slid around her. "What," Faith asked. He nibbled her neck and then her earlobe. "Jamie, you have sound check. Stop," Faith said. "I love you," Jamie said. "I love you too," Faith replied. "Good. You're doing an interview with me. Patrick called and said one of the country magazines is coming to talk to us," Jamie said. "Why me," Faith asked. Jamie kissed her. Not 20 minutes later, hair and makeup showed with a few dresses for Faith. Instead of choosing a dress, Jamie found black leather pants. Faith picked a blouse and got changed. The second Jamie saw her, he almost wanted to rush everyone out of the room.

Faith got her hair and makeup done and Jamie was even more turned on. Once hair and makeup left, that smirk turned into a devious looking smile. "Don't even think it. I checked the schedule. They're gonna be here in the next half hour," Faith said. He slid her hair off her neck and nibbled. "Jamie," Faith said. "If I really wanted to, I could," he teased. "Quit," Faith said. He kissed and nibbled at her neck in the one and only place that would never show. The camera crew started setting up and Jamie still couldn't get rid of that smirk. Faith walked over to the window, intentionally trying to get out of sight for even a few minutes. "Giving me ideas," Jamie teased. He slid his arms around her and heard someone snap a picture. Jamie turned around. "I'm not posting it. It was just a really cute moment," the photographer said. Jamie forwarded it to his phone and deleted it off the man's camera. It actually ended up being an amazing shot. He nibbled the back of her neck again and they called them over for the interview.

"So we heard about a few CD coming out. When's the release date," the interviewer asked. "A little short of a month away. Y'all are gonna love it," Jamie said. "I can just imagine that you're gonna have more of those love songs everyone loves. So what's this we hear about you getting married?" "We did. I talked her into it," Jamie teased. "So how did you meet?" Jamie linked fingers with Faith. "We met years ago. Fact was, she's the only one I ever wanted to be with," Jamie said. "We met at a coffee shop believe it or not. He stole my coffee," Faith teased. "Intentionally," Jamie joked. "We ended up talking and I finally agreed to go out with him after the 20th phone call," Faith joked. "Fact was that no never was an answer I took well," Jamie said. "How long ago?" "Almost 2 years," Jamie replied. He kissed Faith's cheek. "So where was the wedding?" "We had something small. Just family and some peace and quiet. We didn't want anything big," Jamie said. "Any thought about having kids?" "When the time's right, it'll happen," Jamie said. The interview went on for another half hour and the second everyone left, Jamie kissed Faith. The designer gave Faith the clothes and Jamie locked up. "What," Faith asked. "Wear it," he asked. Faith kissed him and went and got changed to head to sound check. They left and headed over to the venue and Jamie kept teasing the entire drive.

He did sound check, still laughing and smirking. When he was finished, Jamie did one or two more phone interviews then took Faith to dinner. "What are you up to," Faith asked. He kissed her and they went and had dinner on the tour bus. Jamie started getting changed. "What," Faith asked. "Need your help with something," Jamie teased. "I bet," Faith said. She switched back into the leather pants and the top she'd been wearing earlier and Jamie snuck up behind her and wrapped his arms around her. "Jamie," Faith said. He turned her towards him and kissed her with a kiss that turned their knees to jelly. Not 15 minutes later, they were making out on the bed in the stateroom. "You have meet and greet," Faith said. He kissed her, biting her lip and pinned her to the bed. "I think you might need rest for later," Jamie teased. "Bet I won't," Faith replied. The kiss got worse. Goose bumps were popping up everywhere. "What I would do with an extra hour," Jamie teased. He got up, pulled Faith to her feet and got ready. They headed back in and he kissed her before he stepped into the meet and greet. Faith sat down with a bottle of water. Jamie was only smiling because of her.

When Jamie got to the last photo he saw Faith. "And look at that. My favorite fan," Jamie teased. He kissed her, devouring her lips and the photographer snapped a picture. "I love you," Jamie said. "Prove it," Faith teased. "Woman, you don't know what you're getting yourself into," Jamie said. "I can guess." He kissed her and she walked him to the stage. "Don't even think what I know you are," Jamie teased. Faith kissed him and he headed on stage. She watched his show from the side stage and Deacon came up behind her.

"Just so damn perfect," Deacon said. "Don't. Deacon I get you're mad but you don't get to..." "You know that Evan is here right? He showed up to my meet and greet and tried to kick my ass," Deacon said. "So that's where the bruise came from," Faith said. "He's coming after you Faith. He's lost his shit. I don't even know the jackass but I can tell. Faith, you aren't safe. He can show up at any damn venue," Deacon said. "I get it," Faith said. "Then why aren't you doing anything," Deacon asked. Faith went over to Alan and gave him the info. She walked back towards the stage so Jamie wouldn't notice anything, grabbing a drink on her way through. Jamie looked back over and saw her with a drink. He headed over to change guitars and kissed her then headed back on. Jamie kept flirting with her then came up with an idea. "There's a new song I was gonna share with y'all, but I thought you guys might like to meet the woman behind all the new songs," Jamie said. The crowd went crazy. He got up and walked towards Faith. She shook her head. He grabbed her hand and walked her onto the stage. "Say hello to my wife y'all," Jamie said as the crowd screamed. Jamie kissed her and grabbed her a stool and he sat down with her. "I wrote this one the second I knew I was marrying this lady right here." He played through the song that had started the career that jetted him to the skies. He finished the song, kissed her hand and walked her back to the side stage. He kissed her again and came out to finish up the concert.

Faith watched the end of the concert and Jamie finished up. He walked towards her and Faith slid her heels off. He gave her a look that she knew way too well. She backed up and when he started walking a little faster, she walked even faster. When he started chasing her, she ran out to the SUV's. He caught up to her, picked her up and leaned her against the waiting SUV. He kissed her and pinned her against the door of the SUV. "You are so grounded," Jamie teased. Faith kissed him and slid into the backseat and Jamie hopped in with her. "Tease," he replied. Faith kissed him and snuggled up to him. "Needed to show my woman off," Jamie teased. Faith kissed him again. They got to the hotel and hopped out, going straight upstairs to their suite. They walked in and Jamie held her behind him. "What," Faith asked. "Hallway. Get Alan," Jamie said.

Faith went into the hall and Alan put her into a separate room. The guys guarded her like she was a jewel. Not 10 minutes later, Faith heard a commotion coming from the hall. Nobody would let her out the door. Faith sat down on the floor and called Emma. "What's wrong," Emma asked. "Something's going on. Evan showed at the concert. Deacon told me," Faith said. "You're the biggest priority to them Faith. Let him handle it," Emma said. "I told him," Faith said. "He's alright. He's doing what he promised," Emma replied. "He's gonna get killed," Faith said. "Take a deep breath. Go slide into a hot bath. Breathe," Emma said. Faith hung up. She heard Jamie almost screaming in the hallway. Faith went to go to him and the guys blocked her into that room. Callon came in and sat with her. "He's fine," Callon said. "Then why is he screaming? Just tell me what's going on," Faith said. "He said to give you this," Callon said handing her a glass and the bottle of Jack Daniel's he'd baited her with. "I'm not touching it until he…"

Jamie came into the room and wrapped his arms around her. Faith didn't let go. "I'm alright," Jamie said. She still didn't let go. "He's in the custody of the cops. They just left," Jamie said. Faith kissed him. "Guess we're stayin in here tonight," Jamie said. He picked Faith up and wrapped her legs around him. He curled up on the bed with Faith. "You trust me right," Jamie asked. "I was scared," Faith said. "He's never hurting you again. You know that right," Jamie said. Faith kissed him. "Nobody is touching us," Jamie said. "Jamie," Faith said. He kissed her. His hands cradled her face and she noticed the bruises and blood. "Jamie, you're telling me what happened and you're talking now," Faith said. She got up and went to go into the hall and was face to face with Alan. "Ice," Faith said. "We got it," Alan replied. He went and grabbed ice and handed it to Faith. "I can walk down there myself," Faith said.

"Take the ice," Alan said. She went back in and put ice into a towel and put it on Jamie's hand. "Shit," Jamie said. "You're going to the hospital if you don't watch it," Faith said. "I'm fine. I already have scars and cuts on my damn knuckles. I'm fine," Jamie said. "Then quit flinching," Faith said. "Distraction helps," he teased. "And so would a drink that you can't have," Faith said. She kissed him and grabbed bandages from her first aid kit from her bag. "I know something that would be better," Jamie teased. "With a messed up hand, you aren't doing anything," Faith said. Jamie pulled her into his lap and kissed her. His hand was still wrapped up with the towel and ice but his other hand was holding her as tight as he could.

"You are just so cute when you're giving in," Jamie teased. "Am not," Faith replied. He kissed her and tackled her to the bed, pinning her down even with the wrapped up hand. "Jamie," Faith said. He kissed her and with his good hand, he undid her leather pants. "Jamie, I swear. You are like a damn teenager," Faith said. He peeled her pants off along with the rest of her clothes then Faith helped him with his. They kicked them onto the floor and he made love to her. It was even better than the night before. His hand killed him but it didn't matter one bit. Being with her was like the best pain killer in the planet.

Faith woke up a few hours later when she heard Jamie cussing up a storm. She slid the hotel robe on and walked into the bathroom. "What are you…Jamie, stay put," Faith said. She got dressed, went and got more ice and grabbed a proper first aid kit. She came back in and cleaned the cuts and gashes up and bandaged his hand. "Faith, I'm fine baby," Jamie said. "Just sit," Faith said. "Or what," Jamie teased. "Or you're sleeping in here," Faith said. He kissed her. "Stop and let me finish this," Faith said. "Faith," Jamie said. She finished taping him up and went back into the bedroom. "Babe, I…" She went back down the hall and went to go into the suite. "Faith," Alan said. "What," she replied. He shook his head. "I'm getting my bag," Faith replied. She went to go into the suite and saw what had happened. There was blood on the glass table and footprints. She grabbed her bag and Jamie's and looked up to see Alan. "What? I can't even come in here alone," Faith asked. "He didn't want you getting freaked out," Alan said. "He's going to the damn hospital. He could have glass in his hand," Faith said. "Then I'm taking him. You're staying here," Alan said. "I'm his wife. Alan, stop treating me like a damn child," Faith said. She turned around and saw Jamie at the door. "I didn't want you freaking out. I didn't want you getting all upset. He came at me and I knocked him to the ground. I ended up cutting my damn hand on that stupid ass table. The cops showed and he pulled a gun on me and them. I didn't want you scared. Do you get it now," Jamie asked. "Right. You're handling it," Faith replied. She dropped his bag and walked down the hall. She locked the door behind her.

"What part of keep her out of here didn't you…" "Jamie, this is on you. She came down here so you two had what you needed. What's the point of hiding it from her anyway? You said she was cool with you handling it," Alan said. "If she sees him, she'll be pissed off as shit. That's why I said to get him out of here and don't let Faith see this." Alan looked and Jamie's hand was still bleeding. "We'll go over to the hospital and get you patched up then you can work on what you're gonna say to her," Alan said. "Get someone here. I'm not leaving unless she's with me," Jamie said. "She's with the guys. She's fine," Alan said. Jamie gave him a look. That look that said don't fight me on it unless you want blood loss. Jamie sat down, brushing the glass off the sofa. "Talk to her. Jamie, just tell her." "Tell her that he tried to shoot me and I had the faster trigger finger? Right. She'll lose it all over again," Jamie said.

Faith sat down and was almost half way through that bottle when Jamie was at the door. "Faith, please," Jamie said. She put her ear buds in and went and had a hot bath. A half hour later, she overheard Jamie cussing up a storm in the hall. She tried drowning out the sounds but she couldn't. Faith got out of the tub, dried off and put her pajamas on. "Faith, please," Jamie said. She stared at that suitcase. Faith put her jeans, a t-shirt and a sweater on, slid her shoes on and put her things in that bag. She called the airport to check on the flights. "Everything is grounded. The weather in Nashville is pretty bad. I'm sorry. Unless you wanted to drive or go to another airport, we can't do much. The weather's actually heading here," the woman said. Faith hung up. She grabbed her things, opened the door and walked down the hall. "Faith," Jamie said. She got in the elevator and went downstairs. She got in the SUV and left. The minute she disappeared into the horizon, Jamie was determined to find her. "Jamie, they just fixed your hand. You aren't driving," Alan said. "Then drive and fast," Jamie said pulling over. Within a half hour, he was two cars behind her. He didn't stop calling her cell. "Babe, please. I know you're mad at all of this but I told you I would take care of it. I didn't want you getting hurt again," Jamie said. An hour later, Jamie figured out where she was going. He saw Faith pull off and he went after her. He got out and walked over to the SUV.

"Faith," Jamie said. He opened the door and saw her crying. "Faith," Jamie said again. She shook her head. "Baby, come out here," Jamie said. "Leave me alone," Faith said. "Baby," Jamie said. "Just…." He kissed her. Faith got out the other door. "Woman, stop," Jamie said. Faith called the airport again. "The weather's clearing. Next flight takes off in 45 minutes. If you can get there…." "I'll be there. I'm all of 5 minutes away," Faith said. She got in the SUV and headed straight to the airport. "You aren't leaving. Faith," Jamie said as she went through security. Faith got on the plane and went home. Not Nashville home. She went back to her mom and dad's.

"What are you doing here," her dad asked. "I just needed a few things," Faith said. Her dad gave her a hug that opened the waterworks. They came in and her mom made them some tea. "I'm not gonna ask what happened. Just tell me he didn't hurt you," her dad said. Faith shook her head. "What happened," her dad asked. "I just missed being me," Faith replied. "I know there's something else," her dad said. "Evan hunting me. Jamie losing it," Faith said. "I'm not asking anything else," her dad said. Not 10 minutes later, Faith saw headlights pulling into the driveway. She got up and went upstairs to her bedroom. "You have to talk to him," her dad said. Faith shook her head. "You know better Faith. You're talking to him and that's that," her dad said.

She heard Jamie talking to her mom and getting caught up. "What did you do to your hand," her mom asked. "Jamie came after her. I dealt with it. I told him that he doesn't get to keep coming after her. Faith saw what happened at the hotel and left. Just tell me she's here," Jamie said. "Drink," her dad asked. "Coffee," Jamie asked. Her dad nodded, poured Jamie a mug and went back upstairs. "Faith," her dad said. "He destroyed a glass table top and there was blood on it. His hands probably had glass in them. I get scaring him off, but scaring me?" Her dad hugged her. "Come and talk to him," her dad said taking her hand. "I can't," Faith said. Her dad walked her down to the living room. Jamie looked up and saw her in one of his t-shirts. "I was worried sick," Jamie said getting up and hugging her. "I'm fine. Jamie you didn't have…" He kissed her and her toes were curling. "You two go upstairs and talk," her dad said. "I'm not…" Jamie kissed her again and walked towards the stairs. They walked into her room and he closed the door so nobody else would hear them.

"I'm not going back there," Faith said. Jamie kissed her. "I get running away from him, but I'm not hurting you," Jamie said. "You destroyed that room," Faith said. "He tried to shoot at me Faith. Was I supposed to stand there and let him? He was trying to kill me to get to you. I'm not letting him hurt you again. You know that. Faith, you said you'd let me deal with it. I did. He's leaving you alone once and for all," Jamie said. "Meaning what," Faith asked. "Doesn't matter," Jamie replied. "Yes it does. Just say it." "The officers that showed? One of them got shot by Evan. They shoot back Faith," Jamie replied. "What did you do?" "Faith, the cops are handling him once and for all. Please," Jamie said. "Answer me," Faith said. "He got shot. After that, I didn't care what happened. I just wanted to make sure that the one thing I did right in this planet was alright," Jamie said. "Meaning what," Faith asked. He kissed her. "Nobody is hurting you. I promised you that. I don't go back on those kinds of promises," Jamie said. "Just go home," Faith said. "Not without you. Faith, you have to let me take care of you. Please," Jamie said. "Right," Faith replied sarcastically. "I'm not leaving without you." "Jamie, just leave me alone," Faith said. "No. Faith, you have to trust that I did the right thing," Jamie said. "He's gonna get ten times worse," Faith replied. "I'm here with you. He's not gonna hurt you anymore." "He's not gonna leave us alone. You know it and so do I," Faith said. "Come home," Jamie said. Faith shook her head. He grabbed her bag. "Jamie," Faith said. He grabbed her hand, walked her down the steps and they said goodbye to her parents. "You sure," her dad asked as he hugged her. Faith shook her head. They left and headed back to the airport. Jamie didn't let go until they were in the air.

"What's going on with you," Jamie asked. Faith went to get up and Jamie held her hand. "Stop trying to run," Jamie said. "I can't even get away to relax for a while. Jamie, whatever happened with you two…" "I love you. That stupid jackass isn't getting between us," Jamie said. "I wanted time Jamie. Time alone to deal with the baby and everything else. I can't keep putting it aside," Faith said. He kissed her. "I'm sorry. Faith, it kills me that all of it happened. On top of it, he's not backing down and stopping. He's going to now. I promise you," Jamie said. "And? He got shot. If he ends up in an actual jail cell, he's still gonna keep coming after me. He has a one-track mind Jamie. The only thing he's concentrating on is getting me back into that house," Faith replied. "Faith," Jamie said. "Just stop."

They landed back in Dallas a few hours later, and Jamie carried Faith into the hotel and put her back in the bed. Faith woke up 3 hours later with Jamie's arms wrapped around her. "Where you goin," Jamie asked. "Washroom," Faith replied. Jamie let go. Faith had a hot shower and freshened up. She got dressed and as she was about to put on some makeup, Jamie got up. "Where you going," Jamie asked. "Why? Forgot my leash," Faith said sarcastically. She went to grab her bag and Jamie stopped her. "You coming to sound check," Jamie asked. "No," Faith replied. She went to leave and saw Alan at the door. "What," Faith said. "Not alone," Jamie said. Faith shook her head. Jamie kissed her shoulder, then got up and showered. He got dressed, grabbed the change of clothes for the show for both of them then they headed out to grab breakfast alone.

"I'm not gonna have to be watched 24 hours a damn day. I deserve privacy," Faith said. "I get you're frustrated Faith. I trying to prevent the Evan crap from happening again," Jamie said. "Go ahead and start it again. I need peace and quiet. Doing that while I'm on a leash isn't what I had in mind," Faith said. "I get it, but for now please just let me take care of this." "Jamie," Faith said. "Fine. Just don't take off again," he asked. "Jamie," Faith said. "Please?" "Fine, but if…" Jamie kissed her. "Come with," Jamie asked. He slid his hand in hers. He talked her into coming to sound check then Jamie got a message from management that an interview was booked for them both in an hour and a half.

"I'm not doing it again. Not after…" "Faith, if we don't someone is gonna say something. The Evan stuff is separate and is staying that way," Jamie said. "And I'm…" "Stop freaking out Faith. We're done for a week after tonight. Then we can go home and take the time to deal with what happened. It's hurting me just as much," Jamie said. Faith shook her head. "Faith, I love you. I always will. Stop thinking what I know you are," Jamie said. "I lost a baby Jamie. I lost it because of the bullshit he's causing. The bullshit he's never gonna stop with. Who's to say that next time all of this isn't gonna happen again," Faith asked. "I love you. Whatever happens next time we get pregnant we'll deal with better. He's not ruining this," Jamie said. "And what happens if we can't get pregnant Jamie?" "Then I'll love you until the air stops. Forever and ever," he said. "We wanted to have…" "Whatever happens we deal with together," Jamie said. He kissed her again. "Means we have more time to practice," Jamie said.

After another interview, Jamie came up with an idea. Whether it was going to work or not was another story altogether. "What," Faith asked seeing the look on his face. "Nothing," Jamie said. He kissed her and wrapped his arms around her. "You suck at lying by the way," Faith said. He kissed her again, devouring her lips. "Come with me," Jamie asked. "And where are we going," Faith asked. He kissed her. "Two hours before I have to be back here. Got a surprise for you," Jamie said. "And what would that be," Faith asked. They got back to the hotel and two robes were laying on the bed. "Jamie," Faith said. "Just slide one on and come with me," Jamie said. Faith did what he asked and they walked into a connecting room to their suite.

When Faith saw the two massage tables, she smirked and shook her head. "What," Jamie asked. She kissed him and laid onto the massage table. An hour and a half later, they were both completely relaxed and almost falling asleep. Jamie got up and slid her robe around her. "Better," Jamie asked. "Would you get mad if I slept tonight," Faith teased. He kissed her. "Unless I'm curled up with you, I'm gonna miss you something fierce," he said. "I'll do my best to wait up," Faith joked. Jamie kissed her and walked her backwards to the bed. "Jamie," Faith said. "Have a half hour," he teased. Faith laughed. He kissed her.

"Dinner?" "Fine, but I'm coming back and going to sleep," Faith said. He kissed her again and they got changed. She slid on a jean skirt and a t-shirt and Jamie slid his sweater over her shoulders. Faith put her boots on and they headed to the concert.

They walked in and grabbed dinner, Jamie got ready to go on and he smirked. "You aren't talking me onto that stage tonight," Faith said. "Why not," Jamie asked. "Clothes," Faith replied. He kissed her, devouring her lips. "Go do your meet and greet," Faith said. One more kiss and he left. Faith sat by the door. As soon as he finished the meet and greet, he pulled Faith into his arms and kissed her. "You have a show to do," Faith said. He snuggled her and nibbled her earlobe. "Before you end up on the counter in the dressing room," Jamie teased. Faith kissed him and walked him up to the stage. He got set up then after another kiss from Faith, he headed back on. She looked and he mouthed the word, "Stay." Faith shook her head. He nodded. Alan brought her over a drink and she saw the smirk on Jamie's face.

As soon as the show was finished, Jamie noticed that Faith wasn't there. "Where did she…" "Waiting in the dressing room," Alan joked. Jamie headed down there and saw Faith curled up on the sofa. He walked in, locked the door and leaned over her, planting a kiss on her lips that would've resulted in one hell of a sex session if nobody else was coming in. Faith got up and he had a smirk ear to ear. "Quit the X-rated brain," Faith said. He kissed her again and they headed out. "And tomorrow we're going home," Jamie said. "Oh really," Faith said. He kissed her and they barely came up for air the entire ride home. They got to the hotel and were halfway down the hall when he got another one of those grins. "What are you up to now," Faith asked. He headed into the room and Faith saw candles in the bathroom. "Jamie," Faith said. "You're relaxing. Tub for two," Jamie said. He kissed her again and slid her sweater off. "Jamie," Faith said. He undid her jean skirt. They both got undressed and slid into the tub together. "I love you," Jamie said. "Are you just sucking up," Faith asked. "I'm helping you relax. You said you needed peace and quiet. This is quiet and relaxing," Jamie whispered. He poured her a drink and handed it to her then opened a soda. "Jamie," Faith said. He nibbled her neck then down her shoulder. "Jamie," Faith said. "What," he asked. "You're trying to seduce me again," Faith said. One of his hands slid under the bubbles. When she realized where it was headed, it was way too late. "Jamie," Faith said. "What," Jamie asked. "Quit," Faith said. She got up and wrapped herself in the towel. She went into the bedroom and put her pajamas on and slid into bed. He blew the candles out and put her unfinished drink on the side table.

Jamie's phone went off at 10am. He looked and Faith was sitting on the sofa. He freshened up and walked into the TV room. "Did you get any sleep," Jamie asked. "No," Faith replied. She finished her breakfast, finished off her juice and went to get up. "I was trying to have a moment together. We were…" "What," Faith asked. "I'm not starting all of this off with a fight," Jamie said. "Then don't," Faith replied. She went and got in the shower. When she finished, she got dressed and did her hair and makeup. She came out of the bedroom and finished packing her things up. "You're that mad," Jamie asked. "First you try getting me drunk so you can get your way then you think that I'm just gonna let go of what happened with him. Jamie, it's not that damn easy," Faith said. "Tell me what you want me to do or say Faith. I don't want to end up fighting with you all the way through the week. We lost a baby Faith. I'm not losing you too," Jamie replied. Faith went to walk out and Jamie grabbed her hand. He pulled her to him and kissed her with a kiss that was so tender, so passionate and powerful that the bag slid right out of her hand.

Jamie wrapped his arms around her and just held her in his arms. "We went through hell Faith. We lived through it. I love you. I was protecting you Faith. I was protecting us. I don't know what you want me to do," Jamie said. "Give me time to get through it. Jamie, I …." He kissed her. "Then let me take you home so we can do this together," he asked. Faith nodded. Jamie kissed her again and they headed to the airport.

When they got back to the house, two cop cars were sitting out front. "Crap," Jamie said. He pulled off to the side. Jamie kissed Faith and hopped out to check out what was going on. "There was a break-in or attempted one. We caught the two people involved. They're both fans," the officer said. "That whole I'm keeping my private life private means nothing," Jamie said. "They're being booked for break and enter and trespassing. Anything else you need us to do," the officer asked. "Did they get in," Jamie asked. The officer shook his head. "That's all I needed to know," Jamie replied. The police cars pulled off and Jamie pulled in the driveway. "Jamie," Faith said. "In the house. I'm not talking about it out here," Jamie replied. He kissed her and they headed inside.

Chapter 10

Jamie came into the house hand in hand with Faith. "What did they say," Faith asked. "Fans being idiots. Tried to get into the dang house," Jamie said. "Now you're determined to get an electrified fence," Faith joked. He kissed her. "To protect both of us. I don't want anyone getting in here," Jamie said. "I figured that," Faith teased. She went to go upstairs and Jamie pulled her back into his arms. "What," Faith asked. He kissed her. Jamie pulled her tight to him, wrapped her legs around him and walked up the steps. He didn't break the kiss and he barely made it up the staircase. They ended up against the wall at the top of the steps. His jeans fell, her skirt slid up and they had hot as hell sex against that wall. They ended up a pile on the floor and they'd barely come up for air. "What are you up to," Faith asked when he finally let up. "Seducing and romancing my wife," Jamie said as he leaned in to kiss her again. They had round 2 on the floor then finally made it to bed and snuggled up together. "I love you," Jamie said. "I love you too. I still don't get why the fans would do something that stupid," Faith said. "Can't run a psych test on them all," Jamie joked. He kissed her shoulder. "Besides. There's only one fan I love." Faith kissed him. "So now that we're home, what else did you want to do," he teased as he nibbled on her neck. "Have a normal day like everyone else," Faith said. Jamie kissed her. "Three options. Bonfire, Horse ride or we start up the fire pit," Jamie said. "Two out of three," Faith said. "Bonfire and the fire pit or bonfire and the ride," Jamie asked. Faith kissed him. "Fire pit and ride," Jamie asked. "Perfect," Faith replied. Jamie leaned over and kissed her, pulling her back around him. "What," Faith asked. He devoured her lips and they were entwined the rest of the afternoon.

They showered and got changed and dressed etc. and headed out to dinner. They were barely even able to let go of each other's hands long enough to have dinner. They were flirting, snuggling and making out all the way through. Jamie finally came up for air. He sent a few text messages to his friends and a half hour later, the bonfire plan was all organized. "Do you want me to bring a drink for you," Jamie asked. Faith kissed him. "Water," Faith replied. He kissed the tip of her nose. They paid the bill and headed back to the house. Jamie put the half-full bottle of Jack in a bag in the back with a couple sodas and some bottled water while Faith got changed. She walked back downstairs in his favorite beat up jeans that she had, a t-shirt and his jacket. "You keep looking like that, we're not gonna make it out of here," Jamie said as he pulled her into his arms. "So if I told you that the black lace…" Jamie kissed her and pinned her against the post by the front door. "We're never gonna get there," Jamie said. Faith kissed him. "We're going," Faith replied. Even one mistaken peek at the black lace lingerie had him beyond turned on.

Jamie opted to take the truck, knowing full well what was bound to happen. They pulled into where his buddies had set up the bonfire and Jamie pulled her into his lap. "What," Faith asked. He kissed her, devouring her lips until they'd started steaming the windows. "Door," Faith said. Jamie shook his head. "Open the door," Faith said. He gave her one last kiss then they hopped out. He didn't let go of her hand. Jamie grabbed Faith a drink and she smirked. "What are you up to," Faith asked. "Seducing my wife," Jamie whispered. "Thought you already did," she replied. He nibbled her ear. His buddies headed over to say hi.

"So you finally showed," Cameron said. "Been touring for months. First chance we had," Jamie replied. "I bet," Cameron teased. When Jamie saw his ex Erica walking towards them, he opted to try and make sure that the ex didn't say anything to piss Faith off. "What's wrong," Faith asked. Jamie kissed her. "Maybe this was a bad idea," Jamie said. "Well look who it is. Long-time no see Jamie," Erica said. "Yeah," Jamie said. He almost white-knuckled Faith's hand. "So I heard someone talked you into settling down," Erica said trying to push buttons. "That she did," Jamie said as he kissed Faith again. "Big mistake Jamie," Erica said. "And why is that," Faith asked. "You need a woman that can handle herself. What are you doing with her," Erica replied. "Being happy. Being as far away from you and your bullshit as possible," Jamie said. He locked up the truck and went off to introduce Faith around to everyone.

"What's wrong," Faith asked. "She's history. Has been since I was in my early twenties," Jamie said. "And the reason she's causing crap now,"

Faith asked. He kissed Faith. "Because I married you. Because I love you more than anything," Jamie said. Faith kissed him. Just as he was about to pull her closer, someone tapped him on the shoulder. Jamie pushed her behind him. "What," Jamie asked noticing his lifelong enemy. He had one arm around Faith protecting her and turned to face him. "What the hell do you want," Jamie asked. "We have unfinished business," the man said. Jamie handed Faith his jacket. She looked at him and he shook his head. Jamie turned around and ended up in his enemy's face.

"What part of stay the hell away from me didn't you get punk ass," Jamie asked. "You're the damn show off. Think you're just so damn important," the man said. "You're getting an ass whooping Andrew. One way or another. Even if I let you win," Jamie said. Andrew took a swing at Jamie. Faith knew better. Jamie was never letting him win. Two punches and Andrew was bleeding. A third and he was flat on the ground with a busted nose, busted out front teeth and two black eyes. "And by the way jackass….. Stay the hell away from me and my wife. Keep the hell away," Jamie said kicking him in the ribs. He turned around and Faith wasn't there. He walked over to the truck and saw Faith making herself a drink. He wrapped his arms around her and kissed her neck. "Come sit by the fire," Jamie said. Faith nodded. He pulled her to him. "I love you," Jamie said. Faith kissed him. He grabbed a soda and they walked over to the bonfire. He sat down with her.

They finished their drinks and snuggled a bit by the fire. "Crappy way to start the vacay," Jamie said. "Doesn't matter," Faith said. He kissed her. "Sexiest woman in the planet and she's my wife," Jamie said. They snuggled then once everyone started crowding them Jamie started to take her home. They walked back to the truck. Faith hopped in and just as Jamie was about to get in, Andrew came up behind him. "Get the hell out of the way," Jamie said knocking Andrew to the ground. Andrew took a swing and Jamie ended up kicking him to the ground. He got back in the truck and took Faith down to the water.

"And what are we doing down here," Faith asked. He undid her seatbelt and pulled her into his arms. She undid his seatbelt. "Now what were you…" He kissed Faith and turned the truck off, leaving just the radio on and moved his seat back. "What exactly was...." He kissed her again and nibble and kissed her neck. He slid his biker jacket off her shoulders, slid it onto the back seat and went for the buckle of her jeans. "Jamie," Faith said. "Skinny dippin or we just hang out in here," Jamie said as he nibbled and kissed her neck so hard it felt like he was drawing blood. "You smell way too good," Jamie said. "Jamie," Faith said. He slid the zipper of her jeans down. Faith kicked her jeans off and Jamie was almost drooling. "You just went all the way out didn't you," Jamie asked. Faith kissed him. Fact being, the minute he finally came up for air, he was past being turned on. They had sex that was past hot, past steaming the windows and he couldn't let go for even a second.

"Remind me to do this more often," Jamie said as they were heading towards round two. "What are you up to," Faith said. He kissed her. "Forgetting the rest of the world and being with the woman I want every second of every damn day," Jamie said. Faith barely came up for air. Two hours later, they were finally exhausted. "Tell me that we still have sodas to keep us awake," Jamie joked. Faith kissed him. "I could always hop out and check," Faith teased. Jamie reached over through the window and grabbed two sodas. He kissed her again. "Someone slipped something in your soda," Faith teased. He kissed her again. "Nope. Just you intentionally teasing me," Jamie joked. "Now what," Faith asked. Jamie grabbed two towels and handed Faith one. "For what," Faith asked. "Come with me," Jamie said. They wrapped themselves with the towels and hopped out of the truck, locking up. Faith saw a beach blanket. "What are you up to," Faith asked. "Swim," Jamie said. They hopped into the lake and ended up splashing around and making out in the perfect water. He picked her up and carried her to the blanket. They wrapped up in towels and snuggled together. "We go riding and have a bonfire just us tomorrow. Sound good," Jamie asked. Faith kissed him. "You me and the peace and quiet," Faith replied. "Home," Jamie said. Faith nodded. He carried her back to the truck, they got dressed (for the most part) then Jamie grabbed the blanket. Ten minutes passed and he hadn't come back. Faith grabbed his handgun, loaded it and hopped out. She went around the corner and saw Andrew with a knife to Jamie's throat. Faith put the gun to the back of Andrew's head. "Either leave him alone or you're gonna have one hell of a headache," Faith said.

"Back the hell off little girl. It's between the men," Andrew said. Jamie looked at her and motioned towards Andrew's left shoulder. The arm that was holding the gun. Jamie tried fighting Andrew and got out of the way of the bullet and Faith shot Andrew's arm. "I said drop it," Faith said. Jamie got up and grabbed the knife. Faith called the police.

"Not exactly what I planned," Jamie said after the police took Andrew away. Faith kissed him. "You sure you're okay," Faith asked. He pulled her that tight into his arms. "You just have that sixth sense about things like this," Jamie asked. "I knew something wasn't right. Just like I always have," Faith said. "I get it," Jamie said. Faith kissed him. "Can we go home?" Jamie nodded. They headed home and Faith fell asleep on the way. Jamie picked her up, locking the truck up, and carried Faith upstairs to bed. He got undressed and slid into bed with Faith. He made sure the alarm was on and wrapped his arm around her. He linked their fingers and Faith snuggled into him. He slid her jeans off. Jamie's leg slid over hers. For the first time in forever, they both slept all night.

Jamie got up the next morning and noticed Faith was in his t-shirt. He smirked. Jamie got up and put on coffee. He made some fresh squeezed orange juice and breakfast and brought it upstairs. "Wake up sexy," Jamie said. Faith opened her eyes and saw breakfast. "Figured you'd be sleeping in," Faith said. He kissed her. "You just looked so dang sexy all snuggle around those curls. Still don't get it. You go to bed with it straight and you wake up with curls like that," Jamie said. Faith kissed him. He handed her the mug of coffee and they curled up together. "So a neighbor of mine said we could take his horses for a ride this afternoon. What you think," Jamie asked. Faith kissed him. "I'll take that as a yes," Jamie teased. "Still have to grab groceries. You have no food left in this house," Faith said. "We'll go groceries then," Jamie said. They curled up together and had breakfast, had a beyond long hot shower then got changed and headed off to get their groceries. Jamie was snuggling her and they were being silly all the way through the store. They got what they needed then Jamie grabbed fresh strawberries and whipped cream, and a package of chocolate covered strawberries. "And what might we need those for," Faith asked. He kissed her then kissed down her neck and nibbled and bit at the mark he'd ended up leaving the night before.

"You are so grounded," Faith said. Jamie looked at the magazines and saw an article about them. He bought it, laughing and they headed out to the truck, groceries in hand.

"It's him," Faith heard when they came out. "Might want to hurry," Faith said. Jamie kissed her. In minutes, the bags were in the backseat. "Oh my god. It's really him," two girls said. Jamie went to get in the truck and Faith looked at him. She hopped out and he linked fingers with him. "Can we get your autograph," the girls asked. "Try to remember. I'm human. Deserve some privacy alright," Jamie asked. The girls nodded. They got his autograph and Jamie opened Faith's door. They got in the truck and headed home, insuring that the two fan girls weren't following in any way.

They pulled into the house, turned the alarm on for the fence and Jamie parked the truck. "What," Faith asked as he gave her the silliest grin. He hopped out, opened Faith's door and kissed her. "Food in fridge first," Faith teased. "Such a tease," Jamie joked. He kissed her again and they brought the groceries inside. They put everything away then Jamie stared nuzzling Faith. She turned towards him and he kissed her, almost pushing just enough to end up having sex on the counter. "Jamie," Faith said. He nibbled at that little spot on her neck. "You do realize that..." Jamie kissed her, picked her up and wrapped her legs around him then walked upstairs and leaned her onto the bed. "Jamie," Faith said. With a growl he kissed her, devouring her lips and started peeling her clothes off little by little. He barely let her up for air. He pulled his shirt and jeans off and curled back up in bed with her. They had sex until they were both forgetting time existed.

Around dinner, Faith managed to finally get up and even with Jamie complaining, Faith got up and made dinner for them. Jamie came downstairs in his beat up blue jeans and wrapped his arms around her waist. "Hungry," Faith asked. He nibbled her earlobe. "Yes," he whispered. Faith fed him a carrot. "Not exactly what I meant," he teased. Faith kissed him and finished making dinner. They curled up together and ate. "My little chef," Jamie said. "You knew I could cook," Faith said. He nibbled her ear. "Best dinner we've ever had," Jamie said.

Faith kissed him. "Still up for that ride," Jamie asked. Faith nodded. They cleaned up, got dressed and headed down for a twilight ride. "What," Faith asked seeing that grin come across his face. "How did I marry such a gorgeous woman? How did I get so lucky," Jamie asked. "Because that's where the road led," Faith said. They were side by side, hand in hand for a little while. "Stop here for a quick second," Jamie said. They hopped off the horses and Jamie tied them up. "What," Faith asked. He kissed her and walked her over to an old oak tree.

"Jamie," Faith said. He pulled out his pocket knife and carved their initials into the side of the tree. "What are you up to," Faith asked. He smirked. He finished carving their names into the tree and stood up. "What," Faith asked. "See this one," Jamie asked. Faith nodded. "This was my mom and dad," Jamie said. Faith smirked. "This one is my aunt Katie," Jamie said. Faith kissed him. "We're gonna be like this forever. You know that right," Jamie said. Faith nodded. He kissed her. "I have an idea," Jamie said. "Which is what," Faith asked. "We go do the big insane crazy wedding that everyone was expecting. This time it's for you and me," Jamie said. "You're kidding right," Faith asked. "No. The big over the top wedding that we were gonna have. What do you think," Jamie asked. "Why," Faith asked. "Because you're the only woman I'm gonna ever marry. I don't want to marry anyone else," Jamie said. "Then why go through another wedding," Faith asked. "So that the entire planet knows. He can't refute it. Nobody can. That means we do things for us from now on. That's all," Jamie said. "We don't need to," Faith replied. Jamie kissed her. "You wanted the big wedding in the beginning. What's different now," Jamie asked. "I don't need it. All I needed was us and a little family and a few friends. We don't need the over the top thing," Faith said. "Wanna show you off," Jamie said. "Then we plan something else. We don't need all the dressed up stuff," Faith said. He kissed her again. "I love you," he replied.

They headed back to the stables. Jamie got the horses settled then he headed back to the house with Faith. "When did you get so excited about weddings," Faith asked. "I just didn't want you having any regrets," Jamie said. "Never will," Faith replied. He kissed her at the light. "Jamie," Faith said. "I love you. I know you wanted the wedding

135

with everyone there," Jamie said. "Don't need it. Jamie, I wanted us to be happy. That's all I ever wanted," Faith said. They got back to the house, got everything locked up and Faith went to grab a sweater. Jamie grabbed some wood from the wood pile out back and started up the fire. He came inside and made Faith a drink then grabbed a blanket or two and walked outside. Faith came out in his jacket and curled up with him by the fire. They talked and talked. For hours Jamie told her about his dreams and how they all changed when he met her. "You remember all the songs I wrote about wanting to take someone down and protecting what you have. That's where it all came from Faith. All the stuff about beating up on people for causing shit or taking them down for making a move on my girl? It was what I was like before you. After you, I wanted to protect and defend you no matter what. That's where it all came from. I told you a long time ago that I wasn't gonna let him hurt you," Jamie said. "Never make a promise you can't keep," Faith replied. "Not with you. Not ever," Jamie said.

Once the fire went out, they headed inside and curled up on the bed. "I'm never jeopardizing us. You know that right," Jamie asked. Faith kissed him. That kiss started a night that he was never ever going to forget. They made love, forgetting about the rest of the world. They were on their own with nobody interfering. Nobody was busting into the house, nobody was guarding them. There was nothing to worry about. For the first time in weeks, Jamie was calm and relaxed. "I'm never letting go Faith. I promise you."

Two weeks later, they were all about to set out when Faith was sick again. "What's going on," Jamie asked. "Flu," Faith replied. He picked her up and carried her to the stateroom and brought her some ginger ale and crackers. "I should probably just stay home," Faith said. Jamie kissed her. "Faith," Jamie said. "I know. Just would feel better being sick at home," Faith replied. Jamie smirked. "Would you stop," Faith asked. He kissed the tip of her nose and grabbed her laptop for her and handed it off. "Thank you," Faith replied. "Have to take care of my baby," Jamie said. He smirked and kissed her. When they finally got to the hotel at the first stop, Jamie kissed her. "What," Faith asked. He kissed her again. "One-track...." He devoured her lips. "Come on sexy," he said. They headed in and got settled in the room. Faith was sick again. "I'm thinking…." "Don't bother," Faith said. "Could be," Jamie said. Faith shook her head. "It's the flu Jamie," Faith said. He kissed her again. "Don't you have an interview or something," Faith asked. He kissed her again, holding her head in his hands. It turned into a half hour make out session.

They had dinner on their own in the trailer. "I promise I won't pull you on stage tonight," Jamie said. Faith kissed him. "Good. I might just go back to the hotel and sleep," Faith said. Jamie shook his head. "Then I'm gonna sit in the back on the sofa," Faith said. He kissed her again. "Nope. This first," Jamie said handing her a pregnancy test. "And where did you find this," Faith asked. "Got one of the roadies to get it for you," Jamie said. Faith shook her head. He smirked. "Determined as shit," Faith said. He nodded and opened the bathroom door. Faith kissed him. "Later," Faith replied. As he was about to turn that one kiss into 100, security was at the door. "What's up," Jamie asked. "Meet and greet in 15 minutes," Alan said. Jamie nodded. Faith got changed and helped him pick out what to wear then walked him down to the meet and greet. She sat at the door while he flirted from across the room. When he was finished, Faith walked him up to the stage. "Leaving me in suspense isn't gonna help you," Jamie teased. Faith kissed him. "I love you," Jamie said. "Love you more," Faith replied. Jamie headed on. Faith watched part of the show then went back to the dressing room.

Faith stared at that box. Just the thought that she might be pregnant scared the crap out of her. She went and took the test, hiding it in her purse. Anyone seeing that now was too much. What if Evan had heard? What would happen next? He'd come after her all over again. Next time, Jamie might not make it through. Faith had to breathe. She went outside and Alan came with her, if only to calm Jamie's worry. "You okay," Alan asked. Faith nodded. Faith was sick again. Alan grabbed her some bottled water. Faith sat until the nausea stopped. "You sure you're alright," Alan asked. Faith nodded and they went back in. Faith sat down by the stage. As soon as he was finished, Faith got up and almost crumbled to the floor.

Faith woke up a little while later at the hotel. Jamie was asleep in the chair. "What are you doing," Faith asked. "Waiting for sleeping sexy to wake up. You alright," Jamie asked sliding over to the bed and sitting with her. Faith nodded. "Did you do it," Jamie asked. She laughed. He handed Faith her bag. "Did you," Jamie asked again. Faith looked in her bag and saw the plus sign on the test. Faith shook her head. "I didn't have time to," Faith said. Faith knew that brushing Jamie off was a mistake, but she didn't know how to take it and didn't even think about how to ensure that nobody would know. "You that worried," Jamie asked. "Look what happened last time," Faith said. "Babe, that was a mistake. It happened. We can't worry that it's gonna keep happening. You're alright. He's not coming near either of us. I love you. If we are, we figure it out from there. We'll work on it together. We'll cut down on the tour dates," Jamie said. "You need to be out there. I'm fine here. We'll get some of the guys to stay there if that makes you feel…" Jamie kissed her. "I meant for when the baby is due. I want us to be okay Faith. Bringing a baby into this means the two of us doing all of this together. I love you," Jamie said. "What if…" Jamie kissed her again. "Nobody is making a move on you or coming near us. Nobody is hurting us," Jamie said. "What if he finds out," Faith asked. Jamie pulled her into his arms. "He's not hurting us ever again," Jamie said. "If he finds out, you know he's gonna come after us again. What then Jamie? What happens next time," Faith asked. "Stop worrying about things that haven't happened yet. When and if it happens, we'll deal with it together Faith. I'm never letting anything happen to you." Jamie cuddled her into his arms. "Faith," Jamie said. "What," she replied. "It's positive isn't it," he replied. Faith nodded. "We're gonna be alright," Jamie said. They both curled back up in bed together. Instead of worrying, Jamie kept picturing what their future was gonna be.

The next morning, Jamie woke up to an empty bed. He got up and saw Faith asleep on the sofa. He freshened up then walked out to her. He leaned over the back of the sofa and kissed her. "You're awake," Faith asked yawning. "What are you doing out here," Jamie asked. "Nightmare. Got some ginger ale and went back to sleep," Faith said. Jamie kissed her. "He's not coming after us," Jamie said. "I know. I'm still gonna be nervous until everything's okay. I don't want to say anything until we pass the three month point. Jamie, if we lose it again I don't want to have to explain it," Faith said. He kissed her. "Not fighting you on that. Never have and never will," he replied leaning in to kiss her.

They got showered and dressed and went to have breakfast. Their bags got loaded onto the tour bus and Jamie snuck them out back. "What," Faith asked. He kissed her and walked her into the bus and a half hour later, they all headed off to the next stop. Faith curled up with Jamie on the sofa. "What's up with you two," Greg asked. "Nothing. Just been a long day," Jamie said. "I should go check emails," Faith said. Jamie kissed her and Faith went into the stateroom and checked emails, leaving the guys to talk.

Faith got a few hours in and Jamie came back there. "How goes the emails," Jamie asked. He looked at her and he knew. "What," he asked. He sat down behind her and saw the email she had stopped at. "Faith, he can't do it. He can't hurt you," Jamie said. "He's going to one way or another. I don't get to have a normal life," Faith said. Jamie kissed her. He read through it himself:

You can't just leave. You really think Jamie throwing a punch is gonna stop me? The cops released me. I want you back in this house one way or another. If I have to drag you back here I will. Then you'll never be leaving. Don't think I can't find you Faith. I always will.

Jamie's blood started boiling. "He's not getting in breathing room of you. I love you Faith. If he even thinks he can get you back there, he's mistaken. He's not touching you. You deserve happy. You... What the hell is he thinking sending that stupid ass email anyway? How can he do that to you," Jamie asked. Faith kissed him. "You'll be safe no matter what. He's not coming here," Jamie said. "This is exactly what I meant," Faith said. He forwarded it to his IT guys and to the police officer dealing with Evan. Jamie deleted it and turned her laptop off. "You okay," Jamie asked. Faith nodded. She curled up in Jamie's arms. Jamie kissed her. A half hour later, Jamie's phone went off. "What," Jamie asked. "He's in custody and after we showed him the truth, he plead guilty. The officer said that he had been off his meds a long while. He's lost it. I asked him why he doesn't let go of all of it and he said that legal or not they were married. Any truth to it," Jamie's buddy asked. "Not one inch of truth. Just make sure he stays in there. Do whatever you have to. We're both sick of having to have bodyguards to help us with all of this," Jamie said. He chatted for a little while longer and hung up. "What did he say," Faith asked. "They have him. He plead guilty," Jamie said. "That's not gonna stop him and you know it," Faith replied. He kissed her. "What if we moved," Jamie asked. "You've lived there for years," Faith said. "We are more important. We go somewhere that has better security. Somewhere we can overhaul any security issues," Jamie said. "We can't just keep running away from it," Faith said. Jamie kissed her.

An hour later, Jamie was getting listings from a real estate agent. "I'm not moving just because of him," Faith said. "We're doing it for us. You and me," Jamie said. "Now you're letting him ruin what we're doing," Faith asked. Jamie kissed her. "What do you think of this one," Jamie asked. Faith shook her head and went in to grab a drink. She opted to sit with the guys. Looking at houses was the last thing she wanted to do. Jamie came back in an hour or so later and handed Faith her laptop. "Let me know," Jamie said. She saw three emails filled with photos and house listings. Faith put her laptop in her bag. "Faith," Jamie said. "I said not now," Faith replied. They pulled in a few hours later to the hotel. Jamie went upstairs and got settled with Faith.

"What's the problem," Jamie asked. "I'm not gonna give into him. I'm not gonna let him win and scare us out of our home," Faith said. "If it means you being safe I'm doing it," Jamie said. Faith grabbed her purse. "Faith," Jamie said. "I'm going out," Faith replied. She grabbed her phone, her coat and her purse and walked out. "Where are you going," Jamie asked following her. "Out," Faith replied. She walked into the elevator and left. Alan was right behind her. Faith went out the front door of the hotel and Alan came out behind her. "Seriously," Faith asked. "Whatever you wanted to do, you're gonna need someone with you. Please," Alan said. "One word to Jamie and I'll kick your backside to the next solar system," Faith said.

Faith went shopping and to lunch and dinner with Alan. "He's called my cell 5 times tonight already. Just go down to the concert," Alan said trying to convince her. Faith shook her head. "What happened that's so damn bad," Alan asked. "Evan threatened me. Jamie went nuts and started saying that we were moving," Faith said. "He was doing it to keep you safe Faith. He loves you," Alan said. "He tells me not to run away from everything then he does this," Faith asked. "He's trying to make sure you're safe. Give him a break," Alan said. "I'm going home," Faith replied. She paid the bill, left the restaurant and booked a flight. She packed and was on a plane just as Jamie was heading on. Alan intentionally went with her, even if it was only to keep a promise he'd made to Jamie. He was keeping Faith safe.

Jamie hit the stage and was in a rare mood. He kept looking and didn't see Faith. He walked over part was through the concert. "Where is she," Jamie asked. "Safe," Callon said. He messaged Alan. Within minutes Alan called. "He's losing it. Where are you," Callon asked. "20 minute layover. She's not coming back to the next few shows. I'm here with her. It's fine," Alan said. "Then you're breaking it to him after the concert," Callon said hanging up.

Faith went back to the house and got settled and Alan started a fire in the fireplace. "You don't need to stay," Faith said. "He'd kick my ass if I didn't. Faith, if you don't wanna go back there that's fine, but me leaving isn't happening. Just give it a break," Alan said. Faith went upstairs and drew herself a hot bath. She slid in, turned on her iPad and played video games then went through emails. She was perfectly fine until an email from Evan popped up again.

Chapter 11

Don't think that you can brush me off. I hope you're enjoying that hot bath Faith.

Faith got up and wrapped herself in a towel and drained the tub, pulled on Jamie's t-shirt and leggings and ran downstairs. "What," Alan asked. Faith handed him the iPad. She walked back upstairs and packed all of her things from the bedroom. "So you believe that leaving is the smart move now? He was trying to save you Faith. You just walked away," that voice said. "I'm taking care of myself like you said Patsy," Faith replied. "Sometimes you need to have someone there with you. If you love him then walk with him," Patsy said. Faith wheeled her bag down the hall and came face to face with Alan. "Where are you going," Alan asked. "Anywhere but here," Faith replied. Alan grabbed her bag and Faith went to grab the other one. "Faith," Alan said. "I have one other one," Faith said. She went back into the bedroom and the door slammed. "Take care of things and stop running. I could do it. Why can't you," Patsy asked. "Because I have a damn baby to think about. He's ruined one already. I'm not letting him do it again," Faith replied. She got the door open and walked downstairs. She headed off in her truck and Alan followed. Faith checked into the Opryland, determined to be away from the house just in case. Alan stayed in the connecting room.

An hour or two later, Jamie called her cell. "Hi," Faith said. "Where are you," Jamie asked. "Staying at a hotel. He got into the house. Alan's here," Faith said. "Come back and meet me," Jamie said. "Not now," Faith replied. "Faith," Jamie said. "I'm fine. I'm staying here. There's extra security and I'm fine." "Please," Jamie asked. "I'm staying here. If I go anywhere else I'll tell you," Faith said. "If he scared you that much then you should be here," Jamie said. "Jamie," Faith said. "Please," Jamie asked. Faith handed the phone to Alan and went back to her bedroom and closed the door. "I'll send you an address. I'll get things moved over there. Stay at the house with her and don't let anyone else on the property," Jamie said. "Will do," Alan replied hanging up.

Alan went into Faith's room. "What," Faith asked. "We're moving somewhere safe. He knows you're here and so does half the damn city. Let's go," Alan said. Faith got changed and they head out the back way. Alan drove in front of Faith and took her straight to the house that Jamie had set up. Faith pulled in and saw the dream house she'd been staring at in architecture magazines. Faith pulled in and Alan pulled in blocking the driveway. He turned on the electric fence. He flipped on the security system with the code that Jamie had given him. Faith walked in and found the sofas she loved with the furniture she'd been staring at for months. "You can get settled upstairs. I have to check on some things," Alan said. "How did all of this get set up," Faith asked. "Jamie did it. He said he wanted you to be safe and this was the backup," Alan said handing her a note that Jamie had sent. Faith opened it:

Faith, I love you. I'm sorry. I told you a long time ago that I was gonna keep you safe. That's when I did all of this. Whatever your reason, at least I know you're safe. I'll be home soon baby. I love you and I always will. Left you a present in the extra bedroom. Was just in case. I set all this up after we got married. I knew Evan might come after you. You're safe here.

Faith went into the extra bedroom and saw a baby blanket and a teddy bear. She shook her head. She closed the door and went into the master bedroom. Faith saw the black satin sheets on the bed. She went into the bathroom to wash her face and found rings sitting on the counter. She looked over and the bed was unmade. Faith walked downstairs. "What," Alan asked. "Who else was here," Faith asked. "I don't know. The place was locked up Faith. You saw that yourself," Alan said. "Then tell me why there are rings on the counter and the bed is unmade," Faith said. Alan went upstairs. He saw the rings. He slid them in his pocket. "Alan," Faith said. "A friend of ours was staying here. Her hubby was a jackass. It's her stuff," Alan said. Faith shook her head. "Faith, don't think it," Alan said. She stripped the bed and threw the bed sheets in a bag. She changed the bed and re-cleaned everything. "Faith," Alan said. Faith looked in the closet and found one of Jamie's suits. "Right. Sure it was a friend. Why are Jamie's things with hers then," Faith asked. "It's not what you think," Alan said. Faith took her things back outside, threw them in the back of the truck and got around Alan's truck and left. Alan made one call. "What happened," Jamie asked. "Her stuff was still here. Faith found it," Alan replied.

Faith got half way to Gatlinburg when she started getting tired. Faith pulled over at a rental that was gorgeous. The views were worth millions. Faith pulled in and talked to the owner and rented the house. It was peace and quiet that Faith needed. She got settled, poured herself a tall glass of ice water and started a fire in the fireplace. Faith had something to eat and curled up on the sofa. An hour later, she was out cold. Faith woke up the next morning and for the first time in a few weeks, she didn't feel sick. Faith took advantage of the feeling and got dressed. She had a long hot shower, got dressed and headed into town to grab some groceries. Faith spent the day being a tourist like everyone else. Nobody noticed anything. Nobody said a word. For the first time in months, she was left alone. Faith grabbed lunch and something for dinner then headed back to the cabin. She got in touch with the necessary people and set it up that she'd be staying until further notice. As she finished signing the papers, Jamie called.

"Where are you," Jamie asked. "I told you I needed time Jamie. Now more than ever I do. I walked in there and someone else's rings were there and whoever she was had been sleeping in that bed. If that's what you wanted, go take it. I'm not picking a damn fight about whoever she was," Faith said. "Faith, it's not what…" Faith hung up. She cleaned up and relaxed. An hour later, she was writing out song lyrics. Three songs worth of lyrics later, Faith made some dinner. She curled up by the fire and watched some TV then saw Jamie's video for the song he'd written for her. The woman in the video looked familiar. When Faith figured out who it was, she turned the TV off and grabbed the ice cream she'd bought as a treat. She flipped in a movie and relaxed. She fell asleep in front of the TV just as the fire was going out. After a few days of peace and quiet, Faith was finally relaxed. She'd spend the day relaxing or writing, go through emails and do work from the cabin then head out and have a quiet dinner without a disruption. Faith turned her phone back on a few days later and saw 30 voicemails from Jamie. She blocked out the location and called him back.

"I've been trying to call you all week. Where are you," Jamie asked. "Jamie, go deal with whoever that woman is. You let her stay there. You wanted me there too. Your harem isn't happening. Just go do whatever," Faith said. "I need you Faith. Please," Jamie said. "Bet you needed her too," Faith replied. "Faith, please just stop," Jamie said. "Who was she," Faith asked. "Kelly Andrews. She's just a friend," Jamie said. "I'm sure she is. And the black satin sheets that had your cologne on them," Faith asked. He was quiet. "That's what I thought," Faith replied. She hung up and went and had a hot bath. Fact was, being away from every inch of the stress was making her feel better. Faith just relaxed and watched TV via her iPad. Once the water turned cold, Faith slid out and got ready for bed. She was having a descent sleep until the nightmares started again. Nightmares about Evan coming after her and killing Jamie.

"You either come back with me or he never sings a damn note again. You are getting in that truck and you're doing what I tell you. You don't, he's gone and so are you. Found the perfect burial plot for you," Evan said in the dream. Faith woke up and her hands were shaking. She checked her purse and her smith and Wesson was still there. Faith took it out and kept it with her. Somehow it was comforting knowing that she had some way to protect herself. Faith tried going back to sleep but she couldn't. She watched TV a while then went for a walk. Faith couldn't calm her system down. She grabbed a peppermint tea and went back up to the cabin. She turned the fire pit on and went and relaxed outside. She wrapped herself in a chenille blanket and sat out there trying to come up with a baby name. Around 2am, Faith turned her cell back on and Jamie called seconds later.

"Just tell me where you are," Jamie begged. "No. Jamie, after everything I've gone through I need time to myself. You have to let me," Faith said. "Just tell me so I know you're okay," Jamie said. "And have you come back out here and drag me out? Jamie just go do whatever you need to. I need to unwind," Faith said. "You're up at this time of the dang night. I know you're not okay," Jamie said. "Stop," Faith said. "No. Faith, I know something's wrong. I can feel it. Come home. You need me even if you're not gonna admit it," Jamie said. "I have to go," Faith said. "No.

Faith please. I need to know you're safe. Just tell me..." Faith hung up. She turned the fire pit off and went back inside. She locked up and flipped the alarm on and curled back up in bed. She fell back asleep and finally slept right.

Jamie couldn't sleep in that bed alone. He would toss and turn. He worried all night long that Evan was gonna find her. When he did manage to sleep, he had nightmares one after another about Evan hunting her down and killing her. Then it hit him. He grabbed the keys and hopped on the plane. "You only have a day or two. We'll meet you in New Orleans. We'll do whatever we need to so you have extra time. If anything happens, call and tell me," Greg said. Jamie gave him a hug and left.

Faith woke up the next morning with morning sickness from hell. She could barely hold water down. After an hour or so, Faith tried to eat but was back in the bathroom sick again in minutes. Faith opted to try to go back to the sofa then finally managed to keep water down. By the time that she finally stopped being sick, it was almost dinner. Faith worked her way from soup to toast. She started feeling sick again when the room started spinning. Faith tried to shake it off, trying to keep orange juice down. Finally she started feeling better. She finally felt better, at least enough to make it to bed. Faith went to turn her phone on and the second it partially turned on, Jamie called.

"What," Faith asked. "I love you," Jamie said. "What do you want," Faith asked. "Did you go to that candy shop you loved," Jamie asked. "What are you talking about," Faith asked. "I'm home Faith. Back in Tennessee. I need you. Just tell me where you need me to be," Jamie said. "Just leave me alone," Faith said. "I can't. Faith, I can't just go back on that tour without you. I need to know you're alright." "I'm fine," Faith replied. "Just tell me where..." Faith ran for the bathroom, dropping the phone and was sick all over again. "Faith," Jamie said. He said it over and over and Faith didn't reply. It was only when he heard her pass out altogether. "Faith" Jamie said again.

Faith finally came to and she was on the sofa and Jamie was unconscious on the chair. Faith opened her eyes. She shook her head and got up. She packed her things and was gone down the road before Jamie woke up. She moved to a different cabin and got settled, as far away from Jamie as possible. An hour later, Faith's phone was ringing. "Where are you," Jamie asked. "I told you Jamie. Space doesn't mean hunt me down," Faith said. "You passed out. The doctor even came to the cabin. He said you were really dehydrated," Jamie said. "Fine. I'll drink more water," Faith replied. "Where are you?" "I'm not coming back," Faith said. "Come meet me then. Faith, I need to know that you're alright. A week and a half. I'm not waiting another day," Jamie said. "Then go home." "I'll meet you at the Greenbrier. Please," Jamie asked. "Then you leave me alone," Faith said. "No. We talk and figure this out. Faith, you can't just take off. We made a commitment to each other." Faith went to hang up. "Seven," Jamie said as Faith hung up. She went towards the kitchen and grabbed a bottle of water. A few minutes later, Faith was sick again. She called her doctor. "Come down to the hospital. Get someone to drive you. We're admitting you," the doctor said. Faith hung up and got in her truck and drove straight to the hospital.

"You need fluids. If you're that sick, something is definitely wrong. Baby is okay," the doctor said. "You sure," Faith asked. "I'm giving this to you so when you're scared or worried you can listen to this to calm you down." The doctor put the stethoscope into Faith's ears and found the baby's heartbeat. Faith smiled. "That baby is alright. You're alright. You need to concentrate on taking care of that baby. We're keeping you overnight to make sure that you aren't dehydrated again. If you're doing better in the morning, you can go home. Somewhere close to the hospital," the doctor asked. Faith nodded. "Anything else you need for tonight?" "Only one request. Not a word to anyone. I don't need anybody coming here and…" "Alright," the doctor said. She got the nurse to bring Faith some more blankets and a better pillow and put a guard on her door.

Jamie went down to the restaurant and sat there waiting until almost 10pm. He called Faith's cell more than once and it always went straight to voicemail. "Faith, you're scaring me. Tell me that you're alright.

Please," Jamie said leaving voicemail number 5. He had a quick dinner then something told him to call the hospital. Instead of calling, he went there.

Faith was asleep with a heavy duty IV. Jamie saw a guard posted outside the door and he went and checked with reception. "My wife is here. I need to see her," Jamie said. "And your wife's name," the receptionist asked. "Faith Gilbert," Jamie replied. "She's in room..." Jamie went straight down the hall to the room with the guard. He peeked in as he passed. "Can I help you," Security asked. "She's my wife. I'm going in there," Jamie said. "Doctor said no visitors at all. Her blood pressure has to stay down period," the security guy said. "I'm her husband." "Sorry sir. Unless the doctor approves it, I can't let you in." Jamie spent an hour and a half hunting down Faith's doctor. "She needs bed rest undisturbed. Her blood pressure was up and she was dehydrated. You going in and picking a fight isn't a good idea. She needs quiet," the doctor said. "She's my wife. She can't lock me out of her damn room," Jamie said. "I can," the doctor replied. Jamie sat outside her door waiting for a chance to come in there.

The next morning, the doctor went in to check on Faith. "Any better," the doctor asked. "Still nauseous," Faith said. "Your blood pressure is down. Baby is happy. We'll give you something," the doctor said. "He's sitting in the hall isn't he," Faith asked. The doctor nodded. "Tell him I was moved when he was asleep. Please," Faith said. "He's not letting you go. Faith, you need to talk to him and straighten out whatever is going on," the doctor said. "I can't. I told him I needed space to deal with everything that's happened," Faith said. "Like what?" "Evan came after me. That's why I lost the last one. I just think it's nuts that I got pregnant again so soon," Faith said. "It happens Faith. You need to deal with things. This Evan guy needs to be part of your history," the doctor said. "Except he keeps pushing his way into my present," Faith replied. "Maybe you should say a prayer and ask for some help." The doctor headed out and ordered another IV and something for nausea.

"Gives you a chance to live that dream. Why can't you just accept your gift," Patsy's voice said. "What am I supposed to do? Let Evan win? I've done what I can do Patsy. I'm fighting my fight," Faith said. "What about making your dreams come true? This couldn't have been your only dream," Patsy asked. "It was the one I wanted a long time ago. I just don't like watching over my shoulder," Faith said. "Then quit looking that way. The past is there for a reason Faith. Leave it there and forget about it no matter what," Patsy said. "What happens when he comes after me this time? What happens if Jamie gets hurt?" "Hurt Evan first." Faith opened her eyes. That voice disappeared. Somehow, Faith felt like she'd woken up from a nightmare. Patsy had given her the best advice.

Faith got up and got dressed and was wheeled out of her room. "Faith," Jamie said. "What?" "I need to talk to you," Jamie said. Faith shook her head. They took her out to her truck. Faith hopped in and headed back to the cabin. As soon as she pulled in, she saw Jamie pulling in behind her. Faith got out. "What," Faith asked. Jamie walked over to her, held her face in his hands and kissed her. He picked her up and carried her into the cabin. "Jamie, just leave me alone," Faith said. He leaned her onto the bed. "Jamie." "Tell me. You ran out the door. You left," Jamie said. "Who was she Jamie? Were you sleeping with her the entire time," Faith asked. He backed off. "How could you think I would even do that," Jamie asked. "Just go," Faith replied. "No. You are my wife. I love you. I always have," Jamie said. "Then why is she staying there? Don't pull the she isn't any more crap. She was staying in that house when you claimed it was for us. I'm not fighting with you about her. I'll take care of the baby myself," Faith said. Jamie kissed her.

He peeled her sweater off then went for her jeans. "Stop," Faith said. "I love you. Whether you believe me or you don't, I'm not walking away from the only thing I ever wanted." "Then you're letting me do what I need to for me Jamie. I'm handling things myself. I need to…" Jamie kissed her again, peeled her jeans off, kicked his jeans to the floor and peeled his shirt off. He made love to her in that bed. Their legs entwined, and Faith at Jamie's mercy again. He kissed her and barely came up for air. When they finally did, Jamie looked at her. "I love you Faith. I couldn't let anything happen to anybody. My cousin was staying at the house. Her husband was beating up on her. I told her to stay there. She left the rings and said after a year or two, to pawn the rings.

Let her ex think she was dead or something," Jamie said. "You don't have to come up with a story Jamie. Just know something. I'm dealing with Evan my own way," Faith said. "What," Jamie asked. "You heard me. I'm doing things my way. You have to let me handle it," Faith said. "He almost raped you in that house. You're not going back there," Jamie said. "Nope. He's coming to me and getting what he deserves," Faith said. "Faith, you aren't putting yourself in harm's way to get back at him. You're having a baby. We're having a baby." "Jamie, I get you wanting to handle this yourself, but you already tried. It's between me and Evan," Faith said. "No you aren't," Jamie said. Faith went to get up and Jamie pulled her back into the bed. "You can't go," Jamie said. "I'm getting a glass of water," Faith said. She got up and grabbed a drink and walked back into the bedroom. "Tell me you still have the gun I gave you," Jamie asked. Faith kissed him. "Somewhere safe," Faith replied.

Jamie didn't let her out of his death grip all night. He'd barely slept for two weeks. She was the key to him being able to sleep. Jamie kissed Faith's neck, nibbling and leaving a mark. "Jamie," Faith said. "My wife. I am not losing you to him. He's not touching you," Jamie said. "He won't be. Don't worry," Faith said. They had sex again and he was almost shaking after. "Making up for lost time," Faith asked. "You're addictive as hell. Please. Just let me go with you," Jamie said. "Or what," Faith replied. He nibbled down her neck. "Don't you have a concert to go to," Faith asked. "Come with me," Jamie asked. Faith shook her head. "The doctor wants me to stay nearby," Faith replied. He kissed her again. "Then we're making the best of every minute," Jamie said as he kissed her again. They barely came up for air. When Jamie finally had to leave to head back to the airport, Faith drove him. "Promise me that you aren't gonna get in any trouble," Jamie asked. Faith kissed him. "I'll call you," Faith said. He kissed her again, biting that mark he'd intentionally made. "I mean it. Don't do something stupid," Jamie said. "Go sing. I'll deal with..." Jamie kissed her again nibbling her lips. "Another week. Then I'm home for 2 weeks. I love you," Jamie said. "Love you too," Faith replied. "Faith." She kissed him again. "Don't get hurt. Don't let our baby get hurt," Jamie said. Faith kissed him again and Jamie hopped on the plane and headed back to meet up with the band.

Faith left and a half hour later got a call. "Yep," Faith said. "We need to talk," Evan said. "True. I'll invite the police. I'll meet you at Bubba Gump's," Faith replied. "Knew that's where you'd be. Ten minutes," Evan said. Faith hung up. She checked the ammo in the two magazines, loaded one turning the safety on and slid it in the back of her jeans.

Faith turned the corner and parked her car at a private lot. She walked down to the restaurant and saw Evan sitting there. "About time," Evan replied. "Talk," Faith said. "You don't get to just walk out," Evan said. "I didn't. You threatened me more than once Evan. You don't get to put hands on me without a gunshot in retaliation," Faith replied. "Sending your man to finish your work," Evan asked. Faith shook her head. "Don't need to," Faith said. "Then we have something we need to finish. "Which is," Faith asked. "I get back what's mine." "Taken," Faith replied. "Either pay up or I take what's mine." Faith heard the officers coming down the road. "And taking what's yours….that entail holding me hostage for another 6 months? Go ahead and try for another one." The minute Evan put his hands on her, the police came up behind him. "I do have that restraining order," Faith said handing it to the officer. Evan was in cuffs for a third violation. It meant at least 6 months jail time if not more. Faith talked to the officers, told them what had happened and what happened at the trailer. "That would be felony assault. We're gonna need to talk to you at the station," the officer said. "Can we do it somewhere else," Faith asked. The officer nodded. Faith gave him the address and went back to her cabin.

An hour or so later, the officer showed to talk to Faith. "We got some information from Evan. Can you tell me about the marriage," the officer said. "What marriage," Faith asked. "You and Evan," the officer replied. "We weren't married. He tried to forge my signature on one. We won the case," Faith said. "So it was a sham on his part then?" Faith nodded. "He tried getting between Jamie and I. He's threatened me more than once. I was held at gunpoint. Jamie was the only thing that got me out of there," Faith said. "Has he put hands on Evan," the officer asked. "Defending me. Evan came after me and tried to hurt me more than once. Can't really blame him. Fact is that Evan is just as crazy as he's ever been. I have a restraining order for a reason," Faith said. The officer asked a few more questions then headed out. Faith went and had some lunch and relaxed a while on the deck. She did her regular email check and found one from Jamie:

The second I got on that plane I missed you already. You sure I can't talk you into coming? This isn't the same without you here. I miss you. Call me when you get home. Tried calling you a couple times this afternoon. Love you forever.

Faith replied back to him.

Left phone at the cabin. Just went for a walk. Love you too.

Not 10 minutes later, Faith's phone rang. "Hello," Faith said. "I wanted to call and apologize for giving you the wrong idea. Jamie really was helping me," the woman said. "The fact that he never told me the place existed and he tried telling me he only got it when my ex started coming after me was what pissed me off whoever you are. Besides. It's really none of your business," Faith said. She hung up. She could feel her blood pressure start to rise. Faith put something together for dinner. As soon as dinner was made, Faith lit a few candles and had dinner in the tub. By the time she slid out, she wasn't just relaxed, she was ready for bed.

Faith went to crawl into bed and her phone rang. "Hello," Faith said. "You need to come down here," Andrew said. "Why," Faith asked. "Plane will be at the airport. Just go." "What's going on," Faith asked. The phone disconnected. Faith slid on her leggings and a sweater, grabbed a bag and threw in a day or two of clothes and toiletries and headed outside. A black SUV sat in the driveway. "Can I help you," Faith asked. "Came to drive you," the driver said. Faith got in her truck and went to the airport. She locked up the truck and turned the alarm on, got on the plane and headed straight to Jamie. An hour later, her phone went off. "Yep," Faith said. "Why didn't you use the SUV I sent," Andrew asked. "Don't need to. What is going on with him," Faith asked. "How far out are you now?" " An hour and we land. The answer?" "You'll see when you get here. It's not good Faith."

The plane landed and Faith headed to the venue and caught the tail end of Jamie's show. "What's wrong," Faith asked when she saw Andrew. "He's been drinking. He hasn't touched a drop in years and tonight, he went through 3 glasses. Nobody is gonna get through to him but you," Andrew said. Faith walked up to the stage with Alan. "What happened to staying at that cabin," Alan asked. Faith looked over at Jamie and saw him flirting his way through the stage. Faith intentionally stayed out of sight.

As soon as Jamie finished on the stage, he walked off grabbing his drink on the way through. When he walked into the dressing room, he sat down and tried calling Faith again. "Faith, please just answer the phone," Jamie said waiting for the machine. "What did you need," the woman said. "I need to talk to her," Jamie replied. "To tell her what? Jamie, let her come to you when she's ready." "You're the one that got between us. What the hell were you thinking? Just because you and Rick break it off doesn't mean you can crash in my house. I asked you to help me find a house, not for you to live in it with the guy you're screwing this week," Jamie said. The woman stormed out. Jamie pressed redial. "Faith, I know you're pissed at me about all of that but I thought...." Faith came out of the bathroom. Jamie looked up.

"Baby," Jamie said. Faith kissed his cheek. "Faith, it wasn't what you think," Jamie said. "What was it? You let her stay in your house and you bring her on tour," Faith asked. "She's dating Greg," Jamie said. Faith nodded. Jamie kissed her and all she could taste was the bourbon. "One more show and you're done for a week and a half right," Faith asked. Jamie kissed her and nodded. "Then you can put the bourbon away," Faith replied. "I just needed a drink. The cops showed up asking a million questions about you and Evan. I just needed...." Faith shook her head and walked out. "Where's the next show," Faith asked Alan. "Scottsdale," he replied. "I'll fly there tonight and check into a hotel. He needs to dry out," Faith said. "He's losing it. Faith, that's why I called you. I haven't seen him like this in years," Andrew said. "Then take the damn bourbon out of his grasp. Letting him sit there and drink is enabling it," Faith replied. Jamie came out of the dressing room and grabbed Faith's hand. "What," Faith asked. He kissed her, pinning her against the wall. "I need you," Jamie said. "And I need you to stop drinking. After what I did today, I don't need to have to baby my husband," Faith said. He kissed her again. "Stay with me," he asked. "Sleep it off," Faith said. He kissed her again. He walked her out to the tour bus and straight into the stateroom.

"What," Faith asked. Jamie kissed her, biting her lip and leaned her onto the bed. "I can't even sleep without you here." "Jamie, you're drunk. You went that long without having one. What the hell," Faith said. "I need you. I can't do this without you here," Jamie said. "Then there's no point in doing it," Faith said. He kissed her. He pinned her to the bed. "Let go," Faith said. "Baby. Please," Jamie said. Faith got up and walked out, got in the waiting SUV and headed to the airport. She flew out and was back on the landing strip in an hour or so. Faith went and checked into the hotel and soaked. A half hour later, Jamie called her cell. "What," Faith asked. "I need you. I get you're mad Faith but walking out isn't helping," Jamie said. "And how much more did you drink after I left," Faith asked. "Six bottles of water," Jamie replied. "What made you think drinking was gonna fix all of this," Faith asked. "The officer told me that Evan came after you. I was dead scared. I thought he hurt you. That's why I was drinking. If something happened to you and I couldn't be there..." "Jamie, stop alright? Just stop blaming the drinking on that. I took care of him Evan. 100% handled. I told you before I was handling all of it my way. He wasn't putting a hand on me again. He's at the police station and being transferred to a federal prison," Faith said. "Baby," Jamie said. "Get some sleep," Faith replied. "Please," Jamie said. "Not tonight," Faith replied. "I love you." "I love you too," Faith replied then hung up.

Chapter 12

Jamie was half asleep when the tour bus pulled into the hotel in the morning. The guys all came upstairs and got settled while Jamie took his time waking up. "He's waking up. Believe it or not he actually went a night without a drink. Whatever you said worked," Greg said. "I said what was necessary. If this is what he's gonna do every time something goes wrong…." "Faith, he went off the deep end. Evan told him in a text that he'd got what he wanted. Jamie assumed it meant that he did something. He thought Evan raped you," Greg said. Faith shook her head. "He thought something happened. Evan texted that at noon. The cops showed asking questions two hours later. It was all he could do to try to stay calm," Andrew said. "If he can't handle it…" "Faith, go down and talk to him. He's sitting in the stateroom scared crapless," Greg said. Faith headed out and went downstairs. She came out to the tour bus and Jamie was just stepping off.

"Faith," Jamie said putting his bag down. "Remember when I told you that you could handle it?" Jamie nodded. "It's been handled. I just got him out of hiding. The cops got the conversation on tape and came out once he made threats. They dealt with him. He didn't touch me other than trying to kiss me. The police have all the information they need Jamie. He's not coming back after us," Faith said. He kissed her. "I love you," Jamie said. "Stop worrying," Faith said. He kissed her again and she still tasted the Jack Daniels. "When," Faith asked. "What," Jamie replied. "Stay," Faith said. She walked onto the tour bus and into the state room and saw the bottle of Jack Daniels. Faith handed it to Jamie. "Faith." "I want to see you dump it. Every damn bottle of alcohol you stashed on that bus is going down the drain." Faith talked to the driver and he went through the bus with a fine tooth comb. They came out with two more bottles. "Jamie," Faith said. "I didn't…" Faith walked into the hotel. Jamie followed and walked into her room. "This is where you went," Jamie asked. "Now. There's the sink Jamie," Faith said. "I thought I'd lost you. Please," Jamie said. "Next time look at the ring on your left hand," Faith replied.

Faith walked to the door. "Baby," Jamie said. "You have a show to be at," Faith said. Jamie went to kiss her and Faith backed away. "Go do sound check or sleep it off. You aren't staying here," Faith said. Jamie kissed her anyway. He picked her up, wrapping her legs around his waist and pinned her to the bed. "Jamie," Faith said. "No. I'm not letting you walk away," Jamie said. "Off," Faith said. He kissed her again. She knocked Jamie to the ground. Faith grabbed her bag and walked out. She talked to Alan and begged him to keep an eye on Jamie and left.

Faith went back to the old house and changed the security codes. She locked everything up and went and got ready for bed. She fell asleep in Jamie's t-shirt. Walking away almost killed her. She had to. After all that time that Jamie had gone without a drop, she's what ruined it all. Evan ruined it. Faith curled up on the bed. It felt so much colder without him there.

Faith tossed and turned all night. She got up in the morning and was sick. Really sick. Faith made breakfast and went and sat in the back. She walked outside and saw Alan pulling in. "So this is where you went," Alan said. "I needed to step away from it. I needed to be somewhere I considered safe," Faith said. "This isn't safe," Alan said. "I got confirmation from the state's attorney that he's in solitary confinement in maximum security. He's not getting out. I'm fine," Faith said. "He's losing it Faith. We tried getting him into the gym to work out. He's losing it altogether." "I'm not going to save him. He said he hadn't been drinking last night then I find out he had bottles stashed. He needs to stop Alan. He chose to stop drinking. He has to choose that again," Faith said. "He needs you. Faith, that's what got him out of it in the beginning. He did all of this because of you," Alan said. "And letting her into the so-called safe house meant what," Faith asked. "Faith, she was in danger. Rick went nuts on her and came after her with a gun. She was scared. Staying at the house was wrong but Jamie didn't know she was there until you said so," Alan said. "And now you're wedging his wars for him," Faith asked. "He's coming home tomorrow. What do you want me to do," Alan asked. "You're his friend Alan. Go take care of him," Faith said.

Alan headed to the airport to meet Jamie. "Where is she," Jamie asked. "She doesn't want to talk to you right now. Jamie, she said to tell you that you made her a promise. What does that mean," Alan asked. "That I wouldn't let her get hurt. I was so freaked out and worried that something would happen to her. The cops show and I was scared that he hurt her," Jamie said. "What made you stop the first time," Alan asked. "Getting her out of that house and devising a stupid plan. I was on edge for weeks. I started going to the gym so I'd be strong enough to take him down altogether." "Then do that. She loves you, but she isn't letting you back in that house when you're drinking Jamie. You promised her back then. Now you have a reason to. She's pregnant. You're gonna have a baby. Protecting that baby is more important than the bottom of a bottle," Alan said. "Where is Faith," he asked. "Not until you stay off it and stay on the horse." "I need her," Jamie said. "And she needs you sober," Alan said.

Jamie sat on the back patio of the cabin that Faith had been at. He could still smell her perfume on the pillow in the bedroom and it was the only place he managed to escape the memories. He sat out there with a coffee then a bottle of water. Dealing with all the stress from Evan had him losing it. Everything he'd spent years doing was falling to pieces at his feet. He looked at his phone then called. "Faith, where are you," Jamie asked leaving a voicemail.

Faith saw his voicemail. She went and laid down for her ultrasound. "Baby is just perfect. Did you want one or two printouts," the doctor asked. "Three," Faith replied. "We need you back here in 4 weeks for another ultrasound to check on the baby. Other than that, you're just fine. Blood pressure is a little high, but you're probably under stress. Nothing new," the doctor said. "Thank you," Faith replied. "You sure you're alright," the doctor asked. Faith nodded and headed home. "You alright," Alan asked. Faith nodded and was pretty quiet the entire drive home. "Faith, you need to talk to Jamie. I know you're upset and everything but you need to. He said to tell you that he's not backing out of that promise," Alan said. "I don't wanna hear it from you Alan. I need to see it. He was always there for me when I needed him. He needs to do this," Faith said. "Let him talk to you. It'll help him. Please," Alan said. "No. For that matter, if he can't handle not drinking there's no reason for him to come…" "Don't even think it," Alan said. He drove Faith to the house where Jamie was. "Alan," Faith said. "Talk to him then we'll go back to the other house," Alan said pulling into the driveway.

Faith got out of the truck. "Baby," Jamie said. "What," Faith asked. Jamie walked to her and picked her up. He kissed her. "Put me down," Faith said. "Where were you," Jamie asked. "Were you drinking," Faith asked. "No. Faith, please," Jamie said. "I'm not having this fight again," Faith said. "Baby, please just come home," Jamie said. "I am. The road doesn't get easier Jamie. If we have kids, they're gonna drive you nuts. You can't just go grab a bottle and drink it Jamie. Handling Evan is just as bad. If you can't do that without drinking, how the hell are we supposed to have a family," Faith asked. Jamie kissed her. "Don't go," Jamie said. "I'm giving you time to fix this Jamie. I'm not going anywhere," Faith said. Jamie pulled her to him and held her tight. "I love you Faith. Whatever I have to do, I can do. I just can't do this without you," Jamie said. "I'm with you, I'm just not staying here," Faith replied. She went to go get back in the truck and Jamie pinned her to the side of it. He kissed her, not letting her up for air. "Stay," Jamie asked. "When you stop I'll be here," Faith said. "Don't go," Jamie said. "I need to do this Jamie. I love you but you have to do this for you and not because of me," Faith said. "I can't do this without you," Jamie said. "You have to," Faith replied. She got back in the truck. Jamie kissed her. "One night," Jamie said. "If you're better by Friday, fine," Faith said. Jamie kissed her. "Thursday night," he asked. "Fine, but…" Jamie kissed her. "I meant it," Faith said. Jamie nodded. Faith left with Alan and headed back to the other house.

Faith walked into the house and made herself some lunch. She brought some out to Alan as well. "What are you up to," Alan asked. "With what? It's 1:30. You need food too," Faith said. "You sure that separating yourself from him is a good move," Alan asked. "I can't just sit there and let him keep ruining everything. It'll ruin his music career Alan. That's the one dream he always had. If he sits and drinks through his career after everything," Faith said. "I get it Faith. Just don't be too rough on him if he is battling it," Alan said. "He needs to take care of it. He was strong enough to fight the temptation before. He can do it," Faith said. "What if he can't? Faith, you promised for good and bad. This is the bad," Alan said. "I'm gonna be there no matter what. I just don't want to have to watch him every ten minutes. I don't want to have to worry about him drinking himself into a stupor," Faith said. "He was worried about you. That's all," Alan said. "From now on, when he's worried, call me instead of letting him go for a bottle," Faith suggested. "I didn't even know he had until I saw him with the bottle in hand. Faith, just give him a break. Just for tonight," Alan asked. "What's the big deal about tonight," Faith asked. "He needs to have you with him Faith. He's a mess," Alan said. "When he handles this once and for all, I'm gonna be there. I can't just let him drink his way through that career. He's been wanting that career most of his life Alan. I can't let him ruin it," Faith said. "He'll do it, but you know he's doing it for you. He loves you Faith," Alan said. Faith nodded. Faith hugged Alan and went back inside to grab her laptop.

Faith turned it on and Alan came back inside. "What," Alan asked looking at Faith. "If he's in custody, how the hell is he able to send emails," Faith asked. Alan grabbed her laptop and ran a trace program he'd installed and hidden on it. "Says it came from Lexington VA. Which means...?" "If he went back there, he'd get off in minutes," Faith said. "Better. He might be in a maximum security jail. They still have access to internet but not email," Alan said. "Well he got access to it. Does it show that it was read," Faith asked. Alan shook his head. "Do what you have to Alan," Faith said. "Conner's on his way here. Do you want me to take it in or did you want to stay here," Alan asked. "I don't want him here. I get having to take it in, but I'm fine here alone for an hour or two," Faith said. "Nope. You're coming with me if you don't want him here," Alan said. Faith left with Alan and headed over to his tech buddy. "Alan explained what the situation was. Give me ten," his computer buddy said. He handed something to Alan and he hid it in his pocket. "What," Faith asked. "Nothing," Alan said. Faith put her hand out. "What," Alan asked. "What is it," Faith asked. "Jamie asked for something and he finished it up," Alan said. Faith just shook her head. "I'll tell you when we're in the truck," Alan said.

Faith got her laptop back, checked to make sure no more programs to track her had been added and they headed out. "Now, whatever that was he gave you…" Alan handed Faith what the tech had handed him. "Seriously," Faith asked. "He wanted it in case you disappear again. He wanted to make sure that he didn't get you back into Virginia again. Faith, he's scared. He did this after the night that Evan got in that fight with him. This was all because he was scared," Alan said. "Then the drinking needs to stop," Faith said. Alan took Faith back to the house. "Now what," Faith asked. Alan handed Faith his cell and saw the text from Jamie:

I'm coming down to the house. Don't say anything.

Faith replied back:

She's not feeling well. Long day. Come Friday

Jamie replied back:

I'm on my way.

Faith handed Alan back his cell phone. "And," Alan asked. "I said Friday. The fact that he still isn't listening means he's still drinking. I want proof or he's not coming in the door," Faith said. She walked back inside. "Faith, he's not gonna go for it," Alan said. "He either does or I'm not letting him in this house," Faith said. "Talk to him," Alan said. Faith shook her head. She went upstairs, locked the bedroom door and curled up on the bed with her laptop.

"Where is she," Jamie asked. "She doesn't want to talk to you. Jamie, she told me to do a breathalyzer," Alan said. "Then do it. I haven't touched a drink in 24 hours. Almost 36," Jamie said doing the breathalyzer without being aggravating. "Faith," Jamie said. "Jamie, she isn't coming down," Alan said. "Then I'm going upstairs," Jamie said. He went upstairs, unlocked the bedroom door and saw Faith asleep on the bed. Jamie sat down on the chair by her bed. "Just let her sleep," Alan said. Jamie shook his head. "Whatever you're doing here, just go," Faith said. "I love you. Faith, don't kick me out of my own damn house," Jamie said. "Then

I'll leave," Faith replied. She got up and went to grab her bag. "Faith, please," Jamie said. She looked at Alan and he shook his head. "How am I supposed to trust that you are sticking to it," Faith asked. Jamie kissed her. "Because I'm choosing you and not the bottle," Jamie replied. "For how long? Until he makes a stupid move? Then what? You gonna go grab another bottle," Faith asked. "I'm gonna grab your hand instead," Jamie said. "How long since your last drink," Faith asked. "Since I got off that plane. I'm not saying I wasn't tempted but you mean more to me than a stupid bottle of Jack. I need you. If it means staying sober, I'll do it," Jamie said. "What if you lost me," Faith asked. Jamie kissed her. "Never happening." "And if you do," Faith asked. "Don't do this Faith. We're not throwing us away." "That's what I thought Jamie," Faith said. She walked downstairs. "Baby," he said. "Go until you figure out what you're gonna do next time. Go talk to someone. Go to a meeting. Jamie, you need to do this for you. Not to hold onto me," Faith said. Alan stepped outside to the patio and Jamie kissed her. He leaned her against the door, locking Alan out.

He devoured her lips. He had been craving that kiss, that taste of her lips for days. Almost weeks. He picked her up, wrapping Faith's legs around him and barely made it up the stairs. "Jamie, stop," Faith said. He kissed her again. Faith got up and walked back down the steps. "Faith," Jamie said. "Go. Jamie, just go," Faith said. Alan heard her and came into the house. "You can't just..." "Jamie, please," Faith said. She went into the office and locked the door. She sat down on the sofa. Something was wrong. Alan came in. "Faith," Alan said. "Take him to rehab. Just away from here," Faith said. "Detox it is," Alan said. He walked Jamie out, put him in the truck and took him straight to detox. "You can't do this," Jamie said. "This is the only way you're getting her back Jamie. She isn't letting you back into that house unless you're completely detoxed. Either am I," Alan replied.

Faith curled up and went back to bed upstairs. Emma came upstairs 15 minutes later. "Faith," Emma said. "What are you doing in town? I thought you went home," Faith asked. "That chick that Greg had dated is history. He talked me into coming home for the days off. Alan called me. Are you okay," Emma asked. Faith shook her head. "Get dressed. We're going out," Emma said. "Why," Faith asked. "The one place that always makes you feel better," Emma said. Faith got dressed and left with Emma.

"We wondered when you'd be back," the box office manager said. "You did mention that I could come back if I ever needed to," Faith replied. "Yes ma'am. Here are the two VIP access passes. If there's anything we can do, please let us know." Faith nodded and went in with Emma. "So what happened with captain creepy," Emma asked. "Got a wire from the cops, and caught him admitting to everything. They dragged him off and Alan hasn't left my side. I just don't understand why Jamie is doing this Emma. I don't understand what pushed him that far. He's gone alcohol free for years. Why now?" "Because the only reason he stayed that way was so he was always able to come help you. He was sitting by that phone every day worried that he was gonna get a call from the damn hospital saying you were on death's door," Emma said. "So he goes and picks up a drink? Emma, that isn't how he ever handled anything." Emma hugged her. Faith swore Patsy was at her side.

"It starts with one drink. You really think it's gonna stop? Look at how he was when you two were fighting. That's how I ended up with bruises and trying to cover them at every performance," Patsy said. "He would never hurt me," Faith said. "Instead he's leaving emotional ones. Hurts just as much," Patsy said. "What am I supposed to do," Faith asked. "Either do what Tammy always said or walk. Stand by your man or Fall to Pieces."

"You okay," Emma asked. Faith nodded. "What if he stayed sober? Faith, you have to give him a chance to make it up to you. He loves you. That's why he was on edge for all that time you were in Virginia. He went as far as getting someone to watch for a call or a text from you. He was that scared," Emma said. "And what happened after that," Faith asked. "He's still on edge. When he got in that fight with Evan and you lost it on him, he went nuts Faith. He was scared that you were gonna disappear. That Evan was gonna keep coming after you. Faith, the man was scared. You have to let it go," Emma said. Faith nodded. "Tell me what you need me to do," Emma asked. "Go and talk to him," Emma said. Faith nodded. She hugged Emma and got up and went for a walk.

"You can let your guard down Faith. You love him that much," Patsy asked as Faith walked back towards the dressing rooms. Faith nodded. "And what are you gonna do next," Patsy asked. "I need him back the way he was. I could trust him and believe him and believe that he's gonna be there. I know it's hard, but he can't just drink his way through this," Faith said. "If you told him to get help, do you think he would," Patsy asked. "Not if it meant leaving me un-guarded. He's still worried even now that Evan is in prison," Faith said. "Then do what's right. Either help him or make him help himself." Faith had this feeling. Everything seemed clear. She went back out into the theater area then sat with Emma a while longer. "Did you figure out what you wanted to do," Emma asked. Faith hugged her and they headed back to the house.

Faith pulled into the driveway and Jamie was sitting on the front porch with a coffee. "Go and talk to him. Faith, this is your chance," Emma said. "He can't just do it for me. Emma, if he wanted this nothing would stop it. Just like him getting me away from Evan. That drink is something he can control Emma. If he doesn't, it shows me that he can't handle all of this," Faith said. "Let me talk to him," Emma asked. Faith nodded. She headed inside and curled up with a cup of tea.

"What happened," Jamie asked. "If you can be strong enough to protect her and to not drink when you were trying to find a way to save her, you can do it now. She's scared he's coming back Jamie. You drinking isn't gonna make her feel any more safe. You need to be the man she married. Drinking like that scares her," Emma said. "I need her Emma. I haven't touched a drink in 36 hours. I barely even drank before that. He came after her every time she's been alone Emma. Every time we're apart, I'm scared that I'm gonna get a call from the police saying I need to identify her body. I can't handle that. Not now," Jamie said. "Meaning what," Emma asked. Jamie shook his head. "What," Emma asked again. Jamie brushed off tears. "We're pregnant," Jamie replied. "She doesn't want anyone knowing right," Emma asked. Jamie nodded.

Emma walked inside. "Faith," Emma said. "What," Faith replied. "He isn't touching a drop again Faith. I can promise you," Emma replied. "Meaning what? Meaning you pulled off a damn miracle," Faith asked.

Emma nodded. "What if it happens again," Faith asked. "Then tell me," Emma said. Faith hugged her. "He loves you Faith. He needed a kick in the ass. That's all." "Thank you," Faith said. "That's what friends are here for. Just don't forget that he's your best friend Faith. Losing you would kill him. It would kill me too. Promise you'll stop making me worry," Emma said. Faith nodded. Emma headed out and Faith headed outside. She walked her to her car and Emma headed off.

"Faith," Jamie said. "You can't just walk away Jamie. You can't just forget it all. I've tried to and I can't. Every inch of me wants him to pay. I need to know that you're gonna be safe. I need to know that I can count on you no matter what. Clouding your head with a drink so you don't worry isn't gonna work. I need you," Faith said. "I'm not doing it again Faith. I'm not losing you," Jamie said. Faith kissed him. "I have to know I can trust you," Faith replied. He kissed her again and picked her up. He carried her to the porch swing and they curled up together. "I'm not leaving us behind Faith. We spent so long trying to keep everything safe. I forgot to keep your heart safe. I broke a promise Faith," Jamie said. "You were as scared as I was Jamie. I got through it and did the right thing. Sitting there drinking because you were powerless to a point isn't helping anyone Jamie. You stopped drinking because you wanted me to be safe. I stayed away because I needed to get past losing the baby. I needed to get my head around it all Jamie. I couldn't hold on to the one thing we wanted more than anything. We need to take care of each other Jamie. Worrying about what's gonna happen next is all part of getting over it. I went down to the Opry this afternoon. I sat there just like I always do. I remembered why all of this happened Jamie. You got me away from Evan. We did it together. We're staying that way," Faith said. Jamie kissed her.

"What are we gonna do about us," Jamie asked. Faith shook her head. "Take care of the baby like you took care of me. Be there," Faith said. "I don't wanna be anywhere else," Jamie said. For the first time in a while, he was calm and didn't need anything other than Faith. Faith curled up in Jamie's arms and wasn't worried about Evan. He was almost a bad memory. Jamie carried Faith inside. He leaned her onto the bed and kissed her. "I'm never gonna be perfect. Promise you'll still love me if

I'm not," Jamie asked. Faith kissed him. "Like you better when you aren't," Faith said. "I'm sorry. I just started losing it when he came after you. I was scared Faith. If you and the baby ever got hurt…" "No more worrying. If I'm here, I'm safe. Alan already said if I had to stay he'd be here," Faith said. "Thank you," Jamie said. "If it makes you feel better that is," Faith said. He kissed Faith and didn't want to ever come up for air. That time apart had almost killed him. "Promise me something," Jamie asked as they came up for air. "What," Faith replied. "We fight him together." Faith nodded and kissed him.

Faith got up around 5 and went downstairs to get something on for dinner. Jamie was still sleeping. Faith put dinner in the oven. She set the table and everything else and told Alan to come inside. "You two okay," Alan asked. "He's trying. That's all I can say," Faith said. "Just give him a chance to prove that he won't hurt you. I saw him Faith. He was a mess," Alan said. "He finally figured out why Alan. If and when this baby comes, it's gonna need us both. Jamie can't run off and have a drink when the baby is screaming. I can't worry what he's gonna do. He knows that," Faith said. "What happens if it happens again," Alan asked. Faith shook her head and went back to making dinner. "Faith, it's gonna happen at some point. You know that," Alan said. "Then I'm gonna lose the only man that ever meant anything to me," Faith said.

Jamie came down closer to dinner and Faith was sitting out on the porch swing. "You okay," Jamie asked. Faith brushed tears away and nodded. "What's wrong," Jamie asked. "Nothing," Faith replied. "You were crying," Jamie said. Faith walked past him and went back inside. Faith was quiet all the way through dinner. Fact was, Alan had a point. "Tell me what's wrong," Jamie asked. "Just thinking," Faith said. When dinner was finished, Faith cleaned up and went out. She went for a drive alone. After what Alan had said, it had her shaken. What was she gonna do if Jamie did stop? What was she gonna do if he couldn't? She pulled over by the lake. The exact spot Jamie had taken her when they'd been on a date. She sat down on the blanket she always had with her.

"What are you doing way out here," Deacon asked. "Peace and quiet for a while," Faith said. "Company," he asked. "If you're trying to start a problem, no," Faith said. He slid his jacket over Faith's shoulders. "If you need to talk, just say it," Deacon said. "My ex keeps taunting him. It's taking its toll on both of us," Faith said. "What did he do," Deacon asked. "My ex came after me more than once then came after Jamie at the hotel. He's in jail for now, but if he ever gets out….I don't know what to do anymore. It's not fair to put him through it all over again," Faith said. "Then move. Leave and disappear," Deacon said. "Jamie and I are married Deacon. It's a nice try, but it won't happen. Too many ways of him getting to us. Even on a floor with triple security he got through," Faith replied. "What are you scared about," Deacon asked. "Having to relive history," Faith replied. "Nobody is hurting you Faith. If it means Jamie and I working together to make you feel better, I'll do it. I hate seeing you like this," Deacon said. "It's gonna be like this until Evan is either put away for good, or he's gone. I hate living like this," Faith said. "Just know that you can talk to me alright? Even if you need to say something you don't want him hearing. I'm here," Deacon said. "I'm sorry for the way things ended," Faith said. "You two are inseparable. You always have been. Getting in the middle of that is just stupid on my part. If you need me as a friend, I'm happy doing that and nothing else. You're just an amazing woman Faith," Deacon said. "I just don't know if I can handle things with Evan. What if he comes after me and really hurts Jamie," Faith asked. "Then I'll take him down myself," Deacon said. Faith gave him a hug and brushed the tears away. "I don't want you worrying anymore. Promise me," Deacon said. Faith nodded. They got up and Faith put the blanket away. Deacon handed her his cell number, opened her door for her and after a quick hug, Faith headed back to the house.

Chapter 13

"Where were you," Jamie asked. "Needed to clear my head. Besides. I grabbed dessert," Faith teased. "I get the ice cream thing, but what's wrong," Jamie asked putting the ice cream into the freezer. "It's nothing," Faith said. "Faith," Jamie said. She went and sat down and went through some more emails. When she saw the one from Alan about Evan, she moved it into another folder before Jamie saw it. "Faith," Jamie said. "I needed to breathe," Faith said. "What is getting you all scared," Jamie asked. "What happens if he comes after us again? What happens when he comes after you," Faith asked. "Nothing is breaking us up Faith. Nobody." "I didn't mean breaking us up Jamie. I mean come after you and tries to hurt you. You know he's going to. When I left and finally got enough evidence against him, I knew that wasn't gonna be the end. He's hunted me down and knows me Jamie. He knows the way I am just like you do. He's never gonna give up," Faith said. "What's the worst that could happen," Jamie asked. "He kills me, you and the baby," Faith said. "That's what you're scared about," Jamie asked. Faith nodded. "Even if I'm gone the guys are still gonna protect you and prevent that from happening Faith. Nobody is doing that to us," Jamie said. Faith walked upstairs. She drew herself a hot bath and slid into the bathtub.

Jamie walked in a half hour later and handed Faith a bottle of water. "What," Faith asked. "Nobody is hurting you again. Not ever," Jamie said. "What happens if he comes after the baby Jamie? What happens when he kidnaps me and the baby? What happens if he hurts or kills you? This baby can't be without a mother and a father," Faith said. "You're panicking. Faith, breathe," Jamie said. "This isn't a panic mode Jamie. This is true. To the core of my soul true. He's already threatened it more than once," Faith said. "He's not gonna be that close ever again," Jamie said. "Psychic? Jamie, it's a reality we're gonna have to pay attention to. It's gonna happen. There's nothing we can do. Should we even bring a baby into this," Faith asked. "A little late for that," Jamie said. "The minute anyone finds out he's gonna know. He's never gonna leave us alone," Faith said. Jamie kissed her. "Tell me what you need me to do," Jamie asked. "Let me be scared. When I say I need peace and quiet, let me have it. I'm scared Jamie. I've been scared since he started this crap. Since I got out of that house. He's never backing off," Faith said. Jamie kissed her. Letting her be that scared and that worried hurt him as much as it did the baby. Jamie drained the tub, wrapped Faith in a towel and carried her to the bed.

He laid down beside her and curled up with her. "Nobody is hurting that baby Faith. Especially not him," Jamie said. He kissed her neck. "Nobody can guarantee that Jamie. Nobody." "I know that because he'd never be able to hurt either one of us. Faith, you're gonna be an amazing mom. Evan is gonna go away and back away. I don't know when but he will. You have to believe that. He's gonna back off Faith. He's not hurting you ever again," Jamie said trying his best to calm her. "What if he hurts the baby," Faith asked. "He'll be 20 feet under in minutes if he does," Jamie said. "You can't just go after him. Jamie, I'm being serious. When he finds out I'm pregnant, he's gonna come after us. You have to know that," Faith said. Jamie kissed her and snuggled up to her, almost pinning her to the bed. "What," Faith asked. "No more worrying. I love you Faith. He's not touching you or our baby. He's not hurting you either." Jamie kissed her again, barely letting her up for air. "I promise you that nobody is ever hurting you like that again. I promised you that Faith and I meant it," Jamie said. "You get why I'm still scared," Faith said. He kissed the tip of her nose. "Nobody is hurting you again Faith," Jamie said again. Faith kissed him. "No more worrying allowed either. You need to take care of you and baby. I'll take care of everything else. Don't keep thinking the worst. You have me and you always will," Jamie said. "Jamie," Faith said.

The towel slid off the bed. He made love to her. Jamie kissed her until his toes curled and made love to the only woman he'd wanted. Fact was, that was the only thing holding him together when she left. The thought of having her back in his arms is what made him stop. Even thinking that it would be the last time he felt her legs wrapped around him, the last time he'd taste her lips, the last time he'd smell that perfume. He couldn't live without that. It was worth the fight. It was worth anything that he had to do. It was worth the fighting with Evan. It was worth every second that he had to wait for her to leave Evan. Jamie kissed her. When they finished, they curled up together and Faith fell asleep in his arms. Jamie's arms slid around her and his hand rested on her stomach, with his hand on the baby.

Faith woke up the next morning and Jamie was kissing her neck. "Good morning to you too," Faith teased. He nibbled her ear. "What," Faith asked. His hands slid up and he leaned into her. "Jamie," Faith said. "What," he asked. "What are you up to," Faith asked. "Making love to my wife. Making up for lost time," Jamie said. He leaned into her again and made love to her. "You have to head into the studio," Faith said. "Have a job to do first," he teased. Every inch of her body was craving him. He wanted her so bad he could taste it. A half hour later, they finally came up for air and they got up and he walked her to the shower. "I have work to do," Faith said. "So do I. Reminding my wife why she's gonna miss me something crazy when I go back out if you don't come with me," Jamie said.

They stepped into the shower and he washed her hair. "What's all the special treatment for," Faith asked. "I screwed things up. Getting in that fight was just stupid. I didn't know she was staying there. I swear. I set that house up for you and me. It was in case we needed somewhere to go to have a little more privacy. I get that you're scared Faith. From now on, you aren't gonna be scared. I love you. I always will. If that means doing things to make you happy, I'll do them," Jamie said. He kissed Faith and bit that spot on her neck. She almost crumbled in his arms. Not 10 minutes later, they finally came up for air and stepped out of the shower. They dried off. "Do you want to come to the studio," Jamie asked. "Had an idea about how to tell my folks and yours if and when," Faith said. "Which is," Jamie asked. "You'll see tonight," Faith replied. He kissed her and wrapped his arms around her. "What," Faith asked. "I love you," Jamie said. "I love you too."

They had breakfast together and he gave her a half hour kiss goodbye then Jamie headed to the studio. "Come down for dinner," Jamie asked. Faith nodded with a smirk ear to ear. Faith cleaned up and headed outside and saw Alan. "Seriously," Faith asked. "Where we off to," Alan asked. "Shopping," Faith replied. Alan laughed and they headed off. They went out to Green Hills and Cool Springs. Faith headed into a few baby stores. "So what's the baby store stuff about," Alan asked. "Just in case," Faith replied. She grabbed two pairs of baby socks, two bibs that said I love my grandma, and two cute little baby shirts that said I love baby and they wandered the mall. "Nice sneaky way of announcing it," Alan said. "We're keeping it quiet. What is he gonna do when he's on tour and I can't go," Faith asked. "You still have someone there Faith. I'll be there or Jamie will or Emma will. She's gonna be back in a few days," Alan said. "What?" "She's coming back. Said that she needed to be here," Alan replied. Faith grabbed her cell and called Emma.

"What's wrong," Emma asked. "So what's this I hear about you coming down here," Faith asked. "So Alan told you. Is that okay," Emma asked. "You're moving here," Faith asked. "I just thought that since you're gonna be home some of the time, he'll flip if you're alone. This way we're both there if you want to stay. Figured it would calm Jamie down a bit," Emma said. Faith smirked. "That mean things are alright," Emma asked. "He's not gonna quit worrying. Especially after what happened in Gatlinburg at that cabin," Faith said. "Whatever happened to that cabin," Emma asked. "Jamie bought it," Faith said. "As long as we don't go down there when you get close to your due date we're fine," Emma said. "You hinting that you want to see that cabin," Faith asked. "I'll meet you at the house on Friday. We can go up and hang out," Emma said. "You seriously think he's gonna go for that," Faith asked. "Good point," Emma joked. "So come on the tour with us for the weekend. It'll give me someone to hang out with," Faith said. "Perfect. I'll see you there," Emma teased. The girls hung up and Faith went home to get some work done. She went through emails, worked on a couple webpages, adding concert photos into their photo sections. Jamie shot her an email at around 4 saying he missed her. Faith smirked. Faith got changed, slid on Jamie's sweater and headed down to the studio.

Faith pulled in and saw Jamie's truck with a black sports car beside it with a plate saying BNG BNG. Faith looked at Alan. "Don't think it. Greg's girl is here too," Alan said. Faith smirked and they headed inside. Faith saw

Jamie sitting on the sofa and whoever the woman was, was trying to slide into Jamie's lap. "My woman is on her damn way. Just go wait on Greg," Jamie said pushing her away and getting up. Alan headed inside. "Have you seen Faith," Jamie asked. "Waiting for you in the hall," Alan said. Jamie came into the hall. "What you doin out here," Jamie asked. Faith leaned against the wall. "Who's the flirt," Faith asked. "Greg's now ex-girlfriend," Jamie said leaning against Faith and linking their fingers. He kissed her, devouring her lips. "I missed those lips," Jamie said. "Good. You can remember them when you get tempted again," Faith teased. "Only one I'm tempted by is my sexy wife. I love her. Pretty much stuck on her," Jamie teased. "Good thing. You knocked her up," Faith whispered. "And until that little baby shows, I get to keep practicing," Jamie joked. He kissed her. "Marry me," Jamie said. "Stop being so silly," Faith teased. "Why not," Jamie asked. "You have a tour to finish. I have work and a 7 and a half month plan to finish," Faith said. He kissed her and walked her into the studio.

"So we just need to finish up those two tracks if we can. We can hand them off to management tonight and see what they think if they're done by 9. It sounds good but there was just something missing," his producer buddy said. Jamie kissed Faith and headed back in to do one more run before dinner. Jamie sang through the song and stared at Faith the entire way through. At the end, the producer played it through again while Jamie nuzzled Faith. "So that's what was missing. Dude, it's good. They'll probably put that as the first track released," his producer buddy commented. "I'm taking my woman to dinner. Want anything," Jamie asked. "Fortune cookie," Greg teased.

Jamie and Faith headed to dinner at a little out of the way place. They snuggled and were joking around together through dinner, grabbed a frozen yogurt and headed back into the studio. He stopped her. "What," Faith asked. "Remember something. No matter where I am, no matter what stage I'm on or what interview I have to do, I love you. Always have and will until forever ends. That's why we were made for each other," Jamie said. Faith kissed him. "Ditto," Faith said. Jamie smirked and kissed her. "So dang cute," Jamie teased. "Infinity times infinity," Faith said. He kissed her again. They headed in and Jamie worked on the last song. The entire things was about falling for someone out of reach. He just stared at her. Once Jamie finished up, he came in and saw Faith sitting on the sofa. He walked over to her and kissed her. They listened to that last track and Faith kissed him. "Like," Jamie asked. Faith kissed him. "We finished," Jamie asked. "You're done for the day yeah," the producer said. "Cool. I'm heading home. Taking this sexy woman back to the house," Jamie said. Faith and Jamie headed out.

They walked into the house and Jamie picked her up and carried her upstairs. "What are you up to," Faith asked. He leaned her onto the bed and snuggled up with her. "What," Faith said. "I think I might just have to snuggle you all night," Jamie teased. "Good thing we got married then," Faith said. "I still think we should do the big thing. Now that we're already married, the press will back down for a while. We can still do the big wedding like you wanted to do at the beginning. What do you think," Jamie asked. "Still determined," Faith asked. Jamie kissed her neck. "I love you. I want us to have it Faith. We're doing this one for the family," Jamie said. "We had the first one for them," Faith teased. "Then we're doing this one because we're never having another one," he said. "I love you Jamie, but the big wedding? We're having a baby. I can't fit into the dress," Faith said. "You can Faith. We give ourselves extra time. Besides. You'd look sexy in a damn potato sac," Jamie teased. "You're funny. Jamie, I can't…" he kissed her, silencing the protesting and the worry she had. "I love you. Stop worrying. We give ourselves extra time. We have a million years of time Faith," Jamie said. He kissed her and they curled up together. "Stop worrying," Jamie said. Faith nodded. He kissed her neck and they turned on a movie. A half hour later, they were both asleep curled up in bed.

Faith got up the next morning and was sick. Way past the regular sick. "Baby," Jamie said. "Something doesn't feel right," Faith said. Jamie came in, handed Faith her leggings and his sweater and he carried her down to the truck. Alan followed them and they went straight down to the hospital. "What happened," the doctor asked. "She was really sick and almost passed out. Something's wrong," Jamie said. He leaned Faith onto the bed in the emergency department, they blocked off that area for privacy and Jamie sat down with her. The doctors came in and put

Faith on IV. They did an ultrasound. "Baby is just fine. What's going on," the doctor asked. "I got up and I was sick. I couldn't stop the room from spinning. There was nothing I could do to stop it. It almost felt like someone slipped something in my drink," Faith said. Jamie went and talked to Alan and Alan called Conner to check out anything that Faith had drunk.

Jamie didn't let go of Faith's hand. Alan came back a half hour later and handed the bottle of water, the glass and the milk. "Thank you," the tech said. Alan went in to check on Faith. "Well," Jamie asked. "Tech chick has it. That would be an explanation," Alan said. Faith finally stopped being sick, but she was still dizzy. The doctor came in an hour or two later and checked on Faith and brought in the lab results. "Well, the bottle of water was laced and so was the milk. Just the milk she had," the doctor said. Alan went down to the house, grabbed the rest of the bottled water and the other jug of milk and brought it down to be checked. Both were laced. "Now what," Jamie asked. "I told you," Faith said. Jamie kissed her.

The police went through the house, checked everything that could be tainted and then went through the other house. No matter what was around, it was checked. They even went through the tour bus. Alan came back and Jamie and Faith were both asleep in the bed. Alan was about to walk out when Faith woke up. "You okay," Alan asked quietly. Faith shook her head. "What did the doctor say," Alan asked. "Did you find out what it was," Faith asked. Alan shook his head. "I know who did it though," Alan said. He headed into the hall and went down to talk to security.

"Babe," Jamie said. "What," Faith replied. "You feeling any better," Jamie asked. "You know who did this," Faith said. "How would he have got anything into that house," Jamie asked. "We weren't always there," Faith said. "He couldn't have…. Faith, don't think it," Jamie said. "Who knows what else is gonna happen," Faith said. "If he did what I think he did, that man is getting his beat down and he's gonna end up 20 feet down. What the hell," Jamie said. Jamie went to get up and the doctor came in. "Well," Jamie replied. "Date rape drug," the doctor said.

"Meaning," Jamie asked. "Whoever it was slipped it into two things they knew your wife would have. Whoever it was, knows her," the doctor said. "Did you give the cops the information," the doctor asked. "We just did." A half hour later, there were police officers guarding Faith's hospital door. "I think it's out of her system. The police are keeping guard until the man is caught," the doctor said. "Where's Alan," Jamie asked. "He said he was going to handle something. He left about a half hour ago," the doctor said. Jamie called him and didn't get an answer.

Alan threw his bag into his truck and took off for that little trailer way off in the middle of nowhere that Evan had held Faith captive in more than once. 9 hours later, Alan pulled into that little shack. He hopped out of the truck, grabbed his gun and walked inside, busting the door in. The wall was covered in pictures of Faith and Jamie. The word 'Mine' was written across them. "That boy is certifiably crazy," Alan said to himself. He walked down the hall and when he stepped into the bedroom, he saw pillows in the shape of a woman with Faith's shirt on one of them. Alan took pictures of everything then went down to the police station to talk to the officers.

"As long as you can guarantee that she's safe there, she can go home. Just be careful with anything and everything you come in contact with," the doctor said. They wheeled Faith out the back and into the truck and Jamie made sure everything else was taken care of. They were part of the way home when Jamie realized it all. "He's here Faith," Jamie said. "What do you mean here," Faith asked. "I got that milk yesterday. Got the bottled water when we went grocery shopping. He's in the house somewhere," Jamie said. "Meaning," Faith asked. "You're staying at the other house until the coast is clear at the farm," Jamie said. "Thanks for making my choices," Faith said sarcastically. "Baby, you two need to stay somewhere safe. Nobody is getting in or out without a ton of security coming after them," Jamie said. He called ahead to security and they did a room to room security check. Anything that could be contaminated was removed. They pulled in and security was doubled, not even counting Jamie's security guys. They got to the house and Jamie carried Faith inside. "I can walk," Faith said. Jamie kissed her. Let me take care of you alright," Jamie said. "Where's Alan," Faith asked. "Went to put a stop to all of this crap," Jamie replied. "He put himself in danger," Faith said. Jamie kissed her and leaned her onto the bed. "Jamie," Faith said. "You need to take care of you alright? Take care of you and our baby. That's all that you need to do right now," Jamie said. "Jamie," Faith said. He went downstairs and grabbed a bottle of water from the bag he brought home. He handed it to Faith and curled up on the bed with her.

"What are we doing," Faith asked. "Just let me and the guys deal with this babe. You have enough to worry about," Jamie said. "I get that, but he's dangerous. He could kill someone. He's already proven it," Faith said. Jamie kissed her. "I love you. Just let me do this. Faith, Alan is taking care of it. Everything is fine," Jamie said. "No it isn't," Faith replied. "Stop. Faith, stop worrying. You're supposed to be relaxing and keeping your blood pressure down. You scared the crap out of me Faith. Please," Jamie said. "I just…" Jamie kissed her. He leaned her onto the pile of pillows and linked their fingers. "I love you. The only important thing right now is you and me. I need you to take care of of this baby Faith. Please," Jamie said. "The only thing that was hurting us was Evan and the bullshit he caused. That's it Faith. I'm not losing you and I'm not losing our baby because he wants what he can't have. I love you Faith. Just listen to me. Please," Jamie said. Faith kissed him. "I need to know he isn't gonna know about the baby. Jamie, please," Faith said. He kissed her. "For today, just let him deal with it," Jamie asked. Faith nodded. "Now rest. You went through some crazy stuff tonight," Jamie said. They curled up together and Faith finally fell asleep. Jamie was right along with her, but only after he turned the security system on.

Faith woke up the next morning still groggy. She cleaned up then went downstairs. She saw Callon sitting on the back deck. Faith made some coffee for Callon, handed him a mug full then made herself some breakfast, attempting to find anything that wouldn't make her nauseous. Faith sat down outside with Callon. "I know what you're asking," Callon said. "Is he alright," Faith asked. "He's working with the police and the state troopers to track him down. One way or another, he's handling it. He's dealing with that nut bar. Nobody is hurting you again. He's as pissed as Jamie is. Just leave him be and let him do what he needs to," Callon said. "Just make sure he's alright," Faith said. Callon nodded. She headed inside and cleaned up the dishes. She logged into her computer and started getting some work done. Jamie came downstairs around 9. "Why didn't you wake me up," Jamie asked. Faith kissed him. Looked so cute when you were sleeping. You needed sleep," Faith said. Jamie kissed her. "How's baby and mom," he asked curling up with her. "Not so nauseous. I'm just wondering what was happening. I had a bad feeling all night that something happened," Faith said. Jamie kissed her. "I'll find out. Just don't worry," Jamie said. He kissed her again. "Jamie," Faith said. She turned towards him. "I want you so bad I can taste it," Jamie said. He leaned her onto the sofa and undid her robe. "Jamie," Faith said. He slid his jeans off and they made love on the sofa. They wrapped themselves up in a blanket and Jamie didn't want to let go.

"What is going on in that head of yours," Faith asked. Jamie kissed her. "I love you. That's what's going on," Jamie said. "I love you too," Faith replied. "What plans do you have?" "Jamie," Faith said. "Was thinking that we could go over to Belle Meade," Jamie teased. "I know what you're thinking," Faith said. "Nope. All I'm thinking is that I need to finish that song," Jamie said. "And that you want to re-do the wedding. Jamie, we don't need to," Faith said. He kissed her. "We're doing it. Please," Jamie asked. Faith smirked. "Come on. Gives you a reason to go find a wedding dress. We can do it on our one year anniversary," Jamie said. "What's really going on," Faith asked. "I love you. I always will," Jamie said. "Jamie," Faith said. "Nobody can refute it this way," Jamie said. "So that's why," Faith asked. "Baby." Faith got up and went upstairs. She showered, got dressed and ready to go and as she was about to leave, Jamie kissed her and pinned her to the wall. "Please," Jamie said. "Why Jamie? What's the point to it? We're already married. We don't need to have another wedding to shut anyone up. If you're doing it to get Evan to stop, he's gonna get ten times worse. If he finds out, no matter where he is he'll show and do something way over the top and you know that. There's no...." He kissed her again and carried her back upstairs. "Jamie," Faith said. "I want us to have the wedding," Jamie said. "Tell me the real reason why," Faith said. "Because I want us to have the giant wedding. I wanted everyone to be there. I wanted to share it with the people we love. The big wedding was what we were trying for in the beginning remember," Jamie asked. Faith went to shake him free. "Faith, please," Jamie asked. "Tell me the real reason." "This way, we can ensure without a doubt that it's legal. All that crap with him saying it wasn't pissed me off. We're doing this once and for all Faith. We're never doing this again." "You're that worried that he's gonna start up again? Jamie, that marriage license he forged isn't legal," Faith said. Jamie kissed her. "I need to do this so we're alright. We need to do this Faith. I love you Faith. Getting him out of the way once and for all is the only thing that's gonna make things better," Jamie said. "Right. Jamie, you need to stop. Even if we got married every day for the next 20 years he would still come. He'd still keep coming. I told you that. Jamie, making a big giant wedding isn't gonna make it better. It's gonna put all of this out there and pull him in to do this all over again," Faith said. Jamie kissed her. "Don't Faith. Please," Jamie said.

Faith went outside to the truck and hopped in then pulled out and headed to the office. When she walked in, Evan was sitting in her office. Faith walked to the reception desk and called the police. Within 5 minutes, the police were at the office and walking Evan out the door. Faith went into her office and saw a note from Evan on her desk:

DON'T FORGET I KNOW HOW TO HUNT. YOU CAN'T HIDE AND YOU AREN'T GETTING FREE OF ME.

Faith picked the letter up with tweezers from her drawer and called the police station. "I'll send someone down to get the letter. He's in shackles and cuffs. He's being put into maximum security and a psych hold at the hospital. If anything happens, or you hear anything from him, contact us directly. We're going to ensure that you have security at all times. He's not getting to you again," the officer said. "Thank you," Faith replied. She walked into Patrick's office and talked to him. "What's up Faith? I saw the officers leave your office," Patrick said. "Evan started making threats. Patrick, I can't be here if he's gonna be allowed to access the office," Faith said. "What do you mean he was here? I broke the contract Faith. He's not on our label anymore," Patrick said. "Then how did he get in here," Faith asked. Patrick walked her to the door and saw Callon. "What's up," Callon asked. "He was here," Faith said. "Then we need to handle this. You're going back to the house. Jamie would snap if

177

he knew," Callon said. "He's in the studio today," Faith said. "Then we're going to the studio. He needs to have you with him or he'll lose it," Callon said. Faith went to leave and heard a gun go off. The bullet went into the wall beside her. Callon got her back into the office and called one of the guys to stay with her. Jamie's friends rallied around her. "This is just getting plain stupid," Faith said. She walked past the guys and went to head out to the truck and another bullet went off. It just missed her. Faith got in the truck and took off. She headed straight home. Faith locked the doors, the windows and any other access, turned the alarm on and went and sat upstairs in the bedroom on the floor.

"What do you mean you don't know where she went," Jamie said when Callon caught up with him at the studio. "Someone started shooting at the office. She took off," Callon said. "Where's Alan? Did he come back yet," Jamie asked. "No. I tried to get in contact with him but he didn't answer. The phone went straight to voicemail."

Alan finally broke free from the shackles and cuffs that Evan had left him in. The first thing on his mind was getting water, the second...... Faith. He left and found keys to a truck, got in and started driving. He stopped at a gas station and found his wallet gone. He went into the glove box and found his wallet. All of this was just getting stupid. Alan found a pay phone and called Faith. "Alan," Faith said. "Are you okay," he asked. He busted into my office Alan. He started making threats. The cops took him into permanent custody and put him in maximum security. What am I supposed to do now? He has someone on his side helping him," Faith said. "I have all the information Faith. I'm on my way back," Alan said. "Hurry," Faith said. "Tell me you didn't go back to the farmhouse," Alan said. "It's the only place I know inside and out Alan." He hung up and Faith sat back down.

"Where is she," Jamie asked. "She didn't go back to the house. She has to be at the farmhouse," Callon said. "Get her out of there. He has a way in," Jamie said. Half the guys headed to the farmhouse, the rest went straight up to the other house. When Faith heard trucks pulling in, her blood pressure shot up. She heard footsteps, the door slamming and the alarm turning off. She heard steps coming up the stairs and walked into the bedroom. Faith looked over and saw two of Jamie's buddies. "Faith, thank God. We're going," they said. Jamie came in and picked Faith up. They took off down the stairs, Jamie put Faith in the truck and they were gone in a matter of minutes. The guys intentionally stayed behind.

"Jamie," Faith said. He kissed her. "I was so worried," Jamie said. "He started shooting Jamie. I don't know how in the hell he managed that when he was in jail," Faith said. "He organized it before that. He had to," Callon said. "I don't understand why he's doing this," Faith said. Jamie kissed her and didn't let go. They pulled into the new house and Jamie walked her inside. The guys weren't leaving anytime soon, and Jamie had no choice. He wasn't staying at the studio when she was going through this. Jamie didn't let go of her. "What if he finds his way in here," Faith asked. Jamie held her close. "Nobody is getting in here and nobody is hurting you again," Jamie said. "Alan called me," Faith said. "Where is he? Nobody's been able to reach him for days," Jamie said. "On his way back here. I told him what happened. I was about to leave and come here when he called," Faith said. He kissed Faith. "I love you. You know that right," Jamie said. Faith nodded. "Baby," Jamie said. "What did he do to Alan," Faith asked. "We'll find out when he gets back here," Jamie said. "What if..." Jamie kissed her. "Until he gets back, we won't know anything. No more worrying," Jamie said. They curled up together and he turned on a movie. "Jamie," Faith said. He kissed her.

Chapter 14

Eight hours later, Jamie heard a truck pull in the driveway. The minute he moved, Faith woke up. She got up and Jamie grabbed her hand. "Don't move," Jamie said. "It's Alan Jamie," Faith said. "Faith, don't. Stay here until the guys handle it," Jamie said. When Faith heard the front door open," she got up. "Faith," Alan said. She went downstairs and Jamie followed her. "Are you okay," Faith asked as she hugged him. Alan nodded. "What happened to you," Jamie asked. "Evan. He came down here thinking that keeping me there was gonna get him that close. Just tell me you didn't get hurt," Alan said. Faith shook her head. I left even when he had someone shooting. I just needed to get out of that office. It was starting to feel like a jail cell," Faith said. "At least you learned that one," Alan teased. "What happened," Faith asked again. "You're talking to the cops," Jamie said. "I needed to make sure you two were alright." He went and grabbed a bottle of water and drank the entire thing. Faith went upstairs and Jamie went and talked to him.

"What happened," Jamie asked. "The ass had me shackled and cuffed and was trying to beat an answer out of me. When I still kept fighting him, he tried to stab me. I snapped. I got him instead. Jamie, the guy is insane. Faith is in danger no matter where she is. The cops can't hold someone like that. He has too many contacts. If he wants something done, he'll get it done even if it isn't him that does it," Alan said. "Meaning what," Jamie said. "Meaning she's in danger even if you're there," Alan replied. Faith heard from the top of the stairs. She went into the bedroom and pulled on Jamie's jacket and her blue jeans. She grabbed her purse and pulled her boots on and came downstairs. "Faith," Jamie said. "If he's gonna do it, let him," Faith said. Jamie grabbed her hand and pulled her back. "You can't put yourself in danger like this," Jamie said. "Faith, just stop. You can't go running out there," Alan said. "I'm dealing with this myself. He's behind bars," Faith said. "Jamie, dude, tell me you aren't letting her do this," Alan said. "I need to make sure he won't do this again. At least I'll know what he's really doing," Faith said. "No," Jamie replied. "I'm going," Faith said. She went to walk out the door and Jamie grabbed her hand. "You aren't doing this Faith. You aren't putting you and…" "I'm going," Faith replied. Jamie picked her up and flipped her over his shoulder. "You aren't going anywhere," Jamie said putting her down on the sofa. "Jamie," Faith said. "No. Faith, you aren't putting yourself in danger. Not now," Jamie said. "I'm the only thing that's going to stop him and I'm the only one who's gonna stop all of this. The police will be there. I'm not gonna put us in danger," Faith said. "I'll take her once I get a shower," Alan said. "No. She wants to go, I'm going with her. You've been sleep deprived for days. You stay here and rest and I'll take her myself," Jamie said. Conner got to the door and saw Jamie. "I'll go with you. If you need me here," Conner said. "Stay here. Keep the house safe. I'm going with her," Jamie said. Conner took them down to the police station himself.

"You aren't serious about talking to him," Jamie asked. "If it ends this, yes," Faith said. Jamie didn't let go of her hand. "You aren't going in alone," Jamie said. "Yes I am," Faith replied. Jamie pulled her into his arms. "You can't put both of you in danger," Jamie said. "I'm doing this. Jamie, I'm the reason he's doing this. You have to just let me handle it. I can do this and put an end to all of it," Faith said. The officers went to walk Faith in and Jamie was left standing behind a one way mirror.

"So you finally showed," Evan said. "What do you want," Faith asked. "You already know the answer Faith. I want back what's mine. You really thought running off would stop me? I can find you wherever you are. You do realize the next time you're alone, I'm gonna be right behind you taking back what belongs to me. You don't get to say no," Evan said. "Really? I get to do and say whatever I want. I'm not a piece of property Evan. I left for a reason. I'm not coming back. You can stop any time now. I'm done Evan. Done watching my back all the time and done being scared. Evan, get the hell over it. I'm not coming back. I never will," Faith said. "Well, one point Faith…that still belongs to me," he said. "Oh really? You think you're ever getting that close again? Just leave me alone or the next time I see you, I'll be burying your backside 20 feet under," Faith replied. She got up and Evan tried to get her hand. "Evan, you wouldn't be able to do anything even if you wanted to. You are gonna be in here for the rest of your living years. You know, you could always overdose," Faith said as she got up and left.

"Faith, you shouldn't have said that," Jamie said. "Let's just see what happens," Faith said. Jamie grabbed her hand and they walked out the door. "He's never backing away. Faith, you pushed things," Jamie said. "And? He does something stupid, he'll get caught. He's not hurting me again," Faith said. Jamie kissed her and they got in the SUV and headed back to the house. "What did you do," Jamie asked. Faith kissed him. "It's fine," Faith said. He shook his head. "No it isn't," Jamie said. "Jamie." "I need you to be safe and to keep everyone safe," Jamie said. Faith nodded. "I'm being serious Faith. You have more than you to worry about." Faith kissed him. "Everything's gonna be fine. You know that," Faith said. "Faith, if he..." Faith kissed him again. They pulled into the house and went inside. "And from now on, no taking off without anyone. You wanna go somewhere, take someone with you," Jamie said. Faith nodded. "Babe, please," Jamie said. "There's no reason to keep this up. He's in jail. He can't make any plans when he's under 24 hour supervision. Jamie, we need to stop worrying," Faith said. Faith went upstairs and drew herself a hot bath. "Faith, please," Jamie said. "We're fine. The more you worry the more he gets the win Jamie. He needs to learn that he can't screw us up. He can't hurt either of us," Faith said. "I love you Faith. If anything happened to you or the baby, I'd lose my mind," Jamie said. "Nothing is gonna happen. Jamie, I promise you," Faith said. He kissed her. "We're going away. Getting away from him and all of this for a while." "Jamie," Faith said. "Babe, we need to. You'll be safe. He won't know where you are and we can breathe for a while. Get a new perspective on this," Jamie said. "Like what," Faith asked. "My secret. We're taking the plane we have for the tour. We can meet them when we're finished," Jamie said. "And where exactly are we going," Faith asked. Jamie kissed her. He grabbed her suitcase and leaned it onto the bed, grabbed his and put it beside it.

"Jamie," Faith said. They packed up. "And when does this plane take off," Faith asked. Jamie kissed her. "When we get there. I organized it while you were in talking to the psychopath," Jamie said. They packed, and Jamie grabbed an extra bag of her things. Enough that would cover for two full weeks. "Jamie, what are you doing," Faith asked. "We're leaving and that's it," Jamie said. "And where are we going? Jamie, we can't just run. I get you're worried. I get you're scared Jamie. I'm not running," Faith said. "Then consider it an overdue vacation. Just so we can wind down and relax before I have to head on," Jamie said. "And what about the studio time? You still have to finish…." Jamie kissed her. "Studio can be on hold. He came after my wife. That's a little more important," Jamie said. "So you're running from life," Faith asked. Jamie kissed her. "Making my wife relax," Jamie said. They left a little while later. Jamie got them onto the plane and they left within the hour. "Jamie," Faith said. "I want you safe for a little while. Walking into the lion's den wasn't exactly a smart move," Jamie said. "He can't hurt me if he's behind bars," Faith said. "He can and he would. Faith, he sent those men after you to kill you. Did you think that was a coincidence," Jamie asked. Faith shook her head. "He'd never kill me Jamie. He wants me period. He's not gonna be able to do much when I'm dead." Jamie curled up with her on the sofa. "So where are we going exactly," Faith asked. "Away from the world for a while. A friend of mine mentioned somewhere we can go that has privacy and a lot of security so we could have some alone time," Jamie said. They snuggled and fell asleep together for the duration of the flight. Jamie woke her up just as the plane was heading in for a landing.

"So where are we exactly," Faith asked. They stepped off the plane and they were at a tiny airport. They hopped onto another plane and a half hour later, Faith saw a small island away from everything. "Jamie," Faith said. He kissed her and they hopped off the plane. Jamie walked her into the house and they met all the people who took care of the house. They chatted then Jamie walked her up to the master bedroom. Just the view alone was gorgeous. "Jamie," Faith said. "Alone time. You and me. This is one of the only places I loved the minute I saw it. We can just be us and have some privacy Faith. Nobody is hurting either of us," Jamie said. Faith kissed him. Faith and Jamie went for a walk by the water for a while then Faith started getting a bad feeling. "Cell phones do work in emergencies right," Faith asked. "Why," Jamie replied. "Just in case," Faith said. "You're freaking me out," Jamie said. They went back to the bedroom. "What," Jamie asked. "If he…" Jamie kissed her. "He's not coming here," Jamie said. "And if he does?" Jamie kissed her. "Stop thinking like that," Jamie said. "Force of habit," Faith teased. Little did she know her gut instinct was spot on.

Faith and Jamie curled up together in bed and just talked. Jamie had all the ideas that his brain could fill. He grabbed his guitar and serenaded Faith. Somehow it calmed her down. Faith fell asleep in Jamie's arms. Fact being Jamie had that gut instinct feeling too.

Around 5am, Jamie woke up. There was something telling him that he was in danger and so was Faith. He grabbed his 9mm from his bag, loaded it and walked downstairs. He saw someone poking around outside and walked out there. When he thought he saw Evan, he took off after him.

Faith woke up a half hour later and heard two gunshots.....then two more. Faith got dressed and ran downstairs. She went out to the back terrace and heard fighting. She went and grabbed the house phone and went outside. Jamie was in an all-out fist fight with Evan. Faith called the police. "What are you doing," Faith asked. Evan went to come after Faith and Jamie grabbed his leg, knocking him to the ground. When his head hit the concrete by the pool, she knew Evan had been knocked out. She looked at Jamie and he was bleeding. "Jamie," Faith said. "Don't. I need to get up," Jamie said. Faith tried to help him up and saw the blood. "Jamie. Oh my god," Faith said. The police showed a few minutes later and Jamie was starting to go pale. "Something is wrong," Faith said. They put him into an ambulance and took him to the hospital. Faith wouldn't wait behind.

The doctors took one look at Jamie and took him directly into surgery when he got there. Evan was in another operating room. Somehow, even with almost cracking his head open, managed to still be breathing. "Just keep him away from me and from Jamie," Faith said. The doctors brought Faith water. "Before he was put to sleep he said we needed to make sure you were alright. Please just let us check you out," the doctor said. Faith shook her head. "I'm staying here," Faith said. "The doctor said he'd come out and update you," the nurse said. Faith nodded. Two hours later, Jamie's doctor came out. "How is he," Faith asked. " First words out of his mouth in recovery were that we needed to make sure you were okay," the doctor said. "Can I see him," Faith asked. The doctor nodded and walked her into the room they had brought Jamie to. He was asleep, but the minute she linked her fingers with his he woke up. "Are you okay," Jamie asked. Faith kissed him. "Come to bed," Jamie said. "You need your rest. I'll be here," Faith said. "Baby," Jamie said. "Just sleep," Faith said. He didn't let go of her hand for anything. The nurse got a bed for Faith and put hers right beside Jamie's. When he woke up almost screaming in pain, Faith was there beside him. The nurse came in and gave Jamie another dose of his pain meds. "You didn't go back," Jamie asked. Faith shook her head. "Babe, you need to rest. The baby..." Faith kissed him. "You rest and I will. I'm not leaving you here," Faith said. "Tell me he's dead," Jamie begged. "I don't know," Faith said. "We need to get out of here," Jamie said trying to get up. "You just had surgery. Stop," Faith said. Jamie leaned over and winced then pulled Faith towards him and kissed her. "Ow," Jamie said. "Then quit getting all flirty. Just because you're so dang sexy does not mean you get to rip stitches," Faith said.

Faith freshened up and sat down with Jamie. "Still hurts," Faith asked. "Got my Tylenol in my arms," he teased. "I think we should go home," Faith said. "Babe." "Jamie, seriously." "I understand why you wanted to go home, but we deserved this," Jamie said. "You need to heal Jamie. You need your own doctor," Faith said. "Promise me one thing first," Jamie said. "What," Faith asked. "That we're making up for this first break we get," Jamie asked. Faith kissed him. "We're going home where I know the doctors and where you know them. Jamie, you can't..." Jamie leaned over and kissed her. "I'll talk to the doctor," Faith said. Jamie nodded and got up and tried to walk to the bathroom without being in pain. Faith stopped and helped Jamie. He kissed her and Faith went out to talk to the doctors.

"He should stay here for a few more days just to make sure his wound is healing. As long as he has access to a doctor when he gets home," the doctor said. "He will," Faith replied. "The other man that came in has requested to see you," the doctor said. Faith shook her head. "The police are guarding his door. If you wanted to go in…" Faith walked away and went back into Jamie's room and helped him into bed. "You okay," Jamie asked. Faith nodded. "Then why are you all shaky?" Faith brushed it off. "Faith," Jamie said. "He's three doors down," Faith said. Jamie almost blew a stitch. He called the doctor in. "Just get my release papers ready. We're leaving," Jamie said.

They left the hospital, got their things from the hotel and headed back home. Faith made sure that Jamie was alright. "At least we're gonna be home. I loved that villa Jamie, but now that he knows.." "Faith, stop worrying. I love you. If it means going as far away from that nut bar as fast as possible then we go. I love you Faith. You're more important," Jamie said. "As long as you're okay with it. I know you wanted to do something alone together. Jamie, I…." He kissed Faith. "We're gonna be home soon enough," Jamie said. "I should probably postpone some of the dates," Faith said. "Nope. I'll be fine," Jamie said. He kissed Faith. She looked up healing time of Jamie's wound and it said a few weeks. "This means that you're not gonna be able to do anything for a while. You'll be in serious pain through a show," Faith said. Jamie kissed her. "I'll be fine. Promise. After I'm gonna feel like shit but I can't cancel shows. Cuts into our wedding time," Jamie said. "Still determined. Go figure," Faith said. They chilled together on the sofa. When they finally landed, Jamie was asleep with his arms tight around Faith. She kissed him and got him up, got his next pain meds into him and drove him back to the house. Alan was there with the guys waiting.

They got Jamie into the house and settled in the bedroom. Faith came upstairs and he pulled her onto the bed with him. "What," Faith asked. He kissed her. "I love you. He's not hurting you anymore. He knows better now," Jamie said. "What are you up to," Faith asked. "Reminding you that I love you," Jamie said. Faith kissed him, grabbed a bottle of water and brought it up to Jamie. "Marry me," Jamie joked. "I already said yes once," Faith said. "Then say yes again," Jamie replied. "Meaning what," Faith asked. He reached over to the bedside table. "What are you up to," Faith asked. "Marry me again. We can have the big wedding, the honeymoon, all of it. Please," Jamie said with that sexy smirk. "Jamie," Faith said. He opened the ring box and Faith saw a pave diamond band.

"Jamie," Faith said. "Yes," he asked. "I'd say yes even if you proposed with a ring pop," Faith said. He kissed her. "Ow," he said leaning back down. "When you get this healed, you can do whatever you want Jamie. You were in surgery yesterday. Bleeding on the patio of that house the night before. Please," Faith said. He kissed her. "Please," Jamie asked. Faith nodded. She changed his bandage then went and had a hot shower. "Faith," Jamie said. She slid a towel around her and dried off. She walked into the bedroom and Jamie handed her the cell phone. "Yep," Faith said. "It's Dr. Barrett. You 're still coming in for that appointment tomorrow right," the doctor said. "Yes. What's wrong," Faith asked. "We were told about what happened to your husband. Did you want him there with you for this one," the doctor asked. "Yes," Faith said. "We'll see you tomorrow then," the doctor said. Faith kept thinking something was wrong. "Is anything wrong," Faith asked. "Yes," the doctor replied. "Police," Faith asked. "Yes," the doctor said. Faith hung up and called the police down to the doctor's office. "Where are you going," Jamie asked. "Just stay here. I'll take Alan with me." Faith kissed him and left.

By the time Faith and Alan pulled in, the cops were all over the place. Faith managed to talk to the doctor. The nurse handed Faith all of her medical information. Faith left and went home. Half way back, Faith started calling doctors. She got someone that would come to the house. It meant a lot more privacy. "That mean we can get them to come out for a tour stop when you have an appointment," Jamie asked. "That means we figure it out as we go," Faith said. Faith kissed him. "Baby," Jamie said. "What," Faith asked. "Ice cream," Jamie teased. "Whipped cream with that I assume," Faith joked. "I swear, if I had enough strength right now, you'd be naked on this bed," Jamie said. Faith kissed him. "Jamie, stop. You can't keep over stressing your injury. You're gonna make it worse," Faith said. Jamie kissed her. "I love you. Just quit playing nurse," Jamie teased. Faith handed him his pain meds. "Faith," Jamie said. She looked over at him. He motioned to her to come closer. "What," Faith asked. He kissed her again. They were making out for a half hour or more. Jamie didn't move but it took all the will power her had not to.

Faith got up, grabbed some juice for him and went back upstairs. She handed Jamie his juice and he wrapped his arms around her. "I love you," Jamie said. Faith kissed him. "I love you too. Jamie, please just rest," Faith said. "I don't need to," Jamie said. "You trying to tell me that it doesn't hurt anymore," Faith asked. Jamie kissed her. It was an intense kiss. One that had both of them losing track of where they were and what they were doing. He made love to her even though it was the last thing he was supposed to do. They curled back up in bed. "I'm telling on you," Faith said. "Bet I can keep you quiet," he teased. "You're supposed to be resting. You aren't gonna heal right if you keep overdoing it," Faith said. Jamie kissed her. "All I need is you," Jamie said. "Take the meds," Faith said. Jamie kissed her. "There you go. Pain meds taken," he teased. "At least rest," Faith said. "Unless you're here with me it's not happening," Jamie said. Faith kissed him. "Fine, but you're sleeping. I have to check emails," Faith said. Jamie kissed her again. "They can wait," he said. "Not when the fan pages are probably going insane right now."

Faith logged into the email and internet. There was over 500 emails. "Told ya," Faith said. Jamie wrapped his arms around her waist and leaned into her. Faith went through all the emails. There were ones from fans left right and center asking a million questions about Jamie. Faith looked at him. "What," Jamie asked. "They all want to know how you are," Faith asked. "Tell them I'm fine and damn happy for extra time with the sexiest wife in the planet," Jamie said. "Then tweet it," Faith said handing Jamie her cell. He logged into his twitter account and shot off a message to the fans:

Hey y'all. I'm healing. Promise. Be back with another awesome song all about this. Don't worry. Wifey is taking good care of me.

Jamie pressed send and Faith laughed. "You seriously sent that," Faith asked. Jamie kissed her. "Baby and I are sleeping," Jamie joked. "What," Faith asked seeing that smirk on his face. "What if I said I was taking care of my babies," Jamie teased. "You want to sleep alone tonight don't you," Faith teased. Jamie kissed her. "Why not," Jamie asked. "Because. I'm not doing that unless we know that Evan can't hurt us," Faith said. Jamie kissed her. "Nobody is hurting us. The guy is still in the hospital." "Jamie," Faith said. "He's not gonna see it anyway." "Jamie. I mean it. Please," Faith said. He kissed her. "When we get to 5 months, we're spilling it," Jamie said. Faith nodded. "Fine. Until then, not a word," Faith said. Jamie kissed her stomach. "Baby. Are you coming to the awards with us," Jamie asked talking to the barely noticeable bump. "What are you doing," Faith asked. "Talking to munchkin," Jamie said. "I didn't give you…" Faith grabbed her purse and handed Jamie the ultrasound. "What's this," Jamie asked. "So you can see who you're talking to."

Jamie kissed Faith. "What," Faith asked. "We make cute little babies," Jamie said. "You haven't met baby yet. How would you know," Faith asked. Jamie kissed her. "As long as they look like you. You're gonna be an amazing mom Faith," Jamie said. "You still aren't allowed to say anything," Faith said. He kissed her again. He pulled her legs around him and pinned her to the bed. "Jamie, you're supposed to be resting," Faith said. He kissed her to silence her and made love to her. Every inch of her was humming and he barely noticed the pain from the gunshot. At that exact moment, Faith was the only thing in the entire world that he wanted.

An hour later, Jamie let Faith up. She got each of them something to drink and came back to bed. Jamie was out cold. Faith put his juice beside him and got dressed. She snuck her laptop out of the bedroom and walked downstairs. She curled up in the office and finished going through the emails. After Jamie's tweet, things had tipped right over. The fans were sending Get Well Soon messages one after another all over twitter. Faith uploaded some of the goofball pictures that Jamie had loaded onto her phone. Faith wrote a little bit of information on what happened to Jamie then finished the last of the emails. Faith got everything put into the system. A half hour or so later, Faith got a call from Patrick. "What's up," Faith asked. "Wanted to say thank you for all the amazing work you're doing. Jamie's fan club alone just got almost a thousand more fans. How you two managed that I don't know." "He sent tweets out. He's just being silly," Faith said. "What happened to him anyway?" "He got hurt fighting with someone. Was a long story," Faith

189

said. "He's back on stage next weekend. Is he gonna be alright," Patrick asked. "He will be. He's just sore," Faith said. "What happened Faith. Really," Patrick asked. "Evan shot him. They did surgery to patch it up and he's supposed to rest it. Everything's alright," Faith said. "He was shot?" "I can't do anything about it now. Evan did it. Evan's in the hospital Patrick. For what he tried to do to Jamie, he deserved to be 6 feet under," Faith said. Faith talked to Patrick a while longer then hung up and headed upstairs to check on Jamie.

Faith walked into the bedroom and saw Jamie wincing. "Jamie," Faith said. "Pulled something the wrong way," Jamie said. Faith checked the time. She grabbed his pain meds, handed them to Jamie and sat down with her. "Where did you go," Jamie asked. "Patrick called to see how you were," Faith said. Faith got Jamie's change of bandages and cleaned everything up. "Tell me that this stops," Jamie said. "That what stops," Faith asked. "That all of this crap and the stress and the pain stops," Jamie asked. "We'll be fine. Your shoulder should be better soon. You're back on tour next weekend," Faith said. Jamie kissed her. "I'm sick of all of this," Jamie said. "I know. It'll be better in a couple days. Promise. You just need to stop getting up and running around. You're supposed to be on complete bed rest," Faith said. He kissed her again and pulled her to him. "I need a sexy wife distraction," Jamie teased. "You need rest," Faith said. He nibbled her lips and kissed her until he'd pulled her into a never ending kiss.

He didn't come up for air or even let go. "Jamie," Faith said. "What," he asked. "Promise me that you aren't gonna go after him again," Faith replied. He kissed her. "I'm protecting my woman," Jamie said. "You aren't gonna to be able to protect me if you're killed going after him." Jamie kissed her. "I'm not going anywhere," Jamie said. "Then stop making me worry." Jamie kissed her again. "Have to be around for a little baby. Plus, I have this sexy ass wife that I don't wanna ever leave. I love you." "I love you too Jamie, but please don't get hurt again. I don't think either of us will make it if you do," Faith said. Jamie kissed her and pulled her into his lap. "Promise me you aren't gonna try to handle him on your own then," Jamie said. Faith kissed him. "I asked you first," Faith teased. "Feeling better?" Jamie kissed the tip of her nose. "Feel better when you're here," Jamie said. "You need sleep. Would you feel better if you were downstairs," Faith asked. He kissed her again and smacked her butt. "Dinner," Jamie asked. Faith nodded. She kissed him then hopped off the bed and went downstairs to grab dinner.

When dinner was almost done, Faith went upstairs. Jamie was in a fight on the phone. "I said no. That doesn't mean keep trying to get it. It's going on the damn CD one way or another. Don't piss me off," Jamie said. Faith kissed his neck. "If he doesn't stop all of this crap…" Faith kissed his earlobe. "She doesn't get to piss me off. I'm keeping that picture in there. She's my wife. It isn't changing. Leave it in," Jamie said. Faith nibbled his earlobe. "Enough. When I can actually get up without screaming, I'll come down and finish the last one. I couldn't figure out a damn ending," Jamie said. Faith went to get up and Jamie grabbed her butt. "Tomorrow," Jamie said. He finally hung up. "Tease," he said as he leaned towards her and devoured her lips. "Jamie. Dinner," Faith said. He leaned her onto the bed. "Jamie," Faith said. He peeled her shirt up. "Food," Faith said. He nodded. They went downstairs and had some dinner. Jamie finally felt better. He taunted Faith while she was cleaning up after dinner then they curled up together. "You feeling better? Really," Faith asked. "Needed a change of scenery. Come for a drive," Jamie asked. "You aren't driving," Faith replied. "So I get to tease you while you drive," he said. Faith kissed him. They got up and Faith walked him to the car. "You sure I can't drive," Jamie asked. "You are taking pain meds. You're staying in the passenger seat," Faith said.

Faith took him for a drive through the back roads and when they got to the Loveless, Jamie talked her into stopping. "What are we doing," Faith asked. "Pie," Jamie teased. Faith shook her head. "Sugar low or what," Faith asked. "Just means a real date night." They pulled in and Faith walked into the restaurant hand in hand with Jamie. They sat down and he ordered peach cobbler and banana cream pie. "Jamie," Faith said. "Instead of the banana, chocolate silk pie," Jamie said. The waitress smirked and went and grabbed their pie and sweet tea. Jamie kissed her. "What are you up to," Faith asked. "Romancing my wife," Jamie said. "I love you too," Faith said. "Just made me realize what I would've lost if I didn't have you," Jamie said. "As long as I don't lose you I'm fine. You scared me to hell and back," Faith said. "I'm not scaring you again. Faith, even if it means a damn bullet proof vest," Jamie said. "How are you gonna do..." Faith started to say. Jamie kissed her. "Nobody is hurting you. Nobody is using me to get to you. Faith, nobody can ever get between us. Even if they think they can, they won't be able to Faith. When you get scared, remember sitting here just you and me. Nobody coming in with guns, nobody coming in with knives or anything else. Nothing is separating you and me. Not until the day we take our last breaths. Even then, we're gonna be right beside each other," Jamie said. They snuggled and had their pie, and once that was gone they headed home. Faith headed back the long route and they got home and were snuggled back up together asleep on the sofa in minutes.

Chapter 15

Faith woke up the next morning and she was in bed. Faith looked over and saw blood on Jamie's pillow. Faith slid her slippers on and went downstairs. Jamie was making breakfast. Faith walked over and changed the bandage on Jamie's back. "And good morning to you too," Faith said. "Was itchy. It's fine now," Jamie said. Faith kissed him. "Baby," Jamie said. "You're not ripping a stitch," Faith said. Jamie picked her up and put her on the counter. "That's why you're bleeding," Faith said. He kissed her and devoured her lips. "Jamie," Faith said. "I talked to the doctor. He wants to check the incision out, but he said it's fine," Jamie replied. "You were bleeding. You had blood on the pillow Jamie. That isn't normal. You aren't doing what the doctor said," Faith replied. Jamie kissed her. "Quit," Faith said. He inched his t-shirt up her legs. "Jamie." "Why are you always trying to get my attention in this t-shirt," Jamie asked. He wrapped her legs around him. He peeled her shirt off and had her arms pinned to the counter. "Jamie." They made love on that counter. A half hour later, they were sitting on the floor and fed each other breakfast. "Promise me that you aren't going to push it anymore," Faith asked. "When the doctor says I'm okay, just listen to him," Jamie said. Faith nodded and kissed him. Jamie kissed her again and they ended up making out on the floor.

An hour later, and after round 2, they got up and showered then headed off to Jamie's doctor's appointment. Jamie teased Faith. "Well, you're healing well. Just don't over-exert the muscles. I know better, but you have to try to stop pushing it. I know you wanna go to the gym, but you can't. Jamie, bad enough that you're playing guitar this short after the injury. Rest. You don't, I'm not okaying you to go back to work. No flying either," the doctor said. Jamie smirked. "He means it," Faith said. Jamie kissed her. "Jamie, I mean it. You need to stop over-doing it. No weights, no lifting. Keep the wound clean and if you need the pain meds, take them. No drinking, no junk food. Take care of you. If you don't feel strong enough to go back to work then you aren't," the doctor said. Jamie nodded. They finally headed home and he was nuzzling and teasing her all the way home. When they got back to the house, Jamie kissed her and pulled her into his lap. "Jamie," Faith said. He peeled her sweater off and was going for the zipper of her jeans when Faith stopped him. "What are you doing," Faith asked. "Making love to my wife." He kissed her again and undid his jeans. "Jamie," Faith said. He devoured her lips, not letting her up for air. They had sex in that truck then he walked Faith into the house and they barely made it to the steps. "Jamie," Faith said. "What," Jami e teased. "What are you up to?" "Nothing," Jamie said. "Talk," Faith said. "Bed and we'll talk." Faith walked upstairs with him.

They curled up in bed. "Jamie," Faith said. "I was scared for you the entire time you two were together. When he pulled that gun, the only thing that flashed before my eyes was knowing that if I died I'd lose you and Evan was never gonna leave you alone. Faith, I was scared. I didn't want to lose you Faith. I didn't want to know that the minute I was gone he was gonna drag you back there. He isn't winning," Jamie said. "I'm married to you Faith. I love you," Jamie said. "He's not coming anywhere near me. Never will again Jamie. I love you," Faith said. "What happens if I die? What then? Is he gonna come back and come after you? Faith, I got shot. I could've been killed," Jamie said. "You're scared. I get that Jamie. Stop thinking what you're thinking. You're not going anywhere," Faith said. "I love you. I know he's never gonna stop Faith. Fact is, if he stops it's because someone killed him. That's the only way," Jamie said. Faith got up and got dressed, went downstairs and grabbed some juice.

Jamie came downstairs and saw Faith curled up in the oversized chair. "Faith." She brushed the tears away. "Baby," he said. Faith shook her head. "I get why you were scared," Jamie said. "I'm right Jamie. I was right. When I told you he'd never leave me alone until he was dead I was right. You wouldn't even let me think it," Faith said. "I didn't want you worrying. Faith, we're having a baby. Any more stress on you isn't good," Jamie said. "So instead you lie to me? Jamie, you aren't indestructible. You got shot and could've died. He's never leaving me alone until he's dead. I have no choice Jamie. Him finding out about the baby is gonna be the death of me and he's gonna come after me until he kidnaps this baby or me with it. He's not leaving Jamie. He never will," Faith replied.

Jamie walked over to Faith and sat down with her. "He's not hurting you and he's not hurting our baby Faith. I don't care what I have to do," Jamie said. Faith got up and went into the kitchen. "Faith," Jamie said. She shook her head. "Don't make me run after you," Jamie said. "I need to know you aren't putting yourself in our way Jamie. You can't just dive onto the sword. You have to let whatever happens just happen. If he comes after…" "He's not touching either of you Faith. I don't care what he tries. He's not. We're having a baby. He doesn't get to hurt my wife," Jamie said. "He's never leaving Jamie. He's gonna come after us. You have to let me…" Jamie kissed her. "Since I'm not allowed to carry you, come with me," Jamie said. Faith shook her head. "Faith." "I'm going for a drive. I'll be…" Jamie kissed her. He leaned her against the sofa. "I'll be home in a little while," Faith said. "No. Faith, the only way you're walking out that door is if I'm coming with you. Stop this," Jamie said. Faith shook her head and walked out the door. She got in the truck and went for a drive.

Faith drove for a while, went down to the farm house then sat outside on the porch swing. "What are you doing back here," Alan asked. "Needed time to breathe." "Faith, I know something else is swimming in that head of yours. Spill it," Alan said handing Faith a soda. She shook her head. "Faith." "I can't just pretend it's not scaring me," Faith said. "He's not gonna get hurt again. Faith, he's a good man. He's a little over-protective, but he's only doing it because he loves you. Faith, just let him do this," Alan said. "He got himself shot. He could've died Alan. I told him that he needed to stop and get someone else to handle it. He won't even listen to it," Faith said. "He's not gonna get hurt again. Faith, if I have to get a bullet proof vest that nobody can see, I will. I'm not letting him get hurt," Alan said. "He's gonna get himself killed. I know that Alan. I also know that Evan isn't gonna stop until one of them is buried. Evan wants it to be Jamie and Jamie wants it to be Evan. Nobody is doing anything," Faith said. "Faith," Alan said. She shook her head and got up. "Faith, you have to let me handle this. It's fine," Alan said. "It never will be," Faith replied. She went to walk away and Alan saw her getting dizzy. He came up behind her as she was about to pass out.

Faith woke up a half hour later and was on the sofa back at the house where Jamie was. "You alright," Alan asked. "What am I doing back here," Faith asked. "You were out cold. You're safer here," Alan said. Faith went to get up. "He doesn't know you're back. He was sleeping," Alan said. Faith got up and grabbed herself a bottle of water. "You sure you're alright," Alan asked. Faith nodded. "Faith, you're allowed to be freaked out. I'll talk to him. I promise," Alan said. Faith nodded and went upstairs. She walked upstairs to check on Jamie and he was sitting on the edge of the bed.

"Alan had to bring you back over here. What happened," Jamie asked. "Nothing," Faith replied. "Faith." "I got dizzy. My head was spinning. That's all," Faith said. "Then why did he have to carry you into the house?" "Jamie, I'm fine," Faith said. "Sit," Jamie replied. Faith went and put her pajamas on. "Woman, you're driving me nuts," Jamie said. "I'm fine Jamie. I was having one of those days alright? I'm allowed to feel like crap. Just leave it be," Faith said. Jamie leaned over and kissed her. "I love you. If you're not feeling well or you're having a damn panic attack, you need to tell me. I am not letting anything happen to you," Jamie said. "Then stop putting yourself in danger," Faith said. "That why you were dizzy," Jamie asked. Faith shook her head. "Faith." She got up and turned the light off. Not 10 minutes later, Jamie turned the bedside light on. "Faith, please," Jamie said. "You have to stop going after Evan. Please just let me handle this Jamie. Let me finish this once and for all." "You're pregnant. Stop freaking out and stressing over what he's doing. Nobody is hurting you. I'm dealing with this. Me. Not you. End of discussion. Nobody is getting near you or the baby. Let me handle this." "You're handling this? You got shot Jamie. If I hadn't been there, you could've died. Do you get that," Faith asked. "Baby," Jamie said. "No. You know that he's not stopping until he gets what he wants. The only one that can stop him is me," Faith said. "No." "I didn't ask you Jamie. That's what needs to be done," Faith replied. "He's gonna be in jail. Attempted murder. He admitted to it Faith. He's not coming near you." " Jamie, enough. You're not putting yourself in danger and getting killed.

You have to be on the damn stage. All I have to….." "Faith stop it," Jamie said. "Stop putting yourself in danger then," Faith replied. Jamie kissed her. Instead of trying to distract her, he devoured her lips. He made love to her. He peeled her teddy off and kicked his boxers to the ground. Making love to her was the only thing that he wanted, and it was the only way he had of getting her to stop trying to deal with Evan alone.

Faith woke up an hour or two later. Jamie barely let her out of his arms. She went into the bathroom and cleaned up. "What are you doing," Jamie asked from the bed. "Washing the makeup off. Besides. I was hot," Faith said. "What's really wrong," Jamie asked sitting up. "You know the only way this will stop is if I handle it and you're still telling me not to," Faith said. "I'm telling you to keep you and our baby safe Faith. That's the only damn thing we can control. We need to take care of that baby. The Evan crap will stop. Let it stay where it is. You need to stop," Jamie said. "You don't get to tell me what to do Jamie. Did you forget that in a week you're back on tour? You get a distraction. I get to sit there and wait for his next move. I get to sit there when you're doing performances. Jamie, just let me…" Jamie kissed her, pinning her to the door. "Don't leave. Faith, don't put yourself in danger," Jamie said. "I'm the only one that's going to end this Jamie. The only one. Alan isn't going to stop him and you won't either. I'm going to go and end this. I'll go down to the jail and talk to him. Nobody can jump through that window. He's not going to hurt either of us. If me talking to him while he's guaranteed to be on his meds puts an end to this, I'll feel a lot better Jamie. I won't be having panic attacks again. Jamie, I need to do this," Faith said. "Answer is no," Jamie replied. "I didn't…" Jamie kissed her and walked her backwards to the bed. "Stop picking a fight and just come back to bed," Jamie said. He peeled her jeans off, slid her shirt off and curled her into his arms. "We'll figure it out in the morning Faith. For tonight, just stop worrying," Jamie said. He flipped the light off and snuggled her.

Around 10am, Jamie woke up to find a note on the pillow:

Doctor appointment. Everything's fine. We'll talk later. Love you.

Jamie got up and called Faith's cell phone – no answer. He waited 20 minutes and called her back. "Good morning," Faith said. "Where are you," Jamie asked. "I told you," Faith said. "Tell me you aren't going to that jail," Jamie said. "I'll be home in a little while. No worrying," Faith said. "Faith." "I'm on my way home." Faith hung up. Not 45 minutes later, Faith was walking in the door. "You went didn't you," Jamie asked. "He's not bugging us again. He knows straight out that if he does this again, he's going to be permanently committed. He even signed off that he'd agree to it. Jamie, he said he'd stop. That's all that matters," Faith said. "What part of stay safe doesn't register? Faith, I don't care if he was in a padded cell and you could talk to him. I said stay away from him. Faith…" "Jamie, it's handled. It's done," Faith said. "You drive me nuts. Did you know that," Jamie asked. "I'm not doing this Jamie. I'm not having a fight with you about this. It's done and handled." "You could've got hurt Faith. We have a baby to worry about," Jamie said. "And now we have one less worry. He's leaving us alone. He's leaving me alone and he's leaving you alone. We don't need to…" "You really think that's gonna stop him? You trust a psychopath," Jamie asked. Faith walked upstairs.

Faith went upstairs and showered. Jamie walked in and slid into the shower with her. He leaned her against the wall. One kiss and Jamie had her legs shaking. The windows started steaming up. He picked her up and had her legs wrapped around him. He made love to her in the shower. He barely said two words. An hour later, the hot water was almost gone and Jamie finally let her up for air. "Jamie," Faith said. "Come with me," Jamie said. He wrapped her in a towel, wrapped one around him and walked Faith to bed. "What are you up to," Faith asked. "Keeping you safe. That's what I'm supposed to be doing," Jamie said. Faith got up and started getting dressed. "Faith." "I'm making something to eat Jamie." He pulled his jeans on and followed her downstairs. "Jamie," Faith said. "I did say to let me deal with it or at least let me find a way so that it's dealt with. Faith, I don't want him anywhere near you even if it's behind a bulletproof glass window," Jamie said. "So I'm supposed to do what you say or else," Faith asked. "No. Don't put that baby in danger. That's all I wanted," Jamie replied. "Well, you don't…" Jamie kissed her. "Please," he asked. "Jamie," Faith replied. He kissed her again. "For my sanity. Please stay as far away from him as possible. That's all I want. You and me being safe." Faith kissed him. "I'm keeping us safe. Stop worrying," Faith replied. "No more taking off then." Faith kissed Jamie. "Studio," Faith asked. "Only if you're there with me." She nodded and Faith made lunch. They had something to eat then went and got changed to head downtown.

"I am capable of doing my own thing," Faith said. "Just come and give me a little extra inspiration," Jamie said. "Meaning," Faith asked. "I have to finish a song today. I still couldn't figure out an ended for it. I came up with two more but that one song is still pissing me off. I have to finish it," Jamie said. "Fine," Faith replied. He kissed her at the light. "Did you take the pain…" "Not taking them unless I need to. I have to get this finished," Jamie said. "Just promise me that if you need them you'll tell me," Faith said. Jamie nodded. They pulled into the parking lot and headed into the studio hand in hand.

Jamie kissed Faith then headed into the studio. He listened through the part of the song he'd recorded and started going through ideas for the end of the song. Faith sat down and a half hour later, Jamie sent her a text:

Never walked away, begged you to stay and I'm grateful every day for the day you said I love you. Sound good?

Faith walked over to him and walked into the studio. "What," Jamie asked. Faith leaned down and kissed him. "I guess that was a yes," Jamie teased. "What's next," Faith asked. "I love you," Jamie teased. "I'm working on emails. I'm not leaving the room," Faith said. Jamie kissed her again and Faith walked back to the sitting area. Jamie got the tail end of the song down. It definitely wasn't what Faith thought it was. He came up with an ending that was more about being protective than anything else. She listened to it and Jamie looked at Faith. She got up and grabbed herself some juice. Jamie walked over to her. "Faith," Jamie said. "What," Faith replied. "Babe, what do you think of it? Really," Jamie asked. Faith nodded. She went to walk away. "Babe," he said. Faith went and sat back down and finished working through the emails.

Jamie went back and worked on some more music. Faith finished up her emails. Jamie came out a few hours later and Faith was sitting in the hall. "Baby," What are you doing," Jamie asked. "Nothing," Faith said. "Baby," Jamie said. She got up and grabbed her laptop. "Faith." "I'm going to get some work done at the office," Faith said. "Baby," Jamie replied. She grabbed her bag and Jamie grabbed her hand. "Faith, what's wrong," Jamie asked. "Go get your work done, I'm gonna work on mine," Faith replied. "Babe, I get you're upset. Stop taking it out on..." "I'm not. I need to get work done," Faith said. He kissed her. "Faith." She headed out and went down to the office.

The minute she stepped in, Faith was completely creeped out. She locked her office door and got to work. Concentrating on what she could do was all that her brain would let her do. She went through emails, faxes and letters. She dove in head first. She did her best to get everything done. When the clock hit 6pm, someone knocked at her office door. Faith looked and saw Jamie's leather jacket. "Thought you were working," Faith asked. He pulled her into his arms and kissed her. "Jamie," Faith said backing off. "Okay, spill it Faith. What the hell did I do," Jamie asked. "You ask me to help you with the song then you flip the entire thing and turn it into a nasty mean song," Faith asked. "That's the way the song was going. I can't just..." "What are you mad at? Me? You know damn well I'm right. I'm the only thing that can stop Evan. I know that's what it's about." "Stop. Faith, it has nothing to do with us. I started it when you first took off and started living with that psycho. I was pissed off. I was scared he was gonna kill you. When I found out he was hurting you it killed me. I was so mad I wanted to rip his throat out. I don't know what else to say Faith," Jamie said. "You are gonna end up having to tell the story of that song. You know that right," Faith asked. "What do you need me to do Faith? Tell them they can't release it?" "Just go back to the studio," Faith replied. He kissed her. "I love you." "Jamie, just stop." "Faith, if I could've killed him at that exact second you wouldn't have had to go through any of this. We would've been together for years by now. He did this to us. You didn't do it," Jamie said.

Faith sat down at the desk. "Stop Faith. Stop being worried that all of it's gonna come out. What happened is between you and me. I love you.

He's not hurting you, and he's definitely not coming anywhere near either of us again. Would you rather that I do that one you were playing around with," Jamie asked. "It's not finished Jamie. You can't just…" He took her notebook and kissed her, sliding the book into his back pocket. "I love you. That's all that matters. Only regret I ever had was that I let you leave and go to him. That's the only one I'm ever gonna have." "It wasn't about letting me do anything. I get to have my own damn choices," Faith said. "Stop getting mad Faith. I kicked myself that I didn't do more to help you. That I didn't say something or do something before you left. That you went through it. I hate that it happened at all. Faith, if I had gone and stayed near you so you had someone to help, none of the other things would've happened. The threats wouldn't have happened," Jamie said. "Just go…" He closed her blinds and kissed her. He sat her on the edge of her desk. "No more leaving. No more being scared of him. No more fighting and fussing." He kissed Faith, almost dropping every item off her desk. Jamie peeled her jeans off and had sex with her on that desk. He picked her up and carried her to the sofa and curled up with her. "Faith," Jamie said as they were catching their breath. "What," Faith replied. "Promise me. No more fighting about him," Jamie said. Faith kissed Jamie. "Up and you're coming back with me. No more fussing over it. I'm not putting it on," Jamie said. "You…" "No. No more picking. I'm putting your song on it instead. The bad ass one you wrote about kicking Evan's butt," Jamie said. "What if…" "Don't try changing my mind either. I love you. Always will," Jamie said.

After round 2, Jamie talked her into walking back into the studio. They walked back in and Jamie kissed Faith. He handed the recording he'd made when he was helping her. They played through it and the guys loved it. Fact was, it was the right song - helped that Faith wouldn't kick his butt over it too. They did two or three runs of the song then did one good take. They came back in to listen after the third take and the producer agreed. It topped the other song. "Why don't we use the other one as an extra track for the deluxe," he asked. Jamie wasn't about to say yes unless Faith agreed. Jamie looked at her. Faith nodded. Jamie walked over and kissed her. "Fine, but we're not doing it on stage," Jamie replied. "Think we need to do this one part over then it's done," the producer said. Jamie kissed Faith, went and did the last tweak of the song and then they all headed to dinner together. When Faith didn't have a drink with everyone else, Greg asked. "Faith, is there something you're not sharing," Greg asked. "Nope. I'm driving home," Faith replied. Jamie's hand slid down Faith's leg. He nuzzled her neck. "Now I know y'all are hiding something. Spill it," Andrew said. "It's nothing. Seriously guys. She's driving. I can't even drink because of the pain meds," Jamie replied. "You're pregnant," Greg said. Faith shook her head. Faith kissed Jamie and got up and went to the bathroom. She came out and Jamie was standing in the hall. "What," Faith asked. "They're the guys. We have to. They're not gonna…" "No. Not until…" Jamie kissed her. "Okay," he replied.

They went back to the table and did their best not to say a word. They finally headed out and Jamie and Faith walked back to the truck. "I love you," Jamie said wrapping his arms around her. "We're still not…" Jamie kissed her, devouring her lips. "Not…" "You definitely need to start wearing a skirt," Jamie whispered. He opened the back door and leaned her in, peeling her jeans off her on the way in. "Jamie, stop," Faith said. They had sex in the backseat. "I think you needed dessert," Jamie teased. "What has got into you tonight," Faith asked. He devoured her lips. "I'll drive home," Jamie said. "Why," Faith asked. "I'm keeping the jeans. You drive then," he teased. He kissed her again and she slid into the driver's seat. "Farm house," Jamie said. "But we…" He kissed her. "Farm house it is," Faith replied.

They headed over there and when they went to pull in, Faith saw the lights on in the house. "Jamie," Faith said. "Just go," he replied. The minute she parked, he took the keys and pulled Faith into his lap. "What," Faith asked. He handed her back her jeans. "Slide them on and come with me," Jamie replied.

Faith pulled her jeans on and Jamie walked her across the cold dirt and into the house. The fire was going and there were candles in the TV room. "Jamie," Faith said. He handed her the box that was sitting on the counter. "What are you up to," Faith asked. "Upstairs and open," he teased. Faith went upstairs and opened it and found a white satin and lace teddy. She knew Jamie's taste. He picked it out. Faith slid her things off and slid the teddy on. She walked downstairs and Jamie had blankets and pillows by the fireplace. "Jamie," Faith said. He turned around in only his jeans and saw Faith. "Wow," he replied. "What? You picked it out," Faith replied. "If you weren't pregnant, you'd be getting pregnant tonight wearing that," Jamie replied. "Think so do you," Faith asked. He walked over to her and kissed Faith. He walked her to the pillows and leaned her onto them, not letting that kiss break. "Had all this planned did you," Faith teased the minute they came up for air. "Romancing the only woman I ever wanted on the entire planet. Damn right I did," Jamie said. "What about…" He kissed Faith again and curled up on the floor with her. "What are you trying to convince me to do?" Jamie devoured her lips. They had hot, intense sex that had every inch of her and Jamie throbbing and Jamie still hungry for more. "What are you up to," Faith asked. "Getting back what we need. Nobody is getting between us Faith. Nobody," Jamie said. Faith kissed him. "I know you're mad that you…" Jamie kissed her. "He's not getting in the middle of tonight either." Jamie pinned her back to the carpet. "Jamie," Faith said. He kissed down her torso. "All mine," he teased. He nibbled at her hip. "Jamie." They made love again and they curled up together. "Best part of this house," Jamie said. "So, once we get closer to the due date…" "Already organized. Got a few color ideas. I know you love that lilac color. The other option is rose or blue. My mom is making a quilt," Jamie said. "You told…" "No. She said she wanted to make one for when we have babies," Jamie replied. Faith kissed him.

Faith and Jamie fell asleep curled up together. Jamie was dreaming about having kids. Faith ended up with nightmare after nightmare about Evan coming after them and taking her and the baby hostage. When Faith woke up from a nightmare, Jamie was holding onto her. "It's alright. It's me," Jamie said. Faith went to get up and Jamie didn't let go. "You're safe. I'm here baby." "I can't tell anyone Jamie. We can't. Not when he can come after us," Faith said. Jamie kissed her. "You're alright. We're fine. The baby is fine. Nobody is hurting you Faith. He doesn't get to have that power over you. I love you." "I need to know he's not gonna have that option Jamie. I need to know he's not ever getting out," Faith said. Jamie kissed her. "In the morning we call. Everything's okay," he replied. He held her close to him and tried to calm her. "I'm here

Faith. Nothing is happening here." "It happened Jamie." He kissed her. "Not anymore it isn't," he replied. He finally managed to calm her enough so she could get back to sleep. Letting go of her wasn't an option. He slept with his arms around her and didn't let go.

The next morning, Faith woke up and they were still curled up on the floor. "Morning sexy," Jamie said. "Just promise me he…" Jamie kissed her. He grabbed the cordless phone and called the officer that he'd talked to. "Was he sentenced yet," Jamie asked. "We have the testimony from your wife. We have yours. Just on that it proves him guilty. He'll be in there a long time," the officer said. "Can you check with them to make sure? We're gonna need more protection if he isn't and he's on bail or something," Jamie replied. "Give me ten and I'll call to confirm," the officer said hanging up. "Jamie," Faith said. "He's not free Faith. You know he's in jail and they're not letting him out," Jamie replied. He kissed her. "Breakfast," Jamie asked. Faith nodded. "Nobody is touching you," he replied. They got up and made breakfast and just as they were about to eat, the officer called. "He's still there. They had to move him to the infirmary. I guess some guy came after him and started beating on him. Tell Faith she's fine," the officer said. "Thanks," Jamie replied. They hung up and Jamie kissed Faith. "Still in a cell. Not getting out for all the money in the world," Jamie replied. "Jamie," Faith replied. "There's no more worrying allowed," Jamie replied. "Meaning what," Faith asked. Jamie devoured her lips. "You want to kick my butt for turning off the phones? Do it. Faith, he's not getting out. I promise you. We're having this baby and nobody is doing anything. Nobody is getting near you and nobody is hurting us or our baby. I promise you," Jamie replied. "So convinced," Faith teased. Jamie kissed her again. "Come with me," Jamie replied.

He walked her upstairs to the storage room where he'd always had all of his guitars or music or even things he'd always planned to put somewhere in the house. He opened the door and Faith saw a crib with bed sheets that looked like sheet music. There was a mobile with music notes and pictures of Faith and Jamie together. There was a white and lilac teddy bear. A stuffed guitar that Faith knew Jamie had a hand in. "And where did you find all of this," Faith asked. "6 sets of bed sheets and blankets, pink blue and lilac blankets and the glider is coming next week. That's what I had always wanted this room to be Faith. Now it's gonna be whether he likes it or not. The security system was upgraded. We have the beginning stuff," Jamie said. "What happens if…." Jamie kissed her. "No more worries alright? We're gonna be okay baby," Jamie said.

They got cleaned up, had breakfast then headed back to the other house. "And what part of the planning am I doing," Faith asked. Jamie kissed her. "Pick the color and we get the clothes and everything else. I just wanted the basics to be here. Nothing is getting in the way this time Faith. I even got a setup for the tour bus. It's gonna be alright," Jamie said. Faith kissed him. He nibbled her ear. "Jamie," Faith said. "I want you so bad I can taste it," Jamie said. "And good morning to you too," Faith said. Jamie kissed her again then leaned her against the kitchen counter. "Jamie," Faith said. As he was about to go for her belt, the phone rang. First his cell then the house phone then Faith's cell phone.

"Yes," Faith said as Jamie started kissing down her stomach. "It's officer Cartwright. We're sending officers to guard you and Jamie. Evan got out," the officer said. "What," Faith replied. "He took off from the infirmary. I know he's headed there. I don't know how he's gonna be able to do it, but that's where he's heading. Where's Jamie's next tour date," the officer asked. "Dallas I think. How would he even know the tour schedule," Faith asked. "Just be very very careful," the officer replied. He hung up and Faith walked away from Jamie. "Baby." "He's out. He got out of the infirmary. Go figure Jamie. The one place that isn't guarded as much and he gets out," Faith said. "Baby." "We're leaving. I don't care where we go, but we aren't staying here Jamie." "You're safer here than anywhere else in the damn planet. Faith, stop worrying," Jamie said. "I can't stop worrying Faith. I'm not going to be able to," Faith said. Jamie kissed her. "We're flying there. No more tour bus. Faith, he's not hurting either of us." Jamie pulled her into his arms.

Chapter 16

The next few weeks, Faith was shaky. She was scared at every turn. She was watching her back, carrying the handgun that Jamie had bought for her. She was beyond grateful that the doctor was coming to them. Just the thought that Evan would find her and where the doctor was scared the crap out of her. Two doctor visits later, the doctor suggested that Faith might need some non-stressful time. It truly was much better timing. Thanksgiving was almost there. "Family thanksgiving," Jamie suggested as they curled up in the state room. Faith kissed him. "Somewhere nobody would expect us to be. He won't know," Faith said. Jamie kissed her. "Then we get to start telling people." Faith kissed him and nodded. His shoulder had finally healed. He curled up with Faith knowing that no matter where they went, Evan was gonna find them. Jamie booked a cabin in Gatlinburg, booked flights for the family and sent the travel arrangements. By the time he finished doing that, Faith was asleep on the bed beside him. He leaned over and kissed her then went to talk to his buddies.

"I mean, if he hasn't found you yet maybe he's just gonna leave it alone," Alan said. "Right. The man shot me to get her away from me. He's gonna keep coming. I got authorization for you from every venue. We're doing thanksgiving at that cabin. I need someone making sure things are safe. Is there anything that cabin needs security wise," Jamie asked. "We got most of the security stuff organized already. We got the electric fencing and the security system all in. Everything's good. We just have to make sure that the coast is clear before you get there," Alan said. "Okay. So, your mom is coming Alan. Deacon, your folks are coming and Callon, your folks are coming. If you need something let me know. Don't say anything to her. She can't do the stress right now," Jamie said. "What's up with her anyway," Alan asked. "You'll find out soon enough. Just don't ask anything alright," Jamie asked. Alan nodded.

Jamie headed back to the stateroom and Faith looked over at him. "What," Jamie asked. "I heard you talking to them. Jamie, I can't keep watching over my shoulder. We need to do something now," Faith said. Jamie kissed her. "Second to putting you in a bubble, you're alright. Faith, we're gonna be safe. The guys can handle it. Trust that," Jamie said. Faith kissed him. "I trust you Jamie. I promise you I do. I just need to know that everything is gonna be okay. I'm gonna be watching over our shoulders forever Jamie. We both know that." Jamie kissed her. "Nobody is hurting either of you or me. No more worrying," Jamie said. "What if he…" Jamie kissed her. "He's not touching either of you." She curled up with Jamie.

They finally got to Gatlinburg for thanksgiving and everything was perfect. Everything was decorated, the cabin smelled like turkey and pumpkin pie. Faith walked in and got the table set and ready and the guys turned on football and made sure the cabin was safe. Everyone came for thanksgiving and before they had dinner, Faith handed out a little bag to each person. Everyone opened them little by little. "What's with the bib? I can't possibly be that messy," her mom joked. Faith smirked. "No," her dad said. Faith nodded. "You're pregnant," Jamie's mom asked. "We're due in March," Faith said. Everyone was up hugging each other and celebrating. After grace was said, they all sat down and had one of the most memorable thanksgivings ever.

The guys finished watching football after dinner and Jamie had a grin ear to ear. Faith walked over to him and he kissed her. "I so totally called that," Alan joked. "Yeah you did. We just had to make sure that we wouldn't miscarry. I know it's stupid, but I didn't want him knowing," Faith said. Jamie kissed her again. "Bath," Faith said. Jamie got a smirk ear to ear. "Finish watching football," Faith said. The guys got the cabin secure while Faith was relaxing. They went back to their cabins with their folks and Jamie double checked to make sure everything was air tight. He got up and turned the football of and walked in and slid into the tub with Faith.

"I thought you were watching football," Faith asked. "I would rather be in here with you," Jamie said. He nibbled her ear and had his hands entwining hers. "I gather everything is safe," Faith asked. "We were watching…" "I know they added extra security," Faith said. "After knowing that he's... "Jamie." "I did it for you to make sure you felt better. Wherever we are, we're safe," Jamie said. Faith nodded. She leaned into his arms. "I love you," Jamie said. "I love you too. I know that things are gonna be better Jamie. I just hope that the police have him back in custody," Faith said. Jamie kissed down her neck. "Did the guys head out," Faith asked. Jamie nibbled her ear. "We're all alone," he said. Faith slid out of Jamie's arms, got up and wrapped herself in the towel. "Where are you going," Jamie asked. Faith kissed him then went and grabbed a slice of warmed pumpkin pie for each of them. Jamie walked into the bedroom and Faith handed the pie to him. "How did you know," Jamie asked. Faith kissed him. "I always loved it." He kissed her. "I love you," he said. Faith curled up in his arms. They had their pie and watched an old movie then headed to sleep.

Faith woke up in the middle of the night with another nightmare about Evan. "He's not coming baby. I promise you," Jamie said. "Did the officer call you back," Faith asked. "I'll call him in the morning. I promise," Jamie replied. He snuggled up to her and wrapped his arms around her. "Everything's gonna be fine. We're gonna have our baby and he's gonna be a bad memory," he said. "What..." Jamie kissed her. "No more worrying." Faith kissed him. "Baby, nothing is ruining this. Nothing."

Faith managed to fall asleep but woke up at 7am. Something told her that something was wrong. Really really wrong. She got up, grabbed the 9mm from Jamie's lock box and went and sat in the TV room. "I figured you'd be here. And look at that. I get her all to myself," someone said. He came up behind her. "Why can't you leave me alone," Faith asked. Evan sat down beside her. "Because you're mine. I got you first Faith. You're not leaving me," Evan said. "Already did. Leave," Faith said. "I want what's mine," Evan said. "You can't have me back Evan. What's done is done." When he leaned towards her to kiss her, Faith put the gun to his chest. "You wouldn't," Evan said. "Did you want to try it? Evan, leave. Go wherever the hell else you want to go. Stay away from me and stay away from Jamie. You don't, you're gonna be in a body bag. Got me," Faith said. "You wouldn't," Evan said. "Don't tempt it Evan. Now," Faith said. She watched him leave. Faith got up and locked up the door he'd got through and double checked the other doors and put the gun back in Jamie's lock box. Faith slid back into bed. She finally slept. Jamie looked over and kissed her neck. She snuggled into him. Jamie couldn't sleep. He watched her finally sleep.

Faith got up the next morning and Jamie was half asleep on the chair by the bed. "What are you doing," Faith asked. "He was here last night wasn't he," Jamie asked. "I handled it," Faith said. "Did he find out you were pregnant?" Faith shook her head. "Well," Jamie said. "I told him to stay away. I grabbed the gun from the lock box," Faith said. Jamie walked over to her and kissed her. "Next time wake me up," Jamie said. Faith kissed him. "We're leaving. He knows we're here," Jamie said. Faith kissed him again. "Shower," he said walking her into the massive bathroom. He washed her hair and they started getting changed. The baby started kicking up a storm. They had breakfast, said goodbye to the family and headed back to the house.

They pulled in and Alan and the guys were already there. "What," Faith asked. "Promise that you'll wake me up next time," Jamie said. Faith nodded. They head into the ranch house and they curled up together in the TV room. Jamie invited the guys in to watch some football. They all headed in except for Alan. Faith kissed Jamie and got up to go talk to him.

"What's wrong," Faith asked. Alan looked over at her. "You shouldn't be out here," Alan said. "What's bugging you," Faith asked. "Is it nuts that I almost feel responsible for you," Alan asked. Faith shook her head. "We're friends Alan. You held my damn hand through stuff that most people couldn't." "When he got into the cabin, I was supposed to be there. My girl kept getting mad that I wasn't giving you two privacy," Alan replied. "Alan, you don't have to put us first. You know that right," Faith said. "You two are family Faith. That baby needs to be safe as much as you two do. I can't just leave." "If you need a break, just say it," Faith said. Alan got up. "What," Faith asked. He walked out the back and walked around the yard. Faith curled up on the porch swing. When she saw Alan walking towards her, Faith got up. She walked down to him and she walked with him. "What," Faith asked. "I know why he's in love with you Faith. I can see it," Alan said. "Meaning what," Faith asked. Alan kissed her. Faith broke away from him. "I…I can't do this," Faith said. She went back into the house and went upstairs. Faith logged into her emails to distract herself. Not 5 minutes later, she heard footsteps coming up the stairs.

"Babe," Jamie said. "Yep," Faith replied. "What's wrong," Jamie asked closing the door. "Nothing," Faith said. "Faith," Jamie said. "I just felt like chilling out up here. You guys relax and watch…." Jamie kissed her. His lips wouldn't let him let go. "I can tell them to go if you want," Jamie said. "You hang with the guys. You deserve some dedicated guy time," Faith said. "What's wrong," Jamie asked. "Nothing. I promise you. I just wasn't in the mood for football," Faith said. "Babies still kicking up a storm," Jamie asked. Faith nodded. "I still can't believe we finally told everyone," Jamie said. Faith kissed him. "Go watch the game with the guys," Faith said. He kissed her again, devouring her lips. "I love you," he said. "I love you too," Faith said.

Jamie headed downstairs and Faith called Emma. "What's up with you," Emma asked. "Now that I can finally tell you the secret you mean," Faith teased. "Well," Emma asked. "We're due in April," Faith replied. "Why didn't you tell me," Emma asked. "We already miscarried once. I just wanted to be sure," Faith replied. "And when are we having your baby shower," Emma asked. "We're gonna be back out on tour in a few weeks Emma. I don't know," Faith said. "I'll plan it then." Faith laughed. It felt right. This time was gonna be better for them both. "So what's up with you and Greg," Faith asked. "It's not. Believe it or not, I've been talking to Alan. We're just friends, but there's something about him Faith." Now she understood what Alan had said. "He has a girlfriend Emm." "I know. I'm just saying. He's a really nice guy Faith," Emma said. She could tell how happy Alan was making Emma. A minute or two later, Alan texted Faith:

Broke it off with my girl tonight. That's why I was walking outside. I'm sorry.

Faith smirked. Emma was chatting her ear off about Alan and Faith couldn't help but smirk. "So what would you think if I moved down there for good," Emma asked. "In town babysitter," Faith joked. "Funny," Emma replied. "Would be kinda good for baby to have a godmother in town," Faith replied. "Really?" "Who else would it be Emma? If it weren't for you pushing us together, I'd be dating Deacon," Faith teased. "You were meant to be with Jamie and you know it," Emma replied. "You think Alan and I could work," Emma asked. "I have a feeling that the godparent thing might glue you two together," Faith said. They talked a while longer and Emma started packing. Faith hung up and checked through emails. Faith replied back to Alan:

Call Emma. She's a good person Alan. You don't deserve one cent less.

Faith checked through the last few emails and came across one from an unknown email address. She opened it and almost dropped the laptop:

I'll get you back. Don't think I won't. A bullet won't stop me. Might as well give in Faith. You know you belong with me – Evan

She slapped the laptop shut. She almost started getting shivers. Faith walked downstairs. She would've killed for a drink. Anything to make her stop shaking. She walked outside walking right past Jamie and the guys. Seeing her like that told him something was really wrong. He wasn't brushing her off again. Jamie walked outside and saw her sitting on the porch swing.

"Spill," Jamie said," sitting down behind her and wrapping his arms around her. "I thought you were watching football," Faith asked. "Talk or I go upstairs and look at what freaked you out." "He emailed me. I don't know how, but he did," Faith said. "Evan," Jamie asked. Faith nodded. "Babe, there's no reason to be scared. He can say whatever he wants but he's not hurting us," Jamie said. "I just wanted to take it all back. I wanted to feel like it didn't happen. Why can't I have that," Faith asked. "Because it did happen. Babe, that's why I wasn't letting you get hurt again. Nobody is putting hands on you but me," Jamie replied. "What if he tries to hurt the baby or take the baby," Faith asked. Jamie kissed her. "Woman, you worry too much. He's not touching either of you," Jamie replied. "Jamie, please. Don't say what's gonna calm me down. I'm being serious. He's this determined to get to me, he's gonna do something," Faith said. "Baby. Look in my eyes. Nobody is hurting you. Nobody is touching that little baby. Nobody. I don't care if I have to Velcro the kid to my leg. He's not hurting either of you," Jamie said. Faith snuggled into him. "He's not. Even if we have to have a bodyguard 24 hours a day. I'm taking care of you two. Stop worrying," Jamie said. He kissed down her neck. "Jamie," Faith said. "Smell so good I could…" He laughed. "That's how I got pregnant. Quit," Faith teased. "Can't get you more pregnant," Jamie joked. Faith turned and looked at him. He kissed her. "Now come inside. You're watching ball. No more stupid emails tonight," Jamie said. They walked in and his hands were on her stomach and he was kissing her neck. They sat down together on the sofa and Alan went outside.

Once the game finished up, the guys headed off to get some shut-eye, leaving Jamie and Faith alone. "What," Faith asked. He nibbled up her neck to her earlobe. "Jamie," Faith said. He nibbled back down and kissed her neck. "What are you up to," Faith asked. "Seducing my wife," he whispered. "Since the guys are right out that door, we should probably…" Jamie kissed her and pinned her to the sofa. "Jamie," Faith said. "Shh," he teased. He kissed her again, devouring her lips until she started feeling light headed. Jamie curled up on the sofa burying both of them in the oversized blanket. "What are you doing," Faith asked. "Hunting," he teased. They didn't come back up for air for an hour. Her silky legs were wrapped around him and he made love to her on the sofa.

After, Faith was curled up in Jamie's arms when his cell started buzzing. "I'm not answering that," Jamie said. He leaned in and kissed Faith again. "Could be something important," Faith said. He kissed her, devouring her lips and making her forget phones ever existed. An hour later, Jamie's phone started ringing again. Faith grabbed it and answered. There was a hang-up the minute Faith said hello. Faith looked at the caller list. "Jamie, who's Kathleen," Faith asked. Jamie put the phone back on the table. "Definitely not important." He kissed Faith. "Jamie," Faith said. He kissed her again. "Doesn't matter," Jamie said. "Yeah it does." "Faith, not now." Faith went to get up and Jamie pulled her back into his arms. "Where you going," Jamie asked. "You gonna tell me who she is," Faith asked. "A friend from high school," Jamie said. "And she has your cell number why," Faith asked. Jamie kissed her. "It doesn't matter. You do," Jamie replied. "Then say it," Faith said. "I saw her at a show. She got a meet and greet and came back to say hi. That's it. Nothing else," Jamie said. He leaned in and kissed Faith and pulled her into a kiss that could've melted metal.

A half hour later, he followed her upstairs and put his phone on silent. They slid into bed together and he kissed her neck. "What are you so worried about? I'm not leaving you. Never," Jamie said. "I don't get why she just hung up. She saw the ring on your hand. That's just…" Jamie kissed her. "Woman, quit fussing and get in this bed," Jamie said. Faith washed off her makeup and Jamie texted Kathleen that he was having some alone time with Faith. When Kathleen messaged him back with a picture of a positive pregnancy test, he called her. Jamie got up and slid out of the bedroom making it seem like he was locking up.

"What in the hell are you trying to do," Jamie asked as Kathleen answered the phone. "You aren't gonna answer then I have no choice Jamie," Kathleen said. "We didn't…" "Jamie, you know damn well we did." "Don't you dare start that crap. You tried it in high school and now you're doing it again. We didn't have sex. I wouldn't have. Besides that, the guys would've killed me 5 times over before I ever did that. Stop with the bullshit," Jamie said. "I want you back," she said. "And I'm married. Get the hell over it. Lose my number," Jamie said hanging up. He turned around and Faith had heard the entire phone call. "Babe." Faith shook her head and walked upstairs. "Faith," Jamie said. He walked into the bedroom and Faith was curled up on her side of the bed with the light off. Jamie got washed up and curled up in bed with Faith. "What," Faith asked when Jamie curled up with her. "We don't go to bed mad. Remember," Jamie said. "You call some chick from high school before bed and you expect me not to be mad," Faith said. "Look at me," Jamie said. Faith turned over and looked at him. "Only woman I'm ever gonna want or need is you. That's why I told her to screw off. Faith, it's nothing. I promise you," Jamie said. Faith nodded. "Babe," he said. Faith nodded again. Jamie kissed her. "It was nothing. Nothing happened. The woman has been trying to get me into bed since high school. When I met you, I didn't look at anyone else and haven't. I love you," Jamie said. Faith nodded. "Baby," Jamie said. "Okay," Faith said. He kissed her. "I mean it," he said. "I know," Faith replied. Getting her to say I love you back wasn't an option. Not tonight. He fell asleep with his arms around her and wasn't letting go for anything.

Jamie woke up the next morning to Faith's phone buzzing. He grabbed it before it woke her up and saw 15 emails from Evan. He read through them. One after another, his blood pressure just went up and up with every email. He went downstairs and Alan woke up. "What's wrong," Alan asked. "This little shit is getting a butt whooping the size of this planet. Find his ass and kick it," Jamie said. "Dude, you look like you're gonna blow any second. Sit," Alan said. "I can't. That little punk is torturing her Alan. The emails are just the tip of it. He keeps doing that I'm gonna lose them both," Jamie said. "I'll get tech on it. You know he can fix anything. Just chill," Alan said sending the emails off to his friend. They were gone from Faith's cell and Alan had a filter in her email in minutes. Anything that came from Evan was going straight to his cell instead. Faith wasn't gonna have to see it at all. Alan handed the phone back to Jamie and he slid it in his pocket. "I know what you're thinking. The Jack isn't in there," Alan said. "I could kick his ass," Jamie said. "Dude, you have the one and only thing he wants. Be grateful you have her. Jamie, she loves you. She left him and you are who she belonged with. You knew it. That's why we were keeping an eye out all the time. Jamie, go be with your wife," Alan said. They gave each other a guy hug and Jamie headed back upstairs. He slid Faith's cell into the drawer and curled back up with her. "What's wrong," Faith asked. Jamie kissed her. "Absolutely nothing. Just was talking to Alan. Go back to sleep sexy wife," he said. He curled up with her and even though the Alan stuff was pissing him off, he knew that he had what he needed right there in his arms.

Faith woke up a few hours later and Jamie was nuzzling her neck. "And good morning to you too," Faith said. "I have the sexiest wife in the entire planet," Jamie said. Faith smirked. "Full of compliments in the morning aren't you," Faith teased. He kissed her. "Marry me," Jamie teased. "Already did," Faith replied. "Every year," he said. Faith kissed him. "Bad dream," Faith asked. Jamie leaned onto his back and Faith curled up with him. "I'm just glad we're where we're supposed to be. Life sucked without you," Jamie said. "You always had me there," Faith replied. "Not until you were in my arms. Faith, I know that he did some stupid shit to you. He never deserved you. I love you. I have since that first day. Life wasn't right without you," Jamie said. Faith kissed him. "So what are we up to tonight," Faith asked. "Opry. You coming with me," Jamie asked. "Can't let you go in there alone," Faith said. "I'm glad you said that," Jamie said as he kissed her. His lips devoured hers and time stopped. "This means I get to show off baby too," Jamie said. "Had to didn't you," Faith asked. He kissed her. "Jamie," Faith said. "What," he asked. He leaned in for another kiss that felt like it lasted for hours. Finally, they both got up and showered. Jamie teased Faith, trying to distract her. "I swear, you are gonna get a butt kick in a minute," Faith said. He kissed her again. "Jamie," Faith said. "We're going shoppin. You need a dress for tonight," Jamie said. Faith shook her head. He nodded. "Jamie, seriously," Faith said. "Best place in the world to do it," Jamie said. He kissed her again, finished getting dressed and headed downstairs. Faith came down behind him carrying her Stetson boots. "Oh no you aren't," Jamie teased. "Don't think I won't," Faith joked. He kissed her and they made breakfast. Alan couldn't help the smirk.

They all had something to eat, the guys hung out and Jamie was determined to find Faith a dress. "I don't have to do this," Faith said. Jamie kissed her. "We're doing it," he replied. They hit a few stores he loved, a few she loved and then Jamie found the dress. "I swear, you are intentionally doing this," Faith teased. Jamie kissed her. They went to head out and a few people were wandering around waiting. Jamie signed a few autographs then they headed out. Jamie took her to lunch then they headed to the Opry for sound check. Faith got a few pictures done. She posted them up and Jamie hopped off the stage. "What," Faith asked. He kissed her. "I love you too," Faith said. He kissed her and hopped back on to finish sound check.

Faith went backstage and made sure Jamie's stuff was all together. "You sure you're alright with a man running your life," Patsy said. "Meaning," Faith asked. "He even has your mail messages. Don't tell me you're alright with him having all the control." "Patsy, I need to let him handle it. I can't just take him on alone. He's my best friend," Faith said. "You know you're having a girl. You gonna let her be like you," Patsy asked. "I'm gonna let her or him be whoever they want to be. As long as they're good people that's all that matters," Faith said. "That man isn't gonna leave you be. Faith, if you need to keep watching your back you aren't gonna be able to relax. I know he loves you, but you can't just let him handle this. You need to do this. Show that little baby that mama is strong. I did it for my girls Faith. They became the most amazing girls ever," Patsy said. "What am I supposed to do," Faith asked. "I'll give you the push. It's your choice Faith," Patsy said. Faith headed back into the sitting area and saw Jamie.

"What you doing all the way back here," Faith asked. "They're doing tours. I don't want anyone interrupting us," Jamie teased. "Doing what," Faith asked. He kissed her. "We're going to dinner and we're staying at the hotel tonight," Jamie said. Faith smirked. "Oh really," Faith said. Jamie kissed her. "Come with me," Jamie said. Faith nodded. They ducked out the back before anyone saw them and they headed over to the hotel. They walked into the room that Jamie had booked and saw sterling and white roses. "Jamie," Faith said. "I had to. Babe, you deserve all of this. I know the stress you went through. He didn't leave you alone. He still won't. I just want you to have down time. I have ball and being on stage with the guys. You don't have the way of doing that other than hanging with Emma," Jamie said. Faith kissed him and wrapped her arms around him. "She's coming in tomorrow. Guess she has a little thing for Alan," Faith said. Jamie laughed. "What," Faith asked. He kissed Faith. "Maybe that's why he's all cheered up," Jamie joked. He flipped on the CD player and their wedding song came on. The song he'd written her all that time ago. They danced and snuggled and kissed until dinner came. "Jamie," Faith said. "Alone. Nobody jumping in the middle, nobody interfering. Just you and me." They had dinner and curled up together a while before hair and makeup came for Faith. "I could have handled it myself," Faith teased. Jamie kissed her and went to get changed.

Faith got her hair and makeup done, slid the dress on and came out. "My wife is one sexy woman," Jamie said. Faith kissed him. "I'm not walking out on the stage like this," Faith said. Jamie smirked. "What," Faith asked. He kissed her again. "Damn right you are. Sexy ass woman and she's all mine," he joked. He slid his jacket over her shoulders and they headed back over to the Opry. "My phone," Faith said. Jamie shook his head. "Not tonight," he replied. They got backstage and Jamie kissed her. "Nervous," Faith asked. "I can't do the circle. You know how many people stood there before me? It's probably haunted," Jamie said. Faith kissed him. "I'll stand there with you," Faith asked. He kissed her and smacked her butt. He walked to the side stage and watched part of the show with her. "I love you," he whispered in her ear. "I love you too," Faith replied. When it was his time to go on, Faith kissed him, rubbed the lipstick off and walked him to the side. He kept an eye on her and played his heart out. At the tail end of his last song, he did what she worried he would. "I want y'all to meet this fine woman I got. Figured where better than the Opry to share our huge news…." Jamie looked at her. Faith nodded. "We're having a baby," Jamie said. Everyone cheered and he kissed Faith on stage. He finished one more song then walked straight over to her and kissed her side stage away from everyone. "Had to didn't you," Faith asked. He kissed her. "That one is live on the radio," Jamie said.

Faith shook her head and he walked her backstage. They hung out with Jason and the other performers that night and Jamie walked her into the dressing room and locked the door. "What," Faith asked. He kissed her, spun her around and leaned her against the wall. He kissed her again and kissed down her neck. "You are so damn sexy," Jamie said. "You sure you weren't drinking," Faith teased. "Nobody is getting either one of you away from me. Nobody. I love you. I'm not letting anyone ever hurt you," Jamie said. "What are you up to?" "Shouting it from the rooftops," Jamie teased. He kissed Faith again then headed out to talk to Jason while Faith freshened up her lipstick.

"You sure she isn't gonna kick your butt for that," Jason asked. "Dude, I've been holding it in for months. I get why she didn't want to say anything," Jamie replied. "Just remember if you don't treat her right, you're replaceable. Dude, if I ever lost my kids it would kill me. I had no choice with anything else. She's a good woman Jamie," Jason said. They went off and chatted about duets and ideas for new music and Faith relaxed. "You love him that much? To let him just blurt that out," Patsy said. Faith nodded. "Don't give up on him Faith. You love him that much it will hurt you just as much," Patsy said. "I know," Faith replied. "I'll try to push him into the right if he falls out. Just tell me," Patsy replied. Faith nodded. She went back into the seats and saw Jamie and Jason chatting away. She grabbed water for her and Jamie and a refill for Jason and handed it to them. "How the hell he lucked out I will never know. Spread some luck my way," Jason said. "You got it," Faith replied. "And if this one screws up, you can come stay with me and the kids," Jason joked. Faith smirked.

The crowd started piling in for the late show. Jamie was talking to Jason until he had to head on stage. When Jamie headed on, Jason sat with her. "So I had a question for you. What would you think about me and Jamie touring? Good move," Jason asked. "I can tell you two would be having a blast," Faith joked. "I mean it. You wouldn't get mad right," Jason asked. "If that's what management decides, I'm not complaining. I've been a fan for a while," Faith said. "Girl, what could possibly be wrong with you? You're a good woman Faith. How'd he luck out," Jason asked. "Long story," Faith replied. "We got time," he teased. "I'll tell you if the tour turns out," Faith replied. "I'm grabbing a drink. You comin," Jason asked. "When he's done. No prob," Faith said. Jamie looked over and winked at her. Faith shook her head. He nodded. She went and talked to Jason a while by the seating in the back.

Chapter 17

"I still don't get how you two met," Jason said. "We met almost 2 years ago. He sorta helped me out with a bad situation. We've been kinda close ever since," Faith said. "I meant what I said Faith. He messes up, I get first dibs," Jason teased. "I'll make a note," Faith teased. "Come with me a sec," Jason asked. "Why," Faith asked. They went into the back, away from everyone, and Jason kissed her. "I meant it," Jason said. "We're…" "I know. Just call me if you need me," Jason said scribbling down his number and handing it to her. He kissed her again and headed back in to grab his guitar and he headed on stage. Faith went over to security and told them to let Jamie know she was going to the hotel.

Faith got to the room and cleaned up. She slid on her pajamas and curled up on the bed and uploaded the new photos to his website. She sent a few over to Jason's management and they uploaded theirs. Faith went and poured herself a drink and flipped on a movie. Jamie didn't make it back for an hour or two. He walked in around 1:30 and saw Faith out cold on the bed. He got changed for bed and washed up. He slid onto the bed and wrapped his arms around Faith. He turned the light and the TV off and looked at her. She was gorgeous when she was sleeping. Even more beautiful when his baby was growing.

Faith woke up the next morning from a kick that felt like something was being ripped. "Ow," Faith said. Jamie was wide awake in seconds. "Babe," Jamie said. "This kid is gonna kick a hole in me," Faith replied. "What can I do," Jamie asked. "Nothing. Baby alarm clock," Faith joked. "You need sleep," Jamie said yawning. "Sleep. I'm going to try to calm this one down," Faith said. She kissed Jamie and he tried pulling her back to bed. "Sleep," Faith replied. She got up and curled up on the sofa and went through emails. Emails went out of her inbox which threw her. She looked through her filters and noticed that one had been added. When she realized what it was about, she went through her others and left it alone. Faith went through the forums about Jamie's Opry show and found nothing but good posts. She flipped on the TV and saw Jason doing an interview. "Well we did find an act for our tour. I can't really tell everyone who it is yet," Jason had said. "Well we are getting the exclusive. Once Jason releases the name, I know all the tickets are gonna be sold out." Faith smirked and decided to start playing up the teasing about Jamie. Faith teased that a major surprise was coming. She teased that Jamie had a new tour coming. Teased that Jamie had a tour mate that people were gonna love.

When Jamie finally woke up, he walked over and saw Faith curled up on the sofa with her laptop. "You okay," Jamie asked. Faith nodded. "Think you just gained a quarter of a million fans in a matter of hours," Faith said. Jamie kissed her. "Bed was lonely," Jamie said. "You were better off sleeping there. I was tossing and turning and I couldn't sleep," Faith said. Jamie kissed her. He looked over and breakfast was waiting for him. He kissed her and sat down and had breakfast. Faith finished up the online stuff and handed the laptop to Jamie. She went and slid into the shower. Faith went to wash her hair and she felt Jamie washing her hair for her. "What are you up to," Faith asked. "Treating my woman right. "I know what you did last night," Jamie said. "Meaning," Faith asked. "You talked him into letting me do the show," Jamie said. Faith smirked. He washed her hair and they got ready to go. "What," Faith asked. "I love you," Jamie said. "I love you too," Faith said.

They headed home and the guys were all together at the house. "What's with the artillery," Jamie asked. Alan pulled him aside and Faith went in. Faith saw the baby blankets like ash on the floor. She went to back out of the house and backed into Jamie's arms. "Why," Faith asked. "We're going. The guys moved things back to the other house," Jamie said. "Why would someone do this," Faith asked. Jamie kissed her. He walked her back to the truck and they all headed back to the other house.

They walked into the house and the guys had made sure everything was secure. Nobody knew about that house and nobody ever would. Faith curled up in the bedroom. Jamie could see that she was scared. She tried telling him she was fine and when Jamie saw her, he didn't know what to do. He found out where Emma was. "I'm on my way," Emma said.

Emma got to the house with baby gifts and it's the only thing that could get Emma out of the funk she was in. The minute anyone told Emma what had happened, she was irate. Mad was an understatement. "Why the hell won't he just leave Faith alone? The man is a dirt bag," Emma said. "Don't hold back," Jamie teased. "Why can't he just leave her alone already," Emma asked. "Because he's being an idiot. He's never backing off," Jamie said. "He is backing off. I don't give a crap what he wants. He's leaving her alone," Emma said. "Meaning what?" "Meaning he is backing off or I'm kicking his butt to mars," Emma said. "I love it when you're around," Jamie joked. He hugged her. "So you're doing the tour with Jason aren't you," Emma asked. "Signing the papers end of the week," Jamie said. "I knew it," Emma said. "By the time the tour starts, baby will be here," Jamie said. "That's gonna mean a big difference," Emma said. "We're not gonna be apart Emma. I promised you when I married her that she'd never get hurt. I promised you that I'd never let her get hurt. She's never going to Emma. I won't let her get hurt." Jamie hugged her. "I'll go check on her and make sure she's okay," Emma said.

Emma went upstairs and Faith was leaned up against the bed curled up. "Faith," Emma said. Faith shook her head. "What," Emma asked. "He's never leaving me alone. Evan is gonna hunt me down like this forever Emma," Faith said. "Faith," Emma said. "He's going to. I'm having a baby. He'll hunt the baby down too. I don't know why he can't just walk away," Faith said. "Let Jamie deal with him then," Emma said. "He shot Jamie. He almost died Emma. He won't stop," Faith said. "Then let the police…" "They did nothing. I'm gonna be in fear the rest of our lives," Faith said. Emma wrapped her arms around Faith. "You're having a panic attack Faith. You have to know that Jamie would rather be killed then let you get hurt. Faith, believe in him. Believe that he won't hurt you," Emma said. "You don't understand Emma. He'd rather kill Jamie and leave me miserable then let me be happy somewhere else," Faith said. "You can't keep doing this. Faith, you can't stress that baby out," Emma said trying another tactic. "If I had just left and never…" "Faith, stop already. Stop," Emma said. Jamie came in and saw Faith in tears. "Baby," Jamie said. "He's never leaving me alone. Jamie, he'd rather kill you and make me miserable then let me be happy without him," Faith said. Jamie picked her up and put her on the bed and curled up with her. Emma went downstairs and called Faith's doctor.

"Let her get it out of her system. She knows that she has to in order for her to keep that baby," the doctor said. "Can we give her anything," Emma asked. "No. She just needs to calm herself. Even if it means leaving for a while," the doctor suggested. Emma hung up and went back upstairs. Faith was asleep in Jamie's arms. "She ok," Emma whispered. Jamie shook his head. Emma went downstairs and made some camomile tea for Faith.

Emma came back upstairs and Faith and Jamie were talking. "He isn't gonna hurt you. Faith, stop worrying," Jamie said. "I'm gonna worry when this baby comes. Jamie, I need to make sure that we're not bringing this baby into hell. I've lived it, but it's not fair for the baby to," Faith said. "Remember what got you out of it Faith? Me. The guys want him to leave you alone as much as I do. We're gonna figure out something baby. I promise you," Jamie said. "What happens when he keeps..." Jamie kissed her. "He's not. Nobody is touching you." Emma put the tea by the bed. "Thank you," Faith said. "We'll figure it all out together Faith. I promise you," Emma said. "I just don't understand why he keeps doing this," Faith said. "To try to win his power back," Emma replied. "I sat there and he just went crazy. I tried to end this crap and he practically..." "Stop thinking about it," Jamie said. "I just don't understand it," Faith said. "He's insane. That's all that can be said Faith. He's not getting better. At some point he'll get himself killed. I love you Faith. Let him go. That's why Alan put that filter on it. I didn't want the emails getting you upset," Jamie said. Faith curled up with him and Emma headed downstairs. She walked over to Alan and Callon. "What's up," Alan asked. "I need you two do help me with something," Emma said.

Emma put dinner together for everyone and they had some dinner together. "Where did Alan and Callon go," Jamie asked. "They'll be back tomorrow," Kevin said. Jamie nodded. They finished up dinner and Jamie went and called Alan. Everything went straight to voicemail for both of them. They relaxed and watched funny movies to relax Faith.

She needed a distraction badly. Jamie got a call around midnight and Emma walked Faith upstairs. "Emma, what was I thinking," Faith asked. "At least you left. You survived it Faith. You ended up where you should've been all along. That's all that matters. He's not gonna keep hurting you Faith. He'll move on to someone else," Emma said. "What happens if he doesn't," Faith asked. "Then Karma will be his punishment," Emma said. Faith curled up and fell asleep. Emma came downstairs. "Did you know where they went," Jamie asked. "I'm ending him coming after her," Emma said. "Emma, you don't know what you just asked. They went there to go after him," Jamie said. "I want him to leave her alone Jamie. The man is asking for a shot to the head. I just want him hurt enough that she can carry this baby. It will kill her if he's what screws this up. She won't make it through Jamie," Emma said. Jamie hugged her.

Faith got up the next morning and saw Jamie asleep in the chair. She got up and walked over to Jamie. She kissed him. Jamie woke up and devoured Faith's lips. He leaned her onto the bed and made love to her without a word being said. After, he got up and went into the bathroom and washed up. Faith walked downstairs. She had breakfast alone then when Jamie came downstairs, she went upstairs. Jamie came back upstairs an hour or two later. Faith was dressed, makeup done and hair done. She slid her boots on and walked back downstairs. "Faith," Jamie said. Faith walked past him, grabbed her purse and cell and walked out the door. She got into the truck and left. Faith went down and got her ultrasound done with the doctor, got printouts of the baby and went out to the mall for a bit. She got a few dresses, some pants and a few tops and headed down to the Ryman. She sat down in the 4th row and tried to think.

"You could've just asked for help," Patsy said. "He's mad. He doesn't get to be pissed over something like that. He was coming after me." "Baby, he loves you but he isn't thinking right. He can't get the control back," Patsy replied. "So now he's gonna practically take it out on me? Did he think I'm the one that created this," Faith asked. "If you want me to help just say so." " How would you help?" "Remind him what he could lose if he doesn't keep acting like an idiot." "Patsy, I can't just walk away from him. He'd go insane," Faith said. "You don't have to leave. Just get him in a situation that he's glad to be alive." Faith shook her head. "Remind him how lucky he is to have you," Patsy asked. "I'll figure out something," Faith replied. "You can talk to me when you need me. I'm not leaving you Faith. I'm here." "I know. Thank you," Faith said.

Faith got up and went down to the office and saw police cars. When she saw Jamie's truck, she turned around and went home. Faith pulled in and saw Evan and Deacon heading into the house. Faith parked and headed inside. "What's up," Faith asked. "Well, we got some good news for you," Alan said. "What," Faith asked. "He's in the hospital. The real hospital. He's not gonna be typing for a while anyway," Conner said. "What did you do," Faith asked. "Handled it," Conner said. "Meaning what," Faith asked. Alan wouldn't look her in the eye. Faith went to go back to the truck and Alan caught up to her. "Faith," he said. "What did you do?" "He's not gonna hurt you Faith. He's staying away from you," Alan said. "Answer me," Faith replied. "Just come back inside," Alan asked. Faith got in the truck and left. She went down to her favorite restaurant and had dinner alone. She was sick of not being in control. She was sick of everyone doing it for her.

Faith finished dinner and went for a walk by the water. She grabbed some ice cream, walked and tried making sense of things for a while. Around midnight, she looked at her phone and saw Jamie had called 50 times. Emma had even started calling. Faith went and checked herself into the Hilton. They even checked her into the same room she'd first stayed in when she had come there with Jamie. Faith curled up on the bed and watched a movie. She went to sleep and tried to really sleep. Nobody was there with her, and she didn't want anyone to be.

Jamie was pacing. "What happened this morning," Emma asked. "Nothing," Jamie said. "Right. She walked out because she was mad for no reason at all right," Emma asked. "I told her we took care of Evan," Alan said. "And," Jamie asked. "She left. She walked back to the truck, got in and left." "And that's the last time any of you saw her," Jamie asked. He was starting to assume the worst. He tried the GPS on Faith's cell and she'd turned it off. He sat down on the step and was trying to figure out where she would have gone. "Jamie," Emma said. "I have to find her," Jamie said. "She's probably doing this intentionally. Let her have her moment. She needs to calm down. She's not in the hospital or anything Jamie. She's fine. Stop thinking that something happened to them," Emma said. He finally went to sleep.

Faith woke up around 9 the next morning. She got changed, did her hair and touched up her makeup and checked out. She headed off and grabbed breakfast then headed back to the house. Jamie was asleep on the sofa. The minute she pulled in, he was awake. He practically ran outside when she pulled in. "Faith," Jamie said. She walked past him and went inside. "Woman, you don't get to disappear and scare the shit out of me," Jamie said. "And there's a ton of shit you don't get to do either," Faith replied. She went upstairs and hung her things up. "So you're not gonna talk to me now," Jamie asked. "You think that hurting him is ending this? You do understand that if you do this it's only gonna make things worse. Jamie, just leave me the…" He kissed her. "Come here," he said. "No," Faith replied. She walked away from him and went downstairs. "Faith," Jamie said. "Leave me alone," Faith said. "I was scared. Faith, I thought…" "Jamie, enough. You don't get to just go after him. It's gonna make him ten times worse. What part of that didn't you understand?" "This isn't about him," Jamie said. "You almost tackle me the minute my eyes open and walk away. Jamie, stop alright. Just stop," Faith said. She went to sit outside and he grabbed her hand. "What," Faith asked. "I was worried alright? I was worried that night that I ended up sleeping in the chair. I was scared that something was going on that I wasn't gonna be able to save you from. I kept thinking that he was gonna come after you and I wasn't gonna be able to do anything. That he was gonna steal our baby." "So you practically tackle me? Jamie, enough. Enough of the stupid excuses," Faith said. He tried to kiss her and Faith pushed him away. "Enough," Faith said. "Faith, don't do this," Jamie said. "Don't do what Jamie? Let his insanity come between us? It already did," Faith replied. She went and started packing up a bag. "You aren't leaving Faith. No," Jamie begged. "I am. I'm ending this crap Jamie. It's over," Faith said. She packed a bag and every time she put something in, he put it away. "Jamie," Faith said. He kissed her. "I get you're mad. Please just let me be with you. I wasn't the one that asked them…" "I was," Emma said.

"What do you mean," Faith asked. "I was sick of him coming after you. Faith, you were losing it. Your blood pressure finally went down. You were out of your mind scared. I wasn't about to let him keep doing that. Faith, you deserved to be free. You went through hell and he kept trying to drag you back. He can't keep doing that and get away with it. I had to do something," Emma said. "And you think that hurting him and putting him in the hospital was gonna fix this," Faith asked. "I thought it would give you time. You need to make sure that the baby is alright," Emma said. "The baby is fine," Faith said handing Jamie the ultrasound picture. Faith walked downstairs and got a bottle of water. "Faith, this wasn't me," Jamie said. "Like that makes a damn difference. You…" He kissed her. "Stop. I fucked up. I shouldn't have…" "Not the first damn time Jamie. Enough," Faith said. "Faith, I was trying to help," Emma said. "I appreciate it, but I can handle him. I'm ending this now. He can't do anything. He's lost it. I'm going and I'm ending this one on one," Faith said. "Oh no you aren't. We're back on tour tomorrow," Jamie said. "I'm going," Faith replied. "No you…" Faith walked upstairs, packed clothes for a day or two and came downstairs. "Faith, no," Jamie said. "I'll meet you. Jamie, I'm doing this. Alone," Faith replied. He tried to grab her bag. "Jamie," Faith said. "No." "I'll go with.." "No Emma. I'm handling this alone. Enough," Faith said. She walked out, got in the truck and headed to the airport. Jamie pulled in behind her with Emma. "Faith," Jamie said. She walked into the airport and got on the plane.

"What the hell is she trying to prove," Jamie asked. "She's trying to fix this. She thinks that going to him is going to stop it all. That it's gonna stop it all. Jamie, she's scared about what's gonna happen." "Emma, she's gonna get hurt. She knows that. He almost raped her last time." "He's in a hospital Jamie. She goes and gets security to tie him to the bed. It's that simple. She needs to do this," Emma said. "Then you get her the hell out of there," Jamie said getting more and more pissed off. "I'll go get her alright? I caused…" "No you didn't Emma. I get that you were trying to help. You're gonna be in danger too if you go," Jamie said. "So you're letting her do this alone," Emma asked. "For now. She doesn't make it back in 24 hours, we're sending Alan there to get her out," Jamie said as they headed back to the house. They got packed up for the tour and Emma packed for Faith. They got on the tour bus and Alan stayed behind. Alan got on a plane just after they left and headed to Roanoke.

"You can talk to him, but don't touch him. His arms are held down for his own protection," the doctor said. Faith nodded and a security officer stayed just inside the door and recorded the conversation. "I knew you missed me," Evan said. "Nope. Not even a little. Wanted to kick your backside to another planet," Faith replied. "Kiss me," Evan said. "Not even if you were the last sleeze on the planet." "Faith, I wanted you back. I love you. Why can't you just come home," Evan said. "I left Evan. That's where I'm staying whether you like it or you don't. Either leave me alone or this is gonna be the least of your worries Evan. You wanna stay here permanently," Faith asked. "Kiss me," Evan said. "The part where I say rot in hell means what," Faith said. "I know you miss me," Evan said. "Evan, I came to say goodbye. That means I'm not coming back. I'm never ever coming back for you. Leave me alone. Leave us alone," Faith said. "I want my wife back," he said. "Evan, I'm not your wife. I never have been," Faith said. "You married me in that field Faith. You said yes," Evan said. "I said we could get engaged. Not married Evan. I never ever would have married you. Right after you said it I tried to leave. Don't you even remember that? You pointed a gun at me," Faith said. "I didn't want you to leave Faith. I wanted us to have that baby," Evan said. "What baby," Faith asked. "That one," he said looking at her bump. "It's mine and Jamie's. I even have DNA tests to prove it Evan. Leave me alone," Faith said. "No. Faith, we had sex at the house," Evan said. "You need some serious medication Evan. I'm not coming anywhere near you and you aren't touching me ever again," Faith said. "I want our baby Faith. It's mine," Evan said. "Goodbye Evan." Faith went to walk out and saw Alan. "What are you doing here," Faith asked. "Getting you home," Alan replied.

Jamie tried distracting himself. He worked on a song like Cuffs but couldn't get it right. He finally found a line that worked and went from there. Emma called Alan and it went straight to voicemail. She sent Faith an email and got a reply. "Jamie," Emma said. He ran to the stateroom and saw Faith's email:

I told you I could deal with it. Tell Jamie to stop worrying. He could've just let me handle this. I didn't need Alan here. He thinks the baby is his. I can't get him to stop but he knows what the truth is. He's just not willing to accept it. He never will. I need a DNA test written up so he sees straight out that the baby isn't his. Tell Jamie to concentrate on a new song.

Jamie replied back:

Faith, get your sexy butt back here. Please baby. Letting him that close is just gonna make things worse. He's gonna keep screwing with you like he did before. Please. You know I can't concentrate unless I know you're safe. I love you. I'm sorry about yesterday. Please. Faith come home.

Emma watched and Faith didn't reply. "I'll keep trying Alan's cell. I can only assume they're on a plane. I hope they are," Emma said. "You see anything come get me," Jamie asked. Emma nodded. Jamie hugged her. He walked back into the sitting area and tried to keep working on the song. Emma emailed Alan. She got a reply a few minutes later:

When she gives him the DNA test, we are leaving. Hopefully that will shut his crazy ass up. I'm sorry you got in shit Emm. Thank you. I didn't want to get you in trouble. I'm the only one that was gonna be able to do anything. I hate what that jackass did. I'll be back soon enough. Please don't be mad.

Emma replied back and talked to Alan for a little bit. An hour or two later, Faith replied to Emma:

I know he's still freaked out. Got a friend to get me the DNA test result form. It's gonna have to suffice. He snapped, but the doctors dosed him. He's going into a maximum security psych ward out of Virginia. They're taking him there by armored truck. He's not getting out and Alan verified the people taking him. I think it's over.

Emma emailed Alan to confirm and went and told Jamie they were on the plane. It was a white lie but one that needed to be said to protect Faith. Jamie nodded and tried to concentrate on work. When they got to the venue, Jamie went straight in and tried to get through sound check. He was checking his cell every 10 minutes. "Jamie, you can't keep checking. It's interrupting sound check," Greg said. "She's dealing with Evan. I'm checking. You don't like it, leave," Jamie said. Greg let it go and they got back to sound check.

Faith and Alan didn't show until almost midnight. When they got to the hotel, Jamie ran over to the door. "Baby. Oh my god. Thank god you're alright," Jamie said. Faith pushed him away. "Faith," Jamie said. "You couldn't trust me to handle it could you," Faith asked. "I needed to know you had backup. That's all," Jamie said. "I was perfectly fine. I handled it. Gave him a dose of reality. He couldn't sit with it so they permanently locked him up. I told you," Faith said. He kissed her. Faith pushed him away again. "Faith, please. You don't understand," Jamie said. She got her bag and went to leave. "No," Jamie said. "I'm not sleeping in here when…" He kissed her, picked Faith up and leaned her onto the bed. He peeled her clothes off. "Jamie, stop." "Baby, I love you. Please," Jamie said. Faith got up. "Don't do this Faith. Please," Jamie said. "You don't trust me to handle this. Jamie, I had a life before you. Do you even remember that," Faith asked. "Don't. Faith, I can't lose you. Not because of him," Jamie said. "Then start trusting me," Faith said. She got her things and went to leave. "Please," Jamie asked again. "I'm going home," Faith replied. "No." "Jamie, until you learn how to trust me…" "I just wanted to make sure that he didn't hurt you like before. That's all. I swear to you," Jamie said. "I…" Jamie kissed her and slid her bag from her hands. "Come to bed. Please," Jamie said. Faith shook her head. He kissed her again. He walked her backwards towards the bed. Clothes hit the floor on the way there. By the time they made it to bed, they were in a kiss that made them both sweat from head to toe. They had sex in bed and he didn't leave her side the rest of the night. He didn't let go.

Faith got up the next morning and saw him asleep. She slid out of bed and checked her text messages. Only one came in:

He had a break last night. Under extreme meds. He won't be hurting you. Any means necessary.

Faith went and had a hot shower and got dressed. She sat down on the sofa and went through the site and checked her email. Nothing major was there for once. Not even the emails that were normally forwarded. She replied back to the text:

Contact if he takes off. Keep him away from phones and computers. Nothing.

Faith put her things together and got organized. "Tell me you aren't leaving," Jamie said. "Only here one night. We have to head out," Faith said. "Faith." "We," she replied. Faith put her things by the door. Jamie had a hot shower and got changed. They headed downstairs and headed out on the bus. Faith sat in the stateroom alone. Jamie went to try and talk to her but she wouldn't say a word. He kept working on the song and Emma tried to talk to Alan away from everyone.

"What happened," Emma asked. "She went in and tore into him. The man is truly nuts Emm. He tried to make a move on her and she basically pushed him away. He tried saying the baby was his. Faith ended it. When she gave him the DNA test, Evan snapped. He didn't get a second to say a word. Trust me. She did the right thing Emm. Jamie's gonna kick my ass for saying it, but she did something to him. She twisted his brain. She made a difference. It might have worked," Alan said. Jamie walked past them and went into the stateroom.

"What," Faith asked. "You talking to me yet," Jamie asked. "Can't just leave..." He kissed her. "Jamie," Faith said. "Woman, quit picking a fight. Kiss me," Jamie said. He devoured her lips. "You don't even trust me. What's the point," Faith asked. "I do trust you. Faith, I wanted to kick that punk's backside. He's dangerous. That's all I was scared about," Jamie said. "And I told you I would handle it. Jamie, you have to let me do this. For my own sanity," Faith said. "Can't just let it..." Faith got up and walked off. "Faith," Jamie said. Faith grabbed a sparkling water and sat down. She went through more emails and Jamie grabbed her laptop. He grabbed her hand and walked her back to the stateroom. "Jamie,"

Faith said. "Stop picking a fight. Stop starting a problem when there isn't one. Faith, I love you. I need you alright. You went there and I snapped because I was scared you weren't gonna come back. Alan volunteered. I didn't send him," Jamie said. "You didn't trust me to handle it," Faith said. "I was scared. I'm allowed to be scared Faith," Jamie said. She went to turn away and he pulled her back into his arms. He kissed her. The scruff he'd grown over 3 days rubbed against her skin. His lips tasted like peach and the kiss he gave her made her feel like she was on fire. He leaned her onto the bed. "Stop picking a fight, stop getting mad and stop…" He kissed her. "Shut it," Jamie said. He kissed her again and devoured her lips. "I love you. I always have and I always will. Quit picking a fight," Jamie said. They hung out and were making out like teenagers the rest of the trip.

When they stopped at the next tour stop, they all hopped out and the guys went in to sound check. Faith organized the interview space and got the meet and greet room set up. When the sound check was done, Jamie walked into the dressing room and wrapped his arms around Faith and kissed her neck. "Interview in 20," Faith said. He kissed her. "Better get ready then babe," Jamie said. "I'm not the one doing…" He kissed her and handed her a suit bag. "What's…" He kissed her and they went and started getting changed. Faith slid into the black leather pants and the sweater. She did her hair and makeup and they headed into the interview together.

They asked a million and one questions then asked about Jamie's news. "What news," Jamie teased. "We heard you divulged some pretty big news at the Opry last week," the interviewer said. "Oh. You mean the news about Faith and I having our first baby. That news. She's due in April or end of March. We lucked out," Jamie said. "And it just works along with the release of the new CD. Just in time," the interviewer said. "I fell for her two years ago to the day. The doctor said near March 20th. That would just be funny if…" Faith kissed him. "Never know what could happen," Faith said. "What happens if you're on tour," the interviewer asked. "We're putting the tour on hold for a month or so around that time. I wanna be there," Jamie said. They answered more questions and as soon as they finished, they got some pictures of Faith and Jamie together. After, they headed off to grab dinner and curled up in the tour bus.

Jamie rubbed her feet after dinner and tried to have some alone time. "What are you doing," Faith asked. "Making sure you're okay," Jamie said. "I'm fine," Faith said. "Your feet were swollen. This will help," Jamie said. They hung out a while together, Jamie got changed for the show and kissed Faith. She walked him down to the meet and greet and he kissed her. He did the meet and greet and as soon as it was done, he walked down the hall and into the dressing room. "What," Faith asked. He kissed her and leaned her against the door. "You have a show," Faith said. "Party pooper," Jamie said. He kissed her again then grabbed her hand and walked her to the stage. "You realize you're white-knuckling my hand," Faith teased. He kissed her when they got to the waiting spot. "What," Faith asked wiping the lipstick off his lips. "No more fighting," Jamie said. Faith nodded and kissed him. "I mean it. No more fighting about him. He doesn't deserve the attention," Jamie said. Faith nodded. He kissed her again and they headed on stage.

Chapter 18

As soon as Jamie finished for the night, they got on the tour bus and left. Jamie wasn't taking any chances. They got on the highway and headed to the next stop on the tour. Jamie fell asleep in Faith's arms listening to the baby. When Alan came in to check on them, he had a grin ear to ear. "What you grinning about," Emma asked him when he walked back over to her. "They're okay," Alan said. "This hasn't been their first rodeo Alan. They've been like this longer than you know. You should see the fight they were in when Faith walked away from him and went to Evan anyway. Trust me. This isn't the first and it's never gonna be the last. They fight. They walk out but they never walk away Alan. They never have." He kissed Emma. "Promise me that we never will," Alan said. "Never will what," Emma asked. "Fall apart," Alan said. "What are you scared about? We didn't do anything wrong. Alan, I couldn't stop what happened. Either could you. We slept together," Emma said. "I…" Emma kissed him. They curled up in Alan's bunk and were making out until the tour bus stopped.

When they stopped, it was almost 6am. They got checked into the hotel for the night and everyone tried to get a little sleep before sound check. Faith got up at 10 when the baby started kicking up a storm. She got breakfast and got a little work done before she had to attempt to wake Jamie up. The minute she leaned onto the bed, he pulled her to him and kissed her. He didn't let her up for air. He made love to her and kissed her from head to toe. "Jamie." Faith said when he finally came up for air. "I don't want to," Jamie said. "We have to," Faith said. "Then you're coming on with me. I'm not letting you out of my arms," Jamie said. He kissed her again before she could say anything. "Shower," Faith said. He got up and followed her into the shower. They showered and Jamie finally let go. "What's wrong," Faith asked. He kissed her. "Jamie," Faith said. "I'm not letting him hurt you," Jamie said. "He's not. He's not getting near me. The doctors said so. He's drugged up Jamie. He's in another state. Somewhere he can't hurt either of us. I just proved it when I was there. It's alright." He kissed her and shaved. Faith did her hair and Jamie handed her brown leather pants and black tee to her. "Jamie," Faith said. "I'm not going on unless you're coming," he replied. Faith kissed him. They finished getting dressed, Faith put on some makeup and they headed over to the venue.

Jamie didn't let go of Faith's hand for a second. He didn't want to. "What's wrong," Faith asked. "I could've lost you. I'm not losing you again," Jamie said. "Stop. I'm here. I'm right here." He started sound check and Faith sat front row so he would know where she was. Whatever had been in that nightmare he'd had, had freaked Jamie out completely. When he finished sound check, Faith walked him into the dressing room. "Jamie," Faith said. "I had a nightmare that he tried to kill you. That he attacked you," Jamie said. "The doctor was there, security was at the door and Alan was just outside the door. He was in cuffs Jamie. Cuffed to the bed. He couldn't even move his hands. It's alright," Faith said. "Promise me," Jamie asked. Faith nodded. "That's why I said not to be worried," Faith said. He kissed her again, devouring her lips. "Jamie," Faith said. He hugged her and held her. She could feel him shaking. "What was the nightmare about," Faith asked. "It wasn't a nightmare," he said. "You're shaking. It was," Faith said. "He had you and killed you. He wouldn't let us be together," Jamie said. Faith kissed him. "I'm right here," Faith replied. "Promise me you won't go there alone," Jamie asked. Faith nodded. He sat down with her and Faith tried to calm him down. Jamie went back to sleep in Faith's arms. She sent a text to Emma and asked her to grab her some dinner. To be super quiet when she came into the dressing room.

A little while later, Emma came in and handed Faith dinner for her and Jamie and two bottles of water. "He okay," Emma whispered. Faith nodded. Faith headed out and told everyone to give Jamie space. That he was asleep. Nobody bothered him until 15 minutes before the meet and greet. Faith woke him up. "You have to go show off on stage," Faith teased. The minute he woke up, he kissed her. "I love you," Jamie said. "I love you too. Babe, you have to go on stage," Faith said. "No sneaking off," Jamie teased. Faith shook her head. I'll be right beside you," Faith said. He kissed her and got changed to head into the meet and greet and kissed her. Faith walked him down and sat outside while he finished up.

Once that was done, he handed two gifts to Faith that were from fans. She walked him down to where he was to head on. He kissed her again and she rubbed the lipstick off. "I love you," Jamie said. "I love you too," Faith replied. "If you aren't…" "I'll be sleeping in the dressing room." He nodded.

Faith finished her dinner and sat down by the stage so Jamie felt better. Faith tried her best to comfort him, but nothing was going to help. She bought Christmas gifts on her iPad, found a few things for the baby and got them. She came up with the perfect gift for Jamie and ordered it, ensuring that it was shipped to Emma's new place. She emailed Emma with the info. Emma smirked and nodded. Faith got a Christmas tree organized. Decorations and everything she needed was going to be there by the time they got home. She let Alan and the guys know what was going on. Jamie didn't know anything.

The minute Jamie walked off the stage, he grabbed Faith's hand and walked her to the SUV and they left. "What," Faith asked. Jamie shook his head. "What," Faith asked. "I can't Faith," Jamie said. "Talk," Faith replied. "She was sitting front row." "Jamie," Faith said. He went to kiss her and Faith backed away.

They got to the hotel and Faith went up in a separate elevator. "Faith," Jamie said as he saw her going into the room. Faith packed her things and went to walk out. Jamie grabbed her bag. "You aren't going," Jamie said. She ripped it out of his hand and walked out. Faith got on a plane and went back to the house. She changed the locks. Jamie called her cell 10 times. Faith didn't answer. She thought about packing everything and leaving and the baby started to kick. Alan called her. Faith wasn't willing to answer anyone. The only person Faith could imagine Jamie talking about was Kathleen. If it was and he had cheated, Faith wasn't gonna make it. This baby wasn't going to.

"Find her," Jamie said. "Security alarm says she's at the ranch. The locks got changed and the code was changed. I can't access anything," Callon said. Jamie went and sat in the stateroom and held onto Faith's pillow. It still smelled like her perfume. He tried to sleep. Nothing helped. He grabbed his guitar and kept working on the song. He was stumped. He needed Faith. He needed her to be there with him. He called the house, called her cell phone. He called everyone he could think of. "Jamie, let her get calmed down," Emma said. "She changed the locks in my damn house," Jamie said. "You can't just leave the tour. Tell me what you want me to do," Emma said. "Nothing will fix this but me," Jamie said. "Well, right now you can't. You need to concentrate on the tour. Say it," Emma said. "Can we get someone to make sure Kathleen isn't really pregnant," Jamie asked. "If she is," Emma asked. "Then I have to talk to Faith. I'm the only one that can fix it," Jamie said. "Alright. I'll go. Promise me you won't take off and try to get her back here," Emma said. Jamie nodded. They dropped Emma at the airport and got her a flight straight back to Tennessee.

Emma landed and headed to Jamie's ranch. He pulled in and saw Faith sitting on the porch swing. "You alright," Emma asked. "He cheated. I went through hell and he cheated. He wasn't scared that Evan was gonna kill me. He was scared I was gonna find out about Kathleen," Faith said. "Faith." "Emma, don't try telling me I'm wrong. I'm right and you know that. How am I supposed to believe in him Emma? He cheated," Faith said. He's losing it Faith. He's trying to prove she's lying," Emma said. "And I'm supposed to believe him? I'm supposed to pretend that nothing has changed," Faith said. "You're supposed to listen to the truth. I am getting it right now," Emma said handing Faith her cell phone. "I got the results. It's a little early to be 100% sure, but it looks like maybe," her friend said. Faith handed the phone back to Emma. "Well," Emma asked. "It's possible. She's doing the amnio to send to Jamie this week. I can get into it after that," her friend said. "When," Emma asked. "Tomorrow at 8am." "As fast as you can," Emma said. She hung up with her friend and went and tried to comfort Faith.

"First he's in love with me and the next he's…" Emma quieted Faith. That promise Jamie had made rang through Emma's head. She made Faith something to eat and sat with her until she was asleep. Emma went back downstairs and called Alan. "She alright," Alan asked. "If that test comes back that it's Jamie's, he's losing her altogether. Make sure it's done by a lab that you can verify. I don't want the tests tainted. Other than wanting to rip his heart out, she's fine," Emma said. "I'll do all of it. Emma," Alan said. "What," Emma replied. "I need to talk to you when we're back. It's not bad. I promise," Alan said. "Sounds good," Emma replied. They talked for a few minutes and hung up for the night. Emma curled up on the sofa and made sure everything was secure and locked up.

Faith tossed and turned most of the night. Her phone rang again around 2am. Faith, half asleep, answered it. "Baby, please," Jamie said. "It's a little late to be begging," Faith said. "Baby," he said again. "I'm sleeping Jamie," Faith replied. "I swear it isn't mine," he said. I'll believe that when I see it for myself," Faith replied. "Faith, please. I need you," Jamie begged. "And I needed what you promised me when we got married," Faith replied. She hung up and turned her phone on silent. A lot of good it did. Faith still couldn't sleep and Jamie didn't let up all night.

Faith went downstairs and Emma was curled up on the sofa. Faith got herself a drink and saw headlights pulling into the ranch. She looked and it was a sports car. "Emma," Faith said. "Sleeping," Emma said. "Call the cops. There's a sports car in the driveway. Jamie would never drive that," Faith said. "Upstairs," Emma said. Faith went upstairs and Emma grabbed her gun from her bag. Whoever it was wasn't alone. Two trucks pulled in behind him. "Where is she," she heard. "Jamie, she's not gonna talk to you," she heard Alan say. "This is still my damn house," Jamie said. He saw Emma. "Please," Jamie asked. "No. You did enough. Go home," Emma said. "Emma," Jamie said. "Go Jamie. I'm not letting you in here. You upset her enough," Emma said. "Open the damn door," Jamie said. She put her gun into the case and unlocked the door. "You upset her I will put a hole in your ass," Emma said. Jamie came inside and walked straight upstairs. "What happened to me handling this," Emma asked. "Rabid dog syndrome," Alan said kissing her.

Jamie went upstairs and Faith had locked the bedroom door. "Faith," Jamie said. "Either you leave or I'm calling the police," Faith said. "You need to come with me," Jamie said. "Leave..." "Faith," Jamie said. "Ow." Jamie found the bedroom key in the top of the closet and came in and saw Faith on the floor. "Faith," Jamie said. "Leave me alone," Faith replied curled up by the bed. "Let me help…." "You wanna help? Leave." "I'm not going," Jamie replied. "Fine. I will," Faith replied. She went to get up and ended up back on the floor. Jamie went to help her and she pushed him away. "Faith, let me help you," Jamie said. "No. You did enough Jamie," Faith replied. She got herself back onto the bed and had some of her ice water. "Faith," Jamie said. "I meant it Jamie. Out," Faith replied. "I know it isn't," Jamie said. "English isn't working. What language do you want? Get out," Faith said. He closed the door and locked it and came back to her side. "I'm not moving. Faith, just admit you need me," Jamie said. "You're the one causing this Jamie. Leave me alone." He got a cold towel and put it on her head. "Jamie. I mean it," Faith said. "And I'm not listening to it. We're doing this together Faith. We find out together. We promised," Jamie said. Faith went to get up and almost fell. Jamie caught her and put her back onto the bed.

"I get you're trying to pick a fight, but you're not supposed to be under stress Faith. Quit picking a damn fight and spiking your blood pressure." "You could have got a woman pregnant and you're fighting with me about blood pressure? Jamie, get out," Faith said. He kissed her. "No." He kicked his boots off and curled up on the bed with her. No matter how hard she tried fighting him, it didn't work. "Just leave me alone Jamie. You cheated. You told me you wouldn't hurt me and you cheated," Faith said. "She's saying I did. Faith, I wouldn't have. I couldn't have done that. You know that," he said. "That's why you're so scared about me being alone," Faith said. He went to try and kiss her and Faith got up. She went downstairs. Jamie came behind her. "Faith." "Get out Jamie. Now," Faith said pushing him out the door and locking it. Faith went to walk back upstairs and almost collapsed. Alan carried her upstairs and put her back on the bed. "I don't want him here," Faith said. "Fine. Let me call the doctor then," Alan asked. Faith shook her head. "If he cheated…." "Faith, stop. Stop thinking about what some stupid deranged fan tried to do. It's not true. He wouldn't and I damn well he won't and I won't ever let him," Alan said. "You were with me Alan. He…." "He wouldn't. Trust me Faith. I have never steered you wrong," Alan said. Faith nodded. "I'm calling the doctor, even if you think you're fine," Alan said. Faith nodded and Emma put a cool towel on her neck and her forehead.

The doctor showed a little while later. She checked Faith over. "Blood pressure spiked. Faith, I told you no stress. Promise me you'll calm the stress down," the doctor said. "I tried. A fan started telling him she was pregnant with his…" "Faith, breathe," the doctor said. "Why would someone do that," Faith asked. "To get Jamie in trouble. Faith, she's not the only fan to accuse a country star that he cheated. Don't let it bother you this much," the doctor suggested. Faith nodded. "If this happens again you're going to the hospital on bed rest. Please," the doctor said. Faith nodded. "I'll talk to him. Just try to close your eyes and sleep," the doctor said. She closed Faith's door and went downstairs. "Is she okay," Jamie asked. "She needs to lower the stress Jamie. I mean it. If she doesn't she's gonna lose this baby. If she doesn't, she'll be on bed rest in the hospital all the way through Christmas." "Thank you," Jamie said. "I meant it Jamie," the doctor said. He nodded and walked her out. "I understand what's happening. It's happened a million times in this town. Just remember that the bigger it gets, the bigger the chance Faith has of not being able to be here. I'm not letting her lose the baby Jamie." He opened the gate and the doctor headed home.

Alan went upstairs. "You okay," he asked. Faith nodded. "I heard what the doctor told him. If it means me staying in this house with you until…" "Alan, I need to make sure that the lab that is doing those results isn't being paid off to make the result the way she wants. I need to…." "Already handled. Got another lab tech on our payroll there double checking the results and re-doing the tests. You'll know Tuesday," Alan said. Faith nodded and tried to get comfortable. "Sleep," Alan said. Faith nodded. He hugged her. "If it's the last thing I do, you're gonna have this baby safe and sound. I promise you." Faith closed her eyes and was out cold in a matter of minutes.

Alan headed downstairs and saw Jamie in tears. "She can't be. She can't. I know that I didn't…" Emma sat there on the other sofa curled up in a ball. "Did you sleep with her Jamie," Emma asked. "Emma, I was drinking. It was a really bad…" Emma got up and went upstairs. She curled up on the bed beside Faith. "Tell me that you didn't actually sleep with her," Alan said. "That's when we were having that fight and I was drinking and…." "Jamie, look at me. If it turns out that it is you better damn well fix it before she finds out. If she finds out you did you're gonna lose her altogether. You know that right," Alan said. "I know....at least I think....no. If I did I wouldn't have done anything without..." "She's gonna kill you. You realize that right," Alan said. "I promise you..." "Just don't Jamie. Don't," Alan said. He went and grabbed himself a drink. "Alan," Jamie said. Alan shook his head. Jamie walked off. "Where are you going," Alan asked. Jamie walked upstairs and sat down on the chair by the bed. He camped out there the rest of the night.

Emma looked over in the morning and saw Jamie. He'd moved the chair so he was sleeping beside Faith. Their fingers were still entwined. She smirked. She had to give it to him. Jamie wasn't letting anything ever come between them. She said a prayer hoping that the fake pregnancy issue was just that. For Faith's sanity, this woman had to be lying. She got up and snuck out of the bedroom. She came downstairs and Alan kissed her and pulled her into his arms. "Didn't know you were up," Emma said as he wrapped her legs around his waist. He kissed her again and walked her into the other spare bedroom on the main floor. He locked the door and curled up on the bed with Emma. Not another word was said. Her clothes slid into a pile on the floor along with his blue jeans. He kissed every inch of Emma and made love to her. He had been craving her all night. An hour later, they finally came up for air. "I'm not losing you ever," Alan said. "What has got into you this morning," Emma asked. "Realized what I would lose if I ever lost you," he replied. He kissed her. "We can't keep doing this," Emma said. "We can do this whenever we want. I'm not losing you," Alan said. "Meaning what," Emma asked. He kissed her again. "Means I'm not letting you go," Alan replied. Emma didn't need to ask another question. There was nothing else for him to say.

Faith woke up when the baby started kicking. Almost instantly, Jamie woke up and was almost kneeling beside the bed. "What are you..." Jamie kissed Faith. "What are you doing in here," Faith asked. "I'm not losing you and we aren't losing our baby," Jamie said. The baby started really kicking and his hand slid onto Faith's stomach and he sat down beside her. "Jamie," Faith said. "I'm not losing you. That's all there is to it Faith. I know I didn't. I know it wasn't me." She went to get up and

Jamie helped her. "Jamie," Faith said. He kissed her again, devouring her lips. "I love you," he said as his forehead met hers. Faith started tearing up and went into the bathroom. She washed up a bit then went downstairs. Jamie followed her and didn't let go of her hand. "Jamie," Faith said. "Don't," he said. "Just let me try to handle this," Faith said. He kissed her. "Just don't walk away," Jamie said. "Don't you have a…" He kissed her. "I get you don't want to be there, but for me," Jamie asked. Faith looked at him. "Please," Jamie begged. She went to shake her head and he kissed her. "We'll know Tuesday. Please," Jamie said. "Fine, but if…" He kissed her. He made breakfast, they had something to eat and Faith and Jamie both went and got changed. They packed up some clothes for Faith and Emma and Alan finally came out of that back bedroom. Not 20 minutes later, they were all heading out and going back to the airport to get to sound check.

Faith barely said a word the entire flight. Jamie didn't let go of her hand. They got to the venue and Faith went and sat in the tour bus and went through email. Emma sat with Jamie and Alan watching the guys do sound check. "You going to check on her," Alan asked. Emma kissed him and got up, heading back to the tour bus. Just as Emma walked in, Faith's phone rang. "Hello," Faith said. "Is this Mrs. Gilbert," the voice said. "Yes," Faith replied. "It's Dr. Martin. You asked me to contact you with those results. I'm calling to confirm. She was pregnant, but there's no chance of Jamie being the father," the man said. "Are you sure," Faith asked. "She lost the child yesterday. She claimed that she was asked to handle the situation by your husband," the man said. Faith looked like she was going to snap. "Is there proof that she's correct," Faith asked. "No. Ma'am, she lost the child last evening at the hospital in New York. Mercy hospital," the doctor said. "Did she tell you to call," Faith asked. "She doesn't know I called. I was told by your investigator to contact you directly," the doctor replied. "Thank you," Faith said and hung up. "Can you get Alan," Faith asked. "What's wrong," Emma asked. "Doctor's name that he talked to."

Emma went and got Alan and asked him. "Dr. Martin. Why," Alan asked. Emma kissed him. "Babe," he said. Emma kissed him again and almost jumped into his arms. Jamie started laughing for the first time in days.

Alan carried Emma out towards the door to the tour buses. She had a smile ear to ear. "What," Alan asked. "Go ask Faith what," Emma said. She walked Alan into the tour bus and saw Faith sitting in the stateroom. "What's up," Alan asked. "What was the doctor's name that you dealt with," Faith asked. "Dr. Martin. He's the guy that Jamie and I know from home. Why," Alan asked. Faith shook her head. "What," Alan asked. "She miscarried first off," Faith said. "Faith," Alan said. "She was asked to take care of it," Faith said. "I just told her if she was bullshitting Jamie she was gonna wish she never said anything," Alan said. "It wasn't," Faith said. "Wasn't what…. Jamie's," Alan asked. Faith nodded. "Then what are you sitting in here for," Alan asked. "Did he sleep with her," Faith asked. "Faith, take the win already. It doesn't…" Faith shook her head. "Faith…" She got up and went to grab her bag. "Faith, stop. He said no. The doctor said it wasn't his. He didn't," Alan said. "If you're making an excuse for him…. Alan, why would he be that worried if he hadn't slept with her," Faith asked. "She came after him when he was drunk. He doesn't remember anything happening Faith. Nobody remembers seeing anything going on," Alan said. "Meaning," Faith asked. "Nothing happened. That's what that means. He passed out. She was about to make a move and Andrew walked in on it. It's fine," Alan said. Faith sat down and put her laptop on her lap.

Emma and Alan went and talked to Jamie. "What's going on," Jamie asked. "Well, you got some serious luck. Kathleen lost the baby and the doc confirmed that it wasn't yours. She still thinks you slept with her. Did you," Alan asked. Emma glared at him. "I passed out. Andrew told me he walked in on her trying to do something. She left. Nothing happened," Jamie said. "You damn well better hope you aren't lying to her," Emma said. "I get you two are protecting her. I promise I'm not ruining this," Jamie said. He walked out to the tour bus and Faith wasn't there. "Where," Jamie asked. "She said she was going for a walk. She hasn't left the secure area," security said. Jamie hopped in the golf cart and went and looked around for her.

He saw Faith's golf cart for the grounds. He went and followed what he thought would be her trail. He walked in and saw Faith sitting in the very back of the stadium. "What are you doing way out here sexy wife of mine," Jamie asked. "Thinking," Faith replied. He sat down beside her. "What," Faith asked. He kissed her. He wrapped his arms around her. "If you're lying to me," Faith said. "I love you," Jamie said. "And if...." He kissed her again and pulled her into his arms. "If nothing Faith. You need to believe me. You have to trust me Faith," Jamie said. "You were with her Jamie. Whether you slept together or you didn't, you were with her. You went on a binge because you were mad. That isn't the right way to handle anything and you know that. I love you Jamie, but I can't keep..." He kissed her. "There won't be. I promise you," Jamie said. "You..." He kissed her again. "Not anymore. No more drinking and no more stupid crap. We go out, we go together or I go with the guys. No more girls trying to get between us," Jamie said. "And if..." "Don't," Jamie replied. "Well," Faith asked. "And if something happens again, it's not gonna involve a woman near me. The guys are gonna be there." "Jamie," Faith said. "You and baby trump it." He kissed Faith. "What are you up to," Faith asked. "Making you feel better. That's all that matters Faith. I need to know that you're okay. I need to know that we're alright," Jamie said. "Jamie, you know why I'm scared," Faith said. "It's not happening," Jamie said. "You said that..." He kissed her. "We are gonna be alright Faith. I'm not going through this. Not ever again," he said. He kissed her again and walked her back to the little golf cart. Hers was gone and Jamie's was sitting there. Faith laughed. "Come for a ride with me," Jamie asked. They hopped in and he wrapped his arm around her and they headed back over to the tour bus.

They got there and Emma and Alan were making out on the bunk. Jamie giggled. "I guess you two made up," Alan teased. "Or you're doing it for us," Jamie joked. "And when exactly did this start," Faith asked. "Long story," Alan said. Jamie had his arms proudly wrapped around Faith. "So you two are looking like you made up," Emma said. "Getting there," Jamie said. Emma looked at Faith. She wasn't looking good. "Faith, are you okay," Emma asked. Faith nodded. Emma walked her into the stateroom. "You aren't are you," Emma asked. "I'm fine," Faith said. Emma grabbed her a bottle of water. "Dizzy or nauseous," Emma asked. Faith ran for the bathroom. "That answers my question," Emma said. Faith came out a few minutes later. "Lay down," Emma said. Jamie came in and kissed Faith. "What's wrong," Jamie asked. "Nauseous," Faith said. He grabbed the ginger ale from the fridge and brought it in to Faith. "Babe," Jamie said. "Probably just all the stupid stress. I'll be fine," Faith said. Jamie kissed her. You aren't hot or anything," Jamie said. Faith nodded. He grabbed an ice pack from the freezer compartment. He wrapped it up in a towel and put it behind her neck. "Jamie, you have a meet and greet," Faith said. "Dinner first. I'll grab some soup," Jamie said. Faith shook her head. "You both need food," Jamie said. He went and got it and brought it back to Faith. "At least try to get ready," Faith asked. He kissed her and grabbed his jeans. "Jamie," Faith said. "Promise me you are staying in bed," Jamie asked. "Fine but…" He kissed her and devoured her lips. They had dinner together then Jamie went and showered and got ready. He put on Faith's favorite shirt and the blue jeans that she'd bought him. He pulled his boots on and sprayed on his cologne. "And tell me why you need cologne if you're just on stage," Faith asked. "Meet and greet. Besides. My wife loves this cologne. That's part of why she got pregnant," Jamie joked. He kissed Faith. He kissed her stomach. "Now munchkin, I'm making a deal with you. Stop making mama nauseous and when you come out we'll have a party for you. Lots and lots of presents but you have to stop making mama sick. Deal," Jamie teased kissing Faith's stomach. The baby thumped almost right where he kissed. "I take that as a yes," Jamie said. He kissed Faith and they finished dinner. He got freshened up and kissed Faith again for luck. "You don't need it," Faith said. He kissed her again then headed on. Callon came and stayed with Faith.

Jamie had a grin ear to ear. It was the first time in a while. He went on stage and he was in rare form. The crowd was roaring the entire night. By the end of the show, Jamie even went as far as inviting Deacon on stage to do the final song with him. Deacon was almost in shock. They finished the last song and the minute the lights went down, Jamie was heading straight back to the tour bus to be with Faith. He walked in and Faith was out cold on the bed. He went to kiss her and she woke up. He kissed her. He devoured her lips. "What are you up to," Faith asked. "Seducing my wife. She loves the shirt, the cologne and the guy wearing it," Jamie said. Faith kissed him. She peeled his shirt off, his boots, his jeans, her favorite boxers and Jamie kicked the door shut. He peeled her sweater off and made love to her. "I want you so bad I can taste it,"

Jamie said. They were in a lip lock for over an hour. They finally came up for air an hour later. The bus had started moving. "What," Faith asked as he kissed her neck and her shoulder. "I'm glad you're feeling better," he teased with a grin ear to ear. "You are such a flirt," Faith said. "Just with my hot wife. She is sexy as hell," Jamie joked. They curled up together the rest of the night. When the bus stopped, Jamie was the only one that noticed.

Jamie got dressed and came out to the hallway. He headed up to the front. "What's up," the driver asked. "Where we at," Jamie asked. " Two hours outside of town. Traffic started getting slow so I turned off. Taking a different route," the driver replied. "As long as we're there before 9," Jamie said. The driver nodded. He went back to the stateroom and Faith had just noticed he was up. He handed her the bottle of water he'd grabbed for them. "Where'd you go," Faith asked. "Wanted to see how much further," Jamie said. Faith kissed him. "Good morning to you too," Jamie said. "So," Faith asked. "Long enough for round two," he whispered. "Back to normal," Faith joked. He snuggled up to her and they fell back asleep. Jamie hadn't slept so good in days. Since Kathleen had caused hell. Since all of that nightmare had started. Jamie fell back asleep with Faith and didn't wake back up until Faith had both of their bags packed and was dressed already. "What are you doing," Jamie asked. "Packing our stuff up to head into the hotel," Faith said. Jamie kissed her and pulled her into his lap. "What," Faith asked. "Last show then we go home," Jamie said. Faith nodded. Jamie kissed her and he got up and threw some clothes on. They all headed into the hotel and Jamie peeled Faith's t-shirt off. "What are you doing," Faith asked when they stepped into the room. He kissed her again and walked her into the bathroom. "Jamie," Faith said. He turned on the hot water and peeled her jeans and lace underwear off. He kicked his jeans off and walked her into the shower.

Jamie washed her hair, she washed his. She washed his back for him and he nibbled on her ears. "You have sound check this afternoon," Faith said. "Means all morning to make use of the bed," Jamie teased. "No. Means interviews this morning. You have to be there at 10:30," Faith said. Jamie kissed her. "Party pooper," Jamie joked. They dried off and started getting ready for the day. "You still have shopping to do don't you," Jamie asked. "So do you," Faith replied. He kissed her. "I know exactly what to get for you," Jamie said. "Red bow's not permitted," Faith replied laughing. "Guess I have shopping to do then," he teased. They finished getting dressed and headed off. Jamie had his interview with a few magazines then they proceeded to do a few photos. "I have to have Faith in a few with me," Jamie said. They agreed. Faith came in wearing one of Jamie's favorite dresses and he had a grin ear to ear. "Did any of y'all notice that the room just lit up," he joked. Jamie kissed Faith. He wrapped his arms around her and Faith had her head on his chest. They snapped pictures. Faith and Jamie were both standing by a window. The picture was beautiful. They snapped until they claimed they found the right pictures. The reporters left and Jamie kissed Faith again. "What," Faith asked. "If we have a baby girl, I want her to be as beautiful as you are. We could have more than one," Jamie said. "Take one at a time alright? If this is any inclination of what's gonna happen when the next one comes, I'm gonna need something to keep the blood pressure down. I can't go through all of this all over again," Faith said. "Don't worry. We can make it together Faith. We always could," he replied. He kissed her again and Faith walked him to sound check. After one heck of a kiss, Jamie got down to work.

Faith checked through her emails and Alan came up behind her. "What's up," Faith asked. "First off, that wasn't the Dr. Martin that I talked to Faith. I checked out who that was, and someone had paid him to say he was that doctor. The doctor is trying to contact you," Alan said. "And," Faith asked. "I'll call. He said he wasn't divulging anything to anyone other than you and Jamie." Faith called and went back towards the dressing room for some privacy. Alan didn't leave her side just in case. "Doctor Martin," Faith asked. "Your name," the doctor asked. "Faith Gilbert," Faith said. "I have the results. I put a rush on them as I knew you would both be eager to get the results once and for all. We confirmed that the baby wasn't Jamie's. She's now 4 months. It's not possible for him to have been the father in any way," the doctor said. "Can you email me the results," Faith asked. "I just sent it to your email. If there's anything else I can do, please let me know," the doctor said. "Thank you," Faith replied. "Most welcome," the doctor said. Alan looked at Faith. Tears fell, but they were happy tears for once. "Faith," Alan said. Faith walked out of the dressing room and walked back into the arena. Jamie hopped off the stage. "You okay," he asked. Faith kissed him. When they came up for air, Faith had a smirk. "What," Jamie asked. "I love you," Faith said. He kissed her. "I'm going down to the hotel for a while. That okay," Faith asked. Jamie kissed the tip of her nose and nodded.

Chapter 19

Faith got back to the hotel. For the first time, her blood pressure was normal and she was completely relaxed. She had a hot bath and finished the ordering of the gifts she needed to. She found a few things for herself then got changed and headed back to the stadium. Faith walked in and headed back to the dressing rooms. When she got there, she heard a woman's voice and Jamie's.

"It isn't mine. I know what you're doing Kathleen. You aren't tearing Faith and I apart. Not ever." "Jamie, we slept together. You know we did. You wanna keep denying that? Afraid Faith would leave if she found out? So what? You aren't the baby's father. Doesn't mean you couldn't have been. Just admit it," Kathleen said. "Once Kathleen. Once. You got me drunk as shit and took advantage. Once. In future, remember who you're dealing with. You don't screw me. You don't get in between Faith and I. You start shit ever again and you'll wish you did lose that baby." Alan came around the corner. Faith shook her head and started walking. "Faith," Alan said. Jamie came out into the hall and saw Faith. "Baby. Faith don't. Please," Jamie said. "You lied Jamie. You told me you…" Jamie walked towards her and Faith turned and walked away. "Faith," Jamie said. "You said you wanted nothing to do with her. You said you banned her from coming back here. I walk back in and you two are in the dressing room together. What? Did you sleep with her again," Faith asked. "It's not…" Faith turned and walked away. "Faith," Jamie said. "Leave me alone Jamie. I'm lowering my blood pressure. You keep coming I'll be in the hospital," Faith said. Jamie sent Alan. "Make sure she's okay. Anything happens you tell me," Jamie said. Alan ran off to catch up to Faith.

Faith was walking and went and sat down as far off as she could. "Are you alright," Alan asked. "My husband was talking to the woman he had an affair with. Just fucking great Alan. Thanks for asking," Faith said sarcastically. "I get you're stressed Faith. What do you need me to do," Alan asked. "Kick her sorry butt back to planet stupid," Faith said. Alan hugged her. "Realistically, what do you want me to do," Alan asked. "Keep her the hell away from me. I see her, this baby is coming out," Faith replied. "Okay. Mommy massage it is," Alan said. He made a few calls and booked Faith a massage to try to calm her and keep her blood pressure down. "At the hotel in an hour. Sound alright," Alan asked. Faith nodded. "He's gonna flip out," Faith replied. "As long as you are safe and calm, that's all that matters right now," Alan replied. He walked Faith back towards the car to take her to the hotel. Faith gave him a hug and she went to the hotel for her massage.

"Where is she," Jamie asked when Alan walked back in. "Hotel. I got her a massage so she can calm down. What did she want," Alan asked. "To cause shit. She succeeded. Just tell me you talked to her," Jamie said. "I talked to her. She's gonna take time to calm down. She needs it. Jamie, she's hanging onto that baby like it's her last hope. When you two have that baby, I don't know what is gonna happen," Alan said. "Don't even think it. She's not leaving me. She's not walking out with our baby," Jamie said. "Then quit causing shit and being an idiot. Kathleen? Really? Like when we were teenagers wasn't bad enough? Stay away from her. Keep away from her. Leave Kathleen in your nightmares. I mean it Jamie," Alan said. "Then tell management to keep her off the meet and greets and ban her from the shows." Alan nodded and went and talked to security and called the label. Jamie called the hotel. "Has she shown yet," Jamie asked. "No," the concierge replied. "When she arrives, can you call me and let me know? Send chicken soup, crackers, ginger ale and a DVD copy of the Notebook up to her," Jamie said. "We will sir," the concierge said. Jamie hung up with him. An hour and a half later, Jamie noticed that there wasn't one call from anyone. He called the hotel back. "Yes sir," the concierge said. "Did she come back," Jamie asked. "She hasn't arrived yet unless she came in the back. I'll call the suite and check," the concierge said putting Jamie on hold. He called the room and got no response. "Sir, she's either asleep or she isn't answering the phone." "Go up to the suite. I need to know she's there. It's important," Jamie said. "I'll call you back in five," the concierge replied. Jamie sat in the dressing room. Five minutes later, he got a call, but definitely not the answer he wanted. "She's not there. She isn't in the hotel. Sir, I don't know what to tell you."

Jamie went over to Alan. "What," Alan asked. "She's not at the hotel. Nobody has seen her. Find her Alan. Now," Jamie said. Alan took off with Callon and they went off to find her. First step – finding out who was driving that SUV. It hit Alan that there was a possibility that Evan could have something to do with it. He hoped he was wrong. Callon stayed at the hotel, Alan tried to access the GPS from the SUV. He found it. It was on a highway headed straight towards Virginia. Alan called in a favor and tracked down a helicopter. Alan hopped on and they managed by fluke to find the SUV. They started trailing it. It was only when it pulled over for a fuel up that Alan had a chance. They landed and Alan ran for the man. He tackled him to the ground. "Who the hell are you working for," Alan asked knowing full well what the answer was gonna be. "This is what I was paid to do. The address to where we were supposed to take her is on the GPS. I swear. I don't know what…." Alan hit him so hard the man was out cold in seconds. He ran over to the SUV and saw Faith with cuffs on her hands and a gag in her mouth. He grabbed the gag out of her mouth and carried her to the helicopter. "So much for relaxation," Faith said. Alan got the cuffs off of her and just as they were about to take off, Alan had a gun to his head. Obviously knocking him out didn't work. "Let go of her," the man said. "She's pregnant. She needs her doctor. Going for a drive somewhere that she's not gonna get the proper medical care isn't gonna happen," Alan said. "She's coming with me or you're going back there in a body bag," the man said. "Really," Alan replied. Not 2 minutes later, the man had a gun to his head. He dropped the gun he had pointed at Alan then raised his hand back up and shot. "Alan," Faith said. Within seconds, the man who had shot Alan was dragging Faith back to the SUV. He finished filling his tank and they left. "You can't just leave him," Faith said. "Shut it or I'll shut it for you," the man said.

Alan got to a hospital and they called Jamie. "What do you mean she's…
" Jamie grabbed his stuff and Faith's and was taken to where the GPS said it was going. The helicopter landed at the end of the area and the police met him. "Sir, you can't just block the area off," the sheriff said. When the SUV started heading into the area, the cops blockaded him in. When Jamie saw the SUV, Faith wasn't in it. The SUV stopped and Jamie dragged the man out. "Where is she," Jamie asked. The man wouldn't

answer him. The police took over. "Divulge where she is or you'll be taking your last breath," Jamie said. "Somewhere safe," the man replied. "Where," Jamie said. "Home," the man replied. Jamie walked towards the police car. "What can I do for you sir," the officer said. "I need a truck," Jamie said. The officer handed Jamie the keys to his truck and the officer followed him. The only place Jamie could think of was that trailer. The second option was that shack in the middle of the forest. Jamie went to the trailer first.

He remembered Faith telling him about Evan complaining about having to fill an oil tank to keep the place warm. That he'd had heaters everywhere to keep them warm. Realistically, he probably could've brought the heaters to the cabin, but he had a feeling. He parked the truck away from prying eyes, grabbed his 9mm out of his coat and walked over to the trailer ever so slowly. The officer knocked. He heard movement and someone trying to talk. Jamie went around the other side to cover the back doors. Just as the officer was about to bust his way in the front door, she saw Evan working his way out the back. Craziest part – he was walking right into Jamie's path. Evan hadn't even got out the door when Jamie had his gun to the back of Evan's head.

"Where is she," Jamie asked. "Who," Evan asked. Jamie punched him and had his hand on his throat in seconds. "Where," Jamie asked again. "No idea what you're talking about," Evan said smugly as the blood trickled down from his head. The officer saw Evan and Jamie. "Tell me," Jamie said. "There's nothing to tell," Evan said. Jamie was about to start the ultimate beat down when the officer stopped him. The man grabbed Evan and cuffed him. Jamie went into the trailer. "Faith," Jamie said. He heard rumbling in the bedroom. He walked in and there was another woman there. Jamie pulled up a picture of Faith. "Have you seen her," Jamie asked showing the woman. "Earlier. We stopped at the cabin," the woman said about to tell Jamie and he took off. Jamie got in the truck and took off to that cabin. That hole in the wall that gave Faith nightmares. The one place she was more scared of then being in that trailer.

"Help me," Faith said. Nobody was there. Not a word was said. No sign of anyone or anything. "Admit you need my help," Patsy said. "Just get me out of here. Please help me find a way to get help," Faith said. "Before you go into labor, stop breathing so hard. Nobody is gonna hear you here. Try to get your hands untied. Faith, going out in that weather isn't safe. Someone is coming. I promise you. Concentrate on what you can do. Breathe. Rest and try to get your hands free. Then you can work on your feet. Faith, you need to make a fire. See if you can find food in the house. Find something to keep you warm. Breathe Faith," Patsy said. Faith found a solution. She kicked the wall until a mirror fell. She grabbed a piece of the broken mirror. She kept rubbing and rubbing until the rope started to loosen. 20 minutes later, she had managed to actually get the rope off from around her wrists. She untied her feet. "Okay. Breathe Faith. Next step, find a way to get warm. Find blankets. Start a fire. Check for food. Try to keep your blood pressure down. Don't start worrying. He's not coming back Faith. I made sure of it. You're safe," Patsy said. "I need Jamie," Faith said. "A few hours ago you were mad at him Faith. I understand being angry about a situation, but you almost walked away. Do you love him," Patsy asked. "More than anything," Faith replied. "Are you going to love him forever Faith," Patsy asked. Faith nodded. "I'm scared. I'm scared that something is gonna happen and I'm gonna be doing this alone. I need him." "Remember when I told you that I would always be there? I'm here. I made sure you knew deep into your heart that you love him. The marriage you two have is strong Faith. Even walking away from each other, you'll always come home to him. His heart is where you belong Faith. I felt that way once. I fought my husband and we picked at each other all the time, but no matter how many times we fought we always found our way back to each other. You two will too Faith. You always have. I'm always going to be reminding you," Patsy said. "I wish I could hug you," Faith said. "Go open the front door," Patsy replied. "What," Faith asked. "Open the door Faith. The person you love is gonna be there. Open the door."

Faith walked to the door and tried finding a way to open it. The door was padlocked with chains from the outside. She found paper. She wrote on it hoping someone would see it. She slid it under the door. She tried cleaning the black spray off a window. Faith heard a car. She realized it was a truck. Her hands started shaking. She hunted through the house and found a rifle – loaded. Faith heard the sound of feet on the front porch. "Faith," she heard. "Jamie," Faith said. He saw the lock on the door. Seconds later, Faith heard a gunshot. She heard the chains drop to the wood. She heard whoever it was grab the note. He tried busting through again. "Babe, stand away from the door if you're in there." Faith sat down on the sofa and the baby started kicking. "Blanket," Patsy whispered. She found stashes of blankets. She opened the cupboard all the way and found a shrine with pictures of her. There had to be hundreds. There was the pictures from the press then tons more that were taken privately. She saw a christening dress and a white wedding dress. It was even in Faith's size – pre baby. She turned and saw a picture of Faith that had been made into a life size board. She started shaking. Faith turned and saw a doll he'd made to look like her. Faith started getting faint. She heard the door open and was about to pass out when someone caught her.

Faith woke up an hour later on the sofa, surrounded by officers, doctors and Jamie was at her side. Faith went to get up and Jamie stopped her. Before she could even say anything, Jamie kissed her. "Are you okay," Jamie asked. Faith looked at him and her eyes started filling. "I know. I saw it. I'm getting you home once the doctors say you're alright." Faith nodded. Faith looked at Jamie. "Baby is fine. I promise." She started crying. "Water," Jamie said. The doctor came over and handed Faith some ice water. Faith had the water and tried to talk. "Jamie," Faith said. "He's been arrested by the state troopers. Nobody is letting him off Faith," Jamie said. "He's gonna…" Jamie kissed her. "Consider it dealt with. He can't hurt you," Jamie said.

"The place is secure now," the officer said. "And," Jamie asked. "He had an arsenal of weapons. You weren't safe here. He has a severe issue with her. He was far past infatuated. The amount of intel he had on Faith was astounding. Someone had to be working with him Jamie. The man that was driving the SUV clammed up. Whatever he was planning was major. Jamie, come with me a moment," the officer said. Jamie walked into a back bedroom and saw a nursery. The room was done in army green, steel grey and white. The crib had been made and repainted into the steel grey. "I want this removed. I don't want her seeing it. For that matter, tear the place down. End of discussion," Jamie said. He walked back into the main sitting room and the EMT put Faith onto a gurney. He rode in the ambulance with her. He wasn't letting her out of his site now that he found her.

The doctors checked her over and took another ultrasound. Jamie sat with her while they showed the picture of that perfect little baby. Jamie had a smile ear to ear. Faith's hand slid onto his. "So baby is okay," Jamie asked. "I can let you know if it's gonna be a boy or girl," the doctor said. Faith shook her head. He kissed her. "For now, we're keeping it a surprise," Jamie said. The doctors checked Faith over officially and they arranged a helicopter for Jamie to get Faith home. "Alan," Faith asked. "He's in the hospital. He'll be alright," Jamie said. "What happened," Faith asked. "I'll tell you when we get you home." They headed straight home and Jamie didn't let go of Faith for even a second.

They got back to the airport and to the house. When they walked in, Alan wasn't there. Emma was curled up on the sofa. "Jamie, the hospital called. They won't say anything to me. I need to know if Alan is okay," Emma said. Jamie made a call and they let her talk to him. "Alan," Emma said. "I miss you too," he replied. Jamie made a call on the house line. Not 10 minutes later, there was a car waiting and Emma was packing. "I'll be home as soon as I can get him transferred," Emma said. "He's being transferred tomorrow. Already set up," Jamie said. Emma hugged him. "Take care of her," Emma asked. Jamie nodded still not letting go of Faith's hand.

"Where do you think you're going," Jamie teased. "To lay down," Faith replied. He pulled her to him and kissed her. "I'm not letting you out of my sight. Never. Not again. What happened anyway," Jamie asked. I got in the SUV and when we started heading the opposite direction, I started asking questions. The car stopped in the middle of nowhere and when I tried to leave, he tied my hands up and my feet. He tried to knock me out and I told him you'd personally kill him if anything happened to the baby. Instead, he gagged me. He had a bag over my head," Faith said. "What happened when you stopped," Jamie asked. "I was sitting in that cabin and almost had a panic attack. Nobody was there. It was cold. I woke up and somehow I managed to find a way to warm up. I heard you at the door and I was trying to get you to hear me. I didn't know what to do Jamie," Faith said. He kissed her and carried her upstairs. He leaned her onto the bed and curled up with her. "He's never coming here again. Nobody is hurting you," Jamie said. "You know he's…" Jamie kissed Faith. That simple kiss turned into making out. Jamie didn't want to ever come up for air. He knew she was safe as long as she was in his arms. When the baby started kicking away, he knew they were alright. He didn't let her out of his arms. They both curled up together and had a nap.

Jamie woke up when his phone started buzzing. He answered. "It's Emma. I wanted to let you know that we're headed back today. He's doing a lot better now. Is it okay if he recuperates at the house," Emma asked. " For what he did, yes," Jamie said. "We're on the next flight back," Emma said. "We'll see you when you get back," Jamie replied. He hung up and curled back up with Faith. "Who…" "Was Emma. She's heading back with Alan. They should be back tomorrow latest," Jamie said. "I wanted.." "When you feel better. Babe, you can barely talk as it is," Jamie said. Faith nodded. He kissed her. "Nap and I'll make you some caffeine free tea," Jamie asked. Faith kissed him. "Two minutes," Jamie said. She came with him. After half a cup of tea, Faith finally started getting her voice back. "Don't push it. Promise," Jamie asked. Faith kissed him. They didn't come up for air again until dinner.

"Hungry," Jamie asked. "Depends on what you're cooking," Faith said. He kissed Faith again and grabbed his cell. He called the guys and asked if they wanted Chinese food. He ordered dinner for everyone and went back to making out with his wife. Dinner showed 45 minutes later and Faith and Jamie turned theirs into an inside picnic. "What," Faith asked when she saw the smile on his face. "I love you," Jamie said. "I love you too. What I would've done if you hadn't…" Jamie kissed her. "No more thinking about it. He's not getting near you again," Jamie replied. "He will find me Jamie. I just pray that he leaves the baby alone." Jamie kissed her. "No more worrying," Jamie said. They finished dinner by the fire and sat and tried to come up with baby names for the next while.

"Come on. Seriously gonna name a baby after Patsy Cline," Jamie asked. "Middle name," Faith said. He shook his head. "Emily, Caroline, Avery," Faith said. "And if we're having a little man," Jamie asked. "Zeke, Jonathan, Duke," Jamie teased. "Logan," Faith said. He kissed her. "If not we just save the name for the next baby," Jamie teased. "Next baby? Jamie, we barely survived him being an ass about this baby. Stop getting so far ahead of yourself," Faith teased. Jamie kissed her and leaned her into his arms. "What are you up to," Faith asked. He kissed down her neck, undid the sweater she'd slid on and kissed right down her torso. He kissed down her right leg. "Jamie, not…" He kissed her again and picked her up. He leaned her onto the bed and was kneeling at her feet.

"Jamie," Faith said. "What," he teased. "What are you thinking in that head of yours," Faith asked. He kissed up her inner thigh. "Nothin," Jamie replied. He kissed her hip. Faith was at his mercy. She could feel his warm breath on her and it for some reason turned her on. He kissed his way up the inner thigh of her other leg. Her toes started to curl and he got a mischievous grin. "What are you up to," Faith asked. One lick and her toes curled. "Jamie," Faith said. He teased until her nails started to dig into the blanket then kissed his way back up her torso and made love to her. For the first time in months he had her attention. He made love to her the rest of the night. Every time his hands slid over her stomach he nibbled that spot on her neck. "Good distraction," he teased. "I missed you too," Faith replied. They curled up together in bed and he didn't let go all night.

When Jamie heard his phone buzzing at 4am, he grabbed it before it woke Faith up. When he saw the caller, he added it to the banned numbers. "Who," Faith asked. "Nobody." He got her back to sleep when he heard someone downstairs. He snuck away and went downstairs and found Emma helping Alan into the house. "You made it did you," Jamie asked. "She alright," Alan asked. Jamie nodded. "Sore throat from yelling but she's okay. I don't know how to thank you," Jamie said. "I'd hug you if my shoulder didn't kill," Alan said. "I got the guys to grab extra ice packs. They're all frozen in the freezer for you," Jamie said. Alan kissed Emma and she went off and got the bedroom set up.

Spirit of Love

"So what happened," Alan asked. "Got to the house and he was holding some other chick hostage like he did to Faith. The cops got him and when he wouldn't say where she was, I knew she was at that stupid cabin. Double padlocked? Anyway, I got through it and Faith passed out. I caught her and got her on the sofa. Thank god I had the brain to contact the EMT and the cops. The man was psycho Alan. His entire closet was like a shrine. Pictures on top of pictures. He had someone following her and following us. I need to know who that is and end this crap," Jamie said. "Already got a name. Scary part is he got himself into the damn crew. The cops are picking him up. He's the ass that picked a damn fight with me last week," Alan said. "I still don't get why he's doing all of this," Jamie said. "She is the only one that ever managed to leave without repercussions," Alan said. "Meaning," Jamie asked. "She ran straight to you. He hates that she moved on with you. That's what's eating him alive," Alan replied. "Why is it that in his pathetic existence, nobody stopped him? Nobody committed the lunatic. Nobody in his family did anything to deter him. If my kid was like that, he'd have doctors round the damn clock Alan," Jamie said. "There's the difference. His mom won't do anything because she's scared of him. His dad is an alcoholic and a nut himself. Trust me. They can't even help themselves." "Any other research," Jamie asked. "She's in love with you Jamie. Promise me that you aren't screwing that up ever again," Alan said. Jamie nodded. "By my side for life," Jamie replied. They gave each other a guy hug and Alan went up to his room to have some long-overdue alone time with Emma.

Jamie went back upstairs and Faith was having nightmares. Jamie slid onto the bed beside her and wrapped his arms around her. "You're home. You're alright," Jamie said kissing her forehead. Faith almost jerked and woke up. "I'm right here," Jamie said. Faith wrapped her arm around him and he could feel her tears. "It's okay baby. I promise you," Jamie said. "I couldn't do anything," Faith said. "Faith, I know you couldn't. Nobody is doing anything like that again. Never," Jamie said. "Why," Faith asked. "He's sick. He gives new meaning to the word sick," Jamie said. Faith kissed him. "Nobody is hurting you ever again. I love you." "I just don't…" Jamie kissed her. "Nobody is hurting you again. I love you baby. Nobody is ever hurting you again. Never," Jamie said.

257

Faith snuggled up to him. "Try to sleep babe. You two both need the sleep," Jamie said. "Promise you aren't leaving," Faith said. Jamie kissed her. "Not even for a split second," Jamie said. He stayed right beside her. Fact was all of this was starting to scare the crap out of him.

They finally got sleep and Jamie got up at 9. He made breakfast, leaving her a note to come downstairs for breakfast. When she didn't come down by 10:30, he went back upstairs. Faith was having a long shower. He went in to check on her and saw Faith crying. He knocked on the shower door and she turned towards him. "What's wrong," Jamie asked. He grabbed her towel and she walked out and right into his arms. "He's not coming near you again Faith. Not now, not ever," Jamie said. "Think I figured out why. That's all," Faith said. He wrapped her in the towel. "What did you figure out," Jamie asked. "When I was with him and lost the baby, he kept saying that he'd find a way. He must think that the baby is his. Even with proof, he's still gonna doubt it. You know how insane he is. It also means that the second this baby is born, he's not gonna stop coming after it. Jamie, we need to…" He kissed her. "The baby isn't gonna be alone Faith. They're always gonna be safe," Jamie said. Faith nodded. He felt the baby start kicking again. "You okay," Jamie asked. "Better now that I'm away from him," Faith said. "Breakfast," Jamie asked. Faith kissed him. She got dressed and came downstairs with Jamie.

Everything was quiet all day. They went for a drive, had lunch away from the fans and the crowds and even got Christmas shopping done. Nobody bothered them. True, it could've been Jamie's buddies blocking the stores, but that's what Faith needed. Normalcy. They went home for dinner and watched a few movies until Jamie's phone started ringing. Seems the press had got wind of what had happened with Faith. That was really the last thing he needed. "What," Faith asked. "Press wants to know what happened," Jamie replied. Faith shook her head. "Babe, they're gonna keep coming if we don't say anything," Jamie said. Faith sat and thought about it. "His name isn't coming into it. It does, he's gonna go nuts and get ten times worse." Jamie nodded. "Good point. I'll talk to Patrick. You okay in here while I talk to him," Jamie asked. Faith kissed him. "Five minutes tops," Jamie said. He kissed her again and went into his office and closed the door.

"We have to say something to the press," Patrick said. "Tell them that someone tried to kidnap Faith. That we caught up to them before they could do anything and the authorities have handled it. End of discussion. I don't want his name brought into it. I don't want his name glorified in the press Patrick," Jamie said. "I get it. They're gonna keep digging and asking, but if we just say it's been handled and that the authorities are handling it, it'll drop faster than a lead balloon. We need to release that new song Jamie. The one you wrote about Faith and protecting her. We're releasing it tomorrow." "Patrick, we aren't using what happened to her to boost the damn song. It's cold and calculated. Leave her out of it," Jamie said. "It's about a man protecting his woman. We're releasing it. There isn't gonna be a video if you don't want it, but we're releasing it. It's the favorite of everyone who's heard it in concert." "Fine, but let me talk to her and warn her first," Jamie said. "You have two days Jamie."

He walked back in to the TV room and Faith was checking emails. He slid the laptop out of her hands and put it on the table. "What," Faith asked. "He wants to release hold onto me. I don't want you upset Faith. I don't want them coming after you and bringing it all up," Jamie said. Faith kissed him. "It's alright," Faith said. He kissed her back. "You sure," he asked. "I know how Patrick's brain works Jamie. It's okay," Faith replied. "What got you all calm," Jamie asked. Faith kissed him. "My husband," Faith said. He didn't let go of her the rest of the night. When Faith finally fell asleep, Jamie started writing. That entire theory of making lemons into lemonade hit him. He finished up the lyrics on the song then snuck out onto the patio and worked on some of the music.

Faith came outside around 3am and heard Jamie playing. He looked over. "What are you doing out here when it's this cold," Faith asked wrapping a blanket around him. "Song idea. Sorta had to run with it when it hit," Jamie said as he kissed Faith. She sat down beside him. Her legs slid into his lap. "Tease," Jamie said. "And damn good at it," Faith teased. He kissed her and slid the guitar to the ground. The kisses went down her neck. "Thought you were playing the song for me," Faith asked. He kissed her, pulled her into his arms and stood up, grabbed his guitar and went into the house. He put his guitar against the door and walked Faith upstairs and onto the bed. The baby started kicking up a storm. He kissed her. "What," Faith asked. "Baby is intentionally kicking you," Jamie joked. Faith shook her head. "I have a feeling she's gonna be just like you," Jamie said. "And how do you know that there's a girl in there," Faith asked. He kissed her. His hand slid onto the baby bump and he asked. "You're a girl aren't you," Jamie teased. The baby kicked. "Told ya," he teased. "What are we gonna do," Faith asked. "Have a little Faith. Hope that things get better, hold on when they don't." "You staying in bed," Faith asked. She heard his shoes hit the floor. "Wouldn't be anywhere else," Jamie said.

Chapter 20

Faith got up around 8 and went downstairs. Emma and Alan were flirting and being two lovebirds. Faith snuck into the kitchen and made breakfast and put out a plate for them. "I didn't even hear you come downstairs," Alan said. "Jamie's sleeping. He was working on something last night," Faith said. "You doing better," Emma asked. "If I ever question him again..." Emma hugged her. "That mean that Evan is leaving you alone," Alan asked. "Nope. He's in the nut house. That's it," Faith said. Emma hugged her again. "He wasn't gonna let you get hurt. Trust me Faith. He's in love with you and not even death could stop it. You two were meant to be together for years," Alan said. "Just took Faith giving in for once to see it. Everyone makes stupid mistakes. I'm just kinda glad that you made it back to where you belong," Emma said. "Took living through hell," Faith said. "So, Alan and I have news of our own," Emma said. "Meaning," Faith asked. Emma heard Jamie coming downstairs. "Now that you two are both here, we can tell you." "Tell me what," Faith asked. "I asked Emma to marry me," Alan said. "What," Faith asked. "We've..." "I knew that's what you were up to. You two have been sneaking around for months," Jamie said. "Jamie," Faith said. He kissed her. "You trying to tell me that you two were sneaking around all this time," Faith asked. "Since Jamie asked me where you were. When you got here, I'd just met Alan," Emma said. "So that's where you went," Faith asked. Emma nodded and Alan wrapped his good arm around her. "So that also means that we're planning a wedding," Faith said. "Another wedding," Jamie said. Faith shook her head. "You're going through with the wedding of the century," Emma teased. "After the baby comes and once I can actually get sleep, yes," Faith said. Jamie kissed her.

They all finished some breakfast then Faith decided to take Emma shopping. "Where you goin," Jamie asked. "Christmas and wedding shopping. You two get to stay home," Faith said. Just as Faith was pulling out, the tree showed complete with decorations and lights. While Faith and Emma went shopping, Jamie devised a plan on how to set the tree up.

"So what shopping do you have left," Emma asked. "Picking up Jamie's present, getting more boxes for under the tree, finding a hiding place…" "So a ton more to do," Emma teased. "And we're getting you an appointment at that bridal salon you wanted to see in New York," Faith said. "I can't do that Faith. The money…" "Jamie won't let me take you anywhere else. He already had me booked in for a date where we have the place to ourselves. You're coming," Faith replied. Emma hugged her and the baby started kicking again. They shopped and got every ounce of their Christmas shopping done then stopped and had lunch. "How are you really," Emma asked. "Still scared. I just don't understand why he can't just leave it be Emma. Why he still thinks that coming after me is the smart thing. I mean trying to kidnap me? That was just stupid," Faith said. "He's disturbed. That I know. I don't get it either Faith. I'm just glad you're home safe," Emma said. They chatted and finished up lunch and headed back to the house. Faith hid the gifts out in the barn out back. There was only one spot to hide them. They came in and the tree was up. Jamie saved a few personal ornaments and the angel for Faith. "What's this," Faith asked noticing a little box. "Open," Jamie said. She opened it and found an ornament with their picture on it from the wedding. She looked deeper in the box and found one for the baby. Jamie kissed her and wrapped his arms around her. "Everyone gets two personal ones," Jamie said handing a box to Emma and Alan. Jamie and Faith hung theirs. Alan opened one – an ornament with a picture of Alan and Emma. The second box Emma opened – an ornament with two rings that Alan had bought. Emma kissed him. "Pretty presumptuous don't you think," Emma asked. Alan kissed her again. Jamie helped Faith put the angel on the tree and they plugged the lights in. "Well," Jamie asked. Faith turned and kissed him.

They had dinner by the tree and tried to figure out Christmas plans. Jamie was intent on everyone being at the house together. Finding hotels that were private wasn't gonna be that hard. Faith called the hotel she knew had high security and managed to get the floor booked for family for the holidays. Faith put an email together and sent it out to everyone they wanted to invite then Jamie decided to plan dinner. "What are you thinking," Faith asked. Jamie looked at Alan. "Turkey and every fixin in the planet," Jamie said. Alan nodded. "Alright then. Massive dinner it is," Faith teased. She checked into getting a turkey. "Babe," Jamie said. "Tough," Faith said. He kissed her. "Stubborn but damn sexy," he teased. "Fine. I'll make some of the veggies then," Faith said. "Or cookies," Jamie teased. "Betty Crocker over here could pull that off in seconds," Emma teased. "Fine. I'm making the cookies and Emma's cooking," Faith joked. Jamie kissed her. They got everything ordered they were gonna need and the guys had a coffee while Faith had cider. When the baby started really kicking, Jamie put his hand on Faith's stomach and rubbed. "Simmer down in there," Jamie joked. They hung out and Jamie and Faith got packed up for the second last set of shows. "You two can stay and chill," Jamie said. Alan smirked. "You need to heal dude. Besides. Private alone time is sorta important after you pop the question," Jamie teased. Faith and Jamie headed upstairs and Alan and Emma went and hung out in the other bedroom.

"You okay with going this weekend," Jamie asked. "Just promise me that nothing is gonna get past security and I'll be fine," Faith said. He kissed her. "Nobody is getting near you. I want you carrying it," Jamie said. "Great. 20 pound purse," Faith said. "Promise me," Jamie said. Faith nodded. "I'm not gonna lose you before Christmas. I'm not losing you period," Jamie said. Faith kissed him and they finished packing things up. "Just promise you aren't giving me a personalized Smith and Wesson for Christmas," Faith teased. "And if I do," Jamie asked. Faith shook her head and laughed. "You would wouldn't you," Faith joked. Jamie kissed her. They finished packing and slid into bed. "What," Faith asked knowing Jamie had a smile ear to ear. "Already got what I wanted for Christmas, my birthday and every holiday in between," Jamie said. "So I can take your presents back," Faith teased. Jamie kissed her. "You aren't taking anything back. You know what I was talking about," Jamie said. Faith kissed him. "And you're never gonna have to return it either," Faith said. They finally went to sleep and tried to catch some shut-eye before they headed out the next morning. Faith made it through the night without a nightmare at all. Jamie got up the next morning and made them breakfast. They had a quick visit with her doctor for a checkup and they headed out.

Jamie and Faith were an hour or two out and the guys all started working on another song. Jamie played with them and got half way into a new song and Faith went to work through the emails. "Babe, remember," Jamie said. Faith nodded. She got most of the emails organized. When she came across some suspicious ones, she forwarded them to Jamie's buddy. Faith finished up and made some more updates to Jamie's site. He came into the stateroom a while later and closed the door. "What," Faith asked. Jamie kissed her. He devoured her lips and snuggled her. "Thought you were working on something," Faith said. "Still working on something. What you doin," Jamie asked. "Emails and updating the site," Faith replied. He kissed her. "And how's baby," Jamie asked. "Kicking and doing a dance," Faith teased. They relaxed for a while then they went in and chilled with the guys. He snuck Faith's music lyric book on the way through.

"Jamie," Faith said. "You come up with lyrics nobody else would. I'm reading them," Jamie said. Faith tried grabbing it out of his hands. He kissed her instead and handed the book off to Greg. "Jamie," Faith said. Greg started going through them while the guys started rehearsing. "Faith, this one is that good," Greg said. "No," Faith said. He handed the book to Jamie. He read through the one that Greg had mentioned and started trying to figure out the song behind it. He played around with it until they stopped for some food. They grabbed something to eat and hung out a while then Jamie started working on her song again. Faith curled up with Jamie and he kept working on the song until it was done. "Well," Jamie asked. Faith smirked. "That's it. I'm gonna scrap it," Jamie joked. "You spent…" Jamie kissed her. They wrote everything out so they could tweak it in studio and Faith went and curled up in the stateroom. Jamie came in a little while later and saw Faith curled up in his t-shirt. "What you doing over there sexy wife," Jamie asked as he slid onto the bed beside her. "Hope," Faith said. "What," Jamie asked. "Baby name," Faith replied. He kissed her. "Easier for girl names," Jamie said. Faith nodded. "Where are you getting the ideas from," Jamie asked. "If she's a girl, she's part of our hope for everything good," Faith said. He kissed her neck. "And if it's a boy," Jamie asked. "J.J. What you think," Faith asked. He kissed her. "Getting all mushy aren't you," Jamie asked. Faith kissed him. "Well," Jamie asked. "What if we go with just the girl baby names," Jamie teased. "Determined about having a girl aren't you," Faith asked. "Thinking that Faith is the perfect name. That's why," Jamie said. "You get the song done," Faith asked. He kissed her. Just as he was about to start snuggling her, Faith felt the bus stop. "Coming to my hotel room," Jamie asked. Faith kissed him. He grabbed their bags and they headed into the hotel and tried to get settled. They curled up on the bed and tried to get sleep.

Jamie got up the next morning and Faith was sitting on the sofa. "What are you doing way over there," Jamie asked. "Emails and checking through to make sure there haven't been any other interview requests for today. Guess you had a good night of sleep," Faith said. "Woman, get your butt over here," Jamie said. Faith put the laptop back in her bag and walked back over to the bed. "What are you doing up so early anyway," Jamie asked. "Had an idea about the baby and I wanted to try and get some info about it," Faith replied. "So what was the idea," Jamie asked. "Trying to find a way to get a crib onto the tour bus. How to transition a bunk into a crib. Got a few ideas from that about what we'd need." Jamie kissed her. "Good plan," Jamie said. "And what are we gonna do when this one comes out? You gonna be okay with me staying home," Faith asked. He kissed her. "You aren't," Jamie said. "And what are we gonna do? Have a way of taking the baby everywhere," Faith asked. He kissed her. "We're getting a new tour bus. The guys came up with it. That way we have 2 staterooms. The baby can sleep in one and we have the other. Babe, staying home alone isn't happening. I can't let that happen," Jamie said. Faith kissed him. "At some point..." He kissed her. "Stop Faith. Nothing is happening," Jamie said. "Jamie," Faith said. "He's not getting anywhere near either of you. Never," Jamie said. "So you're gonna take me and baby with you everywhere? Jamie, it's not realistic," Faith said. "Why," Jamie asked. "Chicken pox, flu, colds, school," Faith said. "Good point," Jamie said. "Exactly. Taking a baby to hotel after hotel isn't a good move Jamie," Faith said. "We'll figure it out," Jamie said. "We should sorta try working on that right now," Faith said. Jamie kissed her. "This little baby is gonna have everything and anything. There isn't gonna be a worry," Jamie said. He got dressed and so did Faith. They hopped back on the bus and headed to the venue. Jamie didn't let Faith out of his arms. "You two are almost making me nauseous," Callon said. "Get used to it," Jamie teased.

They finally pulled into the venue and Faith walked Jamie into the dressing room. "What," Jamie asked. "I'm not going into the interview with you. Not like this," Faith said. "Your pregnant. Doesn't matter," Jamie said. "Yeah it does. Just don't volunteer it," Faith asked. Jamie kissed her. "You're sexy. Second off, nobody puts my wife down. Babe, you're gorgeous. You barely even put weight on. Babe, stop worrying," Jamie said. "I didn't…" He handed her a suit bag he'd got shipped down to the venue. "Jamie," Faith said. He kissed her. He went to go get everything signed in so hair and makeup could sneak into Faith. He came in 45 minutes later and saw her in the outfit he'd bought with her hair done and makeup. "Damn sexy wife I got," Jamie said. Faith turned around. "I'm still not doing it," Faith joked. He grabbed her hand and walked her out to sound check. "No email and no stupid laptop. I wanna see what you think," Jamie said. Faith shook her head and he kissed her. Faith sat down and saw cameras. She figured they'd decided to film part of sound check. Jamie was flirting with Faith the entire way through. As soon as he was done, he hopped off the stage and kissed her. Faith shook her head. "Come," Jamie asked. Faith nodded. They walked right into the interview that Faith was determined not to be in.

They asked about the tour, about the stalking debacle and finally about the baby. "So when are you two gonna be mom and dad," the interviewer asked. "End of March. Perfect timing too. Gives me some time home with these two before the new tour starts in June," Jamie said. "So we heard you've been busy in the studio. A 17 track CD? Why that decision?" "I got a few really good song ideas and it wasn't complete without them. Faith inspires me every day. I couldn't make a CD big enough. I was honestly thinking of pushing it to a double, but I wanted to save a few for the next one. I can guarantee this baby's gonna be like her mama," Jamie said. "So we noticed on a few of the songs that Faith was a co-writer?" "He stole a notebook of mine that I'd had forever. When he saw the lyrics I wrote he just took off and turned them into some amazing songs," Faith said. "So other than your amazing wife, what else got you that inspired," she asked. "Just things that go on with our friends and family. My buddies are like family to us too. I mean, who wouldn't get inspired," Jamie said. They finished up the interview and got a few pictures of Faith and Jamie together then headed off. "Still sexy," Jamie said. Faith shook her head. "Determined," Faith asked. He nibbled her neck. "I like showing you off babe. I'm happiest when you're right here anyway," Jamie said. He kissed her and the baby started kicking up a storm again.

"I had an idea for tonight," Jamie said as they were having dinner with the guys. "What," Greg asked. "A surprise for Faith," Jamie teased. He texted Greg the idea. Greg smirked. "Doable," Greg replied. "Quit with the secrets," Faith said. "Nope," Jamie teased. Faith shook her head. She got up and saw Deacon. Jamie finished up dinner with the guys then noticed Deacon headed straight towards Faith.

"What," Faith asked when she got far enough from Jamie. "He hasn't left you alone has he," Deacon asked. "He's only gonna get worse now. It's almost like it's being thrown in his face. He's gonna keep acting out until he's done. He'll stop," Faith said. "Jamie can't protect you Faith. You know that right," Deacon said. "Can you stop? One ounce of stress and I'm in the damn hospital. Enough," Faith said. "That Evan guy was making threats Faith. Even me. He threatened to kick my ass if I didn't help him get close," Deacon said. "And," Faith asked. "The cops caught him making the threat. Faith, you don't get it," Deacon said. "I do. I'm going to lay down. You hear anything then you tell Jamie and the guys," Faith said. She walked back to the trailer and tried to get sleep.

"What does Deacon think he's…" "Leave him alone Jamie. Nutcase threatened him. Leave it be," Greg said. "Just make sure Faith…" "Already handled. She's having some quiet time on the tour bus." Jamie finished what he was doing then went out to meet her. He hopped on the bus and locked up. He walked back to the stateroom and Faith was going through a few baby books. "What are you up to," Jamie asked sliding onto the bed beside her. "Reading. Looking at what to expect when baby decides to makes its debut," Faith replied. Jamie kissed her shoulder, her neck then nibbled at her earlobe. "What are you up to," Faith asked. "Reminding you of something," Jamie said. "Meaning," Faith asked. "I'm still standing right here. You hurt, I hurt. We're gonna do this together Faith. You'll be fine," Jamie said. "Jamie, It's easy for you. For me, it's like pushing a watermelon through a needle hole. It's painful as hell," Faith said. "You're gonna be fine. Babe, when it comes time we opt for pain meds. That simple. Nothing is gonna go wrong," Jamie said. "I'm almost hoping that I am out cold for it. None of this..." Jamie kissed her and slid the book out of her hand. "Don't need books to tell us what to do. We're gonna do this right Faith. We need help we find it," Jamie said. "Nanny," Faith asked. "Life saver. Babe, please just hear me out on this," Jamie said. "Not now. Jamie. We can't make those decisions right now," Faith said. "Babe," Jamie said. "You have a show to do. I'm just gonna relax back here," Faith said. "Nope," Jamie replied. "Jamie," Faith said. "Fine but you aren't staying here on your own," he replied. Faith kissed him. Jamie finished getting ready and kissed Faith for luck. He went and did sound check then headed on stage. Faith snuck out and watched part of it.

Jamie got every song nailed. When he figured out she was there, the grin went ear to ear. Faith went to sneak out and Jamie almost shook his head. Faith nodded and he gave her a look that said if she didn't stay she was getting a butt kick. Faith went to head back and Jamie started. "So what did you think of that one y'all," Jamie asked. The crowd roared. "Wanna know who wrote it with me? Here she is," Jamie said grabbing Faith's hand and walking her onto the stage with him. "This hot lady is my woman y'all. Songwriter, and one kick ass woman. Anyone ever had someone this amazing? There's only one song I can think of to tell y'all," Jamie said. He sang that song that he serenaded her with more than once. The one that romanced her into his arms more than once. He didn't let go of Faith's hand. At the end of the song, Jamie kissed her and Faith headed back off. She went back to the tour bus and made some tea. She curled up on the sofa and turned on some of the shows she'd taped. She even fell asleep on the sofa.

Jamie came in a short while later. He walked over to Faith and carried her into the stateroom and curled up with her. Faith woke up a little while later while Jamie was sliding her shoes off. "How'd the rest of the show go," Faith asked yawning. "Was better when you were right there. You okay," Jamie asked. "Just tired. The dancer in there is kicking and dancing and has been all day," Faith said. "Well, little munchkin in there. Let mama sleep," Jamie said rubbing her stomach. "Got what we needed for the crib and everything," Faith said. "And," Jamie asked. "A few sleepers and stuff," Faith said. "Babe," Jamie said. Faith kissed him. "Not buying clothes until we need them," Faith said. "Still think we should find out," Jamie said nibbling her neck. "Determined to leak it," Faith joked. "Nope. Baby girl needs her name in there," Jamie teased. "We'll decide in a few weeks. That okay," Faith asked. Jamie nodded. "What if we wait until Valentine's Day," Jamie asked. Faith smirked. "Nobody could top that gift," Faith said. "Well," Jamie asked. Faith kissed him. "Valentine's," Faith said. Jamie snuggled into her. "So are you okay about Christmas," Jamie asked. "Almost done all my shopping too," Faith replied. "Me too," Jamie said. "You started," Faith asked. "Getting there. I went out when you did," Jamie said.

They talked and snuggled. The guys all got settled and tried to get some shut-eye before they got to the hotel. When the bus finally did stop, Jamie grabbed the bags and walked Faith into the hotel. They walked into the suite and Faith saw roses in the bedroom. Faith looked at Jamie. "What are you up to," Faith asked. He kissed her. They went into the bedroom and Jamie got the blinds completely drawn and they went back to sleep in the oversized bed. Jamie didn't let go.

When Faith woke up the next morning, Jamie was talking to the baby. "What are you doing," Faith asked. "Talking to Hope. Just wanted some daddy time," Jamie teased. "And," Faith asked. "Ordered breakfast. Needed to know what she wanted," Jamie joked. "I swear you are gonna spoil the baby before they even come into your arms," Faith said. "Still not convinced," Jamie said. Faith kissed him. She got up and Jamie sat down with her to have breakfast. As soon as they were done, Faith slid into a hot shower. Jamie slid in just as Faith was washing the conditioner from her hair. "So, about Christmas," Jamie said. "What," Faith replied. "Awards and we got invited to do the Christmas special," Jamie said. "We," Faith asked. "We. They're doing a little interview thing with us for it," Jamie said. "Jamie," Faith said. He kissed her. "We'll find a dress and stuff," Jamie replied. Faith laughed and shook her head. "Besides. It's Christmas stuff. It'll get us in the mood for it," Jamie said. Faith kissed him.

Jamie got his sound check finished up, got the interviews finished and came back to the dressing room to find Faith on her laptop. "What are you up to," Jamie asked. "Nothin," Faith said. "Babe," Jamie said. "I'm getting the last of my shopping done," Faith replied. Jamie kissed her and tried to snoop but she'd already shut it all down. "Party pooper," Jamie said. "Nope. You aren't snooping. You're waiting just like the rest of the little kids," Faith said. Jamie kissed her. "Hint," Jamie said. "It'll be in a box under the tree." Jamie shook his head. Jamie hung out with her, they had dinner and hung out for a while before Jamie headed on for the second last show. "You sure you're okay," Jamie asked as Faith opted to put her feet up in the dressing room. "I'm just gonna read. I'm fine. Once my feet go back to normal I'll be okay," Faith said. Jamie sat down and rubbed her feet. "Next time, sit down. Babe, you've been running around all day. Just stop and sit," Jamie said. "Okay. I'll stop and sit right here," Faith said. He kissed her and went in to do the meet and greet. A half hour later, Jamie was heading on stage. Faith kissed him for luck and he was on in a matter of minutes.

Security made sure Faith was safe. When Jamie finished on stage, he walked back in the dressing room to see Faith asleep on the sofa. He sat down beside her and rubbed her feet. They were finally starting to get better. Faith was still asleep. Jamie got Greg to grab her stuff and he carried her out to the tour bus.

Faith woke up a little while later. Jamie was out cold beside her. She closed her eyes and went back to sleep in his arms. It was only when he started kissing and nibbling her neck that she woke up. "What are you doing," Faith asked. "Waking you up. We're gonna be at the hotel in ten. You fell asleep in the dressing room," Jamie said. "Was waiting for you," Faith said yawning. They stopped a little while later and Faith and Jamie headed into the hotel. When they got into the room, Jamie and Faith curled up on the bed and tried to get some more sleep.

Faith got up around 10 and started checking emails. For the first time in a while, nothing other than the meet and greet was on for that day. Faith went and put up pictures from the shows and finished up the last of the updates for the other sites she was responsible for. She got everything finished before Jamie even woke up. She headed into the bedroom and Jamie woke up. "What are you doing up," Jamie asked yawning. "Force of habit. Got my work done for now. Was just going to order breakfast," Faith said. Jamie kissed her. "Good morning to you too," Faith said. Jamie grabbed the menu and ordered them some breakfast. Faith got up and went and hopped into the shower. A little while later, Jamie slid in with her. He washed Faith's hair and making out turned into sex in the shower. "You know what happens at the end of the show tonight," Jamie asked. "You go have a party with the guys," Faith teased. "Don't wanna. Means you and me free and clear until after new years," Jamie said. "Great. I get you being silly for 3 months," Faith teased. "Means I'm coming to every baby appointment and we can shop for baby stuff," Jamie said. "You're just so looking forward to all of this aren't you," Faith asked. Jamie kissed her. "Have been for months," he replied. He kissed Faith and she slid out of the shower. She wrapped herself in the robe and tried to dry her hair. Jamie finished his shower and walked over to her. "What," Faith asked. "I love you," he said as he kissed her neck. "So other than show number 2 million and one, what else did you want to do today since it's the last stop," Faith asked. "Dinner's being catered in special for tonight, we're sleeping in tomorrow and you need to help finish the family Christmas shopping," Jamie said. "You're seriously going shopping," Faith asked. He kissed her. "Tomorrow we are. Today, we're having a me and you day. Nobody disturbing…" Just as he was about to say it, his cell went off. "Yep," Jamie said.

"Three interviews, two telephone interviews then 2 more interviews before the show. They all want the last word Jamie," Patrick said. "What happened to Faith getting to handle that," Jamie asked. "She didn't answer her phone. You two are always together anyway," he teased. Jamie laughed. "Fine, but I'm not having any interviews tomorrow. We have to do that Christmas special and the awards then nothing. Promise," Jamie teased. "Not a problem," Patrick replied. "One thing though. We're having a label party. Couple days before Christmas. You two have to be there," Patrick said. "We will. Send me an email with the times for the stuff today and the details on the party." Jamie finally hung up and Faith started getting dressed. She pulled on leggings and a sweater. "Babe," Jamie said. "No. I'm not doing the interview with you," Faith said. Jamie kissed her. "Pretty please," Jamie teased. Faith shook her head. "Even if I beg," Jamie joked. He nibbled at her neck. "Quit," Faith said. "Come on," Jamie said. Faith shook her head. "Jamie, I look like a damn...." "Sexy wife," Jamie said trying to put her back in a good mood. "No," Faith replied. He kissed her again. He nibbled at her neck, almost leaving a mark. "Jamie, enough," Faith said. "Then come do the interview with me," Jamie asked. "No," Faith replied. He handed her leather pants and black tank to Faith. "Jamie," Faith said. "And the sweater. Come on," Jamie said. Faith shook her head. "You're gorgeous Faith. Nobody even notices unless you let them. Babe, please just..." "Jamie, enough. I don't want him seeing any more than he needs to alright," Faith replied. "Then we're showing him we're stronger than he thinks. That he can't hurt you," Jamie said. "I'm not tempting fate Jamie. Not after that," Faith said. He kissed her. "I'm bringing it with us. The last interviews babe. Then we get you and me time. Nobody else," Jamie said. "He's...." Jamie kissed her again and devoured her lips. He went and finished getting dressed and Faith finished getting ready.

They got on the tour bus and an hour or two later, they were at the venue. Jamie kissed Faith and went in to do sound check bright and early and the rest of the day was booked for interviews. He came into the dressing room and saw Faith. "What," she asked. He handed lunch to her and then prodded at her to do the interviews. Faith shook her head. "Babe," Jamie said. She shook her head again. "I'm not doing it," Faith said. He kissed her and after teasing and taunting her she finally went and got changed. "You're still sexy as hell. I love you," Jamie said. "Jamie," Faith said. "No more after the Christmas thing. I promise," Jamie said. Faith kissed him. "You even think about..." Jamie kissed her. They went into the first interview. Between each one, Jamie made sure Faith had a snack. He was snuggling with her between each and every one. The reporters got a ton of pictures of them together. By dinner time, they had finished all the interviews and Faith and Jamie curled up on the tour bus. They needed time to relax. Jamie finished getting changed to head on and Faith finished up her dinner. "Babe," Jamie said. "What," Faith asked. "Marry me," Jamie teased. "Already did," Faith said. "Again," Jamie said. "Meaning," Faith asked. "On our anniversary," Jamie replied. "May," Faith asked. Jamie nodded and kissed her. "You're ridiculous. You know that," Faith asked. "It's perfect," Jamie said. "We'll talk later." Jamie kissed her and she walked him inside. "What," Faith asked. He kissed her again and went into the meet and greet.

"Jamie Gilbert. What do ya know," a woman said. He looked at her and gulped. "Long time no talk," she said. "Grace, not now," Jamie said. She watched him finish the meet and greet and intentionally waited until the end. He did the meet and greet picture with her and everyone started heading out. "So how have you been," Grace said. "Married. Having a baby with my wife," Jamie said trying to make his point. "We were so good together. What did you go get hitched for," she asked. "Because I did. I'm heading out. Later," Jamie said trying to get out of there as fast as possible. Grace stopped him and kissed him and Callon caught a glimpse. Jamie pushed her away and asked security to remove her. Grace was his weakness. The only one other than Faith. Faith wasn't gonna hear about it and he made sure she wouldn't. "Not a word," Jamie said to Callon.

He came out afterwards and walked over to Faith and kissed her. "I love you," Jamie said. "I know. I love you too." "You watching the show," Jamie asked. "And I'm not going on there. End of discussion. Not gonna talk me into anything else." He kissed her and Faith walked him to the stage. One of the stage guys brought a stool over for Faith. "Determined as always," Faith said. Jamie kissed her again and headed on.

Every song got closer and closer to the last song for the last stop. He sang through them all then threw in a few new ones. He finished that last song and looked over at Faith . She had a smile ear to ear and he walked right over to her. He grabbed her hand and walked her over to the tour bus. They hopped on, everything got loaded up and they started heading home. "What," Faith asked. "I love you. Just promise me something," Jamie asked. "What?" "That I'm gonna have you in my arms the rest of my life. That we're never gonna be apart." "Why are you worried," Faith asked. "I'm not. I'm just saying..." Faith looked at him. "What is running through that head of yours," Faith asked. "Nothing," Jamie replied. Callon looked at him and shook his head. "What," Faith asked. "Just tell her," Callon said. "Tell me what," Faith asked. Jamie kissed her, devouring her lips. The second the kiss broke, he got up and walked her down to the stateroom. "Jamie," Faith said. He shook his head. Faith went to walk back down to talk to Callon and Jamie grabbed her hand. He walked her into the stateroom and closed the door. "Jamie," Faith said. "It's nothing," Jamie said. "Either you talk or you're sleeping on the floor," Faith said. "It's nothing." "Right," Faith replied. She got changed and slid into bed. "Faith." "Either you say it or don't bother sleeping in here," Faith replied. He kicked his jeans and t-shirt off and slid into bed with her. "Jamie," Faith said. He kissed her. She pushed him away. "Say it or you sleep alone," Faith said. "It's nothing. Absolutely nothing," he replied. Faith got up, slid her leggings back on, pulled on a sweater and went and sat on the sofa.

"Wanna know that badly," Callon asked. "Why does he have to have these stupid secrets," Faith asked. "He loves you Faith. He doesn't want you mad. You two get 3 months to yourselves. It doesn't..." "Obviously you saw whatever it was. Tell me," Faith said. "It was nothing," he replied. "Fine. Guy code," Faith replied. She put her ear buds in and watched TV on her laptop. The baby started kicking so hard it felt like her stomach was going to explode. Jamie came out a half hour later and ripped the ear buds out of her ears. He shut her laptop and grabbed her hand. "Let go," Faith said. "An old friend showed and kissed me. That's what happened." "Have you ever slept with her," Faith asked. "It doesn't..." She walked back over to the sofa and sat back down. "Faith," Jamie said. "Have a good sleep," Faith replied. She wrapped herself up in a blanket. "Woman, get your butt over here," Jamie said. Faith watched TV with Callon. He got up and grabbed her hand and walked her back into the stateroom. "Jamie," Faith said. He kissed her. "Bed. Now," Jamie replied. "Then you're..." He kissed her and leaned her onto the bed. "She showed and was stupid as shit. She kissed me. I told her I was married and that we were having a baby and she didn't back off. I walked out and came straight to you. That's all that happened," Jamie said. "If..." He kissed her. "Sleep." Faith tried and she was still mad.

"What's wrong," Jamie asked. "That's what I'm worried about. What I always was worried about," Faith said. "I love you. No more being scared. I'm always gonna run to you Faith, just like you always ran to me," Jamie said. He kissed her and they curled up and tried to sleep.

Chapter 21

All the way through the Christmas break, Faith kept wondering what was next. They booked the hotels, got everyone organized and finished wrapping and buying all the gifts. Faith still wondered if the Grace situation was really what Jamie had said, but she didn't have much choice. The did the Christmas special and it hit the airwaves a few days before Christmas when everyone was starting to show. Everyone started showing in town on Christmas Eve. Faith opted for something Jamie had never had time to do before.

She walked him into the church that she loved. He was hand in hand with her all the way through midnight mass. Afterwards, Jamie opted for a Christmas surprise for Faith. "Where are we going," Faith asked. He pulled up to the back door of the Opry and Jamie walked her inside for a Christmas surprise. "What are you up to," Faith asked. They walked in and Faith saw white rose petals. He wrapped his arms around her and she followed the path. At the end, there was a minister. "Jamie," Faith said. He slid his hand in hers and walked her towards him. "What are you..." The minister started reading the exact words he had at their wedding. Instead, it was renewing their vows. Faith smirked. When it came time for Jamie to say his part, as tradition he wrote his own vow.

"The day we met, I was head over heels with one kiss. That never changed. We have gone through trouble that I couldn't have ever predicted. I thought I was gonna lose you more than once. When I was face to face with the thought of losing you altogether, I didn't know what to do. I knew that no matter what I was never gonna lose you. I was scared that things were too good to be true. I was scared that I was gonna really mess up and you'd walk away. Faith, you never failed me. Even after what Evan did, I was scared that we wouldn't survive it. Every time I look at you we survive things that nobody expected us to. We haven't had things easy and we probably never will. I'm just glad I have someone to ride those rapids with. I have a heart that will love me forever. I never want to take that for granted. I never want us to lose sight of us. Over two years ago today was the day I made the mistake of letting you go. I'm never ever making that mistake again. I promise that I'm gonna love you more every day. I promise that even if we fight, we'll always make up. I'll never take us for granted, and I'll never forget that I could lose you and that being with you is a privilege. An honor that your parents and God gave me. I promise to say I love you every day no matter what. I'll never regret a second as long as I'm with you." Faith brushed tears away. Jamie dried her tears.

"When I met you, I didn't know what to think. How could a guy fall for someone like me? I didn't understand what really brought us together. What kept us together. When I made that mistake of walking away, I didn't know what would happen. When I came out of it and saw you there, I didn't want to let go. I was scared that I'd make another mistake. When we got married, I fell even more. I have gone through fear more than once Jamie. I always knew that we'd have each other. I was proud to never lose you. I knew that I was head over heels when you kept trying to convince me into marrying you. You teased when we first met. When we got married, that was the start of things. That was the start of us. I promise I'll love you forever. That I'll tell you when you're being a pain, I'll pick a fight when needed, and we'll always make up. I'll hold your hand forever." Jamie had a grin ear to ear.

"Now the exchange of rings," the minister said. Jamie pulled them out of his pocket. He slid a pave diamond band on Faith's finger and he handed her his. She slid it on his finger and saw her initials engraved on it. "Love will last forever just like a ring is an unbroken circle. As you stand in the circle of the Opry stage and exchange these rings, know that love is as eternal as the circle of the stage. May your love and this circle be unbroken forever," the minister said. The minister gave Jamie the go-ahead and he kissed Faith. "Congratulations," the minister said. "Thank you for helping me out with the surprise," Jamie said. The minister smirked. "More than welcome," the minister said. Jamie walked him out to make sure he had been paid and Faith sat down by the circle.

"Tell me you're happy," Patsy said. "As long as I never regret any of this," Faith said. "Is he the man you love or the man you're scared to live without," Patsy asked. "Both." "Faith, if you need me, I'm gonna be here. I didn't get to finish raising my girls. It's a regret I took to my grave. Fact was, Charlie and the kids knew every day that I loved them. I have to be happy with that. Faith, the only thing I can tell you is that your daughter is gonna be an amazing woman. She's gonna have his creativity and your heart. Being with him and staying with him is gonna be your choice, but he's your soul mate," Patsy said. "is the baby girl first or second," Faith asked. "Can't tell you. Just know that no matter what, I'm gonna be here to hold your hand," Patsy replied. "Promise me that you'll give me a kick if I screw up," Faith asked. "I won't need to. You have him for that. He loves you Faith. That little girl might give you a few surprises. Don't let him have regrets. Don't have regrets about your daughter either. She'll test you, but she'll need you." "Why me Patsy," Faith asked. "Because you needed me. The only other women I know need me are growing up so fast. Promise me you'll ask when you need something? I'm gonna be here for you and your daughter, and for my daughters. Let them know I love them," Patsy said. Faith nodded. "If you need me, ask me," Faith asked.

Jamie sat at the door in the darkness watching Faith talking to someone he couldn't even see. He listened and realized she was sitting on that circle. The circle he was almost scared to stand on himself. When he heard her say Patsy, it hit him. He'd heard rumors about the Opry being haunted. If Patsy Cline was really talking to Faith, he wasn't about to interrupt her.

"If you need me, you say it. Jamie knows we're talking Faith. I know he does. I sent him to you when you were in danger. I helped you and told him where to come find you. Faith, give him a chance when he screws up. Let him love you and don't run," Patsy said. "Kick him when he screws up," Faith asked. "Oh I will. You'll know," Patsy replied. "Thank you," Faith said. "Love him Faith. Love him like I love Charlie and my babies. Love him like you'll never see him again." Faith looked over and saw Jamie wiping tears away. Faith walked over to Jamie and kissed him. "Home," Jamie asked. "I know you're thinking I've gone nuts," Faith said. "Thank you Patsy," Jamie said. Faith looked at him. "I knew there was a reason. I knew there was someone pushing me to you, but I didn't know it was her. Thank you," Jamie said. He slid his hand into Faith's and walked her towards the door. All the lights went out but the one on that circle. Faith knew it would never go out.

Jamie did a New Year's performance unlike any other. After, he took Faith home and they were inseparable. When Valentine's Day hit, Jamie went all out. There were white and sterling roses everywhere, a few gifts laying around and he wined and dined her all night. They had ginger ale instead of wine and he made her an amazing dinner. He turned on an old romance movie and curled up with Faith on the sofa. For the first time in months, Faith didn't have a care in the planet. She was happy in Jamie's arms. It wasn't until the movie was over that Faith started getting more than just a kick pain. "Babe," Jamie said. "I'm gonna lay down on the bed. This baby is determined as hell to keep kicking until it knocks me out," Faith said. Jamie walked her upstairs and turned the movie on. He rubbed her feet. It wasn't until the pains started coming closer that Jamie started worrying. When they got to 10 minutes apart, Jamie called the doctor. "Get her into the hospital asap. I'll meet you there," the doctor said. Jamie carried Faith to the truck and grabbed the bag he'd packed without her knowing. They got there and Faith was whisked into a hospital room. Jamie wasn't leaving her side.

"Your blood pressure is good, but you're dilating. Faith, if we can't stop the contractions..." "No," Faith said. "Baby will be fine. We bumped your due date up remember? Faith, the baby may be smaller than normal, but the baby will be alright. We may need to keep it in the hospital a while..." "Ow," Faith said. Jamie grabbed Faith's hand. They spend an hour trying to stop the contractions and nothing worked. The contractions started coming every 2 minutes. The doctor washed up. "Baby is coming today," the doctor said. "No," Faith said. Jamie didn't know what to do. "You're 6 Faith. You're having the baby today," the doctor said. Jamie sent a text to Emma, Alan, Faith's folks and his and told them they were at the hospital. To call Emma's cell if they needed help with the travel arrangements. 15 minutes later, Emma was right beside Faith.

Three hours later, Faith was pushing when she heard Patsy. "Told ya so," Patsy said. "Ow," Faith said. "Lean on Jamie if you need him. You're gonna be alright Faith," Patsy said. "Couldn't have just got me pain killers," Faith asked. "Not enough time. Faith, one more push," the doctor said. Two more pushes after that and a baby girl was in the doctor's arms. She was small, but was almost perfect. Faith got to hold her once the doctor was through. "She alright," Jamie asked. "We'll keep an eye on her for a day or two, but she looks pretty darn perfect," the doctor said. Jamie kissed Faith. Emma started crying and hugged Faith. When the doctor was going to take the baby to the nursery to do more tests, Faith looked at Jamie. "I'm goin," Jamie said. He kissed Faith and went. The doctor finished her work with Faith then went down and checked the baby over completely. Jamie was at her side. "Well," Jamie asked. "A day or two in here and you can take her home," the doctor said. "You sure," Jamie said. She nodded. "I need to make sure that nothing happens. I'm putting my own security on this. It has nothing to…" "Understood," the doctor said. "Someone's gonna be here 24/7 until we take her home," Jamie said. The doctor agreed. "Can we take her back to Faith's room," he asked. The doctor nodded. She put the bracelet and everything on Jamie and he walked down the hall with his baby girl in his arms.

Jamie walked in and Faith's folks were there and Jamie's. He slid the baby into Faith's arms. "Well," Jamie asked. "Patricia," Faith said. "Patsy," Jamie said. Faith nodded. "Middle name," Jamie asked. "Hope," Faith replied. He kissed her. "Anything else," Jamie asked. Patricia Hope Emily Gilbert," Faith said. He kissed her. He wrote everything down onto the baby forms and handed the forms to the doctor. They re-did the bracelets and made sure everyone had theirs. Patsy fell asleep in Faith's arms. "Jamie," Faith said. He kissed her. "I know," he replied remembering what Patsy had said when he was determined to find Faith.

Patsy had told him where Faith was, just as she'd helped Faith. "That little girl needs you. She's gonna be a handful, but you have to hold on Jamie. I'll show you where she is. Don't ever take it for granted. Don't take either of them for granted," Patsy had said. "That's how I knew. I loved her before I even met her Faith. That's how I know you're gonna be an amazing mom. Don't ever think you won't. This is how convinced I was," Jamie said. He pulled a little box out of the baby bag and handed it to

Faith. He slid Patsy into his arms. The minute Faith saw the sleeper, she started crying. It was pink, soft and had music notes all over it. "Where did you find this," Faith asked. "Opry gift shop," Jamie replied. He brushed Faith's tears away. "It's all washed babe. The blanket goes with it. I found it the day you told me you were pregnant," Jamie said. Faith kissed him. The baby started to fuss and the nurse came in. "Baby is probably hungry. What did you want to do," the nurse asked. "Try," Faith said. Jamie kissed her. Faith tried and fed the baby while Jamie had his arms around her. There was never a doubt that Faith was going to be an amazing mom. She already was. A little while later, her parents came in with Jamie's and Emma came in with Alan. The guys from the band even showed. They all gushed over the baby and Faith's parents were crying. They all got a few pictures and Faith made them promise not to post anything anywhere. Once everyone headed out, Jamie curled up on the bed with Faith and Patsy and he saw Faith yawning. "You need sleep," Jamie said. "I don't wanna miss a second," Faith said. Jamie kissed her. "Daddy munchkin time," Jamie said. Faith nodded. He slid Patsy out of Faith's arms.

Jamie sat down in the chair beside Faith's bed and had some quality time with Patsy. "I know you were kicking up one heck of a fuss in there. Just so you know, I'm daddy. That sleepy lady over there is mama. Now, no more kickin. Mama loves you something crazy and so do I little bug. I'm never letting you get hurt like she did. Nobody is doing that to you ever. Just promise me that you're gonna be daddy's baby girl forever," Jamie said. "She will," Faith replied. "Woman, get sleep before I come over there," Jamie teased. "So as I was saying, I'm gonna take care of you baby girl. Nobody is ever gonna hurt you and get you mad. I'm gonna teach you how to play guitar, how to write music and writing lyrics. You're gonna have everything Patsy. I promise you that," Jamie said. He looked at her little fingers, her little nose. Jamie realized the one thing he'd been missing all that time. He kissed her little nose and looked up to see Faith smirking and taking pictures with her phone. "What," Jamie asked. "Too cute," Faith said. Patsy fell asleep and Jamie slid her into the crib by the bed. He slid onto the bed with Faith and curled up with her. "We made the perfect little girl," Jamie said kissing Faith's neck. "You say that now. Might change when we're without sleep for 3 months," Faith joked. He kissed her. "So, what would you think if Savannah came and helped out with the baby for a while," Jamie asked. "Why," Faith asked. "So you can get sleep. Babe, we might need it. She's not taking your place or mine. She can help when the tour is going," Jamie said. Faith shook her head. "So we can do us too," Jamie said trying to talk her into it. "Jamie," Faith said. "What," he asked. "I'm not letting someone else raise her. Just..." Jamie kissed her. "She's gonna help," Jamie said. Faith shook her head. She nodded off and tried to get some sleep.

Faith woke up an hour or two later and Jamie was asleep in the chair with Patsy on his chest. Faith tried to get up. As she did, the nurse walked in. "We have to change the baby," the nurse said. "Already did," Faith replied. "And," the nurse said. "Swaddled and back in Jamie's arms. She's fine," Faith said. "We still have to do a little checkup. For the next day or so, we're gonna be checking her out every few hours. Just need to make sure she doesn't have any preemie issues. I'll get the bigger bed put together for you." Faith nodded and tried to relax. Her phone buzzed an hour or two later. Patrick was at the desk and wanted to come in. There was someone there with him. Faith agreed and she heard steps down the hallway. Patrick came in with Jason. Patsy woke up. Faith slid her out of Jamie's arms. Patsy started to fuss and Jason volunteered to take over. "Have a little experience in this," Jason said. He rocked Faith and sang to her until she fell back asleep. Faith had a grin ear to ear. She took video of it and Faith realized what she should've known. "So what's the visit for," Faith asked. "Thought Jason could tell him, but he's..." "I'm awake. That baby girl is so tiring. What's up," Jamie asked. "Combo headlining tour. You and me," Jason said. "What," Jamie asked. "You heard me. Think you can handle that," Jason asked. "That mean that Faith and Patsy here are invited too," Jamie asked. "Definitely," Jason said. "Then is hell yeah alright," Jamie said. Faith had a smirk ear to ear. He slid Patsy back into Faith's arms. "Congrats babes," Jason said kissing Faith's cheek. "She is just dang adorable. I remember when my girls were that little. Wow," Jason said. "So when is the tour starting," Faith asked. "April. Sound good," Jason asked. Faith nodded. "As in beginning of April," Faith asked. Jason nodded. "Sounds perfect," Faith said. Jason hugged her and kissed Patsy's cheek. Jamie and Jason had a quick hug and Jason headed out with Patrick. Faith looked over and there was an envelope for her on the side table. She opened it up and saw a new contract. She read through it while Patsy slept in her lap. Patrick bumped her pay, added more security measures and put a contract in for her pay from the tour with Jamie. She almost laughed. "What," Jamie asked. "Nothin," Faith replied.

A day or so later, Jamie took Faith and Patsy back to the house. The guys finished the baby room and Emma was there with Alan waiting for Faith. They came in and Emma ran right over to Faith. Faith hugged her and put Patsy's car seat on the coffee table. She slid her coat off and slid Patsy into her arms. "Is it possible that she got cuter in two days," Emma asked. "She's gonna be spoiled something crazy," Jamie said. "So what's the big news," Alan asked. "Touring with Jason," Jamie said. "Jason as in Faith's second favorite singer in the planet," Alan asked. Jamie nodded. "That's big. That's more than big," Alan said. Faith nodded. "Beginning of April," Faith said. "That means you're barely home before the tour starts," Emma said. "Long enough that we can get her onto a little schedule. It'll be fine," Jamie said. Faith rocked Patsy in her arms and Patsy started crying. Faith walked upstairs and tried to calm the baby. She decided to cry anyway. Faith sat down in the glider chair and tried to feed her. Seconds later, Patsy was quiet and snuggling Faith. Jamie came upstairs and was leaning on the door jam. "Guess she's hungry," Jamie said. "Shh," Faith said. Watching her with that baby put a smile across his face he wasn't sure he ever wanted to lose. Once Patsy fell asleep, Faith burped her and changed her and slid Patsy into her crib. Jamie wrapped his arms around Faith while Patsy was drifting off. "You are supermom. You know that," Jamie whispered. "She's just so cute when she's sleeping," Jamie said. "Let her sleep then," Faith teased. Faith turned on the nightlight and the mobile and grabbed the baby monitor. They went downstairs and tried to have some grown up time with Emma and Alan.

"So what's gonna happen when Jamie goes back out," Emma asked. "We'll figure it out then," Faith said. "We're getting some help with taking care of her when we're on the road. Found someone," Jamie said. The look on Faith's face said she wasn't hearing of it. Not fighting over it was gonna be the hard part. "So, we're having a little baby shower for you," Emma said. "Emma, please tell me you didn't start…" "We had to. Even your buddies from home are coming. Faith, you'll have fun. We can show her off," Emma said. "Not now," Faith said. "What if we just had something just family here," Emma asked. Faith nodded. Just keep it quiet. No pictures nothing," Faith said. Jamie kissed Faith's cheek. "She's just protective of Patsy. That's all," Jamie said. "I'm sorry, but we can't even trust the press to leave us alone. They'll be all over us for pictures," Faith said. "That photographer that you loved from those pictures we took when we first got pregnant said he'd do the pictures if you wanted," Jamie said. Faith shook her head. "Just what he'd need. More pictures," Faith said. She got up and went upstairs and looked in on Patsy. She was still out cold, but Faith couldn't help it. Faith went through her emails, watching Patsy. Faith got half way through the 400 emails then saw one that just disappeared from her email. She went to try to find it then remembered about the filter Jamie had got one of the guys to put on her email. Just below the one that went missing, Faith saw one from a woman that she'd never heard of.

Faith read through it and started getting really mad. "What you doin in here," Jamie whispered. Faith handed him the laptop, and pushed him out the door. Jamie saw the email and knew the email address. He read it and put the laptop in the bedroom. He went into the office downstairs and made a call. "Long time no talk handsome," Kathleen said. "Now you're emailing my wife," Jamie asked. "You haven't even been here to see him," Kathleen said. "He isn't mine. Woman, leave Faith alone," Jamie said. "Then I'll bring him to you," Kathleen said hanging up. Jamie went downstairs. "What," Alan asked. "Just make sure Faith stays upstairs and out of ear range," Jamie said. "Why," Alan asked. "Just…" "Last time I saw you panic like this…" "Please," Jamie said. Alan walked outside with Jamie. "Why is she coming here? She have a death wish or what," Alan asked. "It's a boy. I don't know what to freaking do alright? Faith will walk out," Jamie said. "What do you need me to do," Alan asked. "Just make sure she doesn't hear any of it," Jamie asked. "Hear what," Faith asked. "Nothin. How's Patsy," Jamie asked. Faith shook her head and walked upstairs. Jamie went back inside and Faith had already gone upstairs. Emma stopped Jamie. "What," he asked. "Whatever you just did, don't go up there. Trust that," Emma said.

Faith put the baby monitor on the side of the tub and slid into a bath. Jamie walked in a little while later. "What," Faith said. "Babe," Jamie said. "Leave me alone Jamie. Just go." "I'm sorry," Jamie said. "I'm sure there's a laundry list of things to be sorry about," Faith replied. Just as Faith was leaning her head back, Patsy woke up. Faith slid out of the tub and Jamie tried to hand her a towel. She grabbed another one, wrapped herself in it and slid on her robe. Faith walked into Patsy's room and saw Patsy. Faith got her up and slid her into her arms. "Now what are you getting all fussy about," Faith asked. She checked to make sure she didn't need a diaper change then opted to curl up with her on the floor. Patsy giggled and yawned. "Are you hungry," Faith asked. Patsy started squealing. Faith fed her and rocked her in the glider. "You know, someday we're gonna rock on that porch swing. You're gonna love that. You're just happy eating whenever you want aren't you," Faith said. Jamie sat down against the wall just outside the bedroom listening to Faith. "What are we gonna do baby? Are we gonna just glide and eat or are we going on a car ride," Faith asked. Jamie went downstairs just as Kathleen was pulling in the driveway.

He pulled his leather jacket on and walked outside. "What are you doing here," Jamie asked. "Introducing you to Jack," Kathleen said. When he looked at her baby, he had Jamie's nose and looked like him. "You can't just show up here. We just brought our baby home Kathleen. You can't just show up," Jamie said. "You know as well as I do that he's your son," Kathleen said. "You can't do that here Kathleen. Not here," Jamie said. "Why? Never told her? I sent you that pregnancy test Jamie. You can screw with those results all you want. He's yours," Kathleen said. "Fine, but I'm not doing anything until the doctor does that test. Kathleen, I just brought Faith and the baby home. Don't do this. Not today," Jamie asked. "You can't just pretend that this didn't happen," Kathleen said. "And I can't pretend that this isn't gonna kill Faith. I need to take care of my wife. That means you leaving her out of this altogether." Only thing Jamie didn't count on was Faith sitting outside on the porch swing when he was saying it.

It was only when Jamie heard the back door close that he realized that Faith had heard every word. He finally got Kathleen to leave and came inside. Alan was sitting on the steps when he came in. "What's up," Jamie asked. He looked beside Alan and saw a suitcase. "Where you off to," Jamie asked. He shook his head and handed it to Jamie. "What's this for," Jamie asked. "You fixed the results? Jamie, you knew that Faith staying with you was teetering on those results. You lied to her dude." "Where's Faith," Jamie asked. "Locked in Patsy's room. Emma's with her. Trust me. You don't want to be face to face with her right now," Alan said. Jamie walked past him and went upstairs. He went into Patsy's room and she wasn't in her crib. He went to walk into the bedroom and heard her giggling and babbling. He tried to open the door and it was locked. "Open the door Faith," Jamie said. He heard zippers. "Faith."

Faith sat and cried on the bathroom floor. She knew it was all too good to be true. Everything had been. Not 10 minutes later, Jamie unlocked the door and came in to see Faith's bags packed. "Where are you two going," Jamie asked. "Go ask your girlfriend," Faith said. She took Patsy and put her in the car seat and walked downstairs. "Faith," Jamie said. Emma put Patsy in the truck and Faith threw her things in the back. "Where are you going," Jamie asked. Faith shook her head and got in the truck. "Faith, you can't just leave. What about Patsy," Jamie asked. Faith pulled out of the driveway and took off. "So they guaranteed not to say a word to anyone," Emma asked. Faith nodded. "That way we're near the Opry. We have everything right there," Faith said. She deposited the cheque the label had given her into her account and headed over to the hotel.

"Faith, just tell me what happened," Emma said. Faith set up the crib for Patsy and gently slid her in without waking her up. "Faith," Emma said. "It's his kid Emma. That Kathleen chick had his kid. That's what," Faith said. "What are you talking about Faith? That's insane. The test results came back negative." "And when she showed with his son who was the damn spitting image of him, he tried to deny it. Emma, the kid looked exactly like him from when he was a little kid. He can't deny that. I'm not gonna sit there while he lies through his teeth about it. All he had to do was tell the truth Emma. He didn't." "You know he called your cell 10 times since we left," Emma said. "Turn the cell off," Faith said. Faith took the phone and turned the GPS off and then turned the cell phone off. "Faith, he is gonna go nuts if he can't get in contact. He's gonna assume…" Faith almost tossed the phone altogether. "Tell me what you need me to do then," Emma said. Faith hugged her. "Just help me with Emma so I can get some sleep."

Faith had a hot bath then slid on a sweater and her leggings. She slid into the bed and fell asleep. Alan called Emma's cell a half hour later. "Hey handsome," Emma said. "Where you two disappear to," he asked. "She's losing it," Emma said. "So is Jamie. I get why Faith's lost it though. She causes shit every time she comes near him Emm. Please just get her to come home," Alan said. "She's not going to. She was looking at freakin real estate Alan. She's not gonna let him…" "We have to find a way baby. Help me figure something out," Alan asked. "As long as it doesn't involve me being in the line of fire and losing my best friend then fine. She's way past being upset Alan. She's so upset she won't even talk," Emma said. "The awards are next week. We need to figure something out," Alan said. "We can't just…" "Take her down to that store Jamie took her to when he got her the dress. I'll get it arranged and we'll get them there together. She has to be at the awards with him or the press will eat them both for dinner," Alan said. "She's gonna lose it," Emma said. "We'll figure it out Emm. I promise. Are you alright?" "Sitting here with Patsy. She's beautiful," Emma replied. "What happens if your plan doesn't work," Emma asked. "Then we're going with him in her place."

Faith was only up once or twice during the night and her and Emma managed to actually get sleep. When Faith woke up around 9am, she saw her cell phone turned on. There was 50 missed calls and 20 voicemails that were all from Jamie. Faith heard one after another of his begging and pleading. Telling her that it wasn't true. Making excuse after excuse about what was going on. Faith erased them and turned her phone off. "What's going on," Emma asked as she woke up. "Nothing," Faith said. She saw Patsy and she was starting to fuss. Faith got up and went and got her and fed her. "Just so damn cute," Faith said. "What did you decide to do," Emma asked. "Be a mom. I need to concentrate on her Emma. That's the only thing I can handle right now," Faith said. She finished feeding Patsy and went and had a shower with the baby in her arms. Faith slid out and got Patsy dressed and bundled her in the blanket and Faith and Emma took her out for a while. "You can't hide from him you know," Emma said. Faith nodded. "Faith," Emma said. "I'm not going anywhere that the press will be all over us. I just need time to breathe and think. That's it," Faith said. She relaxed for the day with Emma without one camera flash, reporter or ounce of stress. They relaxed and had lunch at the Loveless Café, went for a walk through Belle Meade then headed back to the hotel. They walked into the room and sterling and white roses were sitting on the bedside table.

Faith fed Patsy again then changed her and put her down for a nap. "Well," Emma asked. "You can go back to the house if that's what you want Emm. I just can't do it. Every time I think there are no more secrets, one more pops up. I gave him a chance Emm. He lied. I'm not gonna just ignore that." "You still need to talk to him. He is her dad," Emma said. "And he had a baby with her. I'm done Emma. Done." Faith went and started going through emails and Emma hugged her. "Do you need me to stay," Emma asked. "If that's what you wanna do," Faith replied. "You can't just put yourself into seclusion. He loves you Faith. Whatever that woman did, you need to accept his apology. Just talk to him," Emma said. Faith shook her head and called for room service. "Faith," Emma said. "Go and spend some time with Alan. I'm not going back there," Faith said. "You need to..." "If you want to go then go," Faith said.

Emma made her way back to the house just to get Faith more clothes and saw Jamie camped out at the door. "I thought you were with Faith," Jamie said. "I told her I'd grab more diapers and that kinda stuff," Emma said. "Where is she," Jamie asked. "Jamie, she's pissed. She's way past mad. She won't even talk. Jamie, way couldn't you have just told Faith the truth," Emma asked. "Please just help me get her back here," Jamie asked. "Why? So you can lie again? Jamie, you two were fine. She would've accepted it. Instead, you had to lie. She could've handled it then Jamie. Now? You two just had a baby and she's so mad she won't come back even if she needed something. She's pissed Jamie. She's not letting this go." "Just tell me what I need to do Emma. Say it. Anything," Jamie said. "Tell her the truth. Tell her why you were really that scared to tell her. You can't just expect her to be in your arms. She was looking at houses Jamie." "Where is she staying," Jamie asked. Emma shook her head. "She's at the Opryland isn't she," Jamie asked. Before Emma could say anything, Jamie grabbed the bag she was supposed to bring back and pulled out of the drive in his truck. He drove straight to the hotel and found a way to find out Emma's room number. "We can't give out the room number," the concierge said. "The paparazzi is gonna be all over her. I need to make sure she's safe," Jamie said. The concierge thought it through and gave Jamie the info.

Jamie went upstairs and saw the door to the suite. It was the same one they'd stayed at before. Jamie knocked. Faith didn't answer. After knocking again, he heard steps. She opened the door with the chain still on it. "Faith," Jamie said. "Come home," he asked. Faith went to close the door and Jamie wouldn't let her. "She's my daughter too. Faith, open the door so we can at least talk," Jamie said. Faith shook her head and locked the door. "I get you're mad. Faith, one minute she told me it was mine, the next she said she lost the baby. What was I supposed to say? I didn't know who that baby was until I saw him." "Then go talk to her. Go find a way to be with your son and leave us alone," Faith said. Jamie couldn't move. "I need you two Faith. I can't do this without you. Please just open the door," Jamie said. Faith couldn't do it. "I love you Faith. Please open the door. We can talk and figure out what to do," Jamie said. "I know what to do Jamie. You leave. I'm staying," Faith said. He heard Patsy waking up. "Faith," Jamie said. "Leave," Faith said. Faith fed Patsy. "Faith please open the door. She's my daughter too," Jamie said. Faith fed Patsy and barely acknowledged Jamie in the hall. Faith snuggled with Patsy. She cleaned Patsy up and got her changed. Patsy was playing with a stuffed teddy in her bassinet and Jamie tried again. "Babe, please. Just give me a chance," Jamie said. "You already had one. Leave Jamie. Now," Faith said. "No. Open it or I get someone to open it," Jamie said. "Leave me alone," Faith replied. "No. Open the door," Jamie said. She unlocked it and he walked in. He saw Patsy falling asleep in her bassinet and Faith was sitting on the floor in tears. "I didn't..." "Leave me alone Jamie. I mean it. Just go home and I'll take care of her myself," Faith said. "You don't get to do that. She's my baby too. I need you

Faith. Please," Jamie said. Faith shook her head. "Go deal with her. Just leave me alone," Faith said. "You're my wife Faith. Come home."

Chapter 22

Faith spent hours trying to get Jamie to leave. She was exhausted from fighting and was past tired from taking care of Patsy. "Jamie, just go so I can get some sleep while she's sleeping. Go," Faith said. He kissed her. "Stop pushing me away," Jamie said. "Then leave me and Patsy alone. Go and deal with her and your son and leave us alone." "I'm not going home without you. It isn't even home without you," Jamie said. "Go," Faith said. He kissed her again. "You're my wife Faith. I married you not her. I love you. Stop telling me to leave. If you're here then I'm not leaving." Faith shook her head. "Stop getting mad at me Faith. I didn't know. I was as happy as you were when we found out it wasn't. Come home," Jamie begged. "Leave," Faith said trying to push him away. "Stop Faith. Stop pushing me away. Stop blaming me…" "So what? She magically got pregnant? Super sperm that travel through the phone," Faith asked. "Faith," Jamie said. "Just go." "No. Come home. You wanna sleep in another room, fine. You don't want me in the bed with you, fine. You're not staying here. There's a storm coming tomorrow. Just come…" "Get out." He walked over and packed up Patsy's things and Faith's bag. "Jamie," Faith said. He put Patsy into her car seat very gently and grabbed Faith's hand. He walked her out to the truck and put Patsy into the back seat. Faith looked and her truck wasn't there. "Emma took it to the house when she went to talk to Alan." Jamie checked out of her room for her and they went back to the house. Faith still wouldn't get out of the truck and she wasn't letting Jamie take Patsy in either.

Jamie took the bags into the house along with the keys. He walked back out and Faith wouldn't even let him open the door. Finally a half hour later, he got the door open and flipped Faith over his shoulder. He grabbed Patsy's car seat and walked into the house even with Faith fighting him. "Put me down," Faith said. He walked upstairs to their bedroom and put her on the bed, locking the door. "Jamie," Faith said. "You start again, I'm padlocking it. Just stop. I get you're disappointed and I get you're mad. There's nothing I can…" "Yeah there was. Try not screwing around Jamie. Try staying faithful to someone you claimed to

love. Don't give me that bull about loving me either. You cheated
Jamie." Faith unlocked the bedroom door, grabbed Patsy and went into
the nursery. "You can't leave," Jamie said. "Watch me," Faith replied.
She packed Patsy's things, packed the last of the diapers and wipes and
went and started packing the last of her things. "Faith," Jamie said.
"Either you get out of my way or you are gonna be in the hospital," Faith
said. She got her things and Patsy's and went back downstairs. She
grabbed her keys, got Patsy settled and loaded up and pulled out. Faith
left and drove off. She ended up driving towards Dallas. Emma tried to
call then Jamie. Alan then Callon. Faith ignored them all. 10 hours later,
she pulled into the hotel in Dallas. It was away from everyone and
everything. Faith looked outside and saw ranch land. That's what she
needed. Nothing but.

Housekeeping came over to Faith's cabin to make sure she had
everything she needed. "Thank you," Faith said. "She sleeping alright?
We can get some lavender bubble bath if you need it," housekeeping
said. "She's pretty good. She's sleeping a little more every day she's
home. It's fine," Faith said. "Aren't you..." Faith nodded. "Why are you
here?" "Trying to keep it quiet. Please," Faith said. The housekeeper
nodded and left. Not 20 minutes later, the manager was at her door.

"Can I help you," Faith asked. "We wanted to make sure you had
everything you needed. I made sure that security had been kept up to
date. If there's anything you need," the manager said. "Privacy. That's
all. She's not up to sleeping through the night yet. Quiet and privacy,"
Faith said. "That's understandable. Is there anything you might need
while you're here," he asked. "Nothing I can't handle. I just need to be
left alone. I need time to think," Faith said. "Then I'll have dinner sent
down for you. If you want adult company for coffee, just let me know."
Faith nodded. He handed Faith his business card. "I'm here if you need
anything," the man said. "Well, thank you Craig. I appreciate it. I'll let
you know if I need anything. I have to go take care of my daughter,"
Faith said. Craig nodded. He was caught up in those blue eyes. He'd
almost forgot his name. "You alright," Faith asked. "I'm sorry. I'll make
sure the staff keeps things under wraps. If you need me, just call," he
said as he excused himself and slid out.

Faith spent the rest of the day trying to sleep and taking care of Patsy. "You sure you're alright," Patsy's voice asked. "I love him but all that trust just flew out the window. How am I supposed to just trust him again," Faith asked. "If you believe in him, if you love him despite the other things that have gone on, say it. If you love him, do the right thing. Accept him whether he's perfect or not," Patsy said. "He cheated," Faith said. "Do you love him even if he does have another baby?" "The fact that he cheated and lied through his teeth even when he had the chance to come clean? Not like I did." Faith had a bath while Patsy slept. Faith kept her phone on silent and saw 140 missed calls and 20 voicemails, all from Jamie and Emma. She blocked out her cell number and called Emma back.

"Faith," Emma asked. "Can't just leave me alone," Faith asked. "He's going ape shit. Talk to him before he goes postal," Emma asked. "No. He screwed around on me and had a baby with someone else Emma. That right there would be grounds for divorce," Faith replied. "You aren't thinking that. Faith, tell me you aren't…" "Emma, you wanna report back to him? Tell him I'm not coming back," Faith replied and hung up. She turned her phone off and blacked out the GPS on her computer. She checked emails and saw 25 emails off the top from Jamie. She brushed past them and went through the requests from reporters. There was more than one asking for baby pictures of Patsy and Faith with Jamie. Faith went past them. She updated an article or two and some info about the baby then logged out before anyone else noticed.

A few hours left, Faith had just put Patsy down and there was a knock at her door. Faith answered and saw Craig there with Chinese food for Faith. "What's the special treatment for," Faith asked. "Looked like you needed a friend. Being a new mom is a hard thing Faith. If I can help by bringing dinner then I did my good thing for the day," Craig said. They sat down on the sofa and talked and had dinner. "I asked housekeeping to only come when necessary. They're all under confidentiality agreements anyway. You're safe here. We caught a few people nosing around up front. They're gone now," Craig said. "Well, thanks," Faith replied. "Whatever drove you to come out here must have been tough Faith. Must have been something huge. I know you don't want to talk about it.

Just know that if you need a distraction or a cheesy movie, I'm your guy," he joked. "Well, thank you. Honestly, I just needed time with my baby girl. I've been running on empty on the tour with Jamie. When he finally finished, we were still running around. He did the CD release then the promotions. I didn't have time to just relax. When we had her, I knew things were gonna slow down, but they got huge. I didn't know what else to do. I just knew that I couldn't even think straight without some quiet. It's crazy," Faith said. "I'm just glad you considered our resort peace and quiet. We're so far out from everything. Why wouldn't you want to stay downtown," he asked. "More eyes on me. I wanted to disappear into the sunset for a while," Faith said. "I don't wanna pry into whatever it was," Craig said. "It's just stress. A very long story I can't stay awake for," Faith said. "I understand. I was gonna ask. What would you think about going for a ride tomorrow," Craig asked. "I can't really leave the baby here alone," Faith said. "Lunch at the stables then. You can introduce her to the horses," Craig asked. "I'll see how she's doing tomorrow. Craig nodded. "Do me one favor," Craig asked. "What's that? Autograph?" "Don't worry. You're too beautiful to worry." "Thank you," Faith said. Craig kissed her hand and headed out.

Faith went and fed Patsy again then headed to bed herself. Her cell rang one last time and Faith looked over. "Deacon," Faith said. "So where you at," Deacon asked. "Neverland," Faith joked. "Was worried about you. Your man is running around being a royal pain in the ass of everyone. I asked what was wrong. He practically snarled and snapped my head off." "Deacon, leave him be. I'm not home. I went to visit a friend. That's it," Faith said. "I'm heading out to Dallas for a guest spot on a show. If you're around that area…" "Deacon." "I'm just sayin. I never got to see baby…" "Deacon, don't push the button. You will combust," Faith replied. "Fine. If you can get out there, come out and have dinner." "With a baby. Not about to happen." Faith chatted a minute or two more and got off the phone and tried to get to sleep. She was about to close her eyes and heard something at the door. A note was sitting just inside the door:

So, since you don't have a phone, what do you say we go look for one tomorrow? – Craig

Faith went to open the door and he was sitting on the front step. "I do have a phone. I just don't have it on. It's for work and I need a break from it," Faith said. "Then we go hunting for a personal one tomorrow. Faith, truly, I have nothing planned. I'd love to be able to spend a little more time with you." Faith nodded. "Have to make it 10am though. Her nap is at 11," Faith said. Craig nodded. "If I do something right now promise you won't get mad," Craig asked. "Depends on…" Craig kissed her. He leaned her against the front wall of the cabin. Faith broke the kiss and went back inside. She locked the door, washed her face and went to bed.

Faith woke up a few hours later and fed Patsy and changed her then went back to sleep with Patsy right beside her. Faith woke up around 7am and Patsy was squealing and giggling and laughing. Faith changed her and got her cleaned up and changed. She got dressed, got Patsy into her car seat, grabbed herself breakfast and did her hair and makeup and went to leave when she saw Craig on her front step. "Really," Faith asked. "I'm sorry," Craig said. Faith walked past him and went to her truck. "Faith, please," Craig said. "I'm fine going on my own," Faith said. "Please," he asked. "Craig, I'm married. If anyone sees…" He kissed her again. He opened the passenger door for Faith. She got in and hopped into the driver's seat and they headed off to the store to look at cell phones. He handed her the iPhone, then a fancy android. Faith found the one she liked, activated it under her maiden name and made sure it was a completely private number. She headed out of the store and linked the phone into her truck. "Lunch," Craig asked. Faith shook her head. "Craig I get you want…" He kissed her behind the tinted windows of the truck. "Quick lunch," he said. "As long as she sleeps through," Faith replied. "I promise I keep my lips to myself," Craig said.

Faith had lunch with Craig, got some groceries and they went to head back. Craig stopped half way back. "What," Faith asked. He kissed her. Faith pushed him away. They got to the cabin and Faith got Patsy out and grabbed everything. Craig hopped out and Faith grabbed her keys back. "Faith," Craig said. She slammed the door in his face and locked it. Faith put Patsy into her crib and she was asleep seconds later. Faith put the groceries away and figured out what to do for dinner. She went and checked her Nashville phone and Jamie had left a ton more messages. Faith listened to them go from calm to completely irrational. As she was listening to the last message, Jamie called again. "What," Faith said. "Where are you," Jamie asked. "Somewhere with peace and quiet just like I wanted. That's where Jamie. How's your son," Faith asked. "Faith," Jamie said. "Don't alright. Just don't. I have a baby to take care of Jamie. I don't have time to babysit your and keep your dick in your damn pants. That isn't my damn job," Faith said. "Stop being a pain and get your ass back here. Faith, two interviews and they want baby pictures with us and Patsy," Jamie said. "Then introduce them to your son." Faith hung up and went and grabbed herself a big glass of chocolate milk. Her phone buzzed again 20 minutes later. "What," Faith asked. "Come home. Faith, I can't sleep. I can't even concentrate. I need to know where you are." "So you can come hunt me down? Forget it," Faith said. She hung up.

A half hour later, Faith got a call from the Virginia state troopers. She didn't even want to know. "Hello," Faith said. "Mrs. Gilbert, we wanted to let you know. The man by the name of Evan that you have issue with was released from custody. He was supposed to be transferred to another maximum security facility and he escaped. We wanted to ensure that you had security around you and were protected. We were notified of what happened previously." "I understand that. I'm fine. I'm safe and away from anywhere he would even think of. If anything happens, I will let you know. Thank you," Faith said. She hung up and started wondering what to do. She made dinner and tried to unwind. The things kept running through her head about him coming after her. Faith sat down on the sofa and had dinner and a half hour later, Craig was at her door. "What," Faith asked. "I'm doubling security. I wanted to let you know," Craig said. "Might want to triple it. My psycho ex just slid out of federal custody," Faith said. "Then you should move into the main building. Faith, at least come and bring the baby and stay with me. I have artillery training. Please," Craig said. "What exactly are you doing back here anyway," Faith asked. "I came to apologise. Faith, you need somewhere safe to be with your daughter. Please," Craig said. "I'm leaving then." "Just because I kissed you? You're gonna put your safety..." "Been taking care of myself for a long time," Faith said. "Can't just let me help can you," Craig asked. Faith went and started to pack. "Instead of moving closer to security you run? He could run you off the road. Faith, just come stay…" "No." "At my ranch. It's an hour away and far enough from the rest of the planet that you're hard to find. You can have my room. You can stay with Patsy in there. I have triple security. Faith, please," Craig asked. Faith shook her head. "I'm not doing it Craig. I'm handling this the right way," Faith said. "Which is what? Getting both of you killed," Craig asked. Faith packed up the truck and took Patsy to the truck and got her settled. She put the portable crib in the back and locked up. "You can't just disappear," Craig said. Faith handed him the keys. "Fine. Go. Hotel's covered."

Three hours later, Faith pulled up to a gated neighborhood that had triple security. It was somewhere safe. The area was guarded which ended up being perfect. Faith got Patsy settled and finished unpacking. As soon as she was about to sit down, Jamie called her cell again. "What," Faith asked. "He's out Faith. Just come home before you end up getting hurt. Please," Jamie said. "I told you. I can take care of myself. Jamie, just stop trying to make me come back there. You have this plus your son to handle. Worry about that," Faith said. "I need my wife Faith. Come home," he begged. "No," Faith replied. "Fine. The kid is mine. I screwed up and when we were apart I ended up with her. Faith, please," Jamie said. She hung up and activated the blocking on his number. Faith settled in and ensured the security guards and the security system was active. She told the security gate about her ex hunting her. They posted guards at the cabin. Faith settled in and tried to relax for a while. A half hour later, Craig was calling her cell. "What," Faith asked. "You're in danger Faith. You know what he did last time. I'm scared Faith. You and the baby. You need to be home. Please," Jamie said. "Unless you're gone, no," Faith said. "Please," Jamie said. "What phone are you calling me from," Faith asked. "Faith, please." She shook her head and hung up.

Faith finally calmed down after a long bath. She got Patsy dried off and diapered, got her dressed into her pajamas and rocked her. Patsy ended up having one of those nights. She was crying on and off and was past fussy. Around midnight, she finally went to sleep. Patsy was wide awake again at 4am. Faith rocked her and finally got her back to sleep then went back to sleep herself. Around 10am, after two more feedings and changes, Faith got up and tried to have breakfast. Faith's doctor called her. "You're do for miss Patsy's checkup and her baby shots. When can you pop in," the doctor asked. "A week or two. If not, you can always come here. I'm just outside of Dallas for a while," Faith said. "Just let me know when," the doctor said. "Jamie say um, Evan say yes." "Yes that would be fine." "I'll call the police. Just keep him there. Don't say a word." Faith called the police on the other phone and told them where to find her. Faith kept the doctor on the line as long as she could until she could hear sirens in the background. The doctor hung up and Jamie tried calling Faith again. "What," Faith asked. "He took your doctor as a damn hostage," Jamie said. "I'm the one that sent the police Jamie. Me not being there is a better move than anything else. I'm not even in the state Jamie. I have to go. Patsy needs me," Faith said hanging up. She went in and checked on Patsy and she was sleeping peacefully. Faith turned on the monitor and slid into bed. Three or four hours later, Patsy was awake and Faith was feeding her and trying to rock her back to sleep. "What am I gonna do with such a beautiful baby girl? I know you don't understand any of this, but mama's doing what's right baby. Being there right now isn't a good move. Especially not when he's there. Daddy doesn't get it. Being far away from it is the only solution Patsy. The only one that will keep you and me safe." Patsy fell fast asleep. Faith made sure she was dry and slid her back into the crib. She was out cold again seconds later and Faith went and tried to get some more sleep.

Two hours later, Faith heard a commotion outside. She looked out the front and saw police officers outside her cabin. Faith heard her cell buzz and answered. "Hello," Faith said. "Faith, I mean it. Where are you," Jamie asked. "It doesn't..." "Yeah it does Faith. He busted into the other house. The one we had in the gated area. He got in there. If he can do that, he's gonna come after you. Please," Jamie said. "No," Faith replied. She hung up and tried to get sleep. Just as Faith was nodding off, Patsy was awake. Faith curled up with the baby on her bed and Jamie called again. "What," Faith asked. "At least tell me what state you're in." "The US." Faith hung up. Two hours later, there was a knock at her door. Faith slid Patsy back into her crib and answered. "Craig," Faith said. "I needed to know you were alright," he said. "How did you even..." "My cousin is one of the guards. I heard about what was happening back in Nashville. I needed to know that nobody tried to hurt you." "You can't…" Craig kissed her and walked her backwards towards her sofa, kicking the door shut. "We can't do this," Faith said. "You aren't staying here alone. You need someone with you Faith. Just let me do it," Craig said. "I'm married Craig. You can't just show up and…" He kissed her again and picked her up. He wrapped her legs around his waist and pinned her to the sofa. "Craig, let go," Faith said. "Why," Craig asked as he kissed her neck. "Craig, let go," Faith said as she flipped him onto the floor. She got up and opened the front door. "Faith," he said. "You can leave," Faith replied. Craig left but barely made it through the door before he tried to say something. Faith locked the door. An hour later, her phone was buzzing while she was playing with Patsy.

"Hello," Faith said. "Faith, it's Jason. Needed to talk to you. Do you have a few minutes," he asked. "Yes. Can you meet me in town in a half hour," he asked. "I'm sorta not…" "Gaido's. Right on the water," Jason said. "How did you know where…" "Yes," Jason asked. "We'll be there in a half hour." Faith went and got dressed and did her hair and makeup then got Patsy dressed and headed over to the restaurant to meet him. Faith headed in and the place was quiet. "Well hello there beautiful," Jason said. Faith gave him a hug and he saw Patsy out cold in the car seat. "That's always how I got the girls to sleep when they were fussy. She's just so dang cute." "So what's up Jason? I know you didn't ask me to come here so you could see Patsy," Faith said. "That guy that gave you a hard time is all over Jamie. He's made threats and tried to come after him to get to you. Believe it or not, staying here is probably the smart move right now. I'm not gonna report back to him. I just needed to know that you were safe. Jamie's scared Faith. He asked for my help. I'm not like that. You're this scared of that guy, you're better off not saying anything to Jamie." "I'm not trying to hide Jason. I'm trying to take care of me. I don't know what to do anymore. That woman I saw had his son Jason. He lied to my damn face," Faith said. "Everything will be alright. I promise you. I'll get whatever info you needed. Just keep me in the loop. Don't make me worry too," Jason teased. "So how are your girls," Faith asked. "Not bad. I wish I had more time with them. I really do. But this little cutie will suffice. I'm just anxious about getting back on the road. We're doing a few shows before the tour to try out some new material. I really wish you could be there," he said. "Until…" "I know. What if I could find a way for you to be back without anyone knowing," Jason asked. "Still rather be in another area of the country," Faith replied. "We'll figure it out. I'll give you a shout in the morning. Just make sure you're all packed." Faith gave him a hug. They finished lunch and Faith headed back to the cabin.

Faith got back and put Patsy back down for a nap then went and started putting her things together. Faith figured out what to make for dinner and between naps, she managed to finish packing almost everything. Around 6, she got a call from Jason. "What's up," Faith said. "You packed up?" "What's wrong," Faith asked. "The truck is being shipped. It'll be back about the same time we touch ground back in Tennessee. You can stay up at my cabin. At least you'll be in state." "Why are you being so nice about all of this," Faith asked. "Because you need a friend. You got me if you need me." "I meant to ask how things were with your ex," Faith asked. "Single is really good for me right now," Jason said. "You don't have to hand me the keys to…" "I'll come help for a few days. Faith, babies were meant to be a 2 adult project. Trust me. We'll do it together for a while so you can get a descent sleep," Jason said. "I was sleeping," Faith joked. "We'll come up with a better solution. Two heads always were better than one," Jason teased. "Alright, but if I'm putting you out at all…" "Understood. Is midnight alright," Jason asked. "For the flight," Faith asked. "Yeah. That way we're out of prying eyes and stuff. What do you think," Jason asked. "Perfect. Just promise that Jamie…" "Not a word unless you say," Jason said. "See you at midnight then," Faith replied. They hung up and Faith got a weird feeling.

Around 11, Faith got Patsy packed up and got everything loaded into the truck and they headed to the airport. They pulled in and they unloaded everything from the truck into the plane. Patsy slept right through it. They flew straight back to Tennessee, landing at Smyrna instead of Nashville and went up to Jason's cabin. They got unloaded and a half hour later, Faith's truck was dropped off. "Now, let's get her all settled in the nursery," Jason said sliding Patsy effortlessly out of the car seat. He changed her and tucked her into the crib then came out and helped Faith get settled. "What," Jason asked. "You didn't tell him I was here right," Faith asked. "I told him that if I heard from you I'd let him know. I haven't said a word since," Jason said. "I know that I'm gonna be in danger Jason. I just don't want anyone…" He hugged her. "You'll be fine. My 9 is in the lock box here. The code is 225. Security gate at the front is electric. Anyone touches it, they get one hell of a jolt. You're safe. If I'm not here, you're still safe. Nobody is getting in here Faith." She nodded. "You know how damn tempted I am to get your mind off it altogether," Jason said. "With what? Video game battle," Faith asked. "Don't tempt me," Jason said. Faith laughed. "Or what," Faith asked. He gave her a look and stopped himself. He went outside and lit a cigarette. Faith went and drew herself a hot bath and slid in. The tub was perfect. After a while, she slid out and wrapped herself in the oversized towel. She came out and Jason was sitting on the sofa. "What," Faith said. "You walk around in a towel and you're gonna regret it," Jason said. Faith went and slid her leggings and a tank top on. She slid her sweater on and came back out to sit with him.

"So what's really wrong," Faith asked. "Even the same damn shampoo," he said. "What," Faith asked. He walked into the kitchen. "What's wrong," Faith asked. "Faith, I'm not responsible for my actions alright. I love having my girls with me but all of the loneliness is killing me. I can't date without the world being on me like dirt. I can't… " "You can't what?" He kissed her and leaned her against the wall in the kitchen. Faith pushed him away. "I'm sorry," Jason said. "Maybe this was a bad…" "You stay. I'm going for a drive," Jason said. "Stop. I get it Jason. I get what it's like when everything you remembered changes. It's lonely. I get that." "I just miss having a warm body to sleep with. I don't even care about…alright. I do care. I just miss having someone there with me. If being with him makes you feel like crap and you're that mad, why are you staying with him Faith? If he deceived you and hurt you that much, what are you still doing there?" "He got me away from a psychopath. He came and got me out of a situation I couldn't have survived. I've learned Jason. I've learned to lean on him and to trust in him. Now, I just don't know what to do anymore. He cheated and got another woman pregnant. He denied it, then I end up face to face with his son. How am I supposed to react?" "Damn," Jason said. "Exactly. It still hurts." Jason hugged her. "We'll figure all this crap out together. Sound alright," Jason asked. Faith nodded.

Faith took Patsy to the doctor the next morning and she said what Faith already knew. Patsy was perfectly healthy. Faith headed out and managed to get past the paparazzi and they headed back to the cabin. "What," Jason asked. "Thank goodness you didn't go in. The reporters..." "I know. How's baby girl," Jason asked. "Perfect as usual," Faith joked. They grabbed lunch and headed back to the cabin. When they pulled in, there was another truck in the driveway. "Jason," Faith said. "Stay in the truck." He parked around back and walked around front to find out who was there. "What's up," Jason said scaring whoever it was. "Looking for Faith Gilbert. Seen her around," the man asked. "Nope. My kids are here bud. Off the property," Jason said. "I know she's here," the man said. Jason pulled out his gun. "Leave or you leave in a bag," Jason said. "Either she comes out here or you're never gonna sing again," the man said. Faith peeked out and saw that beat up old pick-up truck that she'd seen before. She texted Jason that it was Evan. "Leave her alone. Wherever she is, she's safe. She doesn't need you coming after her. Leave her alone and I won't put you in the ICU," Jason said with his gun point blank at the man's head. "Then you're gonna be fighting a battle you're gonna lose," the man said. "Back off and leave her the hell alone. Got me," Jason said. "Go ahead and shoot. You won't do it anyway," the man said. The gun went off. The man laid on the grass. Jason called the police and told them what happened. Jason came inside and minutes later, an ambulance showed with the police officers. They talked to Jason then talked to Faith. "Do you know that man," the officer asked. Faith handed the officer the restraining order. "You're very lucky Mrs. Gilbert. Very. He put your husband in the hospital. If Jason hadn't..." Faith looked at Jason. "I'll take you," he said. Faith got Patsy into the truck and they went straight to the hospital.

"Where the hell have you....what are you doing here with her Jason," Alan asked. "Long story. What happened," Faith asked. "Evan. He shot Jamie and if we hadn't distracted him, Jamie would've been dead," Alan said. Faith went to go in and Kathleen was at Jamie's side. The minute he saw Faith, he almost jumped out of the bed. "Nice to know you survived," Faith replied. She walked back out of the hospital, got Patsy back into the truck and left. Jason took her out to the lake for a while. Faith had Patsy in her arms and Jason's coat was around Faith's shoulders. He wrapped his arm around her. "I'm sorry hun. I'm so sorry," Jason said. "Now what," Faith asked. "Now you relax and try to make sense of what never has made sense," Jason said. "I need to get the rest of my things from the house," Faith said. "And stay where," Jason asked. "I... I can't just go back. I can't just pretend it didn't happen," Faith said. "Then you're staying at my place. I'll bring the crib from the cabin down there. We'll get things organized," Jason said. Faith nodded. They went back up to the cabin and packed up and left.

After a few days, Faith finally managed to not cry over it. She called work and changed the number, requested that someone else handle Jamie's site and promotion and went back in to work. She got paperwork done on the other artists she was to handle and saw a familiar name. "I didn't think Jason was with the label," Faith asked when she talked to Patrick. "He is now. You know you're still on mat leave." Faith nodded. "Something showed for you while you were out. The single that you co-wrote with Jamie went double platinum," Patrick said. He handed Faith the framed award and Faith went to head out. "You alright," Patrick asked. Faith shook her head and left.

Chapter 23

Faith went downstairs and Jason was signing autographs. "And what are you doing way down here," Faith asked. "Someone wanted to see her mama. Ride home," Jason asked. Faith nodded. She left with Jason and the cameras were going off non-stop. "Watch. That will be all over the papers in the morning," Faith said. "So what did Patrick say," Jason asked. "I know what he's thinking. He thinks that when this blows over I'll be back working with him. I can't just forget it. He has a kid with someone else. You don't get over that," Faith said. Jason's hand slid into hers. "What," Faith asked. "We're going out tonight then," he said. "Surrounded by cameras," Faith said. Jason shook his head. The three of us." "I can't let you mess with..." Jason kissed her at the light. "Stop freaking out and breathe. We're going out somewhere nobody is gonna bug you and nobody is gonna take any pictures of anything. Besides. Miss sleepy back there suggested it," he joked. "Oh really," Faith teased. They pulled into Jason's driveway and he took Patsy in and got her settled. Her phone buzzed. The minute she saw the caller id flash Jamie, she pressed ignore. "Which reminds me. Jamie is going nuts. The man half accused me of trying to break you two up," Jason said. Faith shook her head. One look and Jason knew what was on her mind. "Still pissed," Jason asked. "He's in the hospital and she's at his side with their son and I'm supposed to feel bad?" "Faith, if you want to go talk to him you should. If that what makes you feel better. He's out of the hospital now anyway," Jason said. "What would the point be? He can go live with what's her name and their son. I can't just pretend he didn't do it." "The exact reason why we're going out tonight," Jason said giving her a hug. Faith went upstairs and slid into her jeans then saw a package sitting on the bed. Faith opened it and saw a note from Jamie:

I'm home. Baby, please just come back here. I know you're mad. I know it hurts Faith. I didn't even know that she was pregnant let alone gave birth to our son. I don't love her Faith. I never have. The only person I ever loved was you. Come home. Please. Faith, I miss you.

Faith threw the note out and finished getting changed. "You alright," Jason asked. Faith nodded. "Note from Jamie?" "I don't know what the point is. I don't get why he keeps pushing. There's no point anymore." "Baby girl is wide awake. She said she was ready for dinner," Jason joked. "So did you tell her where we're going?" He kissed Faith's cheek. "Gave her a hint. She guessed all on her own," Jason teased. Faith shook her head. "I bet she did." Jason handed Faith his jacket and they headed out. Patsy was giggling in the car. "She's just so dang cute," Faith said. "Just think about that when we get there," Jason said. "Hint," Faith asked. "Nope," Jason replied. A half hour later, they pulled into one of Faith's favorite restaurants and went upstairs to the more private area. "And we're here because," Faith asked. "Because the minute he started bugging you, you stopped smiling. You need to laugh Faith. You need to try to have fun again. You don't need to watch over your shoulder anymore. Just have fun," Jason said. "And you bring me here," Faith asked. "Nope. Was Patsy's idea. She said you were craving seafood," Jason joked. Faith snuggled Patsy. When she started getting fussy and almost at the point where she was gonna cry, Jason got a bottle warmed up and fed her for Faith. "You do realize that you don't need to do that," Faith said. "You're relaxing. End of discussion." Faith smirked. "Fine," Faith said. She wouldn't let Jason feed her and Patsy got louder. "I got it," Faith said. Jason kissed Faith's cheek. Faith went into the ladies room and fed Patsy. When she came out, Jason had dinner sitting there waiting for her with an oversized fruit juice drink. Faith slid Faith into her car seat and looked at Jason. "What are you up to," Faith asked. "Dinner." They ate and she ended up joking around with Jason all the way through dinner. Once they were finished, they went back to the house and sat out back with a sweet tea and a fire pit. "So here's the deal Faith. Tell me what you need and I'll help you. If you can't be with him, I get it Faith. Trust that. You have to decide what you need to do. I can't do it for you," Jason said. "I needed the truth Jason. He bailed on it altogether and went as far as getting lab techs to clean up his dirty laundry. That isn't right. It never will be," Faith said. "He has a kid with her. It can't be erased and changed Faith. What do you want to do?" "What if I said I didn't know," Faith asked. "Separate until you do," Jason said. "Then what? I can't just…" Jason kissed her. "We.." He kissed her again and pulled her into his lap. "Just tell me what you want," Jason said. Faith went to get up and he kissed her again, harder, deeper until she was getting goose bumps from head to toe. He turned the fire pit off and carried Faith to the sofa. "What are you doing," Faith asked. "Stop worrying and kiss me," Jason said. He kissed her again and as he was about to go for the button of her jeans, Patsy woke up screaming.

"Saved by the baby," Jason said. Faith went upstairs. She changed her then made sure she was fed. Faith put her back to sleep and the minute the door was closed to the nursery, Jason grabbed her hand and walked her into the bedroom. "What are you up to," Faith asked. He kissed her again and walked her backwards towards the bed. "Jason, we can't do this," Faith said. He wasn't hearing it. He didn't let her up for air. When he finally went for the button of her jeans, Faith was already second guessing what they were about to do. Her phone rang. "I'm intentionally turning that thing off from now on," Jason said. Faith went and answered her cell.

"We need to talk," Jamie said. "How's your son doing," Faith asked. "How's my daughter," Jamie asked. "Fine. She's sleeping. What do you want," Faith asked. "I want you to come home before I drag you back here," Jamie said. "Not happening Jamie. Maybe you can try getting shot again and see if she'll give you another kid," Faith replied. "Woman, don't start. What is going on anyway? Patrick told me you backed out of the site," Jamie said. "If we can't even sit in a damn room together, we aren't gonna be able to work together Jamie. I'm not gonna keep…" "Coffee," Jamie said. "No." "Faith, please. We need to talk," he said. "And? Why are you just assuming that I want to Jamie? You got someone else pregnant then you paid someone off so you wouldn't get in trouble? You lied to my face. I am not coming back Jamie. Not when all you do is lie over and over again. You love me? Then stop lying. Stop telling me that you didn't do anything. I saw you two together. I know you Jamie. Well enough to know when there's no point in being together at all." Faith hung up and Jason wrapped his arms around her. She fell asleep crying on Jason's shoulder.

Faith woke up around 4 to feed Patsy and she saw Jason asleep on the glider with Patsy asleep on his chest. Faith took a picture and smirked.

Jason looked over at her. "What are you doin," he asked. Faith smirked. Faith slid Patsy back into the crib and Jason wrapped his arms around her waist. He walked her into the bedroom. He kissed her neck and down her back. "Jason, we can't do…" He turned her towards him and kissed her. "I'm…" He kissed her. He picked her up and carried her back into the bedroom and leaned her onto the bed. An hour later, they finally came up for air. He inched her shorts off and Faith stopped him. "I can't," Faith said. He kissed her again and wrapped her legs around his waist. "Jason," Faith said. He kissed her again. "Just say it," he said. "I want…" He kissed her and ended up making love to her.

It was hot, sexy and something out of a trashy novel you buy in a grocery aisle. Every ounce of her was almost screaming his name. He kissed and nibbled at her until both of them collapsed. "I've been wanting to do that for days," Jason said. "We can't do this," Faith said. Jason kissed her again. "We did. Faith, I don't regret that. We can't just…" Faith got up. She got dressed, grabbed her things and started packing. "What are you doing," Jason asked. Faith got everything packed then threw it in her truck. "You can't just leave," Jason said. "Yeah I can. We shouldn't have…" Jason picked her up and carried her back to bed. "You aren't leaving in the middle of the night like we did something wrong. We didn't do anything wrong," Jason said. Faith went to pack Patsy's stuff and Jason stopped her. "You can't just leave. Where are you gonna go," Jason asked. "Doesn't matter. Evan's dead Jason. I don't have to watch over my shoulder. I get to do what I need to. What I want to. I'm going," Faith said. He kissed her again. "Don't leave. Stay tonight," he asked. "Why," Faith asked. "So I don't run all over town worried about you two. Please," Jason said. Faith sat down on the glider. Jason grabbed her hand and walked her downstairs. "What," Faith asked. "What do you want Faith? Anything. What do you want right now if you could have exactly what you wanted," Jason asked. "For blood not to have to be spilled because of me. For me to not have had to live with the crap that Evan did." "Right now. You choose Faith. Either be with a man who said he loved you and got someone else pregnant or someone who wants to be with you period. Faith, I need you to be alright. Just tell me what you really want right now," Jason said. "I have…" Jason kissed her. "What do you want?" "Jason, I made a commitment. Unless that's over legally, I can't…" He kissed her again. Faith packed Patsy's things, put her in her car seat and they left. The only thing left behind was one single baby blanket. Jason got dressed, put that blanket beside him in his truck and took off to find Faith.

Faith pulled into the street where the ranch was and pulled over. That ranch had been home. Every memory was there. She drove past and it looked abandoned. The trucks weren't there, the lights were off and it looked like nobody had been there in weeks. Faith pulled in, parked the truck and brought Patsy in. The crib was still there, but there was a bottle of Jack on the counter beside it. Faith got Patsy settled, clipped the monitor on her belt and went and finished unpacking. She changed the security codes and locked up. She came upstairs and Patsy was still asleep. Faith went into the bedroom and saw 3 empty bottles of Jack. She cleaned up and around 3am, someone was buzzing at the gate. "Can I help you," Faith asked. "Open," Jason said. Faith opened the gate. She went downstairs and out to the porch. "What are you doing," Faith asked. "You aren't safe here. That's why he isn't here Faith. Can't you see the damn bullet hole? It's right there," Jason said pointing out the hole in the post on the porch. "Faith, please," Jason said. Faith went back into the house. "I get this is where you feel better Faith, but you have to decide what you want. Do you want him or do you want me," Jason asked. "Didn't realize that was an option when he put a ring on my hand," Faith said. Jason kissed her. "If you're staying then so am I," Jason said. He put his bag onto the chair by the door. "What are you doing," Faith asked. "You're staying, so am I." Jason locked up and drew the curtains so nobody would know if they were there. Faith armed the security alarm and went to go upstairs. "Just come and sit and talk," Jason said. "Not if…" Jason kissed her. He turned on the gas fireplace. "Jason, I get.." "Would you let me talk. Faith, I know you are still with him. I know you still love him, but if you want to be happy, you know he isn't gonna help," Jason said. "I need to figure out what to do Jason. I can't just walk away from a marriage. I made a vow to him. I don't take that lightly." "He did. If he didn't that son of his wouldn't exist. Stop giving him chances Faith. Start making you happy and making a home where your daughter can be happy too. You have more than you to think about now," Jason said. Faith got up and went upstairs. She soaked in the tub and when the water cooled, Faith changed and saw Jamie's favorite shirt in the closet. She slid it on and slid into bed.

Faith woke up a few hours later and saw Jason's arm wrapped around her. Faith got up and checked on Patsy. Faith changed her and got her right back to sleep. She went downstairs and sat on the sofa. The sofa was the same one that she had curled up on with Jamie more than once. She looked on the sofa table and saw the picture of her with Patsy when she was first born. Beside it was a picture that someone had taken of the three of them. Faith fell asleep on the sofa.

"I'm going back to the damn house. I can't just sit here. She won't talk to me and if Kathleen starts one more damn time about Faith and I getting divorced…" "Jamie, dude. Chill. The other house is locked up. Nobody is there. You need to just let it go. If you're determined to find Faith, you aren't gonna find her there," Alan said. "Give me the test results," Jamie said. Jamie opened the envelope and for the second time they verified that Jamie wasn't the child's father. "See? She has to listen now." "The doctor said straight out that you can't be over-exerting yourself. Do you wanna burst the damn stitch," Alan asked. "If it means finding my wife? Yes." Jamie got in the truck and drove until he saw the house. He'd had too many memories there with her. He knew the minute the door opened, they'd come back and he'd drown in the fact that he'd lost Faith. He went to go in the gate and it wouldn't open. Jamie buzzed the house. "Hello," Faith said. Jamie thought he was hearing things. "Faith," Jamie said. The gate didn't open.

Jamie went around to the access point for the security gate and fence and opened the front gates with a key. He locked them back up and pulled around and saw two pick-up trucks. He walked to the front door and saw all the curtains drawn. He slid his key into the lock and let himself in. He went to turn the alarm off and Faith jumped up and entered the new code. "You're here," Jamie said. "Temporarily," Faith said. Jamie pulled her to him. He kissed her. A kiss like the first one he ever gave her. A kiss that had her toes curling, her knees turning to jelly and her heart racing like she'd run a mile. He didn't even say a word. He leaned her onto the sofa and wrapped her legs around him. If this was a dream, he was making the damn best of it for as long as he could before he woke up. Not a word was said. Jamie made love to her, devoured her neck and nibbled at that one spot that always made him get his way with her. After, he barely remembered. Whether it was the Jack Daniel's that was still in his system or a fantasy, he passed out on the sofa. Faith went upstairs. She checked on Patsy. She noticed her just waking up. Faith grabbed the bags and left before Jamie woke up, leaving a note with the codes. She left a note by Jason to tell him where she was going. Thank god Jason woke up before Jamie did. He snuck out the door before Jamie was even conscious.

Jamie woke up around noon and saw the note about the codes. "It wasn't a dream," Jamie said. He called Faith's cell and it rang. "Jamie," Faith said. "Where are you," he asked. "He's yours isn't he," Faith asked. "Two tests in a row say no. Faith, he isn't." "I saw you with Kathleen alright? If you want her then..." "Faith, I want my wife. Come home. Please," Jamie said. "Not now. Jamie, you're with her. I know you are. If there was even a tiny chance that..." "There isn't. He looks just like me but he isn't. Two different labs Faith. One that wasn't even in the country. He isn't mine. I need you Faith. I need you and our baby girl. Please. Faith, just tell me what you need me to do," Jamie asked. "You slept with someone else and got her pregnant Jamie. There isn't anything else," Faith said. "You aren't saying what I think you are," Jamie said. "Patrick took me off your site. I'm not gonna be on the tour..." "We're talking. End of discussion. Tell me where to meet you. I'm not letting this go this easy Faith. I love you." "Jamie." "Tell me," he said. "I can't.." "Fine. Meet me at the Hilton. The room we were in when we first got back together. Please," Jamie said. Faith didn't know what to do. "At noon. Please," Jamie said. Faith hung up.

Faith was at a point where no matter what decision she made, she was gonna be hurting someone. Telling Jamie about Jason and what they did wasn't an option, and letting Jamie just brush off what happened wasn't good either. Faith looked over at Patsy out cold and she thought about what that first night was like. The memory of seeing Jamie with Kathleen hit her again. It was like a nightmare that never stopped. Instead of going to the hotel right off the bat, Faith made a move that she was determined to make. Faith sat down at the Opry. Patsy was quiet. "Still need my help don't you," she heard. "What am I supposed to do? Do I go back? Stay with Jason? What? I love him, but I can't go through what I just had to with that woman showing up. You're the one that always kept me on the right path Patsy. You and God are the only two I'd trust to tell me straight. Just tell me what I'm supposed to do," Faith asked. "He put a ring on your finger Faith. You said you wanted to be with him That you needed to be with him. Do you want to be with Jason or do you want to be with Jamie? It's your choice. When I first met you, you were scared and you didn't know what to do. Faith, he loves you. Jason does and so does Jamie. Faith, you're the only one that can make the decision. When you met Jason, he was saving you from Evan. When you got together with Jamie, he had saved you from it. I know that Jason helped, but do you love him," Patsy's voice asked. "I don't know. He cheered me up. Evan came after me and before he made a move he was dead. It scared the crap out of me, but he saved me. Jamie tried for years. He's the one that walked me out that door and kept me safe. I don't know what to do. I look at her and I see Jamie. I see everything we dreamed about having. I look at Jason and it's like he took over where Jamie left off. "I love Jamie. I just…" "Think Faith. Close your eyes and try to picture your future. Who are you with?"

* * *

Jamie sat in that hotel room. He sat on the floor, he sat on the edge of the bed then he sat down in the chair where he'd sat when Faith had first been there with him. The first day where she was having nightmare after nightmare about Evan. He almost wished he'd been the one to shoot Evan instead of Jason. He remembered Faith sitting there. He remembered every stupid fight. Every stupid move he'd made to scare her away like he'd done with all the women before. Nobody had ever got in that close to him. Nobody had let him in like that before. When Faith showed up in his life, he didn't know what else to do other than fall head over heels. The fact that she was making him wait made him think long and hard. He was dead scared she wasn't gonna show. Just the thought of losing his daughter killed him. The thought of not getting to see her first tooth, her first step, her first word. He tried to remember what life was like before he'd ever met her and he couldn't remember it. He called her cell and didn't get an answer. There was only one place he could think of.

* * *

Jason called Faith's cell more than once. It was one thing to take off. It was something else altogether disappearing. He was worried. He tried one last time and Faith finally answered. "What's up," Faith asked. "Where are you," Jason asked. "I need time to think Jason. I get that you're trying to do something good for me but I need to handle all of this myself. Please," Faith said. "Tell me you're not doing what I think you are," Jason said. "I have to go," Faith said. She hung up and Jason started to panic. He was determined to find her. There was only one place she would've gone. He took off and headed straight towards the Opry. That was the one place he thought of. It was the place where she felt like she was home, the one place in the planet where she could be calm and happy.

Faith looked at her daughter. "If you want to be with your husband, you'll go now. If you want to be with Jason, come and sit in my old dressing room," Patsy's voice said. "I don't know what to do," Faith said. "When you asked me for help with your husband, you said that you didn't want to be with anyone else. That you were head over heels. That you couldn't imagine life without him. Is that still true?" "I don't know. He helped me when I needed him. I just don't know what's supposed to happen. I love him but after what he did with that woman, I don't know if I can let it go. What happens when I find out she wasn't the only one he slept with? What happens when more kids come out of the woodwork? I can't just risk that. Not with my daughter here. If I stay with Jason, at least I know he's not gonna do that, but there's no guarantee that things are going to be good. He's divorced. His two kids are crucial to him, but nobody can guarantee that..." "Is Jamie the love of your life?" Faith nodded. "Do you trust Jason that he's not gonna do what Jamie did?" "I don't know what to trust. I just know that all of the things that have been going on recently have to stop. I almost lost her because of that stupid woman. I'm not putting anything above my baby girl. I need to feel secure. I don't know what to do," Faith said. "I'll help," Patsy's voice said.

* * *

Jamie went back to the house. To the one place they had started all of their memories. He sat down on the edge of their bed and saw Patsy's blanket. He slid to the floor and leaned against the edge of the mattress. He sat there and thought about all the memories they'd made there. From that first kiss that turned into the first time they made love, to the first fight, to the day that he put a ring on her finger. He wasn't gonna let those days end. Not for every penny in the planet.

* * *

Jason got down to the Opry and saw Faith's truck. He went to go inside and the doors were locked. He called Faith's cell again and didn't get an answer. Jamie went around to another entrance and got security to let him in. He went in and he swore someone was on stage. He walked in and the shadow was gone. He went backstage and walked through the sitting area and heard a baby. He saw one closed door. He went in and Faith was changing Patsy. "I was wondering where you went," Jason said. "I need to figure this out Jason. I can't just let go of all of this. I need..." Jason kissed her. "Let me take you home," Jason asked. Faith shook her head. "You're just gonna walk away? Faith, what's going on," Jason asked. "I don't know what to do. That's what. Jason, I have a past with him. I have history with him. I love him alright? At least I think I do. I don't know anything anymore. I thought he was the one I was supposed to be with. When all of that happened, I thought that the life I had with him was over. I made mistakes. We made one. I just don't know if I should even be with anyone. Maybe I need to be alone," Faith said. "You need someone to help you with the baby. Just let me be there," Jason said. "Why," Faith asked. "I have two kids Faith. I know what to do. I never counted on wanting to be with anyone. Not after what happened with my ex. I meet you and it's like that entire world flipped upside down. Please," Jason said. "What are you saying," Faith asked. "Just come back to the house with me. Please," Jason asked. Faith shook her head. Jason kissed her. He kicked the door closed and leaned Faith against it. "Faith, stop fighting me and just let me do this. Please," Jason said. "What Jason? Break up my marriage and leave? Walk away from him? He's the one that saved me in the first place. If he hadn't shown, I would've been killed." "And I made sure that he was never gonna hurt you again," Jason said. "I married him. Whether you understand it or not, I married Jamie. We were supposed to be renewing our vows," Faith said. "You either want to be with him or you want to be with me. Just let me do this," Jason said. Faith slipped out of his arms and got Patsy. "Where are you going," Jason asked. "To figure out what the heck to do," Faith replied.

Faith left and took Patsy for a drive. She made sure Patsy was alright and Faith grabbed herself some dinner. When she came out and started the truck, Jamie's song he'd written for her was on the radio. Faith listened then heard Jamie's voice. "So we heard that you'll be playing the Opry again this weekend. You've been doing shows there a lot this year," the interviewer said. "I think I've played there 7 or 8 times this year. I can really say it's an honor. It's never the same without my wife being there with me. I swear, she's the good luck charm. She's the inspiration for a ton of my music from the new CD." "So we heard there was a new huge tour coming up," the interviewer asked. "Haven't signed on anything yet. Honestly, after we had our baby girl I kinda was hoping for a little more time with the two awesome girls." "So you and your wife had a baby girl? What did you two decide to name her?" "After one of the most amazing legends in all of country music. Her first name is Patsy – like Patsy Cline," Jamie said. "And nobody has even got a hint of a picture. When are you two leaking those?" "You'll know." For once Jamie hadn't said anything. "So we heard you were working on a new song. What's the title," the interviewer asked. "In my hand," Jamie replied. Jamie played it and in seconds, Faith's eyes were welling up. She pulled over and realized where she was.

Jamie got back from the interview and sat back down. Right about then, Patsy would be just waking up from her nap. Faith would be running into the bedroom to make sure she was alright and Jamie would have a smile ear to ear. Instead, he was sitting by the bed hoping and praying that

Faith was going to come home. He missed that little girl and he missed Faith. He tried calling Faith's cell and he swore he heard that ringtone he'd set on her cell. Jamie got up and walked downstairs and saw the barn door open. He looked and her cell phone was on the sofa. He looked and he swore he saw Faith's truck. He walked out to the barn and saw Faith rummaging around. "What are you doing," Jamie asked. "Looking for something. I left the bags out here so they could air out after Christmas." "Babe," Jamie said. Faith turned and looked at him. "What are the bags for," Jamie asked. "Jamie, please," Faith said. "You aren't leaving," Jamie said. "I'm working with Jason. I have to..." Jamie kissed her. He barely let her up for air. Faith pushed him away. "You aren't going. Tell me you aren't," Jamie begged. "I thought you'd want to see her," Faith said. "You and her. Faith I want my family back," Jamie said. "You have a family Jamie. You and your son," Faith said. She found the suitcase and pulled it down. "Faith, you can't leave. You can't just rip her out of my life. I don't even know where you're gonna be. Faith, please. I love you. I always have. Just stay." Patsy started fussing and Jamie slid her into his arms and kissed her. "Jamie," Faith said. He rocked her and sang to her and the baby calmed. "I am not letting you two leave. I love you Faith. We belong together. You know damn well I'm right. I need you. Please. Faith, please just stay," Jamie said. She slid Patsy into her car seat and wheeled the suitcases up to the house. "Faith," Jamie said. "I need to breathe Jamie. You have a kid with another woman that you got pregnant while we were together. What am I supposed to say Jamie? That it's alright? It isn't and it never will be," Faith said. Jamie put Patsy into the crib upstairs. "Jamie," Faith said. She was asleep a little while later.

"What," Faith asked as Jamie walked her downstairs. "We're talking until it's settled Faith. I'm not losing you over something she lied about. Here. Take this and tell me there's a reason Faith. Read it," Jamie said. Faith opened up the envelope and saw 3 separate tests done confirming that Jamie isn't the father. "And who did you pay to get this," Faith asked. Jamie kissed her. "I love you Faith. Fine, I screwed up and slept with her. I didn't and there's no way I ever would get anyone pregnant. When we found out you were having Patsy, I was almost in tears. Faith, I'm not letting go of you and I'm not losing my daughter because of what she did.

I can't." "Jamie," Faith said. He kissed her. "No." "Jamie, please. Just let me have time to think." He kissed Faith. He undid her jacket, peeled her shirt off and went for the zipper of her jeans. "Jamie," Faith said. He kicked his jeans off and kissed down Faith's torso. "We can't do this," Faith said. Jamie kissed her then bit her neck in that one spot that always had her turned on. Faith got up. She got dressed and went upstairs. She slid Patsy into the car seat. "Faith," Jamie said as he stood in front of her in his ripped up blue jeans and not much else. "I have to go Jamie. Before we do something we're gonna regret," Faith said. Jamie grabbed her hand before she woke Patsy. "What," Faith asked. He closed the door and leaned Faith against the wall. Look me in the eye and tell me that you don't love me Faith. We got married in front of everyone. We promised forever Faith. Forever doesn't end when some idiot fan gets in the middle." "No. It gets in the way when fans who you slept with start trying to tell you that their son is theirs," Faith said. She went back into the bedroom and put Patsy into her car seat, grabbed the suitcase and walked downstairs. "No," Jamie said. He kissed her. "Don't leave. You want me to go, I'll go. Just stay here. Please. At least I know you two will be safe." "We're fine. I'm staying with Jason for a while at his place. The girls are helping out with Patsy," Faith said. "Oh hell no you aren't. Faith. You're my wife. Staying at his house is just wrong. You're moving your stuff back here and you don't get to say no. You're not going back to his place," Jamie said. "Didn't think I needed to ask permission. I'm going Jamie," Faith said. "She's my daughter. You really don't want to be with me anymore? That what you want Faith? If it is, just say the damn word," Jamie said. Faith went and put Patsy in the truck, put the bags into the back and went to get in and Jamie stopped her. "What," Faith asked. "You don't want to be with me then just say the damn word Faith. I can draw up papers," Jamie said. Faith got in the truck and left.

Chapter 24

"Was wondering where you disappeared to," Jason said as Faith pulled up. Faith walked into the house and changed Patsy and put her down for a nap. She came downstairs and Jason had unloaded her bags. "So you're staying," Jason said. "I don't know. I don't know anything anymore," Faith said. "What's wrong," Jason asked. "He went nuts when

I left. I was trying to leave while he was out and it didn't work. I was getting my suitcases from the barn and he went postal. I need time to think. Is that alright," Faith asked. Jason hugged her. "I'm not gonna put my two cents in. I don't want you getting more upset. I have to go do some promo stuff and do some rehearsals anyway," Jason said. "Thank you," Faith said. Jason hugged her. "If this is what you need right now, I'm never ever gonna say no Faith. If you said you were going back I would understand it. Just know that I'm not pushing you into anything. If you decide that you want to be here with me for good then we decide on what to do. The girls said they wanted to come see Patsy. Is that alright," Jason asked. Faith nodded. "Two cute babysitters. They're more than welcome. Just let me know if you need anything," Faith asked. He kissed her. "I'll call you when I'm on the way back. I can grab dinner. Joe's good," Jason asked. Faith nodded. Jason kissed her. "No more worrying. You have all the time in the planet to figure all of this out. I'm not pushing. Sorta wish you swung this way, but if you don't I'm still gonna be here. Consider this your safe place," Jason said. Faith nodded. "Remember something alright. Even if the entire planet feels way too small, you have the house. If you want, on the weekend we can go up to the ranch. The girls wanted to go fishing. If you want to go, we can…" Faith kissed him. "I'll see you after," Faith said. He kissed her. "If you want to come then tell me. We can go grab lunch or something," Jason asked. "I'm gonna try and get settled," Faith said. "If you need me, just call my cell alright," Jason said. Faith kissed him. "Now go," Faith said. "See you in a few," Jason said. He grabbed his guitar and headed out.

Faith sat there looking after Patsy and all of it hit her. Patsy was squirming around and Faith watched. All the dreams she'd had about having a future with Jamie were sitting in her lap. She had to decide what to do and now was the hardest. She brushed away the tears and Jamie called her. "Hi," Faith said. "You okay," Jamie asked. "I know you're upset Jamie. This isn't what I expected Jamie. I didn't mean for all of this to happen. You know why," Faith said. "Faith, tell me what I need to do. Just say it," Jamie asked. "You cheated Jamie. The one thing you never said you'd do, you did. I saw that boy. He looked just like you Jamie. I can't just ignore that. You know why," Faith said. "Then do me one favor," Jamie said. "What," Faith asked. "Open the gate." Faith went and opened the gate and saw Jamie's truck pulling in. He parked and hopped out and walked right to Faith. "What did you..." Jamie's hands slid to her face and he pulled her towards him. He kissed her and he barely let her up for air. "You can't leave," Jamie said. "I can't just..." "Stop questioning it Faith. Things happened alright. Fact is that things aren't happening ever again. I love you Faith. Just come home so we can work on us again. Please," Jamie asked. "Jamie, you slept..." He kissed her. "Please," Jamie begged. "I can't just come back. Not after all of that," Faith said. "Date." "Jamie," Faith said. "One date. We start fresh for a while. Please," Jamie said. Faith was about to shake her head when Jamie kissed her again. "Where's babe," Jamie asked. "In her crib upstairs. Why," Faith asked. "Just come back to the house. I'm not doing this here. Please," Jamie said. Faith shook her head. "I can't just ignore that Jamie. We made a vow that we'd never cheat," Faith said. "And? You're living with Jason. Tell me that's part of the vows," Jamie said. "Just go," Faith replied. "No. Not unless you're coming with me." Faith shook her head. "Please," Jamie begged. "So you can go do it again? Jamie, I'm not doing this. I'm not just letting all the crap happen. I need to know that I'm alright. That our marriage is gonna work. I can't just walk back in when it's that broken," Faith said. Jamie walked upstairs, slid Patsy into her car seat, grabbed Faith's hand and walked out the front door. "Jamie," Faith said. "Get in the truck," Jamie said. "I'm not going anywhere. Besides the fact that you forgot the bag with her stuff, and my purse and phone and on top of everything, you don't get to tell me what to do," Faith said. "Fine. Pack and meet me at the house at 10." "And what are you doing," Faith asked. "Reminding you why we're together." Faith put Patsy back into her crib and came inside. Jamie finally left, but Faith was left wondering what to do.

Jason came home around 7 and Faith was upstairs sliding Patsy back into the crib. Faith came downstairs and Jason saw her. "Now I dang well know something's wrong. What happened," Jason asked. "Jamie showed. He wants me back there. After him getting that chick pregnant..." "Thought that text said the result was negative?" "He slept with her. He hid it Jason." "We did," Jason said. Faith shook her head. Jason saw the bags still packed. "You're really having a tough one aren't you," he asked. "We both screwed up, but I can't just let that go. She kept coming and coming at him. Who's to say he isn't gonna do it again?" "Then use the tour as a trial basis. The girls are gonna be with me on the weekends when they can. When they aren't, you can chill on my bus. When he stresses you out, you stay with me. That simple," Jason said. "And," Faith asked. "All to yourself. Promise," Jason said. "What about now," Faith asked. "Tell me one thing Faith. If you needed someone and you were in trouble, or scared, who would you call," Jason asked. "You or him," Faith said. "Better one. If she had her first word, would you call him or me," Jason asked. "I'd have to call him," Faith said. "I wish like hell I'd met you first. You know that right," Jason asked. Faith hugged him. "He screws up, you're getting your butt back here." Faith nodded. Jason kissed her and she almost crumbled in his arms. "Kills me that I'm not gonna get to kiss those lips again," Jason said. His hands slid down her back. He kissed her again and picked her up. He slid her legs around him and leaned her onto the sofa. "We…" He didn't want to hear the truth. For once, he wanted to hear that someone wanted him. He'd gone so long without it. "Do you want to be here," Jason asked. Faith looked him in the eyes and nodded. "Going back," he asked. "If it doesn't…" Jason kissed her. He got up, grabbed her hand and led her upstairs. "What," Faith asked. "No interruptions," he said as he closed the bedroom door and put the baby monitor on the side table.

Faith got up an hour later, straightened up her clothes and went to check on Patsy. "Faith, you don't need to explain it. I get why you need to be there with him, but you can stay here. Give yourself some down time to clear your head like you wanted to," Jason said. "Clearing my head would involve not having a guy around," Faith said teasingly. "You saying I distract you," Jason teased. "I need to figure this out. You trying to get me into bed when I'm married isn't helping," Faith said. He kissed her shoulder. "Then I'll warm up dinner and attempt to not distract you," Jason teased. Faith nodded. She fed the baby then headed downstairs. Jason was so good with her. How he managed to eat and hold the baby was something Faith needed to learn. They finished up dinner, Faith cleaned up and Jason was changing Patsy. Faith looked over and she was gurgling to Jason. Faith looked and the baby had a smile ear to ear. "Now if you want to stay here, you can little mouse. Anything you want," Jason said. "I'm sure she'll be able to not be distracted," Faith joked.

"She said she wants to stay," Jason teased. "I bet. She also say that life was full of lollipops?" "Pretty much. She said that she likes being here. What does mom think," Jason asked. "That I still need time. We were just as bad as he was," Faith said. "Difference was you never lied about it. You never hid it and tried to keep it secret. Faith, if he's gonna do it once, he's gonna keep trying to get away with it." Faith went and checked through emails and saw info that one of the papers posted about Jamie on the prowl. He was spotted in a bar or two downtown, drink in hand, with women that Faith had never seen. She sent it to Jamie with the tag:

This is why I think I shouldn't come back.

Faith turned her laptop off. "You look like you're gonna shoot nails. What," Jason asked. Faith shook her head and took the baby upstairs to the crib. Faith went and drew herself a hot bath, locking the bathroom door so she could cry in private. Jason came upstairs a little while later and he knew. "You alright," Jason asked. "I'll be out in a minute," Faith said. She came out wrapped in a towel and Jason saw her eyes all puffy. He pulled her into his arms and just hugged her. "Whatever the hell caused that, it's getting a whooping in the morning," he said. He handed Faith one of his sweatshirts and Faith slid it on and slid on a pair of her shorts. "Well," Jason asked. "If I even say it.." "I know you can't drink, so hot cocoa is gonna have to do it," Jason said. He kissed her forehead and went and made them hot chocolate. Faith sat down on the sofa and laid the baby monitor on the table. He handed her the hot chocolate and sat down beside her, sliding her legs across his lap. "He was out with other people. He was making out with other women. How the hell…" "Okay. Here's the deal. He's acting out and being an idiot. What would you do if you could," Jason asked. "You don't wanna know." "Faith," Jason said. "Kick his butt 10 planets over. I get that he's acting out, but like screwing around and making out with random strangers is a good plan?" "Faith, you know what I'm gonna say," Jason said. "One second he's begging me to come home and the next I see that? He told me he stopped drinking and in every damn picture he was drinking. What's the damn point? There's no way I can damn well do anything. He's not leaving me alone. He's not gonna stop trying to force me to come home." "Then don't." "I can't just…" "Stop worrying Faith. Just let your heart tell you what to do. You need to figure this out Faith. I'm not gonna let you get hurt ever again. He loves you Faith, but if he's gonna do that and hurt you all over again, he doesn't deserve you," Jason said. Faith nodded and finished her hot chocolate. Faith went in and quickly checked on the baby before she went to bed.

Jason walked upstairs after locking up and saw Faith sitting on the bed. "What," Faith asked. "Too damn tempting right now," Jason said. "And why would you say that?" "Long story. Remember that Jason Aldean song? 'This I gotta see' I think. Remember," Jason asked. Faith smirked. "Had to didn't you," Faith joked. "Now come lay down and try to relax. Please. You need to relax. You need sleep." Faith curled up on the bed. "What," Jason asked. Faith snuggled up to him. Jason wrapped his arms around her and fell asleep curled up with Faith. It was the best sleep he'd had in months.

Jamie got up the next morning. A bottle of Jack sat on the table in front of him and he saw a BMW in his driveway. He looked over and a woman he didn't even recognize was making breakfast. "Well good morning," the woman said. "I really need to get ready for rehearsal. I appreciate the breakfast, but I have to go," Jamie said. The woman got re-dressed and he walked her out. "So what are you doing tonight," the woman asked. "Going to try to work things out with my wife. I'm sorry," Jamie said. The woman stormed out and Jamie started kicking himself from that second on. He looked at his cell and saw the message from Faith. "Shit," Jamie said. He went upstairs, showered and went to drive to Jason's. He grabbed two coffees on the way and when he got there, Faith's truck was gone and so was Jason's. He called Faith's cell and got the worst answer. "The number you have called has been disconnected or is no longer in service." He went down to the office and saw Faith's truck right beside Jason's. He walked into the office and Faith was going over paperwork. He went to walk into her office and saw Jason with her. He had Patsy in his arms while she slept. "Faith, we need to talk," Jamie said. "No we don't," Faith replied. Jason slid Patsy into her car seat and he walked Jamie into one of the empty offices. "What," Jamie asked. "She's upset. She's past mad Jamie. She's livid. She barely slept all night. Whatever you did upset her. She doesn't know what to do. You promised her that you'd be faithful and she sees all of the photos and the gossip. She's that upset. I should know Jamie. That's how I lost my damn wife. You need to back off," Jason said. "Then don't touch her. You keep your damn paws off my wife and my daughter. She's never gonna be with you. She loves me. You'd never understand," Jamie said. "Yeah I do. I know better than anyone what that kind of misery looks like. I'm not letting her feel like that again," Jason said. He walked out of that office and went back in to sit with Faith. A few minutes later, Faith headed out with Jason and the baby and they left the parking lot. Jamie didn't even have time to run down the stairs before they vanished.

Faith and Jason got back to the house and he parked her truck in the garage. "I can't believe him," Faith said. Jason kissed her and took Patsy and slid her into her crib. "What the hell possessed him to do that," Faith asked. Jason walked back downstairs, picked Faith up and flipped her over his shoulder and carried her upstairs. He leaned her onto the bed, handed her a pair of leggings and another one of his sweatshirts and kissed her. "What," Faith asked. "We have plans. You, me, munchkin and complete and utter privacy. Sound good," Jason asked. "Depends." "For tonight. Tomorrow we can do the awards." Faith looked at him. "Faith, you'll be fine. We'll go and just hang out. You can bypass the red carpet," Jason said. "Not a good idea," Faith said. "Have to. One night won't..." "Jamie?" "Good point," Jason said. "Besides. If I go with you, the press will be all over us. I can't," Faith said. Jason kissed her. "Then I can always make sure that we're sitting beside Jamie." "Babysitter that's trustworthy. I just don't want all the questions," Faith said. Jason kissed her. "It's up to you what you want to do Faith." "No." "You're leaving it as is," Jason asked. "For now until I can make sense of it." Jason kissed her. "I hate seeing you like this," he said. "He cheated and it's all over every damn magazine and gossip show. One more stupid move and I'm not gonna have a choice." "Come with me." Faith shook her head. Jason leaned over and kissed her. That one kiss lead to a make out session that would make teenagers blush. "I can't keep..." Jason muffled her objections with another kiss that didn't let them up for air for 2 hours. He had his sweater pulled off of her and was about to go further when Patsy woke up. "Stay with me. Faith, just stay here with me. She's used to having us here together. Please," Jason said. Faith kissed him. "Next show," Jason asked. Faith nodded. "Fine, but you're still coming to Vegas with me." Faith nodded. "But if…" He kissed her again. They booked a major suite. "Jason," Faith said. "Romancing you until you forget," Jason said. "Oh really," Faith replied. "If that's what makes you feel better. I hate seeing you all tense and mad," Jason said. Faith kissed him, slid the sweater back on and got Patsy.

"Seriously though. What do you need to find out about all of this? What do you want to do," Jason asked. "I can't…" Just as she was about to say it, Jamie called her. "What," Faith asked. Jason hugged her. "We need to talk," he said. "No. There isn't gonna be talking anymore. I can't Jamie. That trust that took years just got blown sky high. I'm not doing it," Faith said. "Please," he begged. Faith hung up. "Faith, you sure," Jason asked. She got up. "Faith," Jason said. She slid Patsy into Jason's arms and went downstairs. Faith grabbed the breast pump and tried to find somewhere quiet. She read through some articles and found out she was okay with one drink as long as she had enough milk for 2 days for the baby. She stared at the bottle of Jack in Jason's cupboard. She brushed the tears away. She sat down and looked at lawyers. Jason went to come downstairs and heard her on the phone. A half hour later, he heard the phone hang up and he came downstairs with Patsy. "You okay," Jason asked. Faith kissed him. He slid Patsy into her arms. "We're going," Jason said. "Who's gonna…" He kissed Faith and called a friend or two. "What," Faith asked when he got off the phone. He kissed her. "You're coming to the awards with me. Nobody is gonna ask. If they do, we're friends," Jason said. "But…" He kissed her again. "And we can bring her or my ex said the girls want to babysit." Faith smirked. "Decision made. You go get a massage while I'm at the rehearsals. Get all dolled up and look sexy and we go together. Not one question asked." "You sure," Faith asked. "I'm gonna be the only one drooling on the carpet." "You do realize that…" Jamie kissed her and devoured her lips then grabbed them a snack. "What are you doing," Faith asked. "We're having us time. Baby girl told me that she wanted to watch a movie," Jason teased. He kissed her again and walked her and Patsy into the TV room. He grabbed the portable playpen that Faith had upstairs and put a blanket in it for Patsy and slid her in. "You realize she has a crush on you," Faith teased. He kissed Patsy. He leaned into her. "Jason," Faith said. He kissed her again and wrapped her legs around him. "I am not gonna let you get hurt again. Not now, not ever," Jason said. "Meaning what," Faith asked. "You need me, say it." Faith looked at him. "What," Faith asked. "What would you do if I said I wanted you right now," Jason asked as his sweater slid off her body and onto the floor. "We.." He devoured her lips and slid his shirt off. "What are…" He slid her leggings off, kicked his jeans off and made love to her while 'The Vow' played in the background. His kisses were addictive as were her lips to him. They ended up curled up on the floor by the fireplace. He wrapped them in a blanket and curled up with her. "We can't do this," Faith said. "We are Faith. You deserve to be happy. You have to do what's right for you, but I'm not letting you walk back into that. Faith, he blew that chance. He blew what you two had right out of the damn water. You deserve better than that," Jason said. Faith curled up with him and they relaxed a while. Faith got up and got dressed. Just as she finished getting dressed, Jamie called her again.

"What," Faith asked. "I just got served separation papers," Jamie said. "Then sign them," Faith said. "What are you doing? Faith we belong together. Just stop," Jamie said. "No. You slept with a slew of other women Jamie. Don't bother denying it. Whatever trust we had went out the window with your damn senses," Faith said. "Faith, you married me. We promised forever. That isn't changing," Jamie said. "It did. First that woman that said you were her baby daddy, the girl upon girl upon girl people spotted you with. This isn't the way things were ever supposed to be. Just stop. You quit drinking Jamie. All of a sudden you're drinking and getting drunk. Jamie, that wasn't you and it never should be," Faith said. "I don't know what else to do. The silence in this house is killing me Faith. I need you," Jamie said. "I can't Jamie. Not after all of this. I'm staying here. If you wanna see her you can, but I can't do this me and you crap anymore." "Faith, don't do this. Don't just walk away from all of this," Jamie said. "I'm walking away Jamie. I'm going before all the good memories are tarnished. I can't do this." "What about the awards," Jamie asked. "I'm staying home. Patsy and I have plans," Faith said. "Faith, please," Jamie begged. "I don't know if we're ever gonna be able to figure this out Jamie." "Please," he said. "Sign it. If things get better, fine. Jamie we can't keep going on like this," Faith said. "Come home then. Faith, I went out when I realized you weren't coming back." "Try again Jamie. You went out when I wasn't there. You went out when you were on tour and I wasn't there. She showed up at our house with a child and you were worried it was yours. You slept with her. I need to do this Jamie. Please just sign it." Faith hung up and not 2 minutes later, Jason came in and wrapped his arms around her.

"I hate that sound," Jason said. "What sound?" "The one that ends in you being in tears. Just come lay down," Jason said. He curled up with Faith and tried to comfort her. "What did you tell him," Jason asked. "Doesn't matter. He's never gonna listen," Faith said. Jason kissed her cheek. "There's no point in fighting with him. He's not gonna let me do what I need to. He's not gonna leave you alone and he's gonna push until he can't push anymore," Faith said. "You're gonna need that massage," Jason said. "He's the one that started all of this. He's the one that got her pregnant. You came to try and help. That is all it was," Faith said. He kissed her neck. "No more worrying Faith. Let fate handle it. Whatever is meant to happen will. We'll go out and hang out for a while. Nobody is gonna start trouble. We'll go find you a dress…" "Jason, please," Faith said. "Okay. We'll see how you feel tomorrow. Just try to sleep." Faith laid her head on his shoulder and fell asleep in Jason's arms.

Jamie went through the house and no matter how much he wanted to destroy all the memories, he couldn't. He saw the wedding pictures and ended up curled up on the floor. He cleaned the entire house and got rid of every ounce of alcohol. He went and worked out then started putting all the misery into music. He got two songs written by 3am. He got up the next morning, went straight into the studio and recorded them all while they were fresh on his mind. The papers sat on the passenger seat. He wrote out a note and attached it, signed the papers and put them in Jason's mailbox.

Jason headed out first thing to arrange a few things. Faith got up fed Patsy, they had a shower and started getting Patsy ready to go for the day. Jason came back and he wrapped his arms around Faith. "Why are you smiling," Faith asked. "Booked the plane tickets. Got a few people to send over some dresses for you and miss party girl here and there was mail for you. Jason kissed her and he slid Patsy out of Faith's arms. "What," Faith asked. "Open it," Jason said. She opened the first envelope and saw her paycheck from the label. The only other envelope was from Jamie. She opened it and found the note:

I love you. I know why you're mad. Faith, I understand. Please just try to keep an open mind. We both do stupid crap when we're upset. I get why you're staying there Faith. Please just hear me out. One date. Whenever you're ready for it, we have one date and try to start over. The only rule I have is that you give me the chance. I didn't marry you to keep you away from Evan and to keep you to myself. I married you because I've been in love with you since the day we met. That hasn't and never will change. If things don't go wrong with us, we have that wedding that we planned. We did it for everyone else but we can do this for us. Please. I miss you something crazy. Forever, just like I promised.

Faith read it and put it down. "What," Jason asked. "Nothing," Faith said. Jason leaned over and kissed her. "Ready," he asked. Faith nodded. She grabbed some decaf tea and Jason walked her out to the truck. He got Patsy into her car seat and they headed off. "Where are we going," Faith asked. "Down to look at the dresses for you two," Jason said. Faith laughed. They went in and there were adorable dresses for Patsy. Jason handed her his favorite dress and he chilled with Patsy. Faith went and tried it on and it fit like a glove. She looked at it and she looked like she'd never had a baby. Faith slid on a pair of heels and when she walked out, Jason almost fell off the chair. "Well," Faith asked. He slid the baby into her car seat and grabbed Faith's hand, walking her back into the dressing room. "What," Faith asked. Jason kissed her, pinning her to the wall. "So you're liking this one," Faith teased. He kissed her again. "Next," Faith teased. "if I had no self-restraint..." "Go so I can try on the other one I liked," Faith said. He kissed her again and came out and sat with Patsy. Faith tried on 2 or 3 other dresses and Jason picked the first and the last that was one of those dresses that looked like you were naked when you aren't. Both of them looked amazing on her. "Well," Faith asked. "Since we have two shows we have to be at, the two I liked are coming with us," Jason said. "Had to right," Faith asked. Jason kissed her and they headed out the back way. "What are you doing," Faith asked. "I'm not pushing. The flight heads off around 10. We're there by 2 and sound check is 3. While I'm workin, you're doing your massage thing. After, my mom's coming down. She wanted to look after Patsy. I told her we were just friends, so no worrying. She said she misses having little ones. We're staying separate from her," Jason said. "What are you up to then," Faith asked. "You'll see," he said. They got back to the house and packed, headed back to the airport and headed to the awards.

By the time Jason got to the sound check, Jamie was already there and going through things with the stage manager. Jason did his best to stay away from Jamie, but it didn't work. "We need to talk," Jamie said. "Not really. None of my business," Jason said. "Where is Faith," Jamie asked. "Trying to relax. Trying to make sense of things, figure out what to do. She's a mess. I just know her blood pressure is probably maxed out. I'm trying to be her friend. That's it," Jason said. "Then leave her the hell alone. I see you kiss her or make a damn move, I will kick your ass to another planet. She's still my damn wife." Jason let it go. He knew Jamie was fighting a battle he'd already lost. Fact was, when Jamie saw him with Faith, there was gonna be a bloodshed brawl on that carpet.

Faith took care of Patsy and got her massage. She got her hair and makeup done and sat down to feed Patsy. Jason came in when Faith was curled up on the sofa with Patsy in her arms. "Well hello there sexy," Jason said. Faith laughed. "How'd sound check go," Faith asked. "Jamie says hi," Jason replied. "I am so glad I wasn't there," Faith said. "He's gonna be seated on the other side of the stage from us. Far enough that he won't be causing shit," Jason said. "I still don't know about this," Faith said. "You can bypass the carpet." "You know what I'm talking about," Faith replied. "Then we make sure we go through the carpet long before him." Jason kissed her. "We're not taking her. You know that right," Faith asked. Jason kissed her. "She's getting dolled up for her party tonight. She's watching the awards with my mom. They're getting dolled up and staying here," Jason said. Faith nodded. He kissed Patsy. "So what did you want to do for dinner," Faith asked. Not 5 minutes later, there was a knock at the door. Room service came in with a bottle warmer, dinner for Faith and Jason and ice cream for his mom.

Once they finished up with dinner, Jason's mom came in. "My goodness. You look beautiful already," his mom said. "Well, you must be Mrs. Cane. It's nice to finally meet you," Faith said. His mom hugged her. "Call me Eva," his mom said. "Eva, I really appreciate your help with miss fussy tonight. She's been great all day, but she always gets fussy towards bed time." "She'll be just fine. You two go and have fun," she said. Faith showed her where the bottles were etc. and went and started to get dressed. Faith came out in the first dress that Jason was in love with. She slid her heels on, grabbed her purse and got her things into it. She sprayed on a bit of her perfume and came out. "My goodness," Eva said. "Jason's choice." He came out of the other room and saw Faith. "Wow," he said. "Ready," Faith asked. He nodded. Eva played with Patsy, and Faith and Jason headed off to the red carpet. "You ready for this," Jason asked. Faith nodded. They got in the car to head over and Jason made sure that they were free and clear of Jamie. They were driven to the entrance. Jason hopped out and helped Faith. "You can go the back way," Jason said giving her the option. Faith shook her head. He walked her down the carpet. Everyone stopped them and asked who Faith was. "She's a pretty amazing friend." That was the only response he was willing to give. They walked the carpet, Jason did an interview with Faith's hand in his then they headed in. Jason grabbed a drink for himself and a soda for Faith. Everyone and their brother wanted to talk to Jason. It was almost show time when Jamie showed. Jason held Faith's hand. "What," Faith asked. "I'm tearing that off tonight," Jason teased whispering into her ear. "I bet," Faith said. The awards started and Jason linked their fingers.

A half hour in, they came and got Jason to head on for his performance. Faith went with him, ensuring that Jamie would be completely separate from them. Jason kissed her in the hallway before he headed on. "Wish me luck," Jason said. "Don't need it," Faith replied. He kissed her again, they double-checked him for his wardrobe and he went on with the guys.

Security walked her back to her seat. Jason's security guy sat with Faith. Jason did his performance staring right at Faith the entire way through. As soon as he finished, he got changed, grabbed himself a drink and got Faith a refill and got back down to his seat. He got back and kissed her. "Well," Jason asked. "You did good," Faith said. He didn't let go of Faith's hand. When the presenter came up for one of the awards Jason was up for, he held her hand a little tighter. "You'll be fine," Faith said. "And the winner is…..Jason Cane," the presenter said. He kissed Faith's cheek and hugged her then headed on the stage. He intentionally thanked her in his speech. He beat Jamie out of 3 awards. The last and final award, Jamie won. He thanked his wife and his daughter. As soon as he was finished, Faith and Jason headed out. They went to one or two after-party's then went to head back to the hotel. Before Faith could leave, Jamie grabbed her hand. "What," Faith asked. "Dance with me," Jamie said. "No," Faith replied. He pulled her onto the dance floor with him.

"What Jamie," Faith asked. "Why are you here with him?" "Jamie, back off. You screwed half the half- naked women in the planet. I'm here with him because he asked," Faith said. She walked off and Jason walked her out through the cameras. They got back to the hotel and his mom was asleep with Patsy.

"Come with me," Jason said walking her into the bedroom. "Your mom is…" He kissed Faith. He walked her backwards to the bed. "Jason," Faith said. He kissed her again. "She's in the next room." Jason kissed her again and undid her dress. They barely came up for air. Their clothes all ended up a pile on the floor. They had sex. Mind-blowing, out of body experience sex. When they finally came up for air, Faith heard Eva walking around with her to calm her down. "I have…" He kissed her. "No you don't." "She's…" One move and he was inching into round two. "I have to get up," Faith said. "Nope," he teased. An hour later, Patsy was still crying and Jason fell asleep. Faith snuck out of bed, washed the makeup off and came in to check on the baby. "She won't settle," Eva said. "It's okay. She's just being fussy. She needs mama." While Faith fed Patsy, Eva talked to her. "He was so excited when he won. Honestly, he's different since you two met. I don't know what it is," his mom said.

"Think he was just excited. We walked the carpet and everything went great. I think he was more excited than anything about getting any of those awards," Faith said. "I also saw that Jamie thanked you," Eva said. "He's doing his best to win me back," Faith said. "And?" "Not gonna happen," Faith replied. "He's in love with you," his mom said. "I know. Think he might be in love with her too," Faith said with a smirk. "You two talking about me again," Jason asked. "Little miss fussy needed her mama. She was hungry and a bottle wasn't enough. I'm so proud of you," his mom said getting up and hugging Jason. "I still can't believe I got all three," Jason said. "You deserved it. You were great," Faith said. Jason came over and kissed her. "So what did you two do tonight," Jason asked. "She played, we talked, she ate, she had a little bubble bath, we had ice cream and watched you win then she fell asleep for a little while. I guess she sensed when you two came home," his mom said. "I meant to thank you for all of this," Faith said. "I miss seeing the kids this little. Jason's kids are all grown up now." "Never know mom," Jason said.

Chapter 25

Jamie paced in his room. She walked out with Jason, even after everything he did. Then he realized. Everything he had done was the reason she'd left at all. He called the label to see if they could find out where Jason and Faith were. They said it had been a private booking. Jamie was more determined than ever to find her. Little did he know how close she really was. He went to one of the only other hotels he could think of and couldn't get even a hint. Jamie went and sat in his room and tried calling Faith's cell again. "What do you want," Faith asked. "My wife back for one. My daughter in my arms instead of his for two. I need you back Faith. Please just come home," Jamie said. Faith shook her head. "I'm not doing anything Jamie. I'm done. You can go screw the random strangers," Faith said. "That isn't fair and you know it," Jamie said. "I know one thing Jamie. I know that you aren't capable of staying faithful Jamie. You damn well proved it." "Say it to my face then. Kick my ass if that's what you need to do. You have to stop torturing me with this. I fucked up Faith. I get it. I pissed you off and screwed up our lives. I lost it. I just don't get why you get to run straight to him and I don't get to." "Why don't you look in another Jack bottle and see if you can find the answer," Faith said. She hung up and Jamie snapped.

"World war 4 or 5," Jason asked. Faith shook her head. "One interview and we can head out. Sound okay," Jason asked. Faith nodded. "You can talk you know," Jason said. Faith shook her head and went into the bedroom. "Faith," Jason said. Faith started packing and Jason turned her towards him. He saw her eyes filled with tears. His arms wrapped around her. He kissed her forehead. "It's gonna be alright you know. I promise you Faith. I promise it will be." He hugged her until he felt her shaking stop. "Where's munchkin," Jason asked. "Sleeping. What am I gonna tell her? That he's just her biological dad? We can't even sit in a room to figure out how to settle visitation. What am…" Jason kissed her. "We're gonna be okay. We'll figure it out together Faith. Things will get better. I promise," Jason said. Faith hugged him. After the interview he had to do, Jason took Faith, Patsy and his mom and they all headed back to Nashville.

Faith got back to Jason's and Patsy was out cold. "I got it," Jason said. He kissed Faith and went upstairs. He gently changed the baby and slid her into the crib. He came downstairs and Faith was doing laundry. "What are you doing," Jason asked. She brushed tears away. "Woman, what's going on," Jason asked. "One second things are fine. The next they go from liveable to hell. How am I supposed to find a middle ground," Faith asked. Jason kissed her. He grabbed her hand and walked her into the bedroom upstairs. "What," Faith asked. "Lie down," he said. "Jason, this isn't…" He slid her boots off and snuggled up with her. "What," Faith asked. He wrapped his arms tight around her. "Nobody is getting anything Faith. He should know by now that if he wants to see her, he has to stop . Having a kid when you aren't even talking to him makes things a hell of a lot worse. Babe, things are gonna be okay. You'll figure it out Faith. I promise you it'll get easier," Jason said. "Like it's easier for you," Faith asked. "Kills me not having them around all the time. I still talk to them Faith. Every day. Sometimes more than just once. When I miss them, it kills. Seeing that baby makes me happy. Being with you makes me happy. That's what I have to do. I have to accept what I can't change. It's in the bible for a reason," Jason said. Faith kissed him. "Better," he asked. Faith nodded. "Good. I hate seeing you mad," Jason said. "He's infuriating," Faith said. He kissed her again. That one kiss turned into kiss after kiss and goose bumps from head to toe. Just as he was going for the buckle on his jeans, his phone went off. "I could've sworn I left that down…" Faith kissed him and he grabbed the phone. "Baby," Jason said. "Mama said we could come over. We made you something for your awards," his youngest said. "Perfect. Then you can meet Faith and Patsy too," Jason said. "Yay. Daddy, can we stay the weekend," his older daughter asked. "You got it. I'll come over in a little bit," Jason said. "I love you daddy," she said. "Love you too baby. See you in a few." Jason hung up and kissed Faith. "What," Faith said. "Now where were we," Jason said. "You have…" Jason kissed her and Faith started laughing. "What," he asked. "We…" He kissed her and devoured her lips. Faith managed to get up and just as they were cleaning things up, Patsy woke up. Faith fed her and changed her and Jason smiled.

"What," Jason asked. "Go get them. I can think of a few things they're gonna love," Faith said. Jason kissed her. "No more worrying about him," Jason said. Faith nodded. One more over the top kiss and he headed out to get the girls.

Faith got Patsy all settled and the girls showed a little while later. His youngest, Callie, was in his arms when they came in and his eldest, Emily, was hand in hand with him. "You sure you like it daddy," Callie said. "I love everything you two make," Jason said hugging them. Callie hopped out of his arms and Jason introduced them to Faith and the baby. "She's so cute," Callie said. "She's a pretty great little munchkin. I know she was looking forwards to meeting you two. She was so excited she needed two naps," Faith said. Jason walked up behind Faith and wrapped his arms around her waist. "Daddy told me you were staying with him. That mean you love my dad," Emily asked. "Something like that," Faith replied. "That mean you're staying here for good," Emily asked. "We'll see. What's with all the questions," Jason asked. "Don't want you being upset like you were when you and mom weren't together anymore," his daughter said. Emily hugged him and went and played with the baby. "Never gonna be like that again," Jason said. "What if…" Jason kissed Faith. "Not one word." "You two want cocoa or cider," Jason asked. One wanted one, one wanted the other and Faith opted for cider. Jason pulled Faith into the kitchen with him. "What," Faith asked. Jason kissed her, pinning her against the counter and barely let her up for air. Not 10 minutes later, the cider was warmed and the cocoa was ready and he let Faith up. "I want you so bad I can taste it right now," Jason said. "I know," Faith teased. "You are so getting…" "Daddy, can we take Patsy to her crib? She's yawning," Callie asked. "I'll take her up there. You two have some daddy time," Faith said. Callie hugged Faith. "Thank you for making daddy smile," Callie said. "Think that was you two too," Faith said. She giggled then went and sat down and had her cocoa.

Jason kept that grin on his face the entire visit they had with the girls. They had a family movie night the first night and Emily kept looking over at Faith and Jason. "What," Jason asked. "Do you love her dad," Emily asked as Jason was putting her to bed. "Yes," Jason said. "She makes you happy. I miss seeing you happy," Emily said. "I missed it too. She cares about you two," Jason said. He hugged her. "Daddy, can you make her stay," Callie asked. "I'll do what I can. I'm gonna see about her staying." He told the girls he loved them, made sure they were both settled and closed their doors. He went and looked in on Patsy and Faith was rocking her to sleep and feeding her. He leaned against the door jam. Faith looked over and saw that grin that hadn't left his face. She put Patsy into the crib, turned on the mobile and came towards Jason. They quietly slipped out and Jason pulled her into his arms. He kissed Faith, pinning her to the wall and almost devouring her. He barely came up for air until Faith started walking him towards the bedroom. "What is running through your head," Faith asked. "Been wanting you all day and we finally get some privacy so I can devour you head to toe," he whispered. "We..." Before she could even finish her sentence, Jason peeled her bra and her shirt off and was kicking off his jeans. His kisses were becoming a drug to her. "We can't keep..." Even when Faith knew that what they were doing wasn't right, it didn't matter. Jamie signed those separation papers. She could do what she needed to – what she wanted to. Jason made love to her until both of them were completely and totally exhausted. Faith fell asleep in Jason's arms. He was almost covering her. Faith slid the blanket over them and they fell asleep shortly after. It wasn't until Faith woke up 3 hours later that she realized that he was naked beside her. She did her best to keep things quiet. She slid her satin robe on when Patsy woke up for her feeding. Faith snuck her back into her crib and went back to bed. The second she went to grab a t-shirt, Jason pulled her back into bed and devoured her all over again. He made love to her again and then curled back up together. "What," Faith asked. "I hate it when you get up and leave me here all alone." "Missed me that much after 15 minutes," Faith asked. Jason kissed her again. "Miss you after 1 minute." He kissed her. "What," Faith asked. "What if I said I don't want you to go," Jason said. "Where am I going," Faith asked. "Exactly," Jason said. "What are you suggesting," Faith asked. He nibbled and kissed around her neck. "Staying for good. The girls love you and I do. Promise you aren't gonna leave." "Jason." "Or I will have to find a way to convince you not to," he whispered. "You realize we're still..." He devoured her lips. They finally curled up together and got sleep, but Faith knew exactly what he was thinking.

Jason got up the next morning and Faith was still in his arms. He nibbled her neck and she curled into him. "I could stay in bed with you all day and night for years," Jason said. "Except there are three little girls waiting for us," Faith said. "It's 7am. They're still sleeping. I checked." "Meaning," Faith asked. "Come with me," he asked. Faith turned towards him and he kissed her. He helped her up, handed her a sweater and Faith slid her leggings on. Jason slid on a sweater and his jeans and walked her downstairs. "Where are we going," Faith asked. He grabbed the baby monitor and walked her outside. "What?" He kept walking. "What are you…" "So, I'm gonna ask you something. Don't get mad, just listen." Faith nodded and her stomach started getting butterflies. "What if you stayed? Not just for a little while, but for good," Jason asked. "I'm still married. We're separated, but…" Jason kissed her. "What if I wanted you to stay? We stay here and we're happy. No more worrying. No more Jamie causing trouble. You and me. What do you think," Jason asked. "Married. I can't just pretend all of it…" "If I had met you before he did, you'd never have to worry again. You know that right? There wouldn't have been a worry. We…" "We can't have this discussion Jason. I can't just walk away and run off with you." He devoured her lips. "I want you Faith. I want you here. Not just temporarily. I love you." "Jason," Faith said. He kissed her. "Faith, please. Marry me. Please," Jason said. Faith looked at him. "I'm married Jason. Don't you…" He kissed her. "Just between us for now. Please," he begged. "Maybe I should just go," Faith said. He grabbed her hand. "Please," he asked. Faith looked in his eyes. "Marry me. We already know you're better off here. Please," Jason said. "We just…" "I can't help being in love with you. The girls even said last night they hadn't seen me this happy. They both love you Faith. I can't deny it. I can't just put it aside like a bad habit. Please," Jason said. "I'm still married to Jamie. It's not gonna look right Jason. I can't just walk away from a marriage. I.." Jason kissed her again, devouring her lips and barely let her up for air. He picked her up, wrapped her legs around him and leaned her against the back of the shed in the back. "We…" He peeled her sweater off. "We can't…" Her leggings slid down her silky legs. She felt him pull at his jeans and they had sex against that shed. "Marry me," Jason said. "We…can't…" He kissed her again and he could barely even think straight. "We have to go inside," Faith said. "Say yes," he said. "I'm still married. I can't just say yes,"

Faith said. "If you weren't married," Jason asked. "I can't just...." He kissed her. "He signed the separation papers Faith. You can," Jason replied. "Say it." Faith kissed him. She went to walk away. "Faith." "If I wasn't...I don't know." "If you and Jamie weren't together anymore," Jason asked.

The memories of Faith with Jamie flooded her brain. Him rescuing her from Evan, Jamie marrying her in a ceremony of just a few friends and family. It never was the way she wanted it. He talked her into that marriage and that wedding. When she realized that things had gone that far, they were pregnant with Patsy. Faith walked into the house and upstairs to check on Patsy. The girls had her out of the crib, changed and playing on the floor. "Didn't know you guys were up," Patsy said. "Did you say yes," Callie asked. "Dad and I talked about it." "That mean you said yes," Emily asked. "That means we're going to talk. I need to have more time to think about it," Faith said trying to find a way of giving the kids what they wanted. "Please say yes to daddy," Callie said. "I love having you two here. You know that right," Faith said. Emily nodded. "Then tell Daddy yes," Emily said. Faith hugged her. Jason came in a little while later.

Faith called Jamie a little while later. "What's wrong," Jamie asked. "We need to have a talk," Faith said. "Just come down to the house," Jamie said. "No. Not gonna be happening. Just meet me down at riverside," Faith said. "Just tell me what's going on," Jamie said. "See you in a little bit." "At least bring the baby." Faith hung up. She went upstairs to get changed. Faith heard the girls going downstairs. She heard Jason making them breakfast and heard the baby giggling. Faith had a shower and got dressed. Jason came upstairs a little while later and locked the bathroom door. Faith turned around. "Where are you going," Jason asked. "To talk to him and make a decision. I can't..." He kissed her and devoured her lips. "Just promise that when you get back you come with the answer I want," Jason said. "I can't just promise that. I need to do what's right," Faith said. "Then say yes. That's what's right," Jason said. Faith kissed him and finished getting ready. His hands slid around her waist. "What," Faith asked. "I love you. Whether he can handle it or not, I know you're gonna be back in my arms," Jason said. Faith turned. Jason kissed her again and leaned her against the counter. "I have to go," Faith said. He kissed her. "I know. I'm also gonna end up pacing and being worried while you're gone. Just promise me." Faith kissed him again, took a change of clothes downstairs and got Patsy changed. "Where you going," Emily asked. "Patsy wanted to see her daddy. We'll be back in a little while," Faith said. Emily and Callie both hugged her. "Promise," Emily asked. Faith nodded. She slid Patsy into the car seat and headed off.

Faith pulled in and the baby was out cold. Jamie was sitting on the front bumper of the truck. "She grew so much," Jamie said. "So, what I was coming to talk to you about," Faith said. "You're coming home," Jamie said. Faith shook her head. "Faith." "I know you care Jamie, but you cheated more than just once. You got caught once. It got thrown into the spotlight once. How many more times did…" "Faith, you can't be saying what I think you are." "We can't do this Jamie. One date isn't gonna change this. One date isn't gonna turn back time." "Faith, don't. We aren't over. Promise me," he said. "Jason asked me…" "Faith, don't you dare even think it. You aren't leaving me and marrying him," Jamie said. "I'm doing what I need to alright? I can barely even…" Jamie kissed her. "Stop," Faith said. "I'm not losing you to Jason. Never," he said. "You don't get to make that decision Jamie. You screwed half the damn city instead of staying faithful. Want proof? How about TMZ? The Tennessean? Country weekly? That's practically humiliating. You don't get both," Faith said. "Then the past stays that way and you come home." Faith shook her head. "Faith," Jamie said. She shook her head again. "You're staying with him? Seriously," Jamie said. "I am doing what's right. End of discussion," Faith replied. "I'm not losing…" "You can still see Patsy whenever you want. I promise you," Faith said. "One date and I'll leave you be," he said. "I'm not accepting that Jamie. If things don't work then…" "And when you snap out of it? I'm not losing you Faith. You're gonna snap out of it. When you do, you're gonna come back. I'm still gonna be there just like I was when you screwed up and ended up with Evan. I saved you. When Jason turns into another Evan, I'm still gonna be waiting Faith." She nodded. "Just don't jump into a wedding. Please," Jamie said. Faith nodded. He kissed her. A kiss that had her insides melting and every inch of her turning to jelly. "I'm never giving up. Never," Jamie said. "I need…" He kissed Faith again and walked her and Patsy back to the truck. "Jamie," Faith said. He kissed her again. He got Patsy settled and devoured Faith's lips. "Remember," he said. Faith nodded. He kissed her again almost making her too weak to stand and let go. He got in his truck and left before Faith saw the tears.

Faith drove back to the house and saw Jason sitting on the front steps. "What," Faith asked when she saw him. "Girls are watching a movie. Couldn't think straight," Jason said. "Really," Faith said. Patsy started getting fussy and Jason picked her up. She settled right down in his arms. "So did you two talk," Jason asked. Faith nodded. "And?" "If we do, we're having a long engagement. No running off into the sunset either," Faith said. "Meaning," Jason asked. Faith kissed him. "That mean you're saying yes?" "That means I'm thinking about it," Faith said. He kissed Faith. "That mean I get all week to convince you," Jason joked. "I'm thinking. You can't convince…" He devoured her lips. "Say yes." "If I do, we keep this quiet. Deal," Faith asked. "How quiet," he asked. "Nobody but us and the girls," Faith said. "We…" "Jason," Faith said. "For now." "I'll keep thinking," Faith said. He came inside and brought the baby inside. He put Patsy in her crib and Faith came in. "What do I have to do to convince you," Jason asked as he whispered in her ear and wrapped his arms around Faith's waist from behind. "Time," Faith said. "You sure that's all," he asked as he undid the buckle of her jeans. "For now, yes," Faith replied. He bit her neck. "And what…" Jason kissed her and nibbled up her neck to her ear. "I want you," he said. "And the girls are awake," Faith said. He walked her into the master bedroom. "Jason," Faith said. He walked her into the bathroom, pulling her jeans undone. "What…" He kissed her, leaned her against the counter and made love to her. He didn't let up until he almost collapsed on her. Faith got up and went to head downstairs. "Where you going," Jason asked. "To spend time with the girls while they're here," Faith said. "Should cover up that bite mark," he teased. "You…" "Tiny. Not even noticeable except by me," he teased. He bit the back of her neck. "What are you doing," Faith asked. He kissed down the back of her neck. "Quit," Faith said. "They have to go home tonight. School. Know what that means right," Jason whispered.

They went downstairs and Faith saw the girls half-asleep in front of the movie. "That mean that you said yes to daddy," Emily asked. "We're talking about it," Faith said. "When you say yes, can we be here," Callie asked. Faith hugged them. "Movie," Jamie asked. "Number two," Emily asked. Jamie nodded. A half hour into the movie, the girls were out cold. He kissed Faith's neck. "Quit," Faith said. He walked over and carried Emily to her bed then did the same with Callie. He came back downstairs and Faith was putting something together for dinner. He walked up behind Faith and wrapped his arms around her. "What you want," Faith asked. "To hear yes," Jason said. "What are you really doing," Faith asked. "What happened with your talk," Jason asked. "He told me he'd let go if I had one date with him. He just damn well assumed that I'd come back. That's just plain stupid," Faith said. "Do you still love him," Jason asked. "He saved me. He helped me get free of Evan. He gave me my baby. Yeah I love him, but now? I don't trust the feeling anymore. Not with anyone." Jason kissed her. "You can trust it with me." "We can't just run off and get married. You realize how that looks for me," Faith said. "What are you scared for? It's me. I put that permanent hole in his head for coming after you. Faith, I can't just let someone hurt you. That's what he's gonna end up doing if you go back. You know that," Jason said. "I can't just walk away from all of that. He put a ring on my hand Jason. That's not something I take lightly and you know that. Walking away from him altogether... I can't. I just can't do that. He's Patsy's daddy. I can't just walk out on it," Faith said. "Do you love me? I mean really love me. Faith, I have never even met someone like you. You were on my mind from the second we met. I see you with those girls and with Patsy and I fall even harder. Please," Jason asked. "Why? We just started dating. We don't need to rush into this," Faith said. "Then we get engaged and stay that way for a year," Jason said. "You're.." He kissed her. "Marry me," Jason said. "Promise me you won't rush this," Faith said. Jason kissed her again. He picked her up and leaned her onto the kitchen counter. "Say yes," Jason begged. "As long as..." He kissed her. "Say it," he begged. Faith nodded. "Say it," Jason said. "Yes. I'll marry you," Faith replied. He kissed her and they didn't come up for air. He carried her upstairs, into the bedroom and into the master bath. He didn't let her up for air for over an hour. They were pinned to the floor and curled up together among their clothes. "I can't believe you said it,"

Jason said. "Just promise me," Faith said. He kissed her. He devoured her lips. "We should get up," Faith said. He kissed her again. "Up," Faith said. She got up and he kept trying to pull her back to him. "I'm getting dressed," Faith said. Jason got up and kissed her. They got dressed and slid out of the bedroom.

Patsy was just waking up and the girls were stepping out of their bedrooms and rubbing their eyes. When Emily saw the ring on Faith's finger, she got a smile ear to ear. "You said yes," Emily said. "We're keeping things quiet alright? We aren't telling anyone," Faith said. Emily nodded and ran over to Faith to hug her. Callie hugged her too. "Think you two can handle that," Jason teased. "We can't even tell mama," Callie asked. Jason shook his head. "For now, no," he replied. They hugged Jason and Faith went and got dinner finished up. "So, what would you think about going out to dinner," Jason asked. "Tomorrow. Dinner's almost finished," Faith said. Jason kissed her. "What," Faith asked. "Then we're going for ice cream after dinner," Jason teased. He kissed Faith again. The girls were giggling and Jason heard Patsy wake up. He went upstairs and changed her and brought her downstairs. "What," Faith asked. "She said she wanted ice cream." Faith laughed. They finished dinner and cleaned up. As soon as they finished cleaning up, the girls were packed and ready to head home. Jason took them the long route and they stopped for ice cream downtown. Faith slid the ring off her finger and put it into her purse. Jason shook his head. "I told you," Faith replied. He kissed her. They got their ice cream and headed back to take the girls home. As soon as the girls were home, Jason turned towards Faith and kissed her. "Put that ring back on," he said. "Why," Faith asked. He kissed her and put the ring on her finger. "What are you doin," Faith asked. He kissed her and drove out to the lake. "What are we doing out here," Faith asked. He parked the truck and pulled her into his arms. "I'm never hurting you like he did. I promise you you're never gonna hurt again Faith. Nobody is putting hands on you and hurting you ever again," Jason said. Faith nodded. He kissed her and any ounce of doubt she had disappeared. "I love you," Jason said. Faith kissed him. They headed back to the house and snuggled up together. Patsy went straight to bed. "You're never hurting like that again. You know that right," Jason said. "That's what I wish. That Patsy never have to go through that. I don't know. Maybe I should just give Jamie another…" He kissed her. "Jamie who," Jason said.

Faith woke up the next morning and saw 5 missed calls from Alan. She grabbed her cell, checked on Patsy and went downstairs and called him. "What's up," Faith asked. "Whatever you two were talking about has him acting like an idiot. What's going on," Alan asked. "You mean beyond the women he's been screwing around with? I left Alan. I walked out for a reason. Jason asked me to marry him," Faith said. "He what?" "I can't sit there and watch as he self-destructs Alan. He screwed around on me with more than one woman. I can't let that go. Jason was helping me with Patsy and we got closer. He's a good man. We just kinda got closer. He's the one that took care of Evan," Faith said. "Do you even realize what you're doing," Alan asked. "Walking away from the person who caused more stress when it was the last thing I needed? I know what I'm doin g. I'm fine," Faith said. Alan couldn't help it. "He needs you Faith. Even if it's just to maintain his damn sanity. He was drinking again." "And I'm supposed to cure that? He knows what he has to do Alan. He walked away from us before I did." "Faith." "He slept with her. He didn't stop screwing around after that. I'm not gonna be the one sitting at home and trying to look at it blindly. I'm taking care of Patsy and me. He doesn't even regret it," Faith said. "And how do you know that?" "Because he said he'd let go if I went on one date with him. This isn't indecent proposal Alan. He doesn't get to make a stupid move like that." "I'll talk to him. Just give him a chance to win you back before you marry Jason. You don't wanna just go and then end up regretting this," Alan said. "He had the chance. He had more than one Alan. I can't do this with him anymore." "Come meet me for a drink then," Alan asked. "Since you're gonna send him in your place, hell no." "We'll go have coffee then. I'll meet you at the park." "Alan." "You and me. I won't say a thing to Jamie." "You do, you get a butt kicking to the other side of the galaxy." "Faith." "Fine. He shows, that's it," Faith said. "This afternoon. Riverside." "I mean it." They hung up and Faith went upstairs and started getting ready for the day.

Faith stepped out of the shower and went into the bedroom. Jason grabbed her hand and pulled her to him. "What," Faith asked. Jason pulled her back into bed, kissed her and pinned her to the bed. "Where you going," Jason asked. "Meeting. You have rehearsal," Faith said. He kissed her and devoured her lips. "What if I didn't wanna share you today," he asked. "You'd have to cancel rehearsal. The tour is starting soon anyway," Faith said. "Got a new opener," Jason said. "Thought you were getting Jamie," Faith said. "Sorta engaged. Thought my fiancée would be uncomfortable with it. He's opening for Luke. I didn't want you getting flack. Means that we have extra time to relax," Jason said. "I still have…" He slid her satin robe off and knocked it to the floor. "I still have to go," Faith said. He kissed down her neck. He kissed her breast, her stomach, her hip. "I have to go," Faith said. When he nibbled, kissed and licked his way back up her torso, Faith forgot time existed. He made love to her. They were like two happy as hell teenagers. He didn't know what to think, but he knew that he wasn't losing her for even a second. He didn't let her up. "Where are you going," Jason asked. "To talk to Alan. That's all," Faith said. "If you need me, you call. We're downtown to do rehearsal." Faith nodded. "Even better, come over to the studio after your chat. We can do dinner together." "I have to go pick up paperwork from the office anyway. It's not that far." Jason nibbled her neck. "Still can't believe you said yes," Jason said. "Very very convincing," Faith teased. "You sure you're okay? You aren't acting like you," he said. "Just stressed with all the Jamie stuff," Faith said. "Don't let him stress you. We're gonna be alright Faith. We're going out to dinner tonight. You and me and your favorite seafood. You need to get your mind off it," Jason said. "It's off now," Faith said. Jason kissed her. They snuggled a while then got up and Faith started getting dressed. "We can take my truck. The car seat stuff is already loaded in it. Just drop me at rehearsal," Jason said. Faith kissed him. Just as he was about to let her up for air, Patsy was awake again. Jason kissed her again then headed into the nursery to get Patsy. Faith got changed and when Jason came back in with Patsy, he handed her his leather jacket. "What," Faith asked. He kissed her. "I can live without the jacket," Faith said. He kissed her then shook his head. She knew what he was thinking. Part of it got her mad, the other made her remember when a boyfriend's jacket was everything.

Jason, Faith and Patsy had breakfast then headed downtown. "Do you want me to keep her with me," Jason asked. "You have your rehearsal.

She's fine. She's with me. You need to concentrate at rehearsal." Faith kissed him at the light. "I love you," he said. "Love you too," Faith replied. He kissed her and devoured her lips, if only for a moment. She dropped Jason off, he kissed Patsy and Faith then headed in. There was a lump in his throat. Something told him that Faith was in for something really bad. He messaged her a few minutes later:

If you need me, text. I have a bad feeling about this Faith. Please tell me you brought protection.

Faith parked the truck and Patsy was starting to cry. "What's wrong," Faith asked. She knew Patsy was hungry. Faith warmed up the bottle in the truck and fed her. As soon as Patsy finished her bottle, she was asleep in Faith's arms. Faith walked down by the water and sat down on the grass. Patsy slept in her arms. Faith was perfectly fine until she heard someone coming towards her. Faith looked at her cell and saw the message from Jason. She replied back:

Yes I have it. I love you too.

Faith snuggled Patsy and kept her warm. "She finally shows," she heard. Faith turned her head and saw Jamie with Alan. She got up, shook her head and went to walk away. "Faith," Jamie said. "I told you Alan. I said you brought him I was leaving. I'm leaving," Faith said. "Please," Jamie said. "I told you already Jamie. You screwed around. Not just one damn woman either. Dozens. Don't try to play it off either. You screwed up. You chose that. You chose that over me and over the baby. You don't get to keep doing this. I was willing to come home before that. I was in love with you. I just can't do this Jamie. You screwed around even when we were happy. Just leave it be," Faith said. "No. I promised you that you weren't getting hurt. I made you that promise. I'm fixing us." "No you aren't. I'm leaving Jamie. I'm walking out the door and I'm not coming home. I'm not walking back into that house while you're cheating. I'm not. You made your decision Jamie. You chose that. You chose to have girlfriends instead of having your wife. I'm done. We're done," Faith said. She started walking and Alan caught up to her. "You lied. You screwed me over. Don't think I'm gonna be that stupid," Faith said. "He's tipped off the edge Faith. He hasn't slept since you left.

Please. I love you like a sister Faith. I'm not steering you wrong." "No, you just steered his dick wrong. He screwed around and lied. I'm not letting him back." "Faith, hear me out. She's his daughter too. Just let him have time with the baby," Alan said. "No. She doesn't need someone who's like that around her. Second, I damn well don't trust either of you. Knowing him, he'd take her hostage and hold her against me. I'm taking my daughter with me and we're leaving." "Then let him spend time with her here. We talk, he has some dad and daughter time with her." "No. Not after that. Not after he screwed around. She deserves better," Faith said. "Ten minutes." "He moves, he gets a 9 to his head." Alan called Jamie over and slid the baby into his arms. "She grew up so much," Jamie said. "Ten feet. You go one step further you'll never be singing again," Faith said. Jamie nodded. Alan wasn't gonna let him screw this up.

Jamie rocked Patsy and had a dad and daughter chat while Faith was watching intently and talking to Alan. "He screwed up. I get that Faith, but she's his daughter too. He needs time with her too. You need to let him be there," Alan said. "Be where? In a random woman's bed? Screwing someone after he finishes on stage? That isn't gonna be me and I'm not letting Patsy see that. She doesn't deserve that and either do I. Do you know how I found out Alan? Internet. TMZ . TV shows that were all over every damn channel. Do you know how humiliating that is?" "Faith, please. I know he was upset. He was trying to find a way to get rid of the pain. Knowing you left because of that woman's stupid lie, almost destroyed him. He acted out. Faith, he loves you. He loves you so much he can't even function without you. You remember what he was like when he was on tour. He wasn't the same on stage without you. He screwed up. Just give him a chance to make it up to you. Please," Alan said. "No." "Faith, be reasonable. He loves that little girl, and he loves you. He can't turn that off. He won't. Even if he could forget it, he won't. He's begged me for weeks to find out where you are so he can be with you. He wants you two back with him. Faith, just try. Let him try." Faith walked down to Jamie, slid the baby from his arms. "Please Faith," Jamie said. Faith shook her head. "Faith." She slid the baby into the car seat in the truck and went to pull out. Jamie blocked her in. Faith went over the cement barrier, turned the truck around and left to go back to the office. She pulled in, took the baby upstairs with her and leaned her into the portable crib by her desk. Patsy was out cold seconds later. Faith went through her paperwork, got her desk completely organized and cleaned up and they headed over to meet Jason at the rehearsal hall.

Faith walked in and Jason was singing the song she loved. Jason looked at her and got a smile ear to ear. He finished the song then took a break so he could see Faith and Patsy. He walked straight towards Faith and kissed her. "Hey there beautiful," Jason said. "Hey yourself. Patsy missed you," Faith said. He kissed Faith, devouring her lips, and picked Patsy up. She snuggled right into him and clamped down on the neck of Jason's sweater. "How'd it go," Jason asked. Faith shook her head. "Jamie showed with him. He spent some time with Patsy and wasn't more than 10 feet from me. He keeps causing shit. He's not gonna stop until he either gets the baby or me or both," Faith said. Jason kissed her. "He's not getting any of it. You know you two are gonna have to share custody. He's not just gonna let you walk away with her. You two have to figure out visit times. I'm gonna ask you something and you have to promise not to get mad," Jason said. "What," Faith replied. "If things got better, would you ever take him back," Jason asked. "I'm supposed to forget he cheated? That's not forgivable. That's not even forgettable. He ruined what we had. I'm just not letting him push it all aside." Jason kissed her. "That's what I wanted to hear." Jason kissed Faith again. "What," Faith asked. "I love you. That hasn't changed and it never will. We can get married." "Jason. Stop. Just stop and listen to yourself. You promised we'd take it slow." "Why not," he asked. "Because I'm still legally married to him. That's why," Faith said. "You said you didn't want to be with him." Faith shook her head and went to get up. "Faith." She slid Patsy out of his arms and slid her into her car seat. "Faith." "What," she said. "I just want us to..." Faith grabbed the car seat. "Where are you going," Jason asked. Faith went to leave and he ran after her. "I love you. Faith, I want us to be happy and be a family. I need to..." She went to walk out the door. "Faith, don't go," he said. "I'm going home. That's the end of it," Faith said. "Faith." "I'm..." He kissed her. "Two years. Independence day," Jason said. "You realize you're..." Trying to fix us. I get Jamie fucked us up. I get he tried to get you back, but you know where you belong. It's not with him. Faith, you can do anything you want to do, just let me be there." She stopped. "I just want to be with you. That's all. I want you to be happy. I want her to grow up and never have a doubt that we love her. I want you to see how much I love you every minute of the day. I just want us to be together. That's it. You want to put it off for 2 years, fine. You want to just be together without getting married? We can. I don't care if we get married or we don't. I just want you and Patsy to be there." "I can't just…" Jason kissed her. "Guys, I'm heading down for an early dinner with Faith and Patsy. See you in a bit," Jason said. He left with Faith and they headed to the restaurant.

"I promise I'm not gonna push. I just thought…" "I know. I just need to handle this my way," Faith said. Jason kissed her. They sat down to dinner and the baby was out cold. The waitress brought them drinks and they placed orders for dinner. "What you want," Jason asked. Faith ordered and got a bottle warmed up for Patsy. "So other than him acting like an idiot, everything else go okay?" Faith nodded. "He was pushing. Even Alan tried. It's like he expects me to just let it go. How do you let something like that go?" Jason kissed her. "I love you. Nothing is hurting you like that again. You don't understand how much restraint it took to not kick his ass to another planet. He doesn't deserve you Faith. He never did." "Jason, stop alright? He's been my friend for years. He got me away from Evan when I didn't think he was gonna be able to. He kept me safe. Things didn't end the way he wanted, but he never stopped being a friend. Now, things changed, but I'm not gonna be mad and hate him. He cared enough to help me. He just sucks at being married," Faith said. Jason kissed her. "I was married almost 15 years before things tanked Faith. I promise you, when I say those words, I never ever take them back." "You still love her," Faith asked. "It's not the same now Faith. I'm in love with this amazing woman that I'm lucky to have in my life. I don't want anything else."

Chapter 26

After they finished dinner, Jason went back to rehearsal with Patsy and Faith. They watched, cheered the guys on and Jason sang directly to Faith. When they finished up the last little bit, the guys all started heading home and Jason talked Faith into walking on the stage with him. "What," Faith asked. "Pick a song," he said. "Broken," Faith replied. He flipped the recording on and told her to sing it. "I can't." "Sing," Jason said. His hands slid around her. Faith sang through it. When the song was finished, he'd wrapped his arms around her. He nibbled at her neck. He flipped on one of his new songs. "What are you up to," Faith asked. "Seducing my fiancée." Jason turned her towards him and he kissed her. He picked her up and wrapped her legs around him. "We should probably get…" He kissed her again and walked her towards the sofa. "And what might you have in mind," Faith asked. "Can't just kiss you without you thinking we're gonna have sex. Interesting. What if I just devoured you whole right now?" "We'd probably not be able to get off the sofa. We'd have to sleep here. Something tells me that you aren't gonna be able to hold back until we get home." Jason kissed her and undid the buckle of her jeans. He kissed her and kissed her stomach. He nibbled at her hip. "We have to put her to bed," Faith said. He kissed her. "I love you. It doesn't matter where, or when or how but I am not ever giving you up. I love you Faith. I love you and that baby girl. I am not letting anything happen to you. Never," Jason said. "Meaning what?" "Meaning the minute the ink is dry on your divorce, we can tell the world. I know it could be a while Faith, but I don't care if I have to wait decades. I don't care if we never get married. I just want you in my life and in my arms." Faith kissed him. It wasn't until Patsy woke up and started fussing that Jason finally let her up for air. Faith changed her and saw a letter from Jamie. She slid it in her pocket and changed the baby. Seconds later, Jason slid the note out of her pocket. "What," Faith asked. Jason kissed her and went outside to warm the truck up. Faith slid the baby back into her car seat, grabbed the baby bag and her purse etc. then headed back to the house.

They got back to the house and Jason took the baby upstairs and got her ready for bed. Faith went and kicked her jeans and t-shirt off. She slid on her satin teddy, her robe and her slippers then came downstairs. She made some cider for her and Jason and sat down and went through emails. Just as she was getting to the end of the emails, one from Jamie showed:

I get I screwed up Faith. I have tried to find something or some way to replace you in my life. No matter who it is, I can't forget you. I can't move on and try to be a better man like you deserve. That's why I was out with those girls. I need you Faith. I get it. I get you're mad and that it looked really bad. Since you left, I never would let anyone else in my bed. I won't. Nobody is ever gonna replace you in my heart Faith. I love you. I never have ever thought that I'd have to plead my case with you. I thought you'd never leave. I just want back what we had Faith. I want her back and I want us back. I miss having you with me. Please just give me a chance to make this right Faith. I love you. That hasn't changed and it never will. Even if this is the last time that you hear me out, I'm never gonna stop loving you and I'm never gonna stop wanting you in my life. Meet me at the house. Just come so we can talk and figure all of this out. I'm not losing you Faith. I can't just forget what we have. A drink won't make it go away. A nameless woman doesn't change that I love you. I promised Patsy something today. I promised her that she'd never be without me. That no matter what happens, I'm gonna love her forever. That I'm never going to walk away from how much I love her mom. I meant every word to her Faith. I never stopped loving you.

I don't even know how to. I've tried to move on, but I can't. I remember that day when I didn't try to even stop you from going to Evan. I regretted it and hated that day the entire time you were gone. I love you. I love you even when everything is going wrong. Don't walk away Faith. I'll stop everything. I'll stop the world so we can be together again. Please just give it a chance.

Faith was brushing tears away when Jason came downstairs. "What's wrong," he asked. "Nothing. Just a sappy email. She asleep," Faith asked. Jason slid her laptop off her lap, closed it and kissed her. He laid her laptop on the table and slid into her arms. "She's out cold and adorable as always. She fell asleep the minute I put her pajamas on her," he said. Faith kissed him. "From him," Jason asked. Faith nodded. There was no point in lying to him. If things went the way Jason hoped, Jamie would be gone. If things went the way Faith thought they would, she'd be in a triangle for years. "So what did you think about my idea," Jason asked. "Which one," Faith replied. "About after the divorce," Jason said. "Getting way too ahead of yourself. Slow down," Faith said. "You aren't gonna divorce him now? Faith." "Slow down and chill. I just signed the separation papers. Not the divorce papers. Just stop," Faith said. He got up and walked into the kitchen. "What," Faith asked. "You wanna go back to him then go," Jason said. "I never said that. I said that we had to slow down the train Jason. I get you want me away from him and out of his love life, but you have to let me do this. I need to do this the right way. He's gonna end up tying things up just to figure out shared custody of the baby. I have to handle this right or he's gonna draw it out." "Faith, you can get it over faster than that. You know you can. You wanna draw it out." Faith got up. "What," he said. "You're not pushing me to do what you want. I can't just walk out without a fight." "Then fight. End it." Faith shook her head. "What?" "You want me gone, it can be arranged. You don't get to order me around. Makes you feel better you can have the leash back," Faith said. She handed him back the ring and walked upstairs. "Faith," Jason said. She went and checked on Patsy then went into the guest bedroom with the baby monitor and locked the door.

"Faith," Jason said knocking at the door. "Just go to bed," Faith said. "Open," he asked. "Go to bed Jason. Just go." Faith tried to get sleep. She tossed and turned until almost 2am. Finally, she got up and went to check on Patsy and Jason was leaning on the door jam. "What," Faith asked. Jason kissed her. "I screwed up. Faith, I don't want to fight about it. I read that note he hid. He's hoping and thinking that you're coming back. I just need to know that you won't," Jason said. Faith went in and checked on Patsy. Jason went and warmed up a bottle then came up and handed it to Faith. She fed the baby and Jason sat in the doorway. Patsy went back to sleep a little while later. Faith stepped over Jason and went to go back to bed. He grabbed her hand. "What," Faith asked. He kissed her. "I'm sorry," he said. "I get it alright? I get what you want. You just have to understand. It took you almost a year to divorce when you went through this. It's not gonna be that long, but you have to let this play out however it's going to. I'm not going back. I'm not doing anything other than trying to make things right. If you don't trust me to do it, there's no point." He kissed her again. Her toes went numb and he picked her up. "What," Faith asked. He carried her back to their bed and leaned her onto it. He curled up with her. "Just promise it won't be years," he said. "What happened to I'll wait forever," Faith asked. "I want to see that ring on your hand for good." "You promise to let me handle this?" Jason nodded and kissed her again. He kissed and nibbled at her neck. "Jason," Faith said. "As long as I know you aren't leaving me. Just promise me that I'm not gonna lose you like I lost her." Faith kissed him. "We do this together. Just let me deal with him and we're alright." Jason kissed her and devoured her lips. They were making out like teenagers the rest of the night. He made love to her more than once. Fact was, no matter what he said he was still scared. Their love was epic. Jamie had screwed things up good. He wasn't doing it ever. Not if it would mean ever losing Faith.

Jason woke up the next morning and Faith was curled up with him still, but with Patsy in her arms. "Morning sexy," he said. "Good morning to you too. She said she missed you," Faith joked. "I bet. When did she get up," Jason asked. "An hour ago. You sleep," Faith asked. "Sorta. Had a dream about you," Jason teased. Faith kissed him. Patsy started to fuss again. "I got it," Jason said. Faith kissed him. "Ten minutes," he teased. "What," Faith asked. "She'll be out cold in ten," he said. Faith kissed him. He got up and went and did his magic on the baby. Faith's cell went off two seconds after he left the bedroom.

"Yep," Faith said. "It's me. Don't hang up," Jamie said. "What do you want," Faith asked. "Dinner." "Jamie, you can't do this. I get you want things to start fresh, but after all of this they aren't going to. I can't put that aside. Not anymore. I was gonna call you today anyway. We need to figure out custody stuff so you can have time with the baby. I don't want us fighting about it when we go through divorce court," Faith said. "We don't say that word Faith. We can't just end this," Jamie said. "We are. I can't just pretend it didn't happen." "Please." "No. Don't do this. Don't try to play this game. I need to start my life right Jamie. You can't handle this. You proved it. We're better off apart." "Faith, don't do this. Just come to therapy or something. We can try to work this out," Jamie said. "I need to go. Patsy just got up." "Let me have her for the day." "Jamie, stop." "Emma and Alan are still here anyway. Emma can help if I need it," Jamie said. "You take her anywhere or even think about.." "I won't. Please. We can go out for dinner later. We'll talk things through. Faith, please just talk to me." "I'll bring her by around 10. Dinner is out," Faith said. "Please? Faith, one dinner won't kill you. He can live without you for one damn meal." Faith hung up.

Jason came back downstairs and saw Faith. "What now," he asked. "Driving me nuts. He's never backing off. I've had it," Faith said. Jason leaned over and kissed her. "Come with me," he teased. "For what," Faith asked. "Up." Faith walked upstairs hand in hand with Jason. Patsy reached out for Faith and Faith held Patsy's hand. "Now, about that whole stress thing. You don't get to have stress today. No more stress, no more drama and no more bullshit from him. You're gonna have a day of peace and quiet. You, me and Patsy. We're going for a ride," Jason said. Faith walked into the bedroom and saw the tan leather boots that she loved and the beat up blue jeans that Jason had personalized. "What did you do to my jeans?" He kissed her. "And this," he said as Patsy handed her a shirt. In the pocket was a black velvet box. "Open it," Jason said. She opened it and saw two rings. One was her engagement ring he'd bought her, the other was a ring he'd seen and had to get. He slid her ring on her ring finger, the other on her right hand. "Faith," Jason asked. "What?" "Marry me," he asked. "Just promise no more acting like an idiot about Jamie," Faith said. He kissed Faith. "Jamie who?" "I mean it," Faith said. He kissed her. "Marry me and make me the happiest guy in the entire planet," he asked. "He's gonna snap. He's gonna lose it Jason," Faith said. He kissed her. "Miss Patsy said she wanted you to say yes." "I bet she did," Faith joked. He kissed Faith. Patsy grabbed at her hair and Jason started laughing. "I get the long engagement thing. Don't care how long I wait. I just want us," Jason said. "You have that," Faith said. "I meant for real." "I guess you can get your way this time," Faith teased. Jason looked at her. "Meaning," he asked. Faith nodded. "Yes," she said.

The week flew by. Still, nobody knew anything about them getting engaged. That was the way that Faith wanted it. The girls knew but nobody else did. They were barely even apart for more than a few hours. When the tour started, Faith and Patsy were on the tour bus with Jason and his girls. "Found out who was the opener. They never updated it babe. Jamie's opening the first half," Jason said. Faith nodded. First thing that hit her was seeing first hand all the women he'd go after. How many times he'd be with someone else. All of it was hitting her. "What," Jason asked as he finished giving Patsy breakfast. "Nothing. Just realizing why him opening wasn't smart," Faith said. Jason kissed her. "I love you. I get you being uncomfortable baby. I get it. Just remember something – I love you. We're getting hitched as soon as you let me pick a day, and I'm never letting go of your hand. Not for a million," Jason said. Faith kissed him. "Just what I needed," Faith said. He kissed her again then went and slid Patsy into her crib. "What," Faith asked. He walked over to Faith and kissed her, leaning into her. They didn't come up for air for an hour and a half. "Don't we have something to do," Faith asked. Jason kissed her. "Daddy. Can we turn on a movie," Emily asked. "As long as it isn't the one you keep watchin over and over," Jason said. "Fine. Patsy wants snow white," Emily said. "Fine, but you aren't having sodas. Water," Jason said as he leaned in and kissed Faith. "Fine," Emily said.

Jason slid the door closed. "What," Faith asked. He kissed her, devouring her lips. "You know that kiss is damn addictive," Jason said. "Oh really," Faith teased. "Might have to keep it for myself. Just do one thing first," he asked. "What," Faith replied. "Make me a promise. Promise me that nobody but me gets those lips," he asked. "Might have to share with my dad and Patsy," Faith joked. Jason kissed her. He went to peel her sweater off. "What.." He kissed her again, pulled off her sweater and knocked it to the floor then went for her jeans. "We…" "Then we're quiet."

Her jeans fell to the floor along with Jason's, and he made love to her on that bed. He barely let her up for air. "Woman, you are gonna make me forget time," Jason said. "Good," Faith said. He kissed her. "Marry me," Jason said. "Okay," Faith replied. "Then you're all mine," Jason said. "Can we negotiate that part," Faith teased. He kissed her again. "Daddy, can we make popcorn," Callie asked. "The snack one," Jason replied still not letting Faith up. They curled up under the blankets. "What," Faith asked. "Promise me something," Jason asked. "What's that," Faith asked. "That he's not gonna get to you while he's opening," Jason asked. "He's gonna bug us. You know that," Faith said. He nodded. "One good thing is he sure as hell ain't getting you alone even for a second. Not if I'm here. Even if I have to kick his ass every night to remind him," Jason said. Faith kissed him. "You don't need to worry. No kicking butt needed either. You're fine. We're fine," Faith said. He kissed her again. "Good, because I never really got the hang of that sharing thing," he joked. Faith kissed him and they got up. Faith slid her jeans and sweater back on and Jason pulled on his jeans and his sweater and they went and sat back down with the girls.

Jason had his arms wrapped around Faith the rest of the way to the venue. "Daddy, can you play a game with us," Callie asked. "You cheat at candy land," Jason teased. "I do not," she teased. "Yeah you do. Cheated since you were 3," he joked. Faith kissed him. Faith grabbed a game and played with the girls. Jason was kissing her neck and snuggling her all the way through it. "Daddy, are you in love with Faith," Emily asked. "Definitely. That okay," he asked. "As long as you share," Callie joked. He gave the girls hugs and kisses and they ended up playing tag on the bus. Faith made sure Patsy was alright. It almost put a smile on her face seeing her little girl playing with Jason's girls. They were just so cute. Emily was very delicate with Patsy, but there was something to be said about having siblings. Even if they weren't blood, they loved her. Faith put Patsy down for a nap and Jason slid in behind her. "What," Faith asked. Jason kissed her neck. "What," Faith asked again. "They love you like you're their mom," Jason said. "I love them too. I still can't believe how happy Patsy is with them. Gives them someone to play with too," Faith said. "Emily asked if she could keep Faith," Jason said. Faith laughed. "She's growing up," Jason said. "I know. I just don't know what to do with her. She's one lucky little girl," Faith said. Jason kissed her. "What if we got her another little sister," Jason asked. "Getting ahead of yourself," Faith said. "Not even a little," he said. They were snuggling and watching movies a half hour later. When they pulled into the venue finally, they all went in so Jason could do sound check. The girls were coloring and Patsy was sleeping in Faith's arms. Jason couldn't help himself. He sang right to Faith. When he hopped off the stage, Callie and Emily ran over and hugged him. "What you guys doin," Jason asked. "We're coloring," Emily said. "And," Jason asked. "Are you marrying Faith," Callie asked. Jason nodded. "She said yes," Jason said. "So that means that Patsy is our sister now," Callie asked. "What do you think," Jason asked. "Okay," she replied. He looked at Faith and had a smirk. "What," Faith asked. "Nothin," he teased.

The guys finished sound check and Faith took the kids back to the bus. She wanted to avoid Jamie as much as possible. When she went to grab water, Jamie finally caught up to her. "What," Faith asked. "You're seriously marrying him," Jamie asked. Faith shook her head and walked back to the bus. She hopped on and Jason walked out towards the tour bus. "We're talking," Jamie said. "No we aren't," Faith replied. Jason came out just as Jamie was trying to drag her out. "Let go," Jason said. "I need to talk to her. Whether you like it or not, I'm talking to her." Jason got up in Jamie's face. "Leave my fiancée alone," Jason said. Jamie grabbed her hand and tried to pull her towards him. "You heard me," Jason said. Faith grabbed Jason's hand. "I'm handling this," Jason said. She kissed him. "Go and I'll handle…" Jason kissed her. "She's not going anywhere with you," Jason said. He walked Faith onto the bus and closed the door. The minute the door was closed, he kissed Faith. "What," Faith asked. "Tomorrow," he said. "Tomorrow what," Faith asked. "We do it tomorrow." Faith shook her head and walked into the stateroom. "Faith," Jason said. "Guess that whole waiting thing just disappeared," Faith said. "Not when he's pushing. There's no reason for us to wait," Jason said. "Yeah there is. We wait or the answer is no," Faith said. Jason looked at her. "Quit it. You aren't getting your way. I get you want me to marry you right now, but…" He kissed her. "Stop. You want this all immediately. I can't do that. If you can't handle that…" Jason kissed her. "We wait. I get it," Jason said. "You…" "I'm not picking a fight. It scares me that he keeps trying to get in the middle," Jason said. "You're scared he's gonna succeed. You don't believe this is gonna work, why are we…" Jason kissed her. He devoured her lips. "Stop. I get you're scared Faith. Things didn't work out with him. I get you're worried it won't with us. Just try to understand that I know we're gonna be fine. I promise you we will." "I can't just leave him and be with you. He's never gonna leave me alone and he's never gonna stop trying. Maybe we…" He kissed her. "We're gonna be fine. You wanna wait, we wait." He hugged her. "Stop worrying about stuff you can't control. We're alright Faith. We always will be. Doesn't matter if it's now or ten years from now." "Then why…" "Heat of the moment." Faith shook her head. "I'd do it tomorrow if you wouldn't try to kick my ass," Jason said. Faith kissed him and they came out from the stateroom.

His girls were sitting at the table coloring and Patsy was playing around in the crib. "So what movie tonight," Jason asked. "Sleeping beauty," Callie said. "No. ET," Emily said. "Both," Faith replied. They hugged Faith. "Are you still marrying Daddy," Emily asked. Faith nodded. "Then why were you fighting," Callie asked. "Grownups fight baby. Doesn't mean we aren't getting married," Jason said. "But…" "But nothing. You two are still gonna be the cutest bridesmaids in the planet," Jason replied. "But…" "Go get washed up and we'll grab dinner," Jason said. The girls fought over the bathroom and Jason kissed Faith. "Just promise that if things…" He kissed Faith. "They won't. Don't even bother wasting your breath. We're fine and we're staying that way. Got me," Jason asked. Faith nodded. He kissed her one last time and they took the girls to dinner. Patsy slept through it as usual, and Jason made sure the girls ate.

He made a plate up for Faith while she tried to let the baby sleep in her arms. They had dinner, Faith got the girls settled and they opted to come watch part of the show. It wasn't until Faith saw Emma that she understood what Jamie had been trying to do. "Come on Faith," Emily said. Faith went with the girls and Emma followed them. "Long time no talk," Emma said. "I know I should've…" Emma hugged her. "I know. I've seen captain ape shit going nuts at the house. He locked the damn master bedroom Faith. He won't even walk in there. He's lost it," Emma said. "I can appreciate it Emma, but I can't just give in. Jason asked me to marry him. We're getting married. The girls are gonna be bridesmaids," Faith said. "And," Emma asked. "Who else," Faith replied. Emma hugged her. "How's princess doing," Emma asked. "Finally sleeping. The ladies tired her right out," Faith said. "Who's that," Callie asked. "Callie, Emily, this is my friend Emma. Emma, the ladies," Faith joked. Callie giggled and held Faith's hand. "Just what you always wanted right," Emma whispered. Faith nodded. Jason came up behind Faith. She looked at him and he motioned to come with him. "Don't leave their side," Faith asked. Emma nodded and sat down with Patsy in her arms and sat with the girls.

Jason pulled Faith into his arms and kissed her. "What you want," Faith asked. "My woman. The girls alright," Jason asked. Faith nodded. He kissed her again. "I love you," he said. "I love you too. Gonna tell me what you're getting all nervous about," Faith asked. He kissed her. "Promise me that no matter what, we'll never lose each other. Promise," Jason said. "What's going on," Faith asked. "Promise me," he said. "When you tell me why." Jason walked her to the dressing room and locked the door. "What," Faith asked. He kissed her. He devoured her lips and was pulling at her shirt in seconds. "Say it," Faith said. He kissed her. "Jason," Faith said. He had tried to half undress her by then and she stopped him. "Talk," Faith said. He kissed her and silenced her. It was fast, but oh so worth it. "Say it," Faith said as they came up for air. "Can't just want you," Jason asked. "I'm not losing you. What brought all that on," Faith asked. "Nothing," Jason said. "Then why do you look like you're keeping secrets," Faith asked. "Remember when I broke it off with my wife," Jason asked. Faith nodded. Then it hit her. This is where he was when he made a stupid mistake and almost cheated. "She…" Jason kissed her. They got dressed. "She's here," Faith asked. Jason nodded. "I barely even noticed. I just kept thinking about how I was marrying you. How I had the sexiest woman in the planet and I forgot everything." "Then why were you still freaked out?" He kissed her. "Marry me," he asked. "I already said yes," Faith said. "Please," he asked. "And a ring is gonna stop that? Stop worrying. I love you. I'm not going..." He kissed her. "I know," he replied. He slid his hand in hers, grabbed his shirt and his lucky pick and they walked out to the girls. Patsy was asleep, Emily and Callie were watching Jamie and Jamie's eyes were on Faith. It wasn't until he sang 'My Heart' that Faith noticed him looking. Faith shook her head. Jason's arms wrapped around her. Jason was kissing her neck the next time he looked over. At the end of the show, Jamie walked right over to Faith, grabbed her hand and pulled her away. "What," Faith asked.

"You aren't seriously marrying him. Tell me you aren't that stupid," Jamie said. "Tell me that after you screw half the women in Nashville, you aren't trying to tell me what to do," Faith said. She walked off and went up and sat with Patsy, Emma and the girls. "You know, the best part about doing these shows, is having amazing fans. There are 4 right now that are my favorite fans." Faith shook her head. Jason got a smirk ear to ear. "I know y'all are in the dark about this, and I sorta did promise to tell you a secret tonight." The fans went nuts. Makeup came over and touched Faith's hair and makeup up and Jason looked over and smirked. Faith shook her head. He nodded and the smirk turned into a smile. Faith shook her head again. "Well, I know y'all know I was single. Sorry ladies, I'm officially engaged," Jason said. Faith looked at him. "She is one gorgeous woman. I also know that I'm not gonna be single ever again," he said. Callie giggled and hugged Faith. Jason went and grabbed his guitar. "Don't you dare," Faith said. He kissed her then finished up the concert.

"You realize the press is gonna be all over you two," Emma said. Faith nodded. "Don't really have a choice Emm. It's not meant to be a permanent secret," Faith replied. As soon as the show was over, Faith carried Callie and Jason carried Emily. Emma carried Patsy and they headed out to the tour bus. Jamie came up behind Emma and slid Patsy out of her arms. "What do you think you're doing," Jason asked. "I'll take her tonight. She can come with me," Jamie said. Faith shook her head. She put Callie into bed, came out and got Emily and put her into bed. "You don't get to just take her," Jason said. Faith slid the baby out of Jamie's arms. She took her onto the tour bus and warmed up a bottle. Patsy woke up a little while later. Faith changed her then fed her. The baby fell back asleep in her arms and Faith put her down to bed. Faith came back outside and Jamie and Jason were having a fight.

"Leave her the hell alone. I don't care if you think you're getting her back. She doesn't want you. Leave my woman alone," Jason said. "Really? Sorta like you swooping down and stealing her away from me. What the hell. I thought you were my damn friend," Jamie said. "Leave her alone. You wanna be mad, be mad at me. Leave her be." "No. I'm getting my damn wife back. You don't get to steal her away," Jamie said. "She loves me. We're getting married Jamie. She doesn't want to be with you. If she did, she wouldn't have left. You screwed the hell up and ruined things with her. That wasn't on me. Leave her the hell alone," Jason said. "No." "Fine, then you can go to court and fight for an hour of visitation time. You aren't getting that without letting Faith move the hell on," Jason said. He turned around and saw Faith. She shook her head. Jason came over and grabbed her hand. "The girls are sleeping. Enough," Faith said. "I want my life back," Jamie said. "Then go ask one of your girlfriends," Faith said. She walked back onto the tour bus with Jason one step behind. They pulled out a little while later. They went over to the hotel, got unloaded and headed up to the room. They tucked the girls in and slid Patsy into the crib then Jason grabbed Faith's hand and walked her into their bedroom. "What," Faith asked.

Jason devoured her lips. "You do realize that picking fights with him is just gonna piss him off right?" "Just promise that you are gonna be with me. I love you Faith. I'm never stopping that," Jason said. "You need to quit picking fights." "Then you need to slide those jeans off before they're ripped off," Jason taunted. "Jason," Faith said. He pulled at her belt and pulled it off, slid her jeans off and flipped her over his shoulder. He tackled her to the bed. Her black tank top, her black lace bra, her black lace g-string all hit the floor along with his shirt and his jeans and boxers. He made love to her. Time didn't matter. Where they were didn't matter. All that mattered was he had the sexiest woman in the world in his arms and his ring on her finger. He knew that marrying her was going to be hard, especially when Jamie was so completely against it, but he also knew that living without her was something he wasn't prepared for. He loved her so much it scared him sometimes. He wanted her the minute he'd met her. Not even time wore that off. This was the woman he was supposed to be with. Whether Jamie liked it or not, he was marrying Faith. He was going to make love to her every night and remind her every minute of the day that he was her soul mate. "What," Faith asked. Jason kissed her. She forgot space and time. She forgot her history and his. That kiss is what she'd craved her entire life. That kiss that shot lightning down her spine, burned up her insides and had her almost in an out of body state. "I love you," Jason said. "I love you too," Faith replied. They snuggled together in bed and caught some sleep. Jason dreamt of their wedding, and Faith dreamt of the life she had known. Fact was, the minute she'd met Jason, her life had changed. There was no more Evan, no more craziness from her past. It was like it had disappeared the minute he kissed her. He didn't let go of her all night.

Jason got up in the morning to the sound of Patsy crying. He got up, kissed Faith and went to check on Patsy. She reached over for him. "Da," Patsy said. He smirked. He changed her, handed her the teddy bear she was reaching for and came back into the bedroom. "She okay," Faith asked as she yawned. "She did say Da. I can only…" "Da," she said again. Faith smirked. He sat down on the bed and Faith grabbed for Faith's hand. "What you up to little girl," Faith said. "Ma," she said. "She's just so damn cute," Jason said. "Remember back when the girls were this little," Faith asked. "Definitely. They're so cute at this age." "Who's cute," Emily asked rubbing her eyes. "Patsy. I remember when you two were this little," Jason said. "I remember mom telling us about what she used to do when we were little. We always wanted vanilla pudding. She even put it on my pacifier once," Emily said. "And that became the addiction," Jason joked. "Well since you two are awake, I'm going to get up and get a shower," Faith said. Emily took Patsy and they turned the TV on to watch cartoons for a while. Jason slid into the main bathroom with Faith. "What," she asked. He kissed her, picked her up and wrapped her legs around his waist. "We…" He flipped the shower on and walked into it then pinned Faith against the wall. "We can't…" He kissed her and didn't let her up for air. They had hot, passionate, intense as hell sex in the shower and after he washed her hair. "What are you up to," Faith asked. "Never letting go," he replied. "We can't just…" "What," he asked as he leaned her against the bathroom counter. "What are we doing," Faith asked. "Saying good morning, he said as his fingers linked with hers and he held her hands on the counter's edge. "I bet we are. You know we…" He kissed her. "I love you, but we can't just…" He kissed her again. "You're addictive. All your fault," he teased. "I bet," Faith said. "Breakfast," Jason asked. Faith nodded. He kissed her again, almost making her knees crumble, and got dressed. He went and ordered breakfast for everyone just as Callie was waking up. "Morning miss sleepy head," Jason said. Callie snuggled up to him. He kissed her head. "Daddy, can we get the Harry Potter movies," Emily asked. "I'll see," Jason said. Faith finished getting dressed and walked in to sit with them and Callie walked over to her and hugged her. "Morning snuggles. Just what I wanted," Faith said. She picked her up and Callie wrapped her arms around Faith's neck and snuggled her. Faith came and sat down. Jason kissed her then kissed Callie's head. "Ordered you breakfast. We don't have to be down there until 2. What you wanna do," Jason asked. "Toy store for the ladies," Faith said. Jason smirked. "Then we can come back so they can have their movie marathon," Faith said. Jason smirked.

They all headed out and got their movies after breakfast. They managed to sneak in without any interruptions, got their movies and toys and got back to the hotel without anyone saying a word. They came back in and there was popcorn, sugar free sodas and some snacks for the girls. "Daddy," Emily said. "That was all Faith baby. I promise you," Jason said. They ran over to Faith and hugged her. "Give you guys something to do this afternoon. I know you wanted the movie marathon," Faith said. "Thank you Faith," they said. Jason looked at Faith with a smile ear to ear. He took Patsy in and put her down for a nap. By the time her blanket slid over her, Patsy was asleep. Jason turned and Faith was leaning against the door jam. The girls were enthralled with their movie and Jason pulled Faith into his arms. "What," Faith asked. He kissed her.

He pulled her into his arms and kissed her and barely let her up for air. He grabbed her hand and walked her into the bedroom. "We'll be back in a second," Jason said. The girls giggled. "What," Faith asked. He closed the door.

"What's wrong," Faith asked. He kissed her. He devoured her lips and leaned her against the closed door. "I love you. Nothin is ever changing that ever. Marry me. We don't have to do it tomorrow. We can do it in the next few weeks. We…" "Slow…" He kissed her again. "What if we get pregnant," Jason asked. Faith smirked. He kissed her. "Well," he asked. "Then you know, we're gonna have to quit messing around until after we…" He kissed her. That wasn't an option. Not then. "August," he said. "That gives us three months," Faith said. "That gives us three months until we can do whatever we want," Jason said. Faith shook her head. "Well," he asked. Faith kissed him. "End of August," Faith said. He kissed her. He picked her up and carried her to bed and leaned her onto it. "I love you. I love every inch of the sexiest woman in the entire damn planet. I want every inch of you. I want you. It's never stopping," Jason said. Faith kissed him. He was about to start peeling her clothes off when her phone rang. She looked and saw Jamie's number. "Hell no," Jason said.

Chapter 27

"What," Faith asked as Jason undid her jeans and went for her belt buckle. "I want my daughter," Jamie said. "Why," Faith asked. "She's my damn daughter Faith. I get to see her too," Jamie said. "Rules. You can see her, but no stupid idiot girlfriends of the week. End of discussion." "Fine. Then keep her away from Jason," Jamie said. "You don't get rules. I'm engaged Jamie. She said her first words this morning. She said Da to him," Faith said. "She's my damn daughter," Jamie said. "And I'm marrying him. You're the one with half a million girlfriends. Leave it be. End of discussion. You want to have time with her, you can have her for the day and see how things go. Tomorrow. You pick a fight or you don't show to drop her back off to be with me, the police will be kicking your butt." "Fine. See you at 7am." Jamie slammed the phone down and Faith hung up just as Jason was nibbling her breasts. "About damn time," Jason said as he kissed her. A half hour later, they came up for air but Jason wasn't letting her move. One flinch away from round two or three. They did it again and Faith's legs were shaking. "We can't..." "You're not allowed to get back up. We have an hour before.." Faith got up and got changed. "What's that," Jason teased pointing out an intentional mark he left on her breast. "You are so grounded," Faith said. "Nope. This would make me grounded," he said as he intentionally put another mark on her neck. "What are you up to," Faith asked. "Nothin," he teased. He grabbed her jeans and handed them to her. "I swear, you're trying to pick a fight," Faith said. "Not even a little. I'm allowed to want you," he said. "What am I gonna do with you," Faith asked. "Since the girls are with their mom all week, probably a lot," he teased. He kissed her and went and checked on the girls. Faith came out and went and checked on Patsy. She was just waking up and snuggling with her stuffed animals. Faith slid her out and changed her. "Can we stay here," Emily asked. "We have to go after the show anyway baby. You can still have your movies on the bus," Jason said. The girls got packed and Faith finished packing up her stuff, Patsy's and Jason's. He came in a few minutes later and they started heading down to the tour bus. As soon as they got down there, they drove over to the venue and got started on sound check.

Half way through sound check, Jamie's cell went off. He tossed it to Faith and she noticed it was his ex. She looked at him. He nodded. "Hi," Faith said. "Faith right? Can you let me know what flight they're heading home on," she asked. "Not a problem. I'll email it over in a few minutes," Faith replied. "He still finishing up sound check? Kinda late for that isn't he," she asked. "Had a movie marathon with the girls today. He wanted some time alone with them," Faith replied. "I know you're new to all of this, but he did it knowing full well that I was giving Emily the series of the Harry Potter movies for her birthday." "Didn't mention that. She sorta got them this morning," Faith said. "Tell him to call me," she said hanging up. Jason finished up and hopped down to talk to Faith. "What did she want," Jason asked. "She snapped about you getting the Harry Potter series thing then said she wanted to know the flight info for them coming home. I get you two are fighting, but..." He kissed Faith. "We're going with them. I don't want them on a plane alone. She can kiss my ass," Jason said. "And," Faith asked. He kissed her. They went into the back with the girls and Jason started getting ready. "What," Faith asked. He motioned for her to come with him. Faith slid the baby into her crib and went into the bathroom with Jason. "What," Faith asked. He kissed her. "Picking fights and putting me in the middle," Faith asked. "It's no biggie," Jason said. "Meaning," Faith asked. "I told her I was doing it. She was in the middle of a damn date when I said it. It's fine," Jason said. "You don't get to put me in the middle again. Deal," Faith said. He kissed her. "You never were. It's fine. She's just pissed at me. The girls said they wanted to stay with us. That's the only reason," Jason said. "I know, but what's gonna happen when things don't go the way you wanted," Faith asked. He kissed her. "It will baby. We're fine. All that matters is that the girls are fine and so are we," Jason said. He pulled her into her arms. "Nobody in her family is anything like you know who. It's not gonna backfire. I'm talking to her about having more time with the girls during the week. It'll be fine," Jason said. Faith nodded. "Besides. We get lonely, we have options," Jason said. Faith laughed. "Funny," Faith replied. He kissed her. "I love you. We're getting married. We're fine Faith. Nothing else is gonna happen." He kissed her again and they went back into the sitting area where the kids were. "Daddy, can we call mama," Emily asked. "If you wanna tell her what you wanted you can alright," Jason said. "Good. I like the baby," Emily said. She hugged Jason. "Now, if you guys end up staying with me more, you know what that means right," Jason asked. "Still have homework, still have to be good and we get to play with the baby and Faith," Emily said. "Okay," Jason said. They went and called their mom.

Jason pulled Faith back into his arms. "What," Faith said. He kissed her. "We're gonna be fine. You don't need to worry you know. I got this," Jason teased. "I know. Just don't start thinking there's gonna be a wedding in a month. Deal," Faith asked. Jason kissed her. When he heard giggles, he looked over and saw the girls giggling away. "What are you two giggle pusses up to," Jason asked. "Mama wants to talk to you daddy. Patsy was giggling too," Callie said. "I bet," Jason said. He took the phone, kissed Faith and went and made the call while he was finishing getting ready. Not 10 minutes later, Faith heard a royal battle via phone – or at least one side of it. She took the girls and Patsy for some dessert then came back once things got quiet. Faith came back in and put Patsy in her crib and Jason was just stepping back into the room. "Well," Faith asked. He leaned over and kissed her, almost knocking her right off her feet. The girls giggled. "That good," Faith asked. He kissed her again and the girls sat down. Jason walked with Faith, two doors down, to the meet and greet. "She hit the roof didn't she," Faith asked. "Everything will be fine once she calms down. All I did was tell her that we found a way for me to have more time with them. She agreed, but then picked a fight about you." "You do realize that she's doing it because she wants you back right?" Jason kissed her and went into the meet and greet. That was the last concert date for a week or so. Picking a fight before the show wasn't a smart move. As soon as the meet and greet was finished, he walked back down to the dressing room. "You two coming to watch the show," Jason asked. "Can we watch a movie," Callie asked. Jason hugged the girls and kissed them then walked over and kissed Faith. "I'm walking daddy to the stage. I'll be right back. Lock the door behind me alright," Faith said. Emily nodded. Jason pulled her into his arms and kissed her. "What," Faith asked. He devoured her lips. "Tomorrow. The kids are gonna be home and we can have some alone time." "And just what did you have planned with that alone time," Faith asked. "Talking you into a wedding in three months." Faith smirked. Jamie was just walking past when he heard them talking. Jason finally let Faith up for air and they headed up to the stage. Jamie followed them. Jason gave Faith a kiss before he headed on and she sat side stage and watched for a little while. "Tell me you aren't marrying him Faith. Tell me you aren't doing something stupid," Jamie asked. Faith walked past him and went back to the girls. "Faith, you can't just walk off and marry him. You don't know what he's capable...." "Goodbye Jamie," Faith said. He grabbed her arm and pulled her to him. "What," Faith asked. He kissed her. Faith brushed him away and went back to the girls.

When the girls started getting tired, Faith headed out to the tour bus and got them settled. Security stayed with them and Faith went back inside. The second she was through the door, Jamie pulled her off to the side. "Let go of my hand," Faith said. "No. You can't just marry him. He's not the one for you Faith. You have to know that," Jamie said. "I let you be an idiot and make your mistakes. Leave me alone so I can be happy," Faith said. He went to try and kiss her and Faith pushed him away. She went down to the stage and saw Jamie finishing up the last few songs. He looked over and saw her and a smile came across his face. Faith finished watching the show and the second Jason was off the stage, he kissed Faith. "Tour bus," he asked. "With security. They probably have schooled him in Disney," Faith teased. Jason kissed her. He wrapped her legs around him and walked out to the tour bus. They stepped on and the girls were out cold. They let the security man go and not even a half hour later, they were off. Faith and Jamie curled up on the bed in the stateroom. "Home," Faith asked. He kissed her. "Home to an almost empty house. Sleeping in and forgetting the world is there for a while. We're off next week and don't have to go back in until the following Thursday. I plan on talking my sexy fiancée into marrying me. I even picked a date," Jason said. "I bet you did," Faith said. He kissed her, devouring her lips. "June 10," he teased. "Seriously," Faith said. "All you need is a dress and flowers. Everything else we can figure out later. Sound ok," he asked. "We can talk about it later," Faith said. "Yes that hard," he teased. "We can't just run off and plan a wedding like this. The girls are gonna want to be there. We have a lot more to plan then just..."

He kissed her. Not another word was said that night. Faith just wanted to be in his arms. The fact that it included a ring didn't bother her. Faith looked over at him when he was sleeping. "What," he asked. "Nothing," Faith said. "Then close your eyes and come over here," he said. Faith fell asleep in his arms.

Jason woke up a few hours later and checked on the kids. He warmed up a bottle for Patsy and fed her and had a heart to heart with her. He promised her the world and then some. "Nobody is ever hurting you baby girl. I know your daddy loves you. So do I princess. I promise you one thing. I promise you that I'm gonna love you like you're my baby. Mama loves you baby. She really does. I love your mom too. That's never gonna change. Not for all the stars in the sky." Patsy fell back asleep in his arms. He slid her into her crib and came back in to find Faith curled up on the bed still. He kissed Faith's neck. She curled up to him. His arms wrapped around her. He sat there with her in his arms and the only thing that popped into his head was that there was a chance he might lose Faith. He was still scared that Jamie was gonna steal her away. Rushing into getting married wasn't his normal plan. Fact was, Jason was head over heels. He wanted Faith. He was lucky to have even got a chance to be with her at all. "Shouldn't you be sleeping," Faith asked. "Was just thinking. That's all," Jason said. Faith yawned and leaned onto him. "About what," Faith asked. "I'm the luckiest man in the planet. I'm just saying Faith. I don't know how we happened. All I know is that I don't want to lose you. Never." Faith kissed him and he leaned her onto the bed. "What are you really worried about," Faith asked. "Losing you to him. I know it's stupid Faith, but I just keep getting the feeling that…" Faith kissed him. "Whatever the bad feeling is, tell it to stop. He already messed it up. He cheated with woman after woman. He doesn't get to have me back after that," Faith said. "I could end up losing you completely Faith. I can't bare that. That's why I wanted us to get married," Jason said. "That's not exactly the right reasons," Faith said. "I love you. We would've got married anyway. We're fine," Jason said. "Stop worrying alright? Whatever happens, happens. We can't keep being worried that something is gonna happen. We just need to be us," Faith said. He kissed her. "I love you Faith. I get that things aren't being done the right way but I don't wanna wait," Jason said. "I know,

366

but you have to let me figure out what to do with the baby. He hasn't even had one night alone with her. I need to straighten that out with him first," Faith said. He kissed her. "Jason, I'm being serious," Faith said. "He's never gonna let you do what you want. You know that right," Jason said. "I have to try," Faith said. She got up and got dressed. "Faith," Jason said. "I'm going to check on the kids," Faith said. She went and checked the kids and Patsy was awake. Faith slid her out of the crib and sat down to work through some emails. She fed the baby, made breakfast for herself then ate. Jason came out a little while later. "Phone," he said. He handed Faith her cell.

"Hello," Faith said. "I need to talk to you. Alone. Quit picking a damn fight with me about looking after Patsy. I want to see my daughter," Jamie said. "You gonna keep acting like an ass? You need to stop picking stupid ass fights. You want to see her, fine. You don't get to keep making me do what you want," Faith said. "Meaning you choose him over me? Meet me at the house. My bus is right behind his. I'll see you in an hour," Jamie said. "You screw up, don't think it's just gonna blow the hell over," Faith said. "Then you stay with her. We need to talk this out Faith. You want me to be alright with her then stay." "You're acting like an idiot. I know your game Jamie. I come with her and you end up trying to get me back into bed. It's not happening," Faith said. "It's gonna be that easy. If it weren't, you'd be fine Faith. You wouldn't worry about what was gonna happen with us if you knew that you two were gonna stay together. Just come home," Jamie said. Faith hung up. "You done now? You done picking a fight with me? You know I'm right. He's gonna do everything in his power to get you back Faith. That's why I wanted us to get married. I love you, but I'm not losing what we have so he can be an ass. Faith, I want us. I don't want him in the middle of us," Jason said. "Then don't put him there." Faith finished breakfast without another word to Jason.

"So now we aren't talking," he asked. "You done putting him in the middle? Don't tell me it's because you're scared. You're mad that he makes you feel like this. You think it makes me happy that he keeps pushing himself into this? You're letting him push buttons just like I did. I stopped it. You want him to drive you nuts, keep doing what you're doing," Faith said. The baby reached out for Jason. She slid Patsy into his arms and went and had a shower. Jason saw the girls waking up. He made them breakfast and sat down with them. "Daddy, were you and Faith fighting," Emily asked. "Nope. Just having a discussion about some stuff. Faith's daddy wants to see her. Faith and I just know that the house is gonna be real quiet without you two. That's all," Jason said. "If mama says it's okay, does that mean that we get to stay with you," Callie asked. "Yep. Means you get to hang out with baby girl here too. She's gonna miss you two," Jason said. Faith finished getting ready and came out to hear Jason talking to the girls about Patsy. "So that okay with you," Jason asked. "As long as she makes you smile," Emily said. Faith looked at him. "She does. Did y'all pack up," Jason asked. The girls ran off to finish packing up and he got up. "What," Faith asked. He kissed her. "No more fights," he said. "You…." He kissed her again. Patsy was laughing. "No more picking fights," Jason said. Faith nodded. "I get that you want to do this right Faith. Just give me a little leeway here. I never had to deal with something like this," Jason said. "I haven't either. He needs to stop being an idiot, but we can't keep fighting over nothing. Pick the battle," Faith said. He put Patsy into her portable crib. "What," Faith said.

His hands cradled her face. "I love you. The minute we met that first time, I kept hoping for this Faith. I want us to be alright. I get he's gonna be an idiot sometimes but…" Faith kissed him. "Stop picking fights with him. Stop letting him fight with you. Just let him get his crap out and it's done," Faith said. He kissed her with a kiss that could have made anyone forget where they were. "I'm not letting go Faith. Not now, not tomorrow not ever. I can't. I can't let you leave and think nothing of it. The minute you walk back into that house, he's not gonna let go. If it were me, I know I wouldn't. That's why I'm worried." Faith kissed him. "I'm coming home. If he's alright, Patsy stays the night and we see how it goes. I'm not staying there. I know just like you do what he's capable of. Don't worry," Faith said. He kissed her again and the girls came out. They finished up their homework while the bus was heading to where they'd dropped the truck. The girls played with the baby until they stopped. Once they did, they got their bags unloaded and after a good long hug for Faith and Jason and a special one for the baby, the girls headed off with their mom. Jason, Faith and Patsy hopped into the truck and headed back towards the house. Before they pulled out, Jamie stopped her. "What," Faith asked. "Hour and a bit so I can get groceries," Jamie said. "I'll call," Faith replied. She did up the window and they headed out. Jason linked fingers with her. He kissed her hand and they headed straight home.

The minute they pulled in, Jason threw everything into the back, got Patsy into her crib and picked Faith up and flung her over his shoulder. "What are you doin," Faith asked. "Distracting you," Jason said. He leaned her onto the bed and peeled every inch of her clothes off, kicking his off along with it. He made love to her until neither of them could even think straight. Faith finally came up for air over an hour later and Jason wouldn't let her out of bed. "I have to take her," Faith said. Jason leaned in and kissed her again. "I get you're worried, but I'm coming back." "If you don't, I know where he lives," Jason said. Faith nodded. Jason kissed her again. "I have…" "I don't want you to," he said. "Stay right here then. I'll take her over and make sure things are alright then come right back," Faith said. "Takes too long," Jason said kissing her again. "I have to," Faith said. "I know. I'll order dinner. Sound okay," Jason asked. Faith kissed him. He tackled her back to the bed and just as he was about to go for round 2, Patsy woke up. "Fine, but if anything happens, you call me," Jason said. Faith kissed him. He got up with her and had a hot shower in their oversized shower. Faith slid out with him and he went and got the baby ready while Faith got changed.

"Watch your back. He's up to something," she heard. "I know," Faith said. "No Faith. He's been planning a way to get you there. If you really love Jason, don't go," Patsy said. "Or what," Faith asked. "If you love Jason, tell him. You're husband isn't gonna let you leave. You need my help, say it," Patsy replied. Faith nodded. All of it must have looked ridiculous. Faith was talking to someone that had been gone from the world for years. She never did understand why Patsy chose her. She did remember that Patsy never steered her wrong. Not once in the entire time she'd talked to her had Patsy ever done anything but care. A fairy godmother always sounded good, but Patsy guiding her was even better. She valued her opinion above all the others.

Jason slid Patsy into her car seat and Faith came downstairs. "What," Faith asked seeing the look on his face. "Nice move," he said as he noticed Faith had his sweater on. A grin went across his face. "As I told you, he's not causing any issues without getting his butt kicked," Faith said. Jason kissed her. "Before I don't get there…" Jason kissed her again and walked her out to the truck. He slid Patsy into the truck and kissed Faith. Not 20 minutes later, Faith was standing at the front door. She knew Emma and Alan were still there. "Long time no see," Emma said. "Good thing you're here," Faith said. Emma slid Patsy out of the car seat and was giggling at Emma. "Was wondering when you were coming. Good timing though," Jamie said. He looked over at Faith and she was in Jason's sweater. "Faith," Jamie said. "Just don't. As long as Emma is here with you, you're fine with Patsy," Faith said. "Can we at least talk," Jamie asked. Faith shook her head. "Nothing to talk about," Faith said. "Yeah we do," Jamie said. "So you wanting to have time with Faith was a ploy to get me here? Big damn surprise," Faith said. She went over to head out the door and Jamie grabbed her hand. "Just talk to me," he asked. "You have time with Patsy. That's the end of it Jamie. You don't get me back. Not now, not ever and never will ever be happening. Just back off," Faith said. He walked her outside. "What," Faith asked. "You can't be thinking about marrying him Faith. I love you. I have since I saw you. I want to be with you. I don't want us losing each other. I can't do any of this without you. I don't want us to have to share custody Faith. I want my wife back. I'm not screwing this up again Faith. I'm holding on with anything I can find. Please," Jamie said. "You cheated with more than just one person Jamie. You screwed things up with us. You slept with her and were damn convinced that kid was yours," Faith said. "And I told you then that there's no way it was. Faith, please. I love you. Raising this baby apart is killing me. I know you love me too or you wouldn't be fighting with me like you are. We had this fight Faith. We had the fight when you left here to be with him. I said I wasn't letting go and you said you were leaving. It was the biggest mistake I ever made. If I'd stopped you, you never would have had to deal with any of the stress you have. Please just think about it," Jamie said. "Why? You changed Jamie. I left and ended up being with him because he shot Evan. He saved me from it. Evan came after him. He saved me and Patsy. I can't just sit here and say it doesn't hurt. I just know I'm not hurting like that again. I can't be married to someone I don't trust," Faith said. She went back inside, made sure Emma had the baby bag and went to leave. Jamie followed her outside.

"What," Faith asked. "Don't leave," he said. Faith went to get in the truck. He closed the door and pinned her to the truck. He kissed her. His ultimate act of desperation in getting her back and it was killing him. "Don't go. Just stay for a while. I'll get dinner," Jamie said. "I have plans," Faith said. "Stop making this so damn hard," he said. "Right. I'm supposed to make it easy after everything you've done? Go spend time with your daughter. I'll come get her in the morning." "Faith, please. An hour tops," Jamie asked. Faith gave in. She went inside and got Faith settled at the house. Anything other than Patsy was a topic on the 'get your butt kicked if you mention it' list. Once Patsy was settled and playing with Jamie and Emma, Faith left. Jamie went out to catch up to her and she was pulling out of the front gate. He went back inside and tried to have some time with his daughter. Faith pulled into the driveway and Jason came outside to meet her. "And," he asked. Faith kissed him. He picked her up, wrapping her legs around his waist and walked her inside. He locked the front door, walked upstairs and leaned her onto their bed. "Miss me," he asked. "Sick of..." He kissed her again. "He bug you that much," Jason asked. "If he wasn't Patsy's dad," Faith said. He kissed her. "Now back to what we were doing before you had to go," Jason said as he laughed. Just as he was about to undo the buckle of her jeans, her phone rang. "Seriously," Jason asked. Faith kissed him and grabbed her phone. When the call display said Jamie, Faith shook her head. He kissed her and Jason peeled her shirt off and started on her jeans. "Yes," Faith said as she answered. "She's begging for you," Jamie said. "You're her dad. If you're gonna have time alone with her, you have to figure it out yourself Jamie. By the way, nice try," Faith said. "She wants you Faith. Just until she calms..." "No. Jamie, you have to learn how to handle her. Try rocking her in that old rocking chair upstairs. It's almost time for her to eat anyway. Feed her and give her a bath with the lavender bath O put in the bag. Just sing her to sleep." "Faith, please," Jamie said. "I'll call you around 7. If she's still not doing well, I'll come get her," Faith said. "Just come. Faith, please," Jamie said. "No. You aren't being fair about this and you damn well know it," Faith said. "Just come and stay until she calms down." Faith hung up. Jason knocked her jeans to the ground.

Patsy was calmed down and playing a half hour later. "What you making such a fuss about," Jamie asked. Faith snuggled him. "She's not gonna just let you weasel your way in Jamie. She loves him. She's past pissed at you. She's not coming back. I told you that," Emma said. "I'm getting her back Emma. She still loves me and I know it. I screwed up a million times, but I love her. Nothing is changing that." "She's marrying Jason. You can't get in the middle of that. You know it and so do I. Give up Jason. You screwed it up. Faith isn't gonna just leave him." "What if I told her the truth? That Jason isn't faithful and that's the real reason he ended up divorcing his wife? Emma, she belongs with me." "And you aren't one inch better than him. That was in his past. You cheated when you two were married and not just with one woman. You screwed up even more than Jason has. He loves her. That's it," Emma said. "I'm gonna get her back Emma. If it's the last thing I do, We're gonna raise her together."

Faith and Jason had their Chinese food by the fireplace and were cracking jokes and snuggling all night. "What," Faith asked. "I love you. I can tell you how many times I messed up my marriage with her. We started dating when we were practically kids Faith. We weren't grown up enough to understand. We tried to make things work and eventually we just couldn't anymore. Can't say I don't try. I love you. No matter what happens…" "Meaning what? I'm not going anywhere," Faith said. "Faith, I've been there alright. It's easier when it's two of you doing all of it together. No running between houses," Jason said. "What are you saying," Faith asked. "I love you Faith. Nothing is changing that. I put that ring on your hand because I want us to be together, but…." Faith shook her head. "What," Jason asked. Faith got up, got dressed and went downstairs. Jason got dressed and came down a little while later. Faith was sitting on the sofa going through emails. "What," Faith asked. "I didn't mean to get you upset," Jason said. "So you suggest that I'm gonna go back to him? He cheated with more than just one damn woman. He got someone else pregnant Jason. That doesn't go away. That doesn't change. He screwed up. It's not something he can brush under the carpet. I'm not forgetting it either," Faith said. "Babe, I didn't mean to get you upset. I swear. I'm just saying that it's hard as hell raising those kids. When we broke it off, the girls were older so it wasn't so hard. When they're baby girl's age, it's hard. Babe, babies get sick easy. It's gonna be hard babe. It's hard." Faith nodded. "I'm not losing you Faith. Never," Jason said. "Then stop pushing me away. I can leave any damn time Jason. Remember that," Faith said. She got up and Jason grabbed her hand. She pulled away from him and went into the kitchen and cleaned up. Jason came in and slid his arms around her waist. "I'm sorry," Jason said. Faith brushed him off and went upstairs.

Jason heard the water running and poured a drink for Faith. He walked upstairs and handed it to her in the tub. "Thank you," Faith said. "Babe, I didn't mean to get you mad," Jason said. She didn't say a word. Jason grabbed her iPod. "What," Faith asked. "I didn't mean to get you all mad alright? All I mean was things aren't easy. They weren't for me either. She cheated on me Faith. I found out months after that he knew my damn kids. It hurt like crap but it snapped me out of it. It made me move on. Faith, I love you more than anything in the planet. I'm not leaving your side and I'm not losing you. I'm just saying we could end up having to put up with him. He's gonna be part of your life whether you want him to or not. You're both gonna be there her entire life," Jason said. "Meaning what," Faith asked. "Meaning there's always a temptation..." "Get out." "Faith," he said. "Get out," Faith replied. He walked out the door and sat on the bed. Faith came out 15 minutes later, dressed. "Faith." She grabbed her bag and put her stuff in it. "Babe. Please." She packed her bag and got everything, packed Patsy's room and went downstairs. "Faith, please. Don't do this," Jason said. "That worried that I'm gonna end up with him? Really? Worth ruining this," Faith asked. She put the ring in his hand and walked out. "Faith, you aren't leaving." "Yeah I am," Faith replied. She threw everything into the truck and left.

Jason went to come after her and Faith had a 10 minute run on him. He tried to find her but it's like she disappeared. He went over to Jamie's and she wasn't there. He went downtown to the one hotel Faith loved, and there was no trace of her. He called her cell over and over and didn't get an answer.

Faith unpacked and got settled at the hotel. Checking in under another name was the smartest idea she'd had. She got the second bedroom set up for Patsy, curled up on the sofa and tried to relax. "So what are you gonna do now Faith? He loves you, Jason loves you but you know that Jamie is gonna win you back," Patsy said. "He cheated. You don't get to win after that," Faith said. "Faith, that little girl is gonna bring you two back together. Mark my words. I know you're scared Faith. Even accepting that proposal scared you. I was trying to tell you to say no," Patsy said. "I care about him. He's done nothing other than having crappy timing. He brings that up and ruins all of this. That's why he wanted to get engaged so soon. That's why he wanted to run off and marry me. That was just stupid. I can't just be with him because he's scared I'm gonna be with Jamie," Faith said. "Happy you walked out now? Faith, make a decision. You want to be with Jamie and raise your daughter together, or do you want to be with Jason even if he worries every minute that you're gonna leave him for Jamie. I get that you're upset with Jamie, and I get that you're mad at Jason, but you can't just walk away from making a decision. He loves you and so does Jason. It's your decision Faith. I'm gonna be here. Just do what you need to do. Make the right decision Faith," Patsy said. "Give me a sign to help," Faith asked. "You'll get one. Just watch for it. The one that knows you best is the one that you'll choose Faith."

Jamie called around 9. "What now," Faith asked. "I just want to talk to you a while," Jamie said. "We're not together anymore Jamie. You made your decision when you screwed around on me Jamie. That's why I walked out that door. Jamie, I didn't leave because I hated you. I left because I wasn't gonna stay with someone who only wants me when they can't have me," Faith said. "I love you Faith. It was a stupid mistake when we weren't together. That's all," Jamie said. "Jamie, we were. No matter how much you fight this, we were. Go look after your daughter alright?" "Then come over here." "No Jamie. I'm gonna have a bath, get some sleep and come get her in the morning. End of discussion. I'm not having this…" "Faith, come over here. Jason was here. I know you left. Come here," Jamie asked. "I'll see her in the morning," Faith replied. She hung up.

Jason called her cell again an hour or so later. "What Jason," Faith asked. "Just come home. Faith, I screwed up. I'm sorry. I shouldn't have said it. Faith, I love you alright. Come home," Jason said. Faith hung up. She leaned back and tried to sleep. An hour and a half later, Faith heard a knock at the door. She went and opened it, still half asleep. "What are you doing here," Faith asked. Jamie pulled her to him and kissed her. "I'm not leaving here without you," he said. He kissed her again, picked her up and wrapped her legs around him. "What," Faith asked. "I hate being without you. I hate that we're apart Faith. We're supposed to be raising this baby together. Come home," Jamie said. Faith broke away from him. "You're supposed to be home with the baby. Jamie, just go home." "I am. You're home Faith. You. You and me and Patsy is home. I don't care whether we're at the ranch or a cardboard box. I love you. You need to come home," Jamie said. "What I need? Now you're worried what I need? Jamie, I needed a man who wasn't letting go. A man who would be honest and true. You ruined all of it. Every last damn second of it. You wanted to see Faith, see her. Leave me out of it," Faith said. "Faith, stop this. I love you and you know it. Just come home and we can do this together. Babe, I love you. You know that. We can fix this Faith. Please just come home," Jamie said. "No. Good enough answer? No Jamie. No I'm not coming back, no I'm not taking you back and no way in hell do you get me anywhere near you other than dropping Patsy off." Faith went over to the door and Jamie slammed it shut. He cradled Faith's face in his hands and kissed her. He pinned her to the door. He didn't say anything, didn't fight. All he wanted was Faith in his arms in his bed. He wanted their family back. Faith finally pushed him away and pushed him out the door. "Faith, I know why you came here. The hotel is practically empty and you still chose this suite. Open the door and stop being so damn stubborn," Jamie said. "Or what," Faith asked ripping the door open. "Get your room key." "Why," Faith asked. He came in, grabbed Faith's purse, keys and room key. "Let's go," Jamie said. "Where," Faith asked. He walked her down the hall. They went downstairs and he pushed her into the truck. He pulled out and Faith was crying. "Why are you getting upset," Jamie asked. "You ruined our marriage Jamie. You went and got someone pregnant." "Faith, it wasn't mine," Jamie said. "You slept with her and damn well thought it was yours. Just leave it alone Jamie. Just take me back to the hotel," Faith said. "No. We go back to the damn house. We're going home Faith."

Chapter 28

Faith walked back into the house and Emma was asleep with Patsy in her arms. Patsy started to fuss the minute Faith came in. Before it woke Emma up, Faith slid the baby from her arms. She took Patsy upstairs to the nursery and she was wide awake. "Now you know you're supposed to be sleeping," Faith teased. Faith changed her and gave her a bottle and Patsy was white-knuckling her shirt. "You need to come home," Jamie said at the door. "I'm going Jamie. I'm not staying here." "Just stay tonight then. Some of your stuff is still here anyways," Jamie replied. "No," Faith replied. Jamie slid Patsy out of her arms and slid her into the bed and seconds later, Patsy was fast asleep. "Stay tonight. You can sleep in the guest room. You can sleep in the master and I'll sleep in the guestroom. Faith, just stay tonight. You need some time to think." "I need some time alone. Away from you, away from Jason and away from everyone," Faith replied. She kissed the baby and headed out the door. "Faith," Jamie said. She grabbed her stuff and looked at Emma. She nodded and drove Faith back to the hotel. "You okay," Emma asked. "If he can't handle the baby on his own, there's no point in him seeing her," Faith said. "Woman, what crapped in your cornflakes? He tried to get you back. He screwed it up, but he tried. Faith, if you love Jason so much, what are you doing sitting in a hotel room alone? You hate Jamie so much you want to rip his throat out, but you won't do anything. What do you want Faith? What do you want to do with this," Emma asked. Faith ended up crying most of the way back to the house.

They got back to the hotel and Emma smirked when they got to the room. "What," Faith asked. "Same suite Faith. So that idea you thought you couldn't make? Think this is sorta karma telling you what to do. Faith, just take Jamie…" "No," Faith replied. "Then go and straighten things out with Jason. If that's who you want to be with, be with him," Emma said. Faith hugged her. "What," Emma asked. "He'll cheat again Emma. I know he will. He did it once and he'll do it again. I can't go back," Faith said. "Then what about Jason. Is he the one you love Faith? That's the man you want to have beside you the rest of your life? You sure," Emma asked. "What if I said I wanted to be alone?" "Faith, you know how hard it is raising a baby on your own? Do you know what you're saying?" "I'm saying I don't know what to choose. That's what I'm saying. If I stay with Jason, Jamie spends the rest of his life trying to get me back. I end up with Jamie, I'm gonna be watching over my shoulder for the next woman to show up and say she's pregnant. No matter what I do we're screwed," Faith said. "What if I stayed with you for a while? We could find you a place. I could help you with her. Faith, you need…" "She needs me," Jason said standing at the door. Faith walked off and went into the bedroom and Jason followed her.

"What," Faith asked. "Come here," he said. Faith shook her head. "Faith, come here," Jason said. "What do you want? You want me back with him? What?" Jason walked over to her and kneeled down in front of her. "I want you home. Faith, you deserve better than this. You shouldn't have to defend a decision you made. You love me. I love you and no matter how hard I try to find an excuse, I can't get you out of my head. I can't just walk away Faith. I need you. You're the best thing that ever happened to me and those girls Faith. It isn't gonna change when he barks at you and it's not gonna stop if we break it off. I need you. Not some idiotic child who's there for the fame. I need you." "Jason, you're never gonna stop worrying that he's gonna come back. You either want me in your life or you don't." "Woman, listen. Please baby. I love you. Marry me." "Jason." "Faith, look me in the eye and tell me you don't love me," Jason said. Faith couldn't even do it. He kissed her and held her face in his hands. "I love you Faith. I'm not ever turning that off. Please," Jason said. Emma was brushing tears away. "Please," Jason said. Something felt like she was being pushed into his arms. "I…" "You're the only reason other than my girls that I have to wake up every morning. Faith, I love you so much it kills me that I don't have you. Please." "What happens when you do," Faith asked. "I never let go Faith. I'm never going to." "What if…" "There are no other women I could ever be with. Nobody else I want to even look at. I love you," Jason said. He kissed her again. "Please," he asked. Faith nodded. He kissed her again and they barely came up for air for an hour. Emma snuck out with tears streaming down her face.

"Just promise me you won't ever leave," Jason said. Faith kissed him. "Faith," he said. "I couldn't even if I wanted to," Faith said. He kissed her. "Then we're doing this now." "What do you mean now," Faith asked. "No more worrying and watching over our shoulders. The girls have a long weekend in two weeks. Wherever you wanna go," Jason said. "Why are we rushing," Faith asked. "Because I'm not waiting to lose you again." Jason kissed her. "No." "Faith," Jason said. "No. I'm not hopping into a wedding with you. Not now," Faith said. "What are you scared for? Faith, it's me," Jason said. "I know but...no. I want this right Jason. We do this right," Faith said. "Then we wait a month or so. More time. Okay," he asked. "Why are we so rushed," Faith asked again. "We're leaving for the tour in two or three months. I want us to have alone time. I want us to have time to do whatever we want before I start rehearsals baby," Jason said. "We can leave it until..." "No. Faith, I don't want us to wait. I just want us to do this right. I want us to be together Faith. Not another second of waiting either," Jason said. "We can't pull off a wedding that soon anyway," Faith said. Jason kissed her. "Faith," he said. "Give it time. Please," Faith said. Jason kissed her. "Make me a promise you won't start second guessing yourself again. Babe, you deserve to be happy without watching over your shoulder all the time. He screwed up. That doesn't mean that something's gonna happen with us. Faith, you have to know in your heart that I'm not leaving you. I'm never going to," Jason said. "What happens when things get ruined because we are fighting about Jamie? He's gonna be in my life whether I like it or not. I can't just remove him from my life or the baby's," Faith said. "Never would ever ask you to. Faith, I love you. If that means putting up with Jamie being an ass, so be it. I'm not losing you because he won't leave you alone," Jason said. "What happens if we don't work," Faith asked. "Ask me anything about you Faith. You're the only woman I love. Faith, I can't imagine a day without you alright? Tonight was killing me. Please," Jason said. "I can't rush it. I did before and it ruined everything." "We'll figure it out together. However long it takes to get what we want. Promise," Jason said. Faith slid into his arms. "I love you. Even if it takes decades," Jason said. Faith kissed him. "Come home," he asked. She didn't move from his arms. "Just tonight," Faith asked. "Then I'm staying," Jason said. Faith nodded. Faith got changed, Jason got ready for bed and they curled up together. "Couldn't sleep right," Faith teased. "Not without you," he said.

Around 3am, Faith's phone went off. She grabbed it. "Hello," Faith said. "Babe, something's wrong with the baby. She's burning up," Jamie said. "What do you mean burning up," Faith asked. "102. We just got to the ER." That was all Faith needed to hear. She jumped up and started getting dressed. "Faith," Jason said. "Hospital. Now," Faith said. Jason got up and dressed and in mere minutes, they were on the way to the hospital. The minute they were parked, Jason slid his hand in hers. "We..." He held her hand up. The ring wasn't even close to the same as the one he'd given her. This one was a pear shaped diamond with a double eternity symbol on either side of the diamond. It was hand-designed. It wasn't from a catalog, wasn't from a picture. "Jason," Faith said. "Forever no matter what," he said. Faith kissed him. "Now let's get that baby well again," Jason said. Faith brushed away a tear and they headed inside. "The doctor took her straight in," Jamie said. "What happened," Faith asked. "What is he doing here," Jamie asked. "I'm here. Take care of that baby Jamie. Quit causing a problem," Jason said. "I went in to check on her and she was crying and losing it Faith. She was completely losing it. I couldn't calm her down. Then she finally did but she was burning hot. I took her temp and tried the baby Tylenol like you said before and the fever didn't go down. We came straight here." "We who," Faith asked. Emma ducked her head around the corner carrying coffee. "Where's Alan," Faith asked. He was two steps behind Emma. Jason wrapped his hand around Faith's. The doctor came out a few minutes later. The doctor got them to come in and Faith didn't let go of Jason's hand. "What's wrong with my baby," Faith asked. "She has an ear infection. The baby Advil was smart, but she needs an antibiotic. We gave her the big dose and we're gonna see how she does. We put a cool towel on her neck and cooled her down a bit but the fever hasn't gone away altogether. It doesn't look like it has been there a long time. It just flared in the past 24 hours," the doctor said. Jason kissed Faith's cheek. "When can I take my daughter home," Faith asked. "Give us a few hours and we'll see. She's sleeping in the crib now. You can go in, but only you and her..." "Jason's coming with me. End of discussion," Faith said. The doctor nodded and they went and suited up to come and sit with her.

Jamie sat in the hallway and slid to the floor. The tears poured out of him. "Jamie," Alan said. "I lost her. I lost Faith and I almost lost my damn daughter. How can I be..." "Don't. Jamie, it's an infection. It happens. It's alright," Alan said. "I lost Faith. She's marrying him. How am I supposed to just forget the past 4 years? If I'd married her before she made the damn mistake of getting with Evan, I would've been happy and married to her. Now I lose her to him," Jamie said. "If it's meant to be you'll win her back," Alan said. Emma didn't say anything. Alan looked at her and Emma shook her head.

"She'll be okay. I promise you baby. She's gonna be giggling in a day or two. I promise. The girls went through this too Faith. Callie looked this cute babe. When she was in the hospital with a chest infection, it killed me. I was scared. We made it through it and you and I are gonna make it through this too. I promise this one is gonna be stealing all the attention all over again," Jason said. The baby grabbed his hand. The smirk went across his face. "Oh she's fine," Jason teased. Patsy gummed his finger just like she had before. "You should stop scaring mama baby girl. You got her all upset," Jason said. Patsy grabbed her finger and didn't let go. "She wanted her mama Faith. That's it," Jason said. He kissed Patsy's forehead. "Fever feels down," Jason said. He kissed Faith's forehead. "Just a matter of time. I promise you," Jason said. Patsy fell back asleep but wouldn't let go of Faith's finger. Faith curled up in the oversized chair with Jason and sat by her crib. The nurse came in an hour or two later, wrapped Faith and Jason with a blanket and checked on Patsy's fever. "It's down," the nurse said. Jason smiled. "So when can I take her home," Faith asked. "I'll talk to the doctor," the nurse said. Jason kissed Faith. "We're going back to the house tonight. No hotel. Deal," he asked. Faith kissed him. The doctor came in and Faith saw Jamie pacing the hall. The doctor checked the baby over. "If her fever goes up, you bring her straight back here," the doctor said. Faith nodded. "Go tell Jamie," Jason said. Faith nodded and Patsy grabbed Jason's finger again.

"She okay," Jamie said as Faith came out. "Her fever went down. If it comes back up, I'll call you and tell you," Faith said. "Faith, it's my..." "I'm taking her home," Faith said. "She's coming home with me. Faith, if something happens, I need to know what to do. Please," Jamie said. "I want to take her home," Faith said. "Please Faith. I screwed things up with us, but I'm not letting her get hurt. Please just let me take her home." Faith shook her head. "I get you're mad at me Faith. I get you hate me. I know I'm not getting you back Faith. I love you and I love our daughter. Please just let me take care of her tonight," Jamie asked. "If anything…" "I'll call you. She's okay. I promise nothing is happening to her," Jamie said. "If you can't…" Jamie went to kiss her and Faith backed away. She went back into the room. They had the baby all swaddled into her blanket and she was reaching out for Faith. The minute she tried to hand her over to Jamie, the baby was crying and screaming. Faith looked at Jamie. "Fine, but tomorrow…" Faith nodded. Jamie handed her back the baby bag. "I'll bring her over tomorrow if she's better," Faith said. Jamie nodded. Jason slid Patsy into the car seat and they took care of the paperwork and headed home.

Jason saw Faith falling asleep in the passenger seat. He got them home, got Patsy and Faith settled and went to the hotel to get her things and her truck. Faith woke up an hour and a bit later and Jason was just coming in. "Where'd you go," Faith asked. "Hotel," he said. He put her stuff down, put the suitcase of Patsy's stuff down and slid into bed with Faith. "You fell asleep the second that head hit the pillow," Jason said. Faith nodded. "Just sleep," he said. Jason kissed her and wrapped his arms around her. Not a half hour later, the baby was awake. Faith got up and checked on her. The fever was gone but Patsy was starving. Faith fed her and rocked her back to sleep. Patsy was sucking on her finger and finally passed right out. Faith came back to bed and within a minute or two, Jason's arm was wrapped around her.

Once they all finally got some sleep, Jason got up with the baby and made breakfast. Faith came downstairs and saw Patsy giggling in Jason's arms. "Ma," the baby said. "Hello baby girl. What you doing," Faith asked. She nuzzled Jason. Faith got a smile ear to ear. "Having some quality time. She said that she wanted to see your big white dress," Jason joked. "I bet," Faith teased. Jason kissed her. "Sleep okay," he asked. Faith nodded. He kissed her again. They curled up on the sofa and Patsy played on the floor. "Feeling better," Jason asked. "I'm just stressed out. I can't keep dealing with Jamie while he keeps being an idiot. I can't…" Jason kissed her. "I know," he said. Faith curled up with him. "So what we doing today," Jason said. "She's gonna have to see Jamie," Faith said. ""You okay with that," he asked. "Do I have a choice? She needs time with him. She's his daughter Jason." "Then I distract you the rest of the day. We can go to Belle Meade and see if we want to do the wedding there. Just go for a drive even," Jason said. "And how were you planning to distract me," Faith teased. "I have my ways," he joked. Patsy sat up on her own. "Oh my god," Faith said. Jason grabbed her cell and took a few pictures. "Well," he teased. Faith kissed him. "Mama," Patsy said. Faith smiled and got down with her and they had giggle time. After, Faith kissed Jason and he watched Faith while she got dressed and showered. Faith came downstairs and Patsy was laying on Jason's chest on the sofa. Faith grabbed her camera and snapped a few pictures silently. "I know what you're doing Faith. Quit being sneaky," he teased. Faith kissed him and they headed out to Jamie's. They pulled in and Emma came out. "Anything at all happens, you call me and tell me," Faith said. "You need to talk to him," Emma said. Faith shook her head. Not doing it. I've gone through hell enough Emm. I can't put what happened aside. Not now. It's too far past ruined," Faith replied. "What do you want me to say," Emma asked. "I'll come get her at 6. If everything's okay, we'll work on what to do next," Faith said. "I meant about the two of you. Faith, he's losing it. He keeps saying he lost you before Evan. You need to talk to him without any bullshit in the way," Emma said. "Not now," Faith replied. "Faith, he needs you alright? He's been blaming himself all night," Emma said. "Just make sure she's okay." Faith went out to the truck and headed off with Jason. He held her hand in his while they pulled out. "You sure," Faith said. "We'll come back down after dinner and take her home. She'll be fine," Jason said. He kissed her hand.

They pulled into Belle Meade a little while later and walked through the plantation house. It really was beautiful. "Well," Jason asked. "Carriage house," Faith replied. Jason kissed her. "That's what I thought you were gonna say. Pick any day in the next two months," he said. "I still have to get a dress," Faith said. "That's why you're going to the union station hotel to pick one. I'm not coming in. Tomorrow night," Jason said. "And where are you going," Faith asked. "Rehearsal. That way you have the privacy so I don't get to see you in your sexy dress until…" Faith kissed him. "I get it. Just promise this isn't going to be a nationwide moment," Faith asked. He kissed her. Even if you only want 20 people there," Jason said. Faith kissed him. "What if we do it on the May long weekend?" "You're going overboard," Faith said. Jason kissed her. "Fireworks, you and me…" Jason kissed her. "You do realize that you're going way too overboard," Faith said. "We start the tour beginning of July after the 4th. Just means time for us," Jason said. "Fine, but…" He kissed her. "But what," Jason asked. "Seriously tight security. Nobody coming in," Faith said. He kissed her. "Anything you want," Jason said. Faith kissed him. "Not a word either," Faith said. "I have to tell the girls and my ex," Jason said. "Not a word after that," Faith said. He kissed her.

They went and checked out a few cake places, picked out where they wanted the food from and had everything organized except for the flowers, the dress and the minister. It was coming together and even in a short period of time. "So now that it's almost 6, do you want to come have dinner," Jason asked. "We have to pick her up," Faith said. "She's fine. She's with him. Emma's there. Nothing is gonna happen. Come on. We'll go do dinner and go over after," Jason said. Faith nodded and they took off for dinner. It was romance and grown up time. They stopped after and grabbed some frozen yogurt then headed over. "Not a word to him or Emma," Faith said. Jason pulled her into his lap before they hopped out of the truck. "What," Faith asked. He kissed her. "I love you," he said. "I love you too," Faith replied. They hopped out and headed in. Patsy was asleep in Jamie's arms. "Bath," Faith asked. Jamie shook his head. "She conked right out after dinner. She's doing a lot better," Jamie said. "Anything happens tonight, you call me then," Faith said. "What," Jamie asked. "If she wakes up, give her a bath with the lavender stuff. Just warm water. Not hot. If she can't sleep, put on this," Faith said handing a copy of a DVD Jason made for the baby to Jamie. "You sure," Jamie asked. Faith nodded. Jason held her hand a little tighter. "Thank you," Jamie said. Faith nodded. She headed out to the truck with Jason and he pulled her into his arms. "What," Faith asked. "I love you," he said. Faith kissed him. They headed back to the house and Jason was still stunned. "What," Faith asked. "You actually let him have her for the night. What did you do with my woman," Jason asked. Faith kissed him. "Heard what you said. That's all," Faith replied. Jason kissed her. He flipped her over his shoulder and ran her up the steps to their bedroom. "Stay right there," he said as he leaned her onto their bed. "What," Faith asked. "Don't move," he said. She heard the water running. Ten minutes later, he came back in. "Come on," he said. He handed Faith a drink and undid her sweater. "What are you up to?" "Seducing my fiancée. I think she kinda likes it," Jason teased. "Really," Faith asked. He kissed her. They got undressed and slid into the tub.

"I still can't believe you let him have her for the night after everything you went through last night," Jason said. "Like you said. One screw up doesn't mean all the time," Faith said. He kissed her neck and wrapped his arms tight around her. "What you sucking up for," Faith asked. "You know it's gonna get easier right," Jason asked. Faith nodded. I need to know she's safe. That's all. I needed to know it was alright," Faith said. "You got me. You need distraction, you got it. You need someone to hold you in their arms, you know I'm here. I'm not leaving your side no matter what," Jason said. Faith turned and kissed him and put her glass down on the ledge by the tub. "What you doin," Jason asked as Faith straddled him in the tub. "Telling you something. Promise me that you aren't gonna worry anymore about me and him," Faith asked. "I know you two don't belong together Faith. Things are gonna be hard. I promise you. I know you aren't gonna leave. Besides, you do I can come get you back." Faith kissed him. He stood up with her legs still around him and leaned her onto the bathroom counter. "Jason," Faith said. He kissed her and made love to her. It was hot, intense and primal. Like an urge to fight and defend your possessions. After round one, he carried her to bed and they had round 2 and 3.

When they finally did come up for air, neither of them could move. "Promise that this will never stop," Jason teased nibbling her neck. "Sorta need to come up for air and food," Faith teased. "That is so not what I meant. I just want you to be able to tell me anything. I know you get scared Faith. You walk away and try to figure it out alone. Just promise me you'll let me be here." Faith kissed him. "When we get married you can't worry about Jamie. That's the deal. I know that you aren't gonna do anything to cause shit, but I don't want to end up fighting about something I can't do anything about," Faith said. Jason kissed her. "So what time do you have to go to rehearsal," Faith asked. "After I drop you at the hotel to look for dresses," he teased. "And we go get the baby," Faith said. Jason kissed her. They curled up in bed and they just talked and snuggled the rest of the night.

The next morning, Faith was already in the shower when Jason woke up. She came out and he wrapped her in a towel and pulled her into his arms. "Morning sexy," he said. "Good mornin yourself," Faith teased. He kissed her until her toes were almost curling. "Now that's better. Disappeared out of bed before I could seduce my woman," Jason said. "Poor baby," Faith teased. Jason kissed her again. "Shower," Faith asked. "Only if you're coming with me," Jason said peeling her towel back off and walking her backwards back into the shower.

An hour or two later, they were finally dressed and they had breakfast. The second they were done, Faith grabbed more diapers etc. and went down to pick the baby up. "Thanks," Jamie said. Faith nodded. "Fever gone," Faith asked. "She slept like a rock. She was only up once or twice last night. No crying or anything," Jamie said. "Good," Faith replied. "So, next weekend. I'm going to my mom's and I was gonna see if..." "I'll pick her up Sunday night. Not one minute later," Faith said. "8ish," Jamie asked. Faith nodded. Jamie let go. It was the first time he'd managed to let go. Losing Faith was hard enough, but the fact that she was gonna marry Jason killed him a little more every time they showed to get the baby. Faith and Jason pulled out with Patsy a little while later. "So after you pick out a dress, there's a florist coming by. I told her your favorite flowers and stuff and she's coming up with a few ideas," Jason said. "Oh really," Faith said. "Then I figure you'll need to go lingerie shopping then you can come meet me at rehearsal." Faith laughed. "Just have everything planned right out don't you," Faith asked. Jason kissed her at the light. "Just figured we could get it all organized now. Then we can relax and wait for the rest to fall into place," Jason said. "And what else did you plan," Faith asked. "A surprise or two," he said. He dropped her at the hotel after one heck of a kiss. Faith went upstairs to the suite he'd booked and saw a crib for the baby and ginger ale on ice. There was a bottle warmer in the cabinet and everything was just right. Faith got the baby settled and when the dresses showed, Patsy was just starting to yawn. Right behind the dresses was Emma. "I didn't know you were coming," Faith said. "Someone had to look after beautiful over here. You have dress shopping to do," Emma said. Faith hugged her and Patsy held Faith's collar. "He did really good last night with her," Emma said. "Did you help," Faith asked. Emma shook her head. "Alan told him the news," Emma said. "What news?" "We're having a baby Faith," Emma said. Faith hugged her. "When did you two find out," Faith asked. "When I was at the hospital when Patsy got sick. I saw my doctor and she gave me the results," Emma said. Faith hugged her again and Patsy started crying. "What," Faith asked. The minute Faith had her head on her shoulder, Patsy calmed down. "Now go try those dresses on so we can go shopping," Emma said. Faith got Patsy settled and went and started trying dresses on.

Once they got to the third dress, Faith came out and had tears in her eyes. It had the corset top and made her look like a princess. "Well," Faith asked. "If you try on anything else, I'm not letting you buy it. You look beautiful," Emma said brushing tears away. Patsy started fussing and Faith picked her up. Emma took a picture and sent it to Faith's mom and a half hour later, her mom called in tears. Emma handed her the phone. "Well," Faith asked. "Jason," her mom asked. "Yeah. What do you think," Faith asked. "You're getting that dress. You're beautiful," her mom said. "So that's a yes on the dress," Faith teased. "Definitely. Just let me know if you need me to do anything," her mom said. "I will. Just make sure you're here. We're doing this right. No more second chances," Faith said. "We will. Jason emailed us the flight info and the hotel information," her mom said. "When," Faith asked. "The other night. We'll see you a few days before. Give my grandbaby a kiss," her mom said. "I will. I'll even give mama Emma a hug for you too," Faith said. Faith gave the phone back to Emma and slid Patsy into her arms and went and got changed and got the dress altered to fit just right. She came out a few minutes later then the florist showed. Faith picked out three arrangements for the venue, the bridal bouquet and anything else they were gonna need. As soon as that was finished, Faith, Emma and Patsy all headed off to the lingerie store, bottle in hand, and Emma and Faith picked out some sexy lingerie to surprise Jason.

"What do you think," Emma asked when Faith found a few things. "Sorta, but not quite," Faith said. Faith picked out something else and finally came across what she liked. "And," Emma asked. "Perfect," Faith replied. Faith went to pay for the lingerie and the saleswoman handed her a bag. "What's this," Faith asked. "Already taken care of," the saleswoman said. "Really," Faith said almost laughing. "He said whatever you wanted and then a few other things he'd chosen," the woman said. Faith laughed. "Alright then," Faith joked. Patsy woke up and was reaching out for Faith. Faith picked her up and distracted her a bit. They stopped and grabbed some coffee while they calmed Patsy back down then headed down to meet Jason at rehearsal.

They walked in and Patsy was unconscious in her car seat. The second Jason saw her come in, things got really quiet. "What," Faith asked. Jason kissed her. "What's going on," Faith asked. "Nothin. We were just talking," Jason said. "And," Faith asked. Jason kissed her. Faith noticed him intentionally distracting her. "She missed you," Faith said. Jason pulled Faith into his arms. "So what is it that you didn't want me to see," Faith asked as she caught a glimpse of a woman walking out the back. "And who might…" He tried to kiss her but she held him back. "Faith," Jason said. "And the answer to my question," Faith asked. "She's one of Cash's…" "And that's why you smell like perfume," Faith said. "Babe, don't…" Faith turned, grabbed the car seat and the bags and walked out. "Faith, come back in here," Jason said. Faith got in the truck, got Patsy strapped in and left. "Emm, please," Jason said. "You either slept with her or she was trying to make out with you. Pick one," Emma said. "She was trying to make a damn move when I was doing rehearsal. I told her to leave and she tried to kiss me," Jason said. Emma nodded. "Emma, I didn't…" "You want to solve this before that wedding, you better do something big," Emma said. "Just help me out. Tell her I didn't do anything," Jason said. "If I can do anything I will, but she's fuming. How the hell would someone get in here anyway? It's supposed to be closed off?" "No idea. I had fans trying to hop my electric fence Emma. I didn't…" "Fine. One screw up and I'm not helping you again." Emma ducked out and went after Faith in her truck.

Faith got back to the house, put Patsy down after a bottle and went and curled up on her bed. She started going through real estate and her computer shut itself down. "What the?" "Now you can listen Faith. You can keep running from making a decision or you do this. Do you love him or not," Patsy's voice asked. "Yeah, but we aren't even married yet and that's happening," Faith said. "You have to trust someone Faith. He hasn't given you reason at all Faith. Remember, the business means fans. You can't make them leave him alone. They're gonna try to do stupid crap. Fact is that Jason isn't gonna give in. He does, he's getting a swift kick. Faith, just follow your heart. If he isn't it, you know what to do. Jamie is never letting go. Jason is gonna mess up, but he's not gonna cheat Faith." "What happens if it happens again," Faith asked. "He's not going to Faith. You don't believe it, you're better off alone," Patsy's voice said. Faith nodded and tried to relax. She flipped on a movie and just as it was finishing, Faith woke up. She went and checked on Patsy, changed her and brought her downstairs and put something on for dinner. Faith fed Patsy then curled up and had her dinner while going through emails.

Around midnight, Jason still hadn't come home. Faith put Patsy into her crib and went upstairs. A half hour later, Faith was almost asleep and Jason came in. He went in and kissed the baby and came into the bedroom. He walked over to Faith. "So you finally came home," Faith said. He kissed her. There was no coming up for air either. He ended up curled up with her. Faith finally pushed him away. "Faith," he said. "What," she asked. "I came home straight to you. You really think I would go anywhere else?" "Don't," Faith said. "Faith, that was a damn fan. That's not the first damn time one tried to bust in and it definitely won't be the last. I can't just…" Faith got up. "Faith," Jason said. She went in and checked on Patsy. She came out of Patsy's room and Jason slid his hand in hers and walked her back into their room. "What," Faith asked. "I can't just turn that off. I do, nobody buys the CD's. I love you Faith. I'm not screwing this up. I'm not gonna just…" "Whatever," Faith said. She walked downstairs. He came down behind her. "What," Faith asked. "You seriously think that I'd cheat on my woman? Faith, I didn't with her and I am not even looking at another woman. I love you Faith. You can't think that I would cheat. Not now. Not when we spent all this time planning a wedding." "Go do whatever you want. It's gonna be like this there's no point," Faith said. "Faith," Jason said. "Just forget it," Faith said. He picked her up and carried her upstairs. "Put me down," Faith asked. He put her on the bed. "We're not having this fight Faith. I love you alright? Stop worrying Faith. Stop thinking that someone's gonna come between us. There's only one woman I want," Jason said. Faith went to get up. "Faith," he said. She went downstairs. Jason came into the TV room and Faith was curled up on the sofa with a drink. He took it out of her hand, drank it and sat down. "You could just..." He kissed her. "Stop thinking that I'm cheating. I don't want someone else Faith." "And that's why you still smell like perfume." Faith went to push him away. "Stop. Faith, just stop. I didn't do anything. I went to see my girls. That's it Faith." "Then you can quit trying to make me believe you didn't do..." "I didn't sleep with anyone Faith. Please," Jason said. "Get off," Faith said. "Faith, please," Jason said. "Off," Faith said. Jason kissed her. "Stop fightin with me," Jason said. "Then get off," Faith said. She almost knocked him to the floor and got up. She went upstairs and closed the door. "Faith." She curled up on the bed. "I didn't do anything." Faith got up and went into the bathroom. Jason pulled her into his arms. "Let go," Faith said. "No. Look at me Faith. I didn't screw someone, I didn't kiss someone else, and I damn well didn't let anyone do anything to me. Faith, nothing happened. I'm never gonna let something happen. We went through new tour rules Faith. You, me and Patsy. That's the damn rule. Nobody else. A fan tries to get to me, they're stopped. That's it. That's the way it's staying." "Starting after..." "Faith. Stop. Stop being that damn scared. I'm not Jamie and I'm never gonna be." He wouldn't let go. "Faith, I love you. Please," Jason said as he kissed her head. "I love you. Baby please," Jason said. "Jason, what's the point. You want to play around, there's no point in us even bothering," Faith said. "Only woman I want is you. I love you Faith. Just stop. Just come to bed and we can forget this crap," Jason said. "I'm sleeping in the other room," Faith said. "No you aren't," Jason said. "Then I'll leave." "Faith," he said. "Tell me that you wouldn't then," Faith said. He kissed her. "If you're this upset, we get married now. Solves the whole damn problem," Jason said. "Right. Nice solution," Faith replied. "Faith," he said. "Just..." He kissed her again and looked at her. "Faith," he said. "Just give me..." He kissed her again. "Please," he said. "Promise me," Faith said. "I love you. Whatever you want me to do just say it," he said. Faith kissed him. "I need to breathe," Faith said. "Don't go," he said. Faith went outside and sat down on the chaise. Jason let her be then came outside an hour later and handed her a drink and sat down on the chaise behind her. He wrapped his arms around her.

Chapter 29

"I promise you I didn't do anything," Jason said. Faith was in his arms. Patsy was in hers. "Do I get to deal with security," Faith asked. "There's only 7 women allowed backstage. You, Patsy, my mom and yours, my girls and my ex. That's it Faith. I'm not letting you be upset like that again. I'm not losing you," Jason said. Faith nodded. Something warned her that they were empty promises. That's what she knew. Jamie had promised to never leave her side, to protect her and never be with someone else and it all went up in smoke. Now, a daughter that they had to take care of together. The wounds Jamie caused were still in her mind. The pain that he caused still hurt. The fact that Jason erased some of it, was the only thing she could handle. Just tell me what you want me to do," Jason said. "If you cheat, it's done. That's what I want. I'm not gonna sit there when something happens next time. Something happens, I leave with Patsy and I don't come back. I have to…" Jason kissed her. "It's not and it hasn't happened Faith. Never will," Jason said. They fed the baby and he talked her into coming to rehearsal to see for herself. They grabbed breakfast on the way.

They pulled in a half hour later and the guys were warming up. "Just let me know what you think," Jason asked. Faith nodded. He slid Patsy into Faith's arms, kissed her and went on. Patsy curled up in her playpen and played with a few toys. Faith got some emails done while she listened to rehearsal. "Need an opinion. Wasting Time or Hold," Jason asked. "Wasting," Faith said. He smirked at Faith. They tweaked the set list, did a full run through from beginning to end and Patsy slept through in Faith's arms. As soon as it was finished, he hopped down and came over to Faith and kissed her. "I'm thinkin she's getting used to the music," Jason said. "She always did calm down when she heard your stuff or his," Faith said. He kissed Faith again. She slid Patsy into the portable crib. "Well," Kevin asked. "If I didn't get the special treatment, I would've got tickets already. When don't you guys have a good show," Faith teased. "Rain," Jason joked. They went over changes to the website, contest ideas, promo ideas and other ideas for show stuff. "Think we're good.

So, we can go over one last time Monday night before we head out. We do that list for the late night show and I think we're all good," Jason said. Kevin agreed. "So when did you two decide to get hitched," his other guitarist Trent asked. "Just around the May long weekend. Y'all are coming anyway. The invites are comin out. Only one rule – no idiot exes of mine and no drama," Jason said. Faith almost laughed. "So anything else you want to make sure of," Kevin teased. "That you guys know those two songs I told you about," Jason said. "And what songs would those be," Faith asked. Jason kissed her. The guys nodded and gave Faith a hug goodbye. They headed out leaving Faith and Jason there with the baby. "So what's this little plan all about," Faith asked. "Wedding gift for you," Jason said. "Oh really," Faith said. He kissed her and they started getting ready to go. "What," Faith asked when she noticed a smirk ear to ear. "I'm just glad we're okay. That's all. I hate fighting with you," Jason said. "We're gonna have fights. Fact is that we make it through them. That's what really matters Jason. We're gonna have disagreements and stupid dumb fights. It's life," Faith said. He kissed her. "Come here for a sec," he said noticing Patsy still fast asleep. "What," Faith asked. He flipped on a CD and danced with her. "What are you getting all mushy about," Faith asked. "Marrying the woman of my dreams. That's what matters," Jason said. "And?" "No more fighting. Ever." He kissed her, devoured her lips and she managed to get him to the truck.

They pulled into the house a while later and Faith saw the garage open. "What's…You do realize the garage is open," Faith said. He nodded. "Go look," he replied. Faith went in and found the SUV that she'd been staring at since she had Patsy. "Jason," Faith said. "Easier to get her in and out of. Sturdier too. We have the truck for weekends and stuff and the SUV for the rest of the time. It is easier," Jason said. Faith kissed him. He got Patsy and she woke up. Jason slid the car seat into the SUV, and sat Faith down in the driver's seat. "Air conditioned seats for the summer, heated for the rest of the year, plus when she gets a little older, TV in the headrest. Everything you'd want or the baby would need," Jason said. "You could just give me flowers," Faith teased. He kissed her. "I want you to be safe and not have to worry anymore," Jason said. "I'm always gonna worry. I just need to know that I'm not gonna have to watch my back. I need to know that it's not gonna be like…" Jason kissed her. Patsy slid into her arms. "I love you too," Jason said. They headed inside and Faith gave Patsy her dinner. Jason made dinner for them. "What," Faith asked as she gave Patsy a bath. "I had an idea. What if we went down to Georgia for the honeymoon? Somewhere out of the way and away from any stress and stuff. We both need it. We can go and just hang out at a cabin or something. Go in the water, bonfires. The whole thing," Jason said. "So that's what you planned was it," Faith asked. Jason nodded and kissed her. "Lots of room for Patsy to run around, and lots of privacy from the press crap," Jason said. "Good plan," Faith said. "Besides. We could always work on a gift for the girls while we're there," he joked. "And just what kind of gift are you thinking," Faith asked. "One that involves you and me and a lot of practice time. What do you think sexy wife to be of mine," Jason asked. "So either you're trying to seduce me into having a baby with you, or you're just sucking up in general," Faith teased. "Or just wanting you," he said. "Dinner," Faith said. "I may not make it. No restraint at all around you," he said. Faith kissed him. "Bath, bottle then dinner," Faith said. "Then dessert. Should last us until morning," he teased.

The minute they finished dinner, he pulled her into his lap and pinned her to the oversized sofa. "Jason," Faith said. "What," he asked. "What happens after the wedding? I mean what happens if it…" "Don't even think it. I'm never leaving your side Faith. I'm not losing you either. I love you. Even if we're fighting like crazy people for the next 50 years, I'm not leaving you. Faith, when I get married I want forever. I know you do too. Faith, just trust that there isn't gonna be a what's nest. We're never losing this. I just want us to be alright. Just trust that we'll be alright," Jason said. "I'm just…" "Faith, remember that circle be unbroken thing at the Opry," Jason asked. Faith nodded. "That's what the ring is about. Faith, I'm not just doing this so we can be married. I'm doing it because I know we're gonna be forever. I love you. Every inch of me loves you. Just trust that you're not gonna be single again unless I die," Jason said. Faith kissed him. "And I'm not dying anytime soon." Faith kissed him again and they made love on the sofa. They were curled up among the blankets when he got up to grab a drink. He came back and handed her a drink and took a gulp of his. "I love you. I don't know what you're worried about Faith. What we have isn't gonna change," Jason said.

Faith kissed him. "And we're still gonna have a million kids. At least enough practice time to have them," Jason teased. Faith laughed. "Convinced that we're having a baseball team," Faith asked. "As long as you and I are alright. Just hear me out. We can wait for a while right," Faith asked. "Nope. Now's good," he teased. "Jason," Faith said. "Okay fine. The day we start the honeymoon then," he joked. "What happens if we don't work out," Faith asked. "Why are you so convinced," Jason asked. "Because things happen that we can't do anything about. That's why. We both had one marriage go wrong. I just need to know that it's not gonna be a massive mess if it doesn't work. I don't want to leave and I'm not planning on us being apart. I just need…" He kissed her. "You're safe. We're safe. Faith, nobody is hurting us or breaking us up. It's not happening Faith. I love you. I don't get what you're that freaked about," Jason said. "Just let me say it. I know you aren't expecting us to break off. You don't want a divorce any more than I do. I just need to take care of my daughter Jason. We have kids, I need to know that if we break it off, they're alright." "My daughters are fine Faith. Our kids won't be any different. She fucked up and she's still taken care of for life. Faith, I'm not gonna leave. We aren't gonna end up like that. I promise you," Jason said. "I get why you're worried. If god forbid something happens, you aren't gonna need to worry Faith. Not ever. Faith, I'm not gonna divorce you. Not now," Jason said. "And 10 years from now? I don't know what's gonna happen Jason. I just know that I'm not losing you. Faith, we're not gonna end up divorced. I'm not letting that happen." Faith kissed him. "I know. I just think that we need to…" Jason kissed her. "We're not flipping out about something that isn't gonna happen." He walked her upstairs. They curled up in the bed together. "I know why you're worried Faith. Just don't. No worrying. Deal," he asked. Faith nodded and kissed him. "Our little munchkin is gonna be the big sister. We're gonna be a million years old by the time we get sick of each other Faith." She smirked.

Faith got up the next morning and Jason was singing and rocking the baby. She took a few pictures and Jason turned around. "Mama's a superspy," Jason joked. "And what time did she wake up this morning," Faith asked. "Seven. You looked so peaceful I had to let you sleep baby." "Really," Faith said teasing. "And she decided she wanted me to make her breakfast instead. She opted for one heck of a bottle. She was just cute this morning. She wouldn't let go of my hand Faith. Can't help it. She's just so damn cute." Faith kissed him. "So what you up to today," Faith asked. "Got the tux organized, the last part of the wedding stuff and even managed to find a few things I know you wanted but wouldn't ask," Jason said. "Like," Faith asked. "Fireworks in purple and pink. A few other surprises I'm not telling you about until the wedding," he said. "Really," Faith said. "They said we needed to move the date up. A major booking came in. Emma helped me get in contact with some family and we're all good," he said. "Jason," Faith said. "Easter," he teased. "That's in 3 weeks," Faith said. "They said the dress was done too," he said. "Why are we really rushing through this," Faith asked. "Just like I said." Faith kissed him and made them breakfast. "I love you. We don't need the over the top crap Faith. There's only two people that are important. You and me." Faith kissed him again, and they sat down to breakfast.

A few weeks later, Faith's family started to show. Jason's came an hour or two later. Everyone was checked in, settled and on their way to the rehearsal. "Ready for this," Jason asked. "Depends. What happens if something else goes wrong," Faith asked. "Like you finding out mid-way through the wedding that we're pregnant with quadruplets," he teased. "At the rate you were attempting to practice, we could be," Faith teased. "I love it when you talk dirty," he teased. Faith kissed him. Jamie had the baby for a while. He wasn't about to be invited to the wedding. When Faith and Jason got to the rehearsal, Jamie had Patsy in his arms and was talking to Faith's mom. "Great. Just what I always wanted. What the hell is he doing here," Jason asked. "Mom probably just wanted to see Patsy. No picking a fight," Faith said. "Now about that no sleeping together the night before thing...I think we can just bypass..." "No," Faith said. "Babe, we've been living together. We already messed up in the eyes of the church," Jason said. "For me," Faith asked. "You know I'll find a way to kiss you the second you wake up," he said. Faith kissed him. "I know you will. You're having a guy night," Faith said. Jason kissed her. "Nope. Sex with the sexiest woman in the planet instead," he whispered. His hand slid down her back.

They had the rehearsal and it was perfect. They all headed over to Jason's favorite restaurant for a quick dinner. Jason tried to talk Faith into coming home with him. Jason's buddies teased him. "Dude, I'm taking her home and getting Patsy settled," Jason said. "I can handle her. Go have fun," Faith said. Jason kissed her and grabbed her hand, walking her off into a quiet corner. "What you all worried about," Faith asked. Jason kissed her. "Marry me tomorrow," he asked. Faith nodded. He kissed her again, devouring her lips. "You know I'm not gonna be able to get any sleep without you," Jason said. "Something tells me they'll find a way. Just remember what's happening tomorrow. You decide to go to a strip...." He kissed her. "Only woman I want naked near me is you," he whispered. He kissed her one last time and his buddies dragged him off. Faith went back to the house with the girls. "So, what time do you want to get up tomorrow so I can set your alarm," Emma asked. "Ten. Hair and makeup is coming at 11. Not 5 minutes later, Jamie called.

"What's up," Faith asked. "Do you want me to look after her while you're gone," Jamie asked. "We're going to Georgia. We're taking her with us," Faith said. "Faith," he said. "Don't. I'm doing it Jamie. This is what makes me happy." "What if I made you happy?" "Enough," Faith said. "I need you back Faith. You can't just run off and marry him. Not when I'm sitting here waiting for you to come back. You deserve better than that." "Jamie, I deserve someone who doesn't bat an eyelash at every woman he passes. I have that. I know you think I'm gonna just come running back, but I can't do that. Not anymore," Faith said. "I love you Faith. I said it. I can't just let you marry him. We belong together." "Goodnight Jamie," Faith said hanging up. Patsy played with Emma and Sara then Faith got her bathed and put her down to bed. "Still can't believe you look that good after having her," Sara said. "Blame it on Jason. It's just going for a walk every day to be honest. Running around and taking care of her then running around the venue getting things all settled. She's hard enough to handle without the human energizer bunny," Faith joked. They hung out and had some chick flick time then Faith headed upstairs to bed. She curled up on the bed and not 5 minutes later, she got a text:

Just hear me out. Come downstairs so we can talk.

Faith looked at the number and realized who it was. She pulled on her track pants and sweater and came outside.

"Faith, please," Jamie said. "First off, enough. Second, I'm getting married like it or not Jamie. You can't keep thinking that you can get between us," Faith said. "I'm trying to prevent you from getting hurt again Faith. I'm the one that saved you from Evan. I'm the one that protected you. You can't run off and marry him." "Jamie, I'm saying this for the last time. I'm marrying him. Accept it or don't, but it's not changing my decision," Faith said. "Then this will," Jamie said. He went to kiss Faith and she pushed him. "Leave," Faith said. "You still love me Faith. You wouldn't be this mad or this bitter if you didn't. Just come back to the house and we'll find a way to be back together," Jamie said. Faith went back inside and locked the door behind her.

Faith went upstairs, checked on Patsy and slid into bed when she heard her bedroom door lock. Faith opened her eyes and Jason leaned in to kiss her. "Aren't you supposed to be having a guy night," Faith asked. He devoured her lips. "Can't concentrate on that crap. Keep wondering what was in the lingerie bag you wouldn't let me see," he teased. Faith kissed him. "I love you too," she teased. He kicked his jeans off, pulled her into his arms and started nibbling at her neck. "What are you doing here anyway? You're seriously supposed to..." Jason knocked her jeans and panties to the floor. "Wanted my woman," he said. He didn't let her up for air. He made love to her more than once then fell asleep with Faith in his arms. Around 6, Faith woke up. "No," Jason said pulling her back. "Patsy's up. Besides. Thought you didn't want anyone knowing you were here," Faith teased. Jason kissed her, got up and got changed then snuck out. Not 5 minutes later, she got a text:

I love you. The minute that ring gets on your finger I'm not letting go. I know that we're gonna be forever. I can't imagine life without you. I'll see you at the end of that aisle.

Faith smirked. She curled back up in bed and Emma knocked. Faith got up. "What's..." "I know he was here. Nice try though," Emma teased. "She up," Faith asked. Emma nodded. She went and checked on Patsy, changed her and gave her breakfast then curled back up in bed. "You sure about this," Emma asked. "Meaning," Faith asked. "I mean, I thought you and Jamie were gonna be it Faith. You can't just deny that you care," Emma said. "After what happened, I can't just erase it. It hurt Emm. It's just not the same now. That's all. I know he's gonna be there when and if I ever need him, but I love Jason. One day without him and it feels like forever. He knows what to do when I'm mad or upset. Emm, he's a really good man. I love those girls and he loves Patsy. I can't ask for anything better. We're just a perfect fit." "Doesn't mean he's the right one," Emma said. "Yeah it does. When I was with Jamie, I was always watching over my shoulder. He pushed me into a wedding before we were ready. Now, it's just right." Emma hugged her. "All I want is that smile on your face," Emma said.

Around 10, Faith hopped into a shower, brought Patsy with her, and started getting ready. She came down and made breakfast for the girls, had some coffee and started getting ready. The hair and makeup team showed a little while later. By 12:30, they were all done with hair and makeup and Faith slid on her wedding dress. Her mom showed and her dad started crying. "What are all the tears for," Faith asked. "You're beautiful," her dad said. Faith hugged him then saw Patsy in her little dress. "Oh my goodness. Faith, she's so cute," her mom said. "I wanted her to be part of all of it. She loves Emma, so she's carrying her down the aisle." Her mom hugged her and the girls came in. "Wow," Sara said. "Had to. You sure it's not too..." "Faith, you look amazing," Kevin said heading in. "Are you guys supposed to be getting..." He handed Faith a gift from Jason. "I'm goin," Kevin teased. Faith hugged him and he headed off. "Faith," Kevin said. "Silver box on the office desk," Faith said. Kevin headed back to help Jason and Faith sat down and opened the present from Jason. She opened it and saw a diamond pendant on a white gold necklace. It was a teardrop shaped pendant to match her ring. On the back, the words 'Forever Heart' were engraved into the silver. Faith sent a text to Jason:

I just opened the little box. Forever isn't long enough. I love you. That walk down the aisle will be the easiest thing I've ever done. PS I'm marrying you today.

Faith got the flowers and they all hopped into the waiting SUV and headed down to the house. Faith couldn't wait any longer, but hair and makeup did the last touch ups and the photographer started shooting pictures. Her dad came to get her when it was time. "You sure," her dad asked. "Found a guy as amazing as my dad," Faith said. Her dad hugged her and brushed a tear away. "What," Faith asked. "I've never seen you this happy," he said. "Because I found what you and mom have," Faith replied. They headed down to the wedding. Patsy was quiet and the wedding was beautiful. The minute Faith saw Jason, he started crying. The more she walked towards him, the more his hands started to shake. He had on the bracelet she'd bought him. The minute she got to him, he was wiping tears away. Faith handed the flowers to Emma and the ceremony started.

It was like nobody else was there. The ceremony went perfectly....then it came time for their vows. "When I first met you, everything was like a storm around me. I never thought there would be calm and happy. You helped me through the storm and never let go. Life is never perfect, but when we're together, it feels like it is. From the second you talked me into that date, there was something I couldn't resist. You make me happy, you're an amazing dad and I know that the girls and I are lucky to have you. I promise to never let go. I promise to hold your hand through the good and bad, chase away your fears, never let you give in to your doubts and love you with every breath I take. You made my heart strong again. You made me the woman I am standing here before you, and I will never forget the moments we'll always smile about. I promised you then, and I'm never letting that promise be broken," Faith said. He slid the ring on her finger and brushed tears away from his eyes. "When I first met you, I fell hard. My girls thought that I'd lost it. All I knew was that I wasn't letting go. The minute you were in my arms, it's like we just fit. Once all the craziness was over, I was even more in love with you. You are what I've always wanted, all wrapped up in one person. Faith, I love you. I always have, I always will and it will never end. You're an amazing mom. Faith, you inspire me every day. You inspire the music, the feeling that I never want to lose you. I was in love with you before we even met Faith. I promise to love you with every ounce of my soul, to be at your side through good or evil, I promise to hold you in my arms every night and be the only woman I have dreams about each night. I want to be the man you kiss when you wake up, and dream of all night. I promise to be honest, faithful and true to you. I'll never stop loving you. The ring is an unending circle just like the love I have for you," Jason said. Faith almost started to cry and he brushed her tears away. The minister was about to ask if anyone had issue with them getting married and Jason shook his head subtly. "By the honor vested in me by the state of Tennessee, I pronounce you…" "You missed something," Jamie said. "Husband and wife. You can kiss your bride," the minister said. Jason kissed her with a kiss that could've made that room go up in flames. "I love you," Jason said. Faith kissed him. Faith took her flowers in hand and walked down the aisle grabbing Patsy on the way through. They went off with some family and the wedding party to do photos.

When they got back to the venue, everyone was mingling and having a drink. It was just what Faith had wanted. "Better," Jason asked. "Still can't believe we did this," Faith said. "Kinda glad we did Mrs. Cane. We could just skip the party," Jason teased. "We're doing the party. "I love you. You know that right," Jason said. Faith kissed him. "Well Mrs. Cane, I think they might be ready for us. Wanna go in and hang out for a while," Jason asked. Faith kissed him. "Let's get this over with," Faith teased. He kissed her, devouring her lips. They finally came up for air and headed inside. Everyone was there. Within seconds of them coming in, everyone came over and a half hour later, they started dinner. "Still think we should've gone home," Jason teased. Faith kissed him. There were speeches, toasts and more toasts then Jason stood up to do his toast to Faith. "When I met Faith, I swear she knocked me right off my feet. I didn't know whether to kiss her or kidnap her. Luckily, she let me take her out on that first date. What I knew after that first date was that I couldn't live without her. Y'all know what I mean. The music changed the minute she came into my life. All I ever wanted was someone who loved my girls like I did and someone who loves me for just being me. I guess I won on both counts. This woman right here is a blessing that I know I'll never be fully worthy of. I promised you forever Faith. I'm never giving up on that. No matter what it takes. To forever." They toasted then he kissed Faith. They finished up dinner and Jason and Faith got up to cut the cake. "You mess up the dress you're grounded," Faith teased. They had the cake and instead of feeding her cake, he opted to feed her icing. "Best part," he teased. He kissed her and walked her into the middle of the dance floor. The one song started to play, and Faith knew it was part of the surprise. He chose 'Without You' by Keith Urban. Faith kissed him. "Good surprise," Jason asked. Faith kissed him. "Couldn't have been better," Faith said. "I meant what I said," Jason said. Faith kissed him again. "I love you husband," Faith said. Jason kissed her. They finished their dance and Jason pulled his mom into his arms and danced with her. All of it was perfect.

Faith couldn't have imagined a better night. She had her dance with her dad then Jason pulled her back into his arms. "What you want," Faith teased. "My wife. What ya think," he asked putting a smirk of Faith's face. "You did marry me and all," Faith teased. "Another hour or so and we're going," Jason said. Faith nodded and kissed him. "Need you to come here for a sec," Jason said. She looked and the guys were on stage. "What are you up to," Faith asked. He walked Faith over to a chair in front of the stage and kissed her. He hopped onto the stage and the room went quiet. "Remember earlier when I mentioned that Faith inspired a ton of my songs. These are two she hasn't heard yet. I love you baby." He sang the two new songs he'd written for Faith and there wasn't a dry eye in the house. As soon as he was done, he hopped off the stage and kissed her. Faith and Jason hung out a little while longer, got Patsy then Faith threw the bouquet. Emma caught it and Faith, Jason and Patsy left. "So what we doing tonight there husband," Faith teased. "Hotel then bed. We head down to Georgia tomorrow. Thought we could drive, but if you wanna fly, we can," Jason said. Faith kissed him. Faith changed into Jason's t-shirt, gave Patsy a bath and tucked her into bed after a bottle. Jason snuck in after her. "What," Jason asked. Faith kissed him. "Bed," Faith said. He picked her up and kissed her and carried her to bed. "I can walk," Faith teased. Jason kissed her. They curled up on the bed together. "You realize this means you're stuck with me," Jason said. Faith smirked. "Too late to change my mind," Faith joked. Not even 2 seconds later, Jamie was calling her cell. When she didn't answer, there was a knock at the door to their suite. "Seriously," Jason asked. Faith kissed him. "You're not answering that," Jason said. Faith kissed him, got up and slid her robe on. "Faith," Jason said. "Two minutes," Faith said.

Jamie knew it was his only chance. "What Jamie," Faith asked. "We need to talk before you do something really stupid," Jamie said. "You realize we're on our honeymoon as of an hour ago," Faith replied. He grabbed Faith's hand and pulled her into a suite across the hall. "Let go of my hand," Faith said. "Marrying him was stupid Faith. He's gonna screw you over. He already has," Jamie said. "Meaning what," Faith asked waiting to hear his stupid excuse. "Meaning this," Jamie said handing Faith photos. It was picture after picture of Jason kissing another woman. "You wait until now," Faith asked. "I tried to talk to you Faith. You wouldn't listen. Come home," Jamie said. Faith shook her head. She grabbed the photos and walked back into the suite with Jason. "What did he want," Jason asked. Faith got dressed. "Baby," Jason said. She put her dress in the suit bag, put the rest of her stuff and Patsy's into her baby bag and got Patsy. "Where are you going," Jason asked. Faith texted Jamie to ask if he had duplicates. When he replied yes, Faith handed Jason the photos. "That's where I'm going," Faith said. She walked out and went back to the house. She started packing up. By the time Jason got there, Faith's truck was almost packed. "You can't just walk out. Faith, we just got married. We're supposed to be on our honeymoon," Jason said. "Really. And you said you weren't with anyone else. That proves it. I never should've…" Jason kissed her. "I love you. Faith, the past is the past. I can't do…" "Hope you two are happy. Don't pull that crap about you couldn't cheat. You were cheating at a damn hotel and someone saw it. It wasn't that easy I bet. What part was the BS? Rehearsal? What?" "Faith, stop. I love you Faith. I don't want someone else," Jason said. "Find someone willing to put up with a cheat then," Faith said. She put the last two bags into the truck. "You can't walk out," Jason said. Faith went to take the rings off and he stopped her. "You can't get rid of me that easy Faith," Jason said. She got Patsy and they left. "Faith," Jason said. She walked out to the truck, got Patsy settled and they left. Jason was trying to catch up for hours. Faith finally drove to the one place Jason would never think she'd go.

Faith pulled into the cabins that she'd always wanted to go to. When they got to Tybee, Faith almost started crying. She rented one of the cabins for a week or so until she could make sense of what to do. She got Patsy settled and locked up the back of the truck so all her things were hidden. She looked at the rings and took them off. She slid them in her change purse. She started a fire in the fireplace, poured herself a drink and curled up on the sofa. Her phone was ringing for hours. First Jason then Jamie then Emma and Sara then Jason and Jamie again. She ignored it all. Hours later, Faith heard a knock at the door. She got up with the drink in hand. She looked through the peephole and went and sat back down. "Faith, open the door. They told me you were here. We're discussing this," Jason said. Faith put the rings into an envelope, slid it under the door and went and drew herself a hot bath. Faith came out a while later in her robe and Jason's truck hadn't left – either had hers for that matter. She looked out back and Jason was sitting on the steps. She slid on her oversized sweater and leggings. "Just go before it..." Jason turned and kissed Faith. "I love you. Faith, we just got married. Don't do this," Jason said. "I didn't. You did," Faith said. She went back inside and before she could get the door shut, Jason was in the cabin. "Faith, it's not..." "It's not what I think it is? Jason, just go. We can erase this and pretend it didn't happen," Faith said. "No we can't Faith. Please," Jason said. "Just go. I'm not having this stupid fight with you Jason. You promised me. You said it then you turned around and cheated. I'm not blind. Go home. Just leave me alone," Faith said. "Faith..." "No. Take them and do what you want to Jason. They never were meant for me," Faith said. He put them back on her finger. "They're staying there. I told you Faith, I don't walk..." She couldn't get away. She couldn't walk away and he wasn't letting her go. "I don't walk away from a marriage Faith. We can work this out," Jason said. "We can work it out with you signing annulment papers," Faith replied. "We're fixing this," Jason replied. "Leave. Just go home and go screw whoever the hell you want. You wanted to mess around? Go screw who you want," Faith replied. She pushed him out the door and locked it. "Faith," Jason said. She called security for the cabins and they escorted Jason off the premises. Not 15 minutes later, Jamie called her.

"Where did you go," Jamie asked. "Just leave me alone. You wanted me apart from him, you got what you wanted Jamie. Stop gloating," Faith said. "I'm not. I wanted to make sure you were alright. Whether you believe me or you don't, I care Faith. I tried to talk to you before the wedding and you wouldn't hear it. Faith, I love you. Something like that happens, it would kill me knowing that someone could hurt you. It killed me more when Evan pulled that crap. Faith, just let me be there." She sat down and was almost curled up in a ball. She took the rings off and put them on the table. "Come here," Jamie said. Faith shook her head. He walked over to her side of the sofa and slid in behind her, wrapping his arms around her. "Jamie," Faith said. "Movie," he asked. Faith shook her head. He knew she was brushing off tears. He put in the one movie that always got her really good and sat down behind her. His arms wrapped around her. He leaned her head onto his chest and they just sat. A half hour into the movie, Faith got up and went into the bedroom. She locked the door behind her and curled up on the floor.

A half hour later, Faith heard Jamie singing to Patsy to calm her down. He calmed her down, gave her a bottle and rocked her back to sleep from what Faith heard. A half hour later, he knocked at her door. "What," Faith asked brushing her tears away. "Popcorn," Jamie said. "I'm fine. Thanks," Faith said. "Open," he replied. She opened the door and he saw her eyes red. "Baby," Jamie said. "Just don't." She closed the door. Jamie curled up on the sofa. The next morning when he woke up, everything was gone.

Faith got back to Nashville, started house hunting and found the house. She found a hotel where the security level was the top of the top, got a suite under another name and got settled. A few days later, the offer was accepted. Faith ordered the crib she'd wanted and got everything else she'd needed. She moved in without a word to anyone. The house had pristine wood floors, a massive Jacuzzi tub, a view worth every penny and a gourmet kitchen. Faith curled up with a cup of tea and sat in the oversized porch swing on the back balcony. She didn't really care who wanted to find her. She just needed time to breathe. Faith went in after mug number two of her tea and checked her voicemail. How in the world she managed to get 60 voicemails, she didn't know. Most of them were from Jason begging her to come home. The rest were either from Jamie, Emma, Sara or work. She saw a text come in from Deacon:

Now I know something went wrong. Everyone's going nuts. What happened? Call me.

Chapter 30

"If I didn't know better, I'd say you moved," Deacon said. "I did. I'm just in need of new surroundings," Faith said. "So did you find a place?" "Yes. Patsy's settled," Faith replied intentionally not saying a word about any of it. "I heard something happened. You wanna talk," Deacon asked. "No," Faith replied. "Coffee," Deacon asked. Faith hung up. Under 10 seconds to tell him to go away. Faith went through emails and saw over 100 of them from Jamie and Jason. Jamie was determined to see Patsy. Faith knew what that meant. She got Patsy packed up for a day or two, dropped her at Jamie's and he tried getting her to come inside. "I'll come get her Sunday," Faith said. "Aren't gonna say a word are you," Jamie asked. Faith got in her truck and left. She put the rings in an envelope and put them in Jason's mailbox then headed home. She pulled in, made sure the gate was turned on and went back into the house, locking the truck up in the garage. She curled up inside, had a hot bath and turned on a movie. A half hour later, Jason started calling again. Faith turned his calls off and they all went straight to voicemail. It was only when Patrick called that Faith finally answered the phone. "What's up," Faith said. "Office. Tour is starting in two weeks. We need to go over tour plans," Patrick said. "Fine," Faith replied. "See you at 1," Patrick said. Faith went and got dressed and tried to get the red eyes to disappear. She slid on a dress that would've made Jason, Jamie and half the male species pass out and went and headed downtown. She walked into the meeting. "So, here's what we're planning. Faith, I need you doing shots once a week. You don't have to be there every show. Once a week for a few hours. Jamie is opening. That work," Patrick asked. Faith nodded. "Need me for anything else," Faith asked. "Three interviews. They found out you and Jason..." Faith walked out and went into her office and locked the door. Jason went to come in and couldn't. "Open it," Jason said. Faith shook her head. She got the papers and cheques she needed to deposit and put them into her briefcase. She grabbed her work laptop and stepped out. "We need to talk," Jason said. "No we don't actually," Faith said. Not 2 minutes later, Jason was served annulment papers.

Faith went out to her truck and left. Jason caught her pulling out minutes later. Two steps behind her was Jamie.

Faith got half way back to the house and saw Jamie's truck behind her. She pulled over and Jamie pulled up behind her. Faith got out of the truck. "Any reason in particular you're tailing me," Faith asked. "Talk to me." Faith shook her head. "Where's Patsy," Faith asked. "Asleep in the back seat. We can talk Faith. Whatever the problem…" "Go home. I'm going to try and calm down before I kick him so hard my pointy cowboy boots shoot out his forehead." "Promise you'll call if you need me." Faith nodded and went and got back in her truck. Jamie turned around and left her be and Faith went back and curled back up on the porch swing. She deposited her cheques, made dinner and tried to make sense of all of it. A few hours later, Faith heard a car at the gate. She looked and saw Emma. Faith let her in and locked the gate up behind her. "I figured this is where you were," Emma said. "Finally got it," Faith said. Emma hugged her. "I'm so sorry," Emma said. "I lost everyone. Everyone," Faith said. Emma held on a little tighter. "Still have me and Patsy. Even Alan still likes you," Emma said trying to tease. "Everyone cheats. Every damn one," Faith said. "Jackass might be a good term. Emma, I made so many stupid idiotic mistakes. First Evan then Jamie…" "Stop. Faith, you have to let someone do something. Jamie's trying to help. He knows how hurt you are. I get it Faith." "He's making it worse Emma. He's trying to get me back by helping me get through the Jason crap. It's not right." "What do you wanna do Faith," Emma asked. "Forget it? Forget all of it and just be happy? I can't just turn around and date Jamie again. I can't let what happened with Jason get back to me either. Maybe I was just better off with Evan. Wouldn't have had to live through this crap," Faith said. Emma hugged her. "If he hadn't got you out of there, you'd be dead Faith. Stop. You need to stop all of this," Emma said. "What am I supposed to do then? I'm not taking him back Emma. Neither of them," Faith replied. She walked off and went upstairs. "Faith," Emma said. Just as Emma was trying to talk to Faith, Jason pulled into the driveway. "Just…" "Faith, you need to figure it out. You need to make a decision," Emma said. "Fine. My decision is I'm staying fucking single," Faith said.

Jason came to the door. "She doesn't want to talk to you," Emma said. "I don't give a shit what my WIFE wants. We're talking period." Jason walked upstairs and saw the master bedroom door closed. "Open the door Faith," Jason said. "How did you even know," Faith asked. "Because I saw you stare at this damn house every time we drove past it. Faith, just talk to me," Jason said. "Why? Because you wanna tell me it wasn't what I thought? You wanna tell me you didn't screw around now," Faith asked. "Open the damn door," Jason said. "Why?" "Open it or I open it," Jason said. Faith opened the door and he saw her eyes red. "Did you even look at the date on it," Jason asked. "Meaning what," Faith asked. He showed her the picture and it was dated before she was even dating Jason. "Sure you didn't just re-do them to cover your ass," Faith asked. He handed her documentation from the police that showed he was right. "See," Jason said. Faith shook her head. "He's the one causing this Faith. It's not me. I'm not doing anything other than being with you. That's it. Faith, the girls miss you. I miss you. Stop this crap," Jason said. "I'm not going back to that house. This is where I'm staying," Faith said. "Fine. This place is bigger anyway. We'll sell my place and stay here," Jason said. "Why can't you just…" He kissed her. He picked her up, wrapping her legs around his waist and walked her to the bed. "Stop," Faith said pushing him away. "Jason, enough," Faith said. "Woman, I didn't screw around. You know I didn't. Faith, please just stop. I didn't screw around. You know I didn't. Faith, just…" "Stop. Enough," Faith said. She got up and went downstairs. "You're gonna have this damn fight? I didn't do anything. You wanna hit me? Hit me then. Get it overwith. Faith, I can't live like this. I love you. I put these rings on your hand because I wanted forever with you. Not because I wanted one damn day and a lifetime of being miserable. Stop," Jason said. "Just go," Faith said. "No. Not without you," Jason said. "I am home," Faith replied. "Faith, just stop. I need you. Please." "Why?" "Faith, I love you. Don't do this," Jason said. She pushed him away. "No," Jason said. He fought her until she was in his arms. She was still fighting. Emma went outside. It almost killed her seeing Faith like that.

"Just tell me what you want me to do or say or what to fix this," Jason said. "Leave me alone," Faith said. "I can't. I love you Faith. I need you." "And I needed one day out of my life to know that things were gonna be right. That I made the right decision. Instead, I barely get to even be married before things get that fucked up. I needed to know that I wasn't gonna need to worry again. Instead, I was face to face with that. Instead I'm confronted with the one damn thing you promised wasn't…." Jason kissed her. "I swear to you it was before we were together. Faith, it was before I had my show in Dallas when I saw you. It was before the stuff at the cabin. Faith, I love you. Please just come home," Jason asked. Faith shook her head. Jason kissed her again. "Come home. Faith, come home," Jason said. She shook her head and walked out of the room. She walked outside and curled up on the porch swing. Jason almost slid to the floor. "I need you," he said. Faith heard it.

"He's the one Faith," Patsy's voice said. Tears slid down. "I don't know what to do anymore," Faith said. "Then come home," Patsy replied. Faith was almost glad that Jamie had Patsy for a while. She went inside, grabbed her purse, keys and cell. "Faith," Jason said. "You need to go. I have an appointment," Faith said. "Come home after," he said. Faith nodded to get him to leave her be. He left. Faith locked up and went home.

Home never was what people think. In country history, home had always been the Grand Ole Opry. When it was at the Ryman, it was the Mother Church. When they moved it to the Opry, the circle came with them. Every dreamer stood in that circle. Every country artist in history stood there with a dream of making it big. Patsy stood in that circle more than once. No matter who stood there, they always knew that they'd have strength and inspiration in that circle. Even after a flood, it still stood proudly on the stage of the Grand Ole Opry House. That's where she'd first felt Patsy Cline near her – and that's where home was.

Faith pulled into the artist parking, signed in and went in and sat down in the auditorium. "You came home," she heard. Faith turned and swore she saw Patsy sitting beside her. "What now," Faith asked. "When I met Charlie, I was head over heels Faith. He made me so damn happy. We had the girls and I never thought things could get better. I ended up a big country star, but the one thing I missed more than anything was being with my man and my kids. Don't let a stupid dream get in the way of family Faith. If you love Jason, be with him. If Jamie is the one you think you're supposed to be with, do it. Every day that you don't have what you deserve and what you need, is one day you're losing to time. Don't lose time with the people you love Faith. Hold onto it. If I could've been with them again, I never would've left. Instead, I see how my family grew up and tried to move on without me. You don't want to do this Faith. It kills. I love my husband and my kids Faith. I know they're mine. What do you want," Patsy asked. Faith almost kneeled down and it hit her. "I'll give you a push if you need it Faith. Tell my kids that I love them." "Where you going," Faith asked. "To check on my babies." That was the last thing that she heard. Faith walked around and went into the dressing room she'd been in the first time she'd heard Patsy. She saw Jason's necklace sitting on the counter. She'd heard he was supposed to play the Opry that night. Faith went to turn around and saw Jason.

"So this is…" Faith kissed him. As soon as he let her up for air, Faith left and went out to the truck. "Faith," Jason said. "What," she replied. "You coming tonight," he asked. Faith looked at him. "Do-over," he asked. She shrugged and left. Faith got back to the house and two hours later, flowers showed. Faith smirked. The second she saw the card, she had a smile for the first time in a while:

Guess you found your way home. I love you.

Faith put the flowers in water and went upstairs to have a bath. The minute her foot was in the water, her cell rang. "Yes," Faith said. "So what would you think about your husband taking you out on a date tonight? Live music and a few surprises," Jason said. "As long as they aren't bad surprises." "See you at 5." Faith hung up. She slid into the tub and soaked a while then washed her hair. Faith found just the right dress and at 4:30, Jason showed. "What are you doing here so early," Faith asked. "Forgot to do something. Wanted to make sure I didn't forget this time," he said. "Which is," Faith asked. Jason kissed her. He devoured her lips and leaned her against the wall by the entry. "I missed you," Jason said. Faith nodded. "Don't tell me you're still worried," Jason asked. Something told her she was right to be worried.

An hour and a half later and Faith was listening to the radio as they were pulling in. "We just got a major bit of gossip. Jason Cane was caught red-handed with Amanda Hart tonight. Go check out our site if you want to see the pics. The two of them are hot and heavy these days. This isn't the first time either…" Faith got out of the truck at the last light. "Faith," Jason said. She walked into the Opryland hotel and called for a cab. "Faith, you don't get it." She slapped Jason so hard her handprint was on his face. Jason grabbed her hand, walked her into the elevator, up to the suite and into the room without a word. "Let go of my damn hand," Faith said. "Woman, stop being a pain in my ass. Nothing…" Faith stormed out, went downstairs, got into a car to get home and was gone just that fast. Her cell didn't stop ringing. A half hour later, a black SUV showed at her door. "What," Faith asked. "I'm here to take you to the Opry," the driver said. Faith shook her head. "Please don't. As soon as the show's done I'll bring you straight back if that's what you want," the driver said. "I can't," Faith said. He handed Faith a note. Jason was being asked to be a member that night. Faith got in. She was standing side-stage when he went on. Jason didn't see her. When he was asked, he looked over and saw Faith. He tried to get her to come to him and she shook her head. By the time he stepped off the stage, Faith was walking out. He grabbed her hand. "Please," Jason said. "Let go. I was here. I saw. I'm leaving." Jason kissed her, Faith pushed him away and walked out. "Tell me what to do," Jason asked. Faith walked out and left. She went back to the house and curled up by the fireplace. Emma tried to call, Sara tried to call and just about everyone else once news about him being asked to be a member of the Opry hit the airwaves. Faith turned her phone off and tried to relax. She slid into her pajamas and went upstairs when Jamie pulled in.

He had Patsy in his arms and she was out cold. "What are you doing," Faith asked. "Two things. First off, putting her to bed. Second, explaining," Jamie said. Faith took Patsy and the baby bag and almost slammed the door in his face. She walked upstairs, changed Patsy and slid her into bed then came downstairs. "The investigator said they were recent. Faith, Amanda is the one in the picture," Jamie said. "And the reason that they were really older ones and…" "It was. The newer two were the other two Faith. I wasn't lying to you." "Go home," Faith replied. "Faith, I need you to understand," Jamie said. "I do. Now get out," Faith replied. He finally left and Faith turned on the baby monitor. She went and sat down outside and worked on emails. She saw one from Emma. Seconds later, she called her. "Okay. Now I know you're losing it. Faith, talk," Emma said. "Just come over. Don't bother telling Jamie either. The only way I'm talking to him is if its Patsy related. End of discussion." "Faith, he screwed up, but he…" "If you're coming do defend him…" "It's not that. He was trying to protect you. He knew the stuff about Jason was for real Faith. He didn't want you hurting anymore. He was trying to do the right thing. He screwed it up royally, but he tried." "Emma," Faith said. "I know. Faith, I just wanted you to be happy. That's all," Emma said. Faith hugged her. "I'm alone Emm. I have a baby girl with a man I thought I knew, and now I'm alone." "You have me. You have Sara. Faith, Jason is losing it. Jamie already did and he's doing it again. You have to figure out what you want to do Faith. You want to be away from both of them, it's gonna be hard as hell Faith. Jason's not gonna let go. You made a vow," Emma said. "He lied Emma. He straight out lied to my damn face. How am I supposed to stay when I'm surrounded by lie after lie," Faith asked. "Then find a way to get the answer Faith. Jason loves you and so does Jamie. If that's not gonna make you happy…" "I want me back. I wanna be back to the same person I was before the Evan crap. Emma, I can't do this. I need to get out of here for a few weeks or something. I need somewhere to think straight," Faith said. "I'll go with you to help you with Patsy. I won't say anything to Jason. I promise." Faith hugged her. "You're that bad," Emma asked. Faith nodded.

Not even 48 hours later, Faith and Emma left town with Patsy and went to Houston. "Why are we here," Emma asked. "Meaning," Faith asked as she put Patsy down for a nap. "Meaning of everywhere we could go, anywhere in the country…you chose here?" "I need somewhere quiet and away from either of them. This is far away enough that we are. That's all," Faith said. "You seriously that worried that he's gonna come here? Faith, I know you're upset, but…" "This is where I stayed when I needed space Emm. I'm doing this. You have to let me figure this out." Emma nodded. "I'm going to grab some groceries." "Faith," Emma said. "Half hour," Faith replied. She grabbed the keys to the rental and headed to the store. She slid the ball cap on so nobody would recognize her. She got to the store and magazine after magazine was talking about Jason. Some even had shots of Faith with him saying the wedding was a lie. She grabbed what she needed and left. Only one person recognized her, and didn't say anything. "I could deliver next time if you need me to," the woman said. Faith nodded. She got her stuff loaded into the truck. Faith made a few stops on the way back. She grabbed everything else she was gonna need. When Faith got back, Emma was sitting on the porch swing with the baby. "She barely stayed asleep," Emma said. Faith loaded in the groceries, unpacked and put everything away, made herself a drink and came out to the porch swing. Faith slid Patsy out of Emma's arms and rocked her. Patsy was back asleep a little while later. Faith slid her into the crib. "So what's with the man strength drink," Emma asked. "Not breast feeding anymore remember," Faith said. "That wasn't an answer," Emma said. Faith drank it. "Woman, you can't drink them away," Emma said. Faith nodded. She finished the drink and went inside. "What's going on," Emma asked. "I can't deal with the crap that keeps coming. I can't," Faith said. "Woman, divine intervention isn't happening," Emma said. Faith nodded. "I do know that I'm not doing this crap Emm. Jason and I…. there's no point. I can't keep fighting with all of this. I need my life back Emma. I want me. I want back what I was like before. I need to. If it means getting away until I make a decision, I stay here. That's what I need Emma. If you don't get it, I understand." "Just don't run away from it all and try to make new somewhere else," Emma said. Faith nodded.

After a week or two of Jason going nuts trying to find her, he went into rehearsals. "Dude, you're acting nuts. Just because she's gone doesn't mean you flip out on all of us. I get you're upset alright," Kevin said. "I need to find her alright. When I know she's alright I'll be able to concentrate on a damn song," Jason said. "Then go find her. Where's the one place you know she'd go if she wasn't' here," Kevin asked. Minutes later, Jason was getting a plane ticket to Dallas. That's where she had to be. Jason packed up what he needed and went to grab the rings she'd given back to him. They weren't there. He took off anyway, got to the airport and was on a flight in a matter of minutes.

Faith had another drink and curled up on the porch swing. "Faith," Emma said. She relaxed and sipped at her tweaked sweet tea. Emma came out with Patsy all curled up in a towel. "She was demanding to see you," Emma joked. Faith put her tea down. "So what did you want little ducky," Faith asked. "Ma," Patsy said. Faith rocked her and they had a mom and daughter talk. Not even an hour later, Faith heard a truck roaring down the road. She took Patsy inside and gave her a bottle and put her to bed. She came out a little while later and Jason was sitting in the driveway. Faith shook her head, grabbed her drink and went back inside. "Faith," Jason said grabbing her hand. "Can't just leave me alone," Faith said. "We need to talk," Jason said. "I'm done talking Jason. We're getting an annulment." "No we aren't Faith. I'm not losing you," Jason said. "Already did. Hope you and…" Jason kissed her. The tea was knocked to the floor. He picked her up, carried her up the steps right past Emma and into the bedroom. "Put me down," Faith said. "Why? Just tell me why you can't take me back," Jason asked. "Amanda," Faith said pushing him away. The fact that he'd come this far, meant he wasn't letting go that easily. He pulled her right back to him. "Faith, nothing is going on. We are working on a damn song together. That's all," Jason said. "And that's why you've been caught more than once kissing her right? Go mess with someone else," Faith said. "Woman, stop being a pain in my ass. You don't wanna hear this, fine. Listen to the damn song," Jason said handing Faith his iPod. She put the earbuds in. Jason looked at Emma in the hall. "Where are they," Jason asked. Emma handed him the rings. "She's not…" "I know," Jason said.

Faith listened to the song. It was a duet that Jamie had written that he was finally willing to let someone hear. The label had asked him to work with Amanda and help her get her feet wet in the music industry. The fact that she couldn't understand what wedding rings meant, was the only thing that Jamie couldn't stand. She'd made a move over and over again. Jason finally walked off. He wasn't gonna deal with it anymore. He told Patrick that he was done working with her. That he'd had it. "Fine. At least you tried. I know she's…" "A damn flirt and a home-wrecker. Yeah I know," Jason said. "Where is Faith anyway," Patrick had asked during a quick meeting a few weeks prior. Jason walked out. Now, he was face to face with the only woman he wanted or even needed.

She handed Jason his iPod and went to get up. "It's not done," Faith said. "Because I walked out. I told her that she wasn't destroying our marriage. Faith, don't do this. Don't just walk off," Jason said. "You're the one that ruined it. If you'd…" "I didn't do anything," Jason said. "I need my…" Jason kissed her. I'm not living without you," Jason said. "Good line for the song. It's not gonna work on me Jason. I know better," Faith said. He pulled her back to him. "Tell me what I need to do to get you back," he asked. "Stop asking. I fell for a stupid mistake Jason. I married you when neither of us were ready. I get you wanting to rush through it, but…" Jason kissed her again. "I'm not doing this," Faith said. Jason kissed her again. "You're not walking away Faith. I can't let you do that," Jason replied. "Let me? What the hell? You don't have to let me do a damn thing. I get to do whatever the hell I want, whenever the hell I want," Faith said. "Then quit picking a damn fight. I love you alright? I need you. I need us Faith. I know you do too. No matter how much you wanna walk off and leave, you have to just let me be with you. I love you Faith." "And you…" Jason kissed her. "Come home and we can fix this," Jason said.

Faith walked back downstairs. She grabbed her drink and finished it. "Woman, you need to listen to me. I'm not just gonna sit here and let you walk out of my life. I need you Faith. Just come back and we can try to figure this out," Jason said. "There's nothing left to figure out," Faith replied. She went inside and locked the door. "Faith," Emma said. "What," Faith replied. "He's not leaving. He's sitting on the porch. He's not gonna just walk," Emma said. Faith went upstairs and drew a bath, got a refill of her drink and slid into a hot bath.

"She'd never gonna forgive me. It was a damn kiss. I didn't sleep with that stupid little idiot," Jason said. "What do you want me to say," Emma asked. "That you know I'm not gonna hurt her Emma. I need her. Please," Jason said. "It's not my decision to make Jason. I know she was really hurt when Jamie messed up. It tripled when it was you. There is no calming her down," Emma said. "I'll stay here until she does." "Jason, she's not gonna let you be here without a damn fight. You know that," Emma said. "Then I fight until we can't fight anymore. I'm not letting go Emma. It would be like losing a damn limb." "Then find a way to do it without pinning her into a room. You're gonna get her defensive like she was with Evan. Trust me. It's not pretty," Emma said. Jason nodded. "I promise you, I'm not gonna hurt her," Jason said. "And if you break the promise to me," Emma asked. "I'll leave her alone and never look back," Jason said. Emma went inside and Jason heard the tub draining.

Jason went inside and Emma sat down outside and read for a while with her tea. "Why are you even here," Faith asked knowing that Jason was behind her. "Because I'm fighting for our marriage. That's why. I married you because I love you. That doesn't change just because something stupid happens. That doesn't get turned off," Jason said. "What happens when there's no reason to fight," Faith asked. "You keep fighting. I keep fighting. I'm not letting go Faith. I want our marriage to be alright. I want us to be okay. Please," he said. "I can't just..." "I know. Faith, I promise you that I didn't do anything. She's the one that was making passes at me. I love you Faith. Please just stop fighting me," Jason said. "I can't just turn..." Jason kissed her. "I'm not gonna make you do anything Faith. I just want to be with you," Jason said. Faith went to walk away and Jason pulled her into his arms and kissed her. Faith let go and Jason couldn't. "I get you want to be here. I get it. I'm not gonna push," Jason said. "I just need to make sense of some stuff," Faith said. Jason kissed her. "If you want me to stay, I can. Just say the word," Jason said. "I can't do this with...." Jason kissed her. "I love you Faith. Don't make me leave," Jason said. "I can't do this with you here. Jason, I need to think and not have..." "I know. Faith, I need you alright? I love you. I've gone long enough without you. Faith, we were barely even apart a day when we started dating," Jason said. "There's mistake number 2," Faith said. "Woman, stop being such a pain about this. I didn't do anything with her. You want proof, talk to her yourself," Jason said. He dialed and handed her the phone. "Jason," Faith said. "Ask," he said.

"Hello," the woman said on the other end of the phone. "This is Faith," she said. "Faith, I know I messed things up with you two, but..." "But what," Faith asked. "It was a stupid publicity stunt. I didn't mean to get in the middle..." "Did you or didn't you sleep with him? Keep in mind little girl that as of right now, you're apologizing to the entire publicity planet. You don't, I'll rip your career right out of your hands," Faith said. "I didn't. I tried to kiss him and he pushed me away. We slept in the same room because I fell asleep when we were at the recording studio. That's all. I swear Faith," Amanda said. "You're apologizing to the entire press. You realize that right? You have 24 hours," Faith said. She hung up and handed the phone back to Jason. "Faith," he said. She went to walk out of the house and Jason pulled her back into his arms. "What," Faith asked. "I would never have done that Faith. You have to know that," Jason said. Faith kissed him. She told Emma she was leaving. Emma nodded and saw Jason following her. "You can't just let me go to the damn store alone," she said. "No. Faith, I promised you." "What about before then," Faith asked. "Still didn't. Faith, I can't do that and still be able to think straight. I didn't date anyone. I went out with her once or twice. I didn't sleep with her then. Faith, she's not my damn type." He kissed her. "And who is," Faith asked. "You." "Jason," Faith said. "Just stop freaking out. I love you Faith. I'm not messing this up. I'm not losing you. Not when I am so close to getting you back," Jason said. Faith walked off, got in the truck and left.

Jason sat down on the porch. He checked on Patsy and gave her a bottle and changed her. When Faith finally came back in, she walked right past Jason and Emma. Emma wouldn't let Jason get up. "Just let her breathe," Emma said. Faith went upstairs and checked on Patsy and went into her room. She locked the door behind her. Faith curled up on the bed and went through her emails. She saw 15 from Jamie begging her to come home. She replied back with one email:

We're divorced. Stop asking. Don't contact me again unless it's about visiting Patsy.

Pressing send gave her power back to her. She turned her TV on and flipped on an old movie. Emma came inside a while later and heard Faith's TV on. "Well," Jason asked. "TV is on. Not sure if that's good or bad," Emma said. "I love her Emm. I can't stop it. If I did it would be like stopping the fucking weather. I love her," Jason said. "If she starts getting defensive, just come downstairs. You ever hurt her, I'll rip your heart out through your nose with a damn shovel," Emma said. He kissed

Emma's cheek and went upstairs and knocked on the door. If she didn't answer, he knew to back off. When Faith came to the door, he felt a lot better. "You okay," Jason asked. "Got Jamie to screw off. I swear, one more ounce of stress and…" Jason kissed her. "No stress. Gotcha," he teased. "I mean it," Faith replied. "There isn't gonna be stress. Worst you're getting is what to wear to the awards," Jason said. Faith nodded. "Or, could be what to name the next baby," he teased. "Okay, you're grounded. Enough," Faith said. Jason kissed her. "I love you. If that means fighting forever, I'll fight until I can't anymore."

When Emma came upstairs to head to bed, Faith was asleep with her head on Jason's chest and he had his arms wrapped around Faith. Emma closed the door and slid into bed herself. For once, Faith wasn't going to bed upset, mad, angry or anything, and for the first time in a few days, Faith didn't need a drink to calm down. Just as Emma was falling asleep, Alan called her. "How you feeling," Alan asked. "Better. I know I was helping her, but I kinda needed this too. You're so busy trying to help Jamie get her back that neither of us even got time to ourselves," Emma said. "Jamie, believe it or not, is in the bedroom working on music. He threw his phone to shit, but he's writing Emm. Now all I need is my woman here and I'm fine," Alan said. "I'll be back soon I think." "That mean that she finally decided to take Jamie back," Alan asked. "She's curled up in bed with Jason. I highly doubt it," Emma said. "So that's why he threw the phone. I miss you," Alan said. He talked to Emma until she fell asleep.

Faith got up the next morning and Jason's arms were around her. For the first time in a long time, she wasn't sure what to do. "What you worried about," Jason asked. "If it doesn't…" Jason kissed her. "We're gonna be fine. Time I can handle Faith. Fighting with you all the time is something I can't," Jason said. "I just don't understand how he can go from being my protector and my best friend to being a cheat and trying to break us up. I don't get it," Faith said. "He wants you all to himself and doesn't want someone getting in the way. Faith, you told me he was like that when you attempted to date Deacon. It's not gonna change just because it's me," Jason said. Faith kissed him. "I needed you Faith. I'm just glad I have you," Jason said. "I don't know what's gonna happen next," Faith said. "How about we handle whatever it is together," Jason asked. He kissed her forehead and she leaned back onto his chest. "I can tell you're smiling without even looking," Faith said. "I'm just glad we aren't fighting anymore. I hated fighting with you," Jason said. "You can see why I did. What am I supposed to think," Faith asked. "From now on, look me in the eye. Faith, I'm not gonna lie to you. I screw up, I'm still gonna be here. I'm not gonna love you any less even if you screw up. We stay and work on it together. We have to," Jason said. Faith looked at him. "You seriously don't think that we rushed this a little too fast," Faith asked. "Maybe. I don't wanna start over though," Jason said. "I'm just saying," Faith said. "Fine. We take our time this time. I'm not taking that ring off your finger ever again. You do know that right," Jason said. The idea of starting over and Jason running the risk of losing her again wasn't an option. "Faith," Jason said. Just as he was about to try and make a move, Patsy woke up. "You know your daughter has unbelievable timing," Jason teased. Faith got up and went and checked on Patsy.

"What's goin on," Emma asked. "You got in here before me," Faith teased. "Don't have a sexy ass fine man to distract me," Emma joked. Faith hugged her. "Things any better," Emma asked after she turned the baby monitor off. "A bit. Thinking that all the rushing around might be part of all this," Faith said. "Now she has a regret. Mark the day down," Emma teased. Faith finished changing Emma and getting her somewhat dressed. She came out into the hall and was face to face with Jason. "What," Faith asked. "You coming home with me tonight," Jason asked. Faith nodded. "I'm driving back," Faith said. "Woman, you drive me nuts. You realize that right," Jason teased. He kissed her. "I'm not just leavin my truck here," Faith said. "I know. Two days of you driving home isn't gonna be an option though. We're shipping the truck back," Jason said. "Executive decision," Faith teased. He kissed her. Jason finally let her up for air and they all went downstairs. Emma was already starting to get things packed up. "So, the flight leaves at 4. What do you think," Jason asked. "That the plane isn't big enough for everything," Faith teased. Jason kissed her. She slid Patsy into her high chair and fed her. Jason finished his breakfast and started his dessert aka nibbling on Faith's neck.

The Decision is Made

They finally made it back to Nashville that night and the press was all over them. When Faith heard one of them ask if they were just putting on an act, she almost snapped. Jason grabbed her hand and pulled her to him. They got out the door, complete with Emma and Patsy and they headed over to Jason's truck. "Don't listen to it," Jason said. "I swear on my daughter, if all of this was a lie…" They grabbed the bags and got in the truck and were gone 5 minutes later. "What are they talking about now," Faith asked. "Babe, it's fine. I promised you. It's nothing," Jason said. Faith got back to the house and she got that feeling again. Something was wrong and he was hiding something. "Remember what I said," Faith asked. "It's nothing," Jason said. They headed inside and the only thing that changed was there were more teddy bears in Patsy's room. Faith put her down to sleep and walked back into their bedroom. "What," Jason asked as his arms slid around her waist. "I still keep getting a feeling that something's wrong." "Baby, we're fine. Nothing's wrong. You just haven't…." Faith walked back downstairs. "Faith," Jason said. She shook her head. Faith went into the TV room and tried to relax. "Babe, it's late. Just come to bed," Jason said. Faith shook her head. Something told her all of it was a lie. Something wasn't right. Jason pleaded for over an hour. "I'm not…" "Faith, this is just getting silly. Nothing happened," Jason said. Faith grabbed herself a drink and went and sat outside. She clipped the baby monitor on her hip and went outside. Jason came downstairs around 2am and she was still out there. He came outside and saw Faith wiping tears away. Instead of coming outside, he went upstairs and went to bed alone.

Faith couldn't have slept even if she'd wanted to. The feeling was still there that there was something he was hiding. Around 6, Faith went upstairs and grabbed a change of clothes and saw what she feared. Whoever the woman was that he was with, left her clothes behind. Faith saw them drop her truck off. She took the last of her things, Patsy's things and Patsy and got in the truck. She went back to her place. She gave the baby a bath and curled up with her on the porch swing. They had breakfast together, talked and Faith tried to relax. Being away from him was the best thing she did. When she got Patsy down for her nap, Faith finally got some descent sleep herself.

Faith got caught up on work. The phone barely even rang. When she saw an email from Jamie, she picked up the phone. "Thought you said you didn't want to talk at all unless it was Patsy related," Jamie said. "You haven't seen her in two weeks. I guessed," Faith said. "So now that you and Jason…" "Nope," Faith replied. "Meaning what? You finally listened to the truth?" "Meaning none of your business. I'm at my place. End of discussion." "I could come down tonight to come get her. That is if it's okay with you," he said. "Fine," Faith replied. "Faith," he said. "What? Jamie, don't pull that whole 'you're making a mistake' thing again alright," Faith said. "You were. Faith, if I ever got you back…" "Goodbye Jamie," Faith said hanging up. She made lunch, checked on Patsy and cleaned up while Patsy danced around in her playpen. Jamie showed an hour later. "What," Faith asked. "Well, first off, I know damn well that something's wrong. Faith, you came back here with him and you're still here. That tells me I was right," Jason said. Faith shook her head. "You're never gonna stop are you," Faith asked. "Not when it comes to you Faith. I made that mistake once and you left with Evan. I'm not doing it again while you make the stupid mistake of walking away with him," Jamie said. "Have fun with that," Faith asked. He played with Patsy for a little while. "This wasn't an invitation to stay," Faith said. "Woman, tell me why you're still here then," Jamie said. "Bye," Faith said. "Woman, I know you better than you think I do. I know something's wrong. Just say it," Jamie said. "I walked into that house and I kept thinking that there was something he wasn't telling me. I couldn't sleep," Faith said. "Good. The instinct is still there." "Jamie, just stop," Faith replied. "Woman, you had that damn instinct when it was Evan. You made a mistake Faith. I love you alright? No stupid piece of paper is gonna change that. Faith, you know what the right thing is. Stop over-thinking it. You can't sleep and you can't even walk in that room, something isn't right and you know it. Why would you even go back," Jamie asked. "Because we're still married that's why," Faith said. "Not good enough. If you can't sleep, you know that things aren't right. Faith, if it's bugging you that much, there's no reason to keep the charade up."

422

"And what do I do Jamie? What you want? Run back to you," Faith asked. "Do what that voice tells you." "What voice," Faith asked. "I heard you Faith. Before our little girl was even conceived you were talking to Patsy. If that's the name that little voice goes by, listen to her." He saw Patsy starting to nod off. He looked at Faith. He walked over to her and kissed her.

Every inch of those feelings came back. Every emotion she'd felt, every happy moment they'd had together all came rushing back to her mind. He didn't let her up for air. Before she even noticed, Jamie picked her up and walked her upstairs to the master bedroom and leaned her onto the bed. "Jamie, stop," Faith said. "Why," he asked. "I can't do this," Faith said. "Because of that piece of paper," he asked. "Because I know better. Jamie, we don't…" He kissed her again. No clothes hit the floor. It was just the two of them. He didn't care about anything except his woman in his arms and his baby girl. "I love you Faith," Jamie said. She curled up in his arms. "You always knew didn't you," Faith asked. "Told you more than once. Faith, I get you need to do this your way. Just promise me that you aren't gonna just walk away from us," Jamie said. "There's an us," Faith asked. "Always has been. That little spirit you always talk to….she knows Faith. She knows like I do that I'm never ever leaving your side. We're supposed to be together. That's all there is to it," Jamie said.

*   *   *

A few months down the road, Faith went in to check on Jason to make sure he had his itinerary for the day. "You sure I can't talk you out of this," Jason asked. "If this is how it's supposed to be, then it is. I can't change it Jason. I need to do this. You're still my friend," Faith said. He kissed her cheek and hugged her. Faith walked him out to his interview and Jamie came up behind her as she was heading out. "What," Faith asked. Jamie walked her into the arena. He walked her onto the stage and she saw one chair. "What are you doing," Faith asked. "Something I think we needed to do a long time ago." Jamie grabbed his guitar. "Jamie," Faith said. "Just listen for once. Woman, you drive me nuts. You know that," Jamie said. "Thought that's what you loved about me."

Jamie kissed her. "Now stop being a pain," he said. "So what did you drag me out here for," Faith asked. He started playing something Faith hadn't heard. She listened to every word. It was their story. Them falling apart and finding their way back to each other. By the time Jamie finished that song, the stage hands, anyone in the general area and even Jason was listening. As soon as it was done, Jamie looked up at Faith. "Well," Jamie asked.

He saw her eyes all welled up. They were the killer blue that he remembered. It was the color he'd used to be worried to see. "Babe," he said. She brushed the tears away. "You okay," Jamie asked. Faith nodded. She kissed him. "You know I talked you into it," Jamie said. "For once you didn't. You know better," Faith said. Jamie kissed her. "I promised to marry you a million times. You remember," Jamie asked. "Tried to trick me into it a million times," Faith said. "So, I had an idea…." "No," Faith replied. She walked off the stage and went back to check on Patsy. She walked in and Emma and Alan were playing with her. Patsy stood up and managed to walk a few steps to Faith almost alone. "Baby," Faith said. "Mama," Patsy said. Emma had a grin ear to ear. "What you smiling at," Faith teased. Patsy was giggling. They were all happy and when Jamie walked in, Patsy tried to walk over to him. "Well hello there baby girl," Jamie said. Patsy giggled. "Happier isn't she," Jamie whispered. "What are you trying to say," Faith asked. "Nothin," Jamie said. He pulled Patsy up into his arms and kissed her. Patsy hugged him and Jamie had a grin ear to ear. "What," Faith asked. "Nothin," Jamie said with an even bigger grin.

Faith watched Jamie on stage. He sang that song right to her. Things seemed back to the way it was before. There was no stress, no drama, no watching over her shoulder. All there was, was the man who from day one had never stopped loving her. Even when she walked away and was with Evan, he knew she'd come back. Even when Faith had walked away from him and married Jason, he knew they belonged together. When Faith came back to him, he knew there was never gonna be another worry. He never stopped looking at her. His inspiration was back and right at her side. As soon as the concert was finished, Jamie walked over to Faith, handed off his guitar and carried her backstage. He walked into the dressing room and Faith saw sterling roses lying on the counter. "Jamie," Faith said. "What," Jamie asked. He kissed her. "Jamie," Faith said. "I made a mistake once already. I let you leave without fighting like hell. Faith, you are the only woman I ever wanted. Never knew how hard it would be to live without you. It was hell Faith. I'm not losing you ever again. I never should have signed those papers. Faith, I'm not losing my chance again," Jamie said. "What are you saying," Faith asked. He kneeled down. "Jamie," Faith said. "I make you a promise Faith. I'm never letting go of you ever again. Marry me. This time, it's permanent. Please," Jamie asked. "What are you..." He pulled out a ring. It wasn't the one he'd given her the first time. This time, it was a princess cut diamond with a setting that was absolutely perfect. He'd designed it and had seen it done a thousand times. The only difference was that Jamie wasn't letting that ring come off ever again. "Faith, marry me. Please baby. I hate being without you. I always have. Faith, I promised you hears ago I'd never let you get hurt. I'm never going to," Jamie said. "What happens when we implode," Faith asked. "We find the biggest monster glue in the planet and fix it piece by piece. No more walking off, no more running. Marry me," Jamie asked. Faith could hear sniffling. Faith looked at him. "You're never gonna worry about anything. Faith, I'm gonna love anyone like I love you. I never have." Faith looked at him. "Marry me," he asked. Faith nodded. "Faith," Jamie said. "Yes," Faith said. He kissed her. They barely came up for air until Faith heard Emma sniffling. Jamie grabbed Faith's hand and walked her out to the tour bus, and ended up walking into their engagement party bonfire.

"And just when did you plan all this," Faith asked. "Ask Emma," he teased. Jamie kissed her. "This time we do it right," Jamie said. "Instead of what happened last time you mean," Faith asked. "This time, we do it where you wanted, just like we planned last time. This time, we really do it. Faith, I'm not draggin you into that easy quick thing again. I promise you," Jamie said. "How did we end up doing this," Faith asked. "Because you know we belong together. I never doubted it. I know you did," Jamie said. "I never doubted us," Faith said. "Even when you left your heart was still here. It's not allowed to leave ever again," Jamie said. "You so sure of that," Faith said. Jamie kissed her. They curled up together by the bonfire.

"So what's next," Faith asked. "That wedding. You know you left the dress at the house. All we need to do is re-book the venue and stuff anyway," Jamie said. "What did you do? Tell them that we were postponing it," Faith asked. Jamie kissed her, devouring her lips. "That's exactly what I did," he teased. "Jamie," Faith said. "Three weeks when we're on a 2 week break. The first second we have to ourselves, we're doing this," Jamie said. "What are you..." "It's booked," Jamie said. "And what made you think I was gonna say yes," Faith asked. "Because I was never gonna live without you. Besides. That spirit that was always talking to you probably would've kicked your butt if you didn't." Faith kissed him. Jamie heard a song come on the radio and turned it up. "What are you doing," Faith asked. He pulled her to her feet. It wasn't until Faith heard Patsy's voice over the speaker that she laughed. "Told ya so," Jamie said. He intentionally had it played just to get her attention. The song – True Love. He danced with her and held her close. "Marry me," he asked. "What else did you plan," Faith asked. He kissed her again. "Not tellin. And, the ranch is being gutted and renovated. It's gonna be our getaway instead...." Faith kissed him. "What else did you plan," Faith asked. "Honeymoon, our next 3 kids, getting the new truck..." Faith laughed. "What are you up to," Faith asked. "Fixing it. Doing better this time," he said. "Jamie," Faith said. "Marrying the only woman I ever loved. I'm never ever letting go of you," Jamie said. "What happens when I change my mind," Faith asked. "I'll change it back."

Not even three weeks later, Faith was in that dream dress. Her hair, makeup and nails were done, Emma was her maid of honor and Patsy was her flower girl. Faith walked down that aisle and Jamie was in tears. "I love you," he said when she made it to Jamie's side with her dad. Faith had a grin across her face. The ceremony was perfect, right down to the vows. When it came time for him to say his vows, he opted for the simple words.

"When we met, you did nothing but give me a hard time. I let go of the only woman I ever loved, wanted or needed. It was a stupid mistake that I'm never gonna relive. I fell for this woman years ago. Before the singing, before the writing and when I was still dreaming of making it big. When I let go of her, I knew that we'd find out way back to each other. I never wanted anything this much Faith. Never have, never will. I promise to never ever let go again. I promised you forever and I'll promise it every minute of every day from now on. I promise to make you a mom ten times over, to make you laugh, to romance you even when you start getting mad. Forever and a day isn't enough." Jamie's eyes were welling up. "I will never let you forget how much we love each other. I promise to love you until the end of time." Jamie's fingers linked with hers. "Jamie, you never were good at accepting defeat. You kept fighting even when I couldn't understand why. I never could forget you. You changed my life more than once. You saved my life more than once. I know that if you'd never been in my life, I wouldn't be standing here. I wouldn't have our beautiful daughter and I would never know what to do. I've been in love with you since that first day that you hit on me at that bonfire. How was I to know that at that exact second I'd met the man I was supposed to be with forever? I never will forget this man that stands here. How he managed to remember every detail about everything I don't know. He never lost faith. I'm just glad he reminded me to have a little of my own. I promise to pick at you, drive you nuts and love you with every breath. I promise to make you a dad again and to never ever regret anything about us. Forever is a long time, but it's never gonna be long enough," Faith said. Jamie had a grin ear to ear and held her hands just a little tighter. "Now, you two did this before but....by the power vested in me by the state of Tennessee, I pronounce you man and wife....for the last time ever," the minister said. Jamie kissed Faith and it was hot enough to almost make the entire room melt. He slid Patsy into his arms and they walked back down the aisle. They signed off on every inch of paperwork and Jamie didn't let go of Faith's hand ever again.

They got to their reception and Patsy fell asleep in grandma's arms. Jamie walked Faith onto the dance floor and Faith swore she heard Patsy Cline. "I told you Faith. If you love him like I love Charlie, no matter where you go or what you do, that love is never gonna go away. Love him with every breath, every second. Don't ever take a second for granted. Tell Charlie I miss him," Patsy said. Faith nodded. Jamie put on the Patsy song he'd played when he asked her to marry him and danced with his wife. That's the way it was always supposed to be. Even when she walked away, he knew she'd be back. No matter how long it took Faith to realize it, Patsy's spirit, that spirit of love, was always on his side. He was never gonna let Faith regret a moment with him. From that day on, he never did and either did Faith.

ABOUT THE AUTHOR

Sue has been writing since her teenage years. She never takes anything for granted. When she first touched her toe into downtown Nashville, she realized that she'd found her inspiration. Fueled by a love of country music and a history in helping friends through rough situations, she stuck to her writing until she was willing to share a story with the world. Her first novel - Without You - sold hundreds of copies. Driven by her passion, Sue wrote her latest 4 ebooks in a matter of months. Fans have said over and over that her writing is one of a kind.

It's driven by an outside perspective on things close to her heart. Sue was always dreaming of a hero like the men in her novels. Most recently, she's found new inspiration from a chance visit to the Country Music Hall of Fame in Nashville, Tennessee. The ideas never stop flowing with her. She always finds a niche that nobody expected. She's been inspired by some of the top country artists including Jason Aldean, Luke Bryan, Brantley Gilbert, Rascal Flatts, Miranda Lambert and more. What does she do when she goes to Nashville? Opry House tour, The Ryman Auditorium and the Country Music Hall of Fame. Inspiration flows for her where there's music history being made. She's also known for writing while sitting on her favorite pew of the Ryman Auditorium.